WHAT READERS SAY ABOUT *OMAR*:

"...Within pages, I was hooked and anxious to see where the whole adventure would go...I didn't spend much time eating or sleeping for a couple of days. (Thompson is) faithful to the genre in which (he) wrote while asking the reader to give more serious thought to the ideas brought up...a smashing success."

— Earl B. (NH)

"...guaranteed to hold your interest...WARNING!! You'll want more..."

— Roxanne T. (AZ)

"*Omar* is a well-written, well-researched, captivating novel. Craig O. Thompson has mixed politics, advanced technology, diabolically realistic characters into the greatest treasure hunt of all time. Intriguing, ingeniously crafted, excellent plotting all add up to a first-rate story."

— Janet P. (CA)

"...It has to be made into a movie...I'm telling everyone I know about (*Omar*)."

— Chris L. (VT)

"Finished *Omar*...good company during (an) ice storm...I usually find that my reaction to a book I like is a feeling of wanting more, when I reach the last page...and that I want to revisit its characters...I had that reaction to *Omar*!"

— Michael R. (ME)

"...I have just one word for the book. WOW!!! ...I ordinarily read other types of genre, but I couldn't wait to come home from work to dive in."

— Evalyn C. (MO)

"...It is a thriller! What vivid descriptions (he) weaves. I would certainly place (Craig O. Thompson) right up there with Jack Higgins, Stephen Coonts, and Clive Cussler.

— Alan L. (IN)

CRAIG O. THOMPSON

OMAR

A NOVEL

StrataGem Press
Indianapolis

Copyright © 1997, 2001 by Craig O. Thompson, Brightwater Enterprises, LLC
Brightwater Publishing Company™ / StrataGem Press™. First Edition. All rights reserved.

Printed on acid-free paper. Cover design by Harriet McInnis.

Publishers Cataloging-In-Publication Data
(Prepared by Indianapolis / Marion County Public Library and IUPUI Library)

Thompson, Craig O.
    Omar: a novel / Craig O. Thompson. — 1st ed.
        p. cm.

ISBN: (Hardcover) 0-9675207-0-3
        (Softcover) 0-9675207-1-1

1. Oceanographers—Fiction. 2. Shipwrecks—Fiction. 3. Titanic (Steamship)—Fiction.
4. Terrorism—Fiction. 5. Suspense fiction. 6. Treasure-trove—Fiction. I. Title.
PS3570.H59687 O432   2001   813-dc21   00-191553
10 9 8 7 6 5 4 3 2 1   CIP

Brightwater Publishing Company / StrataGem Press
P.O. Box 503, Greenwood, IN 46142-0503 USA

www.brightwaterpublishing.com

Or Contact:
Email: BrightPub@aol.com / FAX: 1-317-883-3603

Published in the United States of America by StrataGem Press,
an Imprint of Brightwater Publishing Company, Indianapolis, IN USA

DEDICATED TO:

All of my family, and to those who encouraged, inspired, and prodded me as a youth to accomplish more than I thought capable of achieving...

Mrs. Theodore Buzanis
Jerry C. Davidson
Bernard L. Hoefer
Betty Lello
Ronald E. Van Tassel
Mr. Wilson (who taught math and danced on his desktop at the same time).

For those who love life
And do not mistreat it.
For those who are endeared to their children
And will protect them at all cost.
For those Christians, Jews, Moslems, Buddhists, and Hindus
Who know we must love one another regardless of our
Religious beliefs.
And for those who know that violence is wrong.

The opposite of love is not hate…it is fear.
Dr. Gerold G. Jampolsky

PROLOGUE

APRIL, 1910

TIRED from the weight of centuries, the gigantic monster could hold no longer. It reached the Western coastline of Greenland and and three thousand years of snow accumulation, coupled with centuries of slow, creeping movement of the glacier, caused the immense iceberg to calve from its parent. It fell to the ocean with a tremendous roar and left behind an enormous glistening icefall on the sheer side of the glacier.

The furious, violent noise of its birth rumbled as an earth-quake and echoed under the cloud cover throughout Jakobshavn Sound. Heard from Dundas in the north to Goldthab in the south, the loud report warned all—a berg of colossal proportions had taken up temporary residency in Baffin Bay.

Perhaps ten thousand tons or more, they thought.

The explosive birth sent shivers up and down the spines of knowing seamen. If measurements had been taken, it would have been charted as one of the largest icebergs of recent history—1100 yards long, 360 yards wide, 190 feet high, at sea-level, and 570 feet, or more, below the surface. Sailing somewhere out there, a berg towered over 19 stories above the waterline—higher than a Cutty Sark's tallest mast. Hidden below was a mountain of ice, in reverse, descending nearly 100 fathoms into the bay.

Sinking from its weight like a capsized ship, the top-heavy berg nearly rolled completely over, uprighted itself, then slowly rocked back and forth, for hours, to find its center of gravity. Enormous waves frothed like mad dogs, as they spread out for miles and pushed back and forth between land masses.

Then, there was silence—until the next calving.

The winds and current helped the berg overcome inertia and gain momentum. Following the northwesterlies, the massive iceberg found a counter-clockwise drift in the currents, and presented a clear, potential danger for anything in its path. With power equal to the force of an ice breaker cutting its course, it sailed through open channels and aggressively blazed its own trail through Arctic floes.

Standing tall among its brothers, the berg sojourned out of Baffin Bay, across Davis Strait, through the Labrador Sea, then out into the open waters of the Atlantic. For nearly two years the leviathan roamed, calving small chucks of ice, along with glacial rocks and sediment—disintegrating bit by bit as it meandered.

————

APRIL, 1912

As silently as it had slipped into the North Atlantic shipping lanes and the warmer waters of the swift Gulf Stream, the iceberg reached the Grand Banks, nearly 500 miles off the coast of Newfoundland. Though melting at a much higher rate, it was still over 100 feet tall at the water line.

During two years of drifting, the sea had sculpted, molded and shaped a primitive battering ram—at first hidden underwater—as though cloaked for a dangerous mission. Though pack-ice had broken off large chunks of the iceberg, the ram had remained intact and, as the berg lost weight, it rose slowly above the waterline—its metamorphosis now complete.

It had wandered and waited. A windjammer with its sails fully set—still towering over 10 stories above water. Below, its cumulus-shaped body quickly deteriorated, as warmer waters exacted their toll.

In an act of defiance, while reflecting the clear starlit night in its towering sail of blackened ice, the berg found an opportunity to strike over the Great North Bank of the Atlantic Ocean, 11:40 p.m., April 14, 1912, at 41°46'N latitude, 50°14'W longitude.

In a deadly execution of might—drawn like a magnet—it rammed the starboard side of a ship, beheaded giant rivets, and split open the vessel with a crushing blow. It fractured and tore through cold, brittle steel plates, and small fissures raced as thunderbolts from one rent plate to the next.

Then, the iceberg silently turned and drifted back into the darkness.

And the *R.M.S. Titanic*, the greatest modern ship in the world, began taking on water.

Most icebergs would have moved on to slowly disappear and die in the warmer waters of their secret North Atlantic graveyard. But the ram had dropped off, and the berg went into an inertial circle. Following the rotation of the earth, it began its disintegration over the wreckage of the *Titanic* as it scattered its glacial ashes on the seabed graveyard below.

———

PART I

NORTHERN IRELAND—MAY, 1995
00:20 Greenwich Mean Time

IAN Harrison and Karen Addams headed back to their village from the Friday night dance at the Presbyterian Church in Belfast. They attended the social every weekend. Ian was accustomed to driving the dark narrow road across the gentle landscape of drumlins and hills, interrupted only by the marshy hollows.

The car windows were partially fogged and, with the defroster only working at half, Ian had split the driver's side slightly to allow more circulation. A cold breeze slipped through, watering his brown-flecked greenish eyes. Karen had snuggled her head against his wide shoulder—her lithe limbs curled across the front seat—and satiny red hair draped gently down his chest.

They enjoyed shocking their families and friends at church socials and other gatherings. Harrison was Catholic and Addams was a Protestant. Close friends thought them an attractive pair. And they were deeply in love.

Though objections were anticipated, Ian had already purchased a ring that Karen wore only when they were alone. They intended to announce wedding plans within the month, as soon as Ian's father was pronounced recovered from his bout with pneumonia.

For now, Karen would just flash her modest gold band in front of Ian's face—Ian swatting back at her hand as though it were an obnoxious fly—Karen laughing and giggling with each little tease.

It was Harrison who first saw the faint glow of lights as they came upon old Albert Bagley's farmhouse. Ian slowed his Ford and gazed out across his fiancée's side of the car. The darkened fields rolled up the hill toward a silhouette of the once abandoned house, at the top of the drumlin.

"Look there, Karen, they must've sold old Bagley's property, eh? There's a glow of lights coming out the backside of the house."

Her sea green eyes searched her mind, as she sat up. "Haven't heard of any sale. Not since the old man died two years ago."

"Maybe they closed out the estate, huh?"

"I doubt it. Mum usually knows of all the goings on with the properties out here. And in the village. She hasn't mentioned anything."

Having passed the entrance, Ian turned the car around on the small Banbridge District road and entered the dirt drive leading to the farmhouse.

"Could be vagrants then," he said, his russet-colored hair tussled by a breeze through the window.

Ian's often adventurous fiancée suddenly was fearful. Her rosy cheeks blanched in the dim light from the dashboard.

"Where are you going. Are you crazy?"

"We'll scare them out when they hear the car. If they don't belong, they'll leave."

"No," Karen insisted, with an intensity that caught Ian by surprise. She grabbed the steering wheel and forced the car to the side of the road. It hit a rut and came to rest at an angle between the drive and an overgrown plot of gravel-filled farmland.

"Damn it Karen. What the devil's gotten into you?"

"I'm sorry, Ian. But it could be anyone up there."

"Yes, Karen, machree. It might be a new family, just moved in. Maybe someone who's fixing up the old farmhouse. It could use it you know." Ian's lean, ruddy face glowed with exasperation.

"I'm frightened out here in the middle of nowhere. Take me home." Her plea was more a demand than a request.

Annoyed at what Karen had done, Ian still gave in to her pleading. "All right. But you didn't have to pull us off . . . "

He put the car in reverse and stomped on the gas. A scraping sound came from the front-end, and the rear wheels dug into soft mud from the previous night's storm runoff.

The headlights had gone out. Ian pulled and pushed on the switch, but both lamps were dead.

"Now look what's happened." He brushed aside his bushy hair and got out to survey the damage.

It was obvious even with the moonless night. His shoes stuck in the mud near the rear wheels. When he surveyed the front-end, he barely saw the Ford's bumper resting on an outcropping of solid glacial drift-covered granite. The front wheels sat two inches off the ground. He put his fingers to a headlamp and almost cut himself on broken glass.

"Look, you stay here. I'll borrow their phone to get a tow. Maybe they've got a tether to pull us out."

"Please Ian, don't go up there. Let's leave the car and follow the main road to the village. We'll return in daylight to pick it up."

"Nonsense," Ian yelled, from twenty yards up the road.

The young man approached the house, cautiously, as he first headed for the darkened front door, then decided, instead, to go toward the direction of the light. It seemed to come from Bagley's kitchen, around back.

Ian had been in the house several years before. The last time was when old Bagley's wife had died. The neighbors had chipped in to hold a small wake for her. Everyone in the village had come out. The Bagleys had farmed their mostly infertile, but fortunately patched, limestone-bearing acreage for over sixty years. Their two boys had moved on to America, and Mrs. Bagley eventually died of a broken heart. "Empty-nest syndrome," someone had said.

Everyone in the village watched Mr. Bagley attempt to keep his farm going. But it was too much for his old bones and, as Ian's father had said, Bagley "upped and died" on the day of his wedding anniversary. That was two years ago and the house had since been closed up tight.

"Hello," Ian called out at the back door. "We're having car

trouble. May we use your telephone?"

He was answered with silence. "Hello? Anyone about?"

The small clapboard farmhouse had deteriorated considerably in the two years since it was last a residence. The back door screen hung precariously from its hinges at a forty-five degree angle.

Ian stood on the top step looking in, with broken glass under foot. The back door window appeared to have been recently knocked out. A cold breeze, crossing the hillside, whistled through the door and Ian felt a chill bite the back of his neck.

"Hello? Anyone here?" He waited, "Hello."

Ian turned the door handle. It was unlocked.

He entered the brightly lit kitchen, stepped on more glass, and noticed an almost empty whiskey bottle sitting open on the counter. But no glasses were present.

Must've been a drifter, he thought. "Looks like he left quickly."

Ian noticed an odor that comes from a house sitting closed too long. And there was a peculiar acrid smell that grew stronger as he moved to an open door across the room.

"Anyone here?" he asked weakly, becoming more nervous about the position in which he had placed himself. He reached through another door, into a darkened room, and felt along the cold wall for a light switch. The smell was now overpowering.

Something's burning, he reasoned. And then it hit him. *Gunpowder! The scent is fresh gunpowder.*

He clicked the switch and, when a bare overhead bulb sprang to life, he was startled to see a man lying chest-down on the floor, bleeding profusely from the back of his head.

"Mother-of-God." Ian recognized the face of the dead man. For years, he had seen this sturdy, cleft-chined face on the front pages of newspapers, on television, and on wanted posters throughout Ulster—Sean Paisley, one of the more notorious of the Ulster Freedom Fighter splinter groups. Hero to some; assassin to others. Maker of bombs, killer of children. Even in peaceful times, he could not show his face in public.

He noticed a crumpled, blood-soaked map sticking out under

the body. Possibly a map of England, but Harrison avoided it.

Ian stood over Paisley for what seemed an eternity, trying to think what to do. Then he heard a gurgling sound.

A chill raced through his bones.

Startled, he turned and focused his eyes across the front room. Another man looked like he had been violently thrown against a timeworn couch. The man's eyes were wide open as he gasped for air. His once-chiseled face was now grotesque, as blood trickled out the corner of his pallid mouth. A massive chest wound had stained his shirt bright red. He lay perfectly still—his arms and legs outstretched—as though caught by surprise.

"John Springer!" Ian proclaimed. Elusive member of the Irish Republican Army. Also wanted for murder, mayhem and numerous bombings, depending on whose side one was on. Another man for whom peace had little meaning.

Here were two arch enemies in the same room, lying in their own pools of blood—a dead unionist and a dying nationalist. Neither had a gun in his hand, though Harrison saw a Smith and Wesson.38 still tucked into Springer's boot. Someone had set them up.

Was this a meeting of splinter groups the British and Irish Parliaments complained about? he wondered.

The gurgling sound continued from the IRA leader. Ian watched his eyes shift and blink ever so slowly, as the man gasped for air and attempted to talk.

Springer struggled to move an arm. He would not give in until he got something across to this young man.

"Mr. Springer," Ian found it odd hearing himself speak so formally to the terrorist. "Don't move. I'll get help."

The terrorist gasped loudly and managed to moan, as if to say, "No! Don't go."

Ian moved closer to the wild-eyed man as he curiously watched him rub blood from his own chest wound onto his index finger.

Disoriented and confused, but with every ounce of energy Springer could generate, he motioned for Harrison to come closer.

As he did so, Springer grabbed Ian's hand and held it to his chest in a griplock only a wrestler could manage.

Forcing Harrison's arm over, and holding it down with his own elbow, the terrorist inscribed letters, in blood, on the palm of Ian's hand. Frightened, Ian realized he could now pull away, but was curious about the message.

Struggling to maintain consciousness, the IRA terrorist dragged his blood-coated index finger across Ian's palm, as a pencil, to write the letter "A." He was losing consciousness as he next wrote the letter "L." Then, before he finished the third letter—a straight line down—his breathing slowed, his eyelids closed and he expelled a last defiant breath. John Springer's arm dropped limp to to his side, and his body slid to the floor.

Ian raised his hand to see a roughly scratched series of three letters, "AL" and an upright line that might have been the beginning of another "L" or "B" or . . .

Suddenly, Ian remembered Karen and raced for the front door. It was nailed shut to prevent intruders. He turned to go back through the kitchen and stopped dead in his tracks.

Karen was cold, sitting alone in the car. She wanted to turn on the heater, but feared someone might hear the engine. Despite her concern, she was relieved to hear footsteps on the roadway. With a fogged windshield, she struggled to see the silhouette of a man walking toward the car. Karen rolled down her window.

"Was there a phone Ian? Did you call for a tow?" her voice filled with anxiety.

There was no answer from the figure now standing near the hood of the car.

"Ian? Is that you?"

Karen Addams was terrified. With no moon to light the night, she barely saw the figure out in front.

"Ian say something, please."

Then, she realized the shadowy person was larger than her fiancé, and fear oozed through her mind.

The figure moved to her side of the car. Out of instinct, Karen quickly locked her door, rolled up the window, then reached over to lock the driver's side.

The man knocked on her window. She was too petrified to look. He knocked once more. Karen slowly turned and forced herself to face him.

In the darkness, she knew the man was not Ian. In fact, he was not Irish. Karim Abdul Khorassani shoved his massive fist through the glass and grabbed Karen by the hair.

She never saw the knife.

WOODS HOLE, MASSACHUSETTS—06:04 EDT

THE phone broke the morning silence. Though an early riser, on the one Saturday Dr. Cary Parker thought he would sleep well past six, the ringing was especially loud and insistent.

A fresh aroma of salt-sea air wafted through a slit left in the bedroom window, and a faint golden sky gave the first hint of a warm spring day.

Victoria reached over Cary. Her graceful olive-bronzed body and long legs followed.

"Hello."

"Mrs. Parker . . . Colonel Bramson. Sorry to bother you so early. Is Doc awake?"

Cary's thighs moved seductively under Victoria. She laughed politely—her sloe, dark hazel eyes luminous.

"He is now."

Bramson, the CIA's Mid-east bureau chief, was a respected intelligence specialist, recruited from the Pentagon by the DCI. He had first approached Dr. Parker for consulting services, when Bramson moved to Langley a year before. And he wanted the ocean-ographer to glide into the provision of underwater support services as soon as he felt comfortable with the agency.

Parker had declined the offer, but did sign on as an advisor with a yet-to-be-determined portfolio. Monthly calls from Bramson allowed Parker an opportunity to get to know him better. They had only met twice.

Split between summer diving expeditions from Woods Hole and his position with the Smithsonian, Dr. Parker had been too busy to attempt other work—even part-time.

To date, Parker had not performed an assignment that might earn him his unwanted "desk" at CIA.

Victoria cast a glance at the moving mass below her and softly pecked Cary on the cheek. He returned the kiss and marveled at how fresh she always looked in the morning.

"It's the colonel."

"Shit," Cary sighed quietly under his breath, and stretched his sturdy, six-five frame out across the bed. With the sun rising a little earlier, Parker's blue, tempestuous eyes caught the light slipping through the drifting curtains.

Victoria smiled, swept disheveled sandy-colored hair from Cary's eyes, and pulled a sheet over their nude bodies in case the girls entered the room. High cheek bones on Cary's sun-browned face gave way to disappointment, and he adjusted the receiver to an exposed ear.

"What's so important on an early, and I stress early, Saturday morning?"

Bramson spoke in an even tone, "You'll want to be in on this. You awake?"

"Yeah," said Cary half-lying.

"They're going down for the Ruby."

Cary searched his groggy mind to interpret the apparently cryptic message. "The Ruby?"

"*The Rubaiyat* . . . the *Great Omar*. Dupont and Taylor have teamed to dive the *Titanic* again. This time they're after the only other priceless relic left."

It took a moment to sink in. *"The Great Omar. . . .* They're going after *The Rubaiyat?"*

"You got it."

Cary sat up on his elbow. His body tensed and Victoria gave him breathing room.

"Those S.O.B.'s just won't give up until every last vestige of the ship is raped."

Victoria looked with empathy at the scientist lying beside her. In an instant, Parker's chestnut tan had turned pale. The ghost had returned to haunt once more.

For eighty-three years, a priceless bejeweled, leatherbound edition of *The Rubaiyat of Omar Khayyam* had quietly rested somewhere at the *Titanic's* gravesite, out over the Grand Banks of Newfoundland, 2077 fathoms from the surface of the North Atlantic Ice Barrier.

An oceanographer and maritime law expert, Parker had supported and applauded the innovative *Titanic* expeditions—the first led by his famous colleagues, Dr. Robert Ballard and Jean-Louis Michel, whose Franco/American project had pinpointed and photographed the initial discovery in 1985; the second led by Dr. Ballard, himself, in 1986. And despite joint efforts by Parker, Ballard and the rest of the Woods Hole team to prevent undersea looting of the gravesite, they were sickened that the ship had, since 1987, been plundered on at least two dozen separate occasions. Mostly by the French and some American investors, and several times by Parker's former partner, Henri Dupont, a Québécois from Montreal.

Parker had joined his colleagues and devoted years, since, in support of a ban on undersea recovery from the *Titanic*, and other ships that could be classified as gravesites.

But salvaging continued, and the original purser's safe, thought to contain over $500,000 in jewels and gold, and the jewel-encrusted *Rubaiyat*, still eluded underwater grave robbers. Referred to as the *Great Omar*, the book, if found, would be worth well over $30 million.

Court battles had raged for years, between profiteer investor groups, for the rights to salvage the *Titanic's* rare artifacts and strip the ship for revenue. Deep-submergence treasure salvors came from every continent when the fever had hit.

Cary had hoped it would be decades, before the court granted permission to either side. But one scurrilous adventurer was finally awarded salvage rights, and he immediately pursued recovery of remaining artifacts and treasure from *Titanic's* gravesite. To complete the job, they would eventually have to destroy the remaining superstructure by cutting it apart, until only a bed of rust was left.

Now, it appeared a free-for-all was about to take place regardless of court orders or court awarded rights.

"But how does this concern you, Colonel? You're Mid-East CIA, not Atlantic operations."

"That's why I called. Section Two informed me that not only is Dupont heading for the treasure...a terrorist plan exists as well. Except they want the *Great Omar* for blood-money."

Blood-money, Cary pondered. "To finance activities?"

"Exactly. And there's a link between the intended terrorist dive and Faheed Al Mar Ragem's group."

"Ragem? The fundamentalist leading terrorist attacks in Egypt?"

"Ultrazealot fanatic, yes. Fundamentalist, maybe."

"I know nothing about terrorists. Why are you calling me?"

"With your background, we're hoping to short-circuit this thing. Ragem's a part of the equation. But it's anyone's guess who'll get there first, especially with Dupont and Taylor hell-bent to go back down."

Go back down, echoed in Cary's mind. *No one was ever supposed to go back!* Bad enough divers had broken their promises to never salvage the *Titanic*. Now terrorists were a factor.

This was too much for so early a morning. Cary sank into his pillow and took a deep breath. He remained silent, hoping the colonel would call someone else.

Bramson broke the silence. "Cary, you have to return to the site before the others."

"Colonel, with all due respect, I'm not about to go down there again. We've promised never to take anything off that ship."

"But we've got to keep both sides from reaching the *Omar*."

"Look, it takes four to six months to prepare for an expedition, charter a ship, schedule equipment, crew."

"You've done it in less . . . "

"We'd never be ready in time. Besides, we've already got our first contract using the new submersibles. I'm assisting a joint American and Russian project to locate a deep bed of manganese nodules. We'll be in the Pacific. Nowhere near the Atlantic, if freshman geography serves me right."

"Call Moscow and postpone it. I can arrange it with the American side."

"Look Colonel, I don't work for the CIA. Remember?"

It was true. Though Parker had signed on with an undetermined portfolio, he was not bound to provide services until more clearly defined. To Bramson, this was the perfect opportunity.

The agency's nearly two-inch thick dossier on Dr. Cary Morgan Parker, underwater archeologist, was well researched:

> Born Los Angeles, CA, September 25, 1954; President of
> See-Life, Inc.—an underwater diving, deep-submergence
> vehicle firm out of Woods Hole, Massachusetts; heads the
> Smithsonian's Department of Oceanography for the Na-
> tional Museum of Natural History, where he splits his time
> and research with Woods Hole Oceanographic Institution.

In the file's summary pages it noted that, following a long dry struggle to finance expeditions and research—with years of proving himself worthy of project funding to establish credibility—Parker's company was well-established and boasted a large list of corporate sponsors (holds major diving contracts with numerous government agencies and private concerns, including the U.S. Navy, British Royal Navy, DoD's top-secret ARPA, General Electric, and the National Science Foundation).

Among other facts, the document listed Dr. Parker as:

> Chair, U.S. Maritime Law Association; U.S. Delegate, Comité Maritime International; contributor to numerous international newsletters, maritime organization legal briefs/case studies; well-paid expert and author of nearly a dozen books on maritime law and archeological accounts of lost ships. Raised in Southern California; excellent physical specimen with few scars or injuries; non-smoker, moderate drinker. Married 14 years; two daughters (Marlow, age 12 and Jessica, age 8); shares avid interest in downhill skiing and scuba diving with wife, Victoria Alexis Parker (born Victoria A. Bettencourt, June 13, 1957, in San Francisco, CA); Victoria holds a B.A. in Art (1979) and M.A. (1981) from Kendall College of Art & Design; was part to full-time diving logistics coordinator and research shipmate at Woods Hole Institute (1981 to 1985); consultant for Suthmann, Collins and Folett, designer of public, institutional, and commercial spaces (1985 to 1989); for the past six years has run her own home-based interior design firm.

Hand-written at the bottom of the last page was a note that read, "Faithful, now."

"My apologies, Doctor," said Bramson. "I understand your feelings. But imagine our position. We now have a dangerous . . . "

"Colonel, we haven't even performed sea trials with our new submersibles. We're still on the Frasca simulator. It'll be weeks before we take the subs two and a half miles down."

"I understand," Bramson said, some sympathy in his voice.

"And the entire Woods Hole fleet is tied up with other projects. Several institutes on the eastern seaboard would give their eye-teeth for your project, not to mention Military Sealift Command."

"With your track record you've been requested, personally, by the director. Besides, M.S.C. can't touch this. It's too sensitive an issue for international waters."

"Never stopped them before."

"Take my word for it."

"The weather won't be in our favor for another two months. The current salvors are holding up until summer. And not even Dupont can dive until then."

"Don't bet on it. Appears your former French Canadian partner has picked up on Faheed Ragem's plan, himself."

"Dupont?"

"Through his contacts in Tripoli."

"What contacts?"

"Every mercenary has contacts," said Bramson. "Look, I'm certain their dive is imminent. Dupont'll dive in the eye of a typhoon if he smells money. We know he approached Clayton Paul Taylor for financing."

"C. P. Taylor . . . "

"They hope to beat Ragem to the punch. I'll bet my next paycheck they won't wait for summer."

"That wealthy jackass will finance anything underwater if he doesn't have to dive, himself."

Clayton Paul Taylor was a wealthy oilman and ruthless investor. Openly rude, sarcastic and inconsiderate of others, "CP", as he was called, regarded the masses as "the little people." Everyone was beneath him—ready to be bought, used, then tossed aside— expendable as crumpled beer cans. A good-old-boy challenged by no one. Rumors lingered of involvement in the Kennedy assassination, but no one tied them with fact. A known racist, some swore he had direct connections with the KKK and the militia movement.

"You know Taylor," said Bramson. "He dislikes anyone who tries to beat him—whatever his game."

Parker felt the cool morning and pulled a blanket over his 208 pound physique. His forty-one years seemed to wear on him—a lifetime from the days when he never dropped the ball as tight-end for Stanford.

Bramson persisted. "I understand your feelings about *Titanic*. But terrorist advisories are quickly becoming a way of life for Americans. If we don't keep those artifacts from greedy salvors, or worse yet, the terrorists, I'd hate to predict the outcome."

"Colonel, I know as little about the location of that book as anyone. In all the dives it's never been located. Let the Navy handle this."

"The Navy's waiting for you to finish development of your new submersibles. I understand you're a little late completing the project. Perhaps I can buy some time."

That stopped Parker cold. He did have a contract with the Navy and Pentagon to develop an entirely new breed of mini-subs—vertical, one-diver submersibles smaller, slimmer, and faster than any ever built. Their planned use: venturing into sea canyon depths never physically reached by man, and reaching secured and classified spaces too small for available manned subs to enter.

Alvin, the submersible used in prior dives, was too large for this type of project. At tremendous depths, smaller subs were needed to access areas aboard sunken submarines and ships that carry top secret equipment or nuclear weapons. Unmanned robotic subs, with photographic and video capabilities were an important part of the equation. And Parker had been one of the leaders in their development.

But experience showed that Parker's high-concept sub would bridge the gap between the need to protect divers at extreme depths, and the necessity to physically explore, locate, or recover objects within smaller windows of opportunity.

That was exactly why Parker's Woods Hole scientific team worked night and day to meet their construction deadline.

"Look," said the colonel, "if you locate *Omar* before the others, you have several choices."

"How's that?"

"You could bring up the relic for permanent display at The Smithsonian, bury it under the sand at two and a half miles below the surface or, destroy it, God forbid, if Dupont or the terrorists get too close."

Bramson waited for a reaction, but got none.

"Naturally, we'd prefer you bring it up. After all, the *Great Omar* was sold to an American and was enroute to its owner when the *Titanic* sank. Conceivably, we could trace descendants and present it personally."

Parker's heart sank at the thought of destroying anything from the *Titanic* for political reasons, let alone to prevent enjoyment of the beauty of an early 20th century artist's work. And this unique binding of *The Rubaiyat of Omar Khayyam* was known to transcend the work of all 14th through 17th century monastic artists who hand bound books—each a work of art.

Bramson interrupted Parker's thoughts. "We need to meet at the Smithsonian tomorrow. I've requested the Boardroom next to your office. Can you make it down by 2:00 p.m.?"

"Sunday?" he sighed. "We're taking the girls to Heritage Plantation. Jessica wants to ride the carousel."

A long silence followed on the other end. Parker waited for a reprieve, but the colonel would not budge. Cary turned to his wife. Though disappointed, Victoria flashed an approving smile at a conversation she suspected was not going their way.

"Tomorrow. Sure. 2:00 p.m."

"And bring your partner, Andrew Calder. Should I phone him?"

"No. I'll see him at the Institute this morning."

"Good. And, Dr. Parker, keep this quiet until we meet."

"Right," Parker agreed, with disgust in his voice.

"Tomorrow."

"2:00 p.m."

The phone clicked off on the other end. Cary looked at the handset as if to say, "Nice talkin' to you."

Bramson was never known for indulging in courtesy. Though

most of his associates respected him as a professional, brusqueness was his trademark.

Cary stared at the ceiling in thought. He had dreaded this moment for years. For over a decade Parker had been embroiled in international maritime law meetings to prevent this occurrence. But the politics of economic zones hampered progress.

We've come so close, he thought. Words from the podium circled his mind as he remembered a recent speech to the IMO. *It's only a matter of time before salvaging historic undersea gravesites will be outlawed. And maritime law will be enforced with internationally supported actions.*

"Henri at it again?" Victoria's soft, dark features highlighted her radiant, expressive face. As they quietly embraced, her auburn hair slid over her breasts.

"Afraid so. This time he's after the *Omar*. The Arabs want it too." He rested his head on his fist. "There's no peace for that ship."

Victoria understood how much it hurt Cary to have Dupont, his former partner, turned diver-for-hire, greedily breaking earlier promises. Before their children, Victoria had sailed numerous projects with her husband and Dupont.

On several occasions, Dupont had attempted an affair with Victoria. Though an independent woman, she loved her family as much as she had loved her days at sea. And though temptation prevailed—in close quarters aboard ship—Victoria ultimately dismissed Dupont's overtures.

Since travel was no longer possible, for weeks at a time, children and interior design projects filled the hours her husband was away. Cary knew of Dupont's advances toward his wife. And since the breakup with his former partner, he had referred to Dupont as "a ketch not fully rigged for sail."

Still, Cary didn't think Dupont crazy enough to attempt an Atlantic salvage expedition in unpredictable weather.

Questions flashed through Parker's mind. *Why do the terrorists want the book? They've the financial wherewithal to finance a trip, but do they have access to deep-sea technology? Who's helping them? How can we possibly dive the mini-subs without sea-trials? Has the* Great Omar *been eaten away by underwater microbes? Or was it buried by sand over time?*

For the moment, Cary was oblivious to Victoria as she stroked her fingers through his thick, sun-bleached hair.

Having never found the *Great Omar* meant salvors would tear apart the hull to locate it at all cost. By today's values, there was no telling how high the bidding might go at Sotheby's or Christie's auction houses—or on the black market—if the book was still intact.

Parker grew restless. He glanced at the clock next to the bed. 6:25 a.m. The previous week had been a rough one. Sleep had not come easy. And he was certain he was in for more sleepless nights.

"Put it out of your mind," said Victoria, her rich, calm tone soothing to the ear. "There's nothing you can do 'til tomorrow."

Cary sighed heavily, but remained silent in thought as his mind raced over the past.

Henri and Cary's joint pledge, supporting Ballard's appeal to never remove artifacts from *Titanic's* graveyard, was more than idyllic promises of two scientists. Much more. They had agreed to respect the spirit of those whose lives were lost in one of the most senseless, tragic episodes ever to occur on the open sea.

Somewhere along the line, Dupont had turned with the other salvors. His desire for a respectable place in history had mutated into the same avaricious desire that had ultimately driven the *Titanic* to its murky doom.

Dupont had shifted his allegiance. Someone at the Québec Institute for Maritime Studies had forced the issue back into Dupont's hands. No longer was there an obligation to preserve historic sites. Stronger than one's sexual appetite, it had become an unquenched, insatiable lusting for treasure—no matter what the price—to finance subsequent research.

Parker considered the future. If only the international community would approve the treaty they had worked on for so many years. They were extremely close. So few objections held them back now. If only . . .

Victoria moved her body closer. She kissed the back of his neck and gently caressed his thighs. He slowly turned to her and forced a smile. Then he kissed her thick, dark eyebrows, her glossy high cheekbones, and soon he found her lips. Vicky could always bring him back when he felt disheartened.

Cary had to be at Woods Hole Oceanographic Institute by 9:00. For now, they would enjoy what few precious moments they could spend together.

———

BAGLEY'S FARMHOUSE, BANBRIDGE DISTRICT, IRELAND 20:40 Greenwich

HEADLIGHTS pierced the fog like cold spears while multi-colored flashing lights reflected off the evening mist, and three Royal Ulster Constabulary police cars warned away the curious. The area was sealed off with police-line tape, to prevent intruders. And ambulances sat at the top of Bagley's road, awaiting word from the medical examiner to claim four bodies.

Rumors had already crisscrossed throughout Ulster, with varied reports of a mass murderer who had stalked the area the night before. But the detectives from Belfast's Castlereagh interrogation center suspected a different type of foul play.

Friends of Ian Harrison—and Karen Addams parents—had reported them missing, upon failing to return from the church social, Friday evening. A search of the region began in earnest by late Saturday morning.

By dusk, investigators had turned up an abandoned, but blood-stained Ford, driven into a marsh across the road from Bagley's

farm. Muddy tire tracks, crossing from Bagley's road, had all but
washed away in a morning rain. Were it not for an inquisitive and
observant passerby, the ghostly tracks may never have been seen.

Soon after, broken headlamp glass was found up Bagley's road.
And the gruesome remains of two Irish terrorists, and a young
couple—nearly beheaded—but lying together in death, were
located in a back room of the musty house.

"I swear to ya', sir," said Shannon O'Dawd, "the last we saw of
them two love birds was when they were making out in Ian's car."

"In the church parking lot," confirmed Erin Rooney. "They
were to be married next Spring. No one else knew."

"Ian's dad is at hospital . . . pneumonia."

Both young men had spent time with Ian and Karen at the
dance, before the couple headed for home.

"Never thought it'd come to this . . . " O'Dawd's eyes were
wet.

Inspector Wickham looked carefully at each of them, then
pulled up the collar on his overcoat as the mist turned into a light
shower.

"You'd better get on home," said the inspector. "Take young
Mr. Rooney here, with you."

Ian's friends turned from Wickham's black Vauxhall and headed
for their car. They heard hysterical crying come from behind the
house.

Karen's parents had arrived shortly before, to identify their
daughter's body. Detective Crumlish stood across the way, attempting to console them.

Glyniss Addams was near collapse. And Lloyd Addams was
beyond himself with grief.

"What happened here, detective?" Mr. Addams said bitterly.
"Who took our daughter's life?"

"The perpetrators have left fingerprints everywhere," said
Crumlish. "But it'll take some time to separate them from any

latent prints left by your daughter or her fiancé."

Mrs. Addams looked at the detective questioningly.

"What do you mean, her fiancé?" said Lloyd Addams."

Inspector Wickham walked over and interrupted, having heard the last remark. He asked Crumlish to assist in the house, then turned to the couple.

"My apologies. Detective Crumlish would not have known you were unaware of their plans. Apparently, it was a secret. Only closest friends knew. It appears your daughter had hoped to tell you when Mr. Harrison's father left hospital." He paused to measure their response. "There's a ring....Still on her left hand. The motive may not have been thievery."

Mrs. Addams wept openly, and Mr. Addams looked harshly at the inspector, "My question has not been answered. Who was involved in our daughter's murder?"

"These are sad times, indeed, Mr. Addams. It appears your daughter and her . . . ah, she and Mr. Harrison tragically stumbled into a terrorist safehouse. We have no idea why they were up here, but something went terribly wrong. We aren't certain what it was, though IRA and UFF splinter groups were both involved."

The inspector hesitated to report signs of other involvement. But closer inspection would hopefully resolve any uncertainties that existed. Until then, it would not be useful to disclose unnecessary information.

Mrs. Addams sobbed uncontrollably, and her husband made a vain attempt to console her.

From inside Bagley's farmhouse, Detective Crumlish stuck his head out the door. "Sir, can you come in? You're wanted by the ME. No sign of a struggle. But we've bagged the hands, just in case."

"Be right there."

"Bagged the hands . . . " said Lloyd Addams. "Our daughter's hands, Inspector?"

"Each of the victims, I'm afraid. Standard procedure. We must check for DNA trace materials—hair, anything foreign under the fingernails, from grabbing or scratching at the culprits."

Wickham pulled a card from his coat.

"We're waiting for the medical examiner to allow removal of the bodies. The coroner will perform an autopsy. And we should be able to release your daughter from the morgue, for interment, by Tuesday. This is my number. Call if you have questions."

He turned to leave, then stopped.

"Oh, an officer will drive you home. You're in no condition to do it yourself." Wickham took Mrs. Addams hands in his and squeezed them gently.

"I truly wish I could be of more help. But, for now, this case leaves more questions than answers. My sincere condolences to both of you."

LONDON—WINTER, 1909

IT had been a cold blustery night. Early morning light, shaded by a still overcast sky, entered the small bedroom of the converted carriage house. Ice had formed on the mullioned windows. And Francis Longinus Sangorski had not slept well.

Even with a chill in the room, a recurring nightmare had caused him to break out in a sweat.

The youngest of four sons of Felix Sangorski, a Polish emigre, and his English wife, Lydia Clark, Francis Sangorski had beaten the odds, coming from common stock to become one of the most successful book binders in England. He and his partner, George Sutcliffe, began their business in a small attic in Bloomsbury, in 1901. Within two years, they boasted regular commissions from the noble-class and were able to move S & S to more spacious premises on Poland Street.

Regardless of their success, Sangorski was haunted by two factors. No matter how thriving his business, he was obsessed with the idea of binding a book the likes of which no one had ever seen; and his recurring dream stalked him without mercy.

"Francis?" his wife whispered softly across the pillows. "Are you all right?"

Sangorski turned to his wife, Rose. Beads of sweat covered his brow.

"You've had that dream again, haven't you?" She blotted his forehead with her nightgown's lace-end sleeve.

He smiled to keep her from worrying.

"It's all right, Rose."   He gently swept back her dark,

waist-length hair.

"Tell me your dream. I feel helpless when you're bothered by that dreadful thing . . . whatever it is."

Sangorski rolled closer to his wife. He thought for a moment, not wanting to alarm her.

"It's nothing, really."

"Oh, codswallop," Rose smiled. "You've said that for two years now."

"There's much on my mind—my work at the bindery."

"Share your dream with me, please?" She looked into his large, square-jawed face. His dark, oval eyes belied the fears of a child. "I share mine with you. It makes me feel better."

Sangorski's eyes creased with a wide mustachioed smile. He relaxed as he gazed into Rose's soft, pink face.

"All right."

With determination, he sat against the sleighbed headboard. "It's curious," he began. "I've dreamt this numerous times, since boyhood. It must come from my fear of water.

"At age four, my father threw me into a pond. He thought a child learned to swim if dropped into water."

"It must have worked. You swim now."

"Actually, mother told me I went straight down. Father just stood there waiting for me to come up."

"What happened then?"

"Mum jumped in after me . . . clothes and all. Then my father jumped in after her," Francis laughed. "Must have been quite a scene. I don't remember it. Only what Mum said. Though I can swim, it must have affected me in some way."

"That was a long time ago."

"It was years before I'd go in the water with friends. Until I was eleven or twelve, I always held my nose when I went under." He glanced at Rose. "Must have looked rather foolish, huh?"

Francis lay his head against Rose's breasts. Though he was only thirty-four, Sangorski's hairline was receding regularly. She gently stroked his thinly covered head.

Rose waited patiently, knowing her husband was having a difficult time.

"For years I've dreamt about drowning. I can't tell if it's in the River Thames, the Trent or at sea."

"Must be that silly pond."

"It's more than that. I'm not drowning as a child. I'm older. There are people around me. But I don't care if I drown."

"You don't care?"

"Well, yes...I care. But it's as if I'm fetching or trying to save someone....Or some thing." Sangorski drifted into thought.

"The dream always begins with friends or relatives. We're together around water. We're drinking bitters and having a good time. Then it gets very cold. I'm in the water, trying to find something, and see everyone around me. Friends scream for me to come back. But I can't. Something pulls me down. I struggle for the surface, still searching for whatever it is. But I'm pulled down."

"What happens then?"

Sangorski looked at his wife. "That's when I wake up sweating like a bloody pig."

Rose preferred he not use such crude language in front of her, but she held back criticism.

"So many things are on your mind, Francis. You're probably sorting them out." Rose tapped him on the head with her knuckles. "There's a new Doctor . . . Freud, I think, who says . . . "

"Wait," Francis jumped from the bed and stood in his nightshirt, barefoot on the cold floor. "I know what it is. That damnable *Rubaiyat*. That's it."

Rose winced. "But you've bound *Rubaiyats* for some time now. Why would that bother you?"

"Not just any *Rubaiyat*, darling. *The Rubaiyat*. The one I've talked to Stonehouse about for the past two years. The greatest of all Omar Khayyam's." He pointed into the air.

"*That's* what I've been searching for in my dream."

Sangorski's mind had focused for months on ways to bring the binding about. Chills surged through his body—rejuvenated by an invisible force.

"I'll convince Sotheran's bookstore of its value to the trade."

"But you've talked to them until you're blue in the face."

"Yet they know the caliber of my work. Even Henry Sotheran himself said as much. And John Stonehouse tells everyone he meets I'm the best book illuminator there is. . . . Well, I must admit, after my brother Alberto. But then John says that of Alberto when I'm not around."

Rose left the warmth of the bed to hug her husband.

"Then try once more. They can't say no forever."

Sangorski's face expressed an excitement Rose had not seen before. Many a dinner party included pleas with his closest friend, John Harrison Stonehouse—manager of Sotherans Antiquarian Bookstore—to commission the finest book ever bound. Stonehouse knew no better master craftsman existed than Sangorski. The Sangorski and Sutcliffe bindery was unmatched among competitors with their book forwarding and finishing skills.

It was Sangorski's unbridled optimism that had attracted Rose to marry him—still as contagious as when they met.

"You bind for King Edward and Archbishop of Canterbury," she said. "Maybe John Stonehouse will commission your *Rubaiyat*."

Sangorski's eyes lit up.

"What would I do without your encouragement?" He brought her to his chest. In one sweeping motion, Francis held her back slightly, looked into her eyes, kissed her and turned to prepare for work.

"This will be the day, I assure you," he yelled from the other room. "Today we'll begin the greatest modern binding in the world, or those bloody bugg . . . I apologize darling. Or those booksellers will wish they'd been bound *themselves* in Morocco leather, gilt in gold, and shipped off to Australia."

———

John Harrison Stonehouse glanced to the street through the tall windows of Henry Sotheran's bookstore. He saw his friend, Sangorski, crossing carefully between the trams and lorries coming out of the nearby Piccadilly Circus. A smile crossed his face at the anticipated visit of his friend.

Stonehouse met Sangorski two years before. They had much in common to bond their friendship. Each loved books as they loved breathing. Both appreciated exquisitely bound and crafted works. And each had a zest and unbounded enthusiasm for their professions.

Stonehouse knew the acclaimed binder had studied with the finest artisans of their time, particularly Douglas Cockerell. Sangorski appreciated the solid business sense in John Stonehouse, and his ability to turn every book sale into an adventure. Both forgave each other's rather large egos and acknowledged the success their egos provided.

Stonehouse glanced out the window, once more, to check the whereabouts of his colleague. Sangorski still paced back and forth, out front. He stopped and sheepishly grinned at the bookstore manager, but made no move to enter. Stonehouse opened one of the large double doors.

"Frank, if you enjoy the cold, you should don a parka and join that American admiral at the North Pole."

"The cold helps me think," Sangorski moved toward the door.

"I should *think* it would make you seek shelter. Come inside, Frank," he laughed. "We'll brew some tea."

Frank, as everyone except his wife called him, was glad to be inside Sotheran's bookstore—each visit a banquet for his soul. The building's design was reminiscent of a small Venetian palace, with features more French and Flemish than Italian. Built of solid Portland stone, without the heavy cornices and projections that gave sanctuary to London's soot, it presented a Gothic effect that portrayed all the good in Edwardian architecture.

Sangorski's heart was warmed when surrounded by thousands

of books, all cared for like children in a nursery. The staff welcomed his visits, always pleased to share the rarest manuscripts or the most famous of autographs.

Dickens, his favorite celebrity author, had shopped at the store most of his life. And, until his death in 1870, Sotheran's had carried all of his books—many of them signed copies. One of the shop's prized acquisitions was his entire library, and a number of his personal effects.

On one occasion Stonehouse had pulled out Dickens' own snuff box and brandy flask. Frank imagined the old author pinching at the snuff, from his finely decorated pocket box, and inhaling the tobacco in a moment of thought.

"Over here, Frank," the managing director interrupted Sangorski's revelry. He had a private office on the lower level, but maintained a ground-floor desk for clientele.

Sangorski moved unhurried between the tables, smelling the combined aromas of fine leather and special paper, touching nearly every book as if saying "hello" to old friends.

"Frank."

"Coming, John."

John Stonehouse had a broad smile on his square-set face. A handlebar moustache accented his strong jutting chin, and serious eyes spoke of years of adventure and travel, in search of rare books on every continent.

"Something's on your mind, Frank."

"Does it show that much?"

"What is it, my friend?"

Sangorski could not raise the courage to speak of the *Rubaiyat*.

"It's the book, is it not?"

The floodgates opened. Frank turned to Stonehouse.

"John, we've known each other for some time. You know there's more in the execution of my work than in the bindings of others. The press reports it at every turn."

"I know each of your bindings become more elaborate and

ambitious an undertaking."

Stonehouse was predisposed by Sangorski's vigor; his passion for his work; and his dynamic personality that made it difficult to say no to anything Frank wanted. John found it odd that a man of this depth and breadth would have such a love for book binding—and the thankless hours it took to create each masterpiece.

"You've seen my designs with the peacock and grape vines. You've said yourself that my rendering of Symonds' *Wine, Women and Song* was the most exquisitely beautiful binding you'd ever seen. I believe those were your words. 'The most exquisitely beautiful.'"

"Yes, I believe I did say that," John smiled. "And it sold immediately." He knew what was coming.

"John," Sangorski took a deep breath. "If that book could be compared to the beauty of Aphrodite, as you also said, then I know you'll compare my *Great Omar* to the glory of Juno."

Stonehouse stepped back as though imagining a magnificent painting not yet there. He spoke grandly, "The *Great Omar*."

Sangorski waited for something more, but Stonehouse prolonged the agony.

"You know I've seen that play, *Kismet*, nearly a dozen times," said Frank.

"Yes, and it's had a heady effect. You've told me of it no less than a dozen times."

"And you've seen my sketches inspired by its scenery and the riot of colors in its designs. Believe me, John, I know this binding would bewitch the Sirens into singing a different song."

Stonehouse laughed. "You're mystically inspired."

"Don't make light of me," Sangorski pointed a thick, blunt finger at his friend. "I've never had the opportunity to accomplish anything so wonderful."

He gazed directly into John's face. "If only someone would commission me to bind Veddar's *Omar Khayyam*.

"Picture *this* Sangorski and Sutcliffe masterpiece in your mind's-eye, John. I've gone over it a thousand times or more, in mine.

"Imagine gold covered inlays, the likes of which you've never seen, each set with numerous . . . no, hundreds of jewels. Rubies and amethysts, topazes, and turquoises. And a bright green emerald to glisten at the reader as he's helplessly drawn into the beauty of my design."

Sangorski leaned back on his heels, emphasizing every word with expansive gestures. His large hands flowed through the air as paintbrushes on a canvas.

"I'll stand three peacocks in the middle of the front cover. They'll be surrounded with more jeweled decoration than has ever been dreamed of before."

Sangorski was totally absorbed in his own world. His trips into the imagination fascinated John. He knew it was just such spirited journeys, over the centuries, that had created masterpieces by other craftsmen like Le Gascon and the Mearnes. He listened intently to the dream.

"Khayyam's *Rubaiyat* is the essence of eleventh century Persia. It's the soul and all-embracing wisdom of one man who understood that essence and who understood the entire process of life from birth to death."

Sangorski went on—oblivious to others in the shop. "In that spirit I'll have symbols of life and death on each cover. The doublures will be cut into sunken panels, richly inlaid with many colored leathers—and more jewels. Gold, will clothe the book like Athena the Virgin, and will peer back from every gilded corner of the binding—green Levant morocco binding. The flyleaves will be in brown morocco, elaborately inlaid and gold-tooled. And . . . "

"More jewels?" John relished gibing his friend.

"Yes. Then I'll complete my design, on the back cover, with a Persian mandolin carved of African mahogany—inlaid with silver, satinwood, mother-of-pearl and ebony.

"And," another blunt finger gesticulated in the air, "with actual strings to be played."

Sangorski looked straight into the eyes of Stonehouse, who now felt chills of excitement.

"John," Sangorski spoke slowly and with resolve, "when you pick up this masterpiece, and hold it dearly in your arms—then, and only then, you'll know you've met up with the world's greatest bookbinder." He waved his finger at Stonehouse once more. "Then you will know, my friend . . . "

John placed his forefinger solidly on Sangorski's chest, almost knocking him off his heels as he interrupted.

"All right, Frank, go ahead and do it."

Surprised at the interruption, but not grasping John's words, Sangorski continued, "I shall use Veddar's Royal Quarto version to . . . "

"Frank. Go ahead and do it! Bind your . . . *Great Omar*." Stonehouse's voice had attracted the attention of everyone on Sotheran's ground floor.

"What? Do you know what you're saying?"

"Yes," John laughed. "Do it and do it well. There's no limit. Put what you like into the binding. Charge what you wish for it. The greater the price, the more I shall be pleased. Provided, of course, that what you do and what you charge will be justified by the result. And the book, when finished, is to be, as you have said 'the greatest modern binding in the world'."

Francis Longinus Sangorski was speechless. He faced his friend and associate, surprised he had finally won the commission.

"These are my only instructions," concluded John Harrison Stonehouse, Managing Director of Henry Sotheran & Company, Bookseller to His Majesty the King.

———

BOARDROOM-NATIONAL MUSEUM OF NATURAL HISTORY
WASHINGTON D.C.—MAY, 1995—14:00 EDT

"BUT, he's got to go down one more time," said Colonel Bramson, CIA's Mid-East bureau chief.

Harold Chapman, Smithsonian's Chief Archivist, agreed.

"If the book's intact we'd have a valuable resource."

"But, Dr. Parker still refuses to . . ."

The carved mahogany double doors flew wide open without a knock. The room went silent as Parker and his partner, Andy Calder, entered. Cary smiled as he glanced from face to face—each looking as if caught in the refrigerator at four in the morning. He knew two of them, and wondered about the third.

"Is this a hornets' nest or what?" said Parker.

Bramson was closest to the doors. An imposing man, he towered over everyone, except Parker. His thinning, closely cropped silver hair gave the impression his head was shaved, and left a wide space between his forehead and the furrowed, bushy eyebrows that drew attention to deep-set eyes and broad, taut lips. With sleeves rolled up and his tie askew, Bramson appeared slightly agitated.

The glass-like finish on the thirty-foot mahogany board table mirrored four crystal chandeliers, and bathed the otherwise dark-paneled room with reflected light. Eighteen hand-carved captain's chairs surrounded the table and filled the room with the rich aroma of fine-grained leather. Nineteenth century oil paintings of eagles, hawks, and other wildlife, were venerably displayed.

Parker observed Chapman standing quietly at the opposite end of the table. Harold was considered a nemesis by most of his colleagues; a sycophant by those who knew him well. Though tall, thin, and mousy in appearance, he was impeccably dressed in a conservative pin-stripe suit. An extremely tight-knotted, solid blue tie gave him a wrinkled neck and a permanent red face.

Parker thought Harold should have been a bookkeeper or accountant. Precise and exacting in his cataloging in particular and in his work in general, Chapman had a passion for anything old and crusty. Artifacts, particularly anything from the *Titanic*, sent him into heat. And this, despite Federal laws prohibiting the display of articles from that ship.

Chapman had been asked to attend at the last moment. Parker waved in resignation, knowing Harold's presence was to pressure him to dive for the *Omar*.

That left a friendly-looking woman standing next to Calder.

"Come in, come in," insisted Chapman. "We were just discussing . . . "

"Uh, that deep-sea dive we spoke about yesterday morning," the bureau chief interrupted. He closed the doors and shook Parker's hand. "Thanks for flying down on short notice."

"Uh, huh," Parker mumbled and helped close the door nearest him.

The colonel nodded to Calder, briefly introduced himself, and motioned for everyone to sit. Parker saw Andy's eyes quickly roll to the ceiling in mock disgust, his usual quick smile withheld. Both chose to stand, having spent hours sitting in airports, a cramped commuter plane, and a taxi from Washington National.

Bramson continued, "Good to see you again, Dr. Parker."

"Anyone who wakes me on a Saturday morning can call me Cary."

"Of course, Cary."

The scientist noted the colonel did not say, *And you can call me Chuck*. Parker would probably do it, nonetheless. He wasn't much for formalities, after all his years aboard submersibles and ships, in close quarters with salty sailors.

"I apologize for my abruptness yesterday. But we have little time." Bramson moved back to the table. "Look, I've told you about Taylor and Dupont's plan to strip the *Titanic*. They want whatever they can pull up in a series of assaults during the next weather window."

Andy's freckled gibbous head turned almost as red as his hair. He looked at Parker as if to say, *Why the hell didn't you tell me?*

Parker's closest ally and Wood's Hole diver, Andrew "Call Me Andy" Calder could be trusted with anything. But Parker had given the colonel his word.

Known for his agreeable happy-go-lucky nature, Andy was well-respected by the entire crew. His leathery weather-beaten face belied the intelligence and warmth found underneath. He had been fortunate years before—having just graduated from San Diego State with his degree in Oceanography—to be hired on at Oceaneering International.

In 1974, OI's development team introduced the one-person, pressurized, submersible suit called *Jim*, named after the 1930's *Lusitania* explorer Jim Jarratt. Calder was with the team when they performed historic dives to 2000 feet in the Arctic. Following another five years as a Physical Oceanographer at Lamont-Doherty, he joined Parker at Woods Hole.

A member of the Woods Hole team for twelve years, Calder was brought into full partnership with their research firm, after Parker's disagreement with Henri Dupont. Unpretentious in his work and personal dealings, Calder supported Dr. Parker's contention that *Titanic* artifacts should be left on the sea floor.

Bramson glanced at Calder, "We're certain Dupont's going after the *Great Omar*. And probably anything else left after recent dives—jewelry, silver, whatever."

"Damn," Calder spoke up. "Now that we're talking about it, I heard something at a party last week. But I chalked it up to Dupont's bravado, trying to save face over his last disaster."

"What disaster?"

Parker stepped in, "South Africa confiscated over fifty million in gold bullion Dupont recovered from a Spanish galleon near Cape Town. They claimed he didn't have a permit. Ended up with a three-million dollar loss for his investors."

"No bravado here," said the colonel as he moved to the coffee pot. "And, there's more."

"More?" said Calder.

After pouring a cup, Bramson held up the pot. "Anyone?"

There were no takers.

"As I mentioned to Cary yesterday, our bureau just learned a group of terrorists also plan to dive the *Titanic*. I asked Dr. Parker not to mention it. What I couldn't say was that FBI and CIA's Mid-East bureau have jointly followed leads into the new Mafioso organization known as STAR. Heard of it?"

All but the woman shook their heads.

"STAR is an international Mafia-controlled group, formed after the Soviet coup. They're buying up black market nuclear arms from former Soviet bloc countries, and selling weapons under the table on a scale that'd make the START Treaty blush."

"Can you imagine rockets for the cost of surplus metal?" the woman broke in, the tips of her fingers leaning against the board-room table. "Nuclear warheads at ten cents on the dollar?"

"Excuse my rudeness," said Bramson. "Dr. Parker and Mr. Calder. Meet Agent Nakamura. Jennifer Nakamura, FBI. Much decorated I might add."

Nakamura greeted them with a polite nod, as they turned to listen to this slender woman—her dark hair in a French braid. To Parker, she was graceful in appearance, dressed in an elegant, yet conservative pastel suit that matched her peach-colored complexion. Serious, dark brown doe-eyes were set apart by a petite nose. And evenly spaced eyebrows complimented her oval-shaped face. Parker guessed her to be five-feet-seven and sensed an extremely self-assured woman. Long, slender fingertips left the table top as she turned with detached precision to make her point.

She stood tall and spoke with confidence.

"Over thirty thousand, mostly Soviet, nuclear weapons have inexplicably disappeared from Eastern European stockpiles."

"Unaccounted for on any government or private list," Bramson inserted.

"Soviet mercenaries will do anything to survive these days. And guess who's taking advantage of it?"

Bramson answered for her, "The Mafia, Ragem—our terrorist friend from the ALFAHAD—and the Yakusa."

"Japanese organized crime?" asked Chapman, in his annoyingly shrill voice.

"Financed by unscrupulous industrialists in Japan," Nakamura confirmed as she took a seat at the table. "Using money funneled across the Pacific Rim. Heavy on the west coast. Moving into the east, with ties to just about all our principal cities."

"What's the connection with the *Titanic*?" asked Parker.

"What I'm about to tell you," said Bramson, "I couldn't reveal over the phone. You've been cleared to receive this information. But it doesn't go outside these doors. Understood?"

They agreed.

"Our operatives in Cairo, Jeddah, and Damascus have been busy these past two years. With the upsurge of radical Islamic fundamentalism and bombings in Egypt and Saudi Arabia, the threat of NBCW— nuclear, biological and chemical warfare—has increased."

Parker and Calder knew of the monthly bombings and shootouts at most of the leading tourist sites—an attempt to trash Eqypt's economy, discourage western tourism, bring Egypt's government to its knees, and create a new fundamentalist state.

"And," Bramson sat at the table, "it's more likely NBCW will reach our homeland. Last week, free-world intelligence agencies were stunned by information our chief asset in Tripoli stumbled upon."

Bramson revealed that top crime bosses, from around the globe, had met with known heads of the Yakusa crime syndicate, in Tokyo, three months before. And that Faheed Al Mar Ragem, leader of the ALFAHAD, also attended, and brought with him two other envoys from the Islamic Brotherhood and the Al-Jama'ah. Bramson reiterated implications for terrorism on American soil, and looked to the FBI agent.

"That's where we come in," Nakamura said, and rose from her chair. "What we've learned went on there is currently being played out, big time."

Nakamura's soft features disguised the toughness she drew upon in her undercover work. She described how Libya, Iraq, and rogue-state terrorist organizations were scrambling for Soviet black-market weapons, as much as the mobsters. And how each organization had signed a blood pact, putting territorial and philosophical differences aside.

"They've agreed," Bramson picked up, "to trade in high-level weaponry, exchange intelligence and, get this . . . share in the financial benefits coming from leads that generate the sale of weapons, or from other capital joint ventures."

"They're privatizing terrorism?" said Parker.

Bramson nodded. "Taking the lead from underworld sidekicks and entrepreneurs like millionaires Osni bin Kamen and Osama bin Laden, who already finance portions of Ragem's terrorist sorties."

"That's bizarre."

The colonel explained how the need for advanced technology spurred the terrorists to breed the peculiar alliance with the underworld—particularly since their agreement would finance forays into terrorist activities abroad.

"Twenty years ago," said Bramson, "it was a gamble to dive for treasure. But with today's technology—technology you helped develop, Cary, it's become an international business."

"And now an underworld enterprise," said Nakamura. "Greed has overridden territorial and nationalist causes."

She glanced at the scientist. "The FBI has assisted CIA's Counterterrorist Center staff by involving our Joint Terrorist Task Force. And we've met with ATF to discuss potential weapons con-traband in and out of the country. Admittedly, with the federal budget cuts we have a hell of a problem on our hands with border control."

"Especially if the ALFAHAD finances terrorist activities on our soil," said the colonel. "Ragem claims he can launch hundreds of suicide missions in less than a week. Their motto is, 'No border will stop us.'"

"So this operation is a trial balloon," Parker confirmed, "and the *Great Omar* is their pilot project."

The Feds nodded in agreement, and the newcomers absorbed the information. Bramson rose and slowly circled the boardroom.

"Most terrorist groups had financial ties to collapsed communist bloc countries, but many supply-lines and fund-raising sources unraveled and dried up."

"I understand that," Parker said. "But what if the *Omar's* been destroyed by microbes? There's not much else left on board. Recent scavengers have seen to that. Except for the purser's safe and the book, divers have stripped the *Titanic* nearly clean."

Chapman sat at the table. "There's still the possibility the Guggenheim diamonds, De Beers shipped, are there. They were worth over twenty-five million when they went down. Imagine what they'd be worth today. And that doesn't count another half million or so in missing passenger jewelry."

You son-of-a-bitch, thought Parker, *you had to bring that up, didn't you?*

"Think of the treasure ships still out there," said Bramson. "If this new syndicate could locate and plunder a vessel like the *Atocha* . . . " he looked at Parker, "What're they pulling from that wreck? A hundred million in bullion and other artifacts?"

"Five hundred million," Parker corrected. "And still counting."

"Governments would kill for a stash like that. Not to mention terrorists. They'd split it ten ways to Sunday and still have enough left for bank accounts in Switzerland."

"Recently the Yakusa," said Nakamura, "through some rather

sophisticated industrial espionage, have developed a new underwater submersible crafted after the ship, the *Yamato*. They've named their new minisub *Yoritomo*."

"You're familiar with Japan's super-conducting silent electromagnetic propulsion system," said Bramson.

Parker nodded.

"I understand it rivals your new tubular system for stealth propulsion. Virtually undetectable by sonar."

"Yes."

"We hear they've miniaturized the *Yoritomo's* system to perform underwater exploration at impressive depths." Bramson downed the last of his coffee.

"And we believe the ALFAHAD will use this new sub to explore the *Titanic*."

"They're already inquiring about other treasure ships," said Nakamura.

"And we think your former partner intends to get there first. We doubt he or his millionaire investor, Taylor, know of the other parties involved."

Parker looked to Nakamura, then at the colonel. "These are dangerous people you're asking us to play with."

"I understand."

"We're just scientists."

"I know," Bramson quietly agreed. "But you're vulnerable to dangerous conditions every time you dive, aren't you?"

"Yeah, but we usually have control over the circumstances. Half-crazed divers don't come at us in the middle of a workday."

Silence invaded the room as the colonel allowed time to mull over the discussion. Then, he spoke up.

"Cary, you're the expert. A lot depends on the success or failure of the ALFAHAD's mission. Imagine a world-wide underground network with nuclear warheads and a battery of missiles strategically placed around the earth—led by fanatical zealots who'll do anything even remotely interpreted as an order from Allah."

"Not to mention," said Nakamura, "what shipments of non-nuclear artillery shells, crates of used AK-47's, and grenades might do. And there's a world harvest of land-mines out there, just waiting to be picked. Traded for loaves of bread these days."

"How far can the terrorists go on their own?" asked Calder.

"The potential's there," said Bramson, slowly tapping a pencil against the palm of his hand. "But predicting the level of world-wide destruction is difficult. At least our government has a modicum of checkpoints to prevent massive armament exchanges with the enemy."

"American companies supplying weapons through Iraqgate would be peanuts," said Nakamura, "compared to an open supply of weaponry on the Eastern European black market. And, with terrorist advisories being issued almost weekly, the odds for another catastrophe are against us."

It's finally come down to the wire, Parker thought.

The existence of an elaborately bejeweled book had been public information since initial discovery of *Titanic's* position. Cary and his colleagues had hoped the binding would be a piece of history never found or touched by human hands.

"They'll never find the book," said Parker, hoping he was right.

"They might," said the chief archivist, wishing to accept it on behalf of the Museum. "You know leather survives at tremendous depths."

Parker looked at him with disdain. "The safe's buried. They'll never get to it. That is, if the book's even in there. Many of the hull walls are paper thin from deterioration. Anyone attempting to enter the ship could be crushed."

"I don't have to remind you, the Japanese have developed a newer version of sidescan sonar. From what we hear in the trenches, it can detect objects inside other objects."

"Yeah," Parker's voice saddened with the reminder that Pacific Rim countries were now receiving more government and corporate money for research than Congress or many Fortune 500 companies would even think of allocating to science.

"Their new device can detect just about anything," Parker said matter-of-factly. "Like a safe hidden in a cargo room or buried in the sand."

"Or a large book inside the safe, if that's where the *Omar* is," concluded the colonel.

"Who's to say someone else might not try again, later?" said Parker. "Can we guarantee these groups won't find another way to finance their nefarious activities?"

"No guarantees," the colonel shrugged. "Especially when you're dealing with criminal minds."

"Or the mind of a fanatic," said Nakamura.

"The CIA's taken a lot of hits lately because of bureaucratic bungling and the lack of reliable information from our own people— not to mention what Aldrich Ames did to our credibility. But I'll tell you this, I know our information is accurate. If we don't prevent this action, you and everyone else in America can kiss your personal freedoms and securities goodbye.

"These fanatics are as suicidal as Kamikaze pilots in World War Two. And if we didn't learn from that what blind faith is, nothing'll teach us how to deal with them."

Nakamura looked directly at Parker. "They believe so strongly their acts of violence against unbelievers will attain the graces of heaven, from Allah, that they'll do anything to show their faithfulness to the *Koran* and its teachings."

"You've got agents capable of handling this," said Parker.

"We have many talented, seasoned people on board at CIA. Unfortunately, some of our newer agents and interpreters, recruited over the past ten years, don't know their asses from holes in the ground. So we're left with a very select crew. And though any one of the oceanographic institutes on the East coast are qualified to make these dives, you're the most capable."

"And best equipped," said Nakamura.

Parker stared at the colonel. He felt ensnared in a dropnet. "If you can't rely on your own people at Langley, the MSC, or the Navy, can I expect you'll bail us out if we get in a jam?"

Bramson tapped his pencil against the top of a chair back and tossed it onto the table. "I won't say 'trust me.' Just believe me. We're putting our reputations on the line. I've culled the best of our staff—the ones I can trust at CIA to follow through."

He stood with hands clasped behind him and stared at a wall diagram of the Smithsonian buildings.

"Cary," Bramson said quietly, "I'd like you to speak with contacts in London. I have a ticket for you to fly out tonight."

"What? You made these arrangements without consulting me?"

Bramson turned around. "I can cancel the tickets. But it won't solve our problem with the terrorists."

Parker could hold his anger no longer.

"Damn it, Chuck. You spring this information with little time to digest it. Then arrangements are made to fly over five time zones without a toothbrush."

"I understand how you feel." Bramson avoided condescension.

"You've wanted me on board for months. And this is how you handle it? Hell of a way to gain my confidence."

"Just make this one trip. Not for me. For yourself. You can't let the terrorists get away with it . . . let alone Dupont. First, fly to London, interview our contacts. Then decide."

Harold Chapman gloated at the end of the table, and Calder futilely searched his mind for an excuse to aid his partner.

"Think of the consequences, if we don't perform a preemptive strike," said Bramson. "We can't give in to Yakusa and ALFAHAD threats."

Parker objected, but wanted to prevent Dupont from returning to the *Titanic*. He forced himself to calm down.

"Dupont's record for scavenging is a given," said Bramson. "But who knows how far the terrorists will go."

"They know you know?"

"Not to our knowledge. The FBI and the CIA have new assets infiltrating the Yakusa here and abroad. Very dangerous assignments. But we've received thorough bits of information over the past few weeks."

Bramson pulled a United travel packet from his briefcase and slid it across the table. Parker's numbness wasn't coming from a submersible in 12,500 feet of icy water.

"Be at Dulles by eleven for check-in. It's a red-eye. You'll arrive at Heathrow at four twenty-five tomorrow afternoon."

"My passport is locked away at home, and I've no clothes."

"A duplicate passport's with your itinerary."

Parker reached for the large envelope, opened it, and laughed. "Oh, you guys are *good*. Where'd you get my picture?"

Bramson ignored the question, "You'll find an American Express card registered in your name. Use it for luggage and clothing. Or anything else you'll need."

"I've only got fifty bucks in cash. I'd need . . . "

The colonel pulled out a stack of money, and passed it to the oceanographer. Parker was running out of excuses.

"This'll tide you over. By the way, Ms. Nakamura will accompany you. She knows as much about this file as anyone. She'll visit with New Scotland Yard while you're meeting contacts about the book. You'll stay at the Claverley Hotel, in Knightsbridge, just down from Harrod's."

"Separate rooms," Nakamura interjected.

"Close to the Tube and cabbies. But stay off the open-topped double-deckers this time of year. Still too damned cold."

"We've arranged meetings with experts in U.K. who know more about the making and shipping of the *Great Omar* than anyone alive. We don't believe the others have used these resources."

"Find out what you don't know about the *Omar*. How it was constructed. The container it was shipped in. Who carried it aboard. Where it was stored versus where it might be resting if it was moved before the ship foundered. Your return ticket is open-ended. Any questions?"

"Am I allowed one last phone call?" Parker said wryly.

"Of course. You'll want to call Victoria."

Parker looked with resignation at Jennifer Nakamura. She smiled almost apologetically.

Calder glanced at his partner and sighed heavily thinking, *Here we go again.* Cary read his sentiments, winked at Calder, and shook his head in disbelief.

"We've completed our business here," said Bramson. "Ms. Nakamura will brief you on the rest of the file."

Harold smiled smugly at the thought of having the greatest modern binding in the world in his own hands.

"One final item," said Bramson. "Mr. Chapman was brought here to prepare for shipping and preservation of any artifacts located. I'm not familiar with the process, nor is Ms. Nakamura."

"As Dr. Parker is aware," the archivist said, "relics must be placed in an electrolysis bath to help items adjust to our atmospheric pressure, after coming from the abyss. It protects delicate items from being destroyed by the heavier oxygen content of the air."

"With that in mind," Bramson went on, "Harold will go along when you sail for the *Titanic*."

Chapman rose to leave, not-so-secretly pleased at the outcome of the meeting. He bid goodbye and hastily left before Parker could catch him.

Andy turned to Cary. "Anything I can do?"

"Get back to Woods Hole. But call John and the crew first. Tell 'em we'll get our collective butts in gear for a series of emergency dives in . . . " Parker looked at Bramson who shrugged an "I don't know exactly when, but soon" shrug.

"Tell them the two *Shelties* and the backup must be readied sooner than anticipated," Parker continued. "Run instrumentation tests before I return. If something critical hasn't arrived in time for installation, get it from the contractors post-haste. Don't tell them everything, yet."

The colonel nodded in agreement.

"Thank God we've had the simulator this past week," Parker continued. "Forget the Pacific program. Concentrate on North

Atlantic diving simulations. I'll do the same when I return."

"Roger that." Calder finally smiled, then turned to leave.

"I want readiness for test dives a week from tomorrow. Check with Woods Hole for booking *Neptune's Knot*. If it isn't available, we'll continue with the simulator."

"Already done," said the colonel. "Spoke with Woods Hole yesterday. The *Neptune* is ours when we need it."

Parker was surprised at Bramson's clout. He had tried to book the oceanographic explorer recently and was told it was not available until August. Something about a *National Geographic* project in the Lesser Antilles.

"What'd you do, Colonel, trade 'em an aircraft carrier?"

Bramson maintained a stoic expression.

"Okay," Parker said, "Andy, make certain Woods Hole knows we have to retrofit their ship for the other two *Shelties*."

"Roger that too. Bye."

Parker turned to Nakamura. "Shall we retire to my office?"

"Lead the way."

"I'd have thought the FBI would know it's location."

"Haven't developed our psychic powers to that extent, yet." Jennifer's eyes glistened, and Parker found her smile disarming.

He turned back to the colonel. "What'll we do about Dupont?"

"Ah yes, the French Canadiénné. I'll arrange a meeting at my office, upon your return. I hear he's in the States right now."

"Good. I've a few things I want to get off my chest. In person."

LONDON—02:45 Greenwich

BRITAIN'S C-13 Special Forces (SAS) fax-machine rang only once in the head office, then clicked to "Receiving" mode. It prepared to dispense a communication from Interpol's Terrorist Counter-Offensive Unit (TE-COU).

The night desk clerk was out getting coffee.

At 57,600 bits per second, the facsimile was conveyed in less than ten seconds. Sharp, clear halftones of perpetrators of mass murder and other terrorist activities stood out below the headlines at the top of the extended "Red Notice" pages.

—FOR IMMEDIATE DISTRIBUTION—
TERRORISTS PRESUMED TO BE IN THE
UNITED KINGDOM

Below were two pictures: the first, a front-faced, computer enhanced view of **FAHEED AL MAR RAGEM, LEADER OF THE ALFAHAD**; the second, a picture of Ragem's top henchman, **KARIM ABDUL KHORASSANI, MEMBER OF THE ALFAHAD.**

A paragraph under Ragem's picture described him as:

> 39 years of age, 6 feet 4 inches, 210 pounds; light brown to reddish hair; brown eyes; gray and brown mustache; master of disguise; armed and dangerous. Hijacked British Airways Flight 1004, with 31 lives lost in on-the-ground shootout, and from explosion of a live grenade; the bombing of El Al Flight 643, 179 lives lost; bombing of Israeli Embassy in Buenos Aires; assassination of Egyptian Ambassador to the U.N., Hamad Khalid; kidnap and murder of two American diplomats, and three British Petroleum executives; and conspiracy to bomb sites in France, Britain, and the United States. Suspected of arranging sale of missiles and conventional armaments between former Soviet states and Mid-Eastern contacts.

To look at Ragem's picture was to see a man who might be an executive with a top Fortune 500 company. His thinning and receding hairline met with a tall forehead. A protruding cleft chin— he had been known to fill in with mortician's putty—and high cheek bones complemented a thin nose, less sharp than most of his contemporaries. Large ears matched his long face. His closely trimmed light brown mustache contained flecks of gray that made him look at least five years older. Deep-set angry eyes and a slightly pouting mouth gave him away, and told of an ominous past rippled with dark and evil secrets.

Under the facsimile's picture of **KARIM ABDUL KHORASSANI**, the description read:

> 38 years of age, 6 feet 6 inches, 265 pounds; cropped, curly black hair; left eye brown, right eye green; full black beard and mustache; large scar on lower left side of neck; armed and very dangerous . . .

The list of assaults duplicated those of Ragem's. But, added to the list were additional crimes of rape and mutilation, sabotage and mayhem.

To the authorities, Khorassani was an amoral psychopathic killer with no sense of right or wrong. Charged with carrying out terrorist activities for the ALFAHAD, Khorassani basked in the glory that came with each assignment. Beyond Ragem's political rationalizations, Abdul had no conscience.

To gaze at his picture was to gaze into the eyes of a man with no knowledge of shame or remorse. His large, wide nose sat atop tightly held lips that filled his huge expressionless face, and was tucked between vacant eyes that shined only when death was close.

A paragraph at the bottom of the sheet read, "**Faheed Al Mar Ragem was sighted in Belfast, then eluded authorities. May have crossed the North Channel. REPORT SIGHTINGS IMMEDIATELY TO INTERPOL, NEW SCOTLAND YARD, OR APPROPRIATE ENFORCEMENT AGENCY. CALL 0171-555-1455 FOR ASSISTANCE.**"

The FAX-phone rang again. An innocuous looking transmission came through from Northern Ireland, reporting the availability of a booklet on terrorist safehouses in rural villages. It covered the transmission from INTERPOL.

The night clerk strolled back to his desk, kicked his feet up, leaned back, and took a catnap.

ABOVE THE ATLANTIC

UNITED Flight 1161 had been cruising at forty-one thousand feet for nearly two and a half hours. For Parker and Nakamura, much of the onboard time had been filled with small talk, obligatory smiles to avoid confrontation, and paging through the airline magazine.

Eventually, Parker put on his headset, tuned into classical music, and pulled out the most recent copy of *Lloyd's Maritime and Commercial Law Quarterly*, taken from his desk. An article on the International Court of Justice and the law of the sea drew his interest— since he was quoted from a case study written several years before.

Nakamura had settled in, first reviewing files from her briefcase, then using the time to relax. Accustomed to commuting between continents on short notice, as a leading expert on underworld gun-running and terrorist incursions into the U.S., Nakamura was constantly on the move between the United States, Italy, Russia and the Mid-East.

"From the Windy City to the world," she would say when friends glamorized her job—imagining her as a tourist on the Mediterranean, or as a visitor to the sphinx of Queen Hatshepsut— totally unaware of Nakamura's time spent in clandestine or otherwise boring meetings.

Jennifer looked at Parker, immersed in his journal. She tapped him lightly on the shoulder, and spoke over the loud humming of the engines.

"I was just thinking . . . "

Parker was irritated at the interruption, but he shifted an

earphone aside.

"What was that?"

"Do you have friends who imagine your job fascinating, though in reality it's routine?"

Parker looked curiously at her.

"You know . . . flying from one place to another. Attending meetings. Then leaving on assignment to a different part of the world—no time to enjoy the scenery."

"I suppose my life's similar. Yes."

"Of course, diving to the bottom of the sea can't possibly be boring."

"It's anything but boring." He pulled off his earphones. "But when I'm two thousand fathoms below the surface, having trouble with equipment, it's generally me against known odds." He turned to face her directly.

"I can't imagine it's routine, confronting criminals and terrorists who hide in dark corners with their thirty-eight super automatics."

"It's all relative isn't it? You put your trust in your crew and equipment, to do your job at two thousand . . . fathoms?"

"At six feet per, that's twelve thousand feet below the surface."

"Well, I trust my fellow officers, equipment, and knowledge of the circumstances won't fail me when something critical goes down. When I'm out there with the underworld, or tracking a terrorist cell, I'm hoping my cover won't be blown, and everything will come down in our favor."

"Sounds stressful. How do you deal with the fear factor?"

Jennifer sat up, crossed both legs in the lotus position, and let her French braid flow out into waves around her shoulders. "I try to rule fear out of my life."

She looked at Parker and smiled, her flowing black hair glistened in the overhead reading light. "I heard Rosa Parks say that once . . . the first black arrested in Selma for refusing to move from the white section of the bus."

"Insightful."

"I imagine you'd react the same, searching for an underwater wreck in complete darkness. Kinda' like me in a dark alley, never knowing what I'll run into."

"Fortunately, we have sidescan sonar when a porthole won't do."

"For me—if under attack, I always rely on the Mozambique Technique."

"What's that?"

"Two shots to the body and one to the head, in case the attacker's wearing body armor. Instinct really."

"With or without sights?"

"Depending on tactical setting, usually without. Most of the time, I've only needed it for target practice."

"I think I'm outgunned."

No doubt, Agent Nakamura led a considerably dangerous life. Though awarded the Medal of Freedom by the President of the United States, at age thirty-four, for voluntary work with impoverished families, and presented many meritorious recognition awards for bravery by the time she was thirty-five, Agent Nakamura took it in her stride.

Proud to be FBI, no matter what the political conflict or scandal at the time, she avoided unethical practices, performed her job well, and let the Senate oversight committee take care of the rest— *not that some congressmen don't need oversight themselves*, she would say when questioned about it.

Raised in Chicago, Jennifer had been a free-spirited tomboy from an upper middle-class family. They owned the most popular Japanese restaurant on Michigan Avenue—just down the street from Orchestra Hall.

Jenny, as all her friends called her, had made a life of befriending underprivileged youth. Many came from Cabrini; others from the remaining old Italian community southwest of the Loop; and from the North side Japanese community.

Her parents encouraged her to attend the Oriental Institute

for Near Eastern Studies, at the University of Chicago. But under a unique Hutchins Plan scholarship program at U. of C., she took an interest in the social sciences and graduated early, with honors, having started there in her junior year of high school. Her Masters in Sociology was completed before age twenty-two.

As quickly as Nakamura made the decision to enter law enforcement, she was accepted into the FBI Academy. Accelerated grade point average, and recommendations from the university president and two senators enhanced her standing.

Sent directly to Quantico for sixteen weeks of basic training, she excelled in the Emergency Vehicle Operator's Course (EVOC) for defensive driving. Skills, quick response, and ability to handle cars at high-speed earned her special attention. Over the years Nakamura returned to Quantico where she took advanced in-service coursework and training in strategy and tactics in counter-terrorism, undercover operations, explosives, weaponry and new technology—areas in which she had expressed intense interest, and for which she displayed strong proficiencies and aptitude.

"I have to admit, I feel like odd man out," said Parker. "Along with CIA, you've obviously had access to my file, and know much more about me than I of you. Frankly, that pisses me off."

Jennifer blushed slightly, knowing she had a very unfair advantage, but could not resist rubbing it in.

"Let's see. . . . Graduated Cum Laude from Stanford, with a B.S. in Archeology in '76, an M.S. in Oceanography in '78, and you completed your Doctorate in maritime law in '81. Somehow, in your spare time, you played tight-end on a two-thirds football scholarship, based on grades and athletic prowess. And you made up the remainder of your educational expenses through summer assignments with Lamont Doherty and other oceanographic institutions."

She touched him lightly on the center of his forehead, "This is a measles pock-mark, and there's a series of red marks on your left side, slightly above the waist—relics of an entanglement with a

Portuguese Man-of-War jellyfish in the Indian Ocean. Your wife . . . "

"All right, enough about me. What about you, Ms. Nakamura? Based on our meeting at the Smithsonian, I suspect you've been involved in a number of mafia cases. Right?"

"I've never counted," she said, hesitant to say too much, since most of her early undercover assignments with the Bureau had centered around mob-related busts in the states of Pennsylvania and Virginia. Except for the Capustroni case. The one that brought her quiet recognition she deserved. . . . And nearly got her assassinated in New York.

"I'll tell you one thing, though. After viewing underworld activities from within the Bureau, I've concluded Chicago's taken a bum rap as the mob-capital of the world."

"With the syndicate's history of under-the-table fixes and rigs over Chicago's fifty wards? Even I know they've held economic and political control for years."

"Tentacles from underworld activities, even within state and local politics, reach every level."

It disgusted Nakamura and made her cynical to think what she had learned of certain politicians.

"Ms. Nakamura . . . "

"I think we're ready for Jenny by now."

"Of course. And call me Cary."

Nakamura smiled broadly, hoping she had dispelled any anger that remained. She found Parker attractive, and wished the trip to be more pleasant.

"Look, Jenny," Parker said with a nervous laugh, uncomfortable at bringing up the subject, "This terrorism thing . . .I'm accustomed to being out on the open sea. Terrorism is another subject. To me, this is something . . . "

"You only read about in newspapers . . . "

"Yeah. Or the evening news. I've never been exposed to this warfare, if I can call it that."

"That's what I'd call it."

"I remember when it was guerrilla warfare."

"A poor-man's war. And that hasn't changed much. But for terrorists—a high return on a relatively small investment."

"You sound like my stock broker."

"I'm serious. We're in the middle of a paradigm shift in the control of weapons of mass destruction. An equalization of the type of Cold War power the super-powers utilized to hold back the opposite side."

"Tools for negotiation."

"Until recently, most world governments wouldn't admit terrorists have gained access and control of the black market weapons stores. Uncontrollable small cells of terrorists are on a nearly equal footing any time they manage to pull off an attack."

"Or use weapons as bargaining chips?"

"Yes. And with help from Hussein or Qadhafi, they're able to distribute biological weapons that could randomly kill more people than conventional warfare. Most aren't aware the Trade Center bomb had a biological attachment that didn't explode. Can you imagine the devastation if it had?"

Nakamura shrugged. "Every time we turn around, Congress cuts the intelligence budget under the guise the Cold War is over and there's no need to monitor the enemy. The perceived enemy, as we understood it during the Cold War, is a ghost. And ghosts come back to haunt. But the true enemy is a poltergeist. . . . One that's ready to pop up from nowhere and destroy our way of life if he doesn't get what he wants."

"God knows I'm not an expert," said Parker, " . . . beyond deep-seated political injustices, from their viewpoint, there's also the constant violence of retribution."

"Exactly. And retribution begets reprisal, that begets retaliation. An entire dictionary of violence has been created to describe the vindictiveness that all-consuming hatred breeds. Before we know it, the hatred runs so deep, a dowser couldn't find it."

A usually upbeat Nakamura was suddenly drained. She leaned her head against the seatback, let out a long sigh, and paused to regain her composure. Parker saw her eyes glisten.

"We refuse to deal with the real issues and understand why a Palestinian or an Israeli—or an Irish Catholic or Protestant—vows vengeance when a member of their family is torn to pieces by shrapnel from a pipe bomb, or from an incendiary device tossed into a crowded marketplace."

"But terrorists approach conflict from a pretty basic stance, don't they?"

"It's more complicated than that. Terrorists from the Mideast are controlled by their psyche. They're predisposed to a subjective and introspective view of the world, because of their personal link with the *Koran*, Islam, and the Prophet Mohammed. For fundamentalists, every thought, each movement, and all decisions made are governed by their religion."

"And their history and politics is their religion . . . "

"Precisely. If all Americans lived that way, I'd give you a Kewpie doll."

Parker sat back. "And that's enough to justify decades of murder and mayhem from one continent to another . . . "

Nakamura nodded.

Time on the plane became less tiresome as Parker and Nakamura debated and discussed related subjects through the night.

The rising sun greeted the wide-body jet as it cruised high over the North Atlantic. Viewing the distant ocean from a cloudless vantage point reminded Parker of their mission—and of the *Titanic*, resting quietly in its own sea of tranquility over 53,000 feet below.

———

PART II

PART 1

HEATHROW AIRPORT, LONDON—Monday
16:05 Greenwich Mean Time

"ANNOUNCING arrival of Air India passengers, flight 461, from Rome, Gate 32. Announcing boarding for Iberia flight 622, to to Madrid, Gate 47. Please have passports and boarding passes available for immediate boarding." The loudspeaker faded into the background of the congested lobby of Terminal 3.

Faheed Al Mar Ragem watched from a safe distance opposite the ticket counters. A cigarette loosely dangled from his lip in mock disinterest, as his calculating eyes measured distances and confirmed escape routes. *The Times of London* in hand, Ragem nodded imperceptibly to signal approval, as each member of his feared ALFAHAD moved into place.

Each had arrived separately from different starting points after their final meeting in Belfast, three nights before. Just before their incident with Irish terrorists over a black market weapons deal, and with an unfortunate young Irish couple who stumbled upon their meeting, their attack plan was reviewed several times to assure its success. Fake passports and other I.D. were foolishly provided by offshoot members of the U.F.F. and the I.R.A., in Belfast——both groups tricked to believe they could trade ALFAHAD for Soviet weapons.

"Announcing arrival of United passengers, Flight 1009, from New York, Gate 14 . . . "

Terminal 3 had been chosen, considering the larger airlines that served western infidel countries. The location had not been chosen for convenience of escape. The Underground and bus system was closer to Terminal 1 than 3. The main roads and highways were blocked with late afternoon traffic. And the peripheral entrance and egress roads were jammed with airport transfer buses, cabbies, lorries and autos waiting to load or unload passengers, baggage and cargo.

Of course, thought Ragem, *much of that will work to our benefit.*

The area would be crawling with security, once the attack took place. Individual escape routes would depend on deception and quick thinking.

It was unfortunate that Emirates Airway and several other third-world airlines operated from there. The occasion chosen for their attack was when the least number of Arabic nationals might be in the terminal. Allah would praise and bless their sacrifice.

"Paging Mr. John MacMillan. Please pick up the courtesy white phone for a message. Attention, Dr. Alistar Benedict, please meet your family at southeast entrance on lower level Terminal 3."

The airport was unusually busy for the season. A beautiful Pakistani mother held her little girl's hand as the woman happily moved across the Plaza to meet her husband. School children from Falconwood gathered with chaperones near Combs Pharmacy. Each had bought sweets following an airport tour. Businessmen entered H.L. Smyth-Clothiers to kill time before departure. Long queues formed at Bureau de Change windows. And hundreds of departing and arriving passengers busily moved from point to point to make connections, meet families, or get to hotels.

The smell of deep-fried fish and chips wafted through the terminal and mixed with the aroma of grilled steaks, hamburgers, and the sweet smells of homemade fudge and Cadbury's chocolate.

This is a coup for the ALFAHAD, Ragem thought. He quietly laughed, deep in his throat, as he reflected for an instant.

The Soviet Union had fallen apart and, except for ethnic cleansing and border disputes, Ragem felt the Russian Commonwealth of Independent States was no longer getting the attention it had first commanded. With the exception of the fundamentalist movement in Egypt, and skirmishes over repatriation of Palestinians in the Gaza Strip, the Middle East was thought to be relatively quiet. This despite continued hampering of the Mideast Peace Accord by assassinations and bombings inside Palestinian and Israeli borders.

Preceding the bombing of the World Trade Center, no one had taken the ALFAHAD seriously. Americans smugly felt their country was untouchable until the Center's bombing scored points for international terrorism. To Ragem it was more of a setback than a victory considering their sloppiness in pulling it off.

Now, the moment had come to signal their intention to pursue assaults on foreign soil—attacks with clear international significance. They would remind the world of their commitment to the cause—and how serious their intent. The media would explode with instant coverage of this incident. And the world would know how truly resolved they could be.

It's been quiet too long, thought Ragem as he casually glanced toward a nearby toy store.

Adnan Rashid had concealed five pounds of Semtex next to a plastic bobbing duck, outside the shop's entrance. Several small children gazed in wonder at the movement of the toy, pleading all the while to "Buy that one, Mummy!" "Get this one, Daddy!"

Four of the toilet facilities had been rigged with plastic explosives to detonate on cue. Rashid had casually left two books, their insides carved out and loaded with bombs, on seats next to The Soap Shop and Healthfood stores. And he carried a briefcase molded from and weighted down with ten additional pounds of Semtex, and a radio transmitter that would set off all bombs as soon as he pushed on the combination lock. He would not go through any of the secure checkpoints, but patiently waited for the assigned moment in the upstairs food court.

The "pregnant" Zaynab sat inside the sandwich bar not far

from the terminal entrance where check-in lines had been backed up all day. Her false stomach would give birth to a satanic explosion within a matter of minutes. Zaynab began to breath deeply, to relax and clear her mind of the world encircling her—hands calmly clasped around her protruding belly full of explosives. Admiring mothers passed by and smiled at her condition.

She and Adnan Rashid felt blessed and honored when they were chosen for the mission. Both would praise Allah moments before their suicide blasts. His will be done.

Only Karim Abdul Khorassani, Atak Abu Rahman, Haji Al-Masud, and Subhi Al-Mamun would have to wait for their ultimate predestined reward. They were spread out just far enough from one another, back-to-back at the center of the terminal, ready to spray a complete circle of death in front of them. No eye contact was needed beyond this point.

As promised, their newly acquired XE-47's would not show up on the metal detector screens if they needed to move through the Linescan X-ray machines. Every piece of the new gun—including bullets—was made of steel-hardened Teflon. The compact XE's had been injection-molded just outside Bromley, England, making it possible to test the small machine gun's "invisible" properties at Biggen Hill Airport before the financial transaction for over 1000 units took place. It also meant the deadly guns would not have to be smuggled into the country. Only out. And that was easy.

Small enough to fit inside large, specially sewn pockets, in the terrorist's baggy-styled Armani pants, the 100-shot detachable magazines spit small, explosive, blunted plastic bullets at an average muzzle velocity of 1390 feet per second—a deadly pace. At point-blank range, there was no worry about effectiveness. The terrorists finally had something to get excited about—a solid, undetectable match for the Israeli Uzi or the old Soviet Kalashnikov.

———

NEW SCOTLAND YARD, LONDON
16.18 Greenwich Mean Time

"GOD almighty!" exclaimed the commissioner of New Scotland Yard. John Lawton placed his phone in its cradle. His usually sanguine face turned ashen. Without removing his hand, he picked up the receiver. A four-digit autodial security code brought up an instant conference call for a predetermined group of local and international forces dealing with terrorism.

Immediately the call was directed to the heads of MI-5 Security, C-13, SAS, all British international airport security departments, and New Scotland Yard's Division Heads. It also connected with local offices for CIA, FBI, Israel's Mossad, and the recently admitted replacement for the KGB elite anti-terrorist Alpha Group, known as the Secretariat for International Investigations (SII)— now with a small out-of-the-way office in Kensington.

Each organization had treaties with Britain and held membership in Interpol. All secured phone lines were picked up before the second ring.

"Lawton here. *BBC* just received an anonymous tape. Damndest development. We've been warned of a possible terrorist attack at Heathrow within the next twenty-four hours. But it must be treated as imminent. Rather bizarre—the warning uses a Sinn Fein code." Lawton's dove gray eyes searched his mind for answers.

"Must be a connection with the Interpol circular we received this morning on Ragem and his ALFAHAD," said the local head of the Mossad. "The piece fits the puzzle. Any more information?"

"We don't know if they're going for planes, people or both," said Lawton. "Anyone pick up anything?"

"T-COU's circular reported Ragem in Belfast yesterday," came a quick reply from the the head of C-13. "But we had a slip-up in the office last night. The Alert didn't get to me until quite late this morning.

"Manchester notified us Ragem has already slipped across North

Channel and made it possibly as far as Birmingham. One of our operatives spotted him at Liverpool's train station, but was eluded by Ragem before help arrived."

"Something's going on," said the voice from MI-5. "There may be a connection between Ragem and the murder of an unlucky young couple who chanced on an IRA safehouse Friday night—their throats slit from ear to ear. Not an M.O. typically associated with IRA. No fingerprints for Ragem. But they found prints for his top lieutenant, Khorassani. Seems there was a joint meeting that went awry. Sean Paisley and John Springer were both mortally wounded. Why U.L.F.'s Paisley was in an IRA safehouse defies logic. But the youth—the unfortunate dead young man, had the letters 'AL' and an unfinished line, in blood on the palm of his hand. The blood-type matched Springer's. Our guess is the 'AL' was Springer's way of saying ALFAHAD before he croaked."

"Not a good sign," said Lawton. "Spread the circular everywhere." Pensively, his fingers combed thick silver hair straight back. "Lawrence, are you there?"

"Here sir," answered Gerald Lawrence, Chief of Airport Security, Heathrow. "The circular's coming in, sir."

"Distribute at once."

"We're inundated with travelers. It'll be a miracle if we spot anyone now. But we'll give it a go."

"If Ragem's involved, he's there. We're activating T-Plan A. Cover every entrance. Have London Control hold all planes. Redirect large airborne to Gatwick and Foulness—smaller planes to Rochester, Southend or Biggen Hill. If fuel's low, work it out best you can. Look for bombs and watch out for sprayguns. Try to hold until SF gets there. But do what you have to do. Don't wait for the rest of this conversation. You know the drill. Go!"

"Done!"

A click on the line and a red light going off on an electronic wall-board signaled Lawrence was already in action.

"Townsend, mobilize SAS to Heathrow. Especially the bomb squad. Take every copter and personnel carrier at your disposal."

"Yes, sir."

"Contact London Transport. Have them slow down the tubes. Block every U.G. entrance and exit from Heathrow Central on out. Be wary of false-looking wigs, mustaches, and other hair pieces. Ragem's a master of disguise. Get him and any of his band alive. But take the bloody buggers down if you must save civilian lives. They're busier than hell out there."

The commissioner checked the giant wall map opposite his desk and continued, "Move Mobile Op to Heathrow's back gate, off Great West at A30, north of Staines Road. We'll keep all priority lines open for you."

"Right, Commissioner."

Another click off the line.

T-Plan-A, short for "Terrorist Attack Imminent—Highest Priority," directed coverage with pairs of soldiers, placed in concentric circles, throughout the entire airport and outlying area. SAS would coordinate personnel from military and civilian police branches. Each group would be staggered no more than 200 yards apart in any direction. Every road in or out of Heathrow would be blocked all the way out for 3 miles.

All airport runways would shut down. Baggage carriers and conveyors would slow, at first, then freeze in place. Airport personnel would be placed quietly on alert with photos of terrorists delivered to all stations.

Ticket issuance would be intentionally slowed to a crawl to allow for counter-to-counter searches and possible identification of the terrorists—if still arriving on site.

As a precaution, every hospital administrator, ambulance company, firehouse and emergency volunteer group would be placed on alert, in case of emergency or casualties. They would be considered as "Tier 2" level security, having no information regarding possible cause. It would be treated as a highly regarded "test situation" until further notice.

"Gatwick, you still there?"

"Yes, sir."

"You know the rules. Follow the plan. You won't have ground forces for backup if they've pulled a switch on us. Get all available security on heightened alert and cover your ass. Your air lanes will double from this moment on. So give your Traffic Controllers shots of adrenaline and caffeine. We don't need any mid-airs right now."

"Already ordered full alert."

"Good going man. Keep me informed."

Another line clicked off.

"Five?" Lawton asked for the MI-5 Commander.

"Sir."

"The Queen's back from Windsor Castle. We don't know how many terrorists are in country, so double your security around the three P's. Use T-Code to access the Queen and Prime Minister. If the press inquires, quote Shakespeare, but hold on anything else. It's 16.21. My god, the rush hour is on. Use the bus lanes. Don't bloody waste time."

As the Plan was implemented, intense security covered the "3-P's" as they were called—The Palace, Parliament, and Prime Minister's residence. SAS moved to the "Royal Triangle," shielding an area roughly from Whitehall and Victoria Embankment at the bend of River Thames, near King's Reach, to points stretching through Piccadilly, and The Mall, then to Knightsbridge, and down Grosvenor Place and Buckingham Palace Road on the north and west sides.

Security would extend over Victoria Street and beyond, on the south, over to and including Lambeth Palace Road, between Lambeth and Westminster Bridges, covering Parliament from the eastside of River Thames.

Lawton was left with the heads of the international bureaus.

"We'll set up field operations and communications at our Mobile base," he said. " . . . just outside Heathrow. Your people know anything new about these buggers?"

Mitchell, of CIA, answered first, "Langley's been following Ragem for the past two weeks. Colonel Bramson's Mideast Bureau thought they had a handle on him. But he played chameleon and disappeared into the woodwork in Oman."

A buzzer interrupted the conference call.

"Yes?" said the Commissioner.

"Sir, Lawrence here. All planes have been redirected and will check in if problems. So far, no alarms in the air. All airport doors are covered and T-Plan is in effect."

Another buzzer.

"Lawton, here."

"Townsend, sir. SF is out in force. The mobile unit should be in place in less than 15 minutes, with communications up within five minutes after arrival. And Underground is taking all precautions."

"Keep me informed."

Back to the directors on line, "We're within minutes of being fully operational. Moshe, anything from your side?"

"Ragem's eluded us completely," said Moshe Levy of Israel's Mossad. "If he was in Belfast yesterday, he's moving quickly to pull this off."

The Russian SII Director broke in, "With Ragem anything is possible. Libya helps float him in and out of heaven and hell whenever he needs assistance. We've not been able to contain either since the Putsch."

Lawton wasn't comfortable expressing what he knew, since the previous Soviet government had funded Ragem through covert operations.

The directors knew Ragem for what he was—one of the coldest perpetrators of violence. He perceived people as entities within a religious or sociopolitical framework, not as human beings. For Ragem and his supporters, even children had no innocence. Calculated assassination, murder, abduction and torture served to coerce the political systems with which they were at odds.

The irony of this potential attack was clear as they were forced to protect vulnerable people and sites of their political houses, modern transportation systems, commerce and international trade—the obvious reasons terrorists were so successful.

Nothing was sacred or safe.

If terrorists could not hold people as hostages, in one way or another they would hold all the playing cards in the western world's deck—weaponry, transportation and communication—at one time or another.

The ease of obtaining weaponry; the smaller scale of weapons; the irony of instantaneous communications and media coverage; the swiftness of modern travel, all contributed to the successful murderous outcomes of terrorist organizations such as the ALFAHAD.

"Frankly, I'm praying it's a hoax," said Ron Bantam, FBI. "Along with your potential for calamity, we've got Agent Nakamura . . . in the air and arriving at Heathrow at any moment with one of CIA's operatives on that *Titanic* project."

"That's right," CIA's Mitchell interjected. "We were to meet with you in the morning."

"Isn't their investigation connected with the ALFAHAD?"

"Ragem's a busy son-of-a-bitch."

"Yes, well, if their plane hasn't landed already they should have been directed on to Gatwick or Foulness," said Lawton. "What's their flight number?"

"Eleven sixty-one. United," said Bantam. "I have a driver at Heathrow waiting to pick them up."

"Better get your driver out of there."

Lawton entered a restricted code into his computer, punched up the international carrier reservation system, accessed United, and entered the flight number.

"Hasn't landed yet. We'll shuttle them from Gatwick. Shall we meet at Mobile Op?"

"We'd be grateful," said Bantam.

"I'll arrange private transport to pick you up. You'd never get by the roadblocks. My secretary will patch you through to the plane. Hold the line."

Inspector Wingate entered the office. "Sir, your helicopter is ready."

"Right." Lawton concluded his conference call, and all lights went off the board as he switched the FBI agent to his secretary.

He glanced across the room at Wingate. "Now it's a waiting game. Let's go."

———

"T-Plan A" took effect immediately. Airport Security Forces instantly received information and took action. Ragem's photo and that of Khorassani came in first, followed by data regarding known accomplices Haji Al-Masud and Atak Abu Rahman. No one was aware of Subhi Al-Mamun, Adnan Rashid, or the "pregnant" terrorist Zaynab's identity—the latter two recently recruited into the organization to serve Allah. Expendable for the cause.

Chief Airport Inspector Clive Harper, assigned to alert international carriers in Terminal 3, moved casually between counters to avoid panicking travelers. Lanky and taller than most, he vigilantly scrutinized every passenger—all the while smiling a broad smile.

Harper approached a counter as the baggage carriers and conveyors slowed, at first, then came to a stop.

A voice came over his MX300 radio earphone. "Sir, confirming power is out to the conveyor systems until ordered otherwise." Harper pressed a button on his portable unit, sending a *message received* double-beep sound back to the senior electrician.

As the whirring from miles of conveyors diminished, a first-level silence was evident only to the inspector and a select few. But as seconds ticked by, passengers noticed the change and questioned anyone official-looking.

Harper spoke intentionally out loud as he proceeded past Air India's counter. "Must be a power outage. I'll get the crew right on it." He repeated the message as he delivered his ID photo sheets to counter personnel.

Passengers were mildly irritated by the thought of any delay in travel plans. Especially at rush hour.

The Chief Inspector's inner strengths had been put to the test before. But this was truly the closest he had come to dealing directly with the possibility of terrorists on his own turf, since he took the position three years before. The IRA bombings in the business district, Victoria Station, South Kensington and some of the other subway stations had been hit by terrorists. Even a Kentucky Fried Chicken shop in Camden.

They had been luckier at Heathrow. Only dummy mortar shells from IRA, so far—and this despite a truce. But the odds had turned against them that some type of fanatic could get through.

Assistant inspectors carried the classified information to various security sectors in Terminals 1, 2, and 4. Counter personnel used the power outage excuse to slow down ticket issuance. Lines backed up toward the main doors as the first announcements emanated from the public address system.

"Ladies and gentlemen, your attention, please. Flight departures have been temporarily suspended until further notice. To repeat, flight departures have . . . "

Passengers looked toward the arrival/departure video monitors, placed throughout the terminal. Fears were confirmed. Virtually every plane was listed as "Delayed." Passengers, with nowhere to go, wearily tolerated the announcement. A few suspected the reason and evacuated the terminal.

United Flight 1161 from Dulles International had begun its descent in preparation for landing at Heathrow when, less than sixty miles out, at seventeen thousand feet descending to eleven thousand, a cryptic two-part message had been transmitted to the flight crew from London Control.

All inbound planes received the same message. One: they were to be on guard against, and check in immediately with any news or indications of terrorist activities, potential highjackings, or suspicious passengers. Two: all large inbound flights to Heathrow would be diverted to Gatwick or Foulness—immediately placed in holding patterns—and classified by fuel status for alternate landings between planes already scheduled for either airport. Smaller planes would divert to regionals.

Captain Rinehart glanced at his flight crew with a questioning look and responded to London Control.

"London, United flight eleven-six-one. Over."

"Go ahead eleven-six-one."

"Uh, roger your inquiry. Negative regarding problems on board. Will keep eyes open. Request new heading and divert frequency."

"Roger eleven-six-one. Amend altitude to flight level one-six-zero. Proceed direct Gatwick when able. Reduce and hold two-five-zero knots for spacing into Gatwick. Over."

"Roger. Level one-six-zero. Able Direct Gatwich at this time," Rinehart confirmed. He took the plane to sixteen thousand feet, changed his heading and reduced speed.

"United eleven-six-one. Contact Gatwick tower at ten miles out on one-six-two-point-one. Over."

"Confirm, one-six-two-point-one. Good day."

Rinehart's navigator plotted the new course and potential fuel consumption to cover delays, noting they had less than three hours of fuel. At ten miles out, Captain Rinehart switched from London Control to the Gatwick frequency.

"Uh, Gatwick. United eleven-six-one on divert from Heathrow. Over."

"Go ahead eleven-six-one."

"Holding at flight level one-six-zero, for further instructions on direct Gatwick heading, at two-five-zero knots. Over."

"Gatwick, roger. Expect holding instructions. Give fuel

status."

"Two plus hours hold, with no problems, if traffic is running on less. Over."

"United eleven-six-one, roger and thank you. Descend and maintain at flight level one-two-zero. Cleared direct Gatwick, hold on the zero-niner-zero radial, right turns, one-five mile legs. Expect further clearance at one-six-five-five Zulu time. Over."

"Confirm EFC of one-six-five-five Zulu. Advise traffic condition. Over."

"Traffic heavy. Expect to hold an hour."

"Gatwick, roger. What's reason for diversion?"

There was a long pause.

"Gatwick, any word?"

"Uh, eleven-six-one, we have little information. Purely precautionary stance, Captain."

"Roger that." Then Captain Rinehart asked one question that gave him more answers than he probably wanted. "Will buses and trains be running?"

"No word on that, captain. Trains on hold. Will inform as we receive new data. Gatwick over."

Captain Rinehart looked at the navigator of their 747 widebody. It was standard procedure to hold trains and buses if suspected IRA activities were occurring. But to check for potential terrorist activities on board planes, then divert from an airport meant something more delicate and dangerous had developed. Rinehart silently prayed there were no live Barometric Improvised Explosive Devices on board—the type that took down Pan Am 103.

Groans and murmurs erupted from the main cabin, following Captain Rinehart's obligatory announcement of the Gatwick divert. Passengers contemplated changes in plans, families and friends waiting on the ground back at Heathrow, or the delay in getting transport.

The Captain continued, "Uh, weather on the ground should be about forty-six degrees Fahrenheit, eight degrees Celsius, winds out of the north at . . . ”

The Captain interrupted his message to receive an encrypted call on a special phone. Then he resumed consoling passengers, hardly missing a beat.

“Northerly winds at ten miles per hour—slightly overcast. Visibility about fifteen miles on the ground. Flight attendants will provide you with anything you need to be comfortable until our arrival. Uh . . . we’ll keep you informed as we, ah, approach our turn for landing.” The microphone clicked off with a burst of static, then clicked back on once more.

“Will the chief flight attendant please report to the cockpit?”

Nakamura turned to Parker.

“What do you think it is?”

“No idea.” said Parker. “Seems a little odd. Didn’t sound like they’re anticipating wind shear.”

“Maybe the IRA issued a new threat.”

“But it wouldn’t make sense to try anything now,” said Parker. “Negotiations have gone too well.”

“Must be serious if they’re diverting to Gatwick.”

“Who’d you say is meeting us at Heathrow?”

“Excuse me,” The chief flight attendant interrupted, whispering loud enough to hear over the jet engines. “According to our seating chart, the two of you should be Ms. Nakamura and Dr. Parker.”

“Yes. May we help you?” said Parker.

“The Captain requests your company in the cockpit. You have a call.”

“May we take it on a cabin phone?” Parker said.

“The call’s directly patched to the cockpit.”

Nakamura threw a questioning look to Parker as she rose from her seat. “Do you know who’s on the other end?” she asked the steward.

“A Mr. Ron Bantam, I believe.”

"The agent arranging for our Heathrow pickup," she said. "Must be new instructions." The three moved to the plane's foresection.

Captain Rinehart greeted them at the cockpit door. He skipped introductions, though he managed to break a friendly smile.

"Come in, please." He glanced down the aisle beyond them, as they entered the cockpit, excused the attendant—asking him to remain close by—then closed and locked the door.

Rinehart handed Nakamura a portable satellite encrypted phone.

"Agent Nakamura, here. Dr. Parker is next to me."

"This is Ron Bantam in London, Ms. Nakamura. Can you hear me?"

"Yes."

"My apologies for the inconvenience you'll be going through. But there are serious problems on the ground."

Agent Bantam explained circumstances involving the anticipated attack and what the British were doing to head it off. With her hand cupped over the phone, Nakamura relayed the essence of the conversation to Parker.

Bantam continued, "I can't greet you at Gatwick, but an SAS helicopter will bring you to Mobile Op for the counter-offensive operation. We'll want to meet with you immediately. You'll be quickly cleared through Customs."

"Any suspects?"

"The ALFAHAD," said the encrypted voice. Nakamura looked at Parker. The captain, monitoring the call for security, glanced up from his phone, knowing they were treacherous.

"Put Dr. Parker on," said Bantam. Nakamura handed over the phone.

"Dr. Parker?"

"I'm listening."

The scrambled voice continued. "Ms. Nakamura will give you the details on our change in plans. Colonel Bramson asks that you continue with scheduled appointments. But be prepared if we have to appropriate your services."

"Understood," he said, uncertain what he could do to help.

"That's all. Don't want to take more air time at Captain Rinehart's expense. Thank you Captain."

"No problem. Over and out." The captain turned to his cabin guests. "We've been through this drill before. We feel helpless, knowing what could be going on down there."

"May be a false alarm," said Parker. "To disrupt services."

"Pray you're right."

Jennifer put her hand on Rinehart's shoulder and smiled, "Just get us safely on the ground, Captain."

Rinehart turned to his controls and checked in with Gatwick.

———

The "white noise" that emanated from Heathrow's miles of conveyor belts had covered a multitude of sins for airport authorities. Now the silence generated a different reaction from Ragem and his accomplices. They knew their plan was discovered. The curiosity of nearby passengers, the seemingly unperturbed actions of terminal employees, together heightened the urgency for quick action.

Out of the newfound silence came the sound of distant sirens. Ragem smiled at the foolishness of the police. *They can't sneak up without their noisy sirens proclaiming their egos*, he thought, and quietly laughed to himself. Outside, gridlock had formed on all inbound traffic lanes. Military, civilian police and other emergency vehicles found it difficult to pass.

From two miles out a pack of SAS manned, Westland Lynx Ah Mk.1 land-based assault helicopters bore down on the airport.

The bearded Ragem glanced at a wall clock across from his post. 4:28 p.m. 16:28 Greenwich. He put his cigarette out in a nearby ashtray, folded his newspaper in half, tucked it under his arm and maneuvered through the crowd—away from the area that would be decimated in less than two minutes.

———

Inspector Harper moved through the line of airport shops, pubs and eating areas. The terminal neared peak capacity as those on business trips competed with tourists waiting for canceled flights. Tired children hung upside down on lounge seatbacks, treating them as monkey-bars. Other children chased siblings in circles to kill their boredom, while parents quietly chastised them for not sitting still.

Irony always confuses the issue, thought Harper as he passed through the crowd. *If we clear the terminal and allow passengers to board for destinations, we might make the mistake of loading on planes designated for destruction. But if we leave them within the confines of the terminal, they could be sitting ducks.*

Harper bumped into passengers rushing in the opposite direction and politely excused himself.

We can't win, no matter what we do. Harper was resigned to reality, as he glanced around. Full evacuation would be the next step.

Sirens grew louder as patrol cars and military vehicles approached Heathrow's four terminals. But late afternoon traffic hampered access, as lines of cars inched over to allow them to maneuver through the gridlocked roads.

Thirty-nine four-bladed rotors whopped at the air around the perimeter of Heathrow's terminals. SAS personnel prepared to be dropped from inside fully loaded twelve-man cabins. They would encircle the airport as planned—for an assault if necessary—to protect each terminal from attack. Pintle-mounted door guns provided protection for the soldiers, and underslung ATGM rocket pods allowed fire-power for larger targets.

As the police neared each terminal's traffic circle, heads turned toward the shrill sounds in anticipation of seeing ambulance attendants enter to help someone with a heart attack, or perhaps something as banal as a political dignitary being shuffled off to a private gate.

Children innocently watched in anticipation of something special occurring.

In Terminal 3, Harper walked into a nearby men's toilet and entered a stall to check for bombs. He reached for the toilet lid to carefully lift it as his radio beeped. He pushed his index finger against his ear piece and struggled to hear an airport security officer call from across the lobby.

"Calling Inspector Harper."

"Harper here," he quietly spoke into his throat mike, hoping not to alarm anyone in the area.

"This is Officer Sheldon. Better get over here right away."

"Identify location. What have you got? Over."

"Sir, I'm next to Healthfoods. Just found a loaded book. The buggers have left us a bomb. Over."

"Damn," said the Inspector, as he quickly moved from the toilet facility. "Clear the area and cordon it off with whatever's available. Notify Mobile Op and call in security to assist."

"Lucky it wasn't boobytrapped."

"I'm heading to meet the bomb squad out front. Do what you can to avert panic. Close the area for inspection and send everyone outside. We don't know how many devices they've set. Evacuate now!"

Harper moved swiftly across the lobby, and radioed the Airport Communications Center.

"This is Inspector Harper," he spoke quickly. "Don't waste time. Get on the All-Call and request an orderly evacuation of all terminals, one through four. Evacuate to the outside immediately."

"Roger."

"Tell them to leave all baggage. Tell 'em it'll all be secured. Repeat the message, evenly, in as clear, concise and relaxed a voice as you can muster until we're certain we've evacuated everyone. The tone of your voice determines order or chaos. Understood?"

"Understood," the CS quickly answered back.

"Go!" Harper almost shouted into the mike.

He turned toward central lobby and looked at the doors, frustrated the patrols had not arrived. He pushed the radio button to check status of emergency crews—then decided he'd better help clear the terminal.

"Ladies and gentlemen," Harper said to nearby passengers, "we must clear the area for inspection, please carefully and quietly move through the outside doors." Harper personally shepherded passengers toward the doors. He pushed the radio Talk button.

"Come in Tower. Harper here. Do you read? Over."

"This is tower."

"Any planes disembarking you couldn't divert or hold? Over."

"Eight, sir. Holding them at the outer perimeter of the field on runway turnouts."

"Good. Don't let anyone out. No disembarking until further notice. Understood?"

"Roger."

A calm voice came over the P.A., "Ladies and gentlemen. It is extremely important everyone move quickly and quietly to the nearest outdoor exit. Leave all baggage behind. Evacuate immediately to the nearest outdoor exit. Your baggage will be secured by airport personnel. I repeat . . . "

At first, travelers hadn't paid attention to Harper, security personnel, or to the announcement. This was no time for a fire drill. In a hurry to get to destinations, the message was not understood.

By the first and second repeat, passengers and guests sensed something was indeed wrong. Confused about leaving belongings behind, most hesitated seconds too long.

Custodial personnel collapsed the giant revolving doors for a quicker egress, and now physically assisted passengers outside. Few were actually nearing the street when it all began.

Near the toy shop with the bobbing ducks and the inspection lines by the sandwich bar, Adnan Rashid and the "pregnant" Zaynab gave one last glance toward the other and smiled. Each turned to the east, raised their eyes toward the sky and proclaimed out loud, "Praise be to Allah. In the name of God, the Merciful, the Compassionate."

Passengers were closer to the exits. But heads turned to listen intently to these two seemingly distant people as they simultaneously proclaimed the same words from the *Koran* from two levels of the airport lobby.

The inspector hurriedly moved through the crowded foyer, as he talked on his radio, and encouraged movement outside. Suddenly Harper bumped into a tall, well-tanned businessman in baggy pants. A newspaper dropped to the floor. The inspector half-apologized as he looked into the dark-eyed face of Ragem, helped him pick up his paper, and rushed on toward the front doors.

Harper turned toward the main entrance as every door filled with uniformed and plainclothes officers. Abruptly, he stopped and remembered the face of the businessman. He turned back to focus on the spot where they had bumped. But Ragem had vanished.

Harper burned with rage. Outside, the sirens bore down on his senses as he madly cussed at himself for being so stupid.

He could not let panic set in. Harper reached for the talk button, to call security. But the sound of rapid-fire machine guns echoed throughout the terminal, and the air became raw with terror as voices were lost in screams.

Harper took a shot in the neck and dropped to the floor.

Instantaneously, two different fingers touched the buttons of the radio-controlled devices and Terminal 3, at Heathrow International Airport, became a Stygian inferno.

———

Four Lynx copters flew in above Terminal 3 as hundreds of people scrambled out the exits, below. Then, the SAS commandos witnessed the first shock wave.

"Holy shit," the lead pilot said. He slugged his co-pilot's shoulder and pointed down.

As if watching a silent movie, in slow motion, the building quaked violently. The next shock wave traveled outward from the middle of the building. Glistening shards of glass exploded into thousands of pieces of deadly shrapnel—and rained on those who had escaped. Steel reinforcement, with concrete still attached, lifted high into the air.

From the air, nothing but the sound of Rolls Royce Gem Turboshafts and beating rotors could be heard as the terminal's midpoint collapsed in on itself. Then, repeatedly, its foundations shook and dust clouds and smoke poured through the roof and out the sides. A gas line exploded, sending fire and concrete slabs straight up toward the copters.

"Get the hell outta' here," ordered the lead pilot. "Bank hard right and watch your sides." Each pilot pulled their joysticks straight back and to the right as they jammed their way up and out of the flying debris.

"Mobile Op, Mobile Op, they've hit Terminal Three. Do you read me? This is Firefox One."

"This is Mobile Op, we read you. Assess damage Firefox One."

"Sir, pulling back due to raining fire. Debris in air. Can't get close enough yet."

"Get down there as fast as possible and assess."

"Understood. Out."

The Lynx copters responded automatically as the 43 foot long British Westlands vacated the airspace over the terminal and landed a safe distance from the gates. Eleven commandos armed with Heckler & Koch MP5 sub-machine guns scrambled out of each Lynx, cleared the rotors, spread out, and took up positions in a safety zone fifty yards from the perimeter of the terminal. Each door gunner remained behind with their L4A4 machine guns, prepared to protect soldiers under cover of fire.

The SAS troops moved in to evacuate those running from the holocaust who escaped from the tarmac side of the building. They were closely scrutinized to be certain none of them were perpetrators. But it did not take long to realize these people were innocent.

———

Ragem, already outside, had run with the panicked travelers as the explosions and gunfire erupted. To any observer, he appeared as frightened as anyone else and blended in with hundreds of terrified people. But Ragem knew exactly where to go.

Security forces were everywhere, yet their minds were on the assault and potential confrontation with anyone carrying a gun or looking suspicious. Ragem and others were directed out toward the street, to clear the area of potential victims.

They hurriedly crossed from the unloading zone to the bus island. Ragem stood with a crowd of onlookers and briefly turned to watch as a secondary gas explosion sent parts of the roof flying toward helicopters coming in over Terminal 3. The entire glass awning collapsed the length of the building, in front of the exits— trapping and killing many panicked travelers.

ALFAHAD's leader maneuvered across the road, and traversed and dodged between the jumbled mass of autos and lorries that were unable to move. To avoid detection, he headed south across traffic, through the parking facility, then cut east on the peripheral road. He calmly walked past three petrol storage tanks, and crossed the street toward the Chapel of St. George.

The terrorist feigned concern to passersby as he walked up the steps toward the chapel and entered the courtyard—its outer-walled brick fence separating the noise of the nearby exit road from the peace and serenity of the small, non-demoninational church. A 16-foot cross stood above him, outside, as he prepared to enter the chapel.

Several men in clerics attire raced out the door and down the street to see what had happened, and to offer assistance and prayers for the victims.

The first explosion took out the toy shop with everything and everyone in the vicinity. A second and third blast in the men's toilets had coincided with the forth and fifth explosions in the women's facilities, two more from the books, and another blast from the belly of a woman. The largest explosion had come from the suitcase and briefcase set on top of a departing family's luggage trolley—lost among other baggage.

Entire crowds panicked and ran, first from the explosions, then from the bullets. As mice in a barrel, mothers and fathers wandered and screamed for their children, only to be shot at from another angle. Men and women gathered families, spouses, or friends as they tumbled under chairs, behind check-in counters—anything to provide protection.

Flames fingered out in every direction. The force of each blast sent walls, pulverized glass, and plastic shards flying through the air into passengers and terminal employees.

Airport furniture and shop displays became hurled projectiles. Ceilings collapsed and gas lines exploded, throwing people and debris a hundred fifty feet from the site.

Automatic sprinklers kicked in, but could not keep up with the hot-burning plastics. Black, acrid smoke enveloped the entire area, making it difficult to see just who was spreading terror through the building.

Lieutenant Colonel Donald Harrigan led his SAS group through the main entrance as bullets came from everywhere. With gas masks and goggles in position, the soldiers threw themselves to the floor, crawling in every direction, hoping to find the source of the mayhem through the thick, pungent smoke.

Quick bursts of fire emanated from a central point across the plaza, but they could not tell if travelers were standing in between them and the terrorists.

Harrigan grabbed the megaphone and screamed into the mouthpiece, "Everyone drop to the floor. Get down immediately. Stay low."

If anyone remained standing, it was now too late. The soldiers opened fire with short bursts from their MP5's toward the source of the machine guns.

The sound of returning fire reverberated hideously throughout the terminal's cavernous rooms and hallways.

At the command from Harrigan, the terrorists had dropped to the floor, knowing the next order would be shoot to kill—them.

Smoke provided cover, as hoped. But their cheaply made Soviet gasmasks made it difficult to breathe in the caustic atmosphere. Accustomed to escaping from dangerous situations, escape routes had been preselected before the attack.

Ragem's four remaining accomplices continued to spread death with their new guns. Masks and night-vision goggles in place, they had positioned themselves far enough from the blast area to be protected, yet close enough to escape routes to get out.

The terrorists aimed at anything that moved, and the XE-47's were deadly accurate—especially at close range.

Travelers screamed and cried in terror as bullets ricocheted off hardened surfaces and careened into bodies. Children shook with fear, not understanding what was happening. Some cried and wandered in the chaos looking for parents.

Before the secondary explosions, air handlers had drawn the smoke-filled air throughout the building. It soon mutated into an eerie, darkened, smoke-poisoned house of terror.

Then the attack was over.

Except for burning fires, and spraying water from sprinklers and broken pipes, there was silence.

To Harrigan, the overwhelming stillness was deadlier than that found during the fiery crash of Pan Am 103 on December 21, 1988. He had been at Lockerby. After the initial shock, there, one could feel the finality of death in the burning fire.

But at Heathrow, silence meant many things. Widespread death and destruction throughout the terminal; hundreds of wounded; women, men and children dying from wounds or the trauma of shock; and, terrorists—still possibly lurking in quiet corners, at airport doors, in hallways, or in tunnels.

Whimpers, guttural moans, and silent cries took hold. Shock had already set in with most victims. And some survivors wandered aimlessly through the decimated, smoke-filled ruins, choking and coughing from smoke inhalation.

Lieutenant Colonel Harrigan turned away from the stench of burnt flesh and the horror of unsuspecting faces—caught in the senseless surprise attack.

———

"Captain Allsworth calling Commissioner Lawton. Do you read? Commissioner, this is Captain Allsworth. Do you . . . "

"This is Lawton," the Commissioner interrupted.

"It's a bloodbath! They've destroyed the entire building sir!" The voice of the police captain reported to Lawton's position in the Emergency Operations Trailer.

"Give your position."

"Just entering Terminal Three, sir . . . inside now. SAS is mopping up. No more gunfire. Get the meds in right away. Ambulances and fire control. Everything we have."

"Anyone alive in the area of the hit?"

"Sir, some moaning and crying. But it's eerie . . . can hardly see a thing in front of us. Power's out and too much smoke. Emergency lights are on, but not doing much good."

Allsworth's patrol followed him into the demolished building. They crept cautiously, nearly on all fours, with thousands of broken glass shards and sharp metal fragments preventing them from getting lower than the smoke.

"Colonel Harrigan, this is Allsworth. Are you there?"

"I read you, Captain."

"Any sign of the terrorists?"

"No. Still reconnoitering. Watch your step. They could be anywhere—or fifteen miles from here. We have a reported crater at the food plaza. Get the fire containment squad in as soon as they pass that gridlocked mess. And send every available medic."

The captain reported back to Lawton at the Emergency Op Trailer.

"Sir, just talked with Lieutenant Colonel Harrigan."

"Yes, Captain, we're picking up your conversations. What are you finding?"

"Sir, it's quite dark. The smoke's just beginning to clear. At first glance . . . "

The captain's voice froze in mid-sentence. "Oh, my God."

"Captain?"

Silence answered.

"Captain?"

Allsworth slowly spoke into his radio.

"Sir."

The captain's voice was measured and noticeably shaken. He attempted to regain composure.

"Sir, I can't begin to describe what's happened. In all my years . . . in all my service, I've never seen anything like this." Tears mixed with sweat as he reported to the commissioner.

"Sir, we have women and children cut in half . . . my God, sir, right in half. A little girl still clutching her doll . . . they're both beheaded." The man fell to his knees, dropped his radio and cried. His voice faded into the raspy sound of radio static amid chatter from other sections of the airport.

"Assess the damage, Captain."

It was several moments before he could respond. "There can't be enough emergency vehicles to handle the bodies. We'll have to triage and conscript autos and lorries to carry the wounded. Wait a minute . . . " Allsworth had been checking victims and recognized someone. "Sir, Inspector Harper's down on the floor.

Wounded badly . . . lost a lot of blood."

Allsworth crouched to his knees and placed his finger to the inspector's wrist for a pulse. Harper moaned and slowly opened his eyes. Relieved, Allsworth moved in closer.

"Lie still 'till we get some help."

"They're here . . . " Harper struggled to get his words of warning out, choking on his own blood.

"Save your energy Inspector. You'll be all right."

"No . . . listen . . . to me. He's in here . . . he's . . . "

"Who? Who's in here?"

"I saw him . . . it was the one . . . in the picture . . . "

"Ragem? The terrorist, Ragem?"

Harper could say no more. He only stared and blinked in agreement. A smile of relief crossed his face momentarily, knowing his message had finally gotten through. Then his eyes glassed over, fixed to the ceiling in a wide-eyed, permanent gaze. A final release of air escaped his chest. Allsworth let go of his hand and closed the inspector's eyelids.

"Allsworth. Report in. Over."

"Allsworth here. Inspector Harper saw Ragem. He was in the building."

"Can you get a description?"

"Sir . . . I'm sorry. That's all the inspector got out before he died. Over."

SAS, local police and NSY investigators had already sealed off the airport and fanned out through the four terminals. Airport firefighters moved equipment in. A disaster grid was mapped. And the beginning stages of triage were implemented.

———

United's Flight 1161 received priority status to land at Gatwick Airport. Escorted past a long queue of jets waiting for gate and disembarkation instructions, the plane was directed to taxi into one of the few North Terminal gates still available.

Parker and Nakamura were whisked off the plane before anyone else and led to a VIP holding area in Customs. Before landing, the plane's captain had informed them of the decimation at Heathrow's Terminal 3. That was all authorities would confirm to scheduled air traffic. Others on board the flight had not been informed.

A modified British Westland AH.Mk.3 helicopter swung over Gatwick's tarmac just outside the Customs office and placed itself in the large white-circled landing zone near the apron. The two side-by-side Rolls Royce Gem turboshaft engines remained on for instant takeoff, and the four-bladed main rotor whipped up a strong wind on the ground.

"Dr. Parker," said the Customs inspector, "your transport has arrived. You've both received clearance. They want you to move out quickly." He placed a sticker on the scientist's luggage.

Nakamura reported her 9mm Sig Sauer P228, but without opening anything for inspection another sticker was applied to her luggage and she was waved through.

Parker thanked the officer, nodded at his companion and grabbed both bags. He and Nakamura were hurried through an automatic sliding door—past the service vehicles to the waiting helicopter.

A soldier approached with a Heckler & Koch Automatic slung over his shoulder and his Browning High Power pistol in its backup holster. He slid open the side-door and, above the din, signaled them to move into the cabin.

"Captain Treadway will transport you to Mobile Op, outside Heathrow," said the soldier. He slid the cabin door closed and insisted they use the bench seat-straps.

The helicopter rose above Gatwick terminal, quickly banked to the north, followed A23 for a short period, then cut northwest toward Heathrow. As soon as they were airborne, the soldier briefly explained what limited knowledge he had about the attack, then returned to the cockpit.

The helicopter banked to the left and leveled off. Parker and Nakamura felt the effects of jetlag and hours of discussion, as they leaned their heads against the padded headrests and closed their eyes. The droning of the helicopter rotors made it difficult to talk, but easier to sleep. The few moments they had to rest came quickly upon them.

Within ten minutes they were startled awake by the overhead cabin speaker.

"This is Captain Treadway. We're approaching Mobile Op. You might want to glance out the starboard window. It's getting dark, but you can see the fires at Terminal Three. Take a look. Then prepare for landing." The pilot clicked off.

Parker and Nakamura unlatched their safety belts and moved to the opposite window. The early evening cloud cover glowed over Heathrow as fires still raged from broken gas lines and residual effects of the bombing.

"Incredible that a small band could do so much damage."

"Look at the World Trade Center," said Nakamura. "Or Oklahoma City."

For the first time Parker fully realized the threat. "And this was done without money they'd have if they locate the *Omar*."

"Or other treasure ships," she said. "Ragem's got access to the world's largest stores of black market guns—everything from Kalashnikovs to weapons-grade plutonium. The more cash, the more damage he can do."

The chopper banked to port and the intercom interrupted, "Prepare for landing. Fasten your safety-harness."

Parker and Nakamura returned to their bench seats, and mentally steeled themselves for what was to come.

———

Ragem silently prayed thanks to Allah. Others had entered the Chapel of St. George to escape danger, and offer prayers before the altar while they awaited word of loved ones.

Police and soldiers had entered the chapel to search for perpetrators. But Ragem took the same reverent position of other mourning petitioners and was overlooked as one who could have committed such a grisly crime.

Deciding it was time to leave, Ragem moved into a hallway. Seeing no one nearby, he checked the door handle of a storage closet. As promised, it was unlocked. He ducked inside, turning the deadbolt lock into place.

Tucked high on a shelf was a plain bag. Inside was a change of clothes, a new hairpiece and mustache for disguise, a mirror, and a battery-powered booklight for changing in the dark. A lined nylon jogging suit, a wind breaker and a pair of tennis shoes—comfortable enough to travel in—were rolled up inside. A thousand British pounds and another thousand in francs was slipped inside an envelope containing a new passport and fake ID's.

Within forty minutes of the attack, Ragem was already moving with the diminished crowds—just down from Car Park 3. A line of vehicles had queued up alongside the terminal's curb after emergency crews had run out of ambulances to carry the wounded.

Authorities had impressed autos and taxis into service as temporary emergency vehicles. And medical and volunteer personnel assisted those who could be moved into the back seats of vehicles for evacuation to hospital. On the backside of the terminal, air ambulances were loaded with critically burned patients, as quickly as helicopters were made available to evacuate to burn wards.

Ragem boldly approached a cabby, holding the door open for a volunteer assisting a wounded young woman into the cab. Ragem appeared distressed as he spoke.

"Are you going to hospital?"

The cabby nodded.

"I'm told my wife and son were evacuated. My car is blocked and I can't get out to reach them." He turned and looked directly into the eyes of the Red Cross volunteer who was already exhausted. "May I ride along and help you take care of this person? Perhaps my family will be there too."

The volunteer looked at the cabby and shrugged thankfully, feeling the strain. "Any help is welcome," she said. "But we won't know to which hospital they're directing us until we're on our way."

"No matter," Ragem walked to the other side of the old FX4 taxi. "At least I will begin my search."

He opened the door, climbed in, and helped spread a blanket over the sedated victim. He pulled down the spare seat, on the driver's divider wall, and sat quietly watching as military, medical, and security personnel sprinted from one place to another. As the driver awaited instructions, Ragem heard sporadic shots echo from deep within the terminal.

The terrorist commiserated politely with the driver and volunteer as a bobby placed a pennant on the antenna of the cab. The officer walked back and looked into the cab's window, then waved the musher into the emergency evacuation lane—cleared through the maze of vehicles.

Oblivious to the pain and moans of the sedated patient, Ragem prayed once more to Allah for the safekeeping of his compatriots and for the souls of the two who had volunteered for their suicide mission.

The black sedan headed north, out of the airport, and eventually pulled out onto M4 Motorway. Its flashers blinked and the pennant waved briskly as it proclaimed an emergency "pass-through," avoiding all security and visual check-points along the way. The driver turned up his CB radio and conversed with someone back at Heathrow. Shortly, he looked back at Ragem through the rear-view mirror, slid his divider-window open, and spoke over his shoulder.

"We've been directed to Ealing General. Should be able to exit at Windmill and head up through Osterley Park. Hopefully your family is there." He smiled into the mirror.

Ragem thanked the driver for his courtesy and the window was pulled closed. Within minutes, Ragem would fade into the countryside. Hours later, he would be spirited across the English Channel to Calais. Then, his routing would take him to Paris, on to Tripoli, and finally into Cairo.

The Red Cross volunteer found it odd that their guest showed little concern for the wounded lady. *But then*, she thought, *he has plenty to worry about, what with his wife and son injured.*

––––––––

Rounds of shots echoed furiously through Heathrow's miles of subterranean tunnels that led from one terminal to another, or to the subway and bus systems.

Karim Abdul Khorassani, Ragem's chief lieutenant, was as sturdy and aggressive as the facsimile had described him—a frightening figure of a man, even from a distance. Taking cover behind a temporary plywood construction wall, erected for repair of a nearby escalator, his XE-47 was still warm from firing at British troops.

Ordinarily, nothing would have been left to chance as Karim Abdul prepared to do battle with anyone who approached him. But having taken the wrong turn in a smoke-filled passageway, Khorassani found himself caught between two tunnels leading to the Underground, and soldiers filtering down from all levels above.

Captain Allsworth and his squadron moved through the intersecting corridors, stepping guardedly down a still escalator—exposing themselves to danger with no cover other than the escalator's metallic walls. They reached the lower level.

"This is Allsworth. We're approaching your sector. What's your status? Over."

Bullets were exchanged and the sound of shots ricocheted through the tile-lined hallways. Allsworth heard screams over the radio.

"Sir," a young soldier reported in, "we've one man caught behind a repair barrier—at escalators leading to Terminals One, Two and Three. Another got away and headed topside. Over."

"Can you smoke him out with teargas?"

"Difficult, sir. Passengers are caught in the cross-fire. If we fire gas, he might come out shooting and hit those trapped in the middle."

"We'll attempt to move in from behind and cut him off from this direction," said Allsworth. "Do what you can to clear out the tourists. Over."

The soldier acknowledged the order and signaled those in his group to move in on the stranded travelers. As with Allsworth's squad, the soldiers had only the upright balustrade of a moving walkway for protection. They crouched low as possible and skimmed along its edge for cover. The long, straight, tube-like tunnel made it difficult to move without being seen. There were no corners to hide behind if the terrorist attacked.

Two families and a businessman were huddled tightly against the walkway handrail thirty yards down as the soldiers advanced toward them.

Suddenly, Khorassani jumped out and fired at anything that moved. Shots flew overhead and pinned the squad down at the opposite end. A soldier took a ricocheted bullet in his left leg, and collapsed. The troops answered back with a barrage of submachine gun fire, and forced Khorassani to take cover.

"All right, everyone," the squad leader yelled out as he reached within 5 yards of the pinned-down travelers, "keep low and move back with us. We'll cover you from behind." He grabbed the hand of a wildly sobbing teenage girl, who held her little brother, and pulled them back behind their line. Other soldiers assisted as the children were taken first; then the women; finally the men. Two soldiers helped them get to the end of the tunnel, and safely around the corridor to a hallway.

The squad watchfully pressed forward. Without warning, Khorassani jumped from the barrier and wildly attacked down the moving walkway, almost doubling his speed. Bullets spit out of his XE-47 at a rapid rate as he headed directly for the soldiers.

A soldier raced back to the end of the moving walkway, reached over its handrail, and hit the emergency stop button. The walkway stopped instantly. Khorassani flew forward, hit his head solidly against the side panels, and tumbled to the floor of the walkway. As he went down, the terrorist took a bullet in his side and one in the left shoulder.

A giant, reincarnated Khorassani stood up, let out a raging scream, and picked up where he left off.

"In the name of Allah, the Merciful, the Compassionate . . ." he yelled over and over as he aimed his machine gun directly at the soldiers and stumbled down the walkway.

The soldiers watched in disbelief as Khorassani took more hits and still moved closer.

Allsworth's squad had worked their way down the other end of the tunnel, to the point where Khorassani had been hiding. Each took position and prepared to fire off a round when Khorassani took one final bullet near the chest and his body slumped over the handrail.

Both squads converged on the terrorist to make certain he was incapacitated.

"My God, good work man." Allsworth recognized Khorassani and was amazed to find him still breathing.

"Any wounded in your group?" he looked at a soldier.

"Three, sir. . . . And a couple of the tourists were injured."

The captain pulled out his radio, "Mobile Op. This is Allsworth."

"Lawton here. Go ahead."

"Dispatch several medics and evacuation teams down here to Tunnel C, Second Level. We've got Khorassani, badly wounded.

Don't expect him to live. And we've civilians and security personnel wounded. Critical you get help down here for at least a half dozen. Over."

"Understood," said Lawton. "Tunnel C. Second Level. Over and out."

Khorassani was the only terrorist in their hands. Near death or not, they had to do whatever necessary to get him to Latham prison hospital. In a sense, he would be held hostage in their attempt to save him. And, hopefully, they would extract information during confinement.

———

Leaving the engines and rotors operating, Captain Treadway gently set his British Westland in a field between a large converted motor home and a fifth-wheel trailer still attached to an oversized Ford pickup.

Looking through the helicopter windows, Mobile Op was awash in bright halogen lights on tall posts. Radar and satellite dishes and various antennae took up most of the two mobile roofs, and extra cables ran in every direction.

Converted American HUMMV's were in various stages of operation—some arriving from the site of the attack, some parked in a state of readiness, others racing out on assignment—performing duties ranging from command post support and medical assistance to communications vehicles and supply cars.

Military and civilian staff scrambled in all directions, and a tight ring of security personnel surrounded the area.

International Press Corps were held at bay a mile from the site. Print and electronic media journalists or photographers would not be allowed near the scene of the attack. Airspace over the terminals had been secured. Those hiring planes and helicopters for fly-over pictures had to do so from more than two miles away from Heathrow's perimeter.

Lawton, a large square-jawed man, emerged from the motor home with two other men. The commissioner held the door open for his aide, Wingate—a tall, lanky fellow.

FBI Agent, Ron Bantam, a nondescript individual with a butch haircut, followed close behind. The three pulled on overcoats as they hurried to the helicopter. Introductions were made, as they sat themselves directly across from Parker and Nakamura.

"Move out, Captain," Lawton instructed the pilot as passengers secured harnesses for takeoff.

"Sir," Treadway saluted and turned for the cockpit.

"Bring us behind Terminal Three, and locate a secured gate ramp."

"Yes sir."

Lawton turned to his guests, skipped any formalities, and got down to business.

"You couldn't have arrived at a more inopportune moment. But we invite your expertise. Ragem was spotted just before the attack, but made good his escape."

"He's a master at that," agreed Nakamura. "Any surviving witnesses?"

"A couple that we know of," answered Lawton. "It's a miracle anyone survived. We've learned there were at least two other accomplices. Possibly as many as six. Can't be certain, until we reconstruct the bombings and attack, or until enough people come forward as witnesses."

"Knowing how Ragem works," said Nakamura, "you can guarantee there were that many for an attack this big."

"What are casualty and wounded counts?" asked Parker.

"Too early to tell. Estimates place the dead at over three hundred. Wounded could come in as high as six hundred or more. Until we pull collapsed walls and ceilings, and get into the craters, we just won't know."

"One crater's depth is nearly twenty-five feet," said Wingate.

Bantam spoke up, "Smoke inhalation killed almost as many as

the attack itself." His mild manner and calm voice belied his FBI position. "Numerous wounded won't last the night."

"The entire airport is shut down," said Lawton, "Created a nightmare with stranded passengers. Terminals One, Two and Four will have limited services after bomb squads clear buildings and the engineers redirect gas, water and power.

"We're still fighting fires—and there're hundreds of passengers in eight planes at runway ends. We can't unload until we've enough service personnel and buses to rescue them."

The intercom interrupted. "Commander, we're approaching Gate Twelve. It's intact. Personnel on the ground will assist you. Touching down in less than a minute. Check your harnesses."

Soon, the five were on the ground and assisted up a set of stairs near the ramp. Portable lights had been brought in, and turbo fans drew the caustic smoke and fumes outside the terminal. One could not escape the haunting feeling the lights created, with ominous shadows cast inside the malformed structure.

Each were given gas masks. The scene was quiet as they stepped over debris. Medical workers and military personnel moved about as they implemented triage, tagged the dead, and marked areas where searchers eventually would dig.

"Over here," a volunteer yelled for assistance. "Two more. We need morphine." Teams of volunteers assisted emergency medical technicians, as those who could be saved were evacuated for triage.

A woman whimpered somewhere in the distance.

The team moved through the rubble, their senses ravaged by the event. Corpses were everywhere. Mutilated bodies caught in an instant of terror. Lives unexpectedly cut short; entire families in pools of blood—clothes ripped from them by the explosive power of plastic bombs; and children's innocent bodies abducted by bullets at close range. It was terrorism in its meanest hour. And each of the adults, hardened mostly by experience, silently wept as they surveyed the devastation.

Lawton carefully stepped over remains of melted restaurant furniture—blown a hundred yards from the food court—and discreetly avoided the remains of dismembered victims.

He glanced around and almost whispered, "I've never understood how anyone could be so treacherous . . . to wish this chaos and mayhem on fellow human beings."

He coughed to compose himself and surveyed the area. "The fires are nearing containment." He signaled his aide to get a report. Wingate moved across the buckled terrazzo floor and headed outside.

"The superstructure's seriously compromised," said Lawton. "Let's move out."

The others nodded in stark agreement.

A bomb squad, close-by, checked for duds and fragments.

"Excuse me," Lawton said to a squad member, "any signs of taggants?"

"None, sir," a woman answered as she sifted through debris.

"Keep us informed if you spot any." He rejoined the group.

"Taggants?" Parker looked at Nakamura.

"Tiny color-coded chips of hardened plastic," she said. "Marked with the explosive manufacturer's location and date of production."

"Not all manufacturers place them in their materials," said Lawton. "But when we find them, it aids in tracing buyers . . . even if stolen."

Where the foodcourt once stood, personnel used sounding devices and other sophisticated sonar equipment to locate those buried alive. Technicians snaked a small robotic camera into a collapsed area, while a group of highly trained labradors—schooled at locating signs of life—and other retrievers trained to find bombs and bomb fragments, were led into sectors where tons of superstructure had collapsed.

"Coming through, please," someone said from behind.

The group stepped aside as medics removed a seriously wounded woman on a stretcher. A volunteer carried the woman's baby—another survivor. She spoke soothing words into the crying infant's blistered ear, softly stroking the baby's head.

The blare of sirens permeated the air from outside as Lawton and his group approached the front plaza. Volunteers moved in a reverent silence, broken only by calls for assistance as other victims were discovered.

Radio transmissions competed for airwaves as emergency calls followed others in quick succession, and static-filled messages echoed throughout the cavernous terminal.

The commander's radio crackled.

"Lawton here."

"Wingate, sir. Bomb squad located a device attached at the three petrol storage tanks near Car Park Two. Attempting to defuse it, and draining petrol into tankers to lessen the chance of a serious explosion if they fail."

"What's its makeup?"

"A large chunk of Semtex and a sophisticated electronic detonator, set for seventeen-thirty. Must have malfunctioned. But they've evacuated the office buildings, next door, as a precaution. Over."

"Keep me informed."

"Understood. Over and out."

The commander looked weary as he shook his head. "My Lord," he turned to the others. "Over twenty-five thousand liters of petrol in those tanks.

"Fifty thousand employees work this airport—three thousand in Terminal Three, alone. And nearly forty-two million passengers pass through each year." Lawton shook his head. "They had to pick a day when all forty-two million were here."

"Watch your step sir," a soldier warned. They approached buckled sections of concrete with jagged steel rebar that had fallen from the roof.

Lawton directed the others around the cave-in, and stepped

through the blown-out frame of a plate-glass window.

As they exited to the street, the devastation was multiplied and strangely set apart by the myriad of flashing lights from every type of emergency vehicle imaginable: ambulances; fire trucks; power, gas and water company vehicles; and military transports—all lit the surrounding area.

Conscripted taxis and autos carried the wounded to hospital. Demolished cars were towed or pushed aside, except where heavy debris had crushed them in place. Pieces of bent metal and melted plastics, pulverized glass, and covered, tagged corpses, not yet removed to the morgue station, filled the area.

Lawton explained their course of action.

"They've cleared most of the pickup zone, reserving two inside lanes for emergency vehicle pass-through, and the outer lanes for temporary hospital and triage. Translators of every nationality were called to assist non-English speaking victims. Some came from the other terminals....Several staff translators were lost in the attack."

Wingate rejoined the party as they moved across the access road. "Commander, we expect the last fire to be out within twenty minutes. And the bomb is diffused at the petrol tanks."

"Thank heaven," Lawton rubbed his tired eyes and shook his head. "Any word on the terrorists?"

"The one in the tunnel—he's shot up bad. Evacuated him to Latham Prison hospital. One got away. And no sign of Ragem or the others."

Lawton was disappointed. He looked at Parker. "If they're here, our troops will find them."

They approached the first tent.

Within thirty minutes of the attack, two large triage tents—complete with cots, operating tables, and medical equipment—had been erected in the access road, across from the terminal. Queues of canvas stretchers, filled with the dead and dying, extended out from the entrance of the first tent.

Walking wounded queued-up for diagnosis next to them. Few held any belongings. A purse; a tiny valise; a small piece of luggage grabbed in the last minute. And those who carried anything held on tight to their possessions.

"Ironically, if the attack had been on a passenger plane," said Lawton, "we'd identify casualties with seat charts. Serious disadvantage, here, considering the randomness of death."

He stopped at the tent. "If anyone's squeamish, remain behind."

Lawton led them through the canvas opening. Screams of pain, moans, and cries for help filled the shelter and tore through the early evening air. Medics quietly tagged every victim and allocated limited resources and personnel.

"We use a universal procedure called simple triage and rapid transport. START for short." He looked to Wingate. "The inspector is much more versed in it than I."

Wingate cleared his throat and took over. "Rescue workers are restricted to performing triage to a minute or less, per patient. And transportation to hospital is stressed."

A doctor assisted a lone woman to a cot. Two loaded stretchers were brought past them. One victim had labored breathing. The other had a deep penetrating wound to his abdomen.

"Once a victim is breathing or ventilated, we've only five seconds to assess the pulse, the need to control bleeding, or administer fluids. If, at the same instant, they can determine patient's mental capacity, they have up to twenty-five seconds to discern ability to follow simple commands."

Occasional shouts of grief and despair broke through the forced and restrained demeanor as reality set in, and some realized loved ones were lost, perhaps forever.

"Under extreme circumstances," said Wingate, "victims are given as fair a chance as priorities dictate."

"Unfortunately," said Lawton, "victims unlikely to survive

trauma . . . severe mental incapacity, age, or mortal wounds, are placed in other areas to await later transport."

They reached the end of the tent and looked toward the shelter for "delayed" or "minor injury" patient categories.

Through the tarpaulin opening, nurses comforted victims and handed out blankets. Since reaction to stress could occur long after a disaster, or within minutes—no matter how normal victims appear during triage—observation for latent signs of shock or psychological problems was critical.

"This may look chaotic, but it's moving well," said Lawton. He turned to the others. "As a kid, during the German bombings, I and my aunt once raced to a road tunnel for shelter, and watched as bombs devastated London."

He was silent for a moment as he glanced around.

"This reminds me of scenes after the Blitzkrieg."

Parker looked grim. "And you thought the terror ended there . . . "

In the second triage tent, one man had queued up for delayed medical assistance. Tagged with a green strip still intact—indicating no emergency transport needed—he was encouraged to wait in the area with those not considered critical.

Haji Al-Masud used the opportunity to plan his next move. Grazed in both shoulders by British troops, Al-Masud had attempted to escape Terminal 3 with Karim Abdul Khorassani.

In Tunnel C, he had dumped an empty XE-47 in favor of a holstered Llama .380, and backed off from his aggressive stance to escape up another tunnel. Back at street level he would have a better chance to elude airport security. Each terrorist was responsible only for himself. And his compatriot, Khorassani, could shoot his way out of any circumstance.

Al-Masud had been mistaken as a panicked tourist, caught in the attack, and was gently led to triage for processing. With little loss of blood, and feigning a mild state of shock, the terrorist was progressively shuttled through the system of checks—certain everyone thought him a victim caught in the crossfire—left only with his valise with "just one night's change of clothes." His tickets and identification, he had explained, were "lost in other luggage in the bombing."

Al-Masud sat on a cold metal folding chair, his small bag held tightly to his chest—one with five more pounds of Semtex, and a yet-to-be-connected detonator. A blanket, wrapped around his shoulders, inadvertently concealed the danger that lay in wait.

Patiently, he awaited an opportunity to prepare his surprise for the infidels. Then, he noticed officials moving through the tent from the other end. Animated in their discussion—from the stance of the group's leader, it appeared he held much authority.

"This is the holding tent for victims in no immediate danger," Lawton pointed out.

"What's the treatment time-line?" Nakamura asked Wingate.

"After the most critical, as we allot personnel from the first tent—all should be released by late this evening. We'll have cots and sleeping bags for those with no place to go."

The group moved to exit at the opposite end of the tent.

"The most serious problems these patients experience," said Lawton, "are shock or psychological trauma—aftereffects of stress from the attack. For some, effects could appear weeks or months later, with mildly detectable, deep-seated depression.

"Others can exhibit bouts of crying, fear and anxiety attacks, or total loss of control. They're a potential danger to themselves and others. It can take months or years of psychological counseling to resolve inner wounds."

Lawton stopped near the exit. "Dr. Parker," he said, "you're a deep-sea diver. In a sense, compare it to the effects of being under water for an extended period. As I understand, with many divers there's a need to overcome nitrogen narcosis effects from deep submergence diving."

Haji Al-Masud listened carefully from his chair.

"Those who don't use the proper mixture of gases," said Parker, "or rise to the surface too quickly, require a recovery period in a decompression chamber."

"Yes. Well, I liken the shock recovery process to a form of mental decompression, purging fears and shocks the body absorbed—to be expelled from the system, like nitrogen bubbles, in order to lead a normal life.

"For some it takes time to calm down the inner-self and overcome disorientation, you might say, through the hyperbolic chamber of their mind."

"Intriguing analogy, Commissioner."

Al-Masud could not believe divine providence had intervened. He had heard of a Dr. Parker in Ragem's discussions regarding salvaging of the *Great Omar*.

Is this Dr. Parker one and the same? But this was too providential. Or, was it? How could he be so fortunate to find himself on this site, at this particular instant?

Allah surely smiles upon me, he thought. And a plan formulated in his mind.

"Commander, we should clear passengers from the planes on the tarmac," Wingate reminded Lawton. "If not, we may have psychological problems to deal with, out there."

"Of course. Let's check bomb squad progress at the other terminals. Perhaps limited disembarkation is possible."

They turned to exit the tent.

Al-Masud knew he had to act at once. *This is the moment Allah has planned. I will be a hero to my people, admired by Ragem, and a glorious example to Allah against the heresies of the world.*

"Dr. Parker?" a voice called out from within the crowded tent.

Parker turned in the direction of the voice.

In an attempt not to startle or intimidate those he approached, Al-Masud slowly rose from his chair—his blanket still wrapped over his shoulders—and warily stepped around two rows of patients in front of him.

Attention was focused as a wooly-haired, tall young man approached. Of chestnut complexion, he had a seemingly cheerful face, with carved cheeks and lantern jaw. A small mistletoe mustache—in two narrow crescents—separated his aquiline nose from round smiling lips. Al-Masud appeared almost Bedouinesque as the blanket-wrapped figure advanced.

"You are the famous Dr. Parker connected with the *Titanic*?" The strapping, clean-shaven young man smiled as he moved toward the scientist.

"Why do you ask?" Parker realized this question had been posed many times before, but not under such circumstances.

"You are the one, are you not?" Al-Masud said with an excited voice.

"Yes, and your name?" Parker reached out to shake the man's hand.

"I am Haji Al-Masud," he said proudly as he dropped the blanket and his right hand emerged. The terrorist jammed his Llama .380 at Parker's right temple. "And I'm from the ALFAHAD. I bring greetings from Faheed Al Mar Ragem."

"Oh, shit!" Nakamura and Bantam reached for their guns and Lawton scanned the tent for security officers.

"I carry a bomb," Al-Masud yelled out. "Set to explode if the level changes more than five degrees."

Screams came from victims surrounding the group. Those who could move panicked and scattered toward the exits.

"Remain where you are," Al-Masud shouted above the frightened crowd, his eyes still focused on Parker. "Or I'll detonate the bomb."

Except for a few who escaped, the crowd froze in place. Some drifted into shock. Others moaned and whimpered out of fear.

Though he was only grazed in the earlier shootout, Al-Masud's right side burned with pain as he held the .380 to Parker's head.

Several soldiers raced in and, seeing what was happening, sighted their rifles on the terrorist.

"Do not fire," Lawton ordered. "He has a bomb." Lawton turned to Al-Masud. "What do you want."

"Nothing more than to take a walk with Dr. Parker," Al-Masud answered and nudged him toward the canvas opening.

Parker glanced at his captor, but cold steel was pushed harder against his temple.

Lawton spoke up, "Look . . . uh, Mr. Masud . . . "

"Haji Al-Masud," he shouted, his eyes shining white with resentment. "Remember that. Haji Al-Masud," and he shoved Parker toward the exit.

"Why don't we just talk this out," Lawton entreated. "We'll provide whatever you need."

The terrorist laughed almost comically.

"Whatever I need, you cannot provide. But Dr. Parker serves my needs exactly, thank you. Now—let us move outside, Dr. Parker. The rest of you are to remain in here. Or," he jostled the valise with his elbow, "in seconds this will take me to Allah, and all of you to hell."

He pushed his hostage out the exit and signaled Parker to head toward the terminal.

Nakamura and Bantam—their key man, who could help abrogate the ALFAHAD, in jeopardy—shot severe glances at Lawton as if to say, *What the hell do we do now?*

Lawton pushed the Talk button on his radio. "Mobile Op. This is Commander Lawton. Clear all lines and patch me to All Call. Over."

"Lines cleared and patched through. Over."

"Attention all personnel. This is Commander Lawton. Listen carefully. . . . We've a delicate complication unfolding. It's imperative all personnel keep your heads and follow strict orders. A terrorist has taken a Dr. Cary Parker hostage. He's being led at gunpoint from the triage holding tent . . . back toward the terminal.

"The terrorist is armed with a pistol and a bomb set to go off if he is taken to the ground, either physically or by a well-placed shot.

"All personnel maintain safe distance and monitor the two from as many angles as possible. Do not . . . I repeat, *do not* attempt to take out the terrorist unless Dr. Parker escapes more than a hundred yards from his captor. Or unless the hostage is mortally shot. Under all circumstances, keep safety of others around them in mind. If they're in a crowd, hold off. Give no excuse to detonate the bomb in a heavily populated area. Over."

He turned to the agents. "Let's go."

The terrorist maneuvered across the terminal access median into the emergency lane's oncoming traffic. Those seeing Al-Masud, with the pistol at Parker's head, slammed on their brakes and held back.

A bright yellow Transfer Service bus sat at the curb in front of the terminal, preparing to evacuate more uninjured passengers to Terminal 2.

"Move!" the terrorist shouted to anyone within hearing distance. Al-Masud shoved Parker toward the front door of the bus as people scattered. "Move!" he shouted again. The two reached the door and stepped up into the bus.

"Leave!" the terrorist screamed at the driver. "Or I'll blow this man's brains in your lap." He laughed loudly at the thought as the driver scrambled through the door.

"In the driver's seat," Al-Masud ordered. "Remember, I have the bomb."

Parker sat and turned to his captor. "Look. I have nothing to do with your mission. Don't hurt more innocent people. Turn yourself in and . . . "

"Shut up and drive to the security gate at the roundabout." He pointed in the direction of the service vehicle maintenance gate, with direct access to the main apron and runway system.

Al-Masud tossed his bag on a seat. It rolled to the floor and the terrorist quickly picked it up.

Parker winced, fully expecting the bomb to detonate. Realizing it was a bluff, he turned to the front, started the bus, and slowly shifted into gear as he thought about escape.

"I know you are connected to us somehow," said Al-Masud as he reached into the bag. "I've heard your name before. Faheed wants you out of his way for future plans."

"You've mistaken me for someone else. You've got the wrong Parker. I'm certain of it."

"No, Dr. Parker, it appears you are the right man at the wrong time, as they say. Wrong for you . . . right for me." He laughed loudly at his own cleverness, pointed the gun up front, and rummaged through the valise.

Parker watched the terrorist in the rear-view mirror as he stepped on the gas. "You don't really have a bomb in there."

"Oh, I assure you Dr. Parker . . . it may not work as I indicated. But this plastic explosive is equal to more than two hundred sticks of dynamite. Do not try any heroics. Just drive to the gate."

Parker had only driven once from the right-side. It felt awkward to shift with his left hand. But he shoved his foot lightly on the gas and the bus lurched down the left-hand lane. Military personnel lined the roadway then cleared back, not certain what to do—their carbines trained on the terrorist, just in case.

Parker hoped there were no itchy fingers as he drove to the north end of Terminal 3. The bus circled the roundabout and stopped at the security gate.

Al-Masud moved to the front and placed the .380 behind Parker's head, indicating to the guards to pull up the barrier arm and roll back the electric chain-link gate.

A guard spoke into a radio, and he obviously received clearance. The barricade went up and the gate slid open. A smile crossed the terrorist's face.

"Drive through," he instructed.

Parker gunned the gas pedal and the bus propelled quickly forward. Al-Masud flew backwards down the aisle as the bus shot ahead. He grabbed the edge of a seat to keep from falling, steadied himself and angrily shot the front windshield out. Parker slowed down.

"Next it will be your brains," the terrorist screamed from the aisle. He raced to the front and rammed his gun into the back of Parker's head. "Drive toward the runways. There are planes with passengers still on board."

Parker slammed on the brakes but the terrorist held an upright support bar. He lurched forward with the bus and remained on his feet.

"You'll have to kill me. I won't take you out to bomb a planeload of passengers."

"You had better think of your family before you try such tricks. Call my bluff and I'll dispatch you quickly. Either way I'll be praised in the name of Allah."

"You'll never make it out by yourself. Not with the armored cars surrounding us."

Al-Masud looked out the windows on both sides. Two lines of Daimler rear-engined Mk.4 Ferrets and FV721 Foxes, now sat thirty yards out on either side, brandishing 7.62 mm. coaxial machine guns, 30 mm. RARDEN Cannons, and Vigilant and Swingfire ATGM's.

"It's obvious you are important to someone," he ranted, "or they would have destroyed us by now. I am not worried about them." He pistol-whipped the back of Parker's head.

"Now drive!" he screamed. "I have to wire the bomb. Make the wrong move and you will surely go up in flames with me."

"I have a choice?"

Parker, his head aching and his mind tired from the journey, knew he had to avert another disaster. He spotted the CB radio and noted the glowing On-light. Slowly, he reached for the microphone and pulled it to his mouth.

"This is Parker," he attempted to say quietly over the hum of the engine. "The bomb is not . . . "

A loud shot pierced the air and exploded into the front of the radio. The CB shattered all over Parker's lap as it sparked, smoked, and died. Parker looked up in the rearview mirror to see his captor smiling.

There's nothing in the CIA's job description about this, thought
Parker.

"Get those copters in the air to back up the Daimlers right
now!" Lawton ordered over his radio as he raced out of the Control
Tower's elevator. "No idea what that lunatic's thinking, but we
won't wait to find out."

He scanned the horizon with night-vision binoculars, then
found the bus.

Four Lynx-3 choppers with enhanced avionics, an INFRARED
Countermeasures system, new night-vision sensors, and a mast-
mounted sight lifted into the air and escorted the service bus onto
the tarmac—one on each side and at both ends—all with their
1364-kg. slung load of anti-tank guided missiles outrigged beneath. Two men in each cabin fed and ran the pintle-mounted
door guns.

"Move in closer," Lawton ordered the lead pilot, "but maintain distance for escape if the bus blows."

He watched the four copters push the envelope of safety, to
gain position, in case they were ordered to take out the terrorist—
or the entire bus. The Daimlers followed alongside.

Lawton and the others watched the bus turn toward the outer
perimeter of the airport.

"Damn," said Lawton. "The bloody fool's heading toward the
loaded jets."

"Commissioner," the air control supervisor turned to Lawton,
"we've still got refueling tankers next to the planes."

"What're tankers doing out there? Don't underground hydrants
refuel planes at each gate?"

"Some were dangerously low on jet fuel, after circling, and
couldn't divert. We thought it best to prepare them for takeoff, if
we had to get them out of here."

"How much fuel in a tanker?"

"They start with five thousand gallons."

"Commissioner, he may try to ram them," said Nakamura. "Or hijack a plane, using the bomb to coerce his way on board."

Lawton turned to the supervisor. "Radio the pilots to evacuate planes immediately. Clear all passengers from the area—toward the fields, beyond the runways. Quickly. And get those tankers out of there."

The air controller radioed an All Call over the emergency frequency setup for the pilots still on the tarmac, and prompt abandonment of the planes began.

"Commander," said the controller, pulling off his headset, "two tankers still have hoses connected to the planes."

"Well, get them *unconnected*." The mike was open and the command was heard.

Agents Nakamura and Bantam pleaded with the commissioner not to allow any ordnance fired, with Parker still on the bus. But Lawton would not hear of it.

"Jeopardizing hundreds of passengers, on the off-chance one man can survive this event, to help stop an entire terrorist organization later is too dubious a plan. If that bus manages to get within three hundred feet of a loaded plane out there, or runs a suicide mission right into the middle of those trying to escape ...well, we can't sacrifice the lives of all those passengers for the life of one man."

The commissioner looked directly at the two FBI agents. "I'm sorry. But the international community will have to deal with Ragem's underwater scheme as it unfolds later. For now, I'll take full responsibility for this action."

He placed his night-vision glasses to his eyes, as though the subject was closed, then pulled them down. "Until we confirm Al-Masud's actual intentions, we'll hold our fire."

The service bus raced across the concrete surface, headed toward the runways. All field lights around the airport's apron, and the visual-approach and glide slope indicator lights along the strips, had been turned off.

The four choppers maintained a steady line of flight along-side. Their searchlights blinded Parker and made it difficult for him to see the centerline stripes and directional markings along the pavement. Even with the bus headlights, in the darkness Parker found it tough determining where the surface ended and the fields began.

To avoid panic, passengers had not been told why they were vacating the safety of the planes. Emergency escape chutes had opened on all jets, and a rushed but orderly evacuation was now taking place. Upon seeing the approaching helicopters, with lights focused tightly on a fast-approaching bus, a sense of urgency over-took the passengers. But as the bus reached the beginning of Run-way 15, it abruptly stopped.

From the tower, Lawton and the others could see it on the tarmac. "What's going on out there?" Lawton radioed to the lead pilot. "Can you see what's happening inside?"

"Commander," the pilot radioed back, "the driver—Dr. Parker— is just sitting in his seat. But the terrorist is moving back and forth up front, looking out the windows. The valise with the bomb is under his arms." There was a pause.

"Now he's looking through the shot-out front windshield, toward the planes. Over."

"Keep on him. Don't let up for a moment."

"Roger that."

Haji Al-Masud barely made out silhouettes of the idle planes on the horizon, some distance down the darkened runway. A quar-ter moon, in a partially clouded sky, provided little light to illumi-nate his potential targets beyond the helicopter's bright directional-specific halogens. Despite the handicap, he spotted an outline of jet fuel tankers sitting next to the jets.

A powerful adrenaline rush passed through his body.

For an instant, Haji pictured his small Egyptian village

southeast of Al-Fayyum—his youngest brother, Nuri, sitting atop a primitive water-wheel's yoke with their gaunt bullock lumbering around the system of buckets and gears; his sister, Um Kawakib, resting under the arbor-shaded porch with her young son on her hip; and his elderly father out in the field, grubbing his one acre berseem crop by hand.

Al-Masud thought of his mother who had died birthing Nuri. And he saw the face of his betrothed, Raijana, whom he had met when he migrated to the city of Al-Fayyum—forsaking the right of marriage to the daughter of his paternal uncle. Raijana had introduced Al-Masud to Faheed Al Mar Ragem, and had assisted him in his indoctrination to the path of the terrorist.

Thinking of Raijana was all Al-Masud needed to prepare for the most rewarding sacrifice he would ever make in praise of Allah. He turned to Parker.

"Too bad you do not know the ways of the *Koran*. For you would understand the beauty of submission and subservience to the one true God . . . Allah." Al-Masud's eyes glazed over. "You would be obliged to cleanse the world of non-believers, such as those we will destroy tonight." He gestured toward the planes.

"And you're about to give a lesson in the ways of the *Koran*," Parker yelled over the copters' din. "No matter what I do, I'm a dead man. Right?"

Al-Masud shrugged. "We accept our fate, Dr. Parker. . . . So should you."

"Has it ever occurred to you," Parker, glanced into the rear-view mirror, "regardless of who is on those planes, many are as devout to their beliefs as you are to Islam?"

"Should that make a difference?"

"Allah has made us all, in his image," said Parker. "Innocent passengers on planes don't make the rules and set policies and laws that affect your people. . . . Politicians do that."

Al-Masud stared back into the mirrored face of the scientist, searching for an ideological response.

"We will blow up the planes," he reasserted. "Faheed will know

I did not fail him, and I, Haji Al-Masud, will have a forum to the world."

"A forum?"

"The crazed media will report this incident, and the world will be reminded that politicians did what served their own self-interests—not what was noble and morally right."

"You son-of-a-bitch! If you excuse what your group did today, and what you're about to do as noble and morally right, you're not only insane, you're . . . "

" . . . psychotic? Deranged?" Parker saw Al-Masud's eyes widen. "You western infidels are all the same. Don't you think we've heard that before?"

Parker felt the gun against his neck.

"Enough of this talk. Drive!" The terrorist looked out a window as sounds of multiple Lynx rotors whopped against the air, and brought him back into action. He edged down the aisle, still looking into Parker's face.

"I will prepare the explosives and the will of Allah will be heard," Al-Masud laughed out loud, his adrenaline pumping more than ever before, as his natural compulsion to kill took over. "Just two more wires to connect." He looked directly at Parker, then shook his gun in the direction of the planes.

"Yes . . . you drive. I will make ready the package."

Al-Masud turned back to the seat, reached into his bag, and began attaching the final wires.

The bag was rigged with a false bottom made of four layers of molded Semtex sheet explosive. Inside the bag, wrapped in a change of clothes, was a hair blower and a calculator—both molded of Semtex. Since carrying the bag was, in fact, carrying the bomb, it was necessary to hook the electric blasting cap, inside, to the timing circuit and power source, then complete the circuit by wiring them to the molded hair blower—a method learned at Abu Nidal's desert training camp in Libya.

Parker intentionally delayed bringing the bus to speed, a mile and a half from Runway 15's end—the longest of the jumbo-jet landing strips. He watched Al-Masud work methodically to make the connections.

Evacuation of the planes moved smoothly enough, under the circumstances, though only half of the passengers had made it out. There were several sprained ankles and friction burns, and one passenger broke a foot coming off a chute too fast, at the wrong angle. Other passengers assisted them into the marshy fields, away from danger.

Like viewing alien ships in the distance, passengers watched the circle of bright lights, above, and the Daimler headlights at the opposite end, following the strangely illuminated bus as it resumed its trek in their direction.

All fuel tankers had disconnected transfer hoses from the planes and cleared the area by dodging across a connector to Runway 14—all except one.

The driver had trouble unhooking the hose connector from the jet. The tower instructed him to detach the other end from his truck, leave the hose behind, and move out. But it had cost him time.

He climbed back into the cab, glanced toward the opposite end of 15 and hair raised on the back of his neck. Four helicopters were glued to a large vehicle moving directly toward him. He had only gained two hundred feet distance from two 747's—still disgorging passengers. And his tanker was three-quarter full.

"Tanker driver, this is Tower. Get the hell out of there!" the radio blared in his cab. "Move out before they take you and the planes together. A bomb's on the bus. We're going to destroy it. Clear the area. Do you read me driver? Over."

"I read, Tower. I read," said the driver. He gunned his foot on the gas pedal, and the truck pitched forward then stalled. The driver turned his key and realized the engine had flooded. He laid off the pedal and tried the starter. The heavy smell of petrol accompanied the continuous engine grinding.

He looked down the runway. Like an apparition, the flying cortege appeared to move in slow motion—with the bomb—as it drew closer.

Once more he hit the starter. Nothing.

Lawton held the mike tightly to his lips, "Get ready to fire. That truck is too close to the planes. It'll take half of 'em out with the jet fuel explosion alone."

"Please Commissioner, give Parker another minute," Nakamura implored. "Just one more."

"We haven't got a minute. They're heading straight for a billion in planes and equipment. Not to mention passengers and crew too close to the jet fuel if it ignites."

Lawton spoke into the microphone. "Move the copters back before firing. We don't know how much explosive that bugger has. Prepare to fire on my orders."

"Yes sir," the lead pilot radioed back. "It's your call, Commander. Over."

Parker realized he was a dead man if his plan didn't work. He knew the pilots, above, would not let them reach the end of the runway. The yellow bus glowed in the lights from the skyward adversaries as driver and aviators picked up more speed and the centerline on Runway 15 blurred into one painted strip.

The cold night air raced through the blown-out windshield, and Parker's eyes watered as the wind cut across his face. He carefully pulled the driver's seatbelt over his shoulder and clipped it home. In the rear view mirror, he watched the terrorist hastily pull out a remote control and draw the large zipper half-closed across the top of his bag.

With sweat pouring from his face, the truck driver turned the key once more. The engine kicked in and he quickly shifted into gear. Slowly, the heavy tanker picked up momentum as it purchased distance from the planes. Approaching the connector to Runway 14, the driver shifted down to make the turn. Suddenly,

the engine died and the truck stalled halfway through the turn—
its tail-end still protruding into the path of the bus. The driver
jumped from his cab and raced across the field in panic.

From Heathrow's tower, the commissioner watched the
helicopters increase their perimeter of safety as they pulled back
from the bus and prepared to fire.

"Ready on my count," Lawton cautioned, waiting and hoping
somehow Parker could stop the bus, or overwhelm the terrorist.

Even in the darkness, silhouettes of hundreds of passengers
still scattered from the planes. Parker had watched the nearly full
tanker as it attempted to clear the area. When it stalled, he knew
what had to be done. In the mirror, Parker saw Al-Masud lift his
eyes skyward—his left thumb poised over the recessed trigger
button on the remote.

The terrorist shouted his prayer to the heavens, "Praise to God,
the Lord of all Being, the All-merciful, the All-compassionate, the
Master of the Day of Doom . . . "

"Ready . . . " Commissioner Lawton repeated, stalling as he
watched through his night-vision glasses. All eyes observed the
transfer bus as it passed the window of immunity.

"Damn it!" Lawton shouted, knowing he had pronounced a
death sentence on an innocent man. He pressed the Talk button,
"Five, four, three, two . . . Jesus!"

Instantly and without further thought, Parker slammed on
the brakes, jammed the steering wheel abruptly to the left, and
aimed the bus off the runway—out into the field. Simultaneously,
the lead helicopter pilot hit the trigger and released an ATGM.

The small solid-fuel rocket, with its miniature wings and aero-
dynamic controls, shot from the underbelly of the aircraft. As the
bus lurched, the rocket missed it completely and slammed into
the runway. An immense rolling ball of flame exploded into the
night sky, and chunks of concrete flew in all directions.

"Hold your fire! Hold your fire," Lawton ordered as he watched the rear of the bus cant sideways.

Haji Al-Masud was thrown to the side, as the concurrent force of the ATGM's near-miss explosion and the momentum from the sliding bus threw its tail-end around in an uncontrollable lunge down the runway. The terrorist hit the seats hard and the remote control flew out of his hand, slid down the aisle, and stuck between a metal seat brace.

Al-Masud was slammed against the opposite wall, hit his head on an upright handlebar and collapsed to the floor.

The intense shockwave from the missile's explosion hit the service bus and the entire left side of its chassis lifted off the ground. The bus careened on its right side tires as its weight fought to remain upright.

Strapped into his seat, Parker was disoriented as the bus spun two full rotations. He struggled to keep his senses as he blindly and anxiously fought for the safety-belt release button.

Quickly, Parker shifted his weight, forced his body to tighten the belt against his chest, and both hands shot up to press the release. The button submitted to pressure and Parker was tossed against the driver's right window. In a competition against time, he held onto the seatback for leverage and struggled to bring his feet to the driver's seat.

Crouching, ready to jump, and holding on for the ride of his life, he looked for an opportunity to thrust himself over the steering wheel—through the open windshield. He felt the bus tilt and knew it wouldn't hold its center of gravity any longer.

The front of the bus slid toward the grassy knoll on the outside edge of the concrete. Parker gathered his energy, used the large steering column for a starting block, and sprang his body through the wide opening.

As he jumped, the back tires of the bus caught the right edge of the runway. The huge metal body lifted off the ground, flipped and rolled over twice, landed on its left side—ripped off its tires— and lunged down the concrete with its undercarriage aimed straight ahead.

Streams of hot sparks followed as the metal chassis scraped against the concrete and headed directly for the fuel tanker, still jutting into its path.

Parker hit the ground hard and rolled wildly several times before coming to rest against an earthen berm. The air was knocked from him and, for a time, he lay dazed in the muddy grass. Then, realizing he had to get far from any explosion—with what strength he had left—he forced himself to crawl up over the berm, slid down the other side, and collapsed.

The bus continued to slide down the runway as smoke and flames erupted from its engine compartment and spread across the underbelly.

Friction won out and the chassis slowed. From the pilots' vantage point, the bus appeared to stop without crashing into the fuel truck. But as it slid to the tanker's rear bumper, it nudged against the truck with sufficient force to puncture the gas tank.

Petrol spilled onto the runway, and snaked along low points as it spread under the bus and beneath the truck.

The helicopters joined standard formation, and the lead pilot took them over the scene—its lights aimed at the vehicles. Having pulled back to avoid flak, the pilots had missed Parker's jump into the darkness.

Searching for signs of life, the pilots did not detect the danger that flowed across the runway.

"Commander Lawton, this is Lead One."

"Go ahead Lead One."

"No sign of movement. Infrared sensors picked up one body— in the middle of the bus. If a second body's in there, it'd show up on the screen. Might've been tossed outside. Await instructions.

Over."

There was a long silence.

"Uh, sir . . . Lead One awaiting instructions. Over."

"I'm sorry, Lead One. Better send a crew down and search the area."

"Will continue to scout. Over."

"Find that second body."

"Understood Commander."

"And be careful. Far as we know, there's still an active bomb down there. Over."

"Roger."

The airman ordered a copter down to perform an on-site search. Two more were sent to scour the length of the runway. And the lead pilot began to circle around the wreckage when something reflected in his lights.

"Let's take it down a bit," he signaled to his co-pilot.

The helicopter hovered closer to the bus as the pilot tightly focused his light below its undercarriage.

"Shit!" He pushed the Talk button and spoke into his helmet mike.

"Move out of here. I repeat, all aircraft clear the area immediately. We're about to have an event on the ground. Coming up and out and banking to the left. Over."

The forward Lynx shot straight up, rotated to port, and proceeded down the runway in the direction of the terminal. The others followed.

"There's petrol everywhere," he radioed. "And the engine's on fire. That tanker's gonna blow skyhigh, any second."

The smell of petrol jarred Haji Al-Masud's senses.

Slowly he regained consciousness and found himself lying amid torn and twisted bench seats. He realized he was alone and had no idea where the bomb's remote control had fallen.

Without regard to injuries, almost methodically, he climbed through twisted remains of the bus in search of his bag and the remote control. Ambient light aided him from the now distant helicopters.

The bomb was jammed under a broken seat, and he couldn't pull it free. Thinking he could set it off manually, Al-Masud reached in for the detonating device. But it had pulled loose and was dumped from the bag during the crash.

In the semi-dark interior of the bus, he braced himself against the upright floor and burned his hand on a hot spot. A pungent odor grabbed at Al-Masud's nostrils, as he realized heat emanated from the undercarriage.

For a moment he thought of living instead of dying. Perhaps he was not meant to die. Dying instantaneously from a bomb, for the glory of Allah, was an honor. Slowly burning to death—or worse, surviving death with third and fourth degree burns over his body was another case entirely.

Somehow he had to escape.

Al-Masud watched flames enter from the engine compartment and through the front windshield. The emergency exit was blocked with wreckage.

The terrorist looked up at exposed side windows, knocked out from impact. He climbed on top of a broken bench-seat to gain height, and stepped on a handrail support post for footing.

Struggling, and in pain, he emerged through a window. His hands grabbed hold of the side panel and, using his elbows to brace himself, inch by inch he pulled the weight of his body up through the opening.

The petrol had worked its way down the entire length of the bus, surrounded the fuel tanker and, somehow, had avoided the flames. Then, out of the surrealistic nighttime scene that unfolded, an ominous whoosh sound overtook Al-Masud's senses and gave birth to the first of four explosions.

The flowing gasoline erupted like a lightning-fast fuse. It started at the engine compartment, raced back to ignite the remaining fuel in the bus petrol tank, flashed under the refueling truck, and instantly set its tires and underbody ablaze.

Al-Masud fought to bring his torso and legs through the window before flames could overtake the entire bus. Then, fire seeped under the collapsed side beneath him and burned through shattered windows, below. He reached for a window bar and sliced his hand on broken glass and twisted metal, but gained leverage and victoriously willed his body up through the opening.

Choking from the caustic smoke, he found himself standing at the rear drive-axle tire next to the tanker. With flames on both sides of the bus, he carefully worked his way down the length of the side panel toward the front, looking for a clear jumping off point.

Within seconds, fiery tires burst, collapsing the tanker's wheelbase from the weight of the jet fuel. As if synchronized, the chassis hit the concrete with a horrendous crash, splitting open the truck's small petrol tank. An intense blast lifted the heavy tanker off the ground—shot remaining petrol across the field like a flamethrower—and weakened the large containment tank on top.

The first explosion caused Al-Masud to lose his balance, slip from the paneling, and fall into the concrete pool of flames. A haunting high-pitched scream—like a wailing siren—emitted from the terrorist as he was instantly set ablaze. Shrieking in pain, his shrill cries were never heard as he blindly ran toward the truck.

The tanker came down against the pavement—its containment tank ruptured—and nearly four thousand gallons of jet fuel ignited in a gigantic moving wave and fireball that rose three hundred fifty feet into the air. It spread out like a phoenix taking wing, and instantly consumed the bus and Haji Al-Masud as it raced across the infield and over the earthen berm on the opposite side.

The remaining bag of Semtex heated to a point of no return, detonated unceremoniously, and dispatched the nearly melted bus carcass into several thousand pieces of debris.

Those in the control tower had watched in horror as the event played out in the distance. The entire night sky momentarily turned to daylight as the succession of blasts illuminated everything in the vicinity. Passengers who had slipped down the escape chutes, but had not yet cleared their planes, raced from the spreading fireball, and scrambled for cover.

Emergency crews and fire trucks, prepared for another disaster, sat on the inner apron awaiting the signal to head out.

"I'll turn over any assistance we can pull from our support operations," Lawton guaranteed the tower's supervisor, as he radioed for backup to be sent to the tarmac. He turned to Wingate.

"Notify triage to be ready for a new set of casualties, in case the area wasn't cleared in time."

"Yes sir." Wingate called out orders on his radio.

"My God I hope we've got the last of those buggers."

Jenny Nakamura looked out toward the burning field and silently cried. Helicopters floated in and out of the drifting smoke as flames spread down the runway, buckled the concrete, and licked at the night sky. *How will we explain this to Cary's family?* she thought to herself.

"Lead One calling Commander Lawton. Over."

"Come in One."

"Sir, the heat's too intense to get up close for our search. There's no sign of Parker anywhere near the runway."

"Keep searching," came the short, curt reply.

"We'll check the perimeter field. He could have been blown beyond the fence. Over."

Lawton turned to Wingate. "Get a line of personnel out there. Search the ground inch by inch."

"Done sir." He moved through the exit and sent a command to muster soldiers and police for the search.

Radio static blared. "Commander. Come in sir."

"Lawton, here."

"This is Lieutenant Putnam, with ballistics, at Terminal Three. So far we've picked up nearly a thousand terrorist gun cartridges.

But they're altogether different . . . appear to be plastic. Hardly anything to them, almost as though they're designed to self-destruct on impact."

"Yes," said Lawton. "That matches what they've pulled from the wounded. We'll be down to take another look. Over."

Lawton put his arm around Nakamura's shoulder and led her out the door. "I'll carry the responsibility for what I've done to my grave. I held off as long as I could."

Nakamura's dark eyes glistened with tears as she turned to Lawton and nodded, knowing all along he was correct in his decision.

"We'll notify Colonel Bramson from Mobile Op just as soon as I meet with ballistics."

"You know, he didn't want to come here. He wasn't even trained for this . . . " her voice faded as the elevator door closed and they descended from the airport tower.

———

Battered and bruised after his jump, Parker had watched the gas ignite under the bus. The spreading fire overtook the tanker, and he knew the area would be decimated. Forcing himself up, Parker struggled for air, and sprinted down a line between the earthen berm and perimeter fence.

He spotted a break and squeezed through to the outskirt.

Just then the force of the radiating blast from the tanker knocked him ten yards across the field and to the ground. Parker looked up as a sea of ignited jet fuel splashed up over the berm, across the fence, and into the boggy grassland—stretching out fingers of searing flame in his direction.

"Damn!" Parker jumped up and pushed his body to outrun the oncoming deathtrap. His left foot caught in the boggy mud and took a shoe. But he raced across the field until he collapsed exhausted, out of danger, as the fire spilled over the area and devoured the shoe.

In the dark, just ahead, Parker had spotted several hundred jetliner passengers gathered together in the cold night air—for safety—some still darting in panic over the fence. The ominous scene reminded him of passengers awaiting their destiny aboard the *Titanic* on that fateful night in 1912.

Slowly he limped toward the crowd, hoping someone would have a radio. Parker heard a voice yell, "There's the terrorist that jumped from the bus."

Several men ran toward him—one with a gun outstretched.

"No!" Parker yelled at the advancing men. "I'm the hostage. Not a terrorist." He collapsed to his knees out of exhaustion. "I'm American."

The group surrounded him and a flashlight shined brightly in his face.

"He's not a terrorist," said the man with the gun.

"Help him up." He dropped the pistol to his side and introduced himself. "Flight Captain Landry. British Airways."

"I'm an American," he gasped for air. "Name's Parker. . . . I was forced to drive the bus."

"You're the one they're looking for?" said Landry.

He took another deep breath. "Right now I'm just looking for a clean bed and two week's sleep. You got a radio, Captain Landry?"

"The emergency coordinator has one. Come, we'll give you a hand." They felt the searing heat from the burning fuel, as Landry reached out and other men lifted him from the ground.

"Let's get you out of this marsh."

The captain looked at Parker. "You need medical attention?"

"I'll be fine." He looked down. "Just some clothes and a new pair of shoes."

Landry laughed. "Be glad that's all you need."

Parker managed a smile.

"We owe you a debt of gratitude," said one of the men. "We were still evacuating passengers. Thought we were goners."

Parker saw lights in the distance. "Have you been in contact with Mobile Operations? I've got to locate Commissioner Lawton of New Scotland Yard."

"Been in touch with Mobile Op from the beginning."

"Get me the Commissioner. My name's Parker," he reminded. "Dr. Cary Parker."

"Parker . . . got it." The flight captain ordered one of the group to forward the message.

Landry and the others assisted a limping and cold Parker—one shoe missing—across the field. And everyone was genuinely pleased to be near the man who saved their lives.

In less than a minute, a Lynx shot across the tarmac to the field and, with little ceremony, evacuated Parker to meet the others in front of Terminal Three. From the helicopter's cabin, Parker was sickened as he witnessed the devastation—lit up by the bright emergency halogens.

The Lynx set down in front of the terminal. Nakamura, Bantam, and Lawton ducked under the rotating blades and rushed to the cabin door as it slid open.

Cary was surprised as Jennifer Nakamura threw her arms around him and hugged tight.

"Thank God you're all right." She looked into his face and brushed his hair back. "We thought you bought it out there." She realized she held on too long and backed off.

Lawton stepped forward and assisted Parker down the steps. "Dr. Parker, I don't know what to say. You were within half a mo of the window closing on you."

"I understand, Commissioner. I expected you to act sooner. Thanks for holding back."

"Ms. Nakamura tweaked my conscience just long enough."

Parker winked at Jennifer.

"Better get you to a hospital," said Bantam.

"No. I need a good night's sleep.

"Let's at least X-ray while the med-van's on site—to be certain you've no broken bones."

"Don't need a pinched lung from a cracked rib," said Nakamura.

They escorted Parker to the van. A physician cleansed and bandaged scrapes and bruises as the films were processed. An enterprising assistant appropriated Parker a new pair of shoes, from the blown out Heel and Toe store inside the terminal. NSY would settle with the owners later.

"Diagnostics show no breaks or fractures," said the physician. "You're extremely fortunate, young man."

"Don't feel so young right now."

"This is a rather atypical welcome to our British Isles," said Lawton, in an attempt to lighten the moment.

"Quite frankly," said Parker, "right now I feel like retreating to my sub and hiding under the deep scattering layer." He glanced at Nakamura. "I've had enough terrorism to last a lifetime."

———

The roads into London were unusually clear for a Monday night, and the forty-five minute taxi drive from Heathrow had been quiet for Parker and Nakamura. Both had tried to nap, but neither could wipe images and smells of death from their minds. Angered and overwhelmed by what he had seen, Parker found he could no longer refuse the mission.

The rubicund, square-jawed cabby had offered Parker his services as a courtesy. "Hell of a way to greet visitors to our country," he had said of the attack. A chiseled, leathery face disguised his sixty-three years—with over four decades as a driver.

The cab turned onto Brompton Road. Its driver wanted to be congenial with his guests. But after directly facing the grim scene at the airport—conscripted to carry wounded to hospital—he hadn't been in the mood to talk much. The taxi would have to be cleaned in the morning, before taking on fares, since bandage cuttings and other medicinal remnants were left behind by the medics.

By 10:30, most of London's main streets were deserted. It seemed anyone not having to be out was watching television, as BBC's continuous coverage of Heathrow's disaster competed head-to-head with CNN International.

The cab passed the still brightly lit Harrod's Department Store, and made a left into old stately Beaufort Gardens, in Kensington. Fifty-foot high elm trees awaited spring foliage and lined the middle of the street.

"Today reminded me of World War II," the driver broke the silence and looked into his rear-view mirror.

"As a boy we'd hide under bridges when German bombs hit. Rather frightening, y' know."

"Still haunt you?" asked Parker.

"Like it was yesterday . . . But today brought back the memories. Sounds mostly." He was silent for a moment as he maneuvered the cab between the parked cars and the median that divided both sides of the four and five storied Regency-styled flats and and small hotels. "I hear warnings just about every day over my CB. A bomb threat here—another there. Y' get used to it, y' know. Slowed down a bit, during the IRA truce. But who knows what's next. . . . Never thought it would happen like this."

The cab turned around at the end of the median and pulled in front of the Claverley Hotel.

"You should sample the bill o' fare at the local pubs, with a pint or two, if ya' know what I mean." The driver looked up, winked in the rear-view mirror, and Parker saw him smile for the first time.

"You'll want to get out around town." He set his flashers and turned to look back through the glass divider. "Wheeler's m' name. John Wheeler. I'd be happy t' take you for a spin any day you're ready."

He jumped out of the driver's side, opened Nakamura's door, signaled Parker to wait, and hurried around to the left side to personally let him out.

Wheeler straightened and looked Parker in the eyes, "Try gettin' into the Ceremony of the Keys at the Tower of London. That's the ticket to get. Kinda' exclusive . . . by invitation only, if ya' know what I mean.

"Ceremony of the Keys . . . " repeated Parker.

"M' wife and I had tickets, years ago, but she came down ill and we couldn't make it. I've tried three times since, and we still 'aven't seen the Ceremony."

"What's it about?" asked Nakamura.

"The guard force of Yeoman Warders—the ones who protect the Tower together with the Queen's foot soldiers—perform the Ceremony by lockin' up the Tower of London and the Crown Jewels, at precisely nine fifty-three every night."

Wheeler assisted Nakamura with her luggage, as they climbed the Claverley's entry steps. "Been doin' it almost seven hundred years," said Wheeler. "Only missed a beat once . . . World War II. Seems a German bomb dropped near the man holdin' the keys. Delayed the lockup about thirty seconds."

"Thanks for your suggestion," said Parker. "And your hospitality. Will you take twenty to treat your wife to dinner?"

The driver held up his hand as if to say *no*. "Don't insult me on your first night in London, now, will ya'?" He smiled.

"We know your name," said Parker. "But this day has separated us from our manners."

"Not to worry."

Parker made the introductions and apologized again. "I may give you a call in the morning," he said. "I have to head out toward Surrey. Do you service that area?"

"M' home's in Surrey."

"Perfect. Talk with you tomorrow." Parker grabbed his Armani bag, purchased at Washington National the evening before— though it seemed like it had already been a week—and limped to the entrance landing.

Nakamura pushed the hotel's security buzzer at the front door. She could see the night desk clerk across the lobby check them out through the well-placed camera just inside the entrance foyer. The lock clicked and buzzed until Parker pulled the door open.

The hotel lobby's Victorian decor was a comforting sight. Jennifer placed her bags on the floor next to the circular velveteen, high-back sofa, and collapsed on its seat.

"I'll need your passport," said Parker.

Jennifer reached into her bag, pulled out her papers, and he moved to the counter.

"Good evening. Dr. Parker and Ms. Nakamura, I presume?"

"How'd you know?"

"We have few rooms. And all other guests have checked in for the night. Besides," the clerk smiled, "we received a call from a Mr. Bramson warning you'd be late."

"Ah, the CIA's checking up on us already," he said to Jennifer.

Nakamura shot him a frown that said *Watch what you're saying.*

"You've come directly from Heathrow?" said the clerk.

"Afraid so," said Parker.

"Had my eyes glued to the telly ever since this afternoon. Terrible tragedy."

Parker nodded.

"We've two lovely rooms down the hall from each other. Didn't have adjoining."

"My *wife* will be grateful," Parker joked.

"Third floor." He handed Parker the keys. "Coffee, tea or cocoa's in the reading room just down the hallway. Complimentary breakfast begins at six-thirty. Under the circumstances, if you sleep in, just call us when you rise."

Parker opened the outer door of the two-person lift and slid the gate back. With aplomb they squeezed into the cramped space, with their luggage, closed the gate and pushed 3.

Nakamura leaned against the wall, closed her eyes with a sigh, and opened them again. Parker knew she felt as he did— thoroughly exhausted and excruciatingly awake.

Both were wired from the day's events. Each had only slept for minutes at a time, since Sunday, yet sleep eluded them.

"I'd hoped to get over jet lag, tonight," said Parker, raising his eyes in disgust. "But I'm too wound up for sleep."

"Same here. Prefer to talk a while?"

Parker checked his watch. "It's five thirty-five at home. Normally, I wouldn't think about sleep for another five or six hours—U.S. time."

"I need to splash cool water on my face and unpack, first."

"I'll call Vickie. Meet you in the reading room in twenty minutes."

The key turned easily enough in the lock, but the thick layers of paint caused the turn-of-the-century door to stick. Cary lightly shouldered the door as he turned the handle, and it gave way. Nonetheless, pain raced to his neck—a result of his tumble from the bus—and he was instantly sorry he hadn't chosen a less macho technique.

More of the lush decorations, seen in the lobby, adorned his spacious room. Large feather bed, ample upholstered chairs, a sitting area with couch and, facing the tall heavily draped windows was a carved rosewood desk and chair—*Probably a campaign relic from India*, he theorized.

Tossing his bag on the bed, Cary sat on its edge, not certain he had the energy to call home. He rubbed his neck and thought of canceling with Nakamura. But he pushed that back in his mind, for the moment, and picked up the phone's receiver.

When Cary was away, Victoria screened calls through the answerphone. Absorbed with architectural renderings, carpet samples, and upholstery swatches, as soon as she heard the familiar, "It's me," she raced for the phone.

"Thank God you're safe. Where are you?"

"Claverley Hotel. You hear about Heathrow?"

"That's all we've seen on TV. They're reporting total devastation. Not much else."

"Just terminal three was hit."

"Good thing your plane was diverted."

"You knew?"

"Colonel Bramson called as soon as it hit CNN. He didn't want me to panic."

"Decent of him. What'd he tell you?"

"Not much. Said he hadn't received intelligence worth noting. Just wanted me to know you and the FBI agent are okay."

Cary volunteered nothing. "Anything new since I left?"

"I won the bid to redecorate the offices at Boston's new City Hall." Her voice was euphoric.

"Terrific. Congratulations."

"I'm excited. And—oh yes, Marlowe got into a scrap with a boy at school."

"Anyone we know?"

"Uh-uh. An eighth grader. Nothing serious. He made remarks about her first bra."

"What'd she do?"

"Got tired of his teasing and slapped him."

"Hard?"

"Damn hard."

"Good for her."

"Yeah, I suppose. Of course, the principal called. She was supportive. Said she discussed the issue with Marlowe and the boy separately."

"How's she taking it?"

"Fine. She's a Parker. What can I say?" Victoria laughed. "But I can't believe I told her young ladies shouldn't do that." She giggled in thought.

"Here's the best part. Want to know what Marlowe said?"

"Sure."

"She stood there with her hands on her hips in disbelief and told me, 'Mother, a woman can't always tend her garden.' Whatever that means. . . . "

Cary laughed hard, but winced from pain, glad Victoria couldn't see him. "You've trained her well."

"Ummm," she answered as they savored the silence between

thoughts.

"Speaking of which—where are the girls?"

"At the Silberman's. Should be home soon. We're having your favorite, tonight—pizza."

"God, that sounds so good."

Victoria's voice became serious, "You're not telling me everything, are you?"

He hesitated. "Just overwhelmed with what I saw, tonight."

She waited for more. "Still aren't going to tell me?"

"Uh-uh."

Victoria knew she shouldn't press. "I miss you, already."

"Me, too."

"By the way, you've got two calls. One from Dr. Senanayake in Sri Lanka."

Cary became more alert. "Haven't talked with Erwin in weeks."

"He's flying to Nice for the Conference on Undersea Recovery."

"Great," said Cary.

"And wants to talk about the new treaty. We had a pleasant talk. The other call was from Paris. A Dr. Levard, regarding the conference."

"That son-of-a-gun."

"I think he wants you to give up your fight for the salvage treaty."

"Of course. The French are dragging their feet on the territorial limit issue for restriction of salvage rights. As I expected, nearly everyone's playing politics as usual."

"Maybe that's your problem."

"The territorial issue?"

"No, you prefaced your remarks with, 'As I expected.' Maybe that's your problem."

"I'm not following you . . . " Cary rubbed his neck, thinking again about canceling with Nakamura.

"You've often told me, 'You get what you expect.' Perhaps it's a self-fulfilling prophecy to *expect* everyone to play politics. Maybe you should *expect* them to settle their differences, regardless of the political outcome—to do what's right."

"I'll put that in my next speech, if you don't mind."

"Long as you credit the author," Victoria said with a chuckle. "When should I pick you up at the airport?"

"Uncertain. But I don't want you fighting traffic into Logan, especially with the kids. I'll catch a limo."

"Can't wait to see you."

"Just a couple of days. . . . I love you."

"Love you, too. Call me tomorrow?"

"Deal."

Cary sighed as he hung up the receiver. Just a couple of days— he hoped. He pushed himself off the bed. As much as he might want to crawl under its covers, he knew he wouldn't be able to sleep until he talked with Nakamura.

Jennifer had changed into a silk jogging suit before coming down to the library. The room was decorated eclectically with two French Rococo sofas, an Irish mahogany side table, and four overstuffed, high-back chairs scattered about. Oriental rugs covered most of the dark hardwood floor.

She mixed a packet of Cadbury's hot chocolate with water, adding four small creamers for a richer taste. Jennifer savored the rich smell as she moved to the bay window, overlooking the Elm-lined Beaufort Gardens. She pulled out a Queen Anne-revival walnut chair, and sat at the leather-topped writing desk.

Wish I felt like sending postcards home.

Jennifer anticipated putting the day's events behind her. She began to focus on pleasant thoughts—a technique she learned years before to maintain her sanity.

Cary pushed open the carved wooden door. He had traded torn clothes for Stanford University sweats, grabbed from his office closet before leaving Washington.

"You look relaxed," he said, noticeably limping into the room.

Jennifer smiled blissfully. "The hot chocolate's with the coffee and tea."

"Tea for me." Parker moved to a Louis XV walnut buffet, measured Sri Lankan tea into a brewing ball, placed it in a cup, and filled it with hot water.

Hanging over the tall mantle above the sculpted marbled fireplace was a sizable painting of Lloyd's Coffee House—the famous old gathering place for marine underwriters.

Parker's eyes circled the room. Portraits of nineteenth and early twentieth century notables peered down from richly gold-leafed, elaborately carved oversized frames—and filled every available wall space.

"If ever eyes stared from walls..." he mused.

Jennifer chuckled, then sipped lightly from her cup. "How's your wife? Worried, I'll bet."

"Saw the reports on CNN. Fortunately, the colonel had enough sense to call."

"You didn't tell her about the bus."

"Thought I'd save that one for three or four years from now."

Nakamura smiled again and rose from her chair in thought. "Still bothered by the mission after what you saw?"

"I've considered our discussion on the plane," he said, and sat on the edge of a sofa. "The part about vengeance and taking away freedoms."

Jennifer nodded and moved closer to Cary.

"After today's disaster," said Parker, "witnessing death and suffering, first hand—not to mention the bus incident—it's difficult not to see these terrorists as anything but criminals."

"They were senseless acts," said Jennifer.

"Committed by fanatics...but just a small percentage out of a race of good people," he said.

"The challenge," said Nakamura, "is to separate those who perpetrate death on the innocent, from those who struggle with life but don't inflict harm on others just because life isn't going their way."

"But even despots believe what they do is for the good of

society. Why not terrorists?"

"It's all perception, isn't it?" she said. "And how they discern the world around them."

"Of course." Parker sipped his tea. "So, as with psychotics, terrorists believe their actions truly resolve their problems—whether Arab, Irish, or American."

"A fine line to walk, but from their perspective, yes. That's not to justify or minimize what happened today. It just allows us to set them apart and attempt to understand their point of view. Then we can deal with the symptoms and, ultimately, the issues."

Both were silent for a time.

"What I can't grasp," said Parker, "are the events in Ragem's life that caused him to react so violently to western society, he'd do anything to show his distaste for it."

"Understand," said Nakamura, "terrorism's been around the Middle East since the first century, when ancient Palestinian Zealots opposed the Romans. In the eleventh century, Christian crusaders were assaulted throughout Persia and Syria by a deadly sect known as the Assassins."

She refilled her chocolate, then sat in the large overstuffed chair next to Cary. "Violence becomes compulsive behavior—a physiological, chemical addiction—like anything that dulls the mind over time....A natural narcotic that desensitizes all ability for rational thought.

"Like alcohol, illicit sex or drugs," she continued, "violence tends to feed on itself and requires more and more just to satisfy what becomes an habitual obsession."

Nakamura suddenly blushed and looked into her cup. "Sorry, I didn't mean to climb on my soapbox"

"It's all right," Parker said, impressed with her knowledge. "But where's the turning point that took Ragem from a young boy to a malicious, unforgiving assassin?"

Nakamura smiled ironically, "Ragem honestly believes, deep in his heart—in his psyche—he's doing what Allah commands. But what compels a person to feel so much hate he'd use deadly force to express opinions in a marketplace? Wish I had the answer."

Her dark eyes burned with the passion of her beliefs. "I got a little carried away." Jennifer's silky voice trailed off into silence.

"Not at all," said Parker. "I'm beginning to understand your reason for success. . . . And the softness under that mysterious cover."

She blushed again, relaxed for the first time, then allowed herself the luxury to slide deeply into the overstuffed cushions. Her eyes felt heavy.

Both stared at nothing in particular as they reflected on the magnitude of their circumstances. The room was quiet. Only the sound of a car pulling away from the curb filtered through from outside. Then, Jennifer sat up in earnest on the edge of her chair, "Have you ever read Plato's *Dialogues* or *The Seventh Letter?*"

"Years ago."

"I ask because . . . why we're in London, all centers around how reliant and fail-safe our intelligence should be for any operation."

She stared out into the room, searching for a thought. "Used to be when terrorists hit an area and captured hostages, the military reaction was to perform a surgical strike on an enemy site—sometimes arriving by ground, occasionally by sea, but often from the air."

"Like Entebbe," said Parker.

"Exactly. Swift retribution accompanied the rescue of hostages before the enemy knew what hit them. It all depended on solid intelligence."

"And the Israelis had the capacity to get it, didn't they?"

Jennifer nodded, "Because of legal handcuffs, it's difficult for us to get critical, accurate intelligence *before* terrorist actions occur, or to make decisive moves on terrorist cells once we know who's included."

"Lack of congressional support, I suppose," he said.

"Budgetary, mostly. . . . The Pentagon can pull dollars like rabbits from a hat, for the war machine, but give the Bureau need-ed financial resources for preventative measures?" Her laughter bordered on sarcasm.

"What about the World Trade Center?"

"We were damned lucky with that," said Jennifer. "Sure, we had our suspicions. But Oklahoma City reminded us we can't jump to conclusions about perpetrators. Their overwhelming stupidity was all we had to lead us through the who-done-it stages. That's the kind of event the FBI can solve with its eyes closed."

"After the fact."

"Yes," she said. "That's better than the cold-blooded sarin gas murders in Japan where no one took responsibility for them. The easiest to solve are the cases where suspects are so myopic, so obviously culpable, they leave evidence or hints of involvement everywhere."

"Or so fundamentally embrace their beliefs," said Cary, "they subconsciously desire recognition by Allah for their deeds against the *perceived* infidels."

"Correct."

"So," he said, "they unintentionally leave affirmations strewn everywhere."

Jennifer considered his statement, "Affirmations—yeah, that says it all. To them, affirmations of their faith. To us, evidence of their guilt."

Cary looked directly at Jennifer. "Then regardless of the cir-cumstances, it boils down to 'us and them,' doesn't it?"

"Afraid so," agreed Nakamura.

"Isn't that too simplified? To say there's no middle ground for negotiation between factions or their philosophies?"

"It's those who oversimplify that we deal with these days," she said. "The fanatic zealot who sees black or white rather than shades of gray."

"So, where does Plato come in?" he said.

"Do you remember Plato's story of the elephant and the blind men?"

"Sure. If a blind man touched an elephant's leg—"

"He might think it a trunk of a tree," she said.

"Yet others might maintain they touched a snake—"

"After touching the trunk or the elephant's tail. That's essentially it," said Jennifer. "That analogy fits within the intelligence community. Without information in its entirety, our intelligence is useless. Often it's too incomplete to give us a true picture about who we're dealing with or looking for, in worldwide terrorist operations."

"So," said Cary, "because of budget, political, or time constraints, administration might interpret existing intelligence as enough to make a decision?"

"Or even complete an existing operation—no matter how weak the source. The control is typically political pressure."

"I often think that's how Colonel Bramson operates," said Parker.

"He means well," said Nakamura. "But CIA and FBI are both guilty of relying too much on electronic surveillance. We've discounted the need for human contact, gut-level intuition, and the type of information we can only get by digging for it—getting our hands dirty. We've only recently returned to that mode with infiltration of international terrorist cells and the local militias."

"Since Oklahoma City?"

Jennifer nodded. "If anything came from that tragedy, it's the fact we've been able to reenter the human phase of intelligence gathering, to protect our citizens *before* perpetrators can act out crimes."

"Talk about exposing yourself to danger," he said.

"But we agreed earlier, danger is relative, isn't it? Undercover agents rely on all forms of surveillance, beyond pure electronics. Disciplined research for one; counter-spies and informants; long hours of observing suspects; and, intercepting messages between those who direct operations and those who carry them out."

"That's how you ferret leads on terrorists in America."

"And that's why we're in London," she said.

Parker glanced at the painting of the old marine underwriters. "I imagine the number one problem is filtering intelligence *between* agencies and congressional committees who deal with it."

"You're catching on fast. They're too territorial to share intelligence for the common good," Jennifer said. "Just too much stovepiping."

"Now there's an interesting term . . . "

"Every agency, whether ATF, DEA, FBI, or CIA, stovepipes information. They send smoke—intelligence—up their own stovepipe . . . through the organization, so it doesn't get shared with other agencies who may be investigating the very same issue. Too often, affairs come down to the wire, only to discover another agency has had the needed information all along."

"But," said Parker, "the fact that CIA and FBI are jointly moving on this operation must mean they've put elbows in the stovepipes."

"That in itself says volumes. Our Central Command is cooperating more with CIA, now. We're sharing data from both central computers, to compare discrepancies between leads and to determine priorities."

"And that increases joint probabilities for success," he said.

"Sure. In the morning I'll meet with terrorism experts at NSY. Then M-5 and M-6 will open files for me to scour. I've no doubt a new wave of terrorism's on its way. In fact, I'm convinced it's already begun. I think there're factions we haven't heard of yet who'll hold the U.S. and the entire western world hostage if we don't act to head them off."

"Think so?"

"High-level government officials blithely dismiss, and even laugh at, the prospect of germ and chemical warfare or nuclear attacks on our own turf."

"Even with nerve-gas canisters in Japan?"

"Even with that," she said. "And who needs a thermonuclear device when you can smuggle radioactive Plutonium Two-thirty-nine and enriched uranium out of the old Soviet Union in tin cans and lipstick cases?"

"To poison water supplies or other dirty deeds," said Parker.

Jennifer glanced at Cary. "On the black market Two-thirty-nine brings in nearly four hundred fifty thousand dollars an ounce. And there are people...organizations buying it."

"Well, you've scared the crap outta me." Parker used both hands to push himself up from his seat. He set his cup on the buffet and limped to the door—stretching his lower back with palms at his waist. "My body aged twenty years today....I'm bruised everywhere."

"Think you're sore now....Wait 'til morning." Jennifer smiled broadly as he opened the door. "I'm a damn good masseuse... "

Suddenly, the edges of Parker's blue eyes were careworn. "A few years ago, I might've had reasons to take you up on that. Maybe another time..."

"Cary."

Parker turned back to Jennifer. "Yeah?"

"I'm really glad you're safe."

Parker flashed a wide smile and winked. "Not half as glad as I." The door swung closed and Jennifer decided to write home, after all.

———

ESHER - SURREY, ENGLAND

THE drive through the countryside was breathtaking. After using all of the morning and the early part of the afternoon to recuperate from the events at Heathrow, Parker arranged for cab owner, John Wheeler, to pick him up at the Claverley Hotel for a ride out to Esher. Wheeler used a borrowed taxi while his was cleaned.

As the black cab pulled up to the estate's entrance, Wheeler looked back at his fare and smiled. "This is it, Doc. Some friend you have here. Must be related to the Queen."

Parker saw the grand entrance and whistled slowly.

Stone walls gracefully curved down from the highest point, at each end of the wrought-iron gate, to form statuesque posts topped with sculptured marble cherubs. Thick, exquisitely trimmed, bright green hedges—looking like they had protected the land since well before George III—extended from each cherub and roamed the outer edges of the property.

Parker opened the cab door and stepped to the gravel. He looked through the gate to the large, imposing Tudor mansion that sat nearly 600 yards from the approach. Tall, carefully shaped rose shrubs lined the driveway. Curved, solid concrete benches were interspersed between the roses and shrubbery that lined the immaculate lawn on both sides.

At the left of the gate an intercom sat under a brightly polished brass plate that held the inscription, *Whitehills*. Parker pushed the button and waited for a response.

No one answered. He pressed the button once more.

"Hello?" came an elderly sounding reply.

"Mr. White?"

"Yes?"

"I'm Cary Parker. I believe you were expecting me."

"Oh, yes, yes. The American. Excuse me for taking so long to get to the speaker box. Drive in, young man."

A buzzer sounded as the gate unlocked and began to open wide. Parker returned to the cab and Wheeler pulled in. Sensing the car had passed through, the gate immediately shut behind them.

The driveway circled in front of the main entrance. Wheeler stopped at the marble steps just as the large mahogany door opened. A tall and imposing elderly man stepped forward.

Parker was struck by the man's wide, enthusiastic smile and a pair of ardent eyes that filled his ample, sagacious face. Though Parker knew him to be in his late eighties, the man moved as if he were fifty. Only a slight stoop of his big shoulders and thinning, pure white hair gave him away. There was a warmth and intensity found only in a person who had a passion for life.

Byron White waved Parker onto the porch. "Come in. Come in, young man. Good afternoon."

Parker arranged to call for the cab in a few hours. As Wheeler drove off for the gate, Parker turned back to the stately gentleman and smiled.

"Mr. White. Cary Parker. How are you?"

"Oh, just glad I'm alive. But no more than you, I'm sure."

The bookbinder extended one of his immense hands to greet the scientist and heartily pulled Parker into the foyer. White's palm and fingers enclosed Parker's entire hand, reminding him of the occasion—as a youngster—when he shook hands with Primo Carnera at the giant boxer's West Los Angeles restaurant.

"You arrived in England about the hour of that dreadful attack at Heathrow, didn't you?"

"I'm afraid so." Parker decided not to discuss the entire episode. "Our plane was diverted to Gatwick. Unfortunately some weren't so lucky. What a tragedy."

"Indeed. Well, I'm glad you're safe my boy. They haven't said much on the telly about the culprits."

"I'm expecting a phone call about that this afternoon. Hope you don't mind."

"Not at all," said White. "So glad you could come. I've much to share."

"I'm honored."

"Actually, it should be the other way around. I've read of your undersea exploits for many years. Along with that Dr. Ballard fellow. I commend you both for your accomplishments."

White put his arm around Parker's shoulder and lead him through an arched alcove, painted with frescoes reminiscent of Raphael's Italian Renaissance style. Fully winged swans pulled at the air to glide across an imaginary blue pond. At the edges of the water were ghostly likenesses of Aristotle, Plato, Copernicus, and da Vinci. Gold-leafed lilies floated in the pond like stars in a sky. It reminded Parker of rare book illuminations he had seen at the British Museum, years before.

They entered a large sitting room and library. Parker took in the 18th century European style decoration—the floors, walls and furniture covered with tapestries. A fire in the marble fireplace crackled and made the room warm and inviting on a cold spring afternoon.

"This is my favorite room, I suppose," said White. "Reminds me of many a book we hand bound and gilt at our bindery. I spend much of my retirement in here—and in my workshop."

"Breathtaking. My wife's an interior designer. I wish she could see this."

"Ah, yes. Well, I regret my wife isn't here to greet you. Eternally shopping, you know."

Parker gazed at the room. Over the mantle and to each side, gold-gilded plaster frames, with vines encircling carved scrolls, enclosed oil paintings of each of the Three Graces. Glass-enclosed barrister bookcases, filled with hundreds of hand-bound books, lined the walls at both ends. Gobelin-style tapestries of birds in flight covered the remaining walls. A Queen Anne style Chinese-lacquer walnut cabinet and a large walnut desk filled the room.

White sat himself in one of the Louis XVth armchairs as he motioned for Parker to sit on the matching couch. "From what I'm told, you have quite an assignment ahead."

"I have."

"When the *Titanic* was first visited, Dr. Parker, I read much in the press about the position you and that Dr. Ballard took regarding the ship as a protected gravesite. I admire your not wanting to bring up the artifacts. And I don't wish to put you off. But I must tell you I disagree wholeheartedly.

"I believe any treasure or valuable artifact *should* be recovered if humanly possible. It does no one any good at the bottom of the sea. I hope you understand my position."

"I've given it a lot of thought lately," said Parker. "Our stance is more in line with archaeologically saving artifacts that provide us with new information—data we might not otherwise have had. With the *Titanic*, most everything on board was already documented. And it's still a gravesite. That's where we differ."

"Of course. But imagine the excitement it would bring to an old man like me, having spent most of my lifetime dreaming about the *Great Omar*, and having made two reproductions myself."

He rose from his chair and picked up a framed color photograph from his desk. "This is my second copy of the *Omar*—taken at the ceremony where I placed it on loan to the British Museum." He handed it to his guest.

In the photo, White stood next to a tall, round mahogany table. He proudly held his copy of the *Omar* binding atop the table, opened out to display both the front and back covers.

On the front cover, three peacocks—two with feathers flowing to a border of inlaid vines and grapes, the other with its feathers proudly unfurled—glowed back from the camera's flash as ninety-seven topazes sparkled from the eyes of the peacock's feathers.

Rubies formed the eyes of the birds, while eighteen pieces of turquoise shaped their crests. Two hundred fifty amethysts formed bunches of grapes, and a hundred eighty-nine olivines, garnets, and turquoises suggested the Persian-design border surrounding the peacocks. A small, carved mahogany model of a Persian mandolin filled the center of the back cover, inset into hundreds of pieces of delicately cut leather. Inlaid with pearl, ebony, silver, and satin-wood, the entire design was encircled by almost two hundred additional jewels.

Parker was taken by the beauty of the photograph. "I've seen old black and white photos of the original *Omar*. But they didn't do Sangorski's designs justice. This is breathtaking."

White looked directly at Parker. "I'd give anything to see the original book brought to the surface, actually. No matter the condition." White drifted off in his revelry as he stared into the photograph.

"I certainly respect your position, Mr. White. It's our intent to locate the book as soon as humanly possible. That is, if it still exists."

"Indeed some of it could still exist. I'm certain of it. The question remains, was the *Great Omar* moved from storage at the last minute before the *Titanic* went down?"

"Do you believe it's still fully intact?"

"It was wrapped and packed to withstand a lot of moisture. Of course, no one ever thought it was necessary to protect it from a sinking ship. They were more concerned about shielding it from moisture content in the air. And particularly keen on protecting its identity on board, because of the jewels."

"Ironic isn't it," said Parker. "They thought more about thievery than the possibility of the *Titanic* going down."

"I confess sinking would never have occurred to me. But there were always thieves on board those ships. Some known. Others under assumed names so they could take advantage of the unsuspecting."

White rose from his chair and moved toward the door. "Forgive me, Dr. Parker. I've been rude. Would you enjoy a spot of tea?"

"Yes, thank you. Ceylon tea?"

"Dyagama, of course," said White as he left the room.

Parker moved to the bookcases at the far end of the luxuriously appointed room. He carefully glided up one of the lead-filled glass doors and parked it under the shelf above. The smell of fine Morocco leather gently wafted through his nostrils. He read each gold-embossed title on the spines of green, brown, white, crimson and other colorful, delicately bound books.

Titles and authors jumped at him from the pages of history.

A multi-volume set of *The Novels of Jane Austen*, dated 1898, stood out in blue half morocco, with ruled gilt on the cover and gilt 'Art and Crafts' style decoration in compartments on the spine. A depiction of Jane Austen, from the portrait by her sister, Cassandra, served as a frontispiece.

Sir Arthur Conan Doyle's *The Adventures of Sherlock Holmes*, dated 1893, contained illustrations by the well-known Sidney

Paget and sat proudly in a protective slip case.

A crown quarto edition of Nathaniel Hawthorne's *The Scarlet Letter*, "with illustrations by Hugh Thomson," sat next to *Letters on Demonology and Witchcraft*, addressed to J.G. Lockhart, Esq., from Sir Walter Scott. Dated 1830, twelve etched plates by George Cruikshank were featured inside.

Parker's eyes, though, were drawn to an 1837 first edition of Charles Dickens' *The Posthumous Papers of the Pickwick Club*—the book that gave Dickens his fame. Bound in green morocco with a decorative gilt spine, a red leather inlay of Dickens' initials was set into the center of the outside cover.

Parker carefully removed it from its velvet-lined fall-down-back box, and opened it to reveal an exquisite miniature of Dickens— placed inside the red morocco doublure for additional ornamentation.

"Did you know the beautiful leather you're handling was soaked in either dog or pigeon dung?" said White as he reentered the chamber.

Parker laughed in amusement. "I'll never pick up another book."

White set a silver tray on the edge of his desk—complete with a lightly chased and filigreed Barnard silver teapot and cream-jug, cake- and sugar-baskets, and Royal Worcester porcelain cups and saucers with tooled gold decoration—all of the Victorian era. The tray held a selection of assorted tea sandwiches, pastries, home baked scones—with Devonshire clotted cream—and strawberry jam.

He poured tea through a hand-held strainer.

"Soaking leather in dung was the only way to free it from its natural greases and from the lime solution used to soak off the hair." He handed a cup and saucer to Parker.

"The process is peculiar to morocco leather. It's considered the best leather for binding books for reference or private collections. Lasts forever."

The bookbinder continued, "Of course, they began using more

scientific methods in place of the dung around the turn-of-the-century. As you can surmise it was a fairly pungent aroma in the early days of tanning." He laughed. "I'm not certain it's improved much since."

White smiled animatedly as he noticed the book in Parker's hands. "*Pickwick Club*. S and S illuminated that one—Sangorski and Sutcliffe, the bindery I worked for and, I should say, managed for thirty-three of my sixty-two years there. Now it's S S and Zed."

"Zed?"

"Ah, yes. You Americans pronounce it as "Zee," don't you? Forgive me, it's S S and Z. They merged with Zaehnsdorf, a formidable competitor of ours for many years. Actually, Joseph Zaehnsdorf founded his London company in eighteen forty-two, long before Sangorski. They moved to Soho in 1890. With the merge, S S and Z is over near Tower of London, now.

"Francis Sangorski, of the original S and S, was the master bookbinder who created the *Great Omar*."

"In partnership with George Sutcliffe, your uncle," said Parker.

"Correct. At any rate, Dickens' *Posthumous Papers* is one of my favorites. Executed in the acclaimed Cosway style, invented by John Stonehouse. A Cosway binding will always have a painted miniature inlaid in gold-tooled morocco leather. Stonehouse managed Henry Sotheran's famous bookstore back then. I believe you'll visit there tomorrow."

"Yes."

White opened the book to the miniature portrait, set under glass in the front doublure.

"Dickens was only twenty-seven when his portrait was done by the world-famous Daniel Maclise. This miniature copy was based on that painting. Many of the miniatures were painted by the prominent copyist, Miss C.B. Currie.

"But the story continues. This same miniature was engraved, at a later date, to become the frontispiece to Dickens' *Nicholas Nickleby*."

"A beautiful piece of work. Must be quite valuable." Parker

handed the book to White.

"I'll never part with it. But in today's market it would be worth around thirty-seven hundred pounds sterling. Slightly under six thousand of your American dollars."

The bookbinder moved to the open case, replaced Dickens and pulled another from the shelf. "This is my favorite. You'll be amazed what I have here."

Parker moved to the bookcase as Mr. White proudly handed him a rich-looking, red goatskin-covered book, dated 1847, and titled *Sonnets* by Elizabeth Barrett Browning.

"Some would say this one is priceless," said White, a gleeful smile on his face. "Turn to the doublure of the upper cover."

Parker opened the beautifully gold- and blind-tooled book. The inside doublures and fly-leaves were of gold-tooled green goatskin. But Parker's eyes were drawn to a small, circular compartment in the center of the doublure. Embossed in a triple circle of gold-leaf was the inscription, "LOCK OF ELIZABETH BARRETT BROWNING'S HAIR," Underneath the circle were the words, "GIVEN TO ROBERT BROWNING BEFORE MARRIAGE."

"I paid dearly for that one. I've never had an affair outside my marriage. But I've loved Elizabeth Barrett Browning ever since my school days." He quoted from Browning, "`...I love thee to the depth and breadth and height my soul can reach, when feeling out of sight. For the ends of Being and ideal Grace... '"

Parker continued the line, "`...I love thee to the level of every day's most quiet need, by sun and candlelight.'"

"Most remarkable." White stood motionless, lost in the memory of years gone by.

"And now you have a lock of her hair," said Parker, amused by the silver-haired man's new-found blush. "That must make your wife jealous."

"Quite the contrary." White glanced over at the scientist. "She's ecstatic this is as far as I got with anyone."

The two men laughed together and moved back across the

room—White holding the small *Sonnets* close to his chest.

"So, Dr. Parker, what can I tell you that you don't already know?" White set the book on his desk, clearly intending to review selected passages later on. He picked up the teapot, refilled each cup, and sat in his chair.

Parker settled into the couch. The afternoon light cast a bright glow across the delicately designed Persian red and gold medallion carpet in front of him.

"We have good reason to believe terrorists are going after the *Great Omar* and any jewelry remaining on board the *Titanic*." He took one final sip of tea and set the cup down.

"No diver has ever come across the *Omar*, despite thorough searches. We knew the book existed but we'd never investigated the possibilities for its method of shipment, storage on board or, for that matter, who the courier was . . . charged with its safety and security."

"If I may, young man," White interrupted, "I believe you should be more aware of *how* the *Titanic Omar* came about. Of course, I refer to it as *Titanic Omar* because of the two copies I've produced, following the ship's sinking. The only existing copy is now under lock and key at the British Museum."

Parker nodded in agreement.

"That way you might gain a better appreciation for its place in history and understand the love and care that went into its binding."

"I understand."

"When I came on board Sangorski and Sutcliffe, in nineteen twenty-four, I was a young apprentice of seventeen. Thought I had the world by the tail and no one could tell me I wouldn't succeed in the bookbinding business. Not even my uncle, George Sutcliffe.

"Imagine. Here I was a strapping young fellow, peering over craftsmen's shoulders, day in and day out, trying to learn all their methods, but wanting all along to do it myself.

"Still, in nineteen twenty-four, twelve years after the sinking of the *Titanic*, hardly a day went by without someone saying, 'This is good work, but you should have seen the *Great Omar*.'"

"Unfortunately, Mr. Lovett, the undisputed master finisher —who had done all of the tooling on the book—died of tuberculosis when I was quite young. The year after *Titanic* sank. But Uncle George and everyone else talked about the binding at every opportunity—Mr. Byrnes, who actually bound the *Omar*, the craftsmen and sewing ladies, and others who had seen the work.

"It was called 'the most magnificent modern binding in the world,' you know. In fact, it's probably taken on more names than any other great book in history. That is, next to the Bible. Some referred to *The Omar* as the 'greatest modern binding in the world.' Others, *The Book Wonderful*. Today, because of my two copies, we tend to call the original the *Titanic Omar* or the *Great Omar*.

"I spent years talking with our staff at the bindery, and to survivors of *Titanic's* disaster. Crew members and passengers ....Anyone in the British Isles who was aboard the *Titanic* itself.

"I spoke with so many people, I felt I'd been there when it happened. I was haunted by the bizarre turns of fate that coincided with both the production of our book and of the *Titanic*. Especially since I secretly intended to reproduce the binding myself. I pieced together how the *Great Omar* had come about and what had ultimately happened to the book. Its genesis and destiny, so to speak."

"Where was Francis Sangorski at this time?"

"Oh, you wouldn't have known, would you?"

"Known what?"

White's eyes lit up. An odd smile crossed his face as he rose and walked to the tea service. Silence took over—but for the crackling fire, and an antique tortoise-shell and gold gilt Markwick Markham clock, on the mantle, that read 4:35 p.m.

White poured another cup of Ceylon tea, offered Parker more, that was declined, and slowly walked over to the window. Backlit by the sun, he appeared as a shadow as he turned to Dr. Parker, sipped his tea and spoke mysteriously across the room.

"The man responsible for the greatest modern binding in the world, designing it, bringing it to life—well, I'll tell you the story." Parker settled back into the chair.

The bookbinder recounted what he had learned about Francis Sangorski—his recurring dream of death by drowning, his obsession with creating the unique binding of *The Rubaiyat of Omar Khayyam*. And how he had charmed his good friend, John Stonehouse, into finally giving his bindery, Sangorski and Sutcliffe, the order to create it. White elaborated how the meticulously designed drawings for the book had taken nearly eight months to produce and two years to carry out.

"The details were so exacting," said White, "that Sangorski's anatomically-perfect human skull illustration was used in medical books for many years after."

White unlocked and pulled open a large drawer at his desk.

"And with the completion of each drawing, I was told, he would share his excitement and enthusiasm with Stonehouse. Amazingly, within three days after finishing the skull design, Sangorski had already completed an ivory and white calf model, just before it was inserted into the *Omar's* back doublure."

He pulled out a thick, oversized envelope, lifted the end-flap, and slid out several folded sheets of heavy tissue.

"I understand the skull had carved ivory teeth," Parker interjected.

"The skull and the snake's head. And an inlaid floral design of poppies growing out of the skull's eye socket. I'll show you."

As he spoke, White carefully unfolded the large sheets of tissue and spread them across his desktop. "When I learned you were coming, I asked S S and Z to pull these patterns from the safe.

"Francis Sangorski's originals," White said proudly.

"The actual designs for the *Titanic Omar*?" Parker rose quickly from his chair and moved beside White.

"They truly are, Dr. Parker. These are the templates,

so-to-speak, used in tooling and tracing the designs on leather. You'll notice they've been used more than once, of course. That's because I made two exact replicas from them."

"The first copy being the one you began in nineteen thirty-two?"

"Took me over five thousand hours and seven years to complete in my spare time. More than five thousand pieces of different colored leather, and over one-hundred square feet of gold leaf— eighteen carat."

White lifted the first design tracing from the desk and held it up. "This was the front doublure inside the cover. As you see, the snake, with its emerald eye, was coiled and enveloped among an apple tree. The solid gold sun radiated through the limbs into the Garden of Eden—symbolic of Life...just as the skull and poppies represented Death."

Parker sifted through the drawings as White described each one. He saw the peacocks and the Persian-style borders of the front cover; the design for the carved mandolin; the repeated allusions to life and death—each matching Veddar's 1884 illustrated version of Omar Khayyam's verse with the intricately decorated front fly-leaf. Delicately inlaid roses were placed in each corner— representing Life. And the back fly-leaf, representing Death, had the poisonous nightshade woven into its corner patterns.

"I'm intrigued by the repetition of life and death symbols," said Parker. "I for one would never have picked the snake to depict Life. And with the rocky history and deaths associated with the book, I'm surprised anyone wants to go after it."

Mr. White spoke deliberately, "I believe most people dismiss it as a coincidence of life...that death and destruction seem to follow the *Omar*. Some have been superstitious enough to suggest it was the book itself that caused the sinking of the *Titanic* and all subsequent deaths.

"Of course, I'm getting closer to my centennial. It would only be a fool who'd think my demise would be ultimately caused by such a work. Especially since I've survived two of my own replicas."

"What happened to your first copy? The one you completed in thirty-nine."

The phone interrupted their discussion.

"Excuse me, Dr. Parker. Phones are a bloody nuisance, aren't they?"

He moved from the couch to his desk. "White residence." He listened intently. "Yes, I'll put him on."

White pulled the phone over to Dr. Parker.

"A Miss Nakamura."

"Hello."

"Sorry to interrupt. How're you feeling?"

"I'll make it. Still rather sore. What's the status from Heathrow?"

"Eleven more on the critical list have died since last night. Five of them children. Smoke inhalation has placed three dozen more passengers on the list. Seniors mostly. And they expect to lose at least fifty to sixty more of the wounded, due to burns or shock syndrome. Still over two hundred sixty unaccounted for—possibly buried in the rubble. They've partially reopened the other terminals. But it could be months before Three reopens—even partially."

"Any more suspects?"

"Clearly our friend Ragem. That terrorist they captured last night?"

"Yeah?"

"One of his group. Khorassani is his name. Seriously wounded, sedated, and under heavy guard at a prison hospital. The police are waiting to interrogate."

"Will he make it?"

"Unknown. He was unconscious when they brought him in. Hasn't come out of it yet. He's joined the wounded on the critical list."

"Any other ALFAHAD?"

"Escaped or among the dead yet to be identified. The forensics field-lab is quite sophisticated. NSY's focusing on the remains of two bodies found at ground zero. Not much left of them."

"Grizzly, huh?"

"Unfortunately."

"How can they possibly determine who's who?"

"Ferroprints, mostly. They're checking for fire-arm imprints on fingers or hands of anyone suspected in the attack, using explosive residue and bullet-hole test kits to tie it all together."

"I understand witnesses survived."

"At least one places a man and a woman in close proximity to two blasts. That's why attention is on the two dismembered cadavers. They performed several field tests, with explosive vapor detectors, concentrating around the blast area. Have you heard the media reports?"

"Not since I left London."

"No one's admitting to it openly, but Libya and Sudan are hinting complicity. Apparently, they've broadcast congratulatory messages all night, to those fighting for the Jihad, through the Islamic Resistance Movement, Hamas."

"Will you visit Khorassani?"

"Tonight or tomorrow. What's your schedule? We need to get together."

"It'll have to be tomorrow. I have an appointment at Sotheran's Antiquarian Bookstore at eight-thirty a.m. Then a brief jog over to the British Museum." He thought for a moment.

"Shouldn't take too long. How about lunch at Wolfe's on Hans Crescent Road, across from Harrod's. My driver said it's quite good." He looked at White who nodded approval.

"Wolfe's it is," said Nakamura. "Perhaps Mr. White would enjoy meeting us there."

"I'll ask."

"How are you getting along?"

"Mr. White's an excellent host."

"I'll be with Commissioner Lawton at NSY, along with Bantam, if you need me. Then I'm Bantam's guest at Stringfellows later this evening. He insisted I get my mind off of yesterday's events."

"Ah, superb restaurant and nightclub, Stringfellow's. Say hello to Peter J. if he's in town. He'll take care of you."

"Peter J.?"

"Stringfellow. Owns the place. I met him a couple of years ago at his New York restaurant. Ask him to set the two of you up with a Butterfly Ball cocktail." Parker winked and smiled slyly at White. "Just be certain you have your life's savings with you and don't plan to go anywhere else afterwards, except the hotel."

"Why's that?"

"It's the most expensive cocktail in the world—Brandy, Maraschino, Grand Marnier and a couple of bottles of Dom Perignon. It'll set you back about four hundred dollars."

"Right," she laughed. "That fits my budget. You staying long?"

"I'll check." He turned to White. "What's our schedule for the rest of the day?"

White thought for a moment. "My wife should be home later. Join us for dinner. We've much to cover."

Parker nodded in agreement, "Could you hear Mr. White?"

"Yes, that's fine," said Nakamura. "I'll see you tomorrow. Noon?"

"Sure." Parker set the phone on the desk.

White opened an elaborately decorated humidor. "Cigar?"

"Thanks, no. Don't smoke."

White closed the box. "Then neither shall I. Nasty habit." White paused as though having second thoughts, then said, "Ironic isn't it?"

"What's that?" said Parker.

"This terrorist problem. In my younger days, I had to struggle and save every tuppence and shilling I could spare, to obtain jewels for my copies of the *Omar*. But others perceive the value of jewels in so many different ways."

"That's what makes the *Great Omar* so intriguing."

"Of course, precious stones are of a highly personal nature to those who can afford to dally in them. Investors seek them to hold and trade on international markets. Individuals purchase jewels because they display status or provide a way to secure one's future."

"And when you think about it,' said Parker, "thieves seek precious stones for all the same reasons."

"I suppose that's true." He laughed at the irony and poured himself more tea. Parker politely refused another cup.

"Before I forget, you and your wife should be our guests for lunch at Wolfe's tomorrow. Ms. Nakamura would enjoy meeting you."

"That's kind of you, Dr. Parker. My wife has scheduled shopping in London. But it would be a good excuse for me to come along." He looked around and whispered, "I hate shopping."

"Then it's a date."

White moved back to his seat and took a deep breath. "Let's see. Where did I leave off?"

"You were telling me about your first replica of the *Omar.*"

"Ah, yes. But let me draw a picture of the times and conditions surrounding the book and its construction. You must understand how this all played into the hands of the *Titanic.* Since I'm a bit of a history buff, I've researched every source I could find over the past seventy-some-odd years.

"You know my connection with the book," White continued, "But regarding the *Titanic,* as I mentioned, I've spoken with many survivors. Met men who built her. Probably read the same books and articles you read about the *Titanic,* before its discovery in the eighties."

"That's quite an accomplishment."

"Yes, if I say so myself," agreed White. "And I've studied most, if not all, of your own books on the subject. Well done, I must say."

Parker smiled at the compliment.

"So, I suspect we could compare notes on the ship. But first

I'll take you back to the days of the *Great Omar*, following Sangorski's commission to construct it.

"I'd enjoy that," said Parker.

"Understand that during most of the two years it took Sangorski and Sutcliffe to produce the *Omar*, the economy of England was beginning to flag. There was considerable disenchantment with the government and strikes were popping up everywhere."

White opened the humidor, out of habit, then closed it.

"Ironically, for the rare book trade and the business of illuminating bindings, the market was fairly brisk in the latter part of the first decade. Royalty still placed orders for magnificent bindings and illuminated vellum pages through our bindery.

"But Americans—rich ones mostly—like the Vanderbilts, Rockefellers, and J.P. Morgan, came in and bought up entire libraries for shipment to America."

"Must've created quite a stir."

White raised his bushy eyebrows. "Some likened it to raping our cultural heritage. But I digress." He moved closer to Parker and looked at him directly.

"Think of the atmosphere at the bindery. With each passing day, a new piece of the *Omar's* puzzle was inserted, and a higher level of excitement generated amongst the bindery staff in anticipation of its completion.

"As the months passed, the book looked more and more as Sangorski had dreamed. And word spread about the *Great Omar's* incomparable beauty and its extremely lavish hand-tooling."

White told Parker of its 1050 jewels embedded in its leather-bound covers, doublures and fly-leafs. He emphasized that nearly 1500 leaves of the finest 22 carat gold-leaf, along with inlaid mahogany, ivory, and mother-of-pearl were implanted into most of the 4967 separate pieces of colored morocco leathers.

White thought for a moment. "They created the most remarkable binding ever designed. But a false sense of security must have surrounded everyone associated with it."

"I don't understand."

"They presumed it'd be snatched up upon completion, for a price that would well reward the owners of the bindery, and Sotheran's, *Omar's* backer. But they didn't take the economy into account. You might even say the economy was the iceberg that sank *Omar*.

"You see, in creating the oversized binding, Sangorski had picked up an undated Original Edition of *Veddar's Illustrated Rubaiyat of Omar Khayyam*. . . . A book measuring thirteen inches by sixteen. Known as a 'quarto' size book.

"They only sold for about three pounds sterling in those days. But it was this *undated* version that probably sealed the book's fate."

"Why would that make a difference?"

"I'll get to that, shortly. It goes back to just before the *Omar's* completion. Mr. Sotheran was quite anxious to have it on display, at his bookstore, around the coronation of King George the Fifth. There were many celebrations going on. And he wanted to show it off to all important people who would visit the shop. But the front cover was still incomplete. So, it only remained at Sotheran's a short while, before it was sent back to the bindery."

"Who worked on the book besides Sangorski?"

"I can't tell you who the sewing lady was—the one who fixed the bands on the outside of the book's spine. Fortunately, times have changed for ladies who work in the trade today. But in those days, those who did the sewing—women mostly—never got credit for their skill, despite their importance to the process."

White thought for a moment.

"Sylvester Byrnes did the forwarding. In other words, taking the sewn book, lacking cover, and attaching it to its binding and spine . . . rounding the corners of the boards, and generally preparing it for finishing.

"George Lovatt was the master finisher, responsible for the

final stage in the binding process—actually gilding and tooling the binding with heated tools. That's where the permanent ornamentation, scrolling, and gold were applied to coincide with the designs you see here."

"But I don't quite understand how the finisher got the design from paper to binding?"

"The technique is simple, Dr. Parker. But the process is exacting, laborious, and time consuming. And only a master craftsman can carry it through. When the finisher uses the working drawing, for the first time, he makes a dent in the paper with his tools. The paper is placed over the cover, and with the tools, the finisher presses them on the lines that make up the design—like tracing, to transfer the design to the leather."

"Like in mysteries, where impressions of handwritten messages are left from torn-off pages of a pad . . . "

"Precisely. In this case, on to the leather or boards upon which thousands of pieces of leather will be applied. When you've taken the working drawing away, you've made a dent where you've pressed the metal tracing tool. So, both the paper and the leather or board has an impression matching the design.

"Once the pattern is transferred to the binding, and the leather is down, the metal finishing tools, with their distinctive designs, are heated to a high temperature and traced over the sheets of gold-leaf to create the brilliant gilding. And with the three *Omar's,* jewels were added for more illumination.

"Any portion of the design not completed in colored leather, was finished with tooling, goldleaf and, of course, a thousand and fifty jewels. It takes superb craftsmen to forward and finish a binding. And Byrnes and Lovatt were the best."

"So, Francis Sangorski designed the binding," said Parker, "created the working drawings for the covers, doublures, and fly leaves, oversaw the mosaics as the leathers were overlayed and glued into place, and generally supervised its completion."

"You've a good grasp."

"But Sangorski never had anything to do with the physical

binding of the book. It was Byrnes and Lovatt who carried out the design on his behalf?"

"Correct. But don't get me wrong. If it were not for Francis Sangorski's foresight and vision, the binding would never have come about. Years later, John Stonehouse, the manager of Sotheran's Bookstore told me—and I quote him directly—'For absolute richness of design and beauty of decoration, it is no exaggeration to say it was the finest, most remarkable specimen of binding ever designed or produced, at any period....Or in any country.'"

White hit the palm of his hand on his desk for emphasis. He looked directly at Parker, "And no man, other than Henry Sotheran, himself, would have been more qualified to state it quite so emphatically."

Both men sat in silence, not realizing the late afternoon sun was already heading for the Celtic Sea.

A car pulled up the gravel driveway. Byron rose from his seat, turned on a desk lamp, and looked out the window as Mrs. White drove around the house to the garage.

"Mr. White, the afternoon's closing in on us, and we haven't had an opportunity to discuss the two *Omar* reproductions you've created."

"Oh I apologize. I tend to digress with my years, you know."

Parker smiled, "Actually, I was going to suggest you share it tomorrow at lunch. So Ms. Nakamura can hear it too."

"Splendid idea. But I'll tell you what . . . I have a wonderful collection of old tools. Some of them are handed down from *Titanic Omar*. May I share them with you?"

"Of course," Parker insisted.

"You shall be my apprentice."

White's face lit up as though he were twenty again, and his energy rebounded.

The bookbinder led Parker to his private workshop at the back of his home. Inside the room, it was as though they had stepped back in time. The furniture consisted of two, hundred-year-old work tables—waist high—with glue pots and several finishing stoves for heating tools, a wooden finishing press, binder and trindles, and a sewing frame.

A wooden chair and stool, both unadorned with fabric, sat ready for a binder to bind. And hundreds of metal gilting tools, lead weights, awls, trimming knives—neatly boxed and racked, according to their use—were placed strategically around the workshop.

White picked up a Backing Hammer and a pair of Nippers. "I still bind a book or two to keep busy. Friends send me their favorites to repair every now and then. Keeps my mind agile." He looked at Parker. "Never could truly retire, you know."

The sweet smell of fine Moroccan leather greeted Parker's senses as he looked around. Beautifully colored sheets of chamois-looking Levant and Hard Grain Morocco were neatly racked on shelves to his left. Labels under each color designated choices from White to Red, with the more exotic Nut Brown, Terra Cotta, Heliotrope, and Royal Blue nesting in between. Other shelves held wooden backing boards and forwarding supplies.

The binder pulled two white workcoats off hangers and handed one to Parker. Looking like scientists ready to discover a new strain of DNA, the two men spent the remaining part of the afternoon as master binder and novitiate—happily plying their trade. White was in his environment, and Parker discovered a fascinating new interest.

Mrs. White interrupted only long enough to be introduced, and she politely excused herself to prepare dinner. She slipped in to make certain they had one more round of tea and scones. Parker found it difficult to refuse their hospitality.

Around eight-thirty, White and Parker would retire to the living room to enjoy a pint or two of fine English Bitters brought in from the local pub in Esher.

The three would enjoy a delightfully prepared seven-course meal around nine o'clock. Smoked salmon would be the appetizer.

Then, a lightly seasoned rice salad with cucumber and radishes would follow. Prime rib served on a bed of asparagus with hollandaise to the side. And kidney pie served with Yorkshire pudding. Finally, a round of caramel custard set in a bed of raspberries would complete the menu.

Following the events of the night before, Parker looked forward to sharing this quiet dinner in the home of newfound friends. There would be little opportunity for such pleasure in the weeks ahead.

LATHAM PRISON HOSPITAL

TWO armed guards stood at attention. They flanked both sides of the door to Room 311—their 9mm. Parabellum, spring-load, automatic submachine guns at the ready. Two additional guards were posted for security, inside the room near the barred windows, as a prison doctor and the supervising nurse monitored Karim Abdul Khorassani.

The terrorist was intubated through the mouth, and on a respirator. EKG lines, stretched to the life-support system, and IV tubes looked like the arms of an octopus were spread out across the bed, carrying NaCl saline solution, blood, and plasmonate. The room was permeated with an antiseptic smell of medication.

The continuous beeps of the life-support monitor and the repeated humdrum "twoosh-donk" sound of the respirator echoed slightly off the linoleum floor. Khorassani's beard and mustache had been shaved before entering the U.K. His black hair had been removed during prep in the emergency room.

Following five hours of surgery, to stop internal bleeding and remove most of the accessible bullets, the patient's condition was downgraded in the morning from seriously wounded to critical. By early afternoon he had lapsed into a deep coma. Despite his condition, he was heavily restrained to the bed. Bandages covered him almost entirely. And another intravenous line fed morphine into his system when needed.

Five bullets had been removed from various parts of his body. At least two more slugs were too close to the spine and other critical points to be removed at all. And more than four hundred stitches had been taken to close wounds where skin had been ripped away or shot clear through.

Severe loss of blood had sent Khorassani into hypovolemic shock almost immediately after he was captured. But orders to perform all necessary procedures to save his life had come from the top. And all precautions were taken to provide security relative to their location.

The head nurse on duty had just taken a pulse and entered it on her clipboard sheet. She checked the wall clock and wrote down 20:41 on the form. This would be the last check before the shift change.

The doctor impassively observed the nurse as she went through the routine checkup. She then took Khorassani's blood pressure.

"Sixty over forty," she spoke out loud for the first time since entering the room.

The doctor acknowledged with a "harumph" and silently observed his patient. He glanced up at the life-support monitor, as it fed back a steady but unchanged report.

A knock on the door preceded Commissioner Lawton, who immediately walked into the room. Bantam and Nakamura followed. Bantam handed a cup of coffee to the doctor and took a sip from his own cup.

"Anything new?"

"Not since you left to eat—well, except for a slight flutter in the eye lids about ten minutes ago. Could have been a reflex response due to head trauma."

"Or he might be coming out?" asked Bantam.

"Anything's possible," the doctor said as he moved aside.

Lawton and Bantam walked over to the bed and observed

Khorassani's assisted breathing. The even hum of the respirator filled the room. Nakamura held back to stay out of the way.

"Well, my friend," Lawton spoke calmly but directly to the terrorist, "you've certainly got good reason to hide from reality. You've caused enough death and terror to last a lifetime." The commissioner moved closer.

Khorassani's bandaged head made an older, large scar on his neck more prominent.

"You were left behind by your own people, Karim Abdul Khorassani. They left you for dead. And they've gone on to plan their next move without you. What do you say to that, my friend?"

The life-support system beeped faster and louder.

Lawton saw Khorassani's eyelids flutter as if in a REM dream state. He turned to the doctor.

"I think we got through to him. His eyes are going nuts under those lids." Bantam shifted aside as the doctor moved in to take a look. He lifted Khorassani's right eyelid. The movement stopped as the terrorist stared blankly to the ceiling. The doctor lifted the left eyelid and received the same reaction.

"Must have been an anomaly." He returned to relax in a chair across the room.

The three civil servants surrounded the bed. Lawton tried once more to get a reaction.

"Your terrorist days are over, Abdul. You're in Latham prison now and there's no escaping this place."

Khorassani's eyes did not move.

"We will have Faheed Al Mar Ragem shortly."

Suddenly, a high pitched respirator alarm filled the room as it screeched its warning in concert with the rapid beeps of the EKG.

The terrorist's closed eyes went berserk as he became agitated, and a groan emanated from his throat. The three agents glanced quickly at each other as if to say, "Did you hear that?" and the doctor and nurse closed in around the bed.

"Ragem's name got the reaction," confirmed Nakamura.

Lawton leaned in closer to Khorassani. "Ragem will be captured soon, and he *and* you will both die with your souls on British soil."

The REM-state reappeared as the life-support and respirator alarms increased in speed and pitch. Then, as quickly as if a shot had been fired, his eyelids opened wide exposing one brown eye and one green. Khorassani stared coldly to the ceiling.

"Ah, Mr. Khorassani," Lawton spoke up. "You recognize the name of your compatriot. Or is it that you're afraid to die where Allah cannot find you?"

Khorassani's eyes instantly pitched to the side and bore into Lawton's face. Lawton smiled with satisfaction. "You'll never see Ragem again. Unless, of course, you tell us where we'll find him."

The eyes icily moved from one person to another.

A cold feeling overtook the room. Those around the bed stared back into the terrorist's grotesquely bandaged face.

Lawton continued, "You've perpetrated your last atrocity on the innocent. You'll only see the walls of a prison. Or inside a casket. You may never see your family, unless you help us find the one who abandoned you. It's Ragem we want. Where is he?"

Khorassani started to smile. Then he felt pain where part of his face had been blown off. He winced and groaned then closed his eyes.

The life-support system beeped wildly. The nurse reached over and pushed a button on the PCA pump. Automatically the drug monitor allocated him 10 milligrams of morphine. The life-support and respirator alarms settled down.

Slowly, the terrorist opened his eyes.

"Why make it difficult for yourself, Karim. Give us your leader and we can negotiate your fate."

Khorassani mumbled gibberish, and everyone leaned toward the bed as he struggled to talk. But the intubation tube from the respirator made it difficult to speak. Again, Khorassani forced his thoughts through the blocked passage of his mouth, the impediment causing his speech to sound muzzy.

Nakamura looked at Lawton. "I think he said, 'May the curse of Allah be upon you.'"

"Oh," said Lawton, staring the terrorist directly in the eyes. "That was considerate of you. You must think us fools to believe Allah would punish us for your sins."

The life-support system beeped faster.

Khorassani tried to propel the intubation tube from his mouth, with his tongue. Lawton looked questioningly at the doctor. The doctor reached over and pulled out the tube. Visible relief crossed over the terrorist's face as he stared individually at each person above him. Then, in a raspish voice, he whispered in broken English.

"You . . . want me to tell you . . . secret hiding place . . . for Ragem?"

No one answered. Khorassani struggled to speak.

"I will . . . tell you . . . one thing . . . only . . . " The beeping sound of the life-support system increased its pace. "There will be . . . a terrible plague . . . death, destruction . . . which you . . . never seen . . . disease and death . . . for Americans and British . . . you wait . . . " He laughed cruelly and choked for air.

The sharp noise of the respirator alarm overtook Khorassani's harangue, and the life-support monitor beeps picked up speed as though heading for a flat-line. Lawton pointed to the intubation tube and the doctor reinserted it down Khorassani's throat.

Nakamura and Bantam glanced at one another to confirm suspicions.

"Satan has led you astray, Karim." Lawton spoke above Khorassani's laughter, "And I believe your *Koran* says that 'whoso takes Satan to him for a friend, instead of Allah, has surely suffered a manifest loss.'" He looked directly at Khorassani, as the terrorist choked again.

"The *Koran* also says that your only refuge will be Gehenna."

Khorassani's eyes raged with anger as they locked on Lawton. The terrorist spit up blood and continued to choke. Then he suddenly went unconscious.

Everyone withdrew from the bedside as the doctor and nurse went into action. "Hand me the epinephrine," the doctor ordered. The nurse picked up a large ampoule and hypodermic needle from a nearby table and passed it across the bed.

The nurse placed suction tubing into Khorassani's throat to clear blood from his passage, while the doctor pulled back the chest dressings, jammed a large needle through the center of the breast, and injected synthesized adrenalin into the heart.

For a few moments the rhythm of the life-support monitor returned to a semi-uniform cadence, as Khorassani's breathing became even and relaxed. Within a minute, a random series of beeps appeared with irregular blips on the monitor. The line between the blips got longer and the rise on each became shorter.

Then Khorassani's eyes opened wide. He glanced directly at everyone. An iniquitous smile overtook his countenance and pierced the shields of those in the room. His eyes widened as though he were experiencing a form of ecstasy and rapture.

Not unexpectedly, the line on the monitor went flat and its elongated beep took over. Khorassani expelled one last, protracted breath as air gurgled through fluids and escaped from his chest and throat.

"He looked rather happy for a man going to hell," said Bantam.

"Frightening, isn't it?" said Nakamura.

The respirator still moaned as Lawton tapped Nakamura and Bantam on the shoulders to signal a withdrawal from the room. The doctor and nurse confirmed the patient's condition, switched off the monitor and respirator, and prepared to order an autopsy.

NORTHEASTERN AFRICA

A sophisticated voice scrambler sat on a table next to the phone. It could be disconnected quickly and was small enough to fit into a briefcase if it were suddenly necessary to go into hiding. The scrambler was an important companion, whether at home or traveling. Stolen from the American Embassy during the Iraqi war, its technology and codes had since been rearranged so as not to be unscrambled by anyone with counterintelligence capabilities.

Four other scramblers had been stolen or bought on the black market, through operatives in eastern Europe and in the Mideast, in order to protect secret conversations between Arab factions closely connected to the ALFAHAD.

Fluttered ringing emanated from the phone with every other hollow pulse of sound. A large, darkly-bronzed hand set down a cup of mint tea and reached over to push three security buttons on the scrambler. Then, in no hurry, the hand picked up the phone's receiver.

"Ahlan," a deeply resonant voice cautiously greeted the caller.

"Ragem?" queried the voice. "You are answering your own phone now?"

"Taari is pissing. Times are rough. What do you want?"

"Khorassani is dead. And so is Al-Masud."

Ragem let out a long sigh and silence followed.

The voice awkwardly explained how Ragem's top lieutenant had proudly served their cause, back at Heathrow, and how Al-Masud had attempted to blow up passenger planes with the transfer bus. By now, Ragem's thoughts were light years away.

Al-Masud was expendable. But Karim Abdul Khorassani had been a childhood friend. They had grown up together as children of poor peasants, in the slums of Cairo. Ragem remembered the laughing, running, and dodging as they stole bread, fruit, or an occasional strip of charcoaled meat from the stands in the thatched-roof market stalls.

Ragem, the faster of the two, had always managed to get away. Khorassani—big-boned and slim, gangling, and forever tripping over himself, as a teenager—got caught every now and then. It was usually up to Faheed to create a diversion that would allow his friend, Karim, to break loose in the confusion.

Eventually, Karim grew out of his gangliness and became taller, muscular, swift, sure and self-confident. Traits any terrorist could use against the enemy. Traits that brought him honor among his people. Along with Ragem, the two built the ALFAHAD into a small but highly respected team of terrorists who could hit a target and disappear before anyone knew with whom they had had an encounter.

Memories of Ragem's closest ally and compatriot flashed before him as if he were reliving the years they had spent together, fighting against political oppression and on behalf of the lives of both their families. Khorassani's, imprisoned by the government or lost to purges of Islamic Fundamentalist uprisings in the ghetto, and Ragem's—all tragically lost except for his brother, Taari—aboard an Iranian airliner accidentally shot down by an American warship.

"Ya akhi," Ragem said. *My brother*, he thought once more, in remembrance of Khorassani—though they were not related.

"I am sorry for your friend," said the voice.

"Why? He is with Allah. Insh'allaah." *God willing* he prayed in silence again.

Faheed Al Mar Ragem had left his childhood behind at a very young age. A large, hirsute young man, even in his teen years, he was compared and known for features that were less angular than a Greek's, yet more sensual than what one might find with a typical Lebanese. His features drew attention and he stood out, at times, when he preferred not to. Hence the necessity for disguises.

Taught to be cunning, deceitful and shrewd, at an early age— just to remain alive—Ragem began leading his small fanatical group of revolutionists in the days immediately following Jamal Nasser's assassination. Their operations left death and destruction in their wake.

Originally well-financed, for years, through his Sudanese, Eastern-European, and Qadhafi's Libyan connections, most of his operational monies were fast drying up. And new links and allegiances were a necessity to remain in operation.

"There is a meeting scheduled at CIA, with Bramson and the diver from Montreal. In two days," said the voice. Parker is to be there."

Ragem's silence implied he wanted more information without asking for it. The voice continued.

"I'm certain they will want Dupont to give up his expedition. But my operatives cannot tell me if they know about your plans for the *Titanic*."

An awkward pause and more silence greeted the caller. The voice was not certain if he should go on. Ragem said nothing.

"Parker is in London. He arrived there with an FBI agent about the time of your attack. They say he was on the airport bus with Haji when it blew up, but reports place him back at Terminal Three after the explosion. The FBI agent's name is Nakamura. Jennifer Nakamura."

"A woman," Ragem broke his silence. "A female FBI agent?"

"Yes. The two are there to learn more about the *Omar*. CIA still wants Parker to dive for the book."

"A female FBI agent," was all Ragem could say. "Miss . . . "

"Nakamura. Ever since Heathrow, she has been asking much about you and the attack. She and Parker will be here at least one more day."

"One more day," he reassured himself with finality. "Good. Arrange for their disposal. That should keep everyone away from our dive."

"I do not wish to provoke my operatives, by pushing too hard."

"Yours is not to decide. Yours is to carry out as ordered."

"They have been good to me. For now, I'm keeping my distance. If they are provoked, I could lose my American visa. I must be careful you know. I must be very careful," the voice rambled.

"You must, my friend," Ragem finally spoke with a measured annoyance in his voice that insisted on complete caution. "You must be extremely careful. Leave no room for error. But you must also do as I request."

"You are not angry with me? You will provide protection if something goes wrong?"

"Allah willing," Ragem evaded a direct answer. "When we get the *Omar* and the lost jewels, we will never want for anything."

He knew how to appeal to the terrorist's cupidity. Both men were greedy. Ragem's own avarice arose from his overwhelming need for retribution against the American and Israeli war machines. And vengeance was as sweet as the millions he would have in his hands in a matter of weeks. Millions to purchase weapons and explosives on the black market, the finest false ID's from Iraq, and training for his soldiers in Libya, that surpassed the zealousness of the word of Allah and His resolve.

The free-lancer was filled with a desire for a lifestyle that secret bank transfers from Ragem could provide. And he would do anything to obtain it.

"I just wanted to keep you informed, Faheed. Rest assured. Your orders will be carried out."

Ragem clicked off the line.

The leader of the terrorist organization slowly moved across the room. He lowered himself to the floor where it was cooler. The heat was stifling. Two overworked ceiling fans squeaked as they pushed the warm air around the room. Beads of sweat dripped from Ragem's forehead and was absorbed by his loosely fitting white galabiyya as he turned on his back.

The white latticed window shutters were closed more to shade the room and keep the afternoon heat out than to shield his wife from viewers on the street.

Until the Russian coup, and the eventual collapse of Ceausescu's government in Rumania, Ragem had maintained extremely close ties with Rumania and the Soviet Union. With the collapse of the Eastern Bloc nations, many terrorist organizations found it increasingly difficult to fund their activities. Ragem's ALFAHAD was no exception. Most of the Eastern Bloc had fallen into hard times. Money, funneled through those countries allied with or a part of the former Soviet Union, was now almost totally nonexistent.

Terrorism was taking on a new look. Former East-German intermediaries were more interested in local struggles to maintain status-quo or to finance renewed racist and Neo-Nazi activities against foreign immigrants flooding the job market.

One bond now holding Ragem's small band together, particularly since the Iraqi-Kuwaiti war, was secret payments channeled from the Saudis just to keep the ALFAHAD out of the way. Ragem's activities were an embarrassment to the Saudi government. In their realm, Palestinian peace negotiations caused many of the ALFAHAD's financial spigots to be turned off.

More desperate than ever, Ragem's only remaining financial source was Arabic oil—Libyan, in particular—where royalties could be used for financing their "holy war." But even that was dwindling. Changes in the geopolitical structure of the Arabic nations were placing a serious burden on the faithful.

Western nations, becoming more self-sufficient with their own oil reserves, helped to modify dependence on the Mid-East oil cartel. Mexico's new discoveries, new fields in Montana and New Mexico, and the reopening of old wells in Texas and California aided in creating a glut on the world market.

Ragem was no longer certain who his true friends were from one day to the next. Only his old friend, the psychotic gun-for-hire terrorist, Abu Nidal, and helping hands from Libya and Iraq, provided meager financial and moral support.

The old ways of operating through the Hizballah—doing business under cover of constantly changing trade names—felt steady pressure through the seemingly endless Peace Initiatives. Abu Nidal had been compelled to join forces with the Iraqi leadership. But rigorously sympathetic to the cause, and one of the few truly loose cannons remaining in the Mideast, Saddam Hussein was more than willing to finance both Nidal's and Ragem's operations.

Ragem sensed he was losing control and had felt obligated to make a statement that would shake up man's perception of fairness—*one that would stop politicians from justifying worldwide discrimination against Arabic cultures.* Maybe world leaders could deny payment for the release of hostages, or luckless victims. "But," he had told his brother, Taari, "once they realize a new movement in terrorism is taking place, the world press will not be able to ignore, and politicians will not deny demands the Arabic world will make."

"The Western world will have to take notice," Taari answered. "First, Heathrow. Next, a series of banks and tourist sites. Then, bridges and main arteries leading in and out of cities."

"And if all else fails, germ warfare," Ragem had said.

Ragem allowed himself to revel on the thought. *The fourth estate will bow down to pressure from the other estates of the realm. The media will have a feeding frenzy, competing over who the culprits might be. Even the Americans won't be certain. After all, it could be one of their own.*

The world's morning shows would provide what the American's call "Monday morning quarter-backing," over pronouncements of indiscriminate slaughterings and other violations of international law. Nighttime media analysts would invent new parallels to replace the tit-for-tat arguments invented by instant-soup journalists. And political pit-bosses would grope for a "hook" to get sound bites on TV and radio.

Now that the PLO had been weakened through the peace negotiations and the Soviet Union could no longer be blamed for every "cold war" scheme taking place around the world, the print and electronic media needed shock-value stories to fill the gaps between earthquakes, hurricanes, serial killers, and rapists. Instant bulletins and we-were-there-first pronouncements would interrupt soap operas to sell the news, in an attempt to outstrip the competitive networks. Even the BBC would wax intense, in portentous discussions about the new wave of terrorism.

Out of the headlines would flow the bylines crediting the latest dispatches from the scenes of the crime. Exclusive reports would editorialize, articles would portray the "new menace," and television and radio talk shows would vent the world's frustrations over such atrocities. Experts on terrorism would be called in to invent new excuses for the failures of government to provide fair and reasonable solutions to the ills of the world.

Yes, thought Ragem, *our cause will get the coverage back that it once had.* He knew the world's networks and news syndicates were too selfish to let the ALFAHAD's actions slip through their hands. Each would scratch and claw at the other to beat paths to the closest broadcast satellite time. "Besides," he laughed, "with too much time to fill, on too many channels, they'll overlook that I'll be using them. And they're too greedy to care.

"*Misery acquaints a man with strange bedfellows*," the Oxford dropout quoted Shakespeare to himself. He smiled at the irony. It seemed to ease the pain of loss.

Ragem's wife, Asma, walked in from the kitchen with his brother, Taari. It was apparent to both that something was on Ragem's mind.

Asma followed the dictates of her husband—veiled, and wearing the traditional ghata head covering—despite being within the confines of her own home. Especially around his brother. Two small children followed close behind. Ragem's daughter, Samar, was just ten. She carried her young infant brother, Samir.

"Was that Zahid on the phone?" Taari asked.

Ragem nodded in distant thought.

"What did he want?"

Faheed looked at his wife, not wanting to discuss the call in front of her.

"We'll talk later," said Ragem.

Not to be shut out of the conversation, Asma spoke up.

"You may talk in front of me. I know what you are up to."

"Insh'allaah," Ragem repeated out of habit.

Her dark eyes spread wide above her hidden smile as she set a tray of dates and a plastic thermos of mint tea on the floor, next to her husband. Her long, black curls fell out of their covering and cascaded onto her shoulders. The gold brocade on her flowing, black dress danced with each movement while she refilled Faheed's cup and turned to serve his brother.

"The news is bad," Ragem spoke softly, still finding it difficult to believe his closest friend was not infallible. He cradled the side of his head in the palm of his hand and stretched out on the bright colored carpet, massaging his left temple as he reclined. Asma knelt nearby and offered him an oblong date. Ragem waved it away.

"Karim Abdul was wounded and captured. He died last night. They will not release his body."

"His spirit is with Allah," Taari said, his defiance difficult to conceal.

"Yes," said Asma, "his spirit is with Allah." She turned back to Ragem. "But you are with us. Praise be to Allah."

"I will never forgive them," Ragem said almost under his breath.

"We will avenge our brother's death," said Taari in a knee-jerk reaction to Ragem's comment. Asma avoided Taari and looked to her spouse.

"You must not harbor these thoughts."

Taari threw a look of disgust at his brother's wife. *She should not be speaking these traitorous ideas.*

Asma knew what was going through Taari's mind, but avoided looking at him directly.

"The *Quran*," she said, "speaks of the unbelievers. It is not for us to decide their fate." Asma moved closer to her husband. "'Allah has set a seal on their hearts and on their hearing, and on their eyes is a covering, and there awaits them a mighty chastisement,'" she quoted.

"Allah has given me that right of chastisement," Ragem shot back.

"No. You have *taken* it . . . upon yourself to judge."

Taari quickly stood up. "I will not hear you speak to my brother in such an impudent tone. In case you've forgotten, the *Quran* also tells us that ' . . . men are the managers of the affairs of women—and those you fear may be rebellious, admonish and banish them to their couches and beat them.'"

Asma shot back at Taari, "You will not speak to me so brazenly in my house, as our guest, or in front of the children."

Ragem raised his hand at his brother and Taari left the room in anger. Ragem rolled to his back and sighed. His daughter, Samar, sensed her father's sadness, pulled back his head covering, and stroked his hair. Faheed closed his eyes, hoped the day would begin anew, and wished to return to his childhood when he and Karim Abdul played simple games in the streets.

Asma stood in silence, not certain how to approach her husband. She turned away as her eyes became wet with fear. Samir crawled to his mother's feet. She picked up the infant, caressed her head against his, and held tightly, hoping the child could hold their world together.

Without looking at her husband, Asma spoke softly, "Faheed, I cannot sit idly by without telling you my thoughts." She waited to see if he would object. There was silence.

"What you continue to do is dangerous. And senseless. I do not understand the anger inside your mind. It binds you as though you are a criminal tied to a flogging post. You strike at your enemies. And they strike back. You strike again and they keep coming back at you."

"Even the *Torah*, given by Allah to the Jews, says 'A life for a life, an eye for an eye . . . '"

Asma turned and faced her husband, straight on. "Can't you believe for a moment that your enemies are just as us. They have children . . . beautiful daughters hugging their fathers and comforting them at times of loss. Little babies like Samir, who know nothing of guns, bombs, or killings. They want to grow up like their fathers. The fathers they think they know."

"Yes, grow up forced to steal food from the marketplace, because fat politicians pass laws that keep our people out of schools and and out of jobs. Why do you think I grew up this way? My family eventually destroyed by an American missile, after spending their life's savings to make the pilgrimage to Mecca. Karim Abdul's family imprisoned by our own corrupt politicians, until they died of unspeakable diseases, chained to urine-stained walls."

Asma spoke with extreme care, "My husband, when you are abroad, there are times I wish you were here with us—a common thief, instead. The authorities would cut off your right hand and your left foot, and you would not be physically capable of doing these things that you do. We would have you with us—a loving father and husband. A father who could watch his children grow up, get married, and raise families. We would not have to constantly move. If you were not doing these terrible things, you could work to throw out the corrupt politicians."

Asma knelt by Faheed's side and placed Samir across his stomach. "You must stop the hate burning inside. You can find other things to think about. Something else to do. Think more of your family," she begged.

"I know of nothing else," Faheed sighed. "I've been doing this for too long."

The black veil covering Asma's face was now stained with tears. She pulled back the veil to reveal her richly burnished features. Her tawny complexion emphasized the slight pouting that always managed to weaken Faheed to his very soul.

Asma bent over to kiss his forehead. She held the kiss until she knew it had burned into his mind. Faheed put his arms around her and gently brought her to his side. Without a word, Samar placed her arms around her mother and the family became one.

"Your children need you to be here," whispered Asma. "Think of your family."

Faheed held her for the longest time. His mind twisted with confusing and conflicting signals that drove him crazy.

"Please, think of your family," Asma kissed his cheek.

The late afternoon sun had already begun its descent over the nearby buildings and sand dunes encircling the city. Inside their house an involuntary darkness had taken over.

At last, the terrorist rose to his elbow, holding Samir close to his chest with his other arm. He handed the baby to his wife, stood up, and walked across the thick Persian carpets. Asma could see he was fighting old battles with himself.

"I am thinking of my family," she could hear him quietly say from across the room. Ragem turned to his wife. "I am thinking of my children.

"First it was the British imperialists who said we must accept change. Now, with these British and American infidels spreading their western ways—women exposing themselves on billboards for colas, and unveiled women on television—do you want our children growing up that way? Wearing short dresses and lipstick? Working and drinking with men as they do in Saudi Arabia?"

Asma glanced to the ceiling. "Allah forgive me for saying this." She gazed into her husband's eyes. "If that was my choice—if I knew I could keep you alive, knowing the alternative to accepting their western ways was your death at their hands, because you chose to fight them, I would drink colas until they rotted my stomach and clothe my children in the skin Allah gave them when they came into this world.

"Let Allah fight the battle. He'll provide for the judgment when the time comes to punish the unbelievers for their deeds."

"Allah says that retaliation—*kisas*, is ours to employ upon unbelievers," said Ragem.

"Allah also told us, through our Prophet, that He has conferred his blessings upon *us*, not on those who have gone astray. For unbelievers, there is no asylum from Allah. But the children, Faheed. Not just our children. Their children, too. I cannot believe Allah is a cruel god. . . . One who would let them suffer at another's hands, for they're too young to have sinned. One cannot hate children and destroy them, Faheed. The children who die have no choice. They're innocent victims."

Asma looked deeply into his eyes, searching for his soul. "It's as though you have a need to hate them in order to survive. And it's eating you like a disease from the inside out."

Ragem turned away from his wife. "Don't judge me by counting victims. We are all victims. Our people have been victimized for centuries. Someone has to stand up for them. And someone must avenge my brother, Karim Abdul Khorrassani. It is written in the *Quran*."

Faheed Al Mar Ragem walked steadfastly to the tray of honey-covered dates, picked up two and shoved them into his mouth, as if to say "subject closed." He poured himself another cup of mint tea and washed down the taste of death that had so quickly risen over his own home.

As the sun set, loudspeakers intoned the Call to Prayer from the lofty minarets at the nearby mosque. Ragem softened his resolve and silently gathered his wife and children onto the burgundy, gold and azur-colored rug. They began to kneel. Faheed put his hands at his baby's side, lifted, and turned him to face Mecca. His wife and daughter knelt closeby.

"We must make the pilgrimage to the Kaaba and the holy well of Zamzan," Ragem spoke to his wife softly as he stared straight ahead.

Asma turned to look at her confused husband, and placed her hand on his. They slowly bowed together until their heads touched the floor in prayer.

———

LAUNCH OF THE *TITANIC*— FOR FITTING-OUT
BELFAST, IRELAND—MAY 31, 1911

THE day was exceptional, lacking the usual fog and cloudy skies. An early morning chill leant a crisp feeling to the air as small and large vessels negotiated across the water. River Lagan would soon be filled with steamers and tugs waiting for the biggest event ever to happen in Ireland.

By 7:30, the *Duke of Argyll* steamer had crossed the channel from England with distinguished guests and invited newsmen. Thousands of festive gawkers would witness the *Titanic's* official launching and observe the immense ship as it moved to its berth for its final months of fitting-out—before the maiden voyage.

"They say the ship'll have a golf course," said a reporter. The natural shoulders of his checked-flannel sack suit gave him an air of expertise that few questioned.

"Truly?" his assistant asked in astonishment. "Where would they put it?"

"Don't know, man." He gazed across the water at the towering steel silhouette, then turned to a rival. "But the *Titanic's* large enough for a golf course, wouldn't you agree?"

"All conjecture," the rival, skeptic reporter protested—his single-breasted, gray-striped worsted showed more wear. "But I'm told it will have dairy cows."

"We'll know in a year when she's properly launched, won't we?" The reporters postulated and moved about the *Argyll* searching for confirmation to other rumors and speculations, of which most were quite outlandish.

By 9:30, spectators covered the prime harbor areas. Entire families made a holiday of it. On each shore, the wealthy and the paupers congregated in their usual cliques, unknowingly personifying every level of society who would fill eight of the decks on the *Titanic*.

Moneyed passengers would eventually reside on the top decks with their opulent life-styles and excessive convoys of servants. Shipping magnates expected second class levels to be occupied by the middle class. Each would spend his life-savings for the thrill of sailing on the largest ship afloat.

Immigrants would fill the steerage section, well below-decks. Dreamers of a better life in America, they would leave most possessions behind to begin anew—hoping to build fortunes out of ashes from their pasts.

The lowest depths of the *Titanic* would become the working bowels of the ship. There, the sweating laborers would stoke the giant steam-engines with dust-laden coal, while electricians powered the mighty generators to activate the first-class elevators, light the ship, and run the Marconi.

But that was a year off.

Harbor Commissioners closed a section of Albert Quay for paying guests. And a fleet of small boats and large ships charged the curious for viewing spots on the water itself.

An unpaid holiday, no one minded. Thousands of poor workers, from Harland & Wolff shipbuilders, watched with pride from piles of timber and coal scattered along the wharf at Spencer Basin. The ship's shell-riveters—the Cloot-men—stood with co-workers, the heater boys and catch boys. Each had a hand at either heating, catching, throwing or hammering over 3 million steel rivets through its inner and outer shells. Wives and children came along for the free show.

Many of the world's richest industrialists and captains of industry would soon dine and celebrate at intimate affairs and gala buffets afterward. It mattered not, since those who sweat and toiled through forty-nine-hour work weeks for just two pounds sterling, physically building monuments to the illustrious Edwardian tycoons—almost as slaves had built the pyramids—would soon return to their meager repasts in modest homes and tenements. Swelling with Anglo-Saxon pride, they knew their place in society.

The black-painted hull of the *Titanic* rested in its massive gantry—its belly empty of the soon to be installed lavish outfittings— waiting to be fed as the bellies of those who had built her. Though the ceremony would be simple, lacking the christening usually associated with such affairs, this was not a time for humility.

By 11:30, expensively outfitted participants and observers covered the shipyard from one end to the other. Irish pride was pardonable, as all eyes gazed at what newspapers would proclaim the day after, "A Masterpiece of Irish Brains and Industry."

It only occurred to a select few, and the financiers who risked their capital on this venture, that most of the money invested in the *Titanic* came from American capitalists. U.S. Steel magnate J. Pierpont Morgan and his Trust—International Merchant Marine— had controlling interest in the group of White Star Line investors.

The bow of the *Titanic* was surrounded by a number of rapidly constructed, bunting-covered observation stands—just meters from the wharf entrance to Harland & Wolff shipyard Queen's Road offices. Distinguished guests were privately received there. Owners, investors, members of the board for White Star Lines and for Harland & Wolff. Political dignitaries. All would eventually parade as peacocks to their reserved seats.

At the center, near the bow, ninety press corps members shared the main grandstand with important guests. Naval architects, port officials, and engineers gathered to celebrate a ship built to be, in reality, part of a new breed—a fleet produced to make money.

The *Titanic* and its smaller sister ship, *Olympic*, represented a line of extravagant transportation launched to compete against older ocean-going liners originally built with safety in mind. Hull design was now dictated by investors' greed, not by naval engineers.

Full double hulls were replaced, instead, by double bottoms.

Safety factors were controlled by cutting costs. Lifeboats were outfitted to meet legal specifications, rather than serve the full list of passengers. Amenities were there to attract and serve the wealthy, at the expense of other lives on board.

Class determined status and social status determined class.

One small grandstand had remained empty until noon. Precisely at 12:00, the photographer's magnesium powder flashpots exploded nearly at once as the main door to Harland & Wolff opened for its distinguished, white-bearded chairman, Lord Pirrie. Jauntily dressed in his vested suit and topped with a yachting cap, he and Lady Pirrie confidently led honored guests to the vacant stand.

Heads and eyes turned to financier, J. P. Morgan, and Joseph Ismay, White Star's powerful chairman and managing director, as they led Belfast's Lord Mayor and other members of the party to their reserved seats below *Titanic's* port bow. The crowd applauded out of respect, though few could identify the dignitaries.

"Joseph," Lord Pirrie spoke to Ismay above the noise, "we must excuse ourselves to make our final inspection."

White Star's chairman, Ismay, nodded in agreement—caught in the glory that was theirs for the moment. J.P. Morgan excused himself from the effort.

"We'll have to make it quick. More for show you know."

"Of course," Ismay replied.

Except for the workers, assigned to last-minute duties in preparation for the launch, Pirrie and Ismay were the only two figures who stood out as they walked the dock in a cursory fashion—heads held high as show horses. No one could be certain they were inspecting anything.

Ismay carried his walking stick and animatedly conversed with Harland & Wolff's chairman. Occasionally, Ismay pointed his walking stick high toward an area of the bow or another section of the ship, as if to say, "We should have put another rivet in there, but no matter."

Edwardian overconfidence guided the day. If something wrong were found at that moment, there was little chance anything would be done. The clock was in motion.

"Look!" a youngster exclaimed from the wharf. "Look at the man." Attention focused toward the rear of the ship.

On the *Titanic's* sternpost, a solitary red flag signaled a "stand clear" warning to the tugs and spectator fleet. It was exactly 12:05.

The ways were set for the ship to glide down the huge stocks of timber and into the bay. Eighteen tons of tallow, train oil and soft soap greased the way for a smooth entry at Spencer Basin. Thousands of spectators felt tremendous anticipation as the time drew near.

Unexpectedly, a rocket fired into the air to announce the five-minute mark. Throughout the bay, talk and laughter turned to whispers. Last minute clanging and banging of tools up and down the wharf, and on board the *Titanic* itself, became silent. The time was 12:10.

The expectation of an exemplary moment was close at hand. Young and old stood together knowing history was being made. The warmth of the early afternoon heightened the excitement. Nothing would dampen the success of the launch.

With a loud whoosh, another rocket signaled the moment for which everyone had been waiting. Total silence took over Spencer Basin. Children held their breath. Parents squeezed their hands tightly in anticipation.

And investors and shipbuilders said silent prayers.

At 12:14 the *Titanic* was officially launched. But the 882-foot, 46,328 ton giant appeared to lay motionless on its stocks. Inertia held on tightly as the massive hulk of steel imperceptibly inched forward. Everyone stood in awe, wondering if the ship would move down the ways. The hush and stillness over the crowd of thousands froze the moment in time.

High above, on deck, the ship's workers perceived slight

movement beneath them. The first to cheer, their joy echoed across the quiet shipyard from building to building and boat to boat. Everyone realized the *Titanic* was moving. The spirited cheering became contagious and grew louder and louder with each inch —then each foot of movement.

The entire section of Albert Quay was awash with cacophonous sounds. Gigantic anchor chains thundered behind to slow the ship as she floated into the water. Ship whistles and boat horns, yelps and hurrahs, laughter and applause mixed with sounds of crackling brace-timbers that had once held the mighty ship at bay.

The vessel gained momentum as it slipped over the well-greased ways. And sixty-two seconds later the *Titanic* floated toward the fitting-out berth, deftly guided by a contingent of tugs.

In the private grandstand, investors breathed a sigh of relief and allowed themselves a cautious smile. Then, Victorian taboos aside, strangers hugged strangers. Children and adults jumped up and down with joy. And laborers gleefully beat co-workers with their caps as the *Titanic* moved to its temporary berth.

———

LONDON—1995

PARKER rose early and took a taxi to the fashionably old Sotheran's of Sackville Street—an Antiquarian Bookstore—in Piccadilly.

He and the shop's manager, Stephen Llorayne, had spent a better part of their morning in the Edwardian-style book shop, confirming much of what Byron White had shared about the *Great Omar* the day before. And Llorayne recounted how his predecessors, in 1912, had prepared the actual packaging and wrapping of the valuable masterpiece for shipment overseas.

All the while the shop's constant background noise emanated from old typewriters, computer keyboards, a persistently ringing phone, and chatter from customers and salespeople. The shop's ambience presented an atmosphere of warmth that made Parker feel welcome and put him in a more relaxed frame of mind.

Following a tea break, Llorayne told Parker about their famous shop, "As far as we can determine, Henry Sotheran Limited is the oldest continually operating bookstore in U.K. Perhaps the world. Seventeen sixty-one is the earliest traced beginnings, through the first Henry Sotheran. He was considered a bookseller *and* publisher in those days."

Llorayne opened a flat-file drawer and pulled a photo of the original shop's elaborately decorated facade—a style consistent with the middle ages and the ecclesiastical period—for which the borough of York was famous.

"The original shop in York, Stonegate, exists today. And," he pointed to the photo, "as you can see, a wooden sign bearing the inscription, *Holy Bible, 1682*, still hangs over the entrance as it did then. York Minster, the largest medieval church in England, is just up the street."

"Our shop's motto is, if we don't carry the book you want, we'll help you find it. We generally succeed," he said proudly, as he handed Parker an exquisite Victorian bound 1850 *David Copperfield*.

"This book is priced at two hundred fifty pounds. Many of our books have been quite valuable. There was a time, if you were a student at a university such as Oxford or Cambridge— because books were so treasured—you had to bring a book with you just to enroll. If you ran amuck, the authorities held your book for recompense."

Parker marveled at the book's beauty. He carefully paged through the edition and handed it back.

"We recently sold a set of letters from Sir Winston Churchill, written in his first year as a Liberal member of Parliament. He was acting on behalf of a Ceylonese man's rights, back in the twenties. The portfolio sold for eighteen thousand American dollars."

Parker's eyebrows raised and he shook his head slightly, as he considered the value of the rare letters. "What type of clientele do you serve?"

"I can't reveal that. We protect identities of our wealthy and not-so-wealthy rare book collectors. That's what makes Sotheran's different. Naturally we get many Royals, a lot of politicians —quite a lot of actors, English and American. All sorts. Much is carried out by mail and fax.

"Famous people come in, but we don't get into bowing and scraping for them. They're grateful for that."

"What's your most unique items sold?"

"Over the years Sotheran's acquired and sold Sir Isaac Newton's personal library, and Dickens . . . he was a regular customer of ours. We bought Dickens' library following his death.

"But most unique? Ahh . . . " Llorayne put his index finger into the air, rose from his desk, and walked over to an imposing wooden and glass case centered against the side wall.

He opened the intricately filigreed doors, pulled out a ribbon-tied folder with a small stack of papers inside, then returned and slid the folder toward Parker.

"This will make your mouth water."

Parker uncovered an 8 X 10 photograph of an elaborately carved, majestic, Elizabethan-style bookcase with a Bust of Shakespeare at the top. Two statuettes of Queen Elizabeth and James I flanked either side in deep embrasures.

The inscription read:

> Book Case made from pieces of timber taken from 40 differ-
> ent buildings connected with Shakespeare's Life and Works.
> The various woods are from 300 to 900 years old.

At the bottom of the photo the inscription read:

> FOR SALE BY Messrs. H. SOTHERAN & CO., Booksell-
> ers to H.M. the King, 43 Piccadilly, London, W., and 140
> Strand W.C.

On the following page was a complete description of the W.C. Prescott Shakespeare Collection that accompanied the large bookcase, containing the complete works of William Shakespeare, "... including the Doubtful Plays and Bibliography ... **EXTENDED TO 95 VOLUMES BY THE ADDITION** of upwards of of **13,000 EXTRA ILLUSTRATIONS** ... "

A Pictorial Key to the Shakespeare Case, showing the exact position of the various pieces of historical timber accompanied the papers. And each part of the *Key Plan* denoted the location from which each piece of timber originated, before the cabinet maker brought it all together.

As Parker glanced over the full-page description with copies of letters of authenticity, he was struck by the note that read:

PRICE, WITH BOOK-CASE £750.

"Sensational," Parker said with a look of disbelief. What year was this sold?"

"The Germans gutted most of our archives when our warehouse burned in World War II. But we believe it was sold within a decade of the turn of the century. Somewhere between the reign of Edward VII and George V."

Parker read aloud from the page of timber extractions, "'Bust of Shakespeare Carved from wood drawn from Parish Church, Stratford on Avon; Four Frieze Blocks, Windsor Castle; Six Panels, Herne's Oak, Windsor Park, the Trysting Place of *Falstaff, Mistress Page*, and *Ford* in the *Merry Wives of Windsor*, Last Act; Six Pieces, Poets Corner, Westminster Abbey.'"

Parker shook his head. "This bookcase would be priceless today."

"No doubt." Llorayne said, then gently placed before Parker two items. "We rarely take these from the vault."

The moment he saw them, he knew what they were.

"Byron White told me of these," he said in awe as he glanced at Charles Dickens' personal snuff box and brandy flask.

"May I?" Parker asked to hold them.

"Certainly. There's a wonderful story about the flask. Dickens had once been in a train accident. He hated trains with a passion, and even campaigned against the proposed underground train system that was to run through his hometown. Following the accident, Dickens carried the flask at all times. 'For medicinal purposes,' Dickens would say, 'to assist in reviving anyone injured in a train wreck.'"

"Of course, these aren't for sale." Parker handed the artifacts to Llorayne.

"Quite so," he smiled. "They're part of our permanent collection."

Parker wished he had a week to browse through the shop. "I need to win the lottery. My tastes are too rich."

Llorayne laughed as he left the room to place Dickens' personal effects in the vault, then returned.

Parker reflected for a moment, took a final sip of tea from his cup, and sat back in the antiquarian chair. "I have a question."

"Of course."

"About the *Omar*."

Llorayne replaced the files and closed, then locked, the glass doors on the wall case.

"Do you believe the *Omar* would be in any shape for recovery, if it were found?"

"I've given that a lot of thought." He returned to his desk. "There was an old shipwreck off our coast, carrying reindeer skins used for boots. Such skins are not a good grade leather. But salvors got this wreck up, and they've actually bound books in that leather. It was pristine when brought from the ocean floor. Remarkably, the leather held up."

"I've heard of that project. As we found with *Titanic*...tanic acid discourages underwater microbes from devouring leather."

"You can actually buy bookmarks made from those skins

in the Queen's Gift Shop at Buckingham Palace. And briefcases have come from them, as well."

"Must be a rough leather."

"Very rough. Obviously not meant for binding books, though some have been. What I'm trying to say . . . it's just possible the *Titanic Omar* might still be in one piece. I'm doubtful, but it's possible."

"At least the bound, jeweled covers, if not the Vedder Edition printed pages . . ."

"True. It was stored, as far as we've determined, in a strongbox. And I've already described how Mr. Stonehouse had it wrapped to protect it from the elements . . . .Yes, anything is possible."

Parker was quiet for a time.

"As you may have heard," said Llorayne, "the *Omar* was completed shortly after King George's coronation."

Parker nodded.

"Around that time our proprietor, Henry Sotheran, decided the shop's manager, John Stonehouse, should travel to America and place it on exhibit. Knowing it would have to pass Customs, Stonehouse shipped the book ahead and made advance arrangements for his own travel and accommodations for New York.

"Two days before going abroad, Stonehouse received a cable from our shipping agents. U.S. Customs had placed a twenty-five percent duty on the book, claiming it too new for exemption. They operated under laws that covered non-dutiable books more than twenty years old. The Original Edition of Veddar's *Rubaiyat*, used in the *Omar* binding, was undated."

"Mr. White mentioned that."

"The Veddar Edition was actually published in eighteen eighty-four...twenty-seven years before Francis Sangorski added his outer binding."

"That would make it duty-free under then existing laws?" Parker took the last bite of a scone.

"That was our company's presumption. But American

Customs officers claimed publishers of the Vedder Edition could have used the same plates to print copies of the book at a much later date. That decision brought the *Omar* within the dutiable period."

"And I suppose neither the bindery nor Sotheran's could prove otherwise, *because* it was an older undated edition of the book?"

"Exactly. That was the book's undoing. And what began as a technicality, mushroomed directly."

"So, if the *Omar* had been released through American Customs," said Parker, "and exhibited to the public, it would have sold for a considerable price and never left America."

"I'm certain of it. The *Great Omar* would have been safe and sound in its new home. . . . And a rare and valuable treasure would have become an icon in its own right as word spread of its existence."

"I gather either your manager, Stonehouse, or Mr. Sotheran refused to pay the duty."

"If Stonehouse had his way, the duty would have been paid. But times were getting tougher in nineteen twelve, and Henry Sotheran vehemently turned down the request to pay duty. He ordered the *Omar* to be shipped back to Forty-three Piccadilly—our shop at the time.

"That was the first irony. But it subsequently set in motion many developments that transpired—the first of which was a rather unfriendly dispute between our owner, Henry Sotheran, and Francis Sangorski, the book's creator."

Llorayne moved a small pile of folders to the edge of his desk. He leaned in closer.

"Mr. Sotheran was fed up with the rising costs of the binding, and was upset when he saw the final bill. But Sotheran wasn't certain what the true cost should have been. You see, our shop was selling rare and rather exquisite books at about one or two hundred pounds each. Occasionally, we might have sold one for three hundred.

"And remember our manager Stonehouse, on his own authority

—knowing it would have been useless to ask Mr. Sotheran for permission—had commissioned the binding by saying that Sangorski could have a blank check to charge what he liked."

"As long as it was justified by the end product," confirmed Parker.

"And," Llorayne agreed, "as Stonehouse had put it, 'the greater the price' the more he would be pleased. But it was Henry Sotheran and Sangorski who clashed about payment. At some point Sotheran obstinately threw up his hands, disowning any further connection with the book, and ordered it to be sold immediately."

Llorayne looked at Parker. "You should understand, Mr. Sotheran was often described as having a retiring disposition, and was considered a fair man in his business dealings. So it was to everyone's surprise when he ordered his manager to ship the *Great Omar* to Sotheby's Auction House to be sold 'without reserve' as he put it."

"How did that sit with Stonehouse? Wasn't he best friends with Sangorski?"

"Story has it that Stonehouse was disgusted with the entire affair. I'm certain he regretted having given Sangorski carte blanche. But there was nothing he could do, short of putting his own job on the line with Mr. Sotheran. He was caught in the middle between his friend, Sangorski, and the man who paid his salary."

"So the book went to auction . . . "

"Yes. And they couldn't have picked any worse timing. In nineteen-twelve our economy was extremely gloomy. On top of a terribly depressed market, one of the worst coal strikes of the period had hit. The national strike went on forever. It devastated those whose lives depended on coal to pay the bills. Even royalty and the wealthy held tight to their purse strings."

"As I recall, Sotheran asked a thousand pounds sterling for the *Omar*."

"Originally, yes," said Llorayne. "In those days the exchange rate would've brought in about five thousand dollars. As Mr. White may have mentioned, the American book collector and book-seller, Gabriel Wells, had offered four thousand dollars to Henry Sotheran—before King George's coronation, and before the *Omar* went to auction. But Sotheran turned it down as too small a price to pay for such a binding."

"But wasn't Wells the American who ended up getting the book from Sotheby's Auction House?"

"That's right. And therein lies another of the many ironies between the tragedy of the *Titanic* and the *Omar*. Mr. Wells had originally offered eight hundred pounds sterling, countering Sotheran's asking price of a thousand, and ended up purchasing the *Great Omar* for less than half its original value. He paid two thousand twenty-five American dollars at auction."

"Considering the outcome, aboard the *Titanic*, it's better he only paid that much."

"Indirectly," said Llorayne, "he saved himself an additional loss of nearly three thousand dollars—quite a large sum in those days."

"Lloyds of London must have insured its trip across the Atlantic."

"One would have thought as much. But that's something we can't confirm. Considering the ship's reputation as unsinkable, they may never have thought of it."

"Remarkable," Parker said. "If they'd just chosen another vessel to ship the book, we probably wouldn't be sitting here today."

Llorayne laughed out loud. "That's the next irony. The auction was held at Sotheby's on March twenty-ninth, nineteen twelve. The book was consigned to another ship on April sixth, just eight days later. But . . . "

"The coal strike?" Parker realized the connection.

"Yes. With the coal strike, freight space was quite unavailable. Ships couldn't get coal, and many vessels languished for months in the harbor. Ships that did have coal were overbooked for space. And the only available sailing was . . . "

"The *Titanic*," Parker said as he stood up, realizing how fate had played its hand against numerous odds and won.

"Even White Star Lines robbed Peter to pay Paul, so to speak. They pulled coal from their less glamourous ships just to send the *Titanic* on its maiden voyage ten days later, April tenth. And if White Star Lines had waited just one day more, who knows what might have happened . . . "

Parker whistled quietly and shook his head.

"Again," said Llorayne, "one could assume a jinx on the book if one attached its unfortunate beginnings to fate. And in the case of Sangorski's patterns, based on his fantasies and Arabian Night's designs from the musical, *Kismet*—fate, destiny, and providence, divine or otherwise—all seemed to merge with the completion of his greatest binding."

Parker found it an extraordinary story and pondered the consequences.

"You know Dr. Parker, I've often played the what-if game about the *Omar*."

"How's that?"

"I ask myself, *what if* Gabriel Wells, the collector who bought the *Omar* at auction, had paid Sotheran's original asking price of a thousand pounds sterling? In all probability, the *Omar* would have been shipped on another vessel . . . "

"At a much earlier date. . . . And survived."

"Or what if Mr. Sotheran hadn't been so insistent the full price be paid. What if he'd swallowed his pride and accepted the lower offer of eight hundred pounds?

"After all, Southeran had to accept Wells' final bid when *Omar* went to auction, and still pay Sotheby's sales commission. The results would've been the same....sold long before *Titanic* was considered for shipment with the courier."

"Harry Widener."

"Yes, the son of a good friend of Wells' who consented to be courier aboard *Titanic*. He was traveling back from Egypt with his parents."

"A young boy as courier?"

"Actually, closing in on his late twenties, I believe. His father, George Widener, was a famous manufacturer of rail cars. No . . . streetcars. Amassed a fortune. His son Harry was involved in his father's business."

"I see," Parker casually sat back in the chair and glanced at his watch. It was 11:50. He rose quickly. "My apologies, I lost track of time. I'm due to meet Ms. Nakamura and Mr. White for lunch in less than ten minutes. Shouldn't have eaten that third scone."

Llorayne smiled, "No fat. I guarantee."

Parker insisted the store manager join them at Wolfe's. The two caught a cab out on Sackville Street and headed across town.

"I'm looking forward to seeing Mr. White again," said Llorayne. "Been a couple of years since we last met."

Caught in their conversation, neither man noticed the black Ford that followed close behind.

———

Nakamura and White arrived at the Hans Crescent restaurant at the same time. The two introduced themselves and secured a booth next to the large plate-glass window looking out on the street. They flagged the scientist and rare book dealer to the table as they arrived.

"What a pleasant surprise," White said to Llorayne. "Haven't seen you since *Omar Three* was presented for display at British Museum."

"Good to see you, Mr. White," Llorayne said as they shook hands. "You look in excellent health."

"Just glad to be alive." White turned to Nakamura, "I tell that to everyone." He smiled broadly. "Keeps me going you know."

Parker introduced the manager of Sotheran's to the FBI agent, and the party took their seats. As they glanced over the menus, Nakamura spoke up.

"Cary, we have a slight change of plans to get to the airport this evening. The terrorist, Khorassani?"

"Ragem's top man . . . "

She nodded. "Died last night. Commissioner Lawton feels the situation could get tense. And we shouldn't rely on public transportation for Gatwick. He's arranged for a Scotland Yard driver, and insisted we take up his offer."

"Considering the circumstances I'd prefer it," he said. "Any word on the other terrorists?"

"Forensics is still involved. Those closest to the detonation zones—suspected of involvement by the level of destruction, around them and their dismembered bodies—appear to be of Arabic extraction."

"But," interrupted Parker, "there could've been innocent Arabic travelers who were victims because of their proximity to the blasts."

"Of course. It's still difficult to establish specifics this early. But there's no question Heathrow was masterminded by Ragem. We suspect he's already out of the country...has been for some time. One thing we know, the bomb signatures don't match IRA."

Nakamura realized she should not discuss so much about the case in front of White and Llorayne, though most of the information had already gone out over the BBC.

"This isn't quite the lunchtime conversation, is it?" Nakamura's dark eyes flashed with apology.

"I understand," said Llorayne. "Between the various fanatic organizations based here, that threaten to blow up something every other week, perhaps we're too cavalier about it. But we steel ourselves against fear or we'd go nuts."

White shrugged his shoulders. "I've seen a lot in my day. Nothing bothers me anymore."

Nakamura smiled and relaxed for the first time since arriving in London.

The restaurant's atmosphere was warm and inviting. They savored pleasing mixed aromas of hearty beef stew, steak, grilled fish and hamburgers. Even Parker was suddenly hungry, again.

A jovial waitress stepped to the table and took their order. And each of the four settled back to enjoy their meeting.

Following the meal, they gave in to temptation and ordered slivers of chocolate mousse cheesecake.

Parker looked at White and Llorayne. "We should tie up loose ends about the *Titanic*. Between the three of us we could recount what we know about the sinking and compare notes on the *Omar*." He glanced at Nakamura. "I'm sure you'll find this interesting."

"Altogether fascinating," she assured.

White nodded, "Happy to share what I know."

"I probably know the least about the ship," said Llorayne. "But I'll chime in when apropos."

White set the scene and recounted what he knew about the last few days—and final hours—of the liner, *Titanic*, as she set out on her maiden voyage. Throughout the discussion, Parker and, occasionally Llorayne, offered information on the circumstances that led to the loss of the ship, and to the loss of the elegant binding.

———

APRIL 10, 1912
11:50 Greenwich

"THE deadliest of all sins is Pride," repeated Samuel Hollis to his wife, Nelda. They stood on the noisy quay, witness to the 20th century's most ostentatious example of pride—the *R.M.S. Titanic*. Samuel's wife nodded in agreement. Even with the sun, she felt a chill as a cool sea breeze mixed the briny smell of the ocean with the scent of oil and burning coal. Nelda Hollis pulled her worn gloves over protruding fingers and was openly glad not to be aboard the largest, unsinkable ship ever.

Ten months of fitting out the *Titanic*, now complete—and sea trials behind her—the liner rested in berth 44 at Southampton's White Star pier, awaiting its scheduled sailing of 12 noon. Sitting at the dock, its horns blasted for all the world to hear. In ten minutes, the *Titanic* would steam into the history books. Everyone standing on both sides of Southampton water was proud.

First it would stop at Cherbourg. Then, Queenstown. Destination, New York.

By 11:00 a.m., London's boat train had deposited the last of its travelers at *Titanic's* dock. The carefree rich mixed for only brief moments with the courageous poor, as passengers waited for their assigned gangways. For most of the rich, this trip would be an experience they had complacently accepted as a necessity of life. For steerage passengers, many felt they had embarked on an adventure of frightening proportions.

Tons of luggage had been conveyed aboard ship—most of it

belonging to first and second-class travelers. Baggage brought by third-class passengers amounted to everything they owned that could be carried on board. Each of the 2227 passengers and crew had found their quarters and temporarily settled in. Unless assigned duties as a member of the crew, nearly everyone found some place on board from which they could watch the imminent departure of their ship.

At 11:55 a.m., all but one gangway had been pulled from White Star's pier, as preparations were made to cast off for the maiden voyage. Much to the dismay of a noncommissioned officer stationed on dock at gangway's end, a drunken surly group of greasers and stokers dashed up to board the ship.

"Stand back," the petty officer commanded the disorderly men, and blocked their way. "She's preparing to cast off."

"Listen 'ere bloke, we have work on board," one yelled, hastening to get by. The others pushed forward with their gear, cussing at the officer.

"It's too late," the petty officer held his ground. "We've taken replacements who came on time."

"Replacements 'e says," someone yelled.

Furious, another stoker jumped out from the group. "I'll replace 'ye, ya' bloody bastard." The group moved forward, challenging the man's authority.

Two seaman raced down the gangway and assisted the petty officer. Harsh words were exchanged and a shoving match ensued. The crew maintained their stance, and the thwarted stokers and greasers left the pier, loudly threatening revenge and secretly regretting their drunken night. Little did they know how fortunate they had been.

With the last gangway removed and sailing permission secured from the harbor master, the seamen released the mighty hawsers from their moorings. And the *Vulcan* and two other tugboats proceeded to draw the liner from the quay.

As Samuel and Nelda Hollis stood with hundreds of others at

the end of the wharf, they watched the *Titanic* move from its enlarged berth. Deep down, Samuel and his wife felt sudden pangs of envy—the second deadliest sin.

By late afternoon, April 14, the air had turned bitter cold. Few people strolled the decks, or even left their cabins. It was an occasion for writing letters, spending moments with families in warm rooms—a quiet time before the elegant social gatherings of the evening to come.

As usual, Captain Smith would prepare himself for his night ahead. On this evening, he would dine as the Guest-of-Honor at a dinner party hosted by the George Wideners. Smith looked forward to such gatherings as much as he did to his upcoming retirement.

At about 7:30 p.m., one of numerous ice warnings, received that day, came from Leyland's *California*, and reported "Three large bergs five miles to southward of us." At 9:40 p.m., a final warning placed the *Titanic* within the specific rectangle covered by a message from the *Mesaba*. It read, "Lat. 42°N to 41°25'N, Longitude 40°W to 50°30'W, saw much heavy pack ice and great number large icebergs, also field ice."

As they had done throughout most of the day, the *Titanic's* crew smugly ignored the warning—though one of the largest lines of ice ever reported continued to be in its direct path. A line of ice, seventy-eight miles long, lay dead ahead.

———

To the quartermaster it looked as though an eerie ghost ship had passed—a fully-rigged, tall-masted windjammer lit by the reflection of thousands of stars cast upon the water on a moonless night. Within moments it disappeared into the darkness.

In the calm waters of the North Atlantic, at 11:40 p.m., April 14th, 1912, the First Class dining room silver, set for breakfast the next morning, rattled slightly.

Few people on board noticed the grazing of the starboard side of the ship, and most went about their business. Lovers resumed private walks on deck. Many passengers continued to sleep below. But to Mrs. Graham and her teenage daughter, Margaret, there was a terrifying noise that sounded like thousands of plate glass windows had broken.

Steward Johnson was certain the ship had dropped a propeller.

Some passengers saw a wall of ice go by their portholes. Chunks of ice fell into James McGough's cabin through his open porthole on A-Deck. McGough knew what it was.

After standing on A-Deck watching the 10-story berg scrape and drop off tons of ice chunks in the water and onto the starboard well deck, some die-hard passengers resumed their late-night games of bridge in the first-class smoking room. Books were read, highballs were consumed. Unconcerned, topside passengers felt the iceberg's impact, but knew the ship was unsinkable.

In the lower third-class depths of the ship, the scraping sound was haunting. Most of the immigrants had never traveled on a seagoing vessel, let alone a ship as massive as the *Titanic*. Unlike the wealthy, above them, everything they owned was on board. But steerage passengers were assured of their safety, before boarding. Indeed, there was nothing to worry about.

After excusing himself from the Widener's dinner party, the ship's captain had checked in briefly with the bridge then turned in early for the night—although this was one of the most critical points in navigating the northerly course.

Smith knew the *Titanic* had been hit the moment the grinding sound was silenced. He raced to the bridge from his nearby cabin.

"What did we strike?" the captain asked of his First Officer.

"An iceberg, sir. I hard-a-starboarded her and reversed engines on full. I attempted to hard-a-port around it, but she was already near at hand. We hit, and I could do no more."

The First Officer confirmed that he had already closed the

emergency doors and telegraphed "Stop" to the engine room. A clawing feeling grabbed at his gut. As chief navigator for the watch, Murdoch peered out from the bridge to starboard and prayed any damage to be undone.

Captain Smith tried to reassure himself, *Nothing can happen to my ship*.

Philadelphians, George and Eleanor Widener, had just gone to sleep in their starboard first-class stateroom, following their dinner party in honor of Captain Smith. Their son, Harry, chosing to remain topside, played cards with Major Butt—President Taft's Principle Aid-de-Camp—and other friends.

George Widener's eyes bolted open as soon as the ship was rammed. Disoriented and still trying to escape the paralysis of deep sleep, he tried to comprehend what had happening.

A new silence overtook the ship—the halting silence one feels when listening for an intruder in the house. Since leaving Europe, the *Titanic* had averaged 21 knots, with its reciprocating engines and one turbine vibrating through the hull as they turned the triple screws driving the ship's propellers. Now the routine, customary noises were gone. The constant, rhythmic sounding engines had stopped.

Widener heard bits of conversation, in the corridor, but could not make out their meaning. He was afraid to wake his wife. She was sleeping soundly.

There appeared to be no urgency to the words slipping under his door.

"Ice . . . " something, they seemed to say.

"Ice . . . " ran through his mind several times. "Ice . . . berg!"

Fear took over. Widener moved across the darkened stateroom, switched on a small desk lamp, then hurried to open the cabin door. The extreme icy, bitter cold had reached the corridors. It chilled him deeply and caught him off guard. But he listened intently.

A steward hastened by, not saying anything. Except for the

distant sound of music drifting from the first-class lounge, the outside corridors were more quiet than ever.

Abruptly, men's laughter cut through the arctic air as sharp scissors. On the well-deck, steerage passengers played a haunting game of soccer with ice chunks from the berg. And echoes of laughter mocked the silence that accompanied the killing of the engines.

Then, the elder Widener heard the confirmation he needed to hear.

"She hit an iceberg," a strolling passenger said casually, noticing the pajama-clad man at the door.

"That cannot be good," replied Widener. "Not when we've been moving at such a clip for the past four days . . . "

The traveler quipped back over his shoulder, "I overheard a crewman back at Southampton say, 'God himself could not sink this ship.' Not to worry, man."

The passenger disappeared down another hallway.

Widener closed the door and pushed the bell to summon their steward. Then, he moved to the edge of his bed. Without hesitating, he quietly pulled a pair of pants over his pajama trousers—attempting not to wake his wife—threw on a robe and slipped into his shoes. He did not stop for socks.

"Gabriel would expect Harry to check on the *Omar*," Widener said of his close friend, Gabriel Wells. Widener's son had been assigned as the courier for the newly purchased book.

Their steward softly knocked at the door, and Widener slipped out into the corridor.

"Thank you for coming at this hour."

"I was still up. How may I help you, sir?"

"They say we hit an iceberg?"

"I haven't confirmed that, sir. Someone else said we might have dropped a propeller. Remain in your room, where it's warm. I'll verify what's happened."

"All right. But please summon my son, Harry. I believe he's up in the first-class lounge with Major Butt. I must see him immediately."

"Right away, sir." The steward politely excused himself and hurried down the hall.

"Ask him to come to his room, not mine."

"Yes sir," the steward replied as he turned a corner and headed for A-Deck.

Mr. Widener returned to his stateroom, unsure what to do next.

"What's the matter George?" his wife asked softly. "Why are you up?"

"I didn't mean to wake you, Eleanor. Go back to sleep. It's nothing." His pure white hair glowed in the soft light, as he pulled the heavy covers and quilt up over his wife's shoulders.

"I heard you send for Harry. Has the ship stopped?"

"It appears we're at a standstill for the moment."

"Why is it so quiet?"

"Might have dropped a propeller. Nothing to worry about. Go back to sleep." He pulled on a silk robe and drew the belt tight.

"Come back to bed soon," Eleanor said, as she placed her head on the pillow in compliance with her husband's wishes. Exhausted from hosting her party for Commander Smith, and with a busy schedule planned with friends the next day, it was not difficult to return to sleep.

The streetcar baron slipped through the door to their son's connecting room. The lights still burning, he crossed to a nightstand set against the wall, pulled open the top left drawer, and fished out a key. The door from the corridor opened.

"Father," a tall, dashingly dressed Harry Widener said, surprised to find him up so late, and in his private room. "I was playing a winning hand when you sent for me. What is it?"

"They say we've hit a berg. What do you know of it?"

"Why yes. Quite impressive," Harry said, pulling a Cuban cigar from his mouth and resting it in a large ashtray on the nightstand. "Too bad you missed it. We felt a jarring of the ship and ran over to the windows for a glimpse. But it was difficult to see anything. So we raced on deck in time to watch this monstrous mountain of ice scrape by. Biggest we've seen the entire voyage. You would'a loved it—must've been a hundred feet or more. Towered over the top deck."

"My God, son, did it do much damage?"

"Of course not. It dropped a bit of ice on the well-deck and some along starboard. But no one's concerned. They say we're perfectly safe." He picked up the cigar and took a large draw. "That's why we returned to the table and dealt out another hand. I had a full-house going. Could'a beat the major."

"Son, I don't want to panic your mother . . . that's why I asked to meet you here." He handed his son the key and pushed the drawer closed. "I apologize for getting into your personal effects. But I feel you should check on the *Omar* for Mr. Wells. And perhaps, move the book from storage to a higher deck, in case we take on water."

Harry almost laughed at the suggestion. "There's nothing to fear, Father. The ship's unsinkable." He drew on the cigar once more and exhaled a large puff of blue smoke.

The elder Widener had been a transportation industrialist too long, and knew that freak accidents do happen. "Don't argue with me Harry. Please do as I ask. Remember, that book is your responsibility, not mine. And you're doing this favor for my best friend."

Harry was properly chastised. "You're right. I apologize." He deposited the cigar back in the ashtray, and grinned to reassure his father. "I'll check on the book lickety-split."

"See if you can raise the chief purser. Ask if the book can go into the captain's strongbox, and verify if the ship is foundering. I still can't understand why we've sat this long in the water, if nothing's seriously wrong."

The young Widener left the room, and closed his fist around the key to a private storage closet on C-deck. No one else, beyond the chief purser, had access to that area.

George returned to his suite and sat in the winged-back chair at the writing desk. The shadows around his owlish eyes grew darker as he awaited news of the ship's condition.

As Harry rushed down the stairs to retrieve the book, passengers converged in the hallways and corridors. They were perplexed. Should they leave their warm cabins or stay inside for safety sake? *There certainly couldn't be any danger on the safest ship in the world.*

Most had speculated the *Titanic* had casually absorbed the piercing thrust upon its hull. But with tons of pressure against it—taxing the strength of the ship's sulfur-ladened plates—the rivets had popped, and the cold steel fractured, like glass, while the ice ripped through it.

In less than thirty minutes, the world's grandest ship lurched forward at its head. The series of catastrophic ruptures caused tons of water to flow in through the *Titanic's* starboard side. And not quite imperceptibly, the bows began to dip forward.

The first scream came from below decks. No one heard it topside.

Those who had too much to drink questioned their minds to see if they should panic. Strains of a waltz came from the band that had positioned itself in A-deck's first class lounge. With the lateness of the hour, few paid attention.

"What do we do now?" a gentleman in the first-class saloon said as he greedily drank down the rest of his hot whiskey and water. He set the empty glass on a gold-gilded table. Even with the table's raised edges, the glass slid to the floor, hit the leg of a chair and shattered.

"Oh my God!" said a young man standing nearby. He and others staggered sideways as the ship deviated from its center of gravity and listed slightly to starboard.

Widener continued to move toward the forward section with

one goal in mind. No longer thinking of himself and the abandoned card game, he had to protect the one unique and valuable item on board entrusted to him.

His parents, the captain, and purser were the only other people to hold the privileged information. The specially bound bejeweled edition of *The Rubaiyat of Omar Khayyam*, enroute to its new owner in New York, rested in its waterproof container in the locked storeroom. But Widener was responsible for protecting it from any serious disaster that might befall the ship.

Gabriel Wells and Mr. Sotheran would expect no less.

Widener passed others in the corridor and noticed them walking slightly uphill as the ship's listing to starboard became more pronounced.

"Does it feel like the bow's dipping forward?" someone said to another.

"I hear the ship's taking on considerable water," the other answered back as they maneuvered the corridor with less than perfect sea legs.

By 12:25 a.m., with little success at raising help with the traditional C.Q.D. message, the wireless operators had already switched to the newer "S.O.S." Following the rule of "women and children first," Captain Edward J. Smith, knowing there was little hope, finally gave the order to fill the lifeboats. It took time for the order to get past a select few, since several of the crew were not immediately informed, and many passengers had not yet received word to abandon ship.

Many expensively dressed men and women—people who had thought their lives secure in their wealth— were now bewildered and disoriented. No one provided advice regarding their situation.

Was the ship in danger? they wondered. *Was this just a practice drill? And why so late at night?*

Somewhere deep in the ship, arguments between steerage passengers and crew took form. Anyone beyond first and second class passengers soon found they must fend for themselves, or experience an insidious form of life-threatening discrimination between the classes.

After contending with crowded corridors and stairwells and, with most passengers now rushing in the opposite direction, Widener reached the door to the storage closet. He glanced down the hallway. With everyone crowding the area, Widener knew he could not retrieve the valuable book without being seen. But there was no time to waste.

He pulled the bit key from his pocket, slipped it into the door's cavity, past the wards, and rotated it until the tumblers engaged. Widener tugged the door open. Though he knew it to be secure, he was relieved to find the large leather bag on the shelf. The book was stored inside a wax-covered, wrapped teak box.

"Water has submerged the boiler rooms up to the first four decks," someone yelled from another hallway. "Everything below E-deck including the racquet court, is under water."

An attractive woman passed by and Widener saw increased panic in her face as she rushed to hug a gentleman who had just come from above.

"I've been at the forward crews quarters," the man spoke out. "E-deck is taking on water."

Passengers questioned anyone with authority regarding the abandonment of ship. But answers conflicted.

Widener quickly seized the leather bag and left the skeleton key behind. He turned and headed back toward the first-class staircase, leading to the Boat-deck and the officer's quarters. Excusing himself as he cut past several slower moving passengers, Widener now understood the impact of the disaster unfolding before him. He would protect the book for which he had been entrusted, then warn his parents of the possible danger.

Off in the distance, wafting down through the Grand Staircase from the first-class lounge, Widener heard the musicians playing strains of a ragtime tune.

Odd, a calamity accompanied by such stirring music, he thought.

The glacial air now permeated every corner of the ship. Widener struggled up sections of the tilting staircase and held tightly to the banister to prevent sliding across the steps. The weight and size of the *Omar* made it more difficult for the courier to maneuver toward each level above.

Lines of passengers proceeded to the boats in a semi-orderly fashion. Panic had not yet set in. Some had found life jackets in their cabins. Others were caught without them. But stewards provided life preservers to those who couldn't return to their rooms. Most believed they would not need them.

As weary travelers entered the top decks, the frigid air reached the main staircase doors and raced to find low spots in the hull.

"Mr. Widener," someone called from behind, then tapped him on the shoulder. "Mr. Widener."

Harry turned to look. Their steward, who earlier had sought him in the lounge, held an armful of life jackets.

"Sir, I've warned your parents to come to the Boat-deck." He shoved a jacket at Widener. "You must meet them there. We've been ordered to abandon ship."

The steward did not wait for a response, but hurried past him and disappeared through a door.

Widener reached the vestibule at the Boat-deck and found it an unpleasant experience to get through. A mass of thoroughly confused families and individuals had congregated at the first-class entrance near the Marconi room.

He watched passengers scramble back and forth, across the deck, as crew determined who would be saved and who would remain behind. Since there had been no required drill following embarkation, none was aware of boat assignments.

Widener hoped his parents had prepared to leave ship. He would search for them as soon as the *Great Omar* was safe.

Across the deck, Widener looked through the sea of faces and spotted Colonel John Jacob Astor and his second wife, Madeleine, patiently awaiting instructions—Astor holding his pregnant wife tightly for protection from the crowd and the polar-like air.

Isidor Straus, one of the partner's of Macy's Department Stores, and his wife, Ida, stood close by. Each had been introduced to Widener and his parents at dinner, two evenings before. It saddened him that new-found acquaintances might lose their lives or be split apart by fate.

"Level off," a crew member shouted instructions to lower a portside boat.

"Pull the rope aft. Careful, mate. Now the stern. All right, level off. Level off . . . "

As Widener headed for Captain Smith's quarter's, near the wheel house, he recognized the wealthy American, Molly Brown, preparing to enter portside boat number six. A young bellboy, no more than 14 years of age, carried an armful of bread-loaves to the boat, then went back for more. Near the first funnel, a dozen men tried to free a collapsible boat from its storage site.

For a brief moment, Harry peered out over the assorted collection of travelers as they gathered with family, banded in their cliques, or stood lonely and apart without friends. Convinced the ship was safer than the small lifeboats, many waited for someone to convince them otherwise.

Harry noticed the new dress code that prevailed—a total and radical social transformation. Some passengers wore their pajamas and robes, others had hastily pulled pants and a shirt—or dress—over their nightclothes. Still others had not yet changed from their evening gowns and tuxedos.

Drab, colorless, and frayed clothes wrapped those who had escaped from steerage. Yet, fur coats covered satin nightgowns as passengers scurried across the Boat-deck...resembling the former pelted creatures that had once inhabited their skins.

Unconsciously, the classes had been liberated from all social values as chic and rakish façades were burst, and their new disguises provided transient asylum.

Widener shook off the eerie sight before him and crossed over to the captain's cabin, holding the jewel-encrusted book and casing close to his chest. The young assistant wireless operator, Harold Bride, was delivering a message to the commander.

"Captain, we're fortunate, indeed. The *Carpathia's* wireless man returned to their radio room to check a time-rush with the *Parisian*. Otherwise, he may not have received our S.O.S.

"They're putting about and heading right for us," Bride said over the clamor. "They promised full speed."

"Wire the *Carpathia* again. Tell them the engine rooms are taking water."

"Yes sir." The young man tacked to leave.

"And Mr. Bride..." The British Marconi employee turned to the captain with a questioning look.

"Tell them the dynamos might not last much longer."

Bride acknowledged the order, excused himself as he bumped into Harry Widener, cut through the crowd, and headed back to assist Chief Operator Jack Phillips in the wireless room.

A whooshing sound emanated from near the Bridge, as Quartermaster Rowe fired the first rocket signaling distress to any passing ships.

Widener approached the captain and spoke quickly.

"Excuse my interruption, Captain Smith, this is the least of your worries. But if the *Omar* can be secured in a waterproof safe, topside, until we return to the ship, I'm certain the owner will be grateful."

"Ah, the young Mr. Widener," Smith remarked to others in his cabin. "Come in. Quickly," Smith almost pulled him through the door. "Wonderful party your parents gave in my honor this evening. Shame it's turned out like this." His voice cracked with emotion.

In the room stood a distracted Bruce Ismay, Chairman of White Star Line; Thomas Andrews, the ship's builder and manager of Harland & Wolff Shipyards; and, First Officer William Murdoch.

"You remember George Widener's son."

Their minds were on other concerns.

"Our chief purser's placing valuables in my strongbox." He directed Widener to the corner safe. The purser had just opened it. He placed small bags, loose jewelry, papers, and intimate size boxes inside for protection—until such time as they could be recovered.

"Had to bring some of the items up from below, what with the water and all . . . " The captain's voice faded slightly.

Widener handed the leather bag to the purser.

"Thank you Captain," Widener said as he turned back to shake his hand.

But Smith was already out the door. At the Boat-deck he offered assistance and used his megaphone to give advice to passengers and crew. The other men followed Smith and dispersed to perform their own assignments. Harry emerged from quarters to search for his parents.

Nine life boats had been launched over the port and starboard sides. At the bows, the *Titanic's* name was nearly covered, and the upper decks began to submerge. Within forty minutes, the forward well-deck was completely under water, with such a heavy list to port that passengers found it difficult to reach and enter the lifeboats.

Henry T. Wilde, the *Titanic's* chief officer, made a quick decision and called out for all remaining passengers to move to the starboard side.

"It'll straighten her up," he reassured. And sure enough, as the passengers banded together and shifted over to starboard, the *Titanic* unwillingly and lethargically reverted to an even keel. The crew returned to loading the remaining boats.

By now, the orchestra had moved to the boat-deck. They continued to play ragtime hits and spiritual hymns—hoping to calm the soon-to-be-disenfranchised passengers who had unwittingly put their faith in corporate folly.

To those who viewed the ensuing disastrous events from the water, the picture was haunting. By 2:15 a.m., the ship was in an ominous downward tilt. Looking on at what was thought to be the most majestic and safest vessel ever to sail an open sea, survivors in lifeboats, and those quickly dying of exposure in the water, were numb with the horror of something they could not wish away.

Treading legs and arms fought with the ocean, in a surrealistic battle to prevail against the elements, as other arms rowed boats to escape the screams of those crying for help.

The ship was ablaze with lights glowing from every porthole and window.

At first, from a distance, survivors in the lifeboats heard subdued and muted sounds of debris falling across decks —striking saloon and cabin walls as they broke apart. Eerie sounds of breakage, as if numerous couples were having spats in houses down the street.

What began as a series of distant noises aboard ship—pieces of crystal and faint sounds of bottles and glasses crashing to the floor— grew louder as the seconds passed. Slowly at first. Then, gathering momentum with deadly force.

Chairs, tables, couches, and statues slid and tumbled across rooms. They fell into stained glass windows and ripped apart ornate sconces, filigreed balustrades, and opulent mahogany and French walnut-paneled walls.

The destruction of the *Titanic* grew. Collisions of heavier objects whose weight or fastenings had initially held them down, broke loose and raced in a stampede to meet the incline. Space heaters, iron bathtubs, gymnasium equipment, pianos, ship boilers and engines were wrenched from their bonds. Aong with tons of coal, they breached their containment areas and explosively fell downward.

Passengers, who less than two hours before had been partying, were now pinned against giant broken mirrors and elegantly decorated walls. Then water overtook the upper decks.

Haunting sounds cut through the icy night air, reverberated across the water, and pierced the vulnerable silence of the sea. Instantly, wailing cries, shrill screams and catastrophic sounds metamorphosed into a deafening roar.

It was like the devil, himself, had upended four city-blocks of Manhattan and dumped everything into one place. The momentum of objects caused multiple blows to the body of the ship, as walls gave way to weight and steerage passengers were crushed and drowned beneath tons of rubble.

At 2:17 a.m., Monday, April 15, 1912—glowing as though a ghost ship—the *Titanic* began its slow plunge for the deep—its stern now rising higher in the air. Many defenseless passengers, swimming from the ship, never saw the first massive funnel as it tore from its supports, toppled from above, and crushed them in the water.

What had started as a series of distant noises became explosive bellows in the darkness. The cacophony grew into a final, violent and raging sound of thunder, as the the hull split in two and the second funnel parted from its base.

In an indelible display, sparks shot from the smokestack's tube and dropped to the ocean like the afterglow of fireworks. An eerie red glow emanated from failing shipboard lights, as the dynamos faltered. Then, as if giving one last sigh, the lights blinked and went out deck by deck as each level submerged.

The aftsection of the *Titanic* continued to rise, exposing its hundred-ton rudder and the three gigantic propellers—frozen in time—never to turn again. As if ashamed, the remains of the once magnificent ship turned in its place, exposed its keel, and hid the grotesque and hideous ending from many of those who were left to tell its story.

Figures surged away from the attacking water as the hull of the *Titanic* rose. And the world's greatest modern ship began its slide into the numbing abyss.

As the two ends of the *Titanic* ripped apart, the forward bow section and its entombed passengers were sent, first, to their grave. Second by second their wailing was silenced, and the foresection slipped quietly into the algid water on its mission of mercy. Those remaining on the rising stern were dazed and confused as they watched events unfold—helplessly and seemingly alone—among hundreds of strangers. Then, husbands and lovers, drinking and dancing partners, children and adults—the poor and the mighty—grabbed at railings and lurched for anything left that might float.

The *Great Omar's* courier, Widener, and his father, George, had earlier bid farewell to Harry's mother as she set out with Mrs. John Jacob Astor and other prominent women in lifeboat number 4. On the upper edge of the fantail, father and son clutched at the ice-cold railing, now rising high above the ocean.

George Widener had spent most of his sometimes venturesome life building streetcars. He had put his faith in all forms of modern transportation, and it had brought him immense wealth. It was said that the Widener name meant as much in Philadelphia as the Vanderbilt name meant in New York. Known throughout the United Kingdom as "the buyer of the Lansdowne Rembrandt, 'The Mill,'" and progenitor of the Widener Gallery of masterpieces in Philadelphia, none of his wealth could save him now.

His son, Harry, twenty-seven and a Harvard graduate, had been primed to take over the famous Philadelphia-based business. Described by his closest friends as "widely liked, very capable, and amiable," the young Widener had many of the traits of his father.

George looked at his son. And he searched his mind, and the black starlit sky, for an answer to his question, *Why?*

Harry gazed out over the pandemonium surrounding them, now oblivious to the screams and cries for help. He could do no more. In the last hour, he, his father, and their friends, Arthur Ryerson and John B. Thayer, had gallantly helped load women and children into the boats. Then, they turned to help each other through the rest of the night. In their personal silence, punctuated occasionally with muted conversation, the men stood calmly together, thoughtful and reminiscent of the past—and of what might have been.

I'm sorry, Mr. Wells, the young Widener quietly thought to himself. He had felt personally responsible for his assignment as the *Great Omar's* courier. A tear froze on his cheek before it could drop to the sea. *Forgive me, Henry Sotheran. Likewise, I have failed you.*

For an instant he thought of Francis Sangorski's vision . . . the most beautiful binding in the world. Only a select few had had the privilege of witnessing its beauty. He told his father of his thoughts, "It appears no one else will ever see Sangorski's grand book and know of its wonder."

The elder Widener slowly nodded his head in agreement. He gazed out into the darkness, hoping to see the outline of his wife, Eleanor, in Boat No. 4.

Grasping the railing tightly, the younger Widener struggled to maintain balance and turned to gaze out over the dark waters The *Titanic's* band had just completed the final strains of a Spanish melody, *Autumn*. It had lilted out over the hundreds of victims to soothe their inner panic.

> *When temptations fierce assault me,*
> *When my enemies I find,*
> *Sin and guilt, and death and Satan,*
> *All against my soul combined;*
> *Hold me up in mighty waters,*
> *Keep my eyes on things above,*
> *Righteousness, divine Atonement,*
> *Peace, and everlasting Love.*

Some would later argue they had heard *Nearer My God to Thee.* But no one mind was focused on the music. The brave musicians had played until it was impossible to play any longer. Their melodies had helped warm the subconscious, covered up the white lies that convinced wives to leave husbands, shaded the horror of pending death, and provided temporary balm to quell the pain yet to come.

The nearly upright stern seemed to howl, *This cannot be!* as it tried to stay afloat, rising at least 15 stories above the water for what appeared an eternity—but could only have been minutes. Teaming masses of bodies appeared to freefall through space into the twenty-eight-degree water. Hands and fingers outstretched to loved ones and imaginary saviors, as they struggled to hold on, or touch goodbye for one final time.

The *Titanic's* aftsection continued to rise. And Harry and George Widener could hold on no longer. Shivering beyond control, their fingers—frozen from exposure—slowly gave way to the weight of their bodies as the upended stern held itself perpendicular to the sea. Without words, the two men looked into each other's eyes. Then Harry's father gazed to the heavens, prayed for God's mercy, and fell silently downward into the salty, foaming cauldron of death. The courier for the *Great Omar* followed.

Stunned by the fall into the glacial-like waters, the elder Widener's prayer was answered. His heart failed instantly, sparing him from the agony of terror that others felt as they slipped between the ice floes. The younger Widener was not as fortunate—his life slowly ebbing, with hundreds of others, as weary, exhausted bodies gave in to hypothermia in the ebony sea. Some released their life jackets and were quietly swept into the abyss.

Screams from the ship were lost to the darkness as the stern sagged hopelessly, lurched downward, and headed toward the depths with the remainder of over fifteen hundred souls still on board the ten million-dollar casket. Almost as quickly as it had begun, the thunderous roaring sounds reverberated across the calm, lonely sea and faded into the distance as though it were a passing storm.

What then came upon the senses of the seven hundred five who would survive in the boats—what all survivors would forever carry to their own graves—were the ominous, helpless sounds from a macabre chorus of wailing voices, emanating from hundreds of mortals lost among the flotsam. An oppressive grief penetrated their spirits as victims begged to be pulled from the glacial waters and wearily struggled for life with cries for which there would be no response. And a penetrating sorrow overtook those in the boats as the catastrophe folded in on itself.

As if in a sepulchral reproduction of *The Last Judgment* . . . the good and the wicked, the impoverished and greedy, the sheep and the goats, those who had faith and those who would find faith, gave way to the archangel's weighing of souls as the devil watched on. And their souls passed, ironically, not through a molten river, but through the frigid waters of the North Atlantic.

———

WOLFE'S RESTAURANT

THOSE who had discussed the fate of the *Titanic* were completely silent. The world around them had disappeared, momentarily.

As though in another dimension, waitresses poured lagers and delivered food to other tables. New customers stepped down from the street-level entrance and animatedly waited in line for seats. Outside, autos and lorries inched by in the traffic. In front of Harrod's Department Store, uniformed valets—in gold-tasseled epaulets—assisted wealthy shoppers in and out of their limos, Rolls Royces and Jaguars.

It all appeared trivial now, up against the backdrop of lives tragically and senselessly lost aboard the world's grandest ship. Then, there was the tragedy at Heathrow. It was almost too much to endure.

For the elderly bookbinder, the respected scientist, the expert on antiquarian books, and the FBI agent, earthly thoughts had given way to a silence that, at once, had bound them together. The power of the past had melded with the present and grabbed hold. And for the longest time it would not let go.

Finally, Parker looked up at White and broke the hush.

"Tell me, Byron, what happened to the *Omar's* creators?"

White suddenly felt the years tugging at his life. He found it difficult to speak. Then he smiled at Parker.

"We've discussed the ironies that plagued the *Titanic*, Dr. Parker. But there are a few more," he sighed. "As we've pointed out, if events hadn't occurred as they did, we might not be sitting here, today."

Jenny placed her hand over White's and squeezed it gently, as she winked at Llorayne. "But, Mr. White, I wouldn't have had an opportunity to meet you."

A broad smile lit up the binder's face. "Fate perhaps? I just wish it were under different circumstances."

"So, there were more incidents?" asked Parker.

Llorayne spoke up. "Who would have guessed, for example, that several years after the sinking, Henry Sotheran would be killed in a motoring accident? And Wells . . . Gabriel Wells, the rich American collector who bought the *Great Omar* at auction, would become the new owner of Sotheran's Bookshop."

"Fate or circumstance?"

"*That* is the question," White smiled.

"The ironies are extraordinary," chimed Parker as he turned back to Mr. White. "However, you still haven't answered my question about Sangorski. I thought he drowned with his *Omar*. But, of course, he never boarded the *Titanic*. At least his name has never been on a list of passengers."

"Ah, yes," said White, glancing at Llorayne. "He was supposed to have boarded the ship, but business commitments prevented him from doing so."

"Fate," Nakamura proffered.

"Coincidence," Llorayne lightly rebutted.

"I should tell you the ending to Sangorski's dream." White smiled. "But first I'll remind you that on the *Omar's* binding there were three peacocks. Remember?"

Parker nodded.

"Some believe peacocks to be a symbol of disaster," said Llorayne. "A sign of fate interceding."

"Just so," said White. "And that, coupled with the signs of life and death—the snake, the human skull with a deadly basilisk serpent stealing from its eye, *and* the field of poppies, all contribute to make the story even more intriguing and full of superstition. Though I'm not the least bit superstitious."

"If nothing else," said Llorayne, "it lends credulity that within six weeks after the *Titanic* went down, Francis Sangorski drowned. And within months after the sinking, George Lovett, who'd been the book's accomplished finisher, died of consumption."

"Tuberculosis?" said Nakamura.

Llorayne nodded.

"You'll recall," said White, "the *Omar's* creator, Sangorski, had a recurring dream." He looked to Nakamura who had not heard that part of the story.

"For years, it is said, he dreamt he was drowning in an attempt to reach for something in the water. Had he in fact gone aboard the *Titanic* and drowned trying to save his book, I suppose psychics would have related the story as a mystical experience warning him not to travel on a ship. However, his recurring dream was fulfilled six weeks after the loss of the *Titanic* and his book. And it had nothing to do with either. That is, short of going on holiday to Selsey Bill, to possibly retreat from the unpleasant memories of the *Titanic* and the loss of his *Omar*."

"Where's Selsey Bill?" asked Nakamura.

"A resort on the south coast of west Sussex," said Llorayne. Directly across the English Channel from Omaha Beach."

"So Sangorski was actually drowned at Selsey Bill?"

"Attempting to save the life of a young girl, we're told. She had gone below the water. He was struggling to find her when it appears he, himself, got caught in the undertow."

"Then Sangorski died a hero," Nakamura half whispered to herself.

"A hero he was, at that," agreed White.

Nakamura sat up straight in the booth. "Cary tells me you've completed an exact replica of the *Great Omar*."

"True," White answered casually. "About five years ago, actually. Took me over fifty years, what with work and all. It's safe in the British Museum now."

"Safe?"

Parker stepped in, "Mr. White has made *two* reproductions of the *Great Omar*. His first replica was . . . " He turned to White. "You explain what happened."

"Yes, well let me tell you how it came about." White said, enjoying any opportunity to share his story.

"Of course," said Nakamura.

Parker and Nakamura continued to listen with fascination, as White's eyes lit up with excitement.

"Unlike today, I was young—seventeen to be precise—when apprenticed to my uncle at Sangorski and Sutcliffe. Even younger of course—still playing on the schoolyard—when the *Great Omar* was born at Eleven Southampton Row." He laughed at the remembrance.

"The Poland Street bindery was a marvelous place . . . so full of history. One could go back a hundred years when one stepped through the door. The furniture and benches—everything was nearly a hundred years old. And the binding procedures were the same as then.

"The firm still has the original wooden press used by my uncle and Sangorski when they began the business. And thousands of finishing tools. The original binding tools for *Winnie the Pooh* are there. And those used for exclusive editions of *Peter Pan*.

"For five years I served my uncle as an apprentice, having learned all thirty-six of the binding operations. Secretly, I felt I was a damn good finisher, as well."

"A finisher?" asked Nakamura.

"I apprenticed Mr. White, yesterday," Parker said. "A finisher performs the last stage in the binding process—the inlay of the leather mosaics, and the precise gilding and gold tooling in the hand work that brings a book to completion."

White nodded.

"And placing gems on specific editions, as with the *Omar*," said Parker.

"Precisely, young man. I was trained to do that as well. So consider my surprise in nineteen thirty-two, three years after I completed my apprenticeship—when rummaging in the old company safe—I found the *Great Omar's* original plans. At first I didn't know what binding they matched. S & S had done many *Rubaiyats*, with similar designs. Not as elaborate, of course.

"But after I unrolled the set of renderings, I studied them for a time. When I saw the drawing of the human skull and poppies, then the mandolin, and three large peacocks, I knew I'd found the treasure of a lifetime. And the more I looked through the drawings, the faster the realization came to me just what I had in my hands."

"Must've been an extraordinary feeling," said Parker

"Of course. As a young man I had seen photographs of the *Titanic Omar* and was told stories about its construction by men who'd actually seen the original work. Mr. Byrnes, a grand old craftsman who actually bound the book, was still with the bindery. Extraordinary . . . yes! Mind you, when the *Titanic* went down with over fifteen hundred lives lost, the loss of the *Omar* received its own separate headlines in the newspapers."

"That's surprising," said Nakamura.

"When the full impact hit me, my heart began beating like a horse at Ascot. There they were—the actual drawings for the *Great Omar*, as created by Francis Sangorski. To me it was like discovering the Crown Jewels. Although Mr. Sangorski had died nearly twenty years before, hardly a week had gone by without someone referring to 'that wonderful binding.'

"Now I had his original working patterns in my hands. I wasn't certain what my uncle would think, if he'd known I'd been rummaging in the safe. So I never said anything about it."

"He never missed the drawings?" asked Nakamura.

"The patterns had been buried in the safe since Sangorski's death. And the years had taken a toll on my Uncle George. He hadn't the energy to reproduce another *Omar*, what with the heartache that came with the original. I don't think anyone ever went looking for the plans before I accidentally pulled them out. Naturally I couldn't hold onto this treasure without Byron White, bookbinder extraordinary, taking a crack at it myself. And I was naive enough to believe I could do it."

He laughed broadly, looked at Nakamura, and sipped his tea. "I was quite cocky in my younger days. Not disrespectful, mind you...remarkably self-assured. This was my opportunity to show Uncle George—and others at the bindery—that I had skills equal to the best. It was always said that no one could match the exquisite tooling George Lovett had performed. He was the master finisher who gold tooled the original *Omar*. But I thought if *he* could do it, so could I. And that's how it started."

"How did you keep Sutcliffe from discovering your plans?" said Parker.

"Realize, our shop was the busiest of the binderies. There was a marvelous clientele. Dukes, duchesses, marquises...all sorts. We had a large work force of sewing ladies, forwarders, finishers, and apprentices all at work on private bindings for King George, Queen Mary, Prince Albert, and other royalty from Buckingham. Even some famous Americans. Uncle George was kept quite occupied managing all that. And since I could only perform work on *Omar Two* in my spare time, it was easier for me to maintain an element of surprise."

"Miraculous it was a surprise at all," said Llorayne. "The binding took Mr. White seven years to complete."

"The initial work—the actual binding—was done at our bindery, after hours. You see, I had obtained another copy of Vedder's *Rubaiyat* . . . the same oversized Quarto book of which the *Great Omar* had been bound.

"I had help from friends with the hand-sewing, the headbanding at the top and bottom of each book, and the gilding of the edges of the leaves. Though sunken panel cut-outs, for protecting the gems, were usually done by a professional mount cutter, I did them myself. Broke seventy-two fret saws before I finished the cover boards.

"Then, Sangorski's drawings were spirited home." There was a glint in White's eyes as he looked at Parker and Nakamura. "I thought as long as they'd been gathering dust, buried in the safe under other drawings and company records, no one would miss them for a time.

"The rest—the actual tooling of the designs, the inlay of the leather, and the placing of jewels was done at home, in the evening. On Sangorski's original book, the musical instrument set in the center of the reverse back cover—the tiny silver and ebony covered mandolin—was made by a professional instrument maker. But for *Omar Two* I constructed my own instrument, after many attempts, and after suffering numerous disappointments. Perhaps it wasn't as good as Sangorski's, but I had the satisfaction of knowing I completed it myself.

"I saved money from my earnings to purchase the gems. And I had help from friends at a firm in Hatton Garden. They enjoyed my work and did all they could to help me. I completed the book in thirty-nine."

"And your uncle's response?" said Parker.

"He was quite proud, actually. And surprised that I could have pulled it off. Sometimes I suspected he must have known. But he never said a word until I laid the binding in front of him. I beamed from ear to ear. When I looked at my uncle, he beamed, as well. And it was the turning point that convinced him I could handle the business upon his retirement."

"Must've been a proud moment."

"Indeed."

"Who bought *Omar Two*?" asked Nakamura.

White raised his eyebrows in resignation. This part of the story was difficult to tell.

"World War II broke out and my *Omar* was considered quite vulnerable, what with the Luftwaffe bombing London and all. It was thought we should place the book in a secure underground vault until the war ended. We had it stored in a lead box, six-floors below ground, in a strongroom on Fore Street. One would think anything to be safe there, regardless of the German air raids in nineteen forty-one.

"As you know, immense areas of the City were razed by the bombing. And Fore Street was not spared. The bombs took out building, strongroom, and book. Once the property was cleared, we were able to get to the underground vault.

"At first, we happily discovered no direct flames had extended into that area and most items had come through. The metal-lined crate, in which my *Omar* was protected, looked to be safe. Unhappily, the vault had been exposed to intolerable heat.

"When we opened the lead case and removed all the protective contents, we sadly found that the leather had melted and had turned into a congealed black mass. Like tar. I worked on the book for seven years and bombs destroyed it overnight."

"Speaking of ironies, in which the entire story of the *Omar* is wrapped . . . " said Llorayne, "had Mr. White's first *Omar* not been stored in the vault, and had instead been left at the bindery . . . "

"You mean the bindery wasn't touched by the bombing?" said Nakamura.

"Not even a scratch," said White.

"So it would've been safe . . . " Nakamura looked saddened to hear of the second *Omar's* demise. She placed her hand over Bryon White's arm and held it there. "How terrible for you."

"You must've been heartbroken," said Parker.

"An enormous shock, to be sure." He sipped on his tea. "But it wasn't without some expectation, what with the War and all. I forced myself to be philosophical about it. All I could do. You see, my home was located outside London. Still, the Germans bombed our area nightly. People lost their houses. Lives were lost. Others maimed for life. And, children were orphaned." White sighed in resignation.

"Just the same, I figured I had my life, my lovely wife, our family—and our home. If my *Omar* was all we would lose, we would be fortunate, indeed."

White had surely lived a full, happy life as he reflected for a moment. His eyes glistened with memories. "There was one bright spot," White went on. "Except for charred turquoise on the binding, all the other gems had survived."

"The musical instrument?" said Parker.

"Miraculously survived, too." He smiled widely. "And at that very moment, I stood over the ruins of the City and held some of the gems in my hand. They caught the glint of the morning sun and I made the decision, then and there, I'd craft a third *Omar*. My resolve was firm. There was nothing but time to stop me. And time it took. Fifty years," he chuckled.

"Next to my work and the love of my wife, it's been the singular motivation that kept me going."

"Where did you get the will to start over?" asked Parker.

"I began my third attempt at binding the *Omar* after the war . . . on the first V-day holiday. I thought it appropriate to do so.

"I first plucked the jewels and the instrument from the mass of melted leather, cleaned them, and carefully saved them for later use. Of course I had to acquire a third copy of Vedder's *Rubaiyat*. And I would have gotten further along but for the effects of my uncle's stroke he'd endured five years before. And the Bindery became more and more my responsibility.

"Following his death, in nineteen forty-three, I was named Proprietor of Sangorski and Sutcliffe. It became a true, full-time job. . . . And for forty years I was unable to work on *Omar Three*."

"Your uncle left quite a legacy," said Parker.

"I was highly honored by it all," White reflected as he sat back into the restaurant booth. "In his many years at the bindery—and long before the *Titanic Omar* was conceived—he'd been responsible for binding fine books, large and small. They've become truly famous throughout the antiquarian book world.

"Where is *Omar Three*?" said Nakamura.

"Happily, even with the superstitions, we've both survived. I completed tooling for it in spring of nineteen eighty-nine. Took me nearly four thousand hours to complete, after I retired in eighty-five." He nudged Llorayne in the side. "My wife teases that the book kept her happy in my retirement. I wouldn't drive her crazy, after all my years at the bindery, since I had something as important as *Omar Three* to accomplish."

"So you stayed out of her way, so to speak?" Nakamura smiled.

"Four thousand hours.   Maybe as many as five . . . " White smiled broadly. "But she was my encouragement through all those years. Otherwise I might never have finished it."

"It sets at the King's Library in the British Museum," said Llorayne. "On permanent loan."

"We have an appointment to see it later this afternoon, Mr. White," said Parker. "Before we catch our plane to the States this evening."

"Wonderful," White exclaimed.

He looked at his watch and rose from the booth. "Speaking of my wife. I'm due to meet her at Harrod's shortly. The afternoon is escaping and you must get to the museum."

"Good to see you again," said Parker. The others stood and retrieved their coats.

"I wish you well," said White. "Hope the material I gave you will be useful. Keep me informed of your progress." He turned to Jennifer. "Miss Nakamura, I've enjoyed your company. You've been quite disarming."

"It's my job," she winked. "FBI, you know."

———

A nondescript Vauxhall touring car headed south on M23 and passed through the low escarpments and chalk hills of the North Downs countryside on its way to Gatwick Airport. The series of seaside resorts dotting the downland of Southern England and the famous white cliffs were the farthest things from Parker and Nakamura's thoughts, at this point. But Sergeant Arledge, the New Scotland Yard driver, felt it courteous to point out the direction if they had time to visit the coast on a future trip.

"I prefer Beachy Head off Seaford, m'self," said the driver. "It's smaller than Dover. Not quite the touristy trade, if ya' know my meaning."

Nakamura, gazing out the left-front passenger window, politely acknowledged the suggestion, covering for Parker who was in the back pouring over *Great Omar* photos and other documents White and Lorayne had given him. Papers were spread on both sides of the seat as he sifted through the information for anything else that might help locate and recognize the gem-covered book. He paid little attention to anything around him.

With the sun setting over the sloping landscape, a radiant blush lit up the small range of hills that surrounded them, casting purple shadows in the low points to the west as the British Leyland car sped on.

"Beautiful, isn't it," said Arledge.

"Uh huh," Nakamura purred in agreement. She didn't want to appear rude, but she was exhausted. Her mind hardly stopped churning since the disaster at Heathrow. And the ride provided an occasion to relax as they cruised toward the airport.

Their car had left city limits, bypassed several suburban communities, and headed through an area filled with small ridges and valleys. Cool water vapor, wisping on breezes from the surrounding seas, mixed with the remaining warmth of the day, condensed in the early evening air, and formed patches of light fog in the low-lying areas.

Absorbed in catching her last glimpse of England, Nakamura—and the driver—had not detected the gray Triumph that dropped back, just past the Purley Way playing fields in South Croydon, as a black Ford took over tracking the Vauxhall.

"This's why I've enjoyed working the drivin' detail for Commissioner Lawton," he went on. "Get to see the scenery. Always changing. Meet friendly people like yourselves." He looked over at Nakamura. "Eighteen years come May."

Nakamura turned from the window and looked at the driver.

"Eighteen years?"

"Come May," he smiled as he glanced into the rearview mirror at Parker. "Your friend sure is engrossed in his work." He looked at Nakamura, then back to his mirror. "I admire someone who can concentrate. . . . Hello? What's this?"

Nakamura saw the driver checking his side-view mirror, then the rearview. "What is it?" She turned around to look out the back window.

"Got someone closing in on m' tail." He checked his speedometer. It read 55 mph. "They could've passed long ago." His grip tightened on the steering wheel. The FBI agent was concerned as she watched Arledge tense up.

Parker looked up for the first time. Nakamura looked out the back. He followed suit. In the remaining twilight, they saw the dark Ford tailgating their car—its lights shining brightly through the rear windshield.

Sergeant Arledge spoke calmly. "Hold on ladies and gentlem'n—we're goin' for a little ride." He pushed his foot on the gas pedal and casually increased his speed by 20 mph. The Ford did the same. Arledge crossed to the far right lane and passed a Bentley in front of him. The other car followed less than 10 feet behind.

Arledge pulled out his loaded Browning 9mm Hi-Power and four clips, released the safety, and set the pistol next to him.

"Better get down, Cary," Nakamura cautioned. "These guys mean business." Parker slid lower in the seat to protect himself and carefully glanced behind.

As the two cars sped on, the Ford moved to the next lane and edged alongside—it's right-hand rear window rolled down. With the approaching darkness, it was difficult to see who or how many were in the sedan.

Suddenly, an automatic rifle rose over the window sill and bursts of fire emitted from its barrel. Bullets ripped off a piece of side molding and shattered the rear-quarter glass window as they zinged past Parker and into the paneling on the opposite door.

"Shit!" Parker exclaimed, brushing off glass.

"Look out! Here we go!" Arledge called out. The NSY driver gunned the accelerator, and the souped-up Vauxhall sped past cars and airport courtesy busses at nearly 100 mph. He hit the siren and pushed another button. The front and back of his car lit up with flashing lights as they raced down the motorway.

The sedan held on close behind, as the two cars weaved in and out of sparse traffic—one directly behind the other.

"Now, Cary!" yelled Nakamura to Parker as she rolled down her window. "Get all the way down. Now!" Nakamura reached to her holster, pulled out a 9mm Sig Sauer P228, and took aim out her window.

Before Parker could move, shots slammed through the back window and lodged in the seatback.

Parker didn't have to think twice as he ducked down, quickly gathered his blowing papers, and shoved them haphazardly into his briefcase.

"You'd *both* better get down," Arledge warned as he grabbed his gun and rolled down the window.

Nakamura ignored Arledge and leaned farther out the passenger window, firing once at the Ford's windshield to judge windage and distance. The bullet glanced off the top of the sedan and she shot five more rounds, this time shattering the windshield. The terrorist's driver and his accomplices recoiled to keep from getting hit. Their car zigzagged wildly as they pulled pieces of windshield off them.

"There're two in front and two more in back," Nakamura yelled above the roar of the engines.

Arledge cut the wheel and switched lanes to protect his passengers.

"Stay down!" he called out. Then he backed off on the gas and lightly hit the brakes to align himself with the gunmen.

Once more, the terrorist's barrel raised and aimed out over the rear side window. Arledge pointed the Browning at the Ford and rapidly fired nine shots into its front and back.

More glass splintered and erupted into the wind and car. A man in the back collapsed as another moved over to take his place. Arledge emptied his clip into the sedan. Three more 9mm Jacketed Hollow Points blew holes through the side doors. And the Ford swerved almost uncontrollably as a bullet wounded its driver. Then, Arledge floored the gas pedal and pulled away.

The Ford swerved, veered toward the center, and slid against the road divider at breakneck speed. Sparks trailed behind as a nightmarish screeching sound emanated from metal against metal. The sedan's driver attempted to regain control and win back acceleration.

"Slam another clip in there, will ya'?" Arledge handed his gun to Nakamura. And she complied.

The Ford pulled away from the divider, back into the fast lane, and began to catch up. Nakamura leaned out her window and fired off seven more rounds. The left-front quarter panel ripped back as another bullet pierced the radiator. High-pressured steam sprayed out from the grille. But the Ford kept coming.

A burst of shots entered the NSY car and demolished the back window—stinging Parker with glass shards. Arledge and Nakamura ducked low. Then shots followed from a pistol in the other car, just missing Nakamura as they flew past her head. She quickly ejected her empty clip and rammed another 13-rounder into her P228.

Steering with one hand, Arledge reached for his radio with the other. "This is Sergeant Arledge in the Gatwick conveyance. We're under attack. Come in. Over."

For a moment it seemed no one was listening. "Come in, please. I repeat . . . "

The radio sputtered, "We have you, Sergeant. Give your location. Over."

"We're under attack on M23 approaching . . . "

Another burst of gunfire interrupted the driver as he looked in the mirror to see the terrorists coming at them again. A bullet grazed his neck and continued on through the windshield. Arledge yelled out and slapped his neck as if going after a mosquito. He raised the mike to his mouth, once more. "I repeat, we are approaching . . . "

Two bullets slammed into the back of Arledge's head and he instantly slumped over the wheel. Blood splattered throughout the car and covered Nakamura.

"Jesus!" she called out as the Vauxhall lunged across two lanes and headed directly for a concrete overpass—Arledge's weight forcing his foot to remain on the throttle. Nakamura grabbed the steering wheel with her left arm as she attempted to extricate Arledge's body from his seat. "Cary, help me get him outta' here," she yelled.

Without another thought, Parker jumped from the seat and reached under Arledge's arms.

"You hold the wheel," Parker yelled, "I'll pull him over." He grabbed Arledge under the arms and pulled.

The radio blared, "Sergeant Arledge, come in. NSY calling Sergeant Arledge. Report please."

There was no time to answer the call. Shots rang out across the motorway as they careened ahead. . . . The Ford raced close behind. Nakamura fought to control the car as she pulled Arledge's foot from the pedal. It quickly slowed and the Ford swerved wildly to avoid crashing into the Vauxhall.

But the sedan rear-ended the NSY car and pushed it into a violent fishtail. It skidded back and forth into the perimeter lane and headed toward the bridge abutment.

Nakamura was thrown to the side. She grabbed the steering column, yanked herself up and seized the wheel. Then she grabbed Arledge's legs and hiked them up. Parker struggled to lift the body's deadweight over the seat top, and it fell with a thud to the back floor well.

Nakamura threw herself into the driver's seat, slammed on the brakes, and the car rolled to a stop just inches from the concrete overpass abutment. Flashing lights brazenly reflected off the bridge supports. And the wailing siren echoed loudly as if caught in a tunnel.

The terrorist's car raced by the Vauxhall, firing as they passed, unable to stop in time. Parker and Nakamura watched as the sedan slowed for three cars to pass, crossed to the outside perimeter lane and slid to a stop 600 feet down the road.

Nakamura grabbed the radio and pushed the button to talk, hoping someone was still listening. "This is Agent Nakamura, FBI. We're under assault. Come in please. Over."

"My God, Ms. Nakamura," a familiar voice came on. "This is Commissioner Lawton. Where are you? Over."

"Commissioner. Thank God. Get some assistance out here ASAP. Arledge is dead. Dr. Parker and I are under attack by . . . "

"Here they come," said Parker.

They saw the rear lights from the terrorist's car move back to the nearest lane—for turning radius—pull forward and reverse direction. Its bright headlights now aimed directly at them. Had it not been dark, they would have noticed the Ford burn rubber from its back tires as it screeched from a dead stop to high speed in mere seconds.

"We're on M23," Nakamura pulled the mike to her mouth, "God only knows where—perhaps fifteen minutes out from Gatwick—heading north in the perimeter lane. Gotta go." She dropped the microphone.

"North?" the radio blared. "What do you mean *north*? Give that to me again." The Commissioner waited for another response. "Ms. Nakamura, come in. Over."

Nakamura checked the motorway for cars, rammed the auto in reverse, and floored the throttle. Simultaneously, she twisted the steering wheel, slammed on the brakes, and the car slid 180 degrees as it reversed direction and maneuvered back into the perimeter lane—facing oncoming traffic. She punched the throttle and the tires laid rubber down the emergency lane.

"Ever driven right-hand side before?" said Parker.

"Only in my dreams!" Nakamura held the gas pedal to the

floor and raced in the wrong direction down M23 at 80 mph. Parker watched the terrorists through the blown out rear windshield. The dead driver lay below him staring blankly to the ceiling.

Nakamura grabbed Arledge's gun from the floor, as she stared over the dashboard to the road. She flicked the safety on and tossed it back to Parker.

"Here," she said. "Join in. There's a fresh clip."

Parker caught the Browning in midair, glanced at it and blanched. "Never shot a pistol before."

"You can handle it, Cary."

"Just target practice," he continued. "With a small rifle."

"First time for everything. I'll drive right-handed on the wrong side, if you back me up from the rear. We've got no choice."

Parker felt the Browning's grip, held it up toward the back window, and released the safety.

"Same principle as a rifle," Nakamura offered over her shoulder. "Aim, hold your arm steady for recoil, and fire. Imagine you've just graduated from Quantico on the Thames," she said. Parker did not see her smile as she looked in the rear-view mirror.

"Shit! My hands are shaking."

"A little scared, myself," said the agent.

Parker looked out over the trunk as the Ford crept up from behind. Bullets ricocheted off the body of the car. Parker ducked from the window, sat up, took aim through the rear, and fired back—getting off three rounds faster than he expected.

"Damn, this thing's got kick." He aimed and shot another three rounds.

"Must've hit something," Parker yelled to the front. "They just weaved all over the place."

Not understanding the danger, oncoming cars in the adjacent lane honked their horns repeatedly, then panicked, as the NSY car and the sedan seemingly raced directly at them. A terrified driver hit his brakes and slid across all lanes. Three cars piled into him and a chain reaction of one collision after another occurred as drivers failed to stop in time. Autos flipped into the air, came down on their roofs, and slid and sparked like fireworks as they rammed others from all angles.

Parker and Nakamura felt helpless. There was nothing they could do to assist as they sped by on an aberrant heading down the side of the motorway.

"This mission is too important to forfeit now," Nakamura yelled to herself as she looked over her shoulder, then into the side-view mirror. Confident at the wheel, despite her inexperience driving right-sided, Nakamura put Quantico's EVOC defensive driving course to work. The car continued to shoot forward as the terrorists gained on them. Then she saw an opening.

"Hold on, Cary. This'll be a rough ride."

In one movement, she cut the wheel hard to the right and the Vauxhall abruptly dropped off the road and plunged down a grassy embankment.

"Holy sh . . . " Parker exclaimed. He hit his head on the roof as the car bounced high into the air with the rough terrain. Then the car punched through an old fenced barrier, slid out onto a country road—running parallel with M23—and barely missed a lone car coming head-on.

Nakamura gunned the accelerator, cut the wheel hard-right, hit the brakes, and flew into an instant one-eighty reverse turn. She assaulted the throttle with her foot and the car fishtailed as it locked into the left-hand lane and sped down the road—the terrorists headed in the opposite direction.

"Yes!" Parker called out. "We've lost the . . . " He stopped and watched the terrorists repeat her daring move. They temporarily hung up on the fencing—cleared it—and raced to intercept them once more.

"Where the hell's the off button for the siren and lights," Nakamura shouted. "We're brightly lit targets in a shooting gallery." Promptly she felt for dashboard switches and the headlights went out.

"Dammit." Then she flicked two other switches. Silence reigned and the bright lights ceased flashing.

"Don't these guys ever give up?" Parker yelled.

Nakamura threw two remaining magazine clips back at him. "Here, you'll need these."

Within seconds the terrorists fired a barrage of shots. Bullets rang off the trunk and rushed past Parker and Nakamura. Parker shot back and missed. Then more fire emitted from the guns behind them.

Instantly, a bullet exploded into their left rear tire and the car veered sideways. The steel rim chewed at the rubber casing as they raced in and out of low-lying, mist-covered depressions. Nakamura held tight and tugged at the steering wheel, as the tire rim pulled them toward a darkened pasture.

Large pieces of rubber soared at the terrorist's car like projectiles. The casing flipped off its metal rim, flew over the hood, and shot through the gaping hole in their windshield.

The Ford swerved violently, but maintained equilibrium. The roar of both engines filled the night as Nakamura kept her throttle near the floor, and the Ford relentlessly followed its prey.

It was difficult to maintain the Vauxhall's speed without losing control. As it lost ground, the black sedan closed in.

Parker saw the front-seat gunman aim out through the sedan's missing windshield and point his gun directly at them. As the gunman prepared to fire, the road dipped into a heavy, fog-filled depression.

"Crap," Nakamura shouted. "I can't see the road."

"And hopefully they can't see us. Just don't run off a curve."

Nakamura strained to look ahead. She searched for signs of a faint line down the middle of the rural road—bore to the center—and hoped no one else would come the other way.

With no one but Allah to admire their efforts, the terrorists never let up. Soon, the rearview lights of their target glowed through the heavy mist, ahead.

Parker saw headlights coming faster toward them. He knocked

jagged glass from the back windshield and took aim. Using the back-side panel as a screen, he placed his arm out over the edge of the trunk for support, steadied his hand, and addressed the moving target.

Unyielding, the terrorist's headlights crept closer. But Parker waited patiently. The faces of two roughly bearded men appeared as ghosts, as the mist thinned, and their features became more distinct. Parker could see the wounded driver—resolute, stubborn, tenacious—aiming his car like it were a spear as the terrorists battled for ground between them.

"Must be getting low on ammo," he said, "or they'd be shooting by now."

"Hope you're right," Nakamura shouted back over the din. She fought to keep the car on a straight path. . . . The steel rim trailed sparks as it carved into the macadam.

As if in slow-motion, Parker watched the despicable face of the gunman in front—his eyes ablaze with arrogance and disdain—as he methodically rose from his seat and came through the open windshield. He lay prostrate over the hood with his XE-47 aimed directly at Parker—ready to sacrifice his life for his cause, if Allah willed it.

Abruptly as it had enveloped the two cars, the fog retreated. And the land sped past as the road carried both cars to higher ground. Then the Ford accelerated as though it had only used half its cylinders. It raced to come alongside, as before, and Parker saw his chance. But not before the gunman saw Parker's arm and pistol, and a burst of shots crossed the trunk, grazing Parker's shoulder.

Without flinching, Parker let off four rounds in quick succession. The gunman flew up from the hood, screamed in pain, and slid off the side. His feet caught the weight of his body on the dashboard, and he hung out of sight over the left fender.

"Yeah!" Parker shouted. He emptied his clip into the side of the Ford as it caught up with them. Then another gunman appeared from the back door window and took aim.

Parker pulled the trigger and nothing happened.

"Damn it," he said, realizing he had not kept track of his ammo and was totally exposed. He instantly dropped to the floor, forgetting Arledge was there.

"Sorry fella," he apologized, "but we're in deep shit." He looked back at the dead officer, "As if you didn't know."

Shots raced through the interior of the car as he felt around for the clips Nakamura had tossed back.

"Watch yourself, Jenny," he yelled, "they're coming up the right side."

"I'm holding on for dear life. You're gonna' have to cover me. I can't grab my gun with both hands on the wheel."

She maneuvered to the right, in front of the sedan, to block its way. But the terrorists veered onto the gravel siding and pushed her from the right rear quarter panel. Her car swerved to the left and back into their lane.

Parker was enraged. He cussed as he located another clip, struggled to find the release, and finally rammed the new cartridges into the butt of the pistol.

He looked up to the window and saw the roof of the Ford as it closed in on them in the opposing lane. Without a second thought, he ascended screaming from the seat, firing bullet after bullet straight out the side window, as fast as his strength allowed.

"You bastards. This is for Arledge, you sons-a-bitches. He never had a chance!"

And neither did the gunman in the back of the sedan—surprised, as he was poised within nanoseconds of pulling his trigger. One of Parker's bullets ripped into his chest. The terrorist flew back with his hand still on the trigger. His XE-47 fired uncontrollably through the windows. It sent a bullet through the front seat, into Nakamura, then wildly shot through the roof of the Ford as the third gunman collapsed.

Nakamura screamed out in pain and slammed on the brakes. The car pitched wildly forward, throwing Parker against the front seat as the terrorist's car passed at high speed, then screeched to a stop 80 yards up the road.

"I'm shot," Jenny said, more to herself, as she forced her left hand to reach over to her right shoulder blade.

"I'm sorry," Cary struggled to adjust himself upright.

"It's not your fault."

"Don't move."

"Damn!" Jennifer cried out, giving in to the pain and anger.

"Hold still," Cary climbed over the front passenger seat. "You'll be all right," he reassured.

"Promise?" she said as she searched his eyes for confirmation.

"Hell yes, Jenny. We'll get you outta' here."

Then, they both heard an engine rev up.

"Get me my gun," Nakamura ordered weakly.

"What?" he said as the Ford sedan slammed into reverse.

"My gun, quickly. You're sitting on it."

Parker hadn't noticed the uncomfortable hard steel until she mentioned it. He grabbed the Sig Sauer. Nakamura took it with her right hand. "Put a fresh clip in yours. You're gonna' need it," she said.

In one motion, Parker reached to the back for the last clip, ejected the old, and slid the new into place.

The Ford picked up speed. Its rear lights glowed as the eyes of a demon, while it viciously raced backwards toward the crippled Vauxhall.

"Aim for the gas tank," Nakamura instructed, as she shoved the P228 over the steering column, balanced her right arm on the dashboard, and sighted the blade and notch. Parker aimed his gun through the windshield.

The rapacious, predatory sedan glared back in their headlights, as it continued its course and reached within 35 yards—nearly half the distance consumed.

"Now!"

Both guns blasted at the sedan. Bullets brushed off the chrome bumper like rain on glass, while they searched for a chink in the armor. But the car relentlessly picked up velocity, doggedly pursuing its quarry. Thirty yards . . . twenty-five . . . twenty . . .

Then . . . KAAA-SAAAAMMP!

Parker and Nakamura watched the nightmarish scene unfold, as first a small pin of fire erupted from under the Ford's chassis. Then, larger flames fingered out from below as it followed the fuel-line across the underbelly to the front and spread to the engine compartment.

Within seconds the entire car lifted into the air, with a tremendous explosion—its momentum still carrying it perniciously toward the NSY car. The force of the explosion blew the driver out of the sedan, and he was thrown to a berm near the roadside. The remaining terrorists were instantly cremated, as the burning chassis slid to a halt barely 30 feet from Parker and Nakamura.

They could feel the intense heat on their faces as both collapsed back into the seat in exhaustion. Then Cary realized he had to assist Jennifer. He sat up and quickly turned to her. She was extremely weak, but conscious.

"We'll get you to a hospital."

"I'll be all right, remember?" She slowly turned her head to him and smiled feebly. "You said so yourself."

Parker climbed out, came around the car, and opened the door.

"Let me take a look."

"No. Help me out of the car."

"You've got to remain still. Lie down until medics arrive. I'll radio for help," he started back around the car.

"Wait . . . " she said. "The radio took a direct hit. It's gone— or we'd have heard from someone by now."

"Damn," Cary said as he searched the rural road for oncoming cars. There was nothing in sight. "We're out in the middle of who-knows-where and M23's nowhere in sight."

Jennifer did not answer. She had willed herself out of the car and walked toward the fiery wreck. The smell of burning tires and plastic was nauseating, as thick black smoke filled the air and billowed upward.

"What the hell are you doing?" Cary spotted Nakamura near

the fire, her gun drawn and ready for anything.

"Just checking." She waved him off, but Parker immediately came to her side. "I saw someone get ejected from the car."

"Yeah. So did I," recalled Parker. The inferno lit everything in close proximity.

They carefully searched the road and discovered a body nearly 50 feet from the burning Ford, lying on a small rise—his left leg twisted behind him. A tree branch had pierced his other leg and impaled him like a lance. The hair had been burnt from his body, now nearly stripped of clothing and covered with second and third-degree burns.

Nakamura gazed into his face and checked for signs of life.

"Looks reasonably dead to me," said Parker. Nakamura bent over to get a closer look, winced from her own wound, and hastily concurred.

"Both his legs appear broken," she said. "He's got multiple contusions to the head, face, and arms."

Parker glanced at Jennifer's shoulder-blade. "My God, Jenny, you're losing a lot of blood. Let's get you back to the car."

"I'm okay."

She turned and walked back slowly, searching the ground for evidence they might salvage.

Parker hesitated for a moment. The fire was slowly burning itself out as the silence of the darkened, pastoral fields took over from what had been a raging blaze. Parker's ears ringed intensely from the close-range shots fired in the car.

He took another step and kicked something. "Hey, Jenny, might be one of those new machine guns they're talking about." He reached to pick it up.

"Don't handle it just yet," she said walking back to take a look. As she approached, she faltered.

"I'm okay," she said.

Cary scolded her as he rushed to hold her up.

"Just help me sit down."

Parker put his arms around her and gently eased her to the

grassy knoll. She felt light-headed and queasy, as she turned pale and cold.

"The smoke from the fire is making me sick." But she knew her body was going into shock.

Behind Parker, the terrorist started to regain consciousness. He was gravely injured from the blast. But the shock of the explosion had numbed him for the fall as he landed limp and dying. Somewhere in his subconscious, voices pulled him back—if only for a moment. He awoke to terrible pain he could not express. His mind told him to accept it and listen carefully. He slowly opened his eyes and gazed up at the darkness . . . *No, not total darkness. There is a light coming from* . . . He forced his head to turn toward the burning car.

From the knoll, in silhouette against the fire, the terrorist could see two figures—a man and a woman. The man was helping the woman. A voice inside told him he still had a mission to complete. Allah was waiting, but he still had a mission . . .

The terrorist struggled to move his right arm. . . . Then his left. He carefully felt around his waist. Extreme pain shot through his entire torso as he tried to lift his thigh to get behind. *Allah, please, let it still be . . . Ah, yes.*

Disregarding the pain, he used part of his strength to pull out a 9mm Hungarian Tokagypt Firebird from behind. He rested for a moment, the gun—a knockoff once used by the Al Fatah—lying on his chest.

Then, he marshaled every ounce of strength and forced himself up on his elbows. He nearly blacked out from the pain but was driven to finish his assignment. *Allah will thank me personally*, he assumed. He put all pain behind him and raised the Firebird.

Parker had searched the Vauxhall's trunk for supplies, and had pulled out a blanket and medical kit. He wrapped Jennifer's wound, placed the medical kit under her feet for elevation, covered her with a blanket, and stood up. He heard a distant sound of helicopters whopping at the air.

"Help's coming, Jenny."

He turned around to explore the horizon and spotted multiple search lights heading from the north.

A violent-sounding scream cut through the air, and Parker turned to see the terrorist sitting straight up, a wild expression on his burned off face—the branch still piercing his leg—and a gun aimed directly at him.

BAM, BAM, BAM!

Parker was startled as shots came from behind, and the terrorist was instantly dispatched.

He looked at Nakamura, holding herself up on her elbow as an aiming support for her 9mm. It was still smoking.

"You're an astonishing woman," he said, surprised she had anything left in her.

"Mozambique Technique . . . " she smiled and collapsed to the ground.

Cary rushed to her side, thinking she was dead. He felt for her pulse, but could not locate it. *Mozambique Technique* . . . his mind thought for a moment. *Mozambique Technique* . . .

"Right," he said out loud, "two shots to the body and one to the head—in case of body armor."

His eyes were wet as he gazed at the woman who had saved his life. "Thanks, Jenny."

"S'okay," she barely whispered, then blacked out.

Parker looked to the sky. Searchlights picked him up from a distance. He waved frantically at four Lynx helicopters, banking overhead, as they searched for a landing spot in the nearby field. The copters landed, sliding doors opened, and armed combat soldiers raced from their cabins to surround the area. The gunships immediately rose to hover in the air and provide light.

A soldier cautiously approached Parker, not certain whose side he was on. He called out above the whine of the copters, "Sir! State your name."

"Dr. Cary Parker—with FBI agent Jennifer Nakamura. She's wounded and needs immediate attention."

"Anyone else alive?"

"Not now."

The soldier called on his two-way radio, listened for a response, then turned back to Parker. "Sir, we'll have help here momentarily." He turned and jogged back to his unit.

Within a minute a Medivac copter landed on the road. After surveying the scene for hidden dangers, the rescue platform lowered and two more armed soldiers left the cabin's side door and stood close by. Then paramedics rushed out of the cabin —their medical supplies and litter in hand.

Another Lynx set its fuselage down at the opposite end of the road. The door slid open immediately on touchdown. FBI Agent Bantam and Commissioner Lawton sprinted to Parker.

"You all right?" yelled Bantam, over the whine of the chopper blades.

Parker looked worn. "Yeah, fine." He pointed to Nakamura.

"How is she?" asked Bantam.

"Doesn't look good. . . . Lost a lot of blood."

The men watched the paramedics assess her condition. Immediately Nakamura's vital signs were checked—measuring blood pressure, pulse, and pupillary action.

Her body was turning cool and clammy. Under the lights, her fingernails began taking on a blue-skin tint. To Parker, she looked like she'd been swimming in cold water for some time.

"Ninety over fifty-five," a paramedic called out to the record-taker. "Pulse irregular and rising."

"Eyes partially dilated," said another.

"Will she be all right?" Parker asked.

"She's in shock," said a paramedic, not looking up. "Her smaller empty veins are shutting down, as the body compensates for loss of blood."

A paramedic introduced two 14-gauge, large-bore IV needles into Nakamura's veins, before they could collapse, and he administered Travenol Ringer's Lactate 9/10 saline solution. Closed-cell foam pads covered the tubing and IV bags to keep them warm. She was intubated for oxygen and her head was wrapped to prevent heat loss.

A woman carefully cut away Nakamura's blouse and Parker's temporary wrapping, to reach the injury. "We have a soft-tissue wound," she said as she inspected the area. "It appears as entry only." She reached for a pressure bandage and applied it to the site. "Her condition is worse than the wound itself."

"Hand me a MAST," one of the men said.

Another man unwrapped a pair of Military Anti-Shock Trousers and, between the two of them, helped gently pull the unique garment over Nakamura's legs. Her torso was shifted to bring the pants to her waist.

She groaned in pain.

Everyone looked at each other, not certain they heard anything in the surrounding clamor. But their simultaneous glances confirmed what they wanted to hear.

"Good sign," the woman called out. She helped inflate the garment's leg pressure chambers to restrict blood flow in the limbs and force more into Jennifer's upper extremities.

Within ten minutes Nakamura was stabilized. Parker, Bantam, and the commissioner watched as she was loaded into the Medivac copter.

"She'll make it," the woman assured.

"Take good care of her," the Commissioner ordered.

The door slammed shut. Within a minute, the Medivac was in the air and racing toward Harley Street Clinic—the best private hospital the commissioner could arrange.

"Let's take a look at your wound, sir." A paramedic directed Parker to one of the ambulances. He let out a hefty sigh and followed alongside.

Parker observed the devastation from the ambulance, as the medic dressed his surface wound. Fire trucks, other emergency vehicles, military security personnel, and New Scotland Yard officers surrounded the burned-out shell, just a short distance from him.

Flashing lights illuminated the entire countryside.

SAS had cordoned and totally sealed off ground and air space within a two-mile radius. Bright lights from a dozen more helicopters covered the area as they circled the perimeter. Additional helicopters remained in the air to ward off media choppers.

"I guess we missed our plane," Parker said wryly, as an EMT completed bandaging his shoulder. He wearily sat on the edge of a gurney near the opened back door of the ambulance. Lawton and Bantam stood nearby.

"Sir," an inspector interrupted. "The fire is out. We're ready to remove and transport bodies—or what's left of 'em."

Lawton signaled approval.

"Uh, Sergeant Arledge's body was removed by ambulance."

"Thank you, inspector."

Two panel-trucks from the morgue were directed through the line of vehicles. Each of the charred bodies would be removed for forensic identification and storage.

Another officer approached Lawton. "Sir, the car is a rental."

"Anything to ID it?"

"There's enough of the plate left and some charred papers in the glove compartment. We'll check agencies for missing cars and match names, signatures, and credit card numbers on paperwork."

"I suspect they'll be false ID's," Bantam interjected.

Lawton nodded to the officer. "Any papers on the two bodies outside the car?"

"Not that we could find, sir."

"It's possible wallets or papers could've been blown off at the moment of explosion," said Lawton.

"We'll scour the road and fields. Come daylight it should be a little easier."

"Right. Thank you," Lawton turned back to Parker. "Are you up to giving details, Dr. Parker?"

Parker shrugged, favoring his left shoulder, and sighed. "Why not . . . " He looked at the EMT for a signal they were finished with him.

"Done, sir. Have a doctor check that shoulder at home."

Parker nodded and climbed out of the ambulance. "How'd you fellas locate us?"

"After Arledge's first call," said the Commissioner, "I called Agent Bantam and we monitored all channels. When Nakamura called in we tried to ascertain your position."

"Then we lost you," said Bantam.

"So how'd you do it?"

"Are you kidding?" said Bantam. "With that car pileup on M23, they had more calls than a UFO sighting."

"You were the first thing out of their mouths," said the Commissioner. "How often do you see *two* cars traveling in the wrong direction on the motorway . . . let alone firing guns at one another. Fortunately, no one was seriously injured."

"Scared the shit outta them," said Bantam.

Lawton walked Parker over to his white Jaguar. It had been dispatched, separately, following his departure from NSY in one of the helicopters. Lawton offered Parker the front passenger seat.

"It'll be warmer in here. And less noise."

Bantam climbed in the back and the commissioner came around to the driver's seat.

The last thing Parker wanted to do was relive the story, as exhausted as he was. But he took his time and explained the entire harrowing experience to the commissioner and the FBI agent—to the closest detail. Parker paid particular attention to commending Sergeant Arledge for his bravery, and his attempt to protect his charges while under fire.

The commissioner's secured phone interrupted. He reached to pick it up.

"Lawton here." He listened carefully, "Patch him through." Keeping his ear to the phone, he looked at Parker. "I asked headquarters to reach your Colonel Bramson. He's coming on line."

Parker wasn't certain he wanted to speak with the man who placed him in this position. He felt as a kid might, waiting to be chastised by his father.

"Yes . . . yes Colonel, this is Lawton. How are you?"

The more he thought about it, the angrier Parker got.

"Well, I must say," the commissioner went on, "we've had some rather trying days, actually." He gave a brief synopsis of the event and apologized for putting his people in jeopardy. Then, he turned to Parker and handed him the phone.

"Wants to speak with you."

Parker hesitated, attempting to control his anger. Then he took the receiver.

"Yes, Colonel?"

"You all right?"

"No. I'm actually pissed beyond belief. What the hell have you gotten us into?"

"Cary, we had no idea things would get this bad. But you can see how important this mission is. Ragem will stop at nothing."

"I'm not trained to deal with these terrorist assholes."

"Look, you won't have to deal with them on this level anymore," Colonel Bramson reassured. "Once you get out on the high seas, in your own niche, they won't be able to keep up."

Parker held the receiver out in front of him as if saying, *Cut the bullshit.* He shook his head and glanced at the commissioner.

"Colonel, I'm too tired to discuss this now. I'll get a plane back tomorrow evening. But for now I need some sleep. And I want to check on Ms. Nakamura at the hospital in the morning."

"No time for that. We have a meeting with Dupont scheduled day after tomorrow. I need you in here fresh and ready for a fight, if necessary. Ms. Nakamura will be in excellent hands."

"But Colonel . . . "

"I've arranged for an F-111. It's sitting on the tarmac at Gatwick, right now. We'll have you in the air in no time. You can sleep on the way back. Besides, Victoria must be anxious to have you home before you head out to sea. Now, give me the Commissioner. We need to speak."

Parker silently handed over the phone to Lawton.

After being reassured that Parker was none the worse for wear, except for his shoulder, the Colonel requested a place for Parker to clean up and ready himself for the flight.

The Commissioner assured Bramson he would place a Lynx and crew at Parker's disposal. Then, the commissioner punched the speaker-phone button and cradled the receiver. A discussion of the best procedure for handling the media followed. A brief statement would go out announcing that, "to their knowledge, all ALFAHAD terrorists, remaining in the U.K., had been shot by NSY police during a high-speed chase."

There would be no mention of Faheed Al Mar Ragem. And due to the sensitivity of Parker and Nakamura's long-range objectives, nothing would be mentioned of their involvement. A special public commendation for Sergeant Arledge's last heroic deed, in bringing the tragic Heathrow episode to a conclusion, would also be issued.

"That'll put the country at ease for a while," the Commissioner said with finality.

———

PART III

CIA - MIDEAST OFFICE - LANGLEY
06:18 EDT

COLONEL Bramson's deep-set eyes moved as if watching Sampras and Chang at Wimbledon. But his head never budged. The CIA Bureau Chief's mouth was drawn tight, creating rows of lines in his face that resembled a Chinese shar-pei. His bushy silver eyebrows furrowed, and he silently gazed as two men exchanged verbal volleys.

Parker could never be as angry as he wanted to be at his former partner, Dupont. Disillusioned, deceived, cheated. Those were emotions Parker felt as he tried to convince him to stay away from the North Atlantic's most famous tomb.

"Damn it, Hank, we've been over this before. You made a personal commitment to me years ago when you promised to uphold the sanctity of the *Titanic's* gravesite. Then you brazenly went after anything that wasn't riveted down and already taken by salvors. Now you're at it again."

"I had no choice, Cary."

"You had no choice," Parker repeated sardonically.

"Oui, my friend." Dupont's square-cut handsome face showed some aging, more from conflict and stress than from his still youthful thirty-six years. Gray already streaked his jet black hair—now drawn into a short-cropped ponytail. And his stubbled chin showed signs of a salt and pepper beard. An inch taller than Parker, Dupont's imposing stature seemed to flag a little, with his now slightly stooped shoulders and protruding paunch.

"There just isn't enough money for scientific exploration

without some type of payback," said Dupont. "You were being pigheaded and Taylor had the money."

"And Taylor is squeaky clean, I suppose."

"Look, I'll admit I was greedy. The pay was astronomical. But if we had not salvaged what was left, someone else would have gone in there."

"Shit, Hank. It didn't have to be you. You know it wouldn't have been me."

"Je sais! I know. I admit it. I've admitted it repeatedly. But that doesn't change the way it is out there."

Dupont was more comfortable with leaky sub batteries at 2200 fathoms than when his old friend attempted, feebly, to filet and grill him into submission. He wondered if Colonel Bramson would finish the job.

"You think you are squeaky clean, Cary," Henri ranted on. "Frankly, I tire easily of your holier-than-thou attitude." He looked at the colonel, expecting cross fire at any moment. Bramson glared back but remained silent, and Dupont turned back to Parker. "You are nothing but an idealist," he sneered. "Idealists have wonderful thoughts about the way everything should be. But my thoughts concentrate on how things are. And right now international law is on my side."

Henri walked to the window and looked out over the still-lighted compound. He turned to face his adversaries and his azure blue eyes cast an intense gaze across the room. "I must tell you, I came here at this ungodly hour in the morning, not because I was ordered, but because I thought we might find common ground."

"Common ground, yes," Parker growled. "Cancel your expedition. Inform C.P. you're not going. Then dive with us to protect what little that's left. We've got to keep the *Omar* out of Third World hands." Parker faced Dupont directly.

"Look, Henri, I've seen first hand what terrorists can do. You can't imagine the carnage—the little children, the unsuspecting and innocent families leaving on holiday. You can't possibly conceive . . ."

"You think me naive?" Dupont coldly interrupted. "I've seen such devastation before. In Québec, we had violence and murder, en masse, when Libération du Québec attempted their revolution. And I've been in France, where terrorist groups grow like the mushroom. I was there when Saint Michel Metro station at Notre Dame Cathedral was bombed. Separatists have bombed the Palace of Versailles, and Corsican liberationists have attacked Paris and southern France." His face grew red with conviction as he went on.

"Do not talk to me about terrorism. In Montreal, and throughout Canada, we still have right-wing racists who vandalize and threaten Jewish targets. I have seen it all first hand."

"Then surely, Henri," Parker spoke calmly, "you must be willing to join us to avert similar events."

Dupont changed the subject. "I have a contract. International law does not prevent me from my right to salvage wrecks. Many countries encourage it. I will carry out my business."

"Which business *is* that, Hank?"

Parker's acerbic tone cut deep. Dupont was clearly uncomfortable. Did Bramson and Parker know all the details of his planned expedition? He suspected not. The tone of the meeting had only changed in level, not in direction. Dupont concluded that most of the meeting was bluff. Though Cary might temporarily accept him as staff aboard their ship, there was little they could do to keep him off the North Atlantic's Grand Bank.

Colonel Bramson broke his granite-like pose and cleared his throat. "Mr. Dupont, you know difficulties can occur out in the middle of the Atlantic."

"Difficulties?" Henri's eyes shot over to the previously silent Bureau Chief.

"Mishaps. Could be life-threatening or do damage to your ship and crew."

"What are you suggesting?"

"I'm not suggesting anything, Mr. Dupont. I'm merely stating the facts of deep-sea fishing."

"You mean . . . accidents happen."

Bramson let him sweat.

"Je suis juste." Dupont searched his mind for the correct translation. "I am right, no?"

"You're a big boy. You've been out there innumerable times. Storms can come from nowhere. A stray iceberg could make it through the early Labradorian summer. Or another vessel might not see you in a fog and ram your ship at flank speed—quite by accident, of course."

"Of course." Dupont couldn't help but smile as he searched his mind for compromise. He was caught in the net and Bramson was pulling him in.

Parker stared at Bramson. This was not the kind of response he expected. But it shut up Dupont for several moments. Parker tried to read the colonel's body language. But the chief was a rock. He admired his ability to appear unmoved. It was one trait he had never been able to develop. *I'm wearing my heart on my sleeve*, he thought to himself, *and Bramson is unyielding*.

"Venez avec nous," Bramson said firmly. "Come with us," he repeated.

Dupont was surprised to hear Bramson speak French. A deadly silence followed.

Parker remained quiet, remembering that the first to speak usually loses. Dupont waited longer, hoping Parker or the colonel would break. They did not yield.

Tiny pearls of sweat broke out at Dupont's hairline.

"C'est bien," Dupont responded, not happy with his own decision. C.P. Taylor would be furious. Not to mention the others.

"All right." The colonel rose from behind his desk and moved directly to shake Dupont's hand. A firm grip signaled to Henri he was safe for now. But he would have to be careful.

"Coffee refill, anyone?" A smiling Bureau Chief moved to the Mr. Coffee at his credenza. Seeing no takers, he poured his sixth cup of black coffee since meeting the two at 5:30 a.m. He looked at his watch and turned to face the two men.

"It's already six twenty-five. I've got a White House world events briefing for the President in thirty-five minutes."

"We'll be on our way," said Parker.

Bramson signaled Parker to wait behind and assisted Dupont to the door where he was met by a security escort.

"I'll call you in a couple of hours," Parker told Dupont.

"Au revoir, Monsieur Dupont," said the colonel.

"Goodbye," he answered back icily.

The solid office door had a sound of finality to it as the latch found home. Bramson sat at his desk.

"I don't know how you trusted that bastard in the first place."

Parker reflected for a moment. "He's changed. He wasn't like that when we first met."

"Funny what greed and avarice will do. At least you can keep an eye on him aboard the *Neptune*."

Clearly, Parker did not look forward to a reunion on board ship.

Dupont passed through the outer office door and was escorted through the labyrinth to the underground parking lot. As he moved silently through the hallways, it occurred to him he should pay more attention to the elaborate security devices and monitoring checkpoints. But his mind was elsewhere.

Plans would have to be altered. *That should only make the mission more intriguing*, he thought. *This new arrangement might actually work out better.*

There was a period, many years before, when Henri looked up to Cary. The man with all the ideas and unflagging optimism. Now he saw his former mentor as weak and indecisive. Someone constantly getting in the way of his plans. *A mouche*, he thought to himself. "Oui," he laughed out loud. "A fly in my face."

The escort stopped and turned to Dupont. "Sir?"

"Nothing, madame. Just thinking out loud."

They passed through security at the main entrance and reached the visitor's section of the parking lot.

"The guard at the gate will take your badge, sir."

"Merci."

The escort turned back for her next assignment.

Dupont wished he could keep the visitor's pass. *I'd make more money with information from here than from all the diamonds and gold ever lost on ocean floors,* he thought to himself as he climbed into his leased Mercedes.

He passed the badge to the guard and laughed at himself for thinking such treacherous thoughts. Dupont's smile turned to a frown when he remembered he would have to talk with Parker in a matter of hours. First he would place several calls. The Mercedes pulled out of Langley, and Dupont wondered if CIA had tapped his phone yet.

GEORGES BANK

NEPTUNE'S Knot had pulled out of Cape Cod's principal port, Woods Hole, at 05:30 sharp—long before most natives exchanged docks between there and Martha's Vineyard or Nantucket. The inlet was quiet. A month would pass before the next solstice would bring back seasonal residents and summer tourists who constantly scurry between the islands.

With the sun rising into a clear sky over Nantucket Sound, it looked to be a singularly beautiful day for the *Shelty's* sea-trial. The scrub oak and snarled, rugged jack-pine glowed against the sand dunes of Cape Cod's elbow as the ship cleared Monomoy Point. Following an unhurried but steady course, *Neptune* moved out into the Atlantic, bearing zero-four-one, with a heading that would place them due east of East Orleans on the Cape.

Parker had waited two years for this day. By 09:40, they were anchored twenty-four nautical miles from the closest landfall, out past the Continental Shelf—halfway between the slope and the looming abyss. The prototype *Shelty* sat just above the deck of the

Neptune, ready to be swung out over the vessel's stern, soon to be lowered for its first saltwater test run.

Parker had named the compact subs after the tiny breed of Shetland Island ponies and miniature dogs. With their one-crew capacity, the *Shelty-class* subs were capable of entering a deep-sea wreck's hold or doorway, or exploring an underwater cave, with a margin of safety never attained until now.

Inside his craft, Parker felt the slight rocking of the *Shelty*, suspended in mid-air between the giant A-frame. Large hydraulic armpads held each side tight and kept the sub from swinging wildly above the open sea.

The scientist loved his new creation and smiled broadly as he glanced at the mini-sub's control panel. He heard the crew, busy at work with activities on board the mothership.

The checkoff list had just been completed when the control center's "prepare for dive" order came over the speaker.

"All systems go," followed.

The command reminded Parker of a launch from Kennedy Space Center. It seemed so natural to have duplicated the process to explore earth's inner-space. Below the surface, Parker and the sea would become one.

A consummate seaman, Parker was alert and ready to take the newly designed one-man submersible to previously unreached depths. For now, the eastern shelf line off Massachusetts would do.

Designed to withstand pressures at nearly five miles beneath the ocean's surface—over 26,000 feet—the mini-sub's technology had come a long way since the days of steel and titanium pressure hulls. The improved and explosively combined Titanium IV/ CeramiK™ alloys were stronger than ever. But with the new quarter-inch thick QQC-multiplex laser diamond-composite applied to their hulls, safety at extreme abyssal pressures was much less a concern than before. The smooth diamond coating gave it added strength and speed. And continuing miniaturization of electronic control and power systems allowed for a significantly scaled down version of the older, larger crafts.

Parker's new vessel would easily fit into the titanium living sphere of the three-man sub, *Alvin*. Used, among other important exploits, to discover and photograph the *Titanic* in the mid-80's, the *Alvin* now resides aboard WHOI's new flagship, *Atlantis*.

Parker hailed his Chief Navigator and Pilot, Holt, on the radio, "John, you getting feed from NavStar on the GPS single board?"

"Globos is picking them up fine. We have four satellites along for the ride," said Holt referring to the new TECOM LN 5000 PC/A SEL, 10-channel Global Positioning System receiver.

Owing to the nature of Parker's upcoming mission, the receiver's navigation engine was especially encrypted with DoD network access—only available to the military—to receive precise, pseudo-random, cryptographic codes from GPS.

Previously, GPS could not transmit encrypted navigational guidance information through deep water without antennas to pick up the signals. The *Neptune* had the antenna, as a surface ship, but the mini-subs had been tied to more conventional means of navigation.

Now, the system was linked on board with experimental Hyperboloidic Acoustic Navigation Translating Software— HANTS—jointly developed between the Naval Postgraduate School and MIT. This new low-band computerized, water-penetrating navigation signaling would network all *Shelties* at once, providing a 3-D fix calculated synchronously with the use of atomic clocks.

The smaller SEL board, installed in the *Neptune's* receiver, allowed the subs to automatically locate and lock into the four closest satellites orbiting at altitudes between 10,000 and 12,500 miles. Instantly, the Globos receiver would relay the *Neptune's* signals into the computer. Simultaneously, it would calculate each sub's position by performing several algebraic equations to provide the necessary fix for PVT—Position, Velocity and Time.

Parker experienced a feeling of movement as the A-frame, holding the *Shelty* aloft, slowly advanced in preparation for lifting the craft up, out, and over the stern. Like a pendulum, the sub was held in a state of suspended animation before returning to its next position in the arc. Hydraulic arms, looking like felt-tipped robotic pool cues, kept it stable.

Suspending a sub over the water, hanging equidistant over the fantail, was a hazardous feat in calm seas or rough. Despite years of experience, Parker felt a twinge of anxiety.

"Uh, guys? Let's not end this before we get started. Deal?" he said.

"Roger." Though everyone smiled at Parker's knowing remark, the mood was too serious to focus on anything beyond the launch. An accidental early release could cause serious physical harm to the twelve-million-dollar sub and its captain. Voices, noticeably business like in their delivery, clicked in and out on the radio—sounding more like preparations for a Mars shot than a diving sequence.

Holt, on the bridge, conferred with Calder in the aft control van as they checked transponders, Global Positioning satellites, confirmed coordinates, and monitored the forward and sidescan sonar readings. The bosun, with his crew of technicians on deck, checked and rechecked the rigging and cables on the traction unit, controlling the umbilical cord. Navigator Vidmar stood by his computerized plotting table as backup for Parker's on-board computer, should he need it.

"Two minutes and counting," Calder announced over the ship's PA system.

"Check." Parker watched through the rear port, over the fantail. Everyone was ready. Then he glanced forward.

"We have a light breeze for launch," Dupont radioed. "Five knots, currently. Ranging four to six."

Small wavelets, with few cresting breaks, gave the ocean an almost glassy, mirrored appearance. Parker was grateful for good weather first time out. He checked his Loran and sidescan once more. All were in order.

The divers were in the water, ready for any emergency.

"One minute and counting."

"Check." Though calm, Parker was anxious to get his new *Shelty* into the water. There was much to prove and approve, considering the $36 million in expenditures for three prototype subs. But he was confident this new breed of Deep Submergence Vehicle would pass the test.

Finally, the giant armature-like frame rose high above the fantail—with *Shelty* suspended in the center. Hydraulic arms pushed the sub directly out over the water, and the overhead traction wheel waited to reel out the umbilical cord as the final countdown began. From port and starboard sides, deck hands held onto critical guy-lines to protect the sub from swinging wildly in a gust of wind—or in potential choppy seas, once the hydraulic arms were pulled back.

From the control van, Calder uttered sweet words to Parker's ears, "Five, four, three, two, one . . . " The large wheel above the *Shelty* played out the cable and the submersible soon touched water.

Divers quickly released the guy-lines and checked for clearance. They performed their obligatory survey for escaping air bubbles that would reveal leaks, and inspected the sail's hatch.

Parker felt natural movement as the ocean hugged at his baby. He smiled with satisfaction from just being there.

"Ready for release?"

"Ready."

In the control van, Calder pushed the console's red button and the umbilical cord unlocked from its hasp.

"We have launch."

Parker experienced the surge that follows every launch. And it was exhilarating.

The divers made certain the umbilical cleared and they backed off as the head diver gave a solid tap on Parker's viewport and displayed a thumbs-up sign.

Previously, the mini-sub would have rolled and pitched with surface waves. This craft displayed a measurable difference. The new multiple gyrostats held her steadier than before. The motion of the sub felt as it should in moderately stirred water. Sea state was between zero and one, and the sub floated easily near the surface—its conning tower rising just enough to clear the water by about two feet.

"Mother?" Parker called to *Neptune's Knot*.

"Mother, here," Calder replied.

"Like floating in a calm pool."

Master audio and video tapes recorded everything, and were synchronized with electronic equipment on board the two vessels, to analyze problems later.

Parker had reason to be happy about the new gyrostabilizers. He developed the smaller system through a grant with the Navy. Tied to an independent experimental, pad-size 20GB computer under his seat, the three gyros—each no bigger than an apricot seed—provided a sense of balance previously not achievable. The computer electronically compensated for the heavier weights typically found in the much larger gyros.

Always the steady hand, Parker pushed slowly on the control. "Okay fellas, guiding *Shelty* into her dive."

"Roger."

"Taking her to ten fathoms. Over."

"Copy."

Quickly, the sub picked up its pace. The new mini-cycloidal jet propulsion system cut the duration of a normal dive nearly in half. The momentum from downward thrust, and the weight of jettisonable ballast, caused the intake valves to naturally force seawater through the funneled ends of the jets, helping to conserve electrical power.

The topside jets drove water in the direction opposite its descent, causing hundreds of miniature corkscrew wakes to push the sub quietly in its intended direction, without churning bubbles to the surface.

"Heaven, I'm in heaven," Parker sang the old Fred Astaire song. "Careful what you sing about, Captain," said Holt, from the mothership. "You don't want that wish too soon."

Parker got a rush from every dive, each experience a new one. Nothing was routine. He had lived much of his youth dreaming of moments like this. It was inevitable he'd push the limits of the sea, alone against the elements, with only himself to account for success or failure. But Parker also knew he depended on the expertise of scores of others to make certain his craft was sound and ready for each trip. And he was confident their combined expertise, developed through years of careful training, would provide the payoff.

"Increasing to three knots. Taking her to twenty fathoms."

"Roger."

"Slope gradient reading at five-five-zero feet."

"Same here."

"Bearing zero-one-zero."

"Copy."

Parker remained close to the surface in the upper mixed-layer. To get a better feel for his craft, he moved the sub farther out over the continental slope—in a line due north from his ship—then remained on a path considerably south of the Wilkinson Divide and west of Franklin Swell.

"*Shelty* here. Gradient increasing. Sonar closing in on one-eight-zero."

"One-eight-zero. Copy."

In the first hour, Parker tested every function of the sub that gave it movement or underwater flight—the thrusters, the aileron controls, and the cycloidal jets. He made quick starts and stops, turns and changes in tack, rolling and banking motions, and tests for pitch and yaw.

"Increasing to six knots. Over."

Basketball = 317-509-4260 (cell)

Booth !!!

"Copy," the quiet response confirmed matching data from the control van.

With the real-time GPS-Hyperboloidic HANTS system, a strap-down Inertial Navigation System (INS) was also tied to a Gravity Gradiometer Navigation System (GGNS). Together, they meshed through the *Shelty's* computer to match Guidance sonar information to stored geographical data, using terrain guidance or natural boundaries to determine position.

Speed-measuring sonar correlated all of the information with Doppler to determine bearings and to automatically project dead reckoning from one point to another. And *Neptune's Knot* would follow *Shelty* on their screens, using the multiple system tie-ins with experimental wireless networked computers.

"Accelerating to ten knots. Descending to fifty fathoms."

"Eight . . . nine . . . ten. Mark," said Calder, watching the duplicate instrument panel and situation display monitors in the control van. "Don't rush it. Over."

Parker smiled. Instantly, the sub turned to port. He maneuvered in a wide arc to starboard and hit half-throttle in a quick maneuver that tested reaction time for moving out of dangerous situations. Then he continued his descent closer to the Thermocline. The temperatures decreased exponentially with the gradually increasing darkness of the water—though the sub would not hit total darkness on the first series of dives.

"*Shelty*, this is *Neptune*. Tracking good on sonar. Looks like she's handling well."

"Maneuvers better than I imagined," said Parker. "Make a note to check the throttle . . . a little sticky. But I think she'll loosen up. Over."

"Copy."

The sub's improved propulsion system employed an attenuated jetstream design emanating from the sides of the vehicle's skin. Speed was amplified tenfold by hundreds of tiny funneled tubes, made from diamond-hard ceramic zirconia—capable of channeling the water fore and aft, topside or below, at high velocity. From this, the craft's improved forward, reverse, dive and ascent propulsion capabilities were enhanced through the hundreds of miniaturized cycloidal-like waterjets surrounding its hull.

"Note, thirty-five fathoms and descending. And," he paused, "mark forty fathoms. Going smoothly. Over."

"Copy. Tracking well." The crew pensively watched the holographic sonar screens as the Shelty continued its descent.

"Coming up on forty-five fathoms. Mark. Forty-six, forty-seven, forty-eight. Slowing her down . . . forty-nine. Mark fifty fathoms."

"We copy, *Shelty*. Looking good," Calder said. "Take a rest, then bring her up."

Parker took two minutes to recheck instruments. He adjusted the oxygen filter and took a deep breath. Breathing in the sub was more comfortable, since experimental membranes—developed by the medical industry—were placed along the midpoint of the sub's waterjet tubing. The hardened membranes served as arteries to absorb air dissolved in the water, as gills would perform the same function for most species of fish. The unique membranes increased the craft's underwater longevity by extracting liquid oxygenous gases from the water, through reversed fractional distillation. It then converted the gases to oxygen, and mixed it with the on board supply for the cabin.

"I'm going to push the envelope on the way up," Parker reported in. "Full throttle this time."

"Uh, Cary, that's not necessary. Over."

"She can handle it. This baby's got spunk."

Calder looked at the technicians in the van. He shrugged a what-are-ya'-gonna-do shrug as crew laughed off the tension.

"We copy, boss."

Parker let his eyes adjust to the semidarkness. The submersible quietly remained suspended at three hundred feet below the surface. A green glow of light, from topside, filtered through the seawater, and Parker allowed himself to be entertained by schools of fish that innocently passed and flash-tacked to a new heading as they sensed the intruder.

Then, he nudged the throttle and the *Shelty* took on life once more. Like a seahorse, it kicked back and surged forward, climbing at ten knots. Then fifteen and twenty.

The water rushed past the sub's viewports as Parker checked his computer for the sonar's plotted DR to Neptune's Knot. He pushed on the throttle.

"Twenty-two knots, fellas. Bearing one-nine-two."

"Roger."

Rapidly he accelerated to thirty knots. He banked to port, forcing the Shelty to almost lie on its side—like crossing his own wake on a water ski nearly parallel to the surface. Then he reversed to starboard and resumed the ascent.

"Got you climbing fast. Watch for surface clutter," Calder needled, referring to their ship lying overhead.

Parker held the throttle steady rather than push too hard too soon. But the *Shelty* raced through its ascent, smoothly accepting the limits as routine.

"Coming up fast, Cary," Andy warned.

"Got a handle on it."

The crew watched the sub accelerate through each level of speed and altitude, flying like a jet through electronic innerspace on their sonar screens.

"Getting close," said Calder. "Better throttle down."

"Got *Neptune* on my screen. Mark at fifteen fathoms . . . ten . . . "

Suddenly, the craft stopped dead in the water, and an underwater wake surged past the *Shelty* like a fast-moving subway. But the submersible held steady, sixty feet from the surface, just fore of *Neptune's* bows.

"What happened," Calder radioed. "You okay?"

"Just testing....This sub stops on a dime."

"Dammit, Cary, don't scare us like that."

"Sorry, partner. But we've got to know her capabilities. Not much time 'til we head for the North Atlantic."

"Yeah, but give us more warning."

"I copy partner."

The control van crew watched their screens in anticipation of Parker's next move. The object on the main color monitor held steady at ten fathoms below the surface. Quickly, Parker increased his speed from zero to fifteen knots, and the object shot across the screen in a straight line underwater, nearly two hundred fifty yards out from the bows.

"Okay, here's your warning, Andy."

Parker's sub took on new life as it flew through seemingly impossible maneuvers. The craft's micro-valvular switching components provided the ability to quickly shift from forward to reverse or port to starboard. And, on sonar, the Shelty appeared to be not of this world.

"If I were an air-traffic controller," said a technician, "I'd be reporting a UFO." The blip on the sonar instantly changed direction, midwater.

"Whoa! Did you see that?" exclaimed Parker after his maneuver put him well beyond *Neptune's* stern in less than eight seconds.

"Sidescan gave us a beautiful picture, *Shelty*," said Calder. Parker heard surprised whoops, in the background, still coming over the speaker from the van.

A sleeker sail with aircraft-like flaps and a more compact current meter were tied by computer to conventional stern and lift propellers. This enhanced the craft's ability to instantaneously maneuver in what were previously difficult turns in tight quarters.

"Nuclear subs would need six hundred yards to duplicate that maneuver," Calder whistled.

"Got that right." Parker said. "Keep an eye out over your port side bow," he requested. "And watch your sonar."

At ten fathoms, Parker headed back toward the ship, performed a three-sixty in another wide arc, under and around *Neptune's Knot*, ascended to five fathoms, then stopped. The crew watched sonar in anticipation as the *Shelty* sat motionless at thirty feet below the surface.

Aiming for topside, Parker adjusted his diving planes and thrusters, suddenly accelerated the sub to full throttle, and sailed under the water at a speed the crew would never have imagined possible.

From the control van, Calder counted the ascent as the mini-sub climbed toward the surface—"Thirty feet, twenty, ten . . . "

Before Andy could call out the next measurement, the *Shelty* soared straight out of the water, like a motorcross cycle flying up and over a hill. The seven hundred cycloidal jets sent out a spray that glowed in the morning sun like the fantail of a giant double-tail-finned goldfish.

"Wahoo!" Parker yelped with excitement as he backed off the throttle. The *Shelty's* diamond-hard surface hit the water ballast-first and scattered small whitecaps as it landed. He cut the thrusters and jets and settled into the water, bobbing slightly, but not pitching heavily as older subs would have—even in mild seas. Then he sat back in his seat with a wide grin on his face.

"Got it out of your system, now?" Calder radioed with a professional detachment that hid his own excitement.

"Roger, wahoo."

In a droll voice, Calder feigned disinterest. "Do we detect excitement on the part of the Captain?"

"Roger, Roger. Better than a number six rapid on the Gauley River. And with ballast still on! Over."

The crew looked at each other in amazement, realizing what had just occurred.

"*Shelty*, *Neptune's* duly impressed," Holt radioed to Parker from the bridge.

"She's handling well."

"Satellite tracking kept close tabs," reported Calder. "NAV

system's holding up. Over."

Though intense concentration was demanded by the mission, the sub's improved satellite navigation and tracking system, coupled with a newly developed computerized acoustic transponder system, provided the team with a genuine sense of security.

For the next hour, the *Shelty* rested in the water as Parker rechecked his instruments and controls, brought up a status report from his computer, and double-checked the data with *Neptune's* on board computations. He took twenty minutes to eat a small packed lunch, as the *Neptune* crew did likewise. Then he prepared for the next sea-trial phase.

"*Neptune*," Parker called back, more relaxed now. "Ready to track a little deeper? Over."

"Ready as ever, Captain." Calder radioed.

"Preparing for descent to a hundred ten fathoms. Bearing three-five-seven, on a direct heading for the southernmost tip of Murray Basin. Over."

Parker focused his mind, set the throttle for three knots, and began descent. After the surface closed over him, he increased speed at the rate of one knot per minute. The light from above dissipated, as he watched his fathometer tick off altitude.

Though unmanned forays into deep-water canyons and gorges of the abyss continued, both the Pentagon and the Navy still felt insecure until they had a smaller manned submersible capable of reaching and rescuing any object at every depth, under most emergency situations. "He wants quick in, quick out," the deputy chief of naval operations for submarine warfare had said of the order from the chief of naval operations, two years before.

Through various development teams, at Woods Hole, millions of dollars had been spent developing and perfecting unmanned robotic visual-imaging devices for safely locating and photographing lost ships, treasures, and military ordnance.

Haley was the precursor to smaller camera robots. Worth over a half million dollars, it was the most prominent among the constantly modified, high-tech, electronic automatons used for scouting ahead, or accessing extremely dangerous underwater sites, without jeopardizing human life. But it was still bulky and difficult to manage at extreme depths. Other Autonomous Underwater Vehicles—AUV's—were in various stages of development, from coast to coast. But Parker's knowledge in this area was touted as the best. And it did not take much convincing, with military brass, to go with his recommendations.

"Your expertise is sought, not bought," Holt repeatedly reminded Parker.

Now, each of the three *Shelty* prototypes was outfitted with a micro-version of *Haley*—tethered still-camera and video units so small they only contained the optic/zoom lenses for the cameras—with micro-valvular jets powerful enough to withstand the strongest currents, yet large enough to prevent lens distortion as they moved through the water. Electronic pulses fed visuals through digital signals transmitted from each lens, over fiber-optic lines built into tethered cables.

With the assistance of on-board computers, images were sent directly to the digital "cameras" and to the video equipment on board each sub. Since they were designed to get cameras between "a rock and a hard place," Parker designated the new robotic lens units as *R.H.P.'s*, after Homer's reference to Scylla and Charybdis, in *The Odyssey*.

Though Parker considered himself an "old salt," nothing prevented his mind from occasionally playing with the fear of implosion. With abyssal level waters 773 times more dense than air, Parker nudged thoughts of implosion—or burial by rock outcroppings—from his mind, and dealt with those challenges individually. Previously learned psychological training exercises helped him push such thoughts further back, where they would be less disruptive.

Arbitrary and capricious dangers, tossed at deep-sea explorers, were a diver's constant companion. Regardless of the danger at reaching such depths, under previously unbearable fields of atmospheric pressure, Parker felt his new design would hold up in the sea's blackest and deepest trenches.

Routine diving twenty-five to thirty thousand feet below the surface would no longer be unthinkable in a *Shetland-class* sub. Interior cabin space was small enough to pressurize quickly, with the design specifically engineered to act as its own hyperbaric chamber.

Tied to the on-board computer, and monitored by another computer on *Neptune's Knot*—with similar techniques adopted for use during space shuttle missions—air mixture and pressurization were constantly adjusted to match the requirements of extended Navy diving tables, to prevent injuries . . . more specifically, nitrogen narcosis, or the bends, during compression in descent, and decompression during ascent.

A realist, Parker recognized it would be more dangerous to rescue anyone caught in the mini-sub, at 25,000 feet below sea level. But with three *Shelties* on line, chances for rescue were increased proportionately.

Designed to operate in a sea state of 6, the subs had numerous safety features, including an ABRT—automated ballast release trigger—designed to operate under extreme flooding situations, or with a loss of hydraulic pressure or electrical power. Each *Shelty* had a built-in locator strobe and beacon, for emergency recovery, and a circular clip-hook implanted into the sub's skin, near the top, in case a tow was necessary.

Parker had long passed the fifty fathom mark attained earlier in the morning and was heading toward the deeper depression of the sea floor. Forward and sidescan sonar reflected the contours on his screen as the sloping gradient sharply increased by degrees.

"*Shelty?*"

"Mother?"

"Talk to me," urged Calder.

"Not much to say. Over."

"Just like to hear the sound of your voice. Keep in touch."

"Enjoying the show," Parker clicked off.

"Roger that."

It was a quiet diversion for him. The undersea's gradual twilight advanced as Parker edged his sub deeper, above the gentle slope of the shelf, and turned on his outside lights. Soon, the submersible approached a shadowy darkness, above the deep scattering layer—where photosynthesis became less important to that part of the underwater food chain—and attenuated light permeated by degrees as it reflected off particles, deviated, and scattered in the water.

The gauges on Parker's instrument panel glowed like the dashboard of his Chrysler, and reflected off the white interior of the sub. He checked the LED readings.

"*Shelty*, come in."

"*Shelty* here."

"We have you approaching a hundred ten fathoms."

"Confirmed," he said.   "I'm surrounded by near-total darkness now—out of the Thermocline and approaching the upper edges of the DSL. Over."

"Creature-feature time," Calder laughed and clicked off.

The submersible hovered at 110 fathoms below the surface as Parker switched off his lights. This was his favorite time. He peered out each viewport to see thousands of bioluminescent sea creatures—plankton mostly—begin to sparkle up close and in the distance. A universe of realtime nautical stars glowed back at Parker's secluded world. It was scenes such as this that put his mind at ease.

"*Shelty*, this is *Neptune*. How does she feel?" a voice from the top crackled over the ceiling speaker.

"Like a dream."

"Roger that."

One of the saltier crew members, topside, joked about a wet dream, and Parker smiled as the radio clicked off.

The sub's walls froze as expected. The biting cold inside would remain a constant 9 degrees Celsius, 48 degrees Fahrenheit, even with special insulation and a newer form of heating system based on the heatpump design. Once the sub reached bottom, on subsequent dives, the water temperature would lie near freezing, with the inside temperature closer to 43 degrees.

The pinging of the sonar and fathometer kept Parker company in the silence of his descent. Outside water pressure increased with a constancy that assured him he was actually descending. Atmospheric pressure stood at over 300 pounds per square inch. At the *Titanic*, outside pressure on the *Shelty's* hull would reach over 5500 pounds psi.

A loud alarm buzzed from the control panel, and pulled Parker back to reality. A bright yellow LED flashed "HATCH LEAK." He looked above and saw moisture drip from inside the sail. Then, a push of a button confirmed the message "HATCH CLOSED AND LOCKED." But the buzzer continued to irritate within the small cabin.

"Copy that one, *Neptune?*"

"Copy," came back a succinct reply. Static clicks punctuated each end of the conversation.

It has to be a malfunction, Parker thought to himself, not needing distractions at this depth. He struggled and reached into the sail to check the hatch's handle. It was as tight as ever. His over-head speaker crackled.

"*Shelty*, you okay?" Calder checked in.

"Hold on. Still checking."

Parker rubbed his finger across the cold surface of the sail, picked up moisture, then licked it. His suspicion was confirmed. No salty taste. He pushed his Talk button.

"False alarm, *Neptune*. Condensation on the walls."

The moisture was within the cabin itself, due to relative warmth inside the craft and the extreme cold seawater outside. It posed no danger. The dampness channeled down the walls and into the small bilge on the floor.

The panel's buzzer was an irritant, however.

"Andy?"

"*Neptune* here."

"How do I shut off this damned alarm?"

"Look to your right. I just installed a small red bypass-button, yesterday. Push to turn off. . . . A second time to reset."

Parker reached over and hit "BYPASS."

"Thanks buddy. The computer should've determined lack of salinity. Didn't we install sensors?"

"Yeah, got 'em at critical openings and joints throughout the craft. I'll check 'em out when you get back."

"What about the present?"

"You're okay. From this point the computer will take false alarm readings into account, bypass and double-check any further moisture detection, and think twice before sending a warning. It's already sent us a message that the program needs a drydock check."

Topside, the crew made note of everything else monitored electronically to that point.

"Heading for a hundred twenty-five fathoms. Bearing three-four-eight. Gonna see what she does out past the slope—closer to the basin."

"Watch those basement rocks," said Calder. "You'll be mighty close at that level. Over."

"Just keep me tight on NAV. Make sure we're in sync, partner. I'm okay down here."

The holographic sonar screen gave Parker a better picture of his surroundings than if the sea were lit with searchlights. Each permutation in the continental margin—its valleys, cliffs, and outcroppings—meshed like three-dimensional pictures. Small seamounts, flat-topped guyots, and other intrusions were easily detected. And Neptune's Knot had the same vantage point.

Out of curiosity, Parker changed direction.

"This is *Shelty*. Coming around to bearing two-seven-one."

He turned back toward the continental slope, rising to the shelf. "Never ceases to amaze me," he muttered into the microphone. "This holographic screen makes the continental margin appear as a pedestal, holding up North America in front of me."

"We copy partner. Damn beautiful sight. Over."

"Adjusting to bearing three-four-one." Parker continued his descent on a new heading due north. He turned on the high-intensity lights and switched on the video-camera. On his monitor he watched the somber uniformity of the ocean's floor rise before him as he came closer to the turbid surface below. The contours of the rising banks, to his portside, did little to break the monotony of the deep-sea environment.

The fathometer showed 112 Fathoms, then 115, then . . .

Aboard *Neptune's Knot*, in the control van, an unseen hand discreetly reached under the console and pushed a button.

Suddenly, without Parker's knowledge, the mini-sub bypassed all programs, kicked into autogyro, and the automatic pilot caused the sub to pick up speed. Instantly, it veered off course.

———

The terrorists had crossed over to America from the north. Entry was even easier since the Congressional budget cuts and a massive shift of funds to *Operation Gatekeeper* on the Mexican border. Legislator's partisan posturing in Washington had cut the budget for U.S. Customs & Immigration by nearly fifteen percent, though the official word from inside the beltway was that only moderate cuts of less than ten percent had occurred.

After all the trouble they went through to obtain forged passports, Ahmed Al-Salih and his two compatriots were blithely waved through without a second glance. Burnout had already reached the overworked Customs officers.

"What fools," Ahmed laughed as they had crossed through the Windsor, Ontario tunnel into Detroit two days prior. "No wonder the Americans do not get along with our countries. They cannot agree among themselves enough to pay for border patrol."

Thoughtful laughter followed from the front passenger, Atak Abu Rahman. Considered the leader of this small band of traveling zealots—each wanted for crimes against most democratic countries of the world—no one was certain what Rahman looked like. Like his leader, Faheed Al Mar Ragem, he had escaped detection through hundreds of disguises and through simple changes of his own facial hair. His specialty was stealing, importing, and transporting explosives. And he was an expert at assembling sophisticated IED's—Improvised Explosive Devices.

Within his family, he was known as a loving father of six children. Yet, in Ragem's ALFAHAD, Atak Abu Rahman was a respected designer of death who had been in on the advance planning to hijack the *Achille Lauro*, and other such acts of terrorism. And he helped devise and carry out plans to murder U.S. diplomats in several mideastern countries.

He was wanted by Germany and Israel for the bombing of an El Al Boeing 747, three years prior, where over 210 people were killed before the plane ever left the ground. Though ultimately blamed for the atrocity, Rahman had managed to escape detection through a series of five stolen cars—each strategically placed for switching five miles apart, in advance of the notorious blast.

Before leaving Britain, two weeks before, Rahman had constructed several explosive devises, including a large belly-pack, which when worn under female clothing, presented the illusion of a pregnant woman. On this trip, twenty pounds of smuggled Semtex, stolen from military stores and hidden in Canada, had been carefully molded under the seats of the rental car. Three XE-47's were hidden inside the door side panels.

Rahman was now in charge of his own plan to lift a newly

developed form of explosive from a U.S. Ordnance Depot. He had learned of this new, lightweight explosive quite by accident. A magazine story, written by an over-zealous American journalist, boasted about newly developed war technology created by the U.S. Army. Mentioned in the article was an explosive, triggered by an electronic signal pitched higher than a dog whistle. What made it unique was the explosive's direct receptivity to the signal, with no electronic wiring, fuses, or other attachments to trigger the device. The article also mentioned the site where the ammunition and detonator was tested.

A few calls to select operatives within the U.S. confirmed the location. Rahman would use the explosives within America's own borders to destroy large institutional buildings and industrial sites— and anyone who happened to be inside or out. And a portion would be smuggled to Iraq for analysis and reproduction by former Soviet explosives specialists.

While in the United States, however, the death team had been ordered to accomplish one other goal. ALFAHAD'S leader, Ragem, wanted one man assassinated—one man who might get in the way of the group's plan to obtain the *Titanic Omar*. This would take precedence once the explosives were obtained.

For now the group would enjoy driving through the lush green rolling hills of southern Indiana. Plans for the next two days would soon come together. And Allah would be proud of their heroic deeds.

Subhi Al-Mamun rode silently in the back seat. A smile of vengeance crossed his face as he was reminded how easy it was to skip over the Canadian border. Though proficient with a gun, Subhi preferred to slit the throats of his enemies with a light-weight dagger, rather than carry a cumbersome firearm. "Allah will be pleased," he thought.

"Hadd"—the right of God—was Subhi's own personal vendetta to carry out unalterable punishments on behalf of Allah, and on behalf of his entire family—killed at the hands of Zionists during a border clash several years before.

Prior to entering the United States through Windsor, the three terrorists had spent the night in a small motel near Tecumseh, Ontario.

Well-dressed, clean-cut, and looking much like a group of international businessmen, they had even slipped into a spontaneous street parade, lead by the Police Bagpipe Band, as the mayor greeted a group of Americans who had taken the ferry over from Detroit for an evening at the Windsor Symphony.

Once across the border, it was easier to blend within the melting-pot of Detroit. A quick run in their rented Taurus took them straight down I-75 to Toledo, and over into Ft. Wayne and Indianapolis to meet with operatives. Finally, they headed on back roads into southern Indiana toward their base near Louisville.

The quiet hills of southern Indiana seemed to glow against the afternoon sky. Miles of timberland mixed with freshly planted fields of corn and soy. And large, rolled bales of hay provided playgrounds for field mice. Horses and cattle roamed open fields that met with old roadside graveyards—occupied by rustic, fallen timbers and time-worn ghosts.

A multi-hued canopy of sunrays, even terrorists could admire, broke through the light cumulus clouds as they passed a catfish hatchery and slipped into the final leg of their mission.

Rahman was driving—stopping suddenly, more often than his nerves appreciated, for not-so-infrequent deer crossing the road. But each stop seemed pleasant. None of the car's occupants had ever seen deer in the deserts of Oman or Syria.

Subhi got out of the car to entice one of the bucks with an apple. It immediately bolted first for Subhi, then for the brush. The terrorist ran backwards toward the car, then tripped and tumbled onto the hood.

Belly-laughs echoed out through the forested hillside from the car's open windows. Subhi looked through the windshield at his partners and laughed back to save face.

It almost made the trip more enjoyable.

As they headed down Highway 60, however, they met up with an enormous 12-point buck defiantly standing its ground in the middle of the road.

Rahman slammed on the brakes. The buck stared into the car and remained unmoved.

"What do I do now?" Rahman said.

"Drive forward," urged Subhi Al-Mamun.

The dark gray Taurus inched forward. The buck stood its ground.

"Use the horn."

Rahman hit the horn twice and the sound blared down the road. Then he moved the car slightly forward. The buck took two steps closer, its wide, hot eyes daring to challenge him once more. The staredown lasted, it seemed, for an eternity.

"Aim for it with the car," said Al-Mamun. "It will move."

Finally Rahman gunned the car directly at the giant stag. It flinched and jumped to the opposite edge of the road. But not before aiming its antlers at the driver's side and leaving a sizable gash the length of the door.

The episode reminded the three men of their mission, and their mood became more serious.

Twenty minutes later they approached the target site.

"Drive moderately," insisted Ahmed. "We do not want to attract attention."

Atak Abu Rahman nodded quietly. Each man took in the sights surrounding them as they casually cruised past the Army-Navy Ordnance Testing Station at Gilbert Depot, just east of Louisville. Congressional budget cuts aside, this small, remote region bustled with civilian and military personnel ever since the increase in activity in the Middle East. Having originally served as a primary development site for Star Wars technology, budget cuts were still replaced by the development of new hi-tech missiles and experimental explosives.

The quiet, mid-afternoon activity was in sharp contrast to the periodic sounds of explosions that emanated daily from the testing of various explosives, mortar, and special weapons.

The rural area endured heavy unemployment in the post-Vietnam phasedown of the early-70's and on into the mid-80's. However, the Pentagon and several top-ranked legislators managed to keep appropriations high for new buildings, and personnel to fill them, in this obscure, but lively, military support center. When Presidents froze hiring at the Pentagon, for political posturing, each administration secretly privatized budget line-items to hide the cost of additional hiring at military sites.

As a result, Gilbert Ordnance Depot never suffered from a lack of manpower.

———

Calder looked at the control van's sonar screen, then back at his controls. A red light flashed on his console. He couldn't tell if Parker had intentionally engaged the autopilot.

"*Shelty*, did you hit auto? Over."

There was no answer.

Aboard the mini-sub, Parker's attention had been drawn to the Autogyro button that had glowed red with the change. He attempted to push it off quickly, upon engagement, but to no avail. The sub veered slightly to starboard and continued its gradual descent. Parker hit the button—no response.

"*Shelty*, I repeat, did you engage auto? We have you on a new bearing zero-five-seven. Over."

"This is *Shelty*. Appears the gremlins are at work. I did not engage, and cannot disengage. Repeat, cannot disengage."

"Hit override."

"Override doesn't work on this one, partner. Trying alternatives. Over."

The topside crew had already jumped to their stations, in response to the glitch. No one had anticipated this problem, however, and they were unsure what to do next.

"I'm hitting our override," said Calder, reaching across the master console. "Be prepared to take back control if this works." He hit the switch. "Anything?"

"Nothing," said Parker, simultaneously attempting to feed new directions into his on-board computer. It was unresponsive.

"He's tracking for the underwater inlet on a direct heading to Franklin Swell," Holt called over the intercom from the bridge. "He'll implode against the swell if he continues his descent."

"Workin' on it," was all Calder could say.

Imperceptibly, at first, *Shelty* began to roll. Then, Parker experienced disorientation, as the sub turned over in a complete loop. Then another. And another, end-over-end.

He compelled himself to relax, knowing he might soon be breathless from centrifugal force. He attempted to control the rolling motion with the diving planes and tried to shut down the cycloidals and thrusters, to ameliorate the problem.

The computer would not respond. The autogyro had taken over completely.

"Andy, I have no control. . . . all micro-valves are operational and jammed. Any ideas?"

"Workin' on it." Calder looked at his crew for suggestions.

"Hurry, 'cause I'm spinning out of control."

"Can you turn off your batteries and drain power?" He waited for a response.

"No go. This thing's locked up tight."

Calder looked at Dupont. "Any ideas?"

Dupont shrugged, "His computer may be shutting down. If there isn't enough memory, it won't accept new commands. Transmit increased memory output to his panel, to buy space in the application for new orders. Then bypass the override and send a kill message to the motors."

Andy did not like Dupont's choice of words, but he thought about it for a split second, then turned back to his computer.

"Hold on Cary, we might have something."

Parker did not respond.

Calder hit his keyboard and opened up the *Shelty's* software application. He brought up the control panel icons and, in a matter of moments, pulled up the memory dialog.

"If we increase the disc cache on Cary's hard drive and allow for more virtual memory, that should give us enough, shouldn't it?" He looked at Dupont for approval.

Dupont nodded.

Calder quickly entered several commands on the keyboard and looked up at the monitor. Sonar displayed *Shelty* still careening farther out through the water. He fed it a new set of directions and pushed Enter.

Sonar painted the same dire picture.

"*Shelty*, your terrain guidance is holding. Do you copy?"

There was no response. "I repeat, *Shelty*. Terrain guidance is holding. Do you copy?"

With the gravitational force of his spin, Parker impelled his hands forward in an attempt to grab for the console and reach the Talk button. But gravity's pull threw his arms back and held them against the cabin wall, above his head.

Again, he willed his right hand toward the button and, slowly, his tensed muscles brought it down toward the console. He gripped the edge of the console with his thumb for a handhold and inched his fingers up toward the button.

With his chest compressed, he struggled to breath and talk, "Sonar shows . . . terrain . . . immediately below . . . but clearing," he said.

"Same here, partner. Hold on. It's bought us some time."

Calder, Holt and the others watched from their stations as the Terrain Guidance Sonar held the sub to the natural boundaries of the sea floor. Even with the wild ride, the computer program matched stored geographical data to Parker's actual position, and kept him above the gradient.

Calder fed commands into the master on-board computer, and punched home the orders. But Shelty continued to skim the Atlantic basin, as it catapulted through the water end-over-end, and headed farther out toward the sloping swell.

Calder pushed the intercom to the bridge. "John, the *Shelty's* getting away from us. Weight anchor at full-speed and track him out over the margin. Bearing zero-four-five. We need to intercept at a line intersecting approximately six-niner degrees, fifteen minutes west by forty-two degrees north."

"You got it," came a quick reply from Holt. And the crew jumped into action as the *Neptune's* cycloidals kicked in and the research ship headed due east to intersect their sub.

Parker sat helpless in his cabin and watched his sonar display near misses from underwater canyon walls, outcroppings, and minor swells rising from the basin.

Slowly, the tumbling submersible shifted through an arc that brought it back around. And it headed in the opposite direction. Continuing to hold onto the console's edge—his strength and endurance waning with every moment—Parker realized what was happening. He pushed Talk.

"We've . . . come . . . around . . . copy?"

Calder was too busy reprogramming to notice the submersible had reversed direction. He looked to the sonar. Not only was *Shelty* coming back, it was ascending.

"Hold on partner," Calder encouraged. "Henri, give me bearings and a DR on rate of ascent."

Dupont fed numbers into the plotting table's computer.

"He's heading directly for the ship," confirmed Dupont.

"Oh shit!" Calder exclaimed. He returned to his keyboard and entered more commands. But the sub continued its heading.

"John," he called to the bridge, "Turn *Neptune* around. The *Shelty's* coming at us. Reverse direction and give us full ahead."

"Reverse at full. Copy."

The ship's alarm sounded, and the deck crew and divers jumped into action—prepared for what might happen next.

Calder's mind raced for solutions as he continued to enter new codes into the computer. Nothing worked.

Neptune's Knot came around bearing west and south toward its original position. And *Shelty* tore through the water like a hungry shark as it bore down on them at full speed.

"Damn it!" Calder hit his fist on the control panel. Then a thought occurred to him.

"Cary, can you open up your console?" He waited for a response, but got only silence. "*Shelty*, do you copy? Can you open the top of your console?"

Still no answer.

"Cary, listen to me! This is your only chance. Get inside the console. Remember the release at center, underneath? I repeat, a release to your console is at the center under the dash. You've got to open it up. Do you copy? Over."

Parker nearly blacked out from blood rushing to his head and from his inability to breath enough air—his lungs compressed from centrifugal force. But his partner's voice called him back. Dazed and confused, he knew he did not have enough strength to reach for the Talk button and open the console.

Got to get to the console. The console, his mind begged.

Inch by inch he forced his arms down toward the console, every second fighting back the forces that held him tightly to his seat. He was dizzy, sick to his stomach, and close to losing consciousness, but his mind pushed him to reach down in front —forcing hands to grasp his pant legs to keep from flying back— as fingers inched forward and up under the dash.

"Cary, pay attention. If you have any stamina left, reach inside the console and rip out the power source and data plugs. Concentrate."

Still no response.

"This is Andy, focus on my voice—open up the console lid and reach inside to the back. You know where they are. The data plug is the large, black, striped-edge plastic connector. And the connector to the power source is the round green plug with the yellow, red and black wires. Rip them out. Do you copy?"

I copy partner, I just can't answer, Parker thought over and over. *I copy partner . . .*

In the control van, everyone's eyes were riveted to the holographic sonar screens. A three-dimensional *Shelty* flew like a bat above the eastern coastal slope, still heading toward the *Neptune* as if it had a homing device. Calder continued to encourage Parker, hoping he was somehow getting through.

Time lost in turning the ship around had allowed the *Shelty* to gain on the larger vessel. And the *Shelty* was traveling twenty knots faster than the fastest speed the *Neptune* could attain.

Parker grappled under the dashboard. Feeling for a catch release, he hit home and pulled up. The console lid crashed up against the hull. The sound startled Parker and his adrenaline pumped faster.

He looked into the console's cavity, and his blurred vision literally doubled the number of wires and connections inside. *Andy said two connectors . . . two connectors . . . black and blue. No black and . . .*he was fading in and out as he reached inside the casement and held onto anything he could find.

Hundreds of wires and cables were fed to scores of components and connectors.

Pull the power . . . pull the power and . . . the data connector.

John Holt hailed the control van. "You guys figure anything out? Sonar's got him only a third of a mile from our hull."

"We're trying to get through," said Calder. "He's not answering . . . may have blacked out."

"Can't you knock out his computer controls from here?"

"We've tried. It doesn't respond to our commands."

There it is, Parker forced his body forward from his seat. *Got to reach the connectors.* But the tumbling sub threw him back. He pushed the limits of his body to grab at the plugs.

"Cary, boost out—boost out! Pull the connectors now!" Calder's voice echoed in Parker's subconscious. "You're close to crashing into the *Neptune.* Pull the connectors, Cary."

"Three hundred yards at 50 fathoms," Dupont reported. "Two fifty at forty fathoms. He's coming up faster."

"Cary . . ."

Parker neared total unconsciousness. Confused and distracted, his head swam with an agitation that bordered on derangement as outside forces pushed the limits of his body.

"Two hundred yards at twenty fathoms," he heard the report in the fog of his mind.

"One hundred fifty, ten fathoms. Seventy-five yards at . . ."

The crew looked across the sea as *Shelty* shot out of the water, thirty feet into the air and flew—gyrating out of control—straight for the hull of the *Neptune.*

"Cary!" Andy yelled into his mike.

"Eeeeyaaahhh!" Parker screamed in frustration and, with all his might fought the gravitational wave—boosted out from the inertial pull—and threw his entire body over the opened console. His eyes focused for one last instant as both hands moved out in unison to grab at the connectors, and seized hold of the fifty-pin ribboned control cable, the power plug, and anything else he could grasp at once. With all his might he ripped at the pinned and soldered wires and cables, and the gravitational pull of the spinning sub threw the weight of his body back against the seat as his fists tore at the console's guts.

Electrical sparks jumped across the inside of the console and arced from one broken solder point to another. In an instant the thrusters and cycloidals shut down.

Parker's cabin went black and filled with acrid smoke.

Shelty flipped twice in midair, 20 feet from *Neptune's* starboard side, then dropped to the sea like a lead weight and sank alongside the research vessel.

An emergency battery kicked in and a small light illuminated the cabin. An onboard mini-computer powered up, sensed the breakdown, and jettisoned all ballast.

Coughing from smoke inhalation, Parker spontaneously collapsed into unconsciousness as his sub gently floated back toward the surface.

"Get him the hell outta there!" Calder ordered over the PA to the deck crew. "Now!" He turned to the intercom, "John, hold her steady."

"Steady as a rock," Holt confirmed. And the muscled, six-three, two hundred thirty pound ship's captain made certain the *Neptune* wasn't going anywhere.

Suited divers were already in the water and in the 15-foot RIB, alongside the sub. On *Neptune's* fantail, the bosun and his crew made preparations to lift the *Shelty* out.

"Get that cable on the retrieval hook," the head diver instructed. Three others bibbed and harnessed rubber bumpers around its perimeter. The head diver balanced himself on top of the bumpers, leaned against the sail, and opened the hatch.

"Hold her down for me. She's bucking like a bronco."

The divers ringed themselves around the bumpers and provided weight to steady the sub. Without the gyros, it continued to bob moderately in the sea as small wavelets broke against its hull.

The hatch was opened and smoke drifted out the top of the sail. The head diver peered inside with a flashlight.

"Dr. Parker, we'll get you outta there. Hold on, sir."

He did not respond.

"Dr. Parker? You okay?" The diver turned back to the others. "Give me the under-arm tether and the small oxygen bottle and mask. Lend me a hand. He's out cold."

The diver straddled the top of the sail and leaned down into the cabin. He strapped the oxygen mask around Parker's face. Then the divers worked feverishly to remove him from the sub. Within ten minutes he was brought into the inflatable and transferred aboard the *Neptune*—revived, but hacking from smoke inhalation and exhaustion.

Holt then adjusted the cycloidal engines, revolved *Neptune's Knot* in place, and positioned the stern to pull *Shelty* from the water. Once on board, damage to the sub, not evident underwater, was quite visible. The severe impact had bent the port and starboard thrusters and ailerons. It would require more than a week to repair.

From a private cabin and, with Parker's permission, Calder placed a shipboard call to Colonel Bramson.

"We have to postpone and maybe even scrub the mission," suggested Calder.

"What're you talking about?" said Bramson, irritated that Parker had not personally called. "Where's Dr. Parker?"

"You might say he's recovering from a near-death experience, Colonel." Calder had no patience for Bramson's gruff attitude, but quickly explained what happened during sea trials.

"We'll never get the damaged *Shelty* ready in time—even with our two backups. The subs aren't ready for deep waters yet. Too many bugs in the software or hardware," he concluded.

"Look, I apologize for coming on too strong. But we've got to reach the *Titanic* soon. I can put all necessary resources behind you. Get you anything you need to effect full repairs, and guarantee working equipment. Just name it, Mr. Calder."

Shit, Calder thought. *This guy doesn't give up.* There was a long silence as the two waited each other out. Andy gave in first.

"I'll . . . I'll check it out with Dr. Parker and the crew," he said, thinking what might be necessary to maintain the schedule. Only days remained before they would load up and head for Newfoundland Ridge and the Somh Abyssal Plain.

"The early prognosis is not good, Colonel. It's possible no amount of money or resources can put Humpty back together—at least not in time to serve your needs."

"These are the nation's needs," Bramson said stoically, "not mine. Let me know A.S.A.P." And the line clicked off.

———

Back on shore, a private call was placed to Dallas. A button was pushed, the line secured, and the receiver lifted.

"Monsieur Taylor?"

"Oui."

"I believe we have taken Dr. Parker out of the loop, as you say."

"How so, Henri?"

"The program disruption worked. Parker's staff is debating whether it was a defect in the software or the hardware. They're not certain which. Cary is under medical care, and one of the submersibles is out of commission. . .damaged beyond immediate repair. They'll never get it working promptly enough to defeat our plans. You'll have the *Great Omar* shortly."

"Did you remove the electronic device?"

"Just an hour ago."

"Anyone suspect foul play?"

"Not a soul, Monsieur Taylor. They're including me in on everything."

"Excellent work, Monsieur Dupont. Keep me informed."

The line clicked off.

———

GILBERT, KENTUCKY

THE gray Taurus slowed on the rural highway as it approached Gilbert Ordnance Depot's North Gate. On the right of the guard shack, two entrance lanes converged into one, and a single lane exited from the Center, left of the small building. Two guards held the post.

A chain-link fence, with curled and razored barbed-wire, stretched from left to right of the gate and meandered some distance to the west. But the fence took a sharp forty-five degree turn to the south, on a knoll just a hundred feet east of the guard house.

At the top of the knoll, a 15,000 gallon propane tank fed a line to heat the guardhouse, two bunkhouses, and some apartments located a quarter mile inside the grounds. Atak Abu Rahman made note of the setting.

As they drove past the main gate, the guards never looked up. Both were reading *Batman* comic books.

The terrorists continued on State Route 23 as though traveling to a distant destination. They followed the fence for eight miles, turned south, then headed toward the village of Gilbert, past the Ordnance Center's West Gate.

Subhi Al-Mamun pointed to large objects out at a distance, across the road—mounds buried in the ground—exposed to public view. He pulled out a Site Map

"Those sodded-over areas?"

The others nodded.

"According to the map, they're weapons storage. Nineteen hundred bunkers. Solid concrete."

As Rahman drove on, more bunkers appeared—hidden among the evergreen pine along occasional jutted outcroppings of limestone strata. Far enough from the road to prevent too much interest, the bunkers protected the nation's largest consolidated collection of heavy guns, artillery, ammunition, special weapons, and support equipment, for maintenance and testing of army and navy weaponry.

Before the sun set, Rahman and his band had traveled the entire perimeter of the Depot boundary, a distance of forty miles. A new experience for these men, they watched large deer herds roam secluded meadows. Occasionally, flocks of mallards congregated on the road, slowing the terrorists.

Of the Depot's six gates, the north entrance provided best access. And even with the small, local population nearby, the Gilbert City Gate had possibilities.

Rahman pulled into the gravel driveway of a service station on the outskirts of Gilbert City. With two pumps out front, it was also a mini-market and tackle shop. Window signs, boasted the area's best night crawlers and red worms, and competed with promotions for fishing gear and chews of tobacco.

Rahman stopped short of the gas hose. He waited, not certain if it was self-service. Just as he opened his door, a lanky man in coveralls came out—a merry smile on his face. A Louisville Cardinals cap concealed most of his uncut brown hair, except for longer strands sticking out from the reversed bill.

"Hey there," said the station's attendant. "Fill 'er up?"

"Please. Thank you," said Rahman, attempting his best British accent.

Unshaven and missing two of his front teeth, a large bump of chewing tobacco protruded from the attendant's left cheek, as if he had a case of the mumps. He spit tobacco juice to the ground. Brown spittle stain drooled from the corner of his mouth, and he wiped it with the sleeve of his shirt.

Rahman had met some interesting people during his overnight stay in Ft. Wayne. But this man was no match for the highly paid government and civil engineers and scientists who worked inside the Ordnance Center.

The attendant reached for the hose, twisted off the gas cap, and latched the handle on automatic.

"Musta' tangled with a pretty good sized buck."

"I beg your pardon?" said Rahman. His partners remained silent.

"That there gash on your car. Musta' been some buck you hit."

"Oh, that . . . well, I have to admit, it scared us to death. Came from nowhere. I swerved to keep from hitting him head-on."

"You ain't from around these parts, air ya?"

"London."

"London? London, in England? Woo-wee. Ain't never met nobody from London. Whatcha' doing in Gilbert?"

"We took the wrong turn-off from Highway 60," said Rahman. "Heading to Nicholasville, Kentucky, to look at English Pleasure horses and a two-year-old stallion."

"You into that there sidesaddle stuff, air ya?"

"No. We purchase them for resale in England. To make a buck as you say in America."

The attendant spit more tobacco juice. It tangled with the rear fender on the way down. "Well, I don't know about that stuff. I ain't got no money to buy horses like you fellers. Since I lost my job at the coal mine, I work two jobs just to feed my old lady and the kids, if you know what I mean."

"What does one do for money around here? Is this farmland?" Rahman feigned ignorance about the largest Ordnance Depot in America's heartland.

"Why, when I ain't workin' here at the station, they got me mopping floors or cleaning toilets at the Depot."

"Train depot?" Rahman and his partners listened carefully.

"Naw, I don't suppose . . . I mean you ain't probably heard a' the Gilbert Ordnance Depot. You all being from that there England."

"No, haven't passed through here before. What do they do at the Depot?"

"Stick around long an' you'll hear it soon enough."

"Hear what?"

"Them explosions, like when they test one a them new bombs. They got all kinds a munitions over there. Shoulda' heard one by now. They's constantly shootin' them off, all day long. Sometimes ya' hear machine guns. Next thing they're poppin' off one a them plastic explosions. You know what I mean? Some new kind they can trigger with a whistle."

"A whistle?"

"Yeah, electronic kind. I seen it laying on a table one night when I was cleanin' Building D. Then I seen them use it one day. I was out drainin' portable toilets in the back pasture area, where they do all the big stuff, ya' know? The only thing they needed to explode the explosion was to blow that whistle."

The attendant held his thumb to his mouth and pretended to blow. "But you couldn't hear it. It looked kinda' like a dog whistle. 'Cept, it's got a small black box on the end.

"This man put the whistle to his mouth, pushed a button on the side, and puffed his cheeks a coupla' times. And KABAM BAM. Blew the shit out of an old building in the pasture. Sent a shitload a shovelers scurryin' up outa' the lake."

"Shovelers?"

"Ducks. Funniest thing you ever seen."

The gas handle clicked off, as he spit on the ground with an emphasis that took the story home.

"I see," Rahman turned to Subhi and Ahmed and smiled. "Must be covered with a blanket of secrecy, experimenting with such ammunition."

"You kidding. They'd soon shoot you dead in the eye, if you tried to get past."

He stood tall, "But I got clearance every night. They're so use to seeing us come in they just flag me through with my cleaning truck." He pointed to a rusted, green '56 Ford F-100 panel truck, at the rear of the lot. Hand-painted on the side panel was the motto, "Sanders Cleaning Sarvice—We Clean Everthing."

"So, you're Mr. Sanders?"

"Yep."

"They certainly trust you . . . at the depot," Rahman said.

"Aw, they done trust me like that there Statue a' Liberty. They know old Sanders won't tell no one. Well, I mean they know I won't tell no one that shouldn't know. Ya' know? I can trust you fellers not to say nothing, cain't I?"

"Of course," said Rahman. "Just passing through. As soon as we get some rest for a day or two. We've traveled all the way from

New York."

Rahman changed the subject. "But that's not as tiring as working two jobs."

"Not so bad going in. But our butts is dragging by one in the mornin', ya know? I close the store at nine, and me and my cousin load up in that there van and head to the Depot. We split up the buildings until we quit about three. Then back here by six to open for them fishermen. Get a catnap 'long about noon."

"Where's the best hotel in the area?"

Sanders laughed. "Hotel?" he laughed even harder. "You want a hotel in Gilbert? Hey fellers, I can direct you to a mo-tel. But there ain't no ho-tel in these parts." He laughed, and more spittle dribbled down his chin.

Rahman got directions to the only motel—rehabilitated clapboard apartments, partially upgraded and reopened after sitting abandoned for two decades. With nearly six thousand employees at the Ordnance Center, the town had to provide housing for employees, and for visitors to the local military prison.

An overnight stay would give the terrorists an opportunity to review orthographic projections of the Center's buildings—copies stolen from Army Avionics and handed over in Ft. Wayne.

The maps and projections included the nine hundred-acre Lake Wildwood, located among a hundred twenty-four square miles of the timber-covered military post. From the drawings, the men knew which lakeside buildings housed the four new electron microscopes, and where the testing chamber was located that simulated over twelve thousand pounds per square inch of underwater pressure. More important, they knew the approximate location of the experimental explosive and whistle triggering device in Building D. And the station attendant had confirmed it.

———

Bramson made good on his promise to Andy Calder. All stops

were pulled and money was no object. Fortunately, additional *Shetland-class* bodies had been fabricated under the contract. After sea trials were complete, nine more mini-subs would be outfitted. Two would go to Lamont-Doherty, three to Scripps, two were headed for Mystic, and two for specialized military use. In less than an hour, an outer shell and thruster units, designated for the military, were pulled aside, crated, and flown from Mesa, Arizona aboard a Hercules L-100 stretch transport plane.

Holt would work his crew through graveyard to gut the damaged Shelty and transfer all parts to the new shell, upon its arrival. Calder spent the waiting period rechecking software programs for any viruses and attempting to locate the troublesome glitch that had thrown Parker's sub off course. They had already searched the ship for signs of sabotage, but nothing had turned up.

Despite a need for more hands, Dupont was not invited to assist—nor was he informed of the maneuvers. In fact, they just preferred not to have him around as they worked through the night.

———

The Gilbert Motel manager, seeing three well-dressed men, decided to give them the best room available. And charged them double the going rate on their stolen credit card.

"Sign here, uh . . . Mr. Hakim." He handed the registration card and a pen to Rahman. "And we'll need your car license so's ya' don't get towed during the night. We get visitors to the prison who park and sleep in our lot without payin'."

"It's a rental, and I can't remember the number."

"Tell you what," the manager looked out the window, "I'll get it from you later and just note it's a gray Taurus for now. We ain't that busy tonight."

"Fine." Rahman improvised a smile.

"They've just finished re-doin' the bathroom," said the manager. "Last guests stole the sink and the pipes. Would've taken the toilet if they'd had time. You fellas stayin' long?"

"Just a day or two," Rahman said. "On our way to a horse show in Kentucky. Decided to drive in from New York to mix business with pleasure. You know, see the countryside."

"Stop by the pharmacy, out on the main road. Got the ol' fashioned rootbeer floats in frozen glasses. Damn good. "

"Thanks," Rahman cut the conversation short and turned for the door.

"There's a body shop—Arnie's—closer in to town, if you're lookin' for one."

Rahman looked quizzically at the manager.

"Body shop?"

"Sanders called me from the Bait n' Tackle. Said you might be comin' by. Said you hit a buck, and might need a body shop."

Rahman affected a slight smile, bothered by the attention given to their car door. "Why, that was kind of Mr. Sanders. Please thank him for us. But we'll have the rental company take care of it upon our return. Good night."

The room had one window overlooking a vacant parking lot, across from a large berm on the perimeter of the property. Curtains, with condensation stains, drooped loosely from a pull-rod. Two queen-sized beds hung low in the middle, resembling sway-backed horses.

"If they ever cleaned this room," remarked Al-Mamun, as they looked around, "it was last Ramadhan."

"We aren't here for the room. Empty the car door panels," said Rahman. "Be careful not to be seen. Time is short."

The three men prepared for the next day, as they removed sub-machine guns, explosives, Soviet-built triggering devices—hidden inside the car—and brought them to the room for assembly.

———

Cary and Victoria had made love slowly to make it an enduring memory. A full moon sent reflections of glimmering light off the pond, through the bedroom's open window, and reflected on the ceiling over their bed. A breeze sifted through the room and casually passed over their glistening bodies.

They held hands, on this last night before Cary's trip to the Conference on Undersea Recovery, in France. From there, he would travel to meet up with his ship and crew for their North Atlantic mission.

Both were silent as they watched kaleidoscopic mutations of light above them. Then, as though moved by an unseen force, Cary spoke hesitantly. Almost in a whisper.

"I want to fall in love again."

Victoria was pulled from miles away. "What did you say?"

Cary's mind was made up about something important. He turned and crossed his bare leg over hers.

"I want to fall in love, again."

Victoria was uncertain what Cary meant. *Was he unhappy with her? Was there someone else? Had he still not forgiven her for her indiscretions with Henri, years before?* She was unable to respond.

Cary gently moved on top of her slim body and lightly kissed first her left eyelid, then her right. Then her temples. She responded naturally by pressing her face harder to his lips. It felt wonderful, but she still did not understand.

"Something's missing from our lives, Vicky. I want to fall in love again, with you."

Relief rushed from head to toe. In the darkness, Cary saw a tear on her cheek. Her eyes opened to see him looking softly into her face.

"Do you remember what it was like when we met?" he said. "What it was truly like? The places we went. The outrageous stunts when we were younger. The stupid things we said. The dawns we greeted after dancing all night."

"My father pounding on your car window, when we fell asleep talking."

Cary rolled onto his back laughing. "At five in the morning . . ."

Victoria giggled seductively as euphoric memories took over.
She was content. But even then, the thought occurred to her, *Could
she be more content?*

"You're demented," she kidded. "You were nuts then and you're
crazy now." Her smile confirmed her recall was as good as his.

Cary stared at the ceiling's dancing reflections, again in thought.
"Vicky, let's not lose our love for each other. I see so many people—
some of our friends—just go through the motions. Somehow they
met, loved, had happy times, then became complacent about their
daily existence. Their work . . . children. Their routine."

He turned to Victoria and glanced into her eyes. An enduring
love came from within, as they stared at each other in the night
shadows of their favorite room.

"We played like children, didn't we," she laughed in thought.

"We were in love."

"And ran down sidewalks holding hands. Well at least I tried
to hold on. You always went so fast."

"We were in love."

"And talked incessantly for hours."

Cary laughed. "We were in love."

Victoria moved closer, nuzzled her nose into his neck, and
pressed her body close to his. "We swam naked at the beach."

"We were in love," Cary hummed.

"We dirty-danced every chance we got."

"We . . ."

" . . . were in love," Victoria silenced him with a kiss, then
looked at him directly, "We're still in love."

"I know," he smiled as his hands found her breasts and began
their final course into the night.

Their breathing was rhythmic, as the bed moved in unison.
Time and space fell far behind. Then, just before their bodies found
it impossible to hold back any longer, Cary whispered, "We'll fall
in love again, when I return from the Atlantic."   As if an

afterthought, "No one lost on the ship had the chance to fall in love again."

He lightly stroked Victoria's hair. "We'll do it for them."

"All right," Victoria whispered.

"We'll dance, sing, run on the beach, and be outrageous just like before."

"Of course," Victoria agreed quietly, then silenced Cary with a kiss.

There was a wistfulness surrounding the climax of their lovemaking. But Victoria's sensitivity to Cary's empathy, for the *Titanic's* lost, went deeper than any melancholy could interrupt.

As if for an eternity, Victoria felt a resurging warmth from within. She clung to Cary tighter than ever as her body, and his, rushed past their memories—and thoughts of what was to come.

———

NICE, FRANCE

POSITIONED on one of the more prominent Mediterranean oceanfronts, the Negresco Hotel had been a familiar address for Cary and Victoria in earlier times. There were reminders of previous stays—Restaurant Rotonde with its famous carousel-horse motif; the stained glass-covered Salon Royal, with its shimmering Baccarat crystal chandelier weighing over a ton; the remarkable Salon Louis XIV, with its 17th century frescoes on the coffered ceiling, imported from the Chateau De Saint Pierre D'Albigny, in the Savoie Region of France; and candlelight dinners at the celebrated restaurant, Le Chantecler.

Doctor Parker's arrival on the French Riviera, was uneventful. The International Conference on Undersea Recovery, at the Negresco Hotel, would begin with a reception in the evening. For now, Parker relished the memories as he settled in.

Parker's antique-filled suite faced the famous Promenade des Anglais on the world renowned Cote D'Azur. Years of heartache in

international negotiations, disappointments and setbacks—
Dupont's broken promises—all were momentarily washed away
by the sight of the crystal clear waters off southern France, and the
rare beauty and luxury of the Negresco.

Parker had positive expectancies for current negotiations over
the control of deep-water treasures, despite negative influences by
delegates representing private interests. Victoria had reminded him
of the adage, "one gets what one expects."
She was right all along, he thought. Now he would expect
delegates to settle the issues at hand and show forward progression
on the proposed treaty.
Parker's schedule would keep him busy during three days of
negotiations. With little opportunity to tour the French Riviera,
he would make certain to savor his favorite pasta and seafood dish,
Tagliatelle Aux Fruits de Mer, at La Coupole Restaurant. Somehow he would fit in a jetboat parasail ride and a visit to the Fragonard
Perfumery, in Grasse, to pick up Victoria's favorite perfumes and
souvenirs for their daughters.

Parker remained confident, regarding the conference outcome.
Adar Al Salaam, however, thought it would be different.
Through the glass doors of the hotel's Bar Le Relais, Salaam
observed Parker, across the lobby in the Salon Louis XIV,
conferring with other delegates on the proposed treaty.

From a distance, groups of scientists discussed the controversial
Dr. Parker, almost as much as their fields of work.
"I admire his tenacity," said the red-haired environmentalist
from Sweden. "He fights for what he believes."
"Dr. Soren, come now," said Dr. Imre, the Hungarian
scientist, "he never knows when he's lost a fight."
"You're both wrong," said Professor Nalda, from Spain. She
set down an empty hors d'oeuvre plate. "Dr. Parker doesn't fight
for anything he believes. Rather, he imagines he fights for what

others believe. Then he can walk away, without guilt, when he knows it's over."

The other two jumped on her statement and a stirring argument ensued.

The American scientist always drew a crowd. Parker, and two leaders in oceanography and maritime law, were surrounded by others as they discussed the draft treaty banning salvage of certain classes of undersea wrecks. They stood beneath one of three Rigaud portraits of Louis XIV, in the Salon bearing his name. The conversation had been animated and sometimes heated.

Parker stood at the center of the group with his long-time friend, Dr. Senanayake, a prominent specialist in undersea archeology, from Colombo, Sri Lanka, and Dr. Georges Levard, of Paris, France, an authority on Admiralty Law.

A large yellow and white Cheshire cat moved unhurried between their feet, as each delegate fought for their point.

"You know as well as I, Dr. Levard," said Parker, "we can no longer allow free-for-all salvaging, especially at today's level."

"But of course, Monsieur Parker. I would have expected you to say that."

"I would expect this organization to display sensitivity for the *Titanic's* survivors and relatives, and to others who might face the same prospects."

"Ah yes. The old discussion about family and friends. Docteur Parker, that argument is wearing thin. Most of the *Titanic's* survivors are dead or nearly so. Their surviving relatives or friends would have few, perhaps vague, memories of any stories they might have heard, let alone memories of the actual event."

"Don't kid yourself, Dr. Levard. Titanic Historical Society members, worldwide, have memorized every detail of the incident, and most related events since. The press documents it regularly."

Parker looked directly at each scientist. "Many of their supporters resent anyone going down there for personal profit. If this treaty isn't passed as written, it could begin a backlash and thrust toward international monitoring, the likes of which you've never seen."

"Gentlemen," Dr. Senanayake interrupted laughing, "let's not have to move this argument into the streets."

Levard and Parker's voices had carried throughout the room. Chagrined, they excused themselves and moved their debate to a window table. Parker glanced around and, out of the corner of an eye, saw quick movement from someone attempting to conceal himself near a column. Thinking it his imagination, he returned to their conversation.

Ambient late afternoon light bathed the enormous fireplace and the salon's burgundy walls. Its glow cast a mellow disposition over their conversation. From across the salon, the terrorist watched and planned his next move.

GILBERT, KENTUCKY

IT was difficult to remain in their small-town motel room for an entire day without appearing too standoffish. Yet, the terrorists would be conspicuous if they wandered around too much. By early afternoon Rahman and Al-Salih decided to visit the local pharmacy for "ol' fashioned rootbeer floats in frozen glasses."

Al-Mamun remained behind. Maid-service was canceled, with the excuse that "Mr. Amir" was not feeling well and needed to rest undisturbed. He used the occasion to attach delayed timing devices, det cords, and pressure-release boobytraps to C4 and Semtex explosives. Then he wired self-adhesive ribbon-charges to fuses for last-minute attachment.

A light knock at the door was followed by a key in the lock. Subhi jumped from his chair and looked through a slit in the curtains, relieved to see his comrades. Careful not to open the door too wide, Rahman glanced at the explosives on the table.

"How is it, my cousin?"

"I have used time wisely. We are ready for tonight."

"Not bad, these rootbeer floats," Rahman said to Subhi, handing him a capped styrofoam cup and plastic spoon. Subhi gladly accepted the drink.

"Are the guns clean?"

"No my cousin. We can do that now."

He pulled out a modified Ruger Mark II, with a small lawn mower muffler attached to the end of its muzzle as a suppressor, and two Walther P38's—older but effective weapons issued to the ALFAHAD, three years before, from PLO munition stores. Then, the XE-47's were brought from under a bed, and the terrorists settled in quietly to prepare for their evening.

Dusk gave way to country-road darkness. At 9:00 p.m. sharp, the lights to the old service station and bait shop clicked off, and Sanders came out the front door. He turned the deadbolt key and closed a metal hasp over its staple, just as a road-beaten '82 Ford LTD skidded to a stop in the gravel—its loud muffler hanging by a wire, and an exhaust cloud gushing out the rear.

"Hey, Bobby Joe," the driver called out, a cigarette hanging from the corner of his mouth.

"Hey, Bubba," Sanders greeted his cousin as he placed a padlock on the door. "Hustle it up."

"Let me park this piece a shit. The Depot ain't going no place." He reversed gear and backed the LTD around the side, next to Sanders' old Chevy panel truck.

"Come on. We're runnin' late." Sanders spit a wad of chew on the ground, opened the driver's door, and jumped into his van.

"Dropped my cigs. Give me a minute." His cousin searched the ground in the dark.

Sanders heard a muffled ping outside and turned to the passenger window. "Get your butt in gear, Bubba. Ain't got no time to waste." He pulled the door closed and shoved his key into the slot. His eyes adjusted to the dark, and through the LTD's windows he noticed a figure bent over toward the ground on the other side. Then the LTD's car door slammed shut.

Bobby Joe sensed something was different in his van. He held his breath for a moment and felt an electrically charged silence in the air. The hair raised on the back of his neck. Someone was in there with him. He instinctively grabbed for the door handle as the passenger side opened.

"You scared the shit outa' me, cuz. What took you so long?" Sanders turned to Bubba...and froze in fear.

Al-Salih, dressed in Bubba's reversed-bill baseball cap and flannel shirt, shoved a .22 caliber Ruger at Sanders' right temple. From the back, Al-Mamun wrapped an arm around Sanders' chest and placed a sharp dagger at his neck. And a voice came from farther back in the van.

"You don't want to make us angry, Mr. Sanders."

"What'd you do to Bubba? And how'd you know my name?"

The panel truck squeaked and shook lightly as Rahman moved to the front brandishing a P38.

"My apologies about your cousin," he said, without a British accent. "I would feel terrible if one of my cousins were shot in cold blood. But there are more important matters we must take care of—with your help, of course."

Afraid to look around, Sanders' mind raced to search for recognition. *Who are these people?*

"If you go about your cleaning business tonight, no harm will come," said Rahman. The terrorists pulled back their weapons.

Then it hit him, "You're the horse fellers, ain't ya'?"

"You're running late, remember?"

"That's it . . . the horse fellers. I told my wife you ain't up to no good. I knew it. I . . . " The cold, suppressed gun rose to his temple once more.

"Mr. Sanders . . . drive."

Bobby Joe broke out in a sweat and his hands shook as he

reached for the ignition. "Please don't shoot. I got five kids ta feed. I ain't gonna tell no one."

"We know that, Mr. Sanders. Just calm yourself and drive to your regular entrance. We know you enter the Ordnance Depot by the North Gate. We followed you last night. No change. Understood?"

"Yes sir, no change. Yes sir."

"Think of your children, Mr. Sanders. And calm down."

"You ain't gonna do nothing to my children are you? 'Cause if you are, you kin just shoot me right here."

"Of course not. Your family is safe—as long as you remain calm and do what we ask."

Just as Sanders had bragged—and Rahman had hoped—the North Gate guards waved them through without a second glance. Their panel truck headed down a heavily wooded road, toward the base interior and the administrative and scientific buildings.

"I hold a site map of the Center," Al-Salih informed Sanders. He unfolded the map and brought out a penlight to check directions. "Do not attempt to deceive us. We know where everything is located."

Sanders shook his head. Somehow he would have to notify authorities.

"What're you fellas after? Their ain't nothing in here you cain't get somewhere else."

"Drive us to Building D." He pointed to the Chemical Formulations building on the site-map, located near an old weapons testing bunker.

The panel truck approached a housing section for military personnel. TV screens flickered through the windows of the one and two-bedroom government apartments as they drove by. Suddenly, a Military Police jeep pulled out and crossed in front of them. Sanders slammed on the brakes.

"Sorry Bobby Joe . . . didn't see ya," one of the MP's yelled out. "Hey Bubba," he waved and drove past.

Sanders' heart raced.

Salih shoved his gun into Sanders' ribs. "Be more careful." He looked back at his map and continued to hold the gun on Sanders. "Lake Wildwood should be coming up on the right. We must turn left on Avionics Avenue...in about two kilometers." He looked at Sanders, "That should be about one and two-tenths miles on your speedometer. Am I correct?"

Sanders nodded sadly. "There's the lake," he confirmed.

The interior highway split just as Salih had predicted, and they headed south. Within a mile the wooded area opened up into a maze of two and three-story buildings and a series of long quonset huts spread out over the equivalent of a square mile. Roads and parking lots for over six thousand civilian and military employees filled the space in between.

"Turn right at Stinger Road and follow it to the cul-de-sac."

"I know the way," Sanders said in disgust.

Gilbert Ordnance Depot—G.O.D., as the locals referred to it—was a catch-all name for the Army-Navy weapons support center. Well paid electronics and weapons engineers designed and tested prototypes for microwave components, acoustic sensors, expendable ordnance and explosives, small arms, and electronic components and modules for jet aircraft and tanks. And the little-known outpost in Northern Kentucky had the highest pay ratio of any center of its type, particularly following Desert Storm.

Sanders, among the lowest paid civilians in Gilbert Village, might have had reason to feel jealous or envious of those who worked full time. But, proud of the work G.O.D. provided in the interest of national security, he took pride in being accepted as part of the team.

The enclosed van turned into the cul-de-sac and drove to the circle at the end. Building D was mostly dark inside, with only two windows on the third floor indicating someone might be working late. As with all facilities on the premises, this structure's entire perimeter was brightly lit for security.

"Is there a back door?"

"Yes, sir," Sanders answered, careful not to offend them.

Rahman signaled to pull behind. Sanders dutifully followed directions. A military jeep and a late-model Saturn took up two parking spaces just behind the rear entrance.

"Open the building door," Rahman ordered Sanders.

Al-Salih, with baseball cap and flannel shirt, grabbed a bucket from the back of the truck and followed—his Ruger Mark II hidden under the shirt.

As they approached the door, Al-Salih realized they needed a magnetic card to enter. He looked at Sanders fidgeting around in his pants pocket.

"Pass card's in my wallet. Musta' fallen out at the shop."

"Mr. Sanders, we can shoot you here and blast the door out ourselves. Which would you prefer?"

Sanders reached deeper into his pocket and laughed nervously, "Well, whatdaya'know. Musta' been mistaken. Here 'tis."

He pointed the card at the reader, but his hands shook so much that he missed the groove. Al-Salih grabbed the card and made a quick pass of it. The door clicked. He pulled it open and signaled the others. Rahman and Al-Mamun grabbed their equipment and left the panel truck for the relative security of Building D.

"Now, Mr. Sanders," said Rahman, his voice in a whisper, "let us remind you we have orthographic projections of this building. We can waste precious moments getting our bearings from the maps, or you can help us save time—and your life—by making yourself more valuable."

"You said you ain't gonna hurt me."

"If you cooperate," he reassured. "Now, in what room did you last see that unusual whistle to activate the new explosives?"

Sanders thought hard. He had only seen it once, several weeks before, and was uncertain on which floor it had been.

"I . . . I think it was the third floor . . . no," he quickly changed his mind, remembering that Dr. Morrison's Saturn suggested he might still be working upstairs as he so often did. The triggering device had been on the first level.

"It should be this way." He moved down the hallway and pulled out his magnetic cardkey. The others followed.

They went through a series of corridors, Sanders taking his time to think it out carefully before making each turn, hoping someone from Security would run into them, yet wishing no harm to any unsuspecting person who might happen along.

Then he led them to a single, nondescript door—no printed title, no numbers—just the words *PRIVATE - Level One Access Only*. And a cardkey slot and palm print reader for additional security.

Rahman noticed the door was of hardened steel. He pulled out a pocket knife and shoved it through the outer, lime-painted drywall, twisted it until it stopped, then cut away a piece. Behind the drywall, the area was reinforced with concrete blocks and, he suspected, steel beams to protect the building from any accidental explosive force. He looked at his partners.

"This is the room," he smiled knowingly.

"There's just one problem," said Sanders.

Rahman waited for him to continue.

"I'm the only one the door will let pass. Each person who enters must have a cardkey and put his hand in this here gadget. If you ain't cleared by security, an alarm goes off when you pass through the 'lectric eye on the other side. And I 'spect you didn't get Bubba's cardkey outta his pants pocket when you killed him." Sanders smiled for the first time. "And I know ya ain't got no security clearance with your palm prints."

The three terrorists spoke angrily in Arabic. Rahman was most upset at their operatives in Ft. Wayne who had not warned them of this technicality. But Al-Salih calmed him down and reminded him they had a diversionary tactic to draw the attention of the post's security. At that point Rahman's demeanor cooled and he looked at the custodian.

"Mr. Sanders, open the door . . . please."

Sanders was worried now. He thought they recognized the futility of their plans. Now he could only do as they asked, to protect himself and his family. He ran the cardkey through the reader, but the green light did not flash. He tried it once more. Still the door remained silent, with no progressive light for the next phase in the security check.

Rahman looked at Sanders like he were a child, grabbed the card, and arrogantly turned it around in front of Sanders' face. Sanders was so distracted he had slid the card through backwards.

Sheepishly he ran it through once more. A green light flashed and a digitized voice came from a small speaker, "Place your left hand on the glass, palm down, in the slot to the right." Sanders followed directions, and the men watched as a light passed under his hand. "Thank you, Mr. Sanders. Have a pleasant evening."

Then, a click and a buzz sounded, and Sanders pulled the door. Al-Mamun held it open as Sanders stood back and the others gazed inside. Rahman looked across to a table with several pieces of electronic equipment in various stages of disarray. Wires, RCA-jacks, and connectors hung almost to the floor.

Next to an oscilloscope lay the experimental triggering device. And at the opposite end of the room was a vault, labeled:

DANGER! EXPLOSIVES!
Do Not Enter Without Protective Gear.

Suddenly, a buzzer sounded. "Mr. Sanders," said the digitized voice, "you have ten seconds to enter and close the door, before lockout."

Rahman and the others were startled by the announcement as they first glanced down the hallway and looked for someone coming in.

"Now who's the fool?" Sanders looked at the terrorists and smiled. "Sorry, fellers." And he jumped through the door, pulling it closed behind him. The buzzer stopped and the door latched tightly as the lock engaged.

In a panic Sanders looked around the room for a telephone. "I know a phone's in here someplace. Where are ya', damn it?"

Scientific clutter signified ordered chaos and filled all table tops, desks, and many parts of the floor—a practice Sanders always resented when cleaning rooms, because he never knew which areas were safe to wipe, dust or mop.

Sanders spotted the phone, buried on a desk, and raced to pick it up. He dialed for the operator.

"This is the Gilbert Ordnance Depot night desk . . . "

"Hello, this is Bobby Joe Sanders in Building D . . . "

"If you know the extension number for the department you desire, please push the four digit number, now . . . "

"Hello, this is an emergency . . . "

"If you don't know the number . . . "

"It's a fuckin' recording . . . " he screamed out to the ceiling.

" . . . please hold and the night operator will assist you."

WCWO radio came on the line with their local country music station interlude.

"My God, what am I gonna do," he cried, "Please someone answer." He pleaded over and over while the music played.

"This is the Gilbert Ordnance Depot night desk, the operator is busy. Please hold for assistance."

Bobby Joe Sanders looked around the room. There were no windows. Only a hinged and vented wall, with selectively placed heat and smoke sensors up near the sixteen-foot ceiling, to vent explosive residue to the outside in case of emergency. No third floor had been built over this section of the building.

"Gilbert night desk," said the operator. But Sanders thought it was a recording. "Gilbert night desk, may I help you?" In his panic, Sanders looked for a way to escape, as the operator disconnected. Sanders listened in again and heard a dial tone.

"Oh fuck!" he cried out and threw the phone across the room.

In the corridor, the terrorists had moved to the opposite end and Rahman counted down, with two remote controls in his hands. "Khamsa, arbaha,talaata . . . "

"What the hell's going on here," a security officer turned the corner at the other end of the hallway and reached for his radio. "Who are you and what are you doing here?"

But bullets from Al-Salih's Walther P38 answered his questions as they raced to their target. The security officer dropped in an instant. His radio fell and slid across the linoleum floor as blood trickled out holes in his forehead.

Rahman picked up the countdown, "Talaata, itneen, wasHid..." and he pushed the two remote radio controls.

For a split second, nothing happened. Then, at the North Gate, two and a half miles away, the 15,000 gallon welded steel tank, recently refilled with an eighty percent load of propane gas, lifted off its pad with four highly charged Semtex explosives set above the two concrete risers.

The tank split and erupted into a ball of flame that turned night into day as it rose in a mushroom shape, two hundred feet into the air, spread across the entrance gate, took out the guard-shack, and headed for the base apartments down the road.

Nearly in unison and almost imperceptibly—due to the force of the propane tank blast—the secured door in Building D imploded into the experimental lab. The terrorists waited for smoke to clear before entering the room, their XE-47's at the ready.

Instantly, sirens and alarms sounded across the military depot, and base security went into action toward the fireball at the North Gate. Though a second alarm rang from Building D's short-circuited door, no one in security noticed two alarms registering at the same moment. The blast at the North Gate gave precedence to all fire-fighting equipment, and security personnel on duty were too curious to check out anything beyond the catastrophic explosion.

"Jesus, will ya' look at that," an MP said to his partner as their jeep headed north on Chaparral Road.

"The north side propane tank just blew," someone reported in by radio. "A guard must've lit up at the shack, and it was leakin'."

"Get the tankers over here pronto," another voice commanded. "The North Gate's history and the fire's moving down through the woods to the apartments."

"Can't get near it," someone else yelled over the frequency.

"Call the Gilbert volunteers. We're gonna need all the help and engines we can muster."

"Evacuate them families outta there now!" Two-way radios crackled with chatter from all directions.

The fire station sounded its alarm, and volunteers raced in from their homes in town, their loose-wired blue lights flashing on car roofs or dashboards.

On the third floor of Building D, Dr. Raymond Morrison had been at his computer, having just configured and entered the final algebraic equations for a new remote laser sensing system. Designed for use aboard satellites, the software application and sensing device would locate and chart SSBN's—decommissioned nuclear powered ballistic-missile submarines—that the Soviets "dumped" into deep waters under Arctic ice, to avoid the expense of nuclear salvage operations.

At the moment of the propane explosion, Dr. Morrison had been drawn to his third floor window. A smaller, secondary shake, unlike the explosive sound-wave, hit the building within milliseconds of the primary explosion. Morrison might not have given it a second thought had he not witnessed the emergency smoke vents fly open in the nearby lab wall below. Something was dreadfully wrong. He needed to investigate.

Quickly, the terrorists moved inside the room. Al-Mamun grabbed Sanders, who had been knocked to the floor by the force of the explosion. Rahman seized the new whistle-shaped triggering device and tossed it to Al-Mamun.

Quietly, like businessmen preparing for an audio-visual presentation to a C.E.O., Rahman and Al-Salih placed four Czechoslovakian ribbon-charges on the vault door and extended the M-60 lighter, six-inch fuse, and twenty-five foot det cord behind an overturned table.

Hidden behind the table, Rahman removed the safety pin, pulled back and released the spring-loaded firing pin, and the primer lit the fuse.

A puff of smoke from the plunger confirmed the fuse was lit. A delay of 10 seconds preceded a connecting spark to the det cord and, burning at 5 miles per second, four separate explosions instantly knocked the hinges and the lock off the vault door. It collapsed outward as planned.

Rahman and Al-Salih raced inside the vault and found a dozen plastic-sealed, corrugated boxes on shelves that read:

DANGER!—CXM-20 EXPLOSIVES
Property of
U.S. Government
Army/Navy Ordnance Testing Station
GILBERT DEPOT

"This is the wireless explosive," Rahman said in triumph. He grabbed a two-wheel cart from the lab and ran it inside. The air-conditioned vault was cool as the two men piled boxes on top of the cart and prepared to load them out to the panel truck.

"Get Mr. Sanders in the truck," Rahman said to Al-Mamun, "and carefully pack that triggering device."

Al-Mamun signaled compliance and grabbed Sanders by the arm. "Move," he said. "And hurry."

The two men hastened down the corridors, backtracking their steps to the entrance. As they approached a closed stairwell, Dr. Morrison, jumping down three steps at a time, slammed opened the stairwell door and ran directly into Sanders.

"Bobby Joe! There were two explosions. Did you . . . " He suddenly saw the panic in Sanders' eyes and turned around only long enough to see the bright reflected flash of a sharp blade. Dr. Morrison dropped to the floor, his neck nearly severed from its torso, and Al-Mamun pushed Sanders down the hallway to the rear door.

"Oh no!" Sanders screamed. "Now what'd ya have to do that for? Dr. Morrison never hurt nobody. Oh no. Oh no," he cried over and over.

"Silence!" Al-Mamun demanded and stuck his dagger at Sanders' back.

Sanders was now frightened beyond belief. Tears streamed down his face as he felt the razor-sharp point of the dagger at his spine.

"Move to the truck!" Al-Mamun insisted, and a terrified Bobby Joe Sanders complied , then was suddenly pulled back. Rahman and Al-Salih followed close behind with eight boxes of the CXM-20 on the cart. The other two were still at the door.

"Military police are running across the grass," said Al-Mamun. "Wait for them to clear."

Rahman glanced at Al-Salih. "You and Mr. Sanders still look like you belong here." He turned to Sanders. "Back your truck to the door as though you are loading out cleaning supplies. Ahmed will make certain you comply, or we take your children with us. Now go!"

Sanders' heart sank as they walked to the truck. He realized no one had paid attention to their movement. Al-Salih opened the rear doors, climbed in, and signaled with his gun for Sanders to follow. The custodian climbed in and moved up to the driver's seat.

"Do not be foolish to attract authorities. Back up carefully." A P38 was aimed at Sanders' head.

Sanders turned the key and the engine kicked over. Too anxious to hear it start, he turned the key again, and the starter screeched loudly across the grounds.

Ahmed slammed the barrel of his gun across the back of Sanders' head. "Don't ever do that again!"

"I didn't think it started. You make me nervous."

"Back up to the door. Now!"

Sanders was extremely careful to put the truck into the correct gear, and the transmission whined quietly as he shifted into reverse. The truck slowly moved toward the building's entrance. When it stopped at the door, Al-Salih grabbed the keys, went to the back, and pushed open the panel doors. Rahman and Al-Mamun threw their guns and supplies into the rear of the truck, climbed in, and pulled the entire cart and eight boxes of CXM-20 inside.

Then, the men sat quietly as they watched military personnel and late-working civilian employees scramble past in their cars, trucks, and jeeps. Within a matter of minutes, the area was relatively quiet, as attention was focused to the north side. Rahman ordered Sanders to follow the longer route to Nimitz Drive, and head out the Depot's East Gate.

———

The sun had risen high over the pine trees when a military jeep pulled to a stop at a clearing just off the main road—next to Sanders' panel truck.

"This is Bobby Joe's."

The MP set the jeep's emergency brake and climbed down. He looked at the corporal, "Let's check it out."

Several hours before, Dr. Morrison's body was discovered in the predawn hours when, after the propane fire was contained, a security officer was reported missing from his rounds. The officer's corpse was found in the corridor of Building D near the blown-out lab.

A few hours later a fisherman, wanting to purchase some bait, came across the body of Sanders' cousin, Bubba, shot through the head and lying in a pool of blood on the front seat of an LTD. And Mrs. Sanders reported her husband missing. It was Mrs. Sanders who recalled her husband's story of a damaged car at the store.

" . . . a gray car," she said, "with three men. A Mustang or Taurus or something . . . small. With a gash in the driver-side door. Bobby Joe said they was staying at the Gilbert Motel," she tried desperately to remember what she could tell the FBI agents.

"He said they was up to no good . . . he thought. Wondered why men saying they was from England, buying horses and all, ain't driving a bigger more expensive car. Ya know what I mean?"

The two MP's stepped from the jeep and carefully approached the old Chevy truck, their UZI's ready. From the highway, a passing car confirmed the Doppler effect as it whizzed by and brought a peculiar silence and serenity back to the area. A bright red cardinal landed on the Chevy's hood and took off for the trees when the MP's approached.

"Listen," the tall lieutenant said. He held up his hand as a halting motion. The two men stopped in place and listened carefully.

"You hear that?"

"Hear what?" said the corporal.

"Someone yelling. Kinda' muffled sounding."

They moved with caution toward the truck's rear doors.

"There it is again. Hear it?"

"Yeah, sounds like someone's inside. Trying to get our attention."

The corporal moved to the door.

"Wait," the lieutenant pulled him back. "Could be a trick."

The lieutenant edged alongside the truck and aimed his submachine gun up through the left rear-door window. The muffled sounds got louder, and the MP slowly worked his foot up on the bumper to get a look inside.

He glanced to the floor of the truck and saw, amid the clutter, someone all tied up and gagged with electrician's tape.

"It's Bobby Joe Sanders." They both looked at the man inside. His eyes bulging in fear—his throat trying to scream words they couldn't understand.

"Let's get the poor bastard outta there," said the lieutenant as he pulled on the rear door handle. "Damn, it's locked." He moved around to the passenger side and tried to open the door.

"It's locked too. Get to the other side."

The corporal ran around the front of the hood to the driver's side door and attempted to pull it open. "Same here. They got him locked up tight." He glanced through the window and called out to Sanders. "Hold on Bobby Joe, we'll get you outta there."

The muffled screams got louder and the truck shook as Sanders struggled to force himself up off the floor.

"He's trying to get up. Maybe he can open it from the inside."

"Naw," said the lieutenant. "He's wrapped like a mummy. Just bust the window out and get his ass outta there. The sun's getting hot and he'll be baked for sure."

The corporal watched Sanders get to his feet and hop toward the front—still yelling from under the tape.

"What's he saying? Can ya' figure it out?"

"The poor sucker's just happy to see us," he laughed. He tapped on the window. "Get back Bobby Joe, I'm gonna knock out the glass. We'll have you out in no time."

Bobby Joe Sanders went berserk as he threw himself up across the front seats and tried to shake his head. But the tape was bound too tightly from his head down and around his shoulders, arms and legs. He dripped with sweat as he tossed about.

"Get back Bobby Joe. You'll get cut by the glass."

The corporal took a stance alongside the driver's door and aimed the butt of his gun at the window. The first hit caused the laminated glass to buckle inward. The second hit crumpled it into hundreds of pieces as the window gave way to the heavy blow and split apart. The young man smiled at his own prowess and reached in for the door handle.

It would not have made any difference which door they opened, since they were all hooked to a series circuit, with four refrigerator-door buttons used as triggers at all opening points. Even the hood was booby-trapped and tied to the rest of the circuitry.

In the split second before the the bomb was triggered, the two MP's finally understood the one word that might have saved them as Sanders' taped mouth uttered a throaty, "Nooooo!"

From one of the military helicopters searching the area for terrorists, two miles south, the pilot looked up to see a massive shockwave skim across the treetops as another fireball burst upward from the clearing and pieces of metal debris scattered for a mile and a half around the perimeter of the blast area. The report shook the entire vicinity, and the helicopter shuddered as the shockwave passed through.

In their rusted, single-wide trailer, Mrs. Sanders held her infant son to her breast. Nine year old Alex, "the sensitive one," as Bobby Joe called him, had his arm around his mother's shoulder —his head tucked alongside her neck as he sat on the edge of the sofa sucking his thumb. The other children were out playing in the yard. The sound of the explosion was near, but no one looked up. After all, Gilbert Depot tested new ordnance every day.

As tears streamed down Mrs. Sanders' face, she knew she would never see her husband alive.

————

MONACO

NESTLED on a headland jutting into the Mediterranean between French and Italian borders, the principality of Monaco provided Parker and other delegates with an evening out, on the last night of their conference. With a lavender and golden tangerine sunset reflecting off the Ligurian Sea, the short fourteen-kilometer train ride from Nice gave everyone a chance to unwind.

A new *Undersea Gravesite Treaty*, completed just hours before required that all delegates introduce it immediately into their respective legislative bodies, at home, to gain support for final ratification at the United Nations. Without giving specifics, Parker had set an imaginary scenario for use of valuable artifacts salvaged by unscrupulous political groups. The fear of such activities was enough to repulse many delegates and helped to gain a majority vote for the treaty.

The margin for approval, worldwide, would be narrow. But Parker was encouraged by adoption of last-minute changes that gave the treaty some teeth and called for timely endorsement. And since Parker would be diving the North Atlantic, his associate, Dr. Ronald McCleary from Scripps Institute, would present the issue to the United States Congress for endorsement. The U.N. delegate would then carry it to the Chamber for presentation and ratification.

Following a lavish reception at the world-renowned Musée Océanographique—near the Palace of Prince Rainier III—Parker joined several colleagues at Albert Quay, near the older quarter of La Condamine, for late-night escargot and paélla at Restaurant du Port. Then, while the richest of the world's wealthy visited the Parisian shops and dined in the exquisite boulevard restaurants, Parker spent the remainder of the evening by the gaming tables at the sometime-infamous Casino, in the district of Monte Carlo.

Condos and high-rises replaced most of the old villas that once stood guard on the edge of the bay. But the legendary, opulent Casino, designed by Charles Garnier, architect for the Paris Opera House, managed to survive a century and several decades since. The Casino sat proudly atop an escarpment at the foot of the Maritime Alps—its famous white walls, rococo turrets, and cupolas of green copper proclaiming its grand, aristocratic place in history.

At just past six a.m., only the fanatic and compulsive gamblers were still drawn to the gaming tables. Common tourists bet scared money on roulette and vingt-et-un, thinking their early-morning strategies would be skill enough. But Baccara continued to attract the largest crowd while millionaires recklessly placed enormous bets that could make J. Paul Getty turn in his grave.

Hours before, the last notes from the Casino's l'Opera de Monte Carlo drifted out over the sea, and a restful quiet—found only in the early morning hours before dawn—floated over the bay as though a veil of peace.

Parker and his colleague, Dr. Erwin Senanayake, stood quietly above the Casino's terraced rampart overlooking the Centre de Congrés and the Mediterranean beyond. Parker's victory the day before had bolstered his energy, strengthened his resolve, and rejuvenated his soul. He took a breath of crisp salt-sea air, and decided it would be just as easy to sleep on the plane.

Parker thought of the last time he and Victoria had waited for a sunrise over this bay—just prior to his discovery of Dupont's attempted affair with her. He erased the image from his mind and would not allow anything to spoil the memory.

The rising sun had not yet crossed over the Italian Apennines, from the Adriatic. But Parker watched the silhouettes of hundreds of anchored private yachts—*some the size of ships*, he thought. He loosened his silk tie and dinner jacket. His friend followed suit.

"Remarkable, isn't it," said Parker, "the wealth represented in just a fraction of those crafts out there."

"Monaco is as they say, 'the world's playground.'"

"Intriguing that the pure Monegasque citizens aren't allowed to gamble."

Senanayake laughed, "Smart, I should say. They take it all from the tourists." He pulled out his empty trouser pockets and chuckled.

"They also pay no taxes."

"There you go, m'n. We're holding the wrong passports."

Parker pointed across the bay, as a copter rose from the Monaco

Heliport beyond the inlet to the Port of Fontvieille.

"In less than an hour, I'll take one of those back to Nice for my flight to St. John's."

"Newfoundland? Where to from there?"

Parker was more tired than he thought, for he had said more than he should.

"Uh, from there I'll be meeting my crew aboard the research ship, *Neptune's Knot.*"

"And?"

"And, we'll be sailing out into the North Atlantic."

"The *Titanic?*

Parker nodded.

"This time of year? Are you crazy?"

Parker could not look Senanayake in the face, "Just some cleanup work I need to do."

"Something's up, isn't it?" He looked directly at Parker. "You were more serious than I thought when you suggested there might be illicit use of salvaged treasures."

Cary couldn't hold back a devilish smile. His friend would pry it out of him if he pressed hard enough, and he changed the subject. "A quick cup of coffee, Erwin? Before I leave . . . "

"A strong cup or two," Senanayake smiled, deciding not to press further. Parker knew that Erwin could be trusted with any information. But the *Neptune's* objective would have to wait.

"It's on me."

The two cut back through the Casino, past the twenty-eight ionic columns and the statue of Hector and Andromache, in the marble-floored entrance hall. Then they headed toward Hotel de Paris, its façade just across from the Casino's garden square.

"Monsieur Parker?" a voice called from behind.

Parker looked back, "Quoi?"

A clerk from the Casino approached. "Monsieur, you are expecting a limousine to the Heliport, n'est ce pas?"

"Oui."

"Heli Aero Monaco telephoned, Monsieur. Your chauffeur will

arrive in twenty minutes."

Parker looked at his watch. It was 6:20 a.m. His flight to Nice International was scheduled for 7:15.

"I checked my bag and briefcase with the concierge. Have the chauffeur take them and meet me at Hotel de Paris, s'il vous plaît."

"Certainement."

He handed the clerk his claim check and a generous tip. "Merçi beaucoup."

"Je vous en prie, Monsieur." The man waved the tip at him and smiled widely, "C'est un plaisir."

Parker and Senanayake crossed Place du Casino, entered the hotel restaurant, and were served immediately. Quiet at first, meditating on events of the past few days, Dr. Senanayake broke the silence.

"You took some hard hits this week."

"Umm," Parker agreed, carefully sipping his hot coffee. "Dr. Levard in particular. I thought he'd never give up."

"He's bull-headed, to be sure."

"But he came around. If not for Levard, we may never have had the final vote to make the treaty retroactive."

"And Dr. Imre."

"Ah yes, the Hungarian poked and prodded all week."

"But by the vote, the potential harm done if we didn't enact the treaty was obvious to him."

"It occurred to me," said Parker, "it's been twenty-five years since the first U. N. Convention on the Law of the Sea. And I marvel at the struggle just to get agreement on matters so basic to global order and international relations."

"Like a constitution for the sea?"

Parker nodded, thought for a moment, then he laughed. "Remember that Bulgarian who chaired U.N.'s Committee Three on the Constitution?"

"Ah yes, Committee Three," Erwin said sarcastically. "The traveling circus where Rolex was out of favor and their primary mission was to wear Patek Philippe watches for jaunts between Geneva, Caracas and the U.N."

"That's the one. And the chairman's name was Yankov. Remember? I always thought his name befitted his position."

Senanayake laughed heartily. Then, he became more serious. "Will we see a constitution in our lifetime?"

"It's been three decades, and we still can't agree on anything beyond causes like Seabed Utilization and Exclusive Economic Zones. At the current rate the U.N. Convention is moving? Perhaps, but with one caveat."

"What's that?"

"A worldwide cataclysmic event that forces every nation to glance in the mirror and admit they're looking at the problem, not the solution."

"Let's hope it doesn't go that far."

"Hell, we've seen Spanish and Canadian warships threaten each other off Newfoundland's coast. If Spain won't admit they're killing off the beds by taking fish too small to lay eggs—let alone fertilize them—how can we expect others to comply?"

Parker was silent for a moment. "I sometimes wish we operated under the Byzantine's codifications."

"Simple and to the point, their Rodian Sea Code," said Erwin, "I'll grant you that."

"Three parts, forty-seven chapters in the longest of the three. . . . And you knew where you stood."

"Today," Parker continued, "with strategic ideas, institutions of maritime law in every nation, and national interests of each state . . . "

"There's a lot of bullshit," Erwin finished the thought. "But with approval of your treaty, it's a step ahead, don't you think? Who knows, maybe the Constitution will be ratified this year, as well."

"I hope so, Erwin."

Parker glanced at the cafe entrance. Out of the corner of his eye, he saw quick movement from someone concealing their presence.

At first Parker paid no attention. Then a heightened awareness kicked in after the events in London with Nakamura, and the mysterious man back at the Negresco Hotel earlier in the week. He wished he hadn't left Arledge's Browning High Power — that Commissioner Lawton had given him—in his bag.

Parker looked back at the door, saw nothing, and thought his paranoia was getting the best of him. He dismissed the feeling and finished his coffee.

A waiter delivered their check.

"You are Monsieur Parker?"

Cary nodded.

"Your limousine has arrived, Monsieur."

"Merçi." He left twenty francs on the table. Senanayake insisted on leaving the gratuity. "You coming?"

"I've five hours before my plane," said the Sinhalese scientist. "Think I'll have another cup."

"You know," Parker smiled wistfully, "I miss the old days."

"You must come to Sri Lanka for a visit. Deepani would love to see you and the girls."

"We're long overdue for curried prawns and stringhoppers. We'd enjoy seeing your family again . . . and a visit to Udarate."

"Yes, the up-country. Next summer?"

Parker thought for a moment. "In time for the Perahera."

"Perfect." The two embraced. "Aeyboo-wan, Mahattea."

"Aeyboo-wan," Parker bid goodbye and headed toward the foyer. "Keep a cold Lion Lager waiting for me."

"Of course."

And Parker was out the door.

———

WOODS HOLE

A car horn had sounded in the Parker's driveway.

"Mom, they're here." Marlowe had yelled from her upstairs

bedroom window.

"Remind the Silbermans about mass in the morning," Victoria's voice got progressively quieter as the girls hopped down the stairs, their backpacks full of pajamas and Nintendo games.

Jessica hugged Victoria at the waist, as Marlowe pecked her mother on the cheek.

"Thanks, Mom."

"I'll pick you up. Ask Mrs. Silberman to call."

"I will," said Marlowe.

"Have fun skating."

The girls ran squealing out the front door, leaving it open wide. Victoria had calmly waved to Joan Silberman. They exchanged sympathetic smiles—Joan's more out of envy—as Marlowe and Jessica bounced into the back seat with their two friends.

"Don't stay up too late," Victoria admonished as an afterthought.

She hardly heard them yell, "We won't!" as the girls giggled loudly, slammed the doors shut, and the car headed back down the private road.

At once, it was quiet. The late spring breeze that usually whisked through the woods seemed to slow to a crawl, though Victoria felt a slight chill surround her. It was always that way when Cary was on the Continent negotiating treaties or consulting with government attachés.

She felt twice as lonely when the children spent the night with friends. *Cary's six hours ahead. He'll call from Nice in the morning*, she thought happily.

For now, she was resolved to keep busy. She had plenty to keep her occupied with the Boston City Hall account. The Lucas project needed catching up. And this was a perfect break for checking new carpet samples in the garage.

She placed Gershwin on the disc player. *Rhapsody in Blue* put her in the mood to dance through the kitchen to the garage. She left the door open for the music to filter through.

In the evening, she treated herself to Johnsonville Bratwurst and pasta, then curled up against thick pillows, in bed, until blurry-eyed from glancing at furniture catalogs. Typically, she would awake at two or three to find the bedside light still on. But this time she told herself enough was enough. It was just past midnight when she closed the Ethan Allen catalogs, touched the lamp, and quickly dozed off.

At first, Victoria didn't hear the smooth scratching of the glasscutter on the outside library door. In her dream state, she imagined one of the turtles had gotten under the patio decking, as they had in the past—its shell scraping against the wood.

The cutter quietly slashed an engraved circle in the glass.

Victoria's eyes opened wide.

Were there voices outside? she beckoned her mind to listen carefully.

A series of small staccato taps. Then a quiet ping occurred as the suction cup pulled the glass from its peripheral circumference. The glass slipped from its holder, fell onto the decking, and splintered into pieces.

Whispers of anger were exchanged outside.

I did hear voices. They seemed unusual in pitch.

Are there two or three . . . or more?

Victoria slowly leaned across the bed for the phone. A catalog slipped off the bed with a loud thud.

Victoria's pulse raced. *My God, where is Cary when I need him?*

There was silence. Both sides listened before deciding what to do next.

A jiggling of the library doorknob.

A security lamp near the patio cast a haze of light through the blinds. Victoria focused her eyes in the darkness to see if other catalogs were ready to fall off the bed. She slowly pulled her legs from under her quilt and nervously reached once more for the handset cradled in the answerphone. It slipped and crashed against the night table.

"Shit." Victoria cried out in a whisper as she groped for the phone. Her entire body shook with fear. *Who's trying to get in? And why?* She hunted for the receiver.

"Please, dear God, don't let them hurt me," she whispered.

She heard the patio decking creak as a shadow moved in front of the double doors leading outside.

An off-the-hook alarm pierced the air from the handset, as she grabbed it off the floor.

"Oh, God, " she quickly muffled it against her breast. The lights inside the touch-tone buttons glared back at her as she dialed 911. She didn't wait for the emergency operator to finish her sentence.

"This is Vicky Parker. Someone's breaking into my house. I'm alone at thirty-eight forty-one Crystal Cove Drive, in Penzance Point. Please hurry. I need hel . . . "

The phone went dead.

"Hello. Hello," said the operator at the opposite end. "Jack, we've been cut off. Run that tape back for me. Quick. Vicky Parker's in trouble."

Jack Akins punched the "Reverse" button on the recorder. He had heard the message too. He was good at this. Jack always bragged he could stop a message on a dime. True to form the message repeated itself as Becky Eastman punched in the direct line to the Falmouth police.

Becky's clear voice broke through the initial static over the radio, "Code ten-thirty-one, slash thirty-three, break-in in progress at three-eight-four-one Crystal Cove Drive. The Parker residence. Victoria Parker in possible distress. Repeat, break-in in progress at three-eight-four-one Crystal Cove Drive. Proceed with caution. Line went dead during nine-one-one message."

Victoria jumped across her bed, for the hallway, as a body crashed through their glass-paneled deck doors. A hand grabbed the end of her nightgown. It ripped like a sheet as she raced down the hall toward the front door.

Two male voices laughed as they screamed back and forth at each other.

Victoria could not understand them. Through the darkness, she saw another figure dart toward her from the hall, converging from the other side of the house.

The foreign voices grew louder and closer.

Victoria raced to the kitchen for the side door. The intruders followed close behind. She reached for the deadbolt knob, slipped, and hit her head on the counter. Her arms knocked over a mixer and set of glass bowls as she tried to prevent her fall. They crashed on the floor and the sound of broken glass reverberated through the house with Victoria's scream.

One man raced past the kitchen island as Victoria rolled away. He sailed past her, stepped on a broken bowl and slid into the cupboards. The other tripped over his partner in the dark and fell near Victoria.

She forced herself to move. Pain shot through her head from a lump rising on her forehead. In the darkness, she found the stovetop grates and tossed them at the two silhouettes as they attempted to get up.

She turned, ran out through the dining room, and headed for the front entrance.

Her mind screamed, *Get to the front door! My God, the door!*

Then she felt hot sweaty hands on her shoulder.

Victoria whipped around and plunged her knee forcefully into her assailant's groin. The man screamed with excruciating pain and doubled over as she grabbed his beard and pushed him into the stair banister. His weight crumpled the railing spools and he went down cursing.

She reached the front door deadbolt. The bolt tumbled into its resting place.

A burly man sailed around the corner into the entryway, saw his friend lying on the floor in pain, and shrieked with laughter.

He waited, looking for the moment to make his move. It was obvious the woman could do some damage.

Indignation took over, in the darkness, as he confronted Victoria. She was out of breath. But with the shadowy light from outside, he read the defiance in her face.

He smiled broadly and warily moved in her direction.

Victoria's hands fumbled for the door handle behind her as she kept her eyes on the approaching madman.

God help me. Please God help me, she cried to herself, not wanting to appear afraid as she gasped for air. Light-headed, from hyperventilation, she forced herself to concentrate on escape.

The man lunged at Victoria and grabbed for her arm. She moved aside and slammed the front door into his head. His sweaty hands lost their grip, and he grabbed his face screaming loudly. Blood trickled from his nose.

Instantly, Victoria turned to run out the door and was jolted by the cold end of an XE-47 pointed directly into her stomach. As if from nowhere, a third man now blocked her way.

Victoria's scream echoed through the surrounding woods and was lost in the sound of waves pounding the beach at high tide.

The terrorist stared at the beautiful woman who had taken out two of his accomplices. He admired her stamina. Certainly, she was capable of hostility and defiance they had not anticipated.

The *Koran* had ways of dealing with contemptible women. But that would come later.

"Ahlan, ya Veektooria, wa sahlan." said Atak Abu Rahman, holding the machine gun tight against her.

Victoria was stunned that he knew her name.

A deep, pained, hearty laugh came from behind her. Out of breath, she turned her head to the entrance.

Though the porch light was on, it was difficult to see the men in the foyer. In the dark shadows of the house, she saw the form of a bearded man as he rocked back and forth on the floor, holding his groin with one hand, and rubbing his head with the other. Another man lay stunned beside him, cussing loudly in Arabic as blood flowed from his nose.

Subhi Al-Mamun spoke from inside. "Our friend said 'Hello, Victoria, nice to meet you.'"

Victoria was petrified, afraid to make any further move. Her head throbbed with pain from her fall in the kitchen.

"Izzayyik?" said Rahman, a wide smile across his bronzed face.

Ahmed Al-Salih struggled up from the floor, came out through the entrance, and rubbed his sweaty, bloodied face with a piece of Victoria's torn nightgown. "He said, 'How are you?'"

Blood dripped from other cuts he received crashing through her bedroom door.

Suddenly, a needle was jabbed into her arm, and she was injected with a heavy dose of Nembutal. Her head began to swim and all went dark. Victoria collapsed, scraping her head against the front steps before she could be caught.

A siren cut through from the distance.

The other terrorist got up immediately and stumbled to Victoria. They gathered her by the arms and legs. She was much taller than anticipated. Sleeker and longer, thought one. Taller than two of them, they discerned. As they lifted Victoria, her nightgown fell in folds between her beautiful legs.

"I wonder what she has under this gown," said one.

"Time for that later, Subhi."

Victoria's arms slipped from Ahmed's hands, in front. Rahman chastised him for being so clumsy, grabbed her under the shoulders, and signaled Ahmed to close the front door. She was whisked into the woods where they had waited several hours before.

Their rented gray Taurus was hidden in the trees. They stuffed Victoria into the backseat of the coupe, climbed in on both sides, and waited. Blood smeared on the seat as Victoria's bruised head fell limp on the cushion.

The terrorists had made their own road through the brush to avoid detection. Now they waited for the authorities to pass, in their rush to approach the house, but doubted the police would be any match for their XE-47s, if discovered.

The sirens grew louder as the police circled up the hillside.

Rahman pushed everyone's heads down as headlights flickered through the trees into the clearing. A police car raced past them. After a moment, a second car drove by.

Rahman counted quietly, "Waahid, itneed, talaata. " He turned the key. The Ford started, and he hit the gas pedal.

Sirens and racing engines covered the sounds of crunching dead branches and leaves under the Taurus' tires. They drove down the hill, past an unmanned guard house for the private drive, and raced out the main entrance. On the primary road, they disappeared quietly into the dark seaside mist.

———

Lieutenant Jim Grimes and Sergeant Frank Peters held their Beretta 92F's at the ready as they carefully stepped over the splintered wooden panes and broken glass, and entered the violated bedroom from the deck.

Grimes located a wall switch with his flashlight and crossed the room. He flicked the bedroom chandelier on with the flashlight's tip, to avoid any prints left behind.

"Jeez, will you look at this mess," he said quietly, "Someone wanted in bad. Check the glass for clothing fibers. Ten-to-one they left something behind."

"The phone's dead, all right." Peters gingerly held the handset and carefully placed it back in its cradle.

Two other officers had entered through the unlocked front door, their Ithaca 20-inch Deer Slayers in hand. Each moved with caution, turning on lights one by one to determine if anyone was left in the house.

Officers Boog and McGuinness edged up the stairs. Finding the second floor untouched, it was apparent no one was home.

"Lieutenant, look at this," said one of the patrolmen, coming in from the hallway. With a pair of tweezers, careful not to disturb more of the evidence, the officer held up a piece of blood-stained silk nightgown.

A patrolman brought in test kits, vials, and other evidence collection material. He taped off rooms where the contents had been violently disturbed by the apparent kidnapping. Outside, the area was cordoned off with yellow crime tape.

"They musta' got Vicky Parker."

"Damn," said Lieutenant Grimes as he holstered his Beretta and clasped his hands tightly behind his back, in thought. The officers walked into the kitchen and met Boog and McGuinness coming in through the dining room.

"Check upstairs for the kids?" said Grimes.

"Yes sir," said Boog. "No sign of 'em. "Their room's are undisturbed. Beds still made."

"No evidence of a struggle upstairs," said McGuinness. "Think they got the kids too?"

"Hope not," said Grimes. "Jeez, what a mess. Frank, get on the radio and call out every unit. Have them keep an eye out for Mrs. Parker and anyone suspicious. She must still be in her pajamas . . . if she's alive. Take this piece of cloth to describe what she might be wearing."

As an afterthought, Grimes said, "Better notify all authorities on the Cape—and call Boston—to be on the lookout for anyone traveling through their area acting odd. We don't know who we're dealing with here."

An officer opened a small paper bag preprinted with an evidence tag. Grimes prepared to slip the cloth inside.

"Wait," said Grimes. "This piece of her nightgown is still damp with blood . . . and something else." He pointed to the stains. We can't put it in until it dries. Prepare the evidence bag and set them together on the kitchen table. Use that point as a gathering site, if it isn't full of fingerprints."

The officer wrote the cloth's description on the front of the bag, for later use.

"Get pictures of everything, and get the sketch artist up here.

Take measurements and dust for prints. I want it all."

"No smell of gunpowder," said Peters. "Musta' just broke in and grabbed her without firing a shot."

"Good sign for now."

"What the hell would they want from the Parker family, Lieutenant?"

"No idea. Stop wasting time and get on that radio."

"Lieutenant. Better come here," another officer called out.

"Boog, check the grounds around the house. Look for footprints, broken branches, mud tracked from another area, anything you can find. Sketch it out if ya' have to."

"On my way, sir."

Grimes hurried to the front entry.

"Watch your step, Lieutenant. Appears to be blood on the front door and on the floor, here," said the officer. "Still damp. A small trail goes out front."

"Clearly fresh." Grimes looked closely, then bent to pick up something with tweezers. "Looks like someone's hair. Thicker than usual. Could be a dog or cat, though." He placed it into a rolled coin envelop and marked it for evidence. "They got a dog?"

"Don't know. Haven't seen one."

"Check it out."

"Yes sir."

"Might be human. Type it all. And scour this area with the mini-filter vac before we dust everything. Don't miss the bedroom. Check for possible rape, just in case." Grimes turned to another patrolman.

"I need a phone." The patrolman went outside to pull a cellular phone from his car.

Grimes returned to the kitchen and glanced at the mess. Then he heard an approaching car. A large stationwagon pulled up in the drive.

"Who the hell's that, this time of night?"

"Is that Dr. Parker?" Sergeant Peters yelled to the front.

"Don't know, sir." They waited for an answer. "No, sir, it's

Mr. Silberman....A neighbor from down the road."

Jack Silberman slammed on the brakes and raced from his car as Grimes came out front. "We heard the sirens and saw your lights. What the hell happened, Lieutenant?"

"Wish we knew. Do you know where Dr. Parker is?"

"He's in France, at a conference. We've got their girls for the night . . . went ice skating with our kids."

"Thank God." he paused, "Is Vicky Parker with you?"

"No. She was spending tonight home with . . . "

"Did you see anyone on the road?"

"No one."

Lieutenant Grimes grabbed the portable phone. They moved back into the house. Silberman followed.

"Watch your step, Mr. Silberman . . . evidence . . . "

The lieutenant punched in some numbers, and tapped his fingers on his holster as he waited for the connection.

"FBI? I need Missing Persons." Turning to Silberman, he said, "You'd better get back and watch those kids. We'll post security outside your home. I think we have something bigger than our force can handle."

MONACO
06:45 GREENWICH

WITH the entire principality less than two square miles, the limo's drive across town was brief. Parker's chauffeur had cut over to Rue Grimaldi, drove past the Palace and Louis II Stadium, then down Avenue des Ligures. In the early morning traffic, it took less than five minutes to reach the Heliport.

The chauffeur popped the trunk, pulled Parker's garment bag and briefcase, and came around to the door. Not accustomed to such service, Parker was already out. He reached for his bag and briefcase and glanced through the sun-glinted windshield of a

Peugeot that pulled up ten yards behind.

Both occupants turned their heads away. But he recognized the face of the driver as the man he had seen while having coffee. And the passenger was the bearded man observing him at the Negresco Hotel, earlier in the week.

Parker took his bags and climbed back into the limo.

"Monsieur?" the chauffeur inquired. "Qu'est qu'il y a?

"Nothing's the matter. Just give me a minute, s'il vous plaît."

"Certainement." Parker closed the door and the chauffeur wondered what his passenger was doing behind the smoked glass windows. Above the street, well-placed security cameras, directly linked to Monaco Police headquarters, saw no unusual activity.

Inside the limo, Parker looked back at the Peugeot. It was clearly the same men. He unlocked the bag and pulled out his gun and three clips. Not ready for another confrontation, Parker wasn't about to let anyone sneak up on him, this time. He removed his tuxedo coat, pulled a holster over his left shoulder and, after checking the clip, tucked the 9mm pistol inside. He put his coat on, shoved the extra clips into his pocket, climbed out of the limo, and turned to the chauffeur with his back to the Peugeot.

"Avez-vous un radio?"

"Oui."

"Appelez un agent," Parker whispered.

"Call the police?" the chauffeur repeated in English to be certain he was serious.

"Now, s'il vous plaît," he quietly begged. "We may have trouble any minute. Uh . . . " He switched back to French, "Urgence."

"Emergency?" the chauffeur confirmed.

"Oui. I'll notify security inside." Parker slightly opened his coat to reveal his holster. "Maintenant. Call now."

He walked through the terminal doors. The limo driver looked behind him then dashed to his two-way radio. Parker looked back through the plate-glass windows and saw the Peugeot was empty.

The limo was still parked in front. He hoped the driver had reached the police, but he could not know a Ruger Mark II—flush to the head—with a rubber baby's nipple over the muzzle, had already silenced the chauffeur before he had a chance to switch to the emergency channel. It happened so quickly, observers in the city-wide camera surveillance room never picked it up.

Inside, the terminal was a flurry of activity with travelers making connections from Nice to Paris and beyond. Others were arriving for short day trips to Cannes, Toulon, and Saint Tropez.

Where the hell is airport security! Parker glanced at his watch. It was 6:55 a.m.

He spotted the Heli Aero Monaco counter and pulled out his tickets. Four passengers were ahead of him. He casually surveyed the terminal for security, and to spot his new set of groupies.

Damn it!

Parker glanced out at the crew on the landing platforms. The deck-operator, sitting in his small cab at the far corner of the pad, controlled the cantilevered landing decks. They had just rolled out on giant steel tracks that balanced and distributed the heavy load, suspended over the water beyond the pilings.

Two conventional twelve-passenger helicopters rested on the upper level—their gimbaled rotor blades hanging limp—after being transported out over the Mediterranean to make room for the day's incoming flights. A third copter—a corporate executive craft—had hovered until the decks were locked into place, and prepared to land on the lower terminal deck.

Parker became impatient when the line had not moved. He pocketed his tickets, bypassed those in front, and walked around the counter.

"Excusez-moi, Mademoiselle. There is an emergency. Je suis en difficulté."

"You are in trouble, Monsieur?"

"Oui. Can you summon the police?"

"What is the matter?"

"I need to speak with security. It's extremely urgent." Parker chose not to display his holstered pistol. He turned and spotted the bearded terrorist coming out of a gift shop. The other was nowhere to be seen.

The attendant looked carefully at Parker, determined he was serious, and picked up a phone. She turned from the counter to prevent alarming customers.

Within thirty seconds two gendarmes approached the counter. The attendant pointed to Parker.

"Monsieur?"

"Parlez-vous anglais? Je parle Français, un peu."

"Oui, I speak English," said one. The other shrugged.

"I'm Dr. Cary Parker, here on business with the International Maritime Organization. Two men may make an attempt on my life. Others could be hurt in the process."

"Monsieur, where are these men?"

Parker specified the direction of the bearded terrorist, but he had disappeared. "Uh . . . there are two . . . one with a beard, wearing baggy pants. The other I can't describe. Except their features are Arabic. One was just . . . "

Shots came from across the concourse.

The gendarme collapsed to the floor in his own blood, while bullets raced past Parker's head and exploded into an electronic flight schedule sign. Parker and the other officer ducked behind the counter, pulling the two screaming attendants down with them. Others screamed in horror.

"Merde alors!" The officer looked at his dead partner and called for assistance on his radio. He looked to Parker for some type of explanation.

"Terrorists." An international word everyone understood.

"Combien?"

"Deux hommes," Parker held up two fingers and continued, "You remain here . . . restez ici. I'll draw them off. It's me they want." Parker pointed to himself, since the Frenchman did not comprehend everything he said. "Lls me veulent."

One of the attendants interpreted for him.

"Non, non," the gendarme grabbed Parker's arm to prevent him from getting shot. And he made another quick call to the station.

Bursts of shots tore at the counter. Screams echoed across the building as travelers ran for cover and others dropped to the floor.

"Mon Dieu! Mon Dieu!" a woman standing in line panicked, and ran directly into the line of fire.

Parker kept low as he peered around the counter. He reached for his pistol and steeled himself.

For a moment there was silence. Then shots glanced off the terrazzo floor.

A terrorist raced toward Parker and shot several rounds. Parker jumped out from the counter, sidestepped a pile of luggage, then sprinted across the concourse to another desk.

"Get down, now!" Parker screamed as he passed by travelers frozen in terror. "Abas, maintenant. C'est dangereux!"

He pushed women and children down to the floor. "Get down. Abas."

Both ruthless men headed in his direction as the travelers scattered. He turned, dropped to his knees, and shot back at the men. Fire was returned as he bounded behind the counter.

Parker spotted a boarding gate and darted for the exit. He turned at the doorway, dropped, fired at the terrorists, then reached for the door. Bullets disintegrated its glass, and he raced through the portal frame and sprinted out onto the lower landing deck.

Hearing the gunshots, ground crew frantically attempted to wave off the executive helicopter that landed on an inland pad. But the pilot had killed the engines and removed his headset—his passengers not yet aware of danger outside the cabin.

Parker jogged across the pad looking for cover.

"Shit." He had lost count of his bullets. "This is worse than counting blackjack cards."

He pulled the clip and tucked it in a coat pocket, per chance a bullet or two might still be inside. Then he jammed a spare magazine home.

Both terrorists followed Parker into the glaring morning sun, their XE-47's aimed out over the decking. Parker heard the 'crack thump' sounds of supersonic bullets zipping over his head and snap-rolled for cover behind an electric cart.

More automatic weapon bursts raked the area. Bullets tore into the cart's frame and blew its tires. Padded seat debris flew into the air and rained down.

Parker lay prostrate, lengthwise from the wheels, in case bullets came under the carriage. "Bramson," he called out to himself, "if I get out of this alive . . . "

Across the deck, anxious passengers didn't wait for the steps to be put in place. Terrified, they jumped to the platform, raced behind the terrorists, and into the terminal.

The gunmen were unconcerned. They were under orders not to let Parker escape.

Parker studied the area around him.

If I get to the upper deck, I can dive the water and disappear among the rocks—if there's room between the rocks for diving. Parker hoped that would leave the terrorists hanging out to dry atop the decking, when the local SWAT Team arrived.

He looked up over the cantilevered landing pads, suspended above the sea, but could not estimate distance. Quickly he pulled off his shoes and tossed them toward the terrorists.

"Wish I'd get through an attack without losing my shoes," he grumbled to himself.

Thinking his shoes to be grenades, with bright sun in their eyes, the distraction was enough to throw off the gunmen's aim as Parker bounded to the upper-level steps. He dropped behind the stairs and sent several rounds of fire at the terrorists. With no cover, they plunged to the concrete.

Parker dashed up the steps, raced ten paces, and hid beside a food-service cart. He calculated the distance behind him.

Thirty yards to the sea.

The two gunmen crossed over each of the pads, as sirens wailed in the distance. Parker stretched out prone on the concrete and peered around the corner of the food cart. He watched the men cautiously move toward the stairs. Then a fusillade of bullets whizzed past him, toward the ocean.

Caught on the outside edge of the upper pads, the deck-controller was trapped in his glassed-in cab with nowhere to run. A stray bullet crashed through the side window, into his neck, and he collapsed unconscious over the control panel. His limp arm forced back the safety-button cover, and the weight of his body disengaged it. Simultaneously, his hand hit the Retract button.

Immediately, a back-up warning buzzer echoed across the bay. Underneath the Heliport, the immense electric motors and gears went into action.

Parker felt the deck jerk slightly and knew he was in trouble. For a moment, the gunmen stood frozen in place, not realizing what happened—as the entire upper section of pads retreated from the sea, toward the terrorists.

Parker knew the more the deck pulled back, the less depth he'd have to dive—to avoid the rocks.

He looked at the controller's cab at water's edge. Then, the two small helicopters at the opposite end.

Not a bit of cover.

"Damn! What's taking the police so long?"

Unyielding, tons of concrete and steel crawled on the tracks as the upper deck approached the terminal—and drew inexorably toward the abandoned helicopter. Police sirens mixed with the warning buzzer, and the sounds became more ominous.

The French gendarme emerged with stealth, through the terminal's side door, looking for an opportunity to bag a gunman. From behind the food-cart, Parker watched the officer move to the executive helicopter, his nine-round MAS pistol in hand.

The terrorists sprinted up the steps to the moving deck, bullets blasting toward Parker. He fired back but, without the right angle, was nearly exposed to a volley of direct hits.

Across the deck, the gendarme used the three-foot-high concrete pads like in a field trench—moving along its edge for cover—popping up to fire as he caught sight of the two men, careful not to get caught in the base of the retreating deck.

Firing off three rounds, the officer hit one of the terrorists in the head and chest, dropping him instantly. The man's gun flew across the deck toward the water.

"Yes!" Parker whooped out loud, seeing the man crumple and twist with the impact of the bullets.

The remaining gunman angrily turned and, from the hip, sprayed his XE-47 like a fire hose aimed across the edge of the decking. Plate glass windows shattered in the terminal and the officer went down with a scream—wounded in the chest, soon to be crushed by the retracting deck.

Parker took advantage of the moment, stepped out from the side of the cart, took careful aim at the back of the terrorist's head, and pulled the trigger three times.

It just clicked, and the terrorist turned around—Parker's arm still holding the empty Browning Hi-Power at eye-level.

"Shit!" Parker threw his gun down and turned pale as a ghost.

The bearded man laughed hysterically as he stepped forward and brought his sub-machine gun to Parker's chest.

"Dr. Parker," he laughed. "The mighty American who would stop the ALFAHAD . . . " His voice became menacing. "I am Sayyid al-Hakim," he beat his chest once with his left fist as he held his sub-machine gun with his right, "You are now food for the Ligurian Bass."

He pulled his trigger hard.

And nothing happened.

"No!" screamed the terrorist—his gun seized up from heat stoppage. He pulled the trigger repeatedly—still nothing. Then Parker jumped forward, grabbed the hot barrel, and pulled al-Hakim to meet a solid knee to the groin. The terrorist released the gun in pain and, with a loud grunt Parker slammed the butt of the XE-47 across al-Hakim's head.

The terrorist first grabbed his crotch, then his face, and slumped screaming to the pad. Parker turned for the other terrorist's gun. But al-Hakim, realizing he had a job to complete, lunged at Parker's legs and brought him down. Both men rolled breathlessly across the concrete. Parker placed a hard right across the man's chin.

Sayyid fell off Parker, rolled to an upright position and dashed for his dead partner's XE-47. Parker struggled to right himself, dived after al-Hakim, and kicked the gun into the water as they both slammed into the upper deck's protective railing.

Parker rammed his fist into al-Hakim's stomach, brought his knee to the man's head as he doubled over, and the terrorist staggered backward.

Parker grabbed the terrorist's shirt, pulled him forward, and hit him with an uppercut to the chin. The gunman's teeth slammed together in a sickening crunch. Then Parker threw him down the steps to the lower level, jumped on top of him—and beat him mercilessly.

But Sayyid al-Hakim's desert-borne stamina helped him recover. With brute force, he knocked Parker back with his feet. Cary went flying toward the edge of the safety railing and the terrorist followed.

Parker gasped in pain as al-Hakim's left foot slammed into his thigh. But he grabbed the gunman's leg, twisted it hard to the right and brought him down over the greased duo-steel tracks.

Al-Hakim felt the vibration of the massive decking as it moved toward him. Parker gasped for air and glanced at the moving slab and wheels.

Immediately the terrorist grabbed the ends of Parker's bow tie and pulled with all his might. He forced Parker over on his back and, with a knee in his stomach, continued to choke Parker as he lay across the rails. From the corner of his eye, Parker saw the upper deck closing in—ready to crush anyone in its path.

At the opposite end, the upper decking had pushed the large helicopter toward the terminal. A fuel tank explosion appeared inevitable. From the terminal, a pilot raced out and jumped inside, while another man ran to pull the wounded officer from the path of the retracting deck.

The helicopter's turbines began to whine, and the terrorist was distracted. In a last ditch effort, Parker gasped for air and rammed his fist into al-Hakim's throat. Caught off guard, the man fell back grabbing his neck—choking and struggling to breathe.

Parker willed himself up from the tracks, grabbed the terrorist with his left fist, and with one last blast of energy, brought his right elbow around to the face. Al-Hakim's head snapped back as he fell across the cold steel rails and under the apron guard.

The train-wheeled truck caught the gunman's shirt sleeve as it rolled forward, and Parker watched helplessly as the man's arm was dragged under the wheel by the mechanism. The terrorist let out a blood-curdling scream as it tugged the remainder of his body completely under the deck and sliced him in half.

"Jesus, God Almighty!" Parker yelled to the heavens, wondering if these pursuits would ever end. He sunk to the steps for rest, then observed they were still moving.

Relentlessly, the upper deck pushed back toward its nighttime parking space. Winded beyond any endurance trial he had ever experienced, Parker gasped for air and turned to the helicopter.

The giant blades slowly rotated, then pitched and bit at the air as they gathered speed. But just as the pilot got lift, the right ski caught on the undercarriage of the runaway deck.

The pilot fought to maintain control, unable to unhook the

ski. He hovered slightly, set down the skis, then edged back in an attempt to break loose. But his rotor blades came dangerously close to the building.

Parker looked toward the control cab at the end of the upper deck. He grabbed hold of a handrail, forced himself to rise, climbed the steps, and tripped and fell to his knees at the top. Then, in a hobbled sprint, he moved across the concrete to the small cab.

He opened the door, edged himself inside, and lifted the dead controller from the panel.

Everything was printed in French, but he forced himself to concentrate and read the markings over the buttons. There were more than he thought—given specific adjustments needed for stormy weather landings and those that allowed the computer program to adjust for pitch and roll of the sea.

He looked back at the copter—its blades within a foot of the terminal. Then he checked the control panel and spotted a red button marked **ARRETEZ**.

"What have I got to lose?" He slammed his fist down on top of the button and heard the machinery shut down. At the same moment there was a noticeable pull as the giant cantilevered slab came to a stop.

Realizing the helicopter was still in trouble, Parker checked the control panel once more.

"Start . . . go. What the hell is the word I'm looking for?" He fidgeted nervously, much too tired and with little energy left to think straight.

He spotted another button marked **AVANCER**.

"Advance . . . that's it!"

He hit the switch and the machinery took hold—moving the upper pads back toward the water.

Parker looked out over the decking. The entire Heliport now swarmed with police and a military SWAT Team—UZI's at the ready as they raced across both levels.

Parker watched the helicopter as it was pulled away from the building—its ski still caught. Then the pilot pushed down on his collective pitch stick, retarded the throttle, and set the craft gently down on the lower deck. The cantilevered section pulled itself away from the ski, and there was a noticeable jerk in the fuselage as it was released.

Parker whistled, "What a pro," and stepped out of the tiny cab. Uniformed officers of all ranks rushed up the steps, over the edges of the slab, and across the deck to see who he was—their guns ready for any perpetrator.

"Here we go again . . . " he mumbled to himself.

Parker leaned against the outside wall of the cab for support, raised his hands high into the air, and slid down to the concrete in complete exhaustion. Slowly, he looked up at the soldiers. "Your timing is uncanny." He smiled sarcastically.

The soldiers looked at each other and shrugged.

HOTEL HERMITAGE, MONACO
09:30 GREENWICH

WEAKENED from lack of sleep, his energy sapped and nerves raw, Parker canceled his flight to Newfoundland and was driven to Hotel Hermitage, Beaumarchais Square, to recuperate from trauma of the attack. Visibly shaken and his tuxedo ripped, blood stained, and in complete disarray, the hotel management rushed him to an inside corridor room, away from the circling traffic, where he might sleep in peace.

He tried to calm himself before placing a call stateside. But it was to no avail. The gun-barrel burn across his left hand was now blistered. A medic had treated and lightly bandaged the burn, but it throbbed as he picked up the phone's receiver. He punched in the call numbers for the secured line and waited several rings, knowing it was only 3:30 in the morning on the east coast.

"Colonel Bramson here."

"What the hell's going on?" Parker all but yelled into the phone.

"Cary?"

"Who else would want to climb through the phone to wring your neck? Come to think of it, there could be legions."

"Thank God. I've been trying to locate you for over two hours." Bramson couldn't get a word in edgewise while Parker related his experience at the Heliport.

The colonel attempted to calm him down. With the Atlantic and part of a continent between them, he knew what he was about to say would take Parker from anger to rage.

"Cary, I can't apologize enough for what you've been through. But you've got to listen, I've . . . "

"Listen, hell—I've been listening to you too long already. For God's sake, Bramson, I was almost killed this morning. For the second time in less than three weeks. And innocent people were shot—all because of our upcoming escapade."

"I understand your ang . . . "

"Anger? Anger! That's not the word for it. Call it ill humor. Resentment, maybe. Hostility, perhaps. Who's kidding who? This entire scheme is moronic. It's sheer lunacy. You've suckered me into this mess. I didn't want to volunteer. And you've managed to place me smack in the middle of every lunatic fringe terrorist in the world."

"But what's important is . . .you've survived. You've outwitted them."

"Oh, thanks. Is this the motivational pep talk I've been waiting for?"

"No. Now shut-up and listen to me."

There was no other way to tell him, under the circumstances. "Victoria has been kidnapped. CIA, FBI and the police are out in force. There's a nation-wide manhunt going on. We'll find her. Your children are okay. They're with a neighbor."

Bramson waited for the rage to come.

There was only silence.

Cary had let the phone drop to his side. He was limp as his mind raced over tracks he had never known, searching for answers that did not exist. His eyes filled with an opaqueness he had not felt since Victoria had given birth to a stillborn boy—and he had had no answers then.

"Cary?" a distant voice squawked from the phone's receiver. "Dr. Parker?"

Cary blindly found himself sitting on the edge of his hotel bed. The energy was gone. He was drained of any ability to respond.

"Dr. Parker? Are you there? Listen to me, please. Cary . . . "

Slowly, Cary was pulled back, as though from a near-death experience. Someone was calling him back. It was too early to give up, too early to abandon hope. "Victoria needs . . .

" . . . your help," said Bramson. "But she needs you to fight those bastards the way you know how. From the deep. Let the authorities find her. You need to locate the *Great Omar*.

"Can you hear me?" Bramson went on. "I know this is diffi-cult. We couldn't have predicted this."

Cary found enough stamina to get the phone back up. "You listen to me," he said, in almost a whisper.

Bramson was actually relieved to hear him speak.

"I'm getting on the next plane. Better yet, you get me an F-16, or a 111, or steal me a fucking MiG on the nearest tarmac. I don't care what it takes, just get me back there. I'll be ready to leave in less than twenty minutes."

"Dr. Parker. You've got to catch a flight to Newfoundland as soon as you're rested. The *Neptune* is enroute to pick you up. Remember? You just can't give up."

"The hell I can't. Your trip to the bottom of the Atlantic is shot full of holes. And I'm not falling into that trap. I'm not going down there with my wife in the hands of some crazy terrorist."

"Cary. Think about what you're saying? Everyone we could

assign, in every agency possible, is looking for Victoria. You can help her more by following through with the *Titanic*.

"Why do you think they kidnapped her? Do you actually believe they want you to dive the *Titanic?* If you come home, you'll play into their hands. They want you home. They hope you won't go after the *Omar*. They pray to Allah you'll come after Victoria and waste precious time while they're salvaging a thirty million dollar artifact they can use for terrorizing and killing more. . . . "

"You son-of-a-bitch. What do you think they're going to do with Victoria? Take her to Disneyland? What fantasy world do you live in? You've been a spy so long you've lost all contact with reality."

"Cary," interrupted Bramson.

"You think they're just going to let her lie there without hurting her, or God knows what . . . "

"Nakamura has been assigned to head up the task force."

There was silence.

"Jennifer Nakamura?" Parker listened now.

"With the resources allocated to her...she'll find Victoria. Believe me, there haven't been this many resources appropriated for a missing-person search since the Lindbergh kidnapping. You can't help her, except by fighting those bastards on your turf. The turf you know and understand best, two-and-a-half miles down."

"You actually believe I can concentrate on a damned jewel-adorned book, possibly rotting on the ocean floor, when my wife is in terrorist hands?"

"You've got to, Cary. First of all, we only suspect it was terrorists. Could be some local burglar who's taken her hostage. You're obligated to find and secure that book before it gets into Third World hands—even if there's a worse-case episode. You can't let Ragem hold the world hostage."

The silence that followed seemed interminable. The colonel could say no more. He waited for a response.

The rage had finally subsided, but the intensity came in a voice that gave chills to a man who already had known the taste and smell of death.

"Bramson, I've been reasonable with you and your requests. But you've broken into the sanctity of my family. Not just my home. You've invaded my family with your reckless adventures. I blame you for what's happened to Victoria. And let me tell you . . .

"Let me tell you. If you don't find my wife, Colonel, you'll wish you could change places with Aldrich Ames. Do you understand?"

Bramson had expected a severe response. He might have said the same had his own wife of thirty-four years been kidnapped. But he could not reply. He was worried, as much or more than Parker, about Cary's wife. He knew what these terrorists were capable of doing.

"Do you understand?" Cary repeated slowly, in as threatening a voice he could engage.

"Dr. Parker, you have my assurances we will find Victoria. That's all I can say."

Cary slowly fumbled for the phone hook and disconnected the man he had quickly grown to resent. Exhausted, he leaned back into the thick pillows on the bed. His tears drained to the pillowcase as he quietly pleaded for help.

———

God help me, were the only words that emanated from Victoria Parker's mind as she struggled out of a drugged stupor. Her drowsiness was heavy and held her to a confined space, like coming out of the deepest sleep. She tried to assess where she was. She had lost track of the days, the hours—the time lost somewhere between then and now.

What happened? How long has it been?

Her shoulders and neck ached and her head throbbed with pain she had never known. She was still as her mind searched for answers. Then she tried to move arms and legs.

Her hands were bound from behind, and legs were tied above

the ankles. She struggled to turn her head. It throbbed, with every movement, as the drug's aftereffects pounded at her senses. Slices of visions passed before her as she fought to remember an encounter with several strange men.

She remembered running, but little else. *I hit someone in the face . . . no, in the . . . who were they? Who are they? Why do they want me?*

A heavy cloth wrapped her head and covered her eyes. It felt and smelled like a cheap motel towel. The odor of thick gaffer's tape penetrated Victoria's senses as she realized it was wrapped around the towel as a binding, and also covered her mouth.

Victoria panicked as she grasped that she could only breath through her nose. Then, she forced herself to calm down.

I've got to control myself. Don't panic. For God's sake, don't panic. Why am I here? Oh, my God, the children, the children. Please someone help me. Cary, why did this happen? Please God, please help me, please . . . her tears were absorbed by the towel.

She tried to call out or scream, but her appeals were muffled by the tape. She fought to keep from blacking out. Fear crept into her mind, and she struggled to chase it away with other thoughts. But it was too difficult to consider her circumstances. Fifteen minutes passed before she felt strong enough to think again.

She felt cramped and cold.

Am I in a car trunk? There's no movement. Maybe its a parking lot where someone will hear me. Victoria kicked against a wall at her back. It sounded hollow. More wooden than metallic. She searched her mind for answers. There was no smell of rubber from a spare tire. Though the space smelled musty as a car trunk might. There were unfamiliar odors. Odors that conflicted with her real-world perceptions. And there was the smell of . . . *of coffee. My God, its coffee.*

There was the sharp smell of weeds, or trees . . . or grass. Not freshly mowed. It was still too early for that. There was a cold and crisp feeling to the air, despite the closed-in, musty feeling of her confinement.

Her eyes searched the darkness behind the binding for more hints. She listened carefully for anything that might give away her location. It was so still, so quiet. Yet, there were sounds. Nearby sounds, but unconnected.

Now she heard the crackling sound of a fire and she smelled the burning of wood as smoke crept through the cracks and filled her nostrils. In happier times, it would have come from camp-outs on the beach. Hot dog roasts with Cary and the girls. Marshmallows fried to a crisp at the end of a bent hanger. But now the smoke told harsher tales. Of distant places, she knew not where.

There was an aroma of cooking—an unfamiliar, spicy smell that grew more pungent as moments passed. Hunger crept upon her. She pushed it aside to think, plan . . . escape.

She listened again. Distant birds chirping. An owl somewhere in the distance. Gurgling, trickling, dripping—continuously repeating sounds.

Water. she thought. *I'm near water.*

Victoria focused on the sounds of water.

Gutter water? She listening intently. *No, too heavy a sound. Too rapid. Rushing. That's it. Too rapid a sound.*

She thought for a moment.

No sounds of waves, like the ocean. Continuous water, rushing water . . . rushing . . . over rocks . . . over . . . no, around branches and tree roots. It must be a stream. Yes. Water in a stream . . . a river.

Victoria gathered her senses, and heard indistinct voices at a distance. She couldn't make out their origin or understand their meaning. They got closer. Maybe they would help her. She kicked about her space—kicking the walls that held her captive. Screaming under the tape that held her silent. Hoping someone would hear her and save her from this torment. The voices were closer. Maybe . . .

No. It can't be. Please don't let it be them.

The voices, the accents...were those of the kidnappers. Suddenly, it came back. Victoria's heart sank as she recalled the break-in. The chase down the hallway. And the attack. Then, she remembered no more. Her head ached and throbbed severely.

The voices approached the area. Then footsteps on metal. Her space shook slightly. Then the footsteps walked on a hollow wooden floor. And the voices were louder. Something was said. . .laughter followed. Metal hinges creaked as a wooden door was lifted out of the way and locked in place with a slip-pin—a rusted nail. Despite Victoria's blindfold, bright light seeped through the towel and she was no longer in total darkness.

"Ah, Mrs. Parker. How are we today?" said a voice with a measured Arabic and English accent.

Victoria pretended to be asleep. Someone roughly nudged her side. She feigned a groggy sound.

"Mrs. Parker. There is no need to pretend you're still under the influence of the drug." Rahman ripped off the thick tape from her mouth.

Victoria yelled in pain, "Damn you!" *No*, she thought, *I won't give them the benefit of* . . .

"Where am I? Who are you. And what in God's name am I doing here?" She tried to see faces through a small slit of light near the tip of her nose. But the angle was impossible.

"In good time," said Rahman. "Shortly, it will all be over."

She knew more than one person was inside. But so far she had only heard one voice.

"All what? What are you talking about? Untie me, now."

"Maybe later, Victoria Parker." She heard him walk away.

"How do you know my name? Why am I here?"

There was no response. Just low whispers from somewhere in the room.

"Please, untie my arms. I'm in terrible pain. Please," she said softly. "At least tie them in front of me, so my shoulders and neck won't hurt so much."

There was no answer.

"I beg of you. In . . . in the name of Allah."

Al-Salih glanced at his two partners and smiled. Each shrugged as they puffed on their Capstan cigarettes. Rahman stirred a pot of fava beans over a woodburning stove. Al-Mamun used his dagger to carve a sharp-pointed stick, from a thick poplar tree branch cut outside their old, abandoned safe-house.

Ahmed ducked under the panel door and over their captive's bunkbed.

"You know of Allah?" he said. Victoria smelled his soured breath and a body odor that hinted of no baths for quite some time.

"I know of the *Koran*," she said softly, hoping for a sympathetic vote.

Ahmed shoved her over on her stomach and began untying her hands. Victoria groaned as she forced her head to the side in order to breath through the towel. She gasped for air and her muscles tightened and cramped.

"Oh, God, please. Quickly, my neck is cramping. Please hurry, please. It hurts so bad."

"Be patient, the knot is tight," said Ahmed. He turned to the others. Subhi, throw me your dagger."

For an instant, two visions flashed in Victoria's mind. One was of relief from a rope cut free. The other was death by dagger, if they had no use for her.

She felt cold metal on her wrists as the rope instantly fell away, and she brought her arms forward.

"Please, do not attempt any foolishness," Ahmed warned. "Or you will be dispatched in the blink of an eye, as they say." He handed the dagger back to Al-Mamun.

A wicked laugh emanated from a corner of the room. Subhi Al-Mamun resumed his whittling. Ahmed took another piece of rope from the floor.

"So, you know the *Koran*?" Ahmed spoke, again, as he wrapped the rope around and under Victoria's waist, to form a belt.

"'In the Name of God, the Merciful, the Compassionate,'" quoted Victoria Parker. "'Praise belongs to God, the Lord of all Being, the All-merciful, the All-compassionate . . . ' I believe that's the way it begins," she continued in an attempt to distract him.

Ahmed tied the rope securely to her hands as he listened to

the Christian quoting Muhammad.

Thank you for small favors, thought Parker as she remembered the magic escape chains her daughter, Marlowe, had received on her twelfth birthday. She recalled the trick behind the escape. *Clasp hands firmly and rigidly, as if around an invisible ball. Aim the elbows out and away from the body so a wider band of rope is required, and to present the illusion that the hands are tightly bound. As the hands are brought in and collapsed together, the rope relaxes and falls off.*

Victoria extended the idea to the "belt-like" rope, wrapped around her waist, as she pulled it slightly away from her body with her wrists—protracting her stomach to give the illusion the rope was indeed tight around her body. It would appear taut until she relaxed. Then it, and the hand rope, could easily be pulled out of when the occasion presented itself.

Now was not the occasion.

"But you have forgotten the last line of the stanza," said Rahman, as he tasted boiled beans from a wooden spoon.

"I'm sorry," she said. "It's been years since my Comparative Religion class at college."

"Let me remind you," said a third voice—the man with the dagger. Victoria heard him rise and step heavily to her side.

"The last line of the first stanza in *The Holy Koran* refers to, '. . . the Master of the Day of Doom.'" Al-Mamun poked his whittled stick-point into Victoria's thigh and startled her.

Ahmed pushed Subhi from her and angrily spoke in Arabic. Several words were exchanged that Victoria could not understand. And it became quiet once more.

The terrorist resumed tying her knots with the rope and completed securing their captive.

"Thank you," said Victoria, in as sincere a voice as she could summon. She rolled her shoulders and slowly turned her head and neck in different directions to relax the muscles. She could not see her captors, but she had found a soft spot in one of them.

"Now, please remove this terrible cover from my eyes," she pleaded.

The request drew laughs as Ahmed closed the drop-down door to the bunk and walked over to the stove.

"At least give me some food," Victoria yelled through the enclosure. "I'm truly hungry."

"Andak li fiTaar 'eeh?" Ahmed asked of breakfast.

"Fuul mudammas," said Rahman.

"Haaga kamaan?"

"Wi 'ahwa walla shaay."

"Give some mudammas to the lady," Ahmed ordered, loud enough for her to hear. "And some tea. The coffee is too strong."

———

PART IV

TARÅBULUS, LIBYA

FORGED from a rocky promontory along the Mediterranean coast-line—part of the old Barbary Coast—the ancient city of Oea, now Taråbulus (Tripoli), is Libya's foremost seaport. The venturesome capital of this principally Moslem, North African country has been a lively center for the processing of fish, the manufacture and trade of building materials, richly woven carpets, popular brands of cigarettes, and for the selling of its citrus, olives, and vegetables.

One Libyan industry, less conspicuous and more deadly, is the breeding and manufacture of biological agents, and the stock-piling and issuance of these infectious, pathogenic microbes for use in territorial and guerrilla warfare.

Tensions generated between Libya and the United States, over the production of biological weapons, and over U.S. trade restric-tions as a result of such illegal stockpiling, was considered stan-dard fare in diplomatic channels. For Faheed Al Mar Ragem, the friction was beneficial. Despite Libya's drastically declining oil revenues and weakness of the Libyan dinar, its interventionist leaning government officials provided Ragem and others, such as terrorist Abu Nidal, with a share of financial backing—and a base from which they could launch activities. And that was the manner of support the ALFAHAD preferred.

Ragem, accompanied by two members of the ALFAHAD, had decided a drive across the coastal highway, to Taråbulus, would be most satisfying as he embarked on this new phase of his life.

Success will be ours . . . with the help of Allah, he hastened to add, as he had slipped into Egypt and eventually crossed over the border into Libya. He had followed the highway past the clear waters of the Mediterranean Sea through Banghâzî, Misrâtah, and on into the new, southwestern quarter of Libya's capital.

The terrorists spent their first night in a guarded suite at the magnificent Jamahiriya Hotel, as personal guests of Colonel Muammar Qadhafi—*Leader of the Revolution*—where they quietly dined with Libya's finance minister, and with Jadallah Tarik, captain of his soon-to-be-turned-over research ship, the *A'isha*.

The following day, Ragem's group was escorted to their converted freighter, sitting among Libya's warships in the Navy shipyard. A light rain, during the night, left the wharf cleaner than usual in the early morning sun. The smell of nearby commercial canneries wafted through the port as the men crossed the gangway to the *A'isha*. A plain green Libyan flag stirred in the breeze, from a mast high above the bridge.

Ragem stood alone on the foredeck and surveyed his new domain. Seventy-five meters in length, with a displacement of 9,575 tons, the twin-screw, diesel-engined *A'isha* was a small, modified freighter with an enlarged, open fantail adapted for launching deep-submergence vehicles. Capable of housing a crew of twenty and a complement of nineteen scientists and technicians, for this trip there would be a full house.

The transformed mercantile ship seemed out of place, sitting among a fleet of ex-Soviet and Yugoslav missile-armed frigates, corvettes and minesweepers. Several gunboats, a patrol boat, and a missile-armed fast attack craft rested nearby. An ex-Soviet diesel-driven submarine was in drydock, across the bay. But Ragem put it all into perspective—his ship would be armed as well.

Along with top secret cargo, deckhands were busy loading crates of large and small weaponry that would be readied for whatever circumstance they might encounter on the high seas.

I could easily grow accustomed to this lifestyle, Ragem thought as he gazed out across the harbor in the direction of Malta. *Perhaps Asma and the children would enjoy a trip at sea one day. We will do more together*, he resolved.

"Mr. Ragem," a voice interrupted.

"Yes?" He turned to see three men approaching.

"Ah, Captain Tarik."

"Mr. Ragem . . . this is Professor Kosuge," said the captain, "the *Yoritomo-class* mini-sub designer."

A slight man of medium build, Kosuge bowed from the waist, his head low, hands at his side. Ragem acknowledged the traditional greeting with an appropriate gesture.

Ragem spoke abstrusely, "I look forward to inspecting your marvel of engineering, Professor. At dinner, last night, Captain Tarik was highly complimentary of your work."

"Thank you Ragem-son," the round-faced professor bowed once more. "You will be very pleased, I'm sure."

"And this is Dr. Hirao, our oceanographer" said the captain. "He just arrived in our country two hours ago."

Too rotund to bend at the waist, the scientist stepped forward and bowed slightly from the chest. His stomach protruded from his polo shirt as his weight shifted. He was already sweating profusely through his clothing.

"Ah, yes," said Ragem, wondering how such a large man could ever explore the ocean in a submersible. "You are the specialist in marine artifacts. Shortly we will have a prize to make your mouth water, Doctor. The *Great Omar*."

"I have heard of this *Omar*," said Dr. Hirao. "Rest assured, it will be in good hands when it is brought up."

"I only expect the best from my associates," said Ragem, "and, of course, fidelity in our relationship aboard this vessel." His eyes pierced their space as if double-edged rapiers had severed the Mediterranean air between them. Since Ragem's reputation preceded him, the engineer and the scientist felt compromised in their work. But both men had already signed an unholy pact to maintain their own reputations in Japan, and each owed his soul and allegiance to the Yakusa.

"Shall I give you a tour of the ship?" Tarik suggested, feeling the tension.

"Of course," Ragem stood back.

"We'll work our way to the fantail where the two subs are stored."

Ragem appeared enthusiastic at the suggestion and, for a moment, his mood became upbeat. "Lead on, Captain Tarik."

The scientist and engineer wondered how deep they were in with this chameleon, Ragem. *Assist him in whatever he needs, and we'll all be rich men*, their superior had told them in Yokohama. *Cross him and you're dead*, they were warned.

Ragem had sized up the captain at dinner the evening before. Of muscular build and tone, a fine frame, and well-tanned, Tarik was too adroit a man to have spent his life as a merchant marine. Ragem suspected, correctly, that Tarik was a soldier of fortune, a remnant of Colonel Qadhafi's Revolutionary Command Council, before it was abolished in 1977—placed aboard the *A'isha* to do the colonel's bidding. Remaining faithful to, and serving the needs of his colonel was paramount on Tarik's mind.

Ragem respected those who were loyal. He also understood that Tarik was not to be treated as the others. For the captain had a direct pipeline to his prime source of funding.

For a brief moment, Tarik's devotion and allegiance reminded Ragem of his closest friend, Khorassani, now dead and in cold storage somewhere in London. It placed a veil of melancholy over the mission. He had so hoped Karim Abdul would have been on the *A'isha* to share in their latest victory. But he shook off the ghost and turned his attention to what was ahead.

The men first moved to the bridge where the captain brought them up-to-date on the latest in navigational and other technology provided by their Japanese partners. The Captain showed

Ragem his cabin—the best on board next to his own—and acquainted the other men with their sleeping quarters. Then they roamed down and across the deck, occasionally ducking into a corridor for a side-tour into the ship's store, the mess, and the converted hold, aft, for scientific research and for protection of the *Great Omar*, once brought on board. Ragem was not made aware of the secured hold, and its secret cargo, below the foredeck.

"Our crew has been at work two weeks," Tarik pointed out. "By all calculations, we should be ready for our voyage by this evening. As soon as the remaining scientific staff arrives." He looked to Kosuge.

"Currently we have six on board," Kosuge reported to Ragem. "The remainder of our eighteen scientists and technicians will arrive on a chartered plane at ten, this morning," he added.

The technical and scientific staff, including the *Yoritomo* pilots and navigators, scuba-diving team, control station/project supervisors, computer technicians, and backup crew had all been assembled in Japan, to provide support for the upcoming dives.

One additional independent observer would board the *A'isha* at the last moment, and join them for the trip. Arturo "The Bear" Gregorio—a member of the Ignazio family from Sicily. And a first cousin to the chairman of the board for *STAR*—the super-secret, underworld dealers in black market nuclear weapons and heavy Soviet ordnance.

The group of men moved amidships and approached the stern. The captain pulled on a refrigerator-style door and crossed its threshold. "Here's our submersible control station," the captain said proudly to Ragem. "Built to exact specifications."

Constructed of four large shipping containers welded together and plunked aft of the crew's quarters, the control station had cramped but adequate room for launch, expedition, and recovery of their underwater vehicles.

The three men stepped inside the highly air-conditioned

room. The cold was a marked difference from the already humid air outside. Four men and a woman were installing electronic components, soldering wires, and testing connections.

"How is it?" Kosuge asked, over the shoulder of an electronics specialist.

Reiko Fujihara could see Kosuge's reflection in her video monitor, "We should have it together and working by late tonight." She resumed her work without waiting for a response.

Banks of monitors, scanning screens, and tracking devices filled the room. A plotting table and navigational equipment sat at the center of it all, next to a plastic model of the *Yoritomo*. The technicians ignored all visitors, knowing they had a deadline to meet.

"Let's not disturb them any longer," suggested Dr. Hirao.

"Yes," said Kosuge, "I will show you our submersibles."

They exited the control room and negotiated their way aft. Mr. Kosuge smiled widely as they approached two *Yoritomo-class* subs, stowed in a makeshift, sheltered berth on the afterdeck.

Tucked up close behind the control station was the latest in Japanese underwater technology—two subs heavily secured to the decking with cables. The larger J10-6M second generation vehicle sat on steel tracks inside its own launch and recovery system rig. The smaller prototype, J10-4.5M, hung like a cocoon above.

"These will bring your treasures home, if other plans fail," Kosuge said proudly. He reached through the flotation launcher and touched the top of the sub's anechoic tiles. "This is our newest and largest *Yoritomo*. Capable of diving over six thousand meters, which far surpasses most other DSRV's."

Ragem looked questioningly at the engineer.

"Deep submergence research vehicles."

"Of course," said Ragem.

"We have named this sub *Kabuki*, because its as rich and visual in its engineering and striking in its styling as is the tradition of our famous dramatic theatre. Notice the mastery of lines and symmetry, the extraordinary beauty and precision of its swept angles, and the harmony of color interpreted in the design. That is

Kabuki. "

"What I see," Ragem interrupted, "are black tiles on a vehicle that must recover the *Omar* and the jewels. I couldn't care less about how you put it together. Just be certain that it works when it must." Though he found it difficult to understand the engineer's interpretation of lines and symmetry, Ragem stepped around the submersible and continued his visual inspection.

Kosuge was angered and insulted by Ragem's arrogant remarks. But he remained quiet and bowed subserviently to the terrorist.

Ragem stepped over steel tracks that extended out from under the submersibles. The tracks ran to the fantail where a large crane supported a device designed to allow underwater, rather than over-the-water, launching.

"This small sub was built first . . . our prototype," said Kosuge, pointing above, in an attempt to recover from the negative encounter. "We call it *Amagaeru* . . . for little frog."

"This is to be used as well?" said Ragem.

"Only as a backup. In case of emergency."

The largest of the *Yoritomo-class* sub's angular fuselage was tucked between highly swept wings. This was not a mini-sub, by some standards. The wing span was twenty feet, with an overall length of nearly fourteen, from nose to tail.

Constructed with an enriched titanium hull, a modified cubic-zirconian outer shell gave it added strength and was overlaid with fibreglass-covered anechoic tiles for stealth. Designed to eliminate nearly ninety-six percent of the electromagnetic visibility feedback that most sonars are engineered to pickup, the DSRV was meant to be physically traced only by coded transponders that converted electronic signals fed directly into a homing device onboard the mothership.

The sub was the paradigm of underwater technical achievement for the darker side of a private industrial complex located in the Pacific Rim—at the highest level controlled by members of the elite organized crime unit, the Yakusa.

"Tell me about this launch system," Ragem pointed to the peculiar cage that surrounded the *Yoritomo*.

"It's an adaptation of a design originally meant for AUV's . . . autonomous underwater vehicles. Unmanned subs. Since we're utilizing a converted ship not originally designed for oceanographic research, we wanted to be certain we could launch these vehicles in most any sea state with a minimal loss factor."

"You see, Ragem-son," Dr. Hirao took over, "the ship and, therefore, the submersible is subject to the influence of roll and heave motion in various states of weather. Any conditions above state-four weather can be extremely dangerous."

"State four is..?"

"A breeze somewhere between seventeen and twenty-one knots, creating pronounced, longer waves than usual . . . uh, one to one-and-a-half meters in height."

"With white caps . . . " added the engineer.

"And a chance of spray," said Hirao. "All combine to make it more difficult for a safe launch."

"You see," continued the oceanographer, "a specially designed research ship can continue to work in rougher sea states, under some circumstances. But we must take into account the differences in using a modified freighter, such as the *A'isha*, versus the use of a research ship specifically designed for deep submergence exploration. This ship was originally designed to cut through storms, not launch vehicles off its stern.

"Above sea-state four, the wind velocity and wave force will cause the *A'isha* to roll and heave violently enough to prompt concern, when sitting idle in the water during a launch sequence. Under these circumstances, if a sub is caught between the ship's decking and the surface of the water during launch, docking, or recovery, it becomes unsafe."

The captain spoke up, "That's why we've not been in a hurry to leave port today. There's a violent storm in the North Atlantic. We must avoid it to protect our ship...and our objective."

"How long a delay?" said Ragem.

"The storm should blow itself out by tomorrow. If we depart late this afternoon, we will clear the worst part of it."

Ragem was displeased. "We will not delay our departure because of a storm."

You don't understand," Tarik said cautiously, "this is no minor weather disturbance. Ships twice the size of the *A'isha* are remaining in port to protect passengers and cargo."

Ragem stared directly into the eyes of the captain, "We *will* leave by twelve hundred hours. Do you understand?"

Tarik glared at Ragem, "All reports say shipping lanes in the North Atlantic are too dangerous. And they're still reporting sightings of icebergs. If we leave earlier than seventeen hundred hours, we could jeopardize our plans."

"Do I make myself clear?" Ragem said in a guttural tone.

Tarik resolved to comply. But he would enter this discussion in his logbook. He knew he was smarter than Ragem, and would lay back on the speed of the ship to delay arrival at the coordinates for the *Titanic*.

"Quite clear, Mr. Ragem."

———

THE NORTH ATLANTIC

"HOW many more hours of this damned storm?" the barrel-chested John Holt yelled in exasperation, to no one in particular, as he piloted *Neptune's Knot* through the thrashing North Atlantic disturbance. An immense uprising swell kept anyone on the bridge from answering. Holt's dark chiseled face was taut from the strain of piloting through what he had called a suicidal mission.

Yet, if anyone was trusted with the helm, it was Holt. As Parker's chief navigator for the past ten years, he was held in high esteem by the crew.

Six years after graduation, with a Master's Degree in Political

Science from Howard University, Holt had traded the politics of Washington for adventure on the high seas. He had found several Washington politicians and their handlers to be " . . . insidious, self-serving phonies with little interest in assisting constituents."

Calder always said it didn't take much to set Holt off when politics came up. With See-Life's team for nearly fourteen years, Holt had told Parker, "It's safer in the pit of an underwater volcano than in a room of congressional staffers. I'd rely on my instincts in a ketch in the middle of a typhoon, before I'd trust those bastards."

Though he had seen too many instances of under-the-table vote buying with Mafia-controlled unions and crime-syndicate bosses, to want to remain in politics, he felt he might have to eat his words, after this storm . . . that is, if they ever made it through.

Holt's rock-hard muscles throbbed with pain as he held tight to the helm and steered a sinuous course. He looked for lulls and windows—to avoid broadsides that had ambushed their ship from every angle for more than twelve hours.

Neptune's Knot moved in lateral motions, back and forth, in and out of the few breaks and troughs that came between hits. Windshield wipers only pointed up the futility of the moment, with their inability to clear the glass for more than a micro-second.

"Can't see a damned thing," Holt yelled over the storm.

Gale force Arctic winds ripped across the Atlantic Ocean, and tore at the research vessel. And the *Neptune* pitched and rolled in the high seas and cold, pelting rain that bombarded the ship.

"Big one off the bows!" Parker called out. "Wedge in between something and hold on tight."

"Brace yourselves!" Holt ordered.

The wave struck directly at the bows and rolled up over the bridge, as tons of seawater covered the ship and darkened its interior. The vessel pitched forward with the downside of a swell, and Holt turned his head quickly left and right to check for potential broadsides—his bronze eyes glowing in the dimmed light of the bridge.

With their Omega life vests donned for the duration of the storm, the entire crew was alert to the danger as wave after wave assailed their ship. Then, two hundred yards of roiling sea surged toward the *Neptune* from its portside, as white foam devoured the dark green sea ahead.

Holt spun the wheel around and guided his ship head-to.

The *Neptune* rose almost vertically as it maneuvered into a potentially backbreaking heading—straight into the wall of water. The bows hit the crest.

Then, water exploded to port and starboard as it cut across the razor's edge, putting a chink into the wave's armor as *Neptune's* full weight carried it out and over the top at full throttle toward another open cavity below.

"Ready to reverse engines," Parker warned. "Ready . . . "

The white foam crashed against the hull with a vengeance and sped along its perimeter in a maddening race to the stern.

"Reverse engines," Parker commanded. "Hold on! Here we go!"

Holt reversed engines over the cavity to slow forward momentum, then spun the wheel hard to starboard in an attempt to ride the trough and come headlong into the next wave at full throttle.

He jammed the throttle forward to gain speed, but the wave crossed underneath, lifting the stern completely out of the water.

The cycloidal engines raced out of control at full speed—pushing only at wet air, until the stern crashed down once more. *Neptune* grabbed at the water and jerked forward in an attempt to meet the wave head-on. But it was too late.

"Beam-to! Starboard!" Calder cried out.

"Hold on. Get a good grip," yelled Holt. His hands turned pale as his grasp tightened on the wheel.

A wall of water, the size of a three story building, hit them broadside and sent everyone flying. The wave grabbed at *Neptune's* surface and exploded like a supernova up and over the ship in an attempt to pass straight through steel. Pushed to a forty-five degree angle, as it fought the laws of physics to survive, the *Neptune's* hawseholes shot water out the sides like fire-hydrants gone amok.

"What's the wind measuring?" asked Parker.

Calder held on tight as he glanced at the Alden radio facsimile, "Fifty-two knots."

The vessel rolled heavily to port, and Calder looked at the machine once more. "Gusting to sixty-three."

"Damn, that's force-ten. What's the Doppler showing?"

Calder checked the screen, "The bad news is we've got at least three hours of this shit left."

"And there's good news?" Parker looked back to the sea, as he held onto the portside window railing.

"Yeah, we should be sitting on top of our old friend by the time the storm dies." Calder forced a smile.

Parker looked out the window, due north. The *Titanic* would be there, as she had been for decades. *No storm could break her up*, he thought. *Just time. . . . And scavengers.* He glanced over at Henri Dupont, but let the thought drop as the ship rose high once more.

The cold, gusty winds had continued from the previous night. The northerly disturbance collided with *Neptune's Knot* ten hours after the ship left St. John's, Newfoundland on a southeast bearing. The weather, caused by a shift of the polar high-pressure zone, had progressively worsened by the hour. Two enormous fronts intersected on top of the ship's position—approaching the edge of Grand Banks—as they followed their heading deeper into the North Atlantic.

Despite a clear morning, no amount of warmth from the sun could have prevented the frigid Arctic winds from rushing south and merging with the warmer elements to form an unstable air mass. By noon, dense, dark nimbo-stratus clouds had quickly materialized overhead. Sheets of rain merged with the green water and the northerly blast to make any sailor caught in the storm think twice about his profession.

"If we weren't so far north of the Equator," said Holt, "I'd swear we were in the middle of a cyclone." He looked at Smithsonian's Chief Archivist, Harold Chapman, who was turning shades of color—mostly pale white. Dupont remained quiet as he grasped the charts table for support.

"We haven't hit winds this bad since the Azores," Calder shouted.

"I'm not worried about the winds," said Parker, as the vessel was slammed from another direction and jarred off course. "It's the wave action that bothers me. And any growlers still lurking out there."

The farther north they traveled, the more likely surviving icebergs could become a threat. And breaking wave forces exerted pressures of over a ton per square foot as they repeatedly punished the *Neptune*. Bergs or waves. Either way, Parker knew it could have calamitous results.

"The waves are wreaking havoc on our *Shelties*."

"Yeah," Calder said above the din, "but we have them tied down better than a specialist in S n' M."

"I worry about their electronics getting slapped around." Parker's voice was hoarse from yelling for so many hours. He stared out over the bridge.

Wave patterns were no longer predictable. The aberrant sea created whitecaps that stretched to the horizon, while the surging ocean undulated like an enormous writhing snake. Bizarre, uncharted boundaries randomly appeared and disappeared, as the helmsman battled to claim sailable territory and the sea offered up a severe pounding.

Holt reversed the propulsion system to back off from an oncoming wave. As the ship plummeted to the low point of a gap between the surging waves, he corrected his position to bring *Neptune's Knot* within range of the *Titanic's* coordinates.

"Bearing one-six-one," Holt blared out. "Can't say how long

that'll hold," he added sarcastically.

Immense patches of foam blew across the water in thick, meringue-like streaks. Holt continued to make small course corrections to buy any smooths he could find between troughs.

Though just past 1300, the day was as dark as the abyss below.

"Wish we'd fabricated sub enclosures," Parker said. "All we need is a deep depression trough and one mammoth wave could knock those babies apart. Especially one carrying a berg." He was visibly concerned.

"Holy Mother of . . . " Calder couldn't finish his sentence as he glanced out the starboard side. The ledge of a swell picked up their stout vessel like a piece of floating bark, and prepared to drop it vertically like a centrifugal ride in a theme park. Only this ride had no waiting line.

"Jesus . . . " Chapman cried.

"Looks as though you got your trough, Cary," yelled Holt.

There was a time, in Parker's youth, when he and his friends would load up pockets of quarters and ride the old wooden roller coaster at Santa Monica's Pacific Ocean Park. They'd shoot through space for hours, without getting off, by shoving their two-bits in the operator's hand, while screaming and laughing, "We're goin' around, again!"

The old dinosaur of a ride would swing them out over the ocean and rip down through the twists, turns, and bone-jarring dips. And the speeding cars shook their insides like an egg beater whipping up an old fashioned earthquake. Since then, Parker's secret thrills had come from finding the most unmerciful coasters in the world—and researching them, as he put it, " . . . for the sake of science."

But science had its limits, as veteran sea legs fought for balance, and an oncoming wave became a backwash on the edge of the giant trough. It opened up suddenly, like a chasm to hell.

Holt held the wheel fast as the ship was tossed high on the lip of the void. *Neptune* floated in space for an eternity, then quickly raced downward as though some unseen hand had pushed its deadweight from a skyscraper.

"Hold on!" Parker yelled, as the ship's bows aimed straight downward and surfed in a seemingly never-ending ride to the bottom.

Everyone grappled for something firm to hold them up, as the boat's floor gave way to open space and stomachs moved into tthroats. For an instant, the crew felt like astronauts in a zero gravity cabin.

Dupont fell against the chart table, hit the back of his head coming down off the edge, and papers went flying. Holt and Calder slammed against the ship's wheel and were pulled to the floor by the momentum of their fall. Everyone else, including Parker, went straight to the floor and uncontrollably slid to the low point.

Then, as suddenly as the vessel had reached the bottom, the bow of the ship dug into the base of the depression, and the opposite side of the monstrous swell surged over the top mast and swallowed the ship.

Chapman screamed in panic and closed his eyes.

The ship's expansion joints creaked loudly as they flexed under high pressure, accommodating the extreme shifts in the arc that the *Neptune* took on between edges of the depression. The vessel's lights blinked off a moment before the emergency lights flashed on, casting an eerie green glow from the swamping sea water as it cascaded down, rushed across the decks like a foaming rabid dog, and fell past the hull on its way to nowhere.

The crew slid in the opposite direction and *Neptune's Knot* abruptly rose to meet the darkened sky as the swell sank from its own weight and moved on.

There was no chance to secure the ship's wheel as it spun wildly on its own. With every ounce of strength Holt had left to battle the forces of nature, he struggled to pick himself up off the floor of the bridge.

"Someone grab the wheel," he shouted wearily.

The ship had turned to port, on its own, parallel with the next swell—an oncoming wave that would severely broadside it if they couldn't come around quickly enough. Parker, Holt and Calder scrambled from their awkward positions to regain steerage.

The swell amplified as it headed toward the *Neptune*, and the three men raced to set the wheel for the ship's course at head-to.

Holt gunned the propulsion system, and momentum carried the vessel up and over the swell just before it could form a tight ridge and break overhead.

The entire crew whooped and laughed off their nervousness, having survived another assault.

"Get the license of that locomotive," Calder shouted, and everyone laughed at the less than graceful positions they had assumed.

"Good as any roller coaster," said one of the crew.

"Cedar Point's *Raptor* has it beat!" kidded Parker. But he turned to glare at Dupont as if to say, *You son-of-a-bitch. If it weren't for you, we wouldn't be out here.*

Dupont ignored the obvious, maintaining balance as he grabbed papers off the floor.

"Hazard a guess on the height of the last one . . . trough to ridge?" Parker glanced at Calder.

"Like I had time to triangulate it . . . " Calder forced a laugh.

"Just a guess?"

"Eighty feet or more, I'd say. Towered at least twenty feet higher than the bridge."

"Eight stories," Parker whistled over the clamor. "Let's hope we don't beat the *Ramapo's* record of twelve."

"Keep your eyes open for the next one," warned Holt. "At the rate we're going we could break any record."

Parker nudged Calder. "After that last ride, we should take another look at our babies."

He turned to help a very seasick Chapman, still struggling to get up from the floor. "Better find a softer place to lie down."

Chapman rushed across the bridge for another disposable bag. And Parker wondered if the once smug archivist was still glad he had come along.

"Let's check the rope safety system, while we're out there."

Calder agreed reluctantly and pulled two still-wet anti-exposure suits off the wall. The two suited up.

"Maintain bearings straight into the winds where you can, John." The *Shelties* were more protected when the waves broke over the bow.

"I'm having a hell of a time maintaining steerage as it is." Blasts of sea and wind bashed against the forecastle and windows of the bridge and made it difficult to be heard.

"Henri . . . relieve John at the helm in five minutes. Get Marshall up here to relieve you in twenty."

Dupont begrudgingly moved next to Holt to assist.

"Hold your speed to one knot while we're out there," said Parker. "Seems worse than it was an hour ago. What's the barograph recording?"

"The glass has dropped another four millibars," said Dupont, "and she isn't bottoming out."

"Crap."

"For God's sake watch it out there," warned Holt.

Parker and Calder cinched up their life vests and hooked up the safety harnesses. As they had done just two hours before, they prepared to inspect the tie-downs on the *Shelties* and the storm roping system on deck.

Calder grabbed two emergency survival kit fanny-packs, and handed one to Parker.

"Take your radios," said Dupont, holding out two. "In case of emergency."

"Thanks," said Calder, taken back by the seemingly unselfish act. He placed his radio in its waterproof pocket. Parker could not look Dupont in the eyes at this gesture of goodwill. It seemed out of character. But he took the radio, slid it into a long pocket and stood at the threshold.

"We'll check in every ten minutes," Parker said.

"Turn on your locator beacons," Holt reminded them. "Just in case . . . "

They were grateful to Parker for investing in a directional-loop receiver system and individual mini-locator beacons small enough to fit on every life vest. In a man-overboard or worse-case setting, if the ship went down, anyone wearing an activated beacon could be located from the air or from ships capable of receiving the signals.

Dupont and another crew member opened the hatch against the winds. To prevent it from swinging away from them and exposing the bridge to wave and spray action of the storm, they leaned alongside the metal door and held the latch tightly.

Parker and Calder quickly stepped over the hatch's threshold to exit the bridge. They were immediately drenched as another wave broke against *Neptune's Knot* with an explosive force.

Dupont was the only one who heard them both yell "Shit!"

FBI HEADQUARTERS
STRATEGIC INTELLIGENCE AND OPERATIONS CENTER

A task force of over two hundred men and women had been assigned to the search for Victoria Parker. Agents for the FBI, and select detectives within numerous local police forces, had spread their search throughout most of New England—heading west through large cities and back-road towns—stretching into Pennsylvania and through the tri-state area of West Virginia, Kentucky, and Ohio. All reports were channeled into SIOC at FBI Headquarters, directly to the desk of Agent Nakamura.

FBI's "Rapid Start" computer system was fed reams of information from interviews conducted from the Canadian to the Mexican borders. When potential links and discrepancies were compared, it spit out a series of promising leads—automatically ranked for SIOC's Central Command to assign leg detail. And investigators had combined forces in the tri-state area, to trace possible connections between the attack at the Gilbert Ordnance facility, an overdue Canadian rental car, and Parker's kidnapping.

A license number, from the Gilbert Motel, matched the missing Taurus; confirmation connected the car and the stolen explosives; then, probabilities increased that the terrorists would slip up and be spotted somewhere along the line. And the noose tightened.

An all-points bulletin went out for the car and occupants: "Report sightings only. Do not take action. Occupants holding VIP hostage. Armed and extremely dangerous."

Brutal weather hampered the search, limiting it to ground only. The same storm, hitting the North Atlantic, had stalled and circled back to the eastern seaboard from Canada on down. With the storm's diameter of over two thousand miles, the entire eastern third of the United States had been deluged with rain. Nakamura and her team had grown impatient with the weather, as they waited for more information.

Then came the break Nakamura needed. The Taurus had been spotted in the Keystone State. Described as a dark gray four door, with a long, deep scratch down the left side, a call to SIOC from a Pennsylvania ranger at Cook Forest State Park placed the car at a secluded campsite—tent and camping equipment conspicuously missing. The ranger reported that when he had driven near the occupants, in the storm-darkened twilight, the car hurriedly left the area, heading north of Cooksburg on Highway 36.

Another report was filed by a highway patrolman, placing the Taurus near Oil City. Then, local authorities followed the car until they lost it in the blinding rain, somewhere between Oil City and Franklin, Pennsylvania—an area of the country with which Nakamura was all too familiar.

While still at DC headquarters, Nakamura had rifled through the new leads, looking for every bit of information to confirm suspicions. Realizing she'd already pulled a double shift, with someone due to relieve her at the SIOC desk, her mind jumped into high gear as memories dictated what she must do next.

With her replacement due shortly, Nakamura felt she could take advantage of her knowledge of the area, and head toward Pennsylvania to follow up on the ranger's sighting.

A gut-level feeling gnawed at her. She knew they were close.

Permission to leave was granted from the SIOC commander. She brought her desk replacement up to speed on the new data and made a call before leaving Washington. Following protocol, she notified the FBI's special agent-in-charge—headquarters city, Pittsburgh—that they were coming into their territory.

A revised all-points bulletin was issued, then Nakamura glanced across the Command Center.

"Mike," she said, "get your gear. We're going for a ride."

Agent Mike Archer—assigned to Nakamura during the Victoria Parker search—grabbed his jacket, checked his holster and clip holder, then picked up his bullet-proof vest. His short cut light brown hair underscored his role with the FBI. Average of build and height, Archer was well within the physical requirements for the agency.

"Where're we heading?" he said, as he pulled on his jacket.

"Western Penn. . . . Those parasites are within our grasp."

Archer stuffed the final half of a Little Debbie Creme Cake in his mouth, grabbed his Remington .870 Magnum 26" short-barrel, and followed his supervisor out the door.

Nakamura could barely see through the windshield of her Cherokee as she and Agent Archer pulled off Interstate 80 at Clarion, Pennsylvania, and picked up Highway 322, heading northwest toward Franklin. Knowing of the terrorist's connection with the Mafia's organization, STAR, and having traced the terrorist's path on a map, Nakamura's intuition had reminded her of a past investigation. The two agents now inched their way through the storm in search of an old Mafia hideout.

Jennifer had taken a catnap while the square-jawed, freckled agent drove the first leg out of Washington. Archer slept most of the way after that.

Nakamura's peripheral vision saw two arms stretch toward the car roof.

"You awake?"

"Coulda' slept another hour or two . . . " Archer yawned.

Nakamura strained to see rural street signs through the rain-drenched windshield, "You know, if I'm right, these guys have borrowed an out-of-the-way safe house from the mob."

"All the way out here?"

"Wait'll you see this place."

Rain and hail beat so hard on the car roof it was difficult to talk at normal conversational tones.

"What's so special about it?"

Nakamura smiled, "You'll understand when we get there. We'll call in the HRT once we confirm the safehouse."

"Hope we can find it in this mess."

If Nakamura's hunch proved worthless, there would be no further loss of time on the part of other agents. Though road-blocks had been set up at key points, nothing had been reported since the last sighting.

The Cherokee turned off the main highway onto a side street.

"If I didn't know the area," Nakamura said, "I never would've seen the road signs."

"Hear you spent a couple of years out of Pittsburgh."

"Three, actually. Assigned to Western Pennsylvania . . . Venango County in the north to Allegheny, in the south. Traveled the area so much, I bragged I could drive blindfolded from Highway 70 up to 80, and the back roads in between.

Nakamura reflected for a moment. "Whenever I was caught on the road, between stakeouts, I visited my favorite tourist site—DeBence's Antique Music Museum, in Franklin. It'll have to wait for now."

The rain battered their windshield, and the rhythm of the wipers brought back memories of the old museum's collection of musical antiques.

"Spent many hours at DeBence's winding the hundreds of music boxes, putting nickels in the nickelodeon, and listening to the ol' brightly colored calliope." She looked over at her new partner. "You rookied in Charleston, West Virginia?"

"Yeah, two years." Guileless green eyes sat squarely over his sharp nose, and exuded the enthusiasm he shared with Nakamura for service with the Bureau. "Matter of fact, we heard your name a couple of times in our office . . . when you and Agent Bridges pulled off that big Customs bust outside Pittsburgh."

"That's where we're heading now."

"Yeah? Whadayaknow."

Pennsylvania had been one of Nakamura's many proving grounds as a young agent. It was ironic that this trip had become an extension of an earlier experience. She was treated as an equal among fellow agents, and was respected for her ability to intelligently outsmart the criminal. Still, she was not certain this would be one of those opportunities.

The overworked ventilation system on their GSA-issue, Jeep Grand Cherokee fought the rain's humidity to keep the inside windows from fogging up. Seized in a drug bust, six months before, the 220 horse V8 Cherokee provided a versatile car for this work. With these road conditions, Nakamura and Archer would need it.

Lightning pierced the darkness and had taken out power for hundreds of homes and businesses in the area. Many roads were flooded from the heavier than usual downpour. As the two agents approached the outskirts of Franklin, Nakamura turned onto Pone Lane, worked her way through several darkened country roads, switched onto South Penn Road, then slowed to a crawl as she looked for an old marker from her past.

Barely able to see the sides of the road, an object caught

Nakamura's eye.

"There she is . . . "

"We there?"

"Just the beginning." She put the black Cherokee in reverse, set her bright lights toward the side of the road, and plugged a hand-held spotlight into the lighter socket.

"Aim this near that dirt road over there." She indicated an area that could barely be seen, let alone driven.

They caught a glimpse of the long abandoned, bent rail-track mailbox—marking a worn gravel road Nakamura had traveled before.

"Thank God for small favors," she said as she switched off the country radio station, found on the dial about fifty miles back. Nakamura reversed the car ten more feet to clear the entrance. They left the relative ease of driving on drenched macadam for the luxury of a gravel road that had not been graded in over four years.

"Just like Chicago's eastside," she said, as the Cherokee rode high over time-worn, water-filled ruts. "Better check your seat belt."

The Jeep bounced back and forth as its full-time, four-wheel drive grabbed the rough road and each wheel dug deep into the trench-like depressions. Water splashed high to the sides, then returned to hide the potholes once more.

"Jeez," said Archer. "Forget the four-wheeler. We should've come in here with a road grader."

The winding, gravel road continued on for nearly two miles, as the FBI agents took the Cherokee first past a fire-gutted single-wide trailer, sitting off its foundation, then by an old log cabin with its front door missing. The headlights cast eerie shadows from bent limbs of trees leaning over the road from too much rain.

"Jesus!"

Suddenly, Nakamura slammed on her brakes. The car slid nearly ten yards on the wet gravel, narrowly avoiding a doe and her fawn as they raced across the road for cover.

"You okay?" Archer looked at Nakamura.

"Yeah . . . that got the adrenaline going." She laughed it off and slowly hit the gas pedal. The car picked up speed and the two agents continued on.

The road thinned and curved downhill for another mile where it came to a split. Nakamura stopped the car and thought out loud.

"The north fork leads down to the Allegheny. The northeast fork divides to a rise that overlooks the river. Both circle down to the site."

"I'll trust your judgment on this one."

She turned the wheel and headed for the rise.

Barely able to see the gravel road, Nakamura relied on the grassy-covered berm between the two tire ruts, to restrain her wheels. At the top of the hill, the slope gave way to a flat-topped, tree-lined ridge overlooking the riverbank below.

"There's a clearing between the trees." Archer pointed to the right.

Nakamura slowed down and, exhausted, pulled over and turned off the lights and engine. The rain beat as war drums on the Cherokee's cold metal shell. It was obvious the fury of the storm and several hours driving through it had taken its toll on both agents.

"Let's rest a few minutes," said Nakamura, "and hope for a break in the storm's intensity."

"Fine with me."

"A topo map is in the glove compartment." She switched on the overhead light.

Archer rummaged through the papers and pulled out several maps. Nakamura selected *Venango County Terrain* and glanced at it to get bearings.

"By rights, we should be just about here." She pointed to a spot on the chart, and pulled out a Magellan GPS 2000 satellite navigator. "If memory serves me, the safe-house should be near the river, less than a mile down this hill."

Nakamura punched map coordinates into the GPS navigator,

hit Enter and, within seconds, was uplinked to the Global Positioning System. Four satellites caught the signal, answered it, and the hand-held computer calculated and pinpointed their exact position. Then, a graphic navigation screen displayed longitudinal and latitudinal data that matched the site.

"Okay," said Nakamura. "Cloud cover or no . . . this confirms it. Daylight should prove us twice right."

Archer continued to scan the map.

Tired from the drive, Nakamura leaned against the headrest and sat quietly with her eyes closed, trying to clear her mind for what might come next.

———

THE NORTH ATLANTIC

THE bridge hatch slammed shut behind Parker and Calder as the northerly tempest struck the ship's hull. The two clicked their hasps to safety ropes and slowly worked their way down the catwalk steps to the fantail.

Parker shouted over the wind, "What happened to prudence and humility to determine a mission's risk?"

"Prudence and humility?" Calder yelled back. "Your friend, the colonel, shot that to hell when he rented this ship."

"We've passed any level of acceptable risk for ship and crew. But it'd take as long to get back out as it took to get in."

"I vote we tell Bramson to shove this mission up his ass," Calder said, straining to see through the constant spray of water and foam.

"Yeah, right . . . " Parker wished. He stopped halfway down and put his arm up. "Hold it," he yelled and pointed out to the next wave. "Incoming, port astern." Both checked their rope hasps, sat back into the steps, put their heads down, grabbed hard to the railings, and prepared to be sacked.

Anticipation was as bad as the hit. Even with insulated wetsuits, temperature of the water combined with the windchill and made it less than a joyful experience. Both watched the wave approach—defying the wind's direction—heading rapidly for them, abaft of port.

Holt came about so the ship could quarter into the wave. But the vessel slipped into a slight trough, and the wave crested fifteen feet over the stern, cascaded over the next deck and headed for the bridge.

As the foaming water approached Parker and Calder, the *Neptune* rose on another swell and the wave backed away, as though retreating in fear.

"Yes!" the men laughed in unison, all the way down the steps.

The two felt compelled to check the *Sheltie's* tie-downs and *Neptune's* rope system and draglines. Before the storm had taken hold, sheathed-rope walking systems were erected on every deck to prevent losing anyone overboard. Large squares of ropes fanned out in all directions. Viewed from above, the ship resembled an archaeological dig for Jurassic bones.

Six warps and knotted draglines floated alongside port and starboard, and three more trailed as far as two hundred feet aft of the vessel—if someone washed over the side.

It took Parker and Calder thirty-five minutes to reach the fantail, between wave assaults and inspection of the roping system. Regardless of exposure suits, their faces were cold and stung from the constant onslaught of saltwater spray and buffeting winds.

Shelties One, Two and *Three* rested upright in their cocoon state, in deck-bolted, pod-like seats that resembled enlarged soft-boiled egg cups. Stabilized for the ride, the submersibles were wrapped in thick canvas, tightly lashed to each other, and heavy-duty steel cables extended out to the hydraulic A-frame.

A cross current of swells rose to meet each other, just fore of the stern, and collided in midair directly over the subs. The waves crashed with a frightening noise against the *Shelties*, then receded from the ship.

Parker moved farther aft.

"Are they holding?" Calder shouted from behind, still checking ropes.

"Appear to be okay from here." With the combined roar of sea and storm, they could barely hear one another.

"Good thing we triple-lashed 'em," Calder yelled back. He lagged behind to retie a loose section of the roping system.

"Be there in a minute."

Parker continued toward the *Shelties*. From a distance the submersibles looked fine. But something appeared unusual, as he approached the A-frame. A loose, bolted U-clamp, securing a steel cable to a deck stanchion, shifted back and forth with each movement of the ship. Parker quickly moved in—alternately hasping the harness and sliding across lengths of rope, ducking under crossovers, and rehasping where necessary.

He leaned in to inspect the clamp. The cable's tension had held, but the bolt securing the cable to the frame had been cut through. The bolt's ends had arched outward, with the cable's clamp ready to pop off. And with each plunge the ship took, the clamp pulled farther from its base.

"Andy, we've got a problem," Parker shouted back to Calder. Retying a section of rope, Calder could not hear above the storm.

Another wave broke across the deck. Parker lost his footing and slipped. But the harness held and he grabbed a rope to pull himself up. The stern of the ship rose with the next swell as Parker struggled to pull out his radio. He looked toward Calder and pushed Talk.

"Andy, there's a serious problem. Copy?"

Calder looked up from his work and waved back.

"Someone's cut a U-clamp bolt. It could let go any minute. Bring new hardware with a wrench and hammer. Hurry, before the cable cuts loose!"

Calder signaled "okay," and turned toward the storage room.

Suddenly, a wave broke over the starboard side and knocked the U-clamp from it's base. The steel cable snapped like a cracked whip and raced by Parker's face. He jumped back as the clamp ripped through his vest and wetsuit and tore across his chest.

Parker screamed out in pain as the cable whipped around, once more, and sliced through the rope securing him to the harness.

He fell back from his weight, the safety hasp slipped off the cut end of the rope, and Parker slid toward the edge of the ship.

"Andy!" Parker called into the radio before it fell from his hand and washed overboard.

Calder whipped around at the sound of Parker's voice and saw his partner grab hold of a second cable as another wave crashed over them.

Parker tried to snap onto the cable but couldn't recover from the ship's pitching and yawing. He grappled for another rope, but the stern reacted like a plane recovering from wind shear. As it rose, his arms dropped with the gravitational pull.

Calder disregarded all caution, unclipped his hasp, and raced over and under what now were obstructions. He cussed at the ropes and frantically tried to pull his radio from its pocket.

"Hang on, Cary," he screamed out, knowing he couldn't be heard. Another swell approached them both from the portside bow. Quickly, he snapped his hasp onto a rope, grabbed hold, and waited to be slammed.

"Hold on," he yelled and pointed to the cresting wave.

The breaker exploded over them and inundated the deck. To Parker, it looked like the force of Hoover Dam broke loose and flooded toward him.

"No!" Calder screamed as he watched the wave lift Cary up and over the stern. A bright orange lifevest was all he could see disappear over the fantail.

"Man overboard." Calder shouted into his radio. "Man overboard. Stop engines, Denny. Cary's in the water. Do you copy? Hold our position."

"All stopped," Denny Marshall confirmed.

"We're suiting up, Andy," Holt radioed back to the stern. "Get the marker in. Can you spot him? Over."

"Can't see a damn thing. He could be two feet from us or two hundred in these swells. Over."

"If he latched onto a dragline, we'll pull him in."

The bridge heard the radio communication from Parker before he was lifted from the ship. Despite seriously affected visibility, from above, they had helplessly watched as a bright orange vest faded into the dark waters.

First Officer Marshall had relieved Dupont of the helm. Holt instructed Marshall to hold a stationary position with the cycloidal propulsion system. The ship's computerized navigation technology locked in on NavStar and maintained its precise position, allowing for drift to compensate for Parker's anticipated movement in the rolling seas if he missed a dragline.

Holt pushed his stop watch to track elapsed time, then turned to the communications specialist.

"Notify ships in the immediate vicinity. Planes can't help unless the weather settles down. Tell them the ship is okay, but we've used the marker for high seas and heavy drift.

"Are we getting a signal from his locator beacon yet?"

The C.S. had tuned in 243 megahertz frequency to locate Parker's beacon, simultaneously monitoring 406 megahertz for the large marker beacon.

"I have him on 243, sir. Trying to get placement."

"Andy," radioed John. "We have his beacon. Did you find the emergency gear? Over?"

"I've tossed in the beacon canister, life raft, and strobe poles."

"We're on our way, Andy. Stay on line 'til I get down there." Holt turned to his crew.

"Everyone assigned to an action station . . . move! And for God's sake be careful."

Holt and ten other crew members raced to spread out around the ship. They promptly tested the trailing ropes for weight and attempted to gain visual contact with Parker. But severe wave action created heavier drag on the knotted ropes, and imitated the pull of a human—making it difficult to tell if anyone was there until the tip of each rope end was exposed. ˙

While the crew donned wetsuits and vests, Calder had tossed over an inflatable raft and a half dozen strobed man-overboard pole lights—two over the stern, two portside, and two more starboard. The raft and strobe poles were tied to ropes to be pulled in, if Parker could get to one safely.

The one-watt floating radio distress canister signal could be picked up by the COMPASS-SARSAT satellite system, and processed to other rescue ships close by, if assistance was needed in a full search of the area.

Calder, visibly shaken, met up with Holt amidships.

"Any sign of him, Andy?"

"The waves are cresting too high and foam covers everything. I've yelled for him repeatedly. But there's nothing."

"You did what you could."

"If only I'd been with him, I could've kept him from going over."

"You don't know that, Andy. Stop blaming yourself. We saw it from the bridge. There was nothing you could've done after the cable snapped."

Holt handed Calder a battery-powered megaphone. "Call out in fifteen-second intervals. Call his name, slowly, every fifteen seconds. Then listen for fifteen seconds. You know the drill. We're getting his locator beacon, and we'll follow whatever signals we pick up."

Secured to a rope, Calder hailed for Parker. Despite the winds, the megaphone hauntingly echoed back at him as *Neptune's Knot* maintained its position and the storm held it's line.

Son-of-a-bitch, Parker thought, fighting to keep his head above the constantly changing surface. Cold salt water stung at the wound on his chest, making it difficult to move, as he desperately searched for a drag line. He could still see the ship only twenty yards out and watched as Calder raced to the rails. Neither one could hear the other.

Parker twisted in place and reached out, ready to grab at anything that came by. "Where are you?" he yelled. Then something whipped by his neck—and he grabbed at it.

"Yes!" His gloved hand managed to gain hold. But his hands—still blistered from gun-barrel burns—could hardly wrap around the trail line as he slipped further.

"Hold on, baby." He choked on seawater and spit it out. "Hold on," he continued to encourage himself, though the pain was excruciating.

The drifting ship pulled the line through his fingers like a ski tow, and the coarse fiber burned through his gloves to his palms and fingers. Feeling for knotted breaks in the rope, he slowly tightened the grip, let the rope float under his armpit, and his other hand searched behind his back to pull it around him for anchored support. Soon, he caught a knotted section and found himself dragging behind the ship—first tossed high, then plunged down with each swell.

"Damn!"

He swallowed water and came up choking—spitting out water—unable to wipe blowing foam from his eyes.

Remain calm, his mind repeated again and again.

As Parker evaluated his situation, he listened for directional calls, but the storm was too intense. He could scarcely hear the locator beacon on his vest, let alone calls from the ship. And in the turbulent waters it would do no good to disperse dyemarker.

Strobe-pole lights flashed eerily against the rain and echoed off the low-lying clouds, indicating additional rescue points—and somewhere out there was a raft. But there was no way Parker would let go of the rope. And climbing into a raft in this storm was like riding a cruise missile with a defective guidance system.

Though he had lost sight of the ship, Parker hoped he wasn't more than a hundred feet away. He was confident the crew would find him soon enough. But water entered his wetsuit through the gash at his chest, seeped in through his partially exposed hands and, with his face uncovered, Parker began to suffer from exposure to the thirty-eight degree water.

Mild hypothermia had already set in.

Parker glanced at the water around him. Even in the dark he could see red. I'm bleeding like a stuck pig...his mind told him, as it began to wander, not particularly caring to remain conscious.

Between onslaughts from the sea, the *Neptune's* crew continued their search as the ship attempted to maintain bearings.

Holt stood amidships. He looked at his stopwatch, then called on the radio, "He's been in six minutes. Any signs? Over."

All spotters had nothing to report. Two of the longer ropes had yet to be pulled in.

"Keep your eyes peeled," Holt shouted back.

"Bridge to Captain Holt," the C.S. called.

"Holt, here."

"Sir, the locater beacon seems to place Dr. Parker out beyond the stern. I think he's on a longer dragline. The signal remains fairly static, aft, whipping port to starboard with the swells."

Holt pushed Talk, "Andy, did you get that?"

"I copied. Send more crew astern to help on these last two lines."

"Roger that."

Holt directed four crew aft.

With each new length of rope exposed above the waterline, Calder and the others anxiously watched the ocean for some sign of Parker.

"Sir, the outer rope has more drag than the others," the bosun yelled over the gale winds.

Calder was encouraged by the report. Holt fought the storm and rushed to the fantail to help pull the weight. Length by length, the starboard-side rope was carefully drawn over the stern—each measure between knots giving further rise to hope for Parker's safety.

"Sir," the bosun shouted, again, "I see bright colors . . . a vest, thirty yards out, floating to port."

All eyes turned to port and tried to spot Parker through the bitter-cold rain.

". . . . No, he's directly astern, now."

"I see him," said Calder. "Get him in before we lose him!"

"All rescue crew report abaft, at once!" Holt radioed, then picked up the pace with the dragline.

All available crew raced across the deck.

For an instant, between swells, the *Neptune* appeared to Parker as a ghost ship. Not certain if he was hallucinating, Parker looked up again. But as he rose and sank with the next swells, there was nothing.

He barely had enough strength to hold on. *They'll be back. They'll be back*, he repeated. And it brought him hope to fight for consciousness.

Then he saw the flashing strobes again. And the ship's lights. And he found himself pulled closer to the hull as voices beckoned him from somewhere in his mind . . .

"Cary, hold on. We'll pull you in. Grab the ring . . . grab the ring . . . "

"Get that grappling ring out closer to him," Calder yelled to the crew. But the swamping water made it difficult to reach out beyond the edge.

"Toss out another buoy," Holt ordered.

A crew member grabbed a second ring buoy and, holding onto the slack end, performed a perfect underhand toss, slightly beyond Parker, then inched it toward him.

"Watch yourself," Calder warned, "Stay hasped. We don't need another crewman overboard."

Parker slipped his right arm through the buoy—then his left.

"Denny," Holt radioed to the bridge, "give a short burst on the forward starboard cycloidals to push her closer."

"Done, sir," the radio blared.

The ship inched to port as the quiet-running cycs propelled the hull closer to Parker. The swells pushed back, but the ship held its course.

"Stop engines," Holt confirmed to the bridge.

"All stopped," the radio replied.

The bosun managed to slip the grappling ring over Parker's head and under his arms, then tightened the loop.

"Loop three more ropes for a roll-aboard," Calder ordered.

Three more crew secured ropes to the A-frame, looped them to hang in the water, then slipped the ropes from Parker's feet, up and under his body. The loops were positioned under Parker's calves, hips, and waist—tightened with his arms inside—and cinched up to place him prone with the edge of the fantail.

"Okay, roll him up here and pull with everything you got!"

Calder saw the gash across Parker's wetsuit. He pointed to a crew member. "Get a litter here, pronto."

Holt, Calder and those close by, picked up the pace. They fought to hold balance as angry swells beat against the stern and whipped up the waters around the nearly unconscious Parker.

By inches, he was gently lifted from the water and rolled up over the side.

Looking sallow, Parker realized he was back on board and weakly glanced around.

"You okay?" Calder shouted as they raced to secure him before he could backwash over the side.

Parker looked at the ropes, "I'm a little strung out," he feebly winked and smiled—his teeth chattering like castanets.

"Hasn't lost his warped sense of humor," Holt said as he assisted Parker into a plastic Stokes litter. He saw Parker's chest wound. "You gotta stop shaving below the neck, sailor. Doc will take a look at that."

Several crew assisted the litter to Parker's cabin. Holt and Calder followed behind.

"You're shivering. Good sign," said Calder. "Initial chilling only. The body's still producing heat."

"Any other sign of hypothermia?" asked Holt.

"Yeah," Parker shivered. "Help me get out of this crap, will 'ya? I gotta pee."

"Good sign!" Calder and Holt high-fived each other and laughed at their mutual diagnosis.

"Shaking or not," said Holt, "I ain't gonna hold it for you."

"Mild case," said Calder as he helped Holt strip off Parker's safety harness and flotation vest. "You'll be all right as soon as you get warmed up."

Parker shook uncontrollably as his two comrades first stripped off the top of his wetsuit, then the remainder. The cabin was not much warmer than outside as Holt tossed him some towels and threw a blanket around him.

"Lucky that wound didn't go deeper," Calder observed.

"Looks like the salt water cleaned you out."

They struggled to stand up as the ship heaved in the choppy sea. But the ferocity of the storm and the surging waves finally subsided in intensity. And they were optimistic they had been through the worst of it.

Parker returned from the latrine, still shaking vigorously.

The ship's doctor cleaned and bandaged his wounds, and proclaimed him more physically fit than a Marine. He prescribed a stiff shot of whiskey and a good nap in a sleeping bag with two extra blankets over him. Then he left the three men alone.

Parker sat on the edge of his bunk, blankets around him. He downed a straight shot of whiskey, then was quiet for a time.

Calder and Holt didn't want to press him, until he felt like talking.

Parker asked for another whiskey and downed it immediately. He looked at the ceiling and breathed out deeply—more serious than the two men had seen in months.

"How're the subs?"

"Under control," Calder responded. "A crew is installing a new clamp as we speak."

"It was sawed clear through . . . " Parker looked at Calder, then at Holt. "The bolt was cut clean in the middle."

"You're certain?" said Calder.

"No question about it."

"Why do you suppose . . . "

"Why?" Parker laughed. "Why not? Everyone else seems to be in on this mission. Why not place a saboteur onboard?"

"You think it's Dupont?" said Holt.

"I can't imagine him to be that stupid. Everyone's watching him like a hawk, as it is."

"Captain," a voice interrupted over the intercom.

"Holt here."

"Sorry to interrupt. Sir, we just reached the fortieth parallel. You asked me to keep you notified."

"Thanks. Tell me when we hit forty-one. I'll be in my cabin."

"Yes sir." The intercom clicked off.

Holt looked at Parker. "Won't be long before you get to kiss your old friend hello."

Parker nodded, still shivering.

"We'll be doubly careful," said Calder. "I'll assign a trusted sailor to check everything bolted down."

The two men excused themselves and went back to their cabins to change.

Parker was more unsure than ever whether he wanted to greet the *Titanic* once more . . . especially under these circumstances. But he put off thinking about it until he was rested. He climbed into his sleeping bag and adjusted blankets around him. By the time Parker's chills abated, he was comatose with sleep.

———

It was the silence that awakened her.

For a moment Nakamura opened her eyes and felt as though

she were on the wrong side of a strange bed, wondering where and what time it was. Then it hit her. She sat up and realized she had dozed off in the car.

"Damn." She looked over at Archer, who was smiling.

"You were really out."

"You shouldn't have let me sleep so long."

"I hate to tell you, but it hasn't been that long. Thought I'd let you catch up."

She looked around, but the windows were fogged.

"Sounds like a lull in the storm."

"Stopped a couple of minutes ago."

Using the long sleeve of her old University of Chicago sweatshirt, she rubbed a clear space on her side window. The rain had eased to a drizzle and the wind had died to a respectable velocity. Sounds of the rain-swollen Allegheny River ascended from below. Nakamura checked her watch. Only twenty minutes had been lost. It was now 21:19.

"Shall we move out?" said Archer.

"Sure."

He reached over the backseat, grabbed two bullet-proof vests, and handed one to his partner.

They slipped the vests over their heads, careful to tuck in the pant flaps, then tightened the two Velcro straps on each side. They readjusted their shoulder holsters, checked their Sig Sauer P228 double-action pistols, put on the leather mag carriers with two extra clips, and pulled their heavy nylon jackets over everything else. Nakamura grabbed her baseball cap and tucked her hair inside.

"Hand me four more clips," she said. "Just in case . . . "

Archer reached into the glove compartment, pulled out more 13-round loads, and both slipped the extra magazines in the side pockets of their FBI-issue jackets.

Nakamura pulled up her right pant cuff and tightened the holster straps holding her leg-gun. A two-inch barreled, blue S&W 38 Bodyguard Airweight was holstered to her leg, for backup.

The Remington semi-automatic shotguns remained in the ceiling-mounted gun rack, if needed later. Nakamura handed Archer the magnetized flashlight off the base of the dashboard and grabbed another off the seat. She clipped a cellular phone to her belt and switched off the ringer.

"Let's do it," said Nakamura. Both agents opened their doors. The driver's side was out of alignment as metal scraped metal and reverberated loudly through the trees. Nakamura winced at the noise.

"Hope the river concealed that." She eased out of the driver's seat, slid to the wet ground, and her boots sloshed in the mud. Both locked and closed their doors, as quietly as possible, then followed the road on foot.

The roadway followed the natural curve of the hillside as it mirrored the extended flood plain of the river bed below. With every sopping step, Nakamura and Archer gingerly lifted and placed their feet to avoid breaking twigs or branches that might be under foot.

About seventy-five yards from the car, Nakamura stopped.

"This path curves down and slopes around the hillside," she whispered. "Lets move off the trail to the undergrowth at the edge of the cliff."

"I'll follow your lead."

Though the higher ground allowed for better runoff, both agent's boots were already water logged. The light drizzle, chilled air, and water-filled ruts made it more difficult to focus on locating Victoria Parker. As the gradient grew steeper, sounds of the river intensified.

Nakamura felt a heightened awareness that came when she sensed they were close to resolving a case. Her inner-consciosness and perception of everything around her became more focused, despite the darkness. And she relaxed, knowing her instincts would now take over.

Archer tended to be more left-brained in his approach, but

deferred to his partner, because of her reputation for instinctive reasoning.

"Won't be long, now, Mike . . . just around the next curve and down about fifty yards."

The incline leveled off once more. The tree-lined edge dissipated, met the road, and became more gravel-filled and noisier with each step. Their only saving grace was the loud spring runoff that gave the Allegheny River its speed, to cover their approach.

"Rain's picking up, again." Archer looked up, but could see nothing in the pitch-black darkness as he felt heavier drops on his face.

A bolt of lightning hit in the distance, and within seconds the area was deluged with a hard-pounding cloudburst. Knowing they were close to being exposed, Nakamura switched off her flashlight and signaled Archer to do the same. Carefully, the two felt their way to the abandoned, trackless railroad bed that once followed the river.

Then they saw it in the darkness—light slipping through the edges of covered windows.

The same abandoned safe-house where Nakamura had broken the drug ring three years before—the old red caboose. Brought in years ago by a company responsible for a dredging project on the river, the caboose had been left behind at the completion of the job. Slightly above the bank of the river bed, the rail car sat in the middle of nowhere, as if returned and dropped after inspection by an alien spaceship. A remnant of days gone by that even aliens had rejected.

Lightning flashed and the caboose stood out like a surreal skiagram—its surroundings caught between shadows and a blazing white sky.

"Intriguing," Nakamura said over the thunder. "Lights on in an abandoned caboose. They've pulled a line from that pole over there."

"Vagrants?"

"Doubt it."

The two slowly edged their way toward the safe-house. As they stealthily moved across the road, Nakamura kept her eyes trained on slits in the covered caboose windows, to detect movement inside.

Unexpectedly, she hit something hard. The impact echoed out over the river as she realized she had not paid attention to her up close movements.

"My god, the Taurus," she whispered.

Then the rain stopped, as quickly as it had begun, and both agents watched the caboose entrances. Nakamura and Archer heard voices, then movement on the hollow floor inside. They ducked behind the dark gray car, now bathed in partial moonlight through breaking clouds.

"Dammit," whispered Archer.

"Of all times for the clouds to part, it had to be now." Nakamura tightened her body in toward the wheel base.

"Wonder how many there are," said Archer.

"We may find out soon."

The front door creaked open and light spilled from the inside. A tall bearded man stepped out on the platform and looked toward the car. Something was said from inside.

A male voice, both agents registered the thought.

"Di'ii'a waHda," the other answered reticently.

He probed the misty night with a flashlight as the rolling clouds cast moving shadows over the area. The flashlight sounded the darkness around Nakamura's feet, but she remained still— with Archer pressed solidly against the door panel, next to her. The circle of light expanded up into the trees, then over toward the river. Nakamura carefully leaned forward and under the front bumper, hoping the terrorist was distracted enough not to see her.

In the light cast from inside the rail car, she saw the reflection of an UZI-like spraygun hanging from the man's neck. *Two men so far . . . and assault weapons*, she noted.

Then the man stepped off the platform and walked toward the car. Nakamura pulled back and signaled Archer. The glow from the flashlight got brighter and wider as the man approached the hood and spread the beam over the area.

His shoes pushed at the gravel as each step got closer. Both agents reached for their Sig Sauers and had them halfway out when the footsteps halted and paused for what seemed an eon. Light passed through the car windows above them, then the man turned and headed to the safe-house entrance.

Nakamura sighed in relief as he went inside and closed the door.

"That was close," she whispered.

They could barely hear questions asked and answers given, from the distance, and could only guess at their meaning.

After waiting a respectable period, Nakamura tapped Archer on the shoulder. They slowly rose to move around the car. But Nakamura's left foot had fallen asleep in the crouched position, and her leg almost gave out from underneath as she reached the driver's side.

"Crap!" she whispered in anger. "Just what I need." She massaged her leg and shifted her weight to the right side while she waited for circulation to return.

Then the door to the caboose opened, once more. Nakamura dropped like a dead weight and rolled under the car as Archer ducked back behind the other side.

———

Parker had slept soundly for almost five hours. The change from a severely heavy sea to calm waters helped him obtain a more restful sleep, despite underlying pain from his chest wound. Too anxious about the mission to stay below and, with the clearing weather, he had to get topside before he went stir-crazy. He felt well enough to leave his cabin, regardless of doctor's orders.

Neptune's Knot sat quietly and alone in the gently heaving water, at 41°43'55"N latitude, 49°56'50"W longitude, directly above the remains of the *Titanic's* bow section. As he stood on deck, Parker stared out at the calm sea. Elongated reflections of late evening stars were almost hypnotic.

Surrounded by the haunting of over 1500 lives, lost eight decades before, he could never shake the feeling that came the night the ship's graveyard was first discovered.

He imagined Captain Smith on his megaphone—begging the lifeboats to return for more passengers and the silent screams of men, women and children caught in steerage, with no chance to escape their fate, as the bow split from the stern and sped toward the deep seabed.

Cary envisioned the wealthy, stoic men standing on the aft section of the stern. Astor, Strauss and the others left behind with their last expensive cigars . . . resigned to their pending cold death as they calmly chatted with one another. And Harry Widener— lonely with his thoughts of failure to carry out his assignment— willing to take responsibility and blame for a loss for which he was not culpable.

Over conjured sounds of debris sliding downward, crashing violently against collapsing walls and bulkheads, Parker was still haunted by his thoughts of children clinging to parents in the frigid waters.

Cary now ached for Victoria and their daughters. He hit the railing with his fist and the inner pain disappeared momentarily. Though his guilt of helplessness on the open sea prevailed, it was easier to dwell on the hauntings than to think about his wife and the terrorists.

The hauntings took over once more. His mind often pictured how it must have appeared when the stern—the remaining half of the *Titanic*—froze vertically in the water during its last moments, as if taking one final look around. Solid, as though a proud British soldier staring directly at the face of death . . . first straightening his coat and saluting with honor. Then slowly, steadfastly, and knowingly moving toward his final resting place.

Once there was a finality to it all. Now Parker prepared to carry out what he and others had promised never to do—remove artifacts from the ship they had vowed to protect from desecration. His anger returned. It was Dupont who had forced the issue years before, and Parker resented him deeply.

"You've broken out in a cold sweat," interrupted Calder.

Startled, Cary turned to his friend and forced a smile.

"Are the ghosts visiting again?"

"Some more alive than others." Parker wiped the sweat from his neck and face. He had allowed himself to dwell too long on the past.

"You're wanted in the control room. Radar's picked up a small ship moving in."

"What's their range?

"Two hundred fifty miles out. Bearing zero-eight-nine."

"The *A'isha?*"

"Possibly."

Cary thought for a moment. "Any word from Bramson on Victoria?"

Calder shook his head, afraid that any word might be terrible news.

Parker let out a long sigh. "Get Dupont to the control room. We need to review tomorrow's dive plans immediately."

"He's already there. He's been looking through just about everything."

"The computers?"

Calder nodded.

"Damn it. I told him to ask me before he accessed our computers." Parker moved quickly to the stairs leading to the control room on the lower deck.

"I asked him if he had clearance to get in."

"What'd he say?"

Andy imitated Dupont's accent, "We're all partners in this, are we not?"

"Partners, hell, I'll partner his . . . "

Dupont threw open the control room door just as Parker and

Calder arrived. "Ah, mon ami. I was coming to look for you. We may have visitors."

Calder watched the two engage.

"Yeah. Well listen to me, Henri. We had an agreement. Remember? You need information from the computer, you ask for it."

"Je suis désolé," Dupont attempted to look contrite.

"The hell you're sorry. Cut the crap, Henri."

Calder moved into the control room and closed the door behind him.

"Look," said Parker, "I don't want you on board this ship anymore than you enjoy being here. But it's a fact of life. You're here and you operate under my rules now. No more raping and pillaging of the *Titanic*. No more broken promises. Just work at what you do best. Locating artifacts. You've certainly had plenty of practice. Pourriez-vous comprendre ceci?"

"Understood," answered Dupont, not wanting an argument at this juncture.

"Good. For my part, I'll attempt to remain civil. Especially in front of the crew. I expect you to do the same. But don't give me an excuse to nail you to a bulkhead. I've had years of practice being pissed off about your broken promises."

"Again, I am sorry, mon ami."

"And stop calling me your friend. We're no longer friends, Henri. Just do your job and this will be over soon." Parker pulled the control room door open and stepped in. Dupont turned to go back in as the door slammed in his face. He looked around to see if anyone was watching from on deck. Seeing no one, he shrugged, pulled on the refrigerator-door handle and stepped over the threshold.

Though the control room was naturally dark, it was ablaze with video screens, sidescan sonar, a green-screened Loran, brightly lit computerized X,Y plotting tables, advanced global navigation systems, and multitudes of equipment designed to monitor the three *Shelties*.

"What've we got on the screen?" asked Parker.

"Looks like fishing partners moving in soon," said Holt.

The sonar coordinator spoke up, "Her signature is more like a moderate-sized merchant freighter."

Holt stepped in, "A passing Navy frigate just reported a ship, fitting that description, headed this way. Said her name was the *A'isha*. And its flying a Libyan flag."

"Also said that the stern looked to be converted with a new type of crane," said Calder. "Appears to be the type used for self-enclosed launchers."

"This must be the *A'isha*," said Dupont, pointing to the radar screen.

Parker looked at both of them. "How do we know?"

"The Navy ship said that for as large as the ship is, it's sitting fairly low in the water," Holt reported.

"Oui. They must be carrying heavy cargo," said Dupont feigning interest.

"Like a Japanese mini-sub," said Parker. "Or two."

"That'd be my guess," said Holt.

"But that in itself wouldn't be enough to weigh her down," said Calder.

Something bothered Parker. But he could not grasp the meaning.

"Have you attempted radio contact?"

"We're waiting for your orders, Captain," said Holt.

Parker was ready to give the order, then had second thoughts. "Let's wait 'til they're within our vicinity. By then we should have a better idea who they are. Get Bramson on the phone and order up photos from one of his fancy satellites."

———

For the moment, the rain had subsided but clouds remained. Nakamura heard more voices from her vantage point, hidden under the terrorist's rented car, while Archer listened carefully from the other side. A shorter man moved out to the edge of the metal platform. Then she heard his pants unzip. And the backlit silhouette urinated over the platform.

Oh fine! A burlesque show, too, Nakamura thought in disgust. Inside the caboose, two male voices laughed and kidded the man outside. Archer could not see the terrorists, but knew what must be going on.

That's three, Nakamura tallied in her mind. *Dammit, how many more?* she wondered. *Is Victoria even in there? These guys are Arabic, though that isn't reason to convict them. Given their weapons, these jerks could be the Ordnance Center terrorists.*

Nakamura had one up on them. She had been in the rail car before, recalled the layout, and visualized the inside. *To the left of the front entrance . . . two open bunks. A third enclosed area doubles for storage or another bunk. An unusable toilet in the middle—given this command performance—and, before the rear door and platform, a small kitchenette. At the entrance on the right is a nook with sitting area and table. More storage and a closet . . . then the open area, across from the kitchenette, with a large pot-belly stove. Two electric hurricane lamps hung from the ceiling.*

The terrorist returned indoors and Nakamura, covered with mud, slipped out from under the Taurus. She looked through the car windows, at Archer, now standing at the other side, then turned her flashlight on the driver's door. A long gash down the side confirmed the stranger's identity. She was at once elated and frightened for their hostage. So far, there was no sign of Victoria.

"Dear God, let her be safe," she whispered. Archer came around to meet her. "Look at this." She shot her flashlight at the gash on the door, then turned it off.

"That's it," said Archer.

"Given the lateness of the hour, we can presume everyone's together. Did you see their UZI's?"

"Yeah, but they're different."

"A knock-off. I saw them in London."

"It would help to know where each terrorist is, inside, regardless how small the caboose."

Nakamura explained the rail car's layout to Archer. And many questions raced through their minds—questions that had to be answered to prevent jeopardizing the hostage's life. *Are they bundled around the stove? Does one keep watch while others sleep? How tired or agitated are they? How fit for combat? Could they be tricked to get them outside? What if the caboose is booby-trapped with explosives, if discovered?*

Archer moved near the car trunk as Nakamura searched for evidence through the windows. Discarded chip bags and empty soda cans littered the floors and seats. She moved to the rear.

Archer pulled out his "faux keys," as he referred to them. After groping through several, he selected one to fit the trunk.

Nakamura stopped him.

"Wait a second."

Archer froze in place.

"Remember the van reported near the Ordnance Center?"

"The van?"

"Yeah, exploded with pressure triggers attached to the doors."

"Shit, that's right."

"If the trunk's booby-trapped . . . or the car itself . . . "

Nakamura thought for a moment.

"I didn't see any hookups under the car. But that wasn't my worry at the time."

She scanned the undercarriage with her flashlight. There were no signs of explosives, wires, or timing devices.

"If the car's rigged, it's in the trunk or under the hood."

They had no choice. Both crouched low to avoid an upward force of an explosion. Archer inserted the pin into the keyhole and, after some jiggling, popped the lid—holding it down until they were ready to leap aside if need be. They turned their faces away from the trunk, uncertain if they were sweating from nerves or wet from the rain. Slowly Archer raised the lid. The hinges squeaked as the cover rose. Nakamura and Archer froze, turning only to look at the caboose.

"Thank God," she whispered, checking the rim of the trunk for delayed boobytraps or wire triggers. She shined her light into the car's trunk. Her eyes widened and adrenalin pumped as never before.

"Bingo!" she whispered.

Laying across the compartment was a torn and bloodstained negligee that matched the section the police discovered at the Parker's home. Nakamura picked up the nightgown, folded it and shoved it under her jacket.

"At least there's no body in the trunk," remarked Archer.

"Good sign . . . "

They glanced at what had been underneath.

"What do we have here?" Archer said.

Two sub-machine guns sat on top of corrugated boxes.

He picked one up. It looked remarkably similar to a Mini-UZI, but used a modified J-clip to increase magazine capacity to sixty rounds. With their flashlights, they saw the entire knockoff weapon was made of a sturdy, hardened plastic, right down to the padded butt and silencer/hand-grip.

"Same as the assault weapons confiscated after Heathrow," Nakamura confirmed as she grabbed a clip from a box over the wheel well and rammed it into the handle. She took three extra magazines and slung an XE-47 around her neck. Archer did the same.

Then Nakamura noticed eight boxes marked:

DANGER!—CXM-20 EXPLOSIVES
Property of
U.S. Government

Army/Navy Ordnance Testing Station
GILBERT DEPOT

"Holy crap," Nakamura looked to the rail car, then back to the trunk. "These are the missing bomb materials from Kentucky."

They had been warned the experimental explosive was a hybrid of earlier RDX formulas. Along with plasticizer and filler compositions that gave it a detonation rate of over 30,000 feet per second—enough cutting action to instantly sever steel girders or other structures like a hot knife through butter—there was one big difference . . . a secret ingredient mixed into the formula that rendered it useless without the unusual triggering device.

Nakamura lifted one of the boxes. "There's enough plastic to blow another Trade Center!"

"Too much to carry back to the Cherokee."

"Close it up for now."

Archer reached for the trunk lid. Something else caught Nakamura's eye.

"Wait a second . . . "

Tucked in a recess of the trunk was an object they had missed. The toy-like component resembled a dog whistle with a small black box at the end.

"The wireless detonator," she recalled. All agents had been cautioned not to push the button on the side of the unit, or test the whistle's capacity if anywhere within three hundred yards of the explosives.

The weather front had circled around on itself, as the wind picked up once more, and bolts of lightning raced across the sky.

"If we can't carry this out of here, we can keep them from using it." Nakamura placed the peculiar looking whistle in her jacket pocket. Archer secured the trunk, and they looked toward the rail car.

"What the hell is a caboose doing out in the middle of

nowhere?" Archer quietly remarked.

Indeed, an anomaly—a trackless, bright red caboose sitting in the mud and weeds, hidden between clumps of trees where once invincible railroad tracks had dominated the Allegheny's banks.

Thunder roared continuously through the river valley and the sky opened up with an intensity usually reserved for Southeast Asian monsoons. Incessant flashes of lightning created a surrealistic background with the river water flowing in stages, like an old-time movie. And the caboose kept getting closer, like a bad dream, as the two agents moved toward the safe-house.

With intermittent lightning, she could see remnants of the drug bust . . . old bullet holes in the safety-glass windows and between large metal rivets in the sides of the caboose. As they circled the area, Nakamura rechecked the entrances and windows while Archer watched for any surprise that might come from the doors at either end. Two windows on each side, three at each end at the platforms, and two each on the front and back sides of the roof cap. Except for light emanating from the cap windows, all others were covered with plywood from the inside.

Archer moved to the river-side of the caboose, and Nakamura checked the side closest to the trees. Air vents on the cap were closed, and smoke rose from the old metal chimney that vented the pot-belly stove.

A loud thunderbolt startled the agents as lightning hit a nearby tree. *God, keep the lightning from those explosives*, Nakamura prayed.

Archer came around the end of the rail car.

"You okay?" he whispered.

"Yeah. . . . Anything?"

"Nothing."

"Wait by the car and cover me," said Nakamura. "I'm going under to give a listen."

"Right."

Archer headed for the Taurus.

An overwhelming smell of electricity, coupled with that of

wood abruptly turned to charcoal, sent chills down Nakamura's spine. She had confronted deadly firearms and nefarious criminals face-to-face. But she feared and respected the power of Mother Nature more than the most vicious deviant she had ever known.

Mother Nature . . . and small wild animals, she thought, as she crawled through the brush, took the XE-47 from around her neck, and pulled herself between the rail car wheels and the underbelly of the caboose. *Hope there're no snakes or spiders under here.*

With the caboose sitting near an incline, a stream of water ran beneath and directly under Nakamura. The cold pierced her clothing, and she wondered if their actions could result in a safe rescue. Lightning hit again and its thunder echoed furiously through the valley.

Weeds and bushes surrounded the caboose and gave cover as Nakamura focused on the activities inside. Over the din of river and storm, she heard voices of men through the thin wooden floor, as they reacted to one another in unintelligible, sporadic bits of conversation. An occasional laugh punctuated their discussion. She listened for what seemed an eternity. But the agent picked up no sign of a female voice.

Then she heard a different sound—movement directly above her—accompanied by a sharp bang against the rail car wall. Thunder masked what she thought was a moan, and Nakamura focused carefully. The sound wasn't from someone walking. It was more of a shifting . . . an adjustment. And the knocking sound—an object hitting it, *like an unconscious knock of an elbow against a shower wall*, she thought. She listened intently for other hints of movement and did not have to wait long.

The shifting occurred once more. And another sound.

It was *a moan I heard.*

Then, more Arabic conversation, footsteps, and mock laughter.

Nakamura stuck her hands into the mud and pushed her head up between the steel joists, to get her ear as close to the floor as possible. A spider web wrapped across her face and she brushed it away, frantically, hoping it had long since been abandoned.

The footsteps stopped directly above, followed by sounds of a creaking door. *The enclosed bunk!* she thought.

"Ah, Mrs. Parker. We have awakened again."

There was no response. Only a moan blending with the storm. But for the first time in a week, Agent Nakamura was elated.

"We must go back to sleep." The door creaked shut above, but a loud moan—a drugged woman attempting to speak, interrupted closure.

"What do you want, Mrs. Parker?" an impatient voice said.

There was a long pause as Victoria Parker struggled to speak.

"Please . . . "

"Yes?"

"It's . . . cold and . . . wet . . . in here."

"It's raining outside. It cannot be helped." The door began to close.

"No," Victoria almost screamed out. The door squeaked open, again. "No, I must...I...have...to go...my bladder really hurts."

"It is too wet and dark outside. You must wait."

"No!" Victoria's voice was stronger and defiant, then softened. "Please . . . I won't try to escape . . . please," she hesitantly begged. "Besides . . . no one else is . . . crazy enough to be out in this weather."

Is that an understatement or what? Nakamura thought.

The men conversed back and forth, and more laughter followed. The floor creaked loudly as a terrorist helped the frail hostage from her bunk and provided support as she gained strength enough to walk outside.

Victoria collapsed upright on the edge of the closet-like bed, until everything stopped spinning around her. She looked up at her captor and forced a smile.

"I'm all right," she felt queasy. "Give me a minute . . . to gain enough strength to walk." She looked at the XE-47 hanging around the terrorist's neck and knew she could not escape. She was in no condition to fight off these men.

"Come," Ahmed Al-Salih took her elbow and helped her up.

From under the rail car, Nakamura heard heavily shuffling feet move the length of the floor. The door opened at the opposite end. Al-Salih and Victoria moved out onto the platform.

Archer watched furtively, from behind the auto, as light spilled outside and two men emerged. His gun rose automatically for the head of a terrorist.

Yes! I can take them both out, he thought, as he prepared his mind for any eventuality. Then he looked closely and realized one of the figures was . . . *something strange*, Archer watched the pair carefully . . . *a woman in men's clothing!* He relaxed his trigger finger, watched carefully for their next move, and thought of Nakamura—now caught under the rail car.

"Please untie me so I can adjust my clothes." In place of her nightgown, Victoria Parker was dressed in a pair of men's pants and a shirt, so she could not be spotted according to the original description. A cap covered her hair to complete the deception.

Al-Salih loosened her bindings. "Do not attempt anything foolish." He tapped his machine gun.

"What could I possibly do in this rainy mess. All I want is to pee."

"I will watch you from here."

"Must you? In America this is private."

Salih's upper lip curled in a strange smile, then he turned slightly away. "I will still be watching." Standing under the platform awning, he pulled out a pack of Capstan's and lit one up.

Victoria carefully stepped down into the driving rain and limped around the caboose. She shivered as she hid behind a large bush near a clump of weeds, at the wall opposite Nakamura. The agent rolled over, crawled beneath the flooring to the other side, and attempted to get Victoria's attention without startling her.

"Vicky, can you hear me?" she whispered out loud. "I'm Agent

Nakamura," But ambient sounds prevented Parker from hearing.

"Vicky," she repeated louder.

Victoria shrieked in surprise as she turned to see a muddy face hidden under the rail car. From afar, Agent Archer heard the scream and prepared for the worse.

"What is the matter?" Ahmed Al-Salih asked from the platform.

"Nothing. Nothing. I . . . I stepped on a sharp rock. I'm okay. I'm all right."

The terrorist turned back to his cigarette. And Victoria moved closer to the caboose.

"I'm Agent Nakamura, FBI. We'll get you out of here."

"Cary's friend . . . the London trip?"

"Yes," the agent whispered.

"Thank God! I'm sorry."

"It's okay . . . "

"No, I mean, I'm sorry . . . I'm glad you're here. But I have to go really, really bad," she said crying from the pain and from an emotion she never thought she would feel, realizing she now had a chance to escape.

"It's okay. You'll be all right, Vicky. How many are there?"

"Three."

"All with guns?"

"Ahmed . . . at the end, has a machine gun. Another man . . . ah, Subhi . . . the big one, has a dagger. And the other carries a pistol. There may be more guns . . . I just don't know."

"Do they ever leave?"

She struggled to speak, "Someone stays behind. . .when they need supplies. . . .I hear their car drive away, but there's still movement in the caboose. And once I think Rahman tried to . . .or wanted to rape me while the others were gone. I was drugged, but kicked like hell. The others came back and he stopped."

"What did you say?" the terrorist stepped off the platform and moved toward Victoria. Archer maneuvered toward the front of the Taurus to shoot, if necessary.

"Just talking to myself. I had to go so bad, I'm delirious with excitement. Please go back," she cried.

Salih stood in place, attempting to make sense of her comments, then laughed and climbed back out of the rain.

Nakamura moved closer to Victoria so they could talk without being heard. "Go back inside and cooperate. Keep from getting tied up, if you can. Are you in immediate danger?"

"They've threatened to kill me . . . if I try to escape. I've had a knife at my neck and guns at my head several times."

"We'll have you out by morning. Conserve your energy. You'll need it."

"What should I do?"

"Nothing, now. I'll call for a rescue team. We'll be back."

Victoria wept silently and reached out to touch Jennifer. "Thank you. Oh, God thank you," she whispered.

"You're a strong woman, Mrs. Parker." She squeezed Victoria's hand for reassurance. "We'll get you out."

Victoria adjusted her clothes as she stood to leave. She glanced under the rail car, to confirm it wasn't a drug-induced hallucination, but the agent had crawled away.

When the two went inside, Nakamura climbed out from underneath. Her foot hit something upright and she turned to see what it was. She pulled out her mini-light and focused it up and down a half-inch pipe. A small cable ran out of the top and into a hole through the wall.

"A phone line," she whispered to herself in amazement. "They've rigged up a damned phone line."

She tugged on the cable to test slackness, and it gave from the pipe. She pulled up six inches, cut the line with a pocket knife, and shoved the end of the wire back into the conduit so the cut would not be evident. Nakamura headed for the treeline and signaled for Archer to join her.

"Did you see her?" Nakamura asked.

"Yeah. Make contact?"

"She's in pretty bad shape."

Nakamura explained what she had learned, then reached for her cellular phone.

"Time to call for backup."

Archer held the flashlight as Nakamura dialed headquarters to request the H.R.T. She put the phone to her ear and there was no sound. She hit the numbers again and pushed SEND. No response.

"Dammit!" The rainwater had shorted out the phone.

Quickly, they headed up the road to call from her car.

———

LANGLEY

COLONEL Bramson put down the receiver and the secured line disconnected. He hit the Intercom and entered four digits.

"Imaging. Mitchell here."

"This is Bramson, in Mid-east. I have a time-critical request. Has NIMA got anything flying over the North Atlantic right now?"

""Surveillance or recon?"

"Prefer the two, but I'll take what I can get."

"You need high-res imaging or real-time quick-look TV?"

"How about both? I need to pick up the eyes of a fly on a ship— covering an eight hundred mile range due east of the Grand Banks, heading west off the northwest tip of Africa."

"The KH-14 can perform high-res thermographic imaging anytime," said Mitchell, "but we'll need daylight to pull better real-time recon. That is, if you want to know what's happening with the fly. And a Landsat can x-ray your objective. You want normal protocol or a direct feed of our TECHINT?"

"We'll do the interp and analysis of the technical information.

Once you establish target, direct it to me. Then I'll want an encrypted downlink to feed to the *Neptune* for our own interp. Of course, any information you provide will be appreciated."

Normal protocol would have been to pick up any encrypted raw technical data from a satellite, and feed it to the appropriate specialists at CIA for interpretation, collation, analysis, evaluation and, finally, dissemination to appropriate parties from the White House on down. In this case, Bramson reserved the right to reverse the order, with dissemination directly through his office, from his own group of experts.

He gave the imaging specialist last known bearings and coordinates for the reported ship. There was a pause while the IS checked positioning and coordinates for available satellites in that region.

"The closest KH Recon won't be around until morning. Landsat has a satellite coming over the Mid-Atlantic Range in about ten minutes but . . . SPOT, the French sat, has the best photographic resolution and just passed through there a half hour ago. Transmits six thousand lines per picture, but it won't complete another revolution for an hour. Hold on a second . . . "

Bramson tapped his fingers impatiently on his desk as the IS called up more information on the computer.

"Colonel, NRO has its new SS, launched last month, and just launched a powerful black 8X sat two days ago. I'll check availability. They'll eat the other sats for breakfast. And the shuttle *Discovery* is still up for two more days . . . testing JPL's third generation AIS, on board."

Bramson was encouraged. The Airborne Imaging Spectrometer could measure over two hundred bands in the infrared wavelengths alone, not to mention near-infrared and all visible color bands. And the "black" SS and 8X spy satellites were so secret, they were shielded from most other offices at CIA and NRO.

"They can get you the fly's footprints if you want 'em," Mitchell added.

"Forget the fly—give me a ship called the *A'isha*. Merchant freighter, Libyan flag. Covered in canvas to hide their cargo. I want to know shape, size, and mineral content if you can see through canvas."

"These days, we can see inside the captain's cabin and count the crabs on his balls," Mitchell bragged.

"Just give me results as fast as possible." Bramson gave Mitchell the *A'isha's* last reported coordinates and clicked off.

In a series of strategic moves, discrete simultaneous actions took place under an activity code assigned to Project Noble. From the space shuttle, Discovery—orbiting earth at a height of 22,000 miles, and traveling at 17,500 mph—an astronaut aimed the Airborne Imaging Spectrometer at the Atlantic Ocean for an unplanned seek-and-find mission, then fine-tuned the large instrument to the *A'isha's* coordinates. Capable of detecting and measuring infrared radiation bands at one million million cycles per second, it focused simultaneously on all the mid, medium and long-wavelength IF bands to see what it could pick up.

In three separate orbits, a Landsat satellite, the NRO SS and the new 8X spy satellites focused their powerful equipment and locked on to the Libyan ship, now sailing at flank speed at 45°02"14"N Latitude and 47°20'24'W Longitude, heading west toward the Grand Banks. Imaging the *A'isha* from seven specific visible and invisible wavelengths of light, the Landsat analyzed and identified the metallurgical content of items stored in and out of crates and under canvas coverings and tarps on deck. Aboard the super-secret NRO SS and 8X "black" satellites, two billion dollars in equipment cut through remaining cloud cover with special radar, photographed their target, eavesdropped on communications, and began transmitting extremely high resolution images back to earth.

At Langley, the encrypted data fed from established NRO and CIA downlinks, as the IS monitored the initial information and quickly scanned it for what Colonel Bramson might miss. Then he picked up his phone and hit Intercom.

"Bramson."

"This is Imaging. Your data is coming through. Ready for me to transfer?"

"Go ahead."

"Would you prefer my initial analysis, Colonel?"

"Please."

Mitchell remained on the intercom. On several video consoles hanging from Bramson's ceiling, pictures of the *A'isha* took form, as several wide-angle shots scanned across the monitors. The IS split the screens between the Discovery's Airborne Imaging Spectrometer and the three satellite images.

"Fortunately, the night sky doesn't deter us here," Mitchell said over the intercom. "Cloud cover is lessening but could make it difficult when we bring up the KH sat in the morning. But most cover has left the scene since the storm pulled out."

The top picture zoomed in to expose the starboard hull and decking of the vessel. "As you see, Colonel, the *A'isha* is a mercantile freighter. Approximately two hundred fifty feet in length, with a displacement of slightly under, ah . . . ten thousand tons. Take a look at its wake . . . twin screw. And thermographic radiation shows diesel-engines."

The spectrometer slowly panned across the deck like a camera. "They've modified the ship. Take a look at the enlarged, open fantail."

There was a pause as Bramson watched an image zoom even closer. "Wouldn't that area typically have a higher gunwale across the stern."

"Exactly." Mitchell continued his scan. "Not much activity at this hour. But look at this, Colonel, our first signs of life."

The colonel found it fascinating that projections of human forms could be seen through walls—in this case steel hulls and bulkheads—by picking up the natural emissions of infrared bands of radiated body heat. It had often occurred to him, if the Germans had perfected thermography, in the days of Hitler, Anne Frank might never have written her diary. And many more Jews would have been murdered under the Third Reich, through the use of thermographic detection.

It's fortunate they didn't have the technology, he thought.

Bramson watched the glowing bodies on his screen, as green revealed most of a human life form. Blue signified cooler areas of each body. And various levels of yellow, gold, and bright red were the more active head and brain centers.

"We have two people occupied on the bridge, and three still working in a large box-like room near the aft-section of the ship." The IS used his electronic pointer. "Look at the electromagnetic waves of color emanating from there. Must be loaded with heavy electronics. They've got some powerful stuff. Want more definition?"

"Probably mission control for their mini-sub. But we'll let Dr. Parker confirm that. Actually, I'd like a body count, if we can determine total personnel on board."

Mitchell shifted an electronic pointer to different sections of the main deck. "Do you see the six . . . uh, must be armed guards stationed fore and aft?"

"Yes."

"They're packing Mini-UZI's. Makes them stand out. From the looks of things, most everyone else is asleep, except for someone down in the engine room." Mitchell thermographically scanned the various cavities of the ship, counting human life forms.

"If types of quarters are any indication, you've got . . . hard to tell, actually, with the stacked bunks . . . looks like some are sleeping in awfully close quarters. Given all that equipment, and resting bodies in the larger cabins, I'd say there's somewhere around nineteen or twenty staff and crew on board."

"I'd concur with that," said Bramson. "Let's take a broader look at the ship itself. I'd prefer to see what it's carrying beyond passengers and crew."

"The sat images on your bottom screen?"

"Yes?"

He pointed toward the stern. "We're getting high readings indicating large amounts of titanium and some type of modified cubic-zirconia, and . . . a fiberglass mixture of some sort. Possibly an anechoic blend with a high sound absorption coefficient."

"Must be their submersibles, with anechoic tiles to negate underwater sonar detection."

"Can't confirm, since they're inoperable, with few electromagnetic waves emitting from them. They're stored in a stacked position, the smaller of the two on top . . . and the larger . . . in some type of framed container. Probably reinforced steel. And rails lead out to the stern."

The specialist pointed to another area, amidships. "These must be wooden crates."

"How can you tell?"

"Not much active infrared radiation. But you can see metal hinges and screws. If we had better resolution . . . wait a second."

Mitchell tightly focused the imaging from the new sat.

"Look at the 8X image. See those tiny black dots?"

"They're long nails in slats, at similar points along each case. We're getting high metallurgic content from their insides." The specialist paused and adjusted the wavelength readings.

"Damn, they're packing quite a wallop. That's not scientific equipment in those crates. It's ordnance." He closed in on the crates and refocused the screen. "I'd say they could be semi-automatics . . . machine guns . . . and, Jesus, look down at the bottom. They've got hand-held missile launchers in there."

"These guys are serious fishermen."

"I hope your research ship . . . what is it, the *Neptune?*"

"*Neptune's Knot.*"

"Hope it doesn't get in *A'isha's* way. Could do some damage."

Bramson was silent for a moment. "With all this ordnance and the armed guards, they're up to something else—beyond diving for treasure and protecting their position."

Mitchell scanned the decking further. "I'll take another look around and get back to you."

"Before you do, encrypt what we have, uplink it to our satellite, and send it to the *Neptune*, will you? Code Zebra, Zebra,

Four, Eight, One. Channel five."

"You got it."

"I'll fax a warning that it's coming."

Both men clicked off their lines, but the shuttle and satellite feeds remained on Bramson's consoles. Bramson poured a fresh cup of coffee, went to his computer, and kept one eye on the imaging screens as he prepared a message for the *Neptune*.

Mitchell ordered up more scans of the *A'isha* in various bands of infrared. The clarity of the satellites provided detailed images of items, no bigger than six inches, as they scanned from one end of the ship to the other.

Then, the earth-bound transmissions focused on the forward hold of the ship. And the thermographic images changed from one wave length to another, like an out-of-control mood ring. Mitchell fine-tuned his equipment and searched for clues the ship might yield on additional contents.

The surreal images focused on a group of double-walled canisters located at the rear of the forward hold. The high-resolution imaging came through chillingly clear.

Bramson looked back at his screen. Five canisters appeared as black images, similar in shape to large metal milk cans from a dairy. But Bramson's attention was drawn more to the brightly-glowing red, gold, and yellow-to-pure-white halo-effect that radiated from each of the containers. Eight other canisters, stored nearby, radiated less in cooler blue-greens, with splotches of red and gold meshing about. They almost seemed alive.

In two different rooms at CIA—Imaging and Mideast office—Mitchell's and Bramson's blood ran cold.

————

THE NEPTUNE

HOLT wanted to get enough sleep in preparation for the morning dive to the *Titanic*. But the cabin intercom startled him from his dream-state.

"Captain, sorry to disturb you. Incoming fax," the voice said. "Looks important."

"Yeah, yeah. Be right up." He forced his tired body from the bunk. With the rude awakening, it took him a moment to get his bearings. The glare from his overhead light almost blinded him as he read his travel clock.

"Two fifteen! Shit, can't a fella get some sleep around here?" He pulled on his clothes and a jacket and tramped up to the bridge.

"This better be good or you'll walk the plank," he growled as the first officer handed him the message.

"You asked me not to disturb Dr. Parker."

"Sometimes I'm just too nice." Holt glanced at the fax from Colonel Bramson. "We've got satellite pics coming in. I'm going down to the van. Better get Cary and Andy up after all."

Holt had been in the DSV control room for about three minutes when Parker and Calder entered.

"What's up?" said Parker.

The Colonel's downlinking satellite photos of the *A'isha*. We're just getting our first look-see." The three men glanced at the monitor over the main control panel as a series of colored lines fed out on the screen.

"This confirms what we've heard," mused Parker. "A rather innocuous ship. Standard merchant. Converted for research. Look at the fantail."

"Did some cutting, it appears," said Calder.

"Are we getting this on tape?"

"Yes, sir" said a technician. "Here's another angle."

"There's the *Yoritomo-class* sub . . . correct that, subs. See that cage there, with the larger framework below the cocooned sub above? Their primary *Yoritomo* rests inside that launcher."

"A launcher?" said Holt.

"Developed by the Chinese," said Parker. "Saw it demonstrated at the World Convention of the Sea in Sydney, several years ago, though this launcher is bigger." He pointed at the monitor. "The tracks, leading to this double-armed, hydraulic crane, allow the launcher to be rolled out with the sub inside its cage, and it's lifted up and out over the water with the U-boom."

"Interesting concept," said Holt.

"The launcher and sub are lowered together and submerged to a depth of at least a hundred feet below the surface . . . using this flotation device, slightly above it, to keep it in a force state of zero buoyancy."

"To cut down on the heave and roll motion between the crane's boom tip and the rolling ship," said Calder.

"Correct. That cuts the wave length in half, below the surface, and creates a smoother launch. Their ship's higher freeboard requires it. Too much space between water and deck."

"We overcame that on the *Shelties* with our new gyros."

"Right. Still, this is a viable system. It was initially developed for unmanned vehicles. They've obviously converted and enlarged it for a manned launch. The trap doors on top of the launcher are for pilot entry into the sub."

"Yeah," said Holt, "but how do they get the *Yoritomo* in and out at underwater depth?"

"The ship's control van releases the umbilical cord, the front and back side arms, then the locks within its framework. Think of it as pulling out of your garage. When work is done, sonar and TV cameras guide the submersible back into place for lifting the launcher on board. And voila!"

"Hey, we got a new picture coming in," Holt interrupted. "A thermographic print."

"They've analyzed the metallurgical content of the subs." Calder read from the screen. "Says here, 'enriched titanium inner hull, with a modified cubic-zirconian outer shell.'"

"Adds tensile strength underwater," said Parker.

"And they've overlaid it with anechoic tiles."

"Rubberized fiberglass to absorb sonar. It'll be difficult to see her below. Judging from everything around her, I'd guess the larger sub has an eighteen to twenty foot span, wing tip to wing tip, and somewhere between thirteen and fifteen feet bow to stern."

"Here's another shot."

"They've enhanced it with highlighted circles around some crew members . . . uh, oh. Their packing weapons."

"The same machine guns used at Heathrow," said Parker. "Those things get around."

"Surprised?" said Calder.

"No. But it confirms Ragem's involvement."

The ship's special phone rang. "A satellite call's coming in. Could only be Bramson at this ungodly hour."

"Who else would get us out of bed like this," said Parker as he picked up the handset.

"*Neptune* here. You want it . . . we dive for it."

"You getting my pictures?" said Bramson.

"Got 'em."

"Wait'll you see what's coming next."

"What do you have?"

"Watch your screen. We've got serious problems." Another series of thermographic prints scanned down the monitor. It was a bizarre looking, almost eerie, sight of thirteen mild to heavily glowing objects.

"What'd you do, find us a ghost ship?" kidded Parker.

"I wish it were that simple. It's almost as apocalyptic."

"Don't beat around the bush. What the hell is it?"

"We matched the IF readings color for color to the computer records for analysis, and we believe that ship is pulling double duty. Five of those objects appear to be canisters of smuggled weapons grade plutonium, Pu239, and enriched uranium, U238."

"Damn," Parker whispered under his breath. "Well, that takes care of this mission. See you back in port in a few days, Colonel." The crew looked at Parker.

"I'm afraid it's not that easy," Bramson continued. "We'd go after them immediately if it weren't for the other eight cans."

"Pray tell."

"Dr. Parker. . .Cary, they've also got bacteria stored in that forward hold. Biological warfare. We haven't yet been able to classify specific microorganisms. But we know they're pathogenic in nature."

Parker was stunned and could only listen as Bramson continued. "We've no idea if Ragem's in on this part, or whether an official in the Libyan government combined two missions. Either way, someone's moonlighting. We suspect the ship's captain might be in on it. The A'isha's under the command of Captain Jadallah Tarik, with direct connections of the highest order in the Libyan government."

"Wonderful. Are we supposed to do a jig now?"

"We believe the ship will head somewhere toward a Western European port, once its mission in the North Atlantic is complete. We may have to let them make a connection, to determine who's involved and break whatever link they've set up. But we don't believe they'll use any of those canisters for your mission.

"It's too valuable a cargo to deploy out there. And the variables are too inconsistent for them to take a chance with the mid-Atlantic's changing winds and currents . . . at least as far as nuclear or biological agents are concerned."

"Are those assumptions supposed to put us at ease?" asked Parker. "Apparently you're not familiar with the science of chaos. We're not dealing with linear systems of predictability here. The more you expect the pendulum to swing in your direction, Colonel, the sooner your expectations lose their validity."

"I understand how you feel, Cary. But remember why you're out there. I wanted to let you know what we're up against. It's only fair. But let us do our work, while you do yours."

Parker pulled the handset from his ear and cupped his hand over the mouthpiece, briefly explaining what Bramson had revealed. Holt, Calder and the others looked to the TV monitor—this time with a seriousness that belied their new-found fears.

"Cary?. . .Dr. Parker? You still there?" Parker heard the electronic voice paging him from the earpiece.

"Yeah. Yeah, I'm here."

"Look carefully at the photo. It appears they've set up a small lab in the rear hold."

"Possibly an electrolytic bath for the artifacts."

"The canisters are in a restricted hold below the foredeck. A smaller one that looks quite secure. As long as they remain there, you're perfectly safe. But you'll have to watch out for armed guards, if the *A'isha* gets too close. They've got heavy-duty ordnance in crates on board."

"More smuggled items for sale?"

"Probably. We'll keep our satellites and the shuttle focused on the *A'isha* as often as possible, to make certain those canisters don't get pulled out of the hold. If they do, we'll pull you out immediately."

"Any word on Victoria?"

"We've developed strong leads, and Nakamura is presently following up. We'll get her back."

Parker remained silent in thought.

"Did you get that?" said Bramson.

"Yeah. Got it. And I'll hold you to it."

"You've got my word."

Parker was filled with quiet rage as he hung up the handset. So far Bramson's word had held little water.

———

ABOARD THE *A'ISHA*

FROM five miles out, Faheed Al Mar Ragem gazed at *Neptune's Knot* through night-vision glasses. He disliked placing himself in jeopardy. But he felt compelled to keep an eye on the proceedings while both ships worked for his benefit.

The radio sputtered.

"This is *Neptune's Knot*, requesting identification of approaching ship. This area is protected. Over," bluffed Holt.

The radio crackled with persistence and Ragem asked the captain to respond.

"This is . . . fishing vessel," the pilot responded, bluffing back in clipped English. A cynical smile crossed Ragem's face.

"What is your name? Identify the name of your ship, over."

"Please, repeat . . . do not understand."

"This is *Neptune's Knot*. This area is a protected salvage site. You are not authorized for entry. Please identify and move your vessel to another site. Over."

"Please to identify . . . fishing vessel. We fishing vessel. Have right to international waters."

A long silence followed from *Neptune's Knot*. Then Parker took the mike from Holt.

"This is Dr. Cary Parker, Ragem. You might be surprised to know I'm still alive . . . after Monaco. It's obvious you can't get competent help these days."

There was more silence. Ragem continued to listen.

"We know you're aboard the *A'isha*, Faheed. And we know why you're here. Do not . . . I repeat, do not attempt to move in on this site, or there will be serious consequences. Over."

Ragem laughed heartily as he left the bridge. Captain Tarik replaced the mike on its hook. Unless Parker and his ship were to display cannon, their plan would remain intact.

———

Just before dawn—in a polar, sun-sychronous orbit—five hundred seventy miles above the surface of the earth, the KH-14 high-resolution reconnaissance satellite, the size of a small bus, adjusted its electro-optical sensors and positioned itself in space in preparation for initial real-time imaging and additional scanning of the *A'isha*.

Politely termed *observation* satellites, the KH series spend much of their existence spying from on high—providing electronic intelligence to the military. The most effective use came during the Gulf War. More recently, they were maximized for observation of troop movements in Iraq; subsequent redeployment of watchdog forces in Jordan and Kuwait; the servicing of NATO and United Nations objectives in Bosnia; monitoring the Soviet dismantling of nuclear weapons sites; various border insurgences; arsenals in several countries; and for the observation of Colombian and Mexican drug cartel operations.

Automatically, the KH-14 satellite adjusted its huge Perkin-Elmer camera, focused its finely ground lenses to the assigned coordinates, and performed another target *search and find* over the Mid-Atlantic Range. The extremely high resolution, multi-spectral, electro-optical sensors were ready for cryptographic signals to direct its next series of moves—to transmit real-time data to its ground stations.

As part of CIA's Project Nobel, three more imaging specialists were assigned to keep a twenty-four hour watch on the *A'isha*. And Colonel Bramson knew he would get little sleep from this point on.

———

Nakamura and Archer returned undetected to the Cherokee, where they uplinked with a communications satellite to FBI headquarters, reported their discovery, and requested the H.R.T.. Archer switched on the Tracor radio locator, tied in with Sat-Nav, to pinpoint their location. Then they changed into dry clothes and, while one kept watch, they split about four hours sleep between them.

Sunrise just began to filter through the parting clouds when a snapping sound awoke Nakamura and startled Archer.

"What was that?" Nakamura rose quickly from the backseat, grabbed her Sig Sauer, and looked out the fogged-up windows.

To their relief, a magnificent twelve-point buck emerged

through the heavy underbrush. It stopped, turned its immense head to the car, stared inquisitively at the large metal intruder, then disappeared into the thicket.

"Rise and shine," Archer said, as if in boot camp.

Nakamura yawned, stretched and stared blankly for a moment at the road in front of them.

The two agents discussed what was ahead. How could they draw the terrorists away from the safe-house, without threatening Victoria's life? And how close was the hostage rescue team?

"Punch in headquarters, will ya?" said Nakamura.

Archer opened up a channel on the secured radio, and punched in some numbers. He passed the mike to his partner.

Nakamura reached over the front seat. "This is WF2D. Anyone else awake? I repeat, WF2D requesting ETA on H.R.T. Over."

The radio hissed for a few seconds.

"WF2D, this is HQ. Checking on your request. Please hold for ETA confirmation. Over." The radio hissed back once more.

"WF2D, we have confirmation on H.R.T. WF12C and WFT4 are just landing by chopper at airfield. Picking up more there—factor six—joining the H.R.T. at lube site within the hour." The message confirmed that agents Mifflin and Arberry were arriving, at that moment, at Pittsburgh International. Six more agents would join them, and together they would meet and form the Hostage Rescue Team at Oil City.

"Have you got a satellite fix on the area? Over."

"Position confirmed. DR coming in clear. You should see backup roll in by zero eight hundred. Over."

Nakamura looked at her watch. It was now 06:50.

"Tell 'em to keep noisy equipment away from the immediate vicinity. Especially the chopper. It's extremely quiet out here. We need absolute stealth or we could spook quarry and cause harm to subject. Over."

"Understood. Will relate to team. Anything else? Over."

Nakamura looked to Archer. He shook his head.

"Not for the present. Over and out." Archer switched off the radio and left the car to stretch out. Nakamura reached back into her knapsack, tore the wrapper off a peanut butter Breakbar, and opened the top of her thermos.

"Snack?" She offered a Breakbar and poured coffee for Archer.

The coffee was barely tepid as they washed down their abbreviated breakfast. Then Nakamura climbed out of the car and wandered over for the temporary seclusion of the bushes. Archer took the other side of the road.

A slight fog, feeling more like a fine drizzle, had settled into the area, as the sun fought with the clouds for control. Eventually, a new warmth took over as the mid-spring day arrived. It appeared the weather would be in their favor.

Knowing the rescue team was on its way, both agents readjusted their bullet-proof vests and mag carriers, and quietly prepared for the next phase. They would remain at the car until backup arrived, then direct the H.R.T. to the site. Nakamura pulled their shotguns from the interior roof-mounted rack and handed one to Archer. They adjusted their Zeiss 3-12X56 T, 9.2/3.3 F/V scopes and broke open the 12 gauge Remington rifled slug loads. Their Sig Sauers were re-checked and holstered.

Finally, they pulled jackets over their vests, made certain additional clip loads were still in their pockets, and took their last sips of coffee.

A woman's scream abruptly interrupted the serenity of the morning and echoed up the hill from below. Then another scream—this time muffled.

The two agents shot quick glances at one another.

"Victoria's in trouble." Nakamura tossed her cup into the car, grabbed her shotgun, and moved quickly down the road toward the caboose. Her sixth sense told her the hostage situation had intensified.

Archer locked the car and caught up.

The screams had melted into the surrounding forest and were absorbed further by the ambient sounds of the river.

"What about the H.R.T.?" Archer whispered as they picked up the pace.

"Can't wait, now. Something's escalated below. Mrs. Parker could be in imminent danger."

The gravel became heavier on the trail, and they entered the woods for cover. The embankment was thick with twisted pine trees and shrubbery fighting for space with the taller hickory, black walnut, and ash.

Both were careful not to snag their clothing as they ducked and turned through the maze of vegetation. And their Remington .870 semi-automatics were held vertically at their sides to prevent hanging up on branches.

The incline was steeper and slippery as they approached the downslope of the ridge. Storm runoff cascaded over the hillside, to combine brown organic humus with mud, as the shrubs thinned out toward the edge. Through the copse, they saw the bright red caboose just above the wet access road that divided the river from the forest's edge. Across the way, the rain-swollen Allegheny sped noisily through its curves and around each bend as it raced to meet the Monongahela to form the Ohio.

Nakamura saw movement in the distance and silently pointed for Archer. They bent down to avoid being seen. With her binoculars, she spotted the three terrorists accompanying Victoria up from the river, south of the rail car.

Victoria's hands were bound in front and the rope continued around her waist. Her mouth was now covered with duct tape. One terrorist brandished a long knife. Two held their guns out as they pushed Victoria toward the safe-house. She appeared wildly distraught.

"Shit," whispered Nakamura. "This would've been perfect timing for the hostage team to hit." She wished they had called for help earlier.

"They'll be here soon," Archer reassured.

Suddenly, Nakamura's right foot slipped out from under her. She reached to grab the closest tree, but her left foot caught a large, snaking root and she tumbled forward, hitting the ground hard with her chest. A loud gasp emitted from her lungs as the impact expelled her breath. Archer was over too far to help.

The men looked to the ridge and saw movement as Archer dropped for cover. Then Ahmed Al-Salih frantically pushed Victoria to the rear caboose platform, and through the door, as the other two raced toward the ridge with an XE-47 and a knife poised for attack.

Nakamura pushed her body into the decaying woodland floor, took a deep breath to recover, and held what was left. It would be difficult to escape after twisting her ankle on the root.

Archer lay silently nearby, Sig Sauer in hand. He waited for an opportunity to assist and hoped not to have to defend their position before help arrived.

Subhi Al-Mamun and Atak Abu Rahman guardedly approached the hillside and edged their way up the slippery rocks. The terrorists were so close, Nakamura and Archer could hear them breathe.

The agents knew that as long as Victoria Parker was inside with one of the men, they could not take these two. Nor were they ready to give up so easily. Nakamura's shotgun was lost in the brush behind her. Slowly, she reached to her holster for the Sig.

Her hand wrapped around the cold, blue steel. But as she pulled the gun out, a branch snagged her jacket and shook the bush nearby. Mamun spotted movement out of the corner of his eye, stood up, and shot a round of bullets into the trees. Unexpectedly, a large buck came charging out of the thicket and raced straight down the hill for the terrorists. In hysterical laughter, the two men hastily slid down and turned to run, as the deer charged from behind.

"Thank God," Nakamura gasped heavily as she took in several deep breaths to recover. Archer inched toward her.

Al-Mamun swung around and ran backwards, aimed in the direction of the buck, and pulled the trigger. But his foot slipped on wet rocks and he fell back into a mud pit, shooting up toward the sky. Rahman tried to grab Al-Mamun by the collar and slipped into the mud next to him.

The buck halted in its tracks and stared defiantly at the two dolts as they laughed at their predicament. Al-Mamun aimed his gun at the buck and pulled the trigger. But the mud had jammed the mechanism.

Angry, Al-Mamun tossed the gun into the brown ooze and stepped on it, pushing it below the surface as the two helped each other up—Rahman still holding his XE-47 away from the mud.

"All right!" Archer mused. "One gun down. One more to go."

"And the knife," said Nakamura.

She had learned to respect those who used knives as a weapon. They watched in amusement as the men walked toward the Taurus—caked from head to toe like mud wrestlers. For the moment the terrorists appeared deceptively less dangerous.

Mamun checked his pants pocket, pulled out keys, and reached for the car trunk keyhole.

"Damn," said Nakamura. "They're going for replacements. And their extra guns are in my car."

The terrorist slipped the key into the slot and turned it. The trunk lid popped open.

———

An early morning quietness surrounded the *Neptune*. Nearly one hour before, Parker had climbed through the top of the mini-sub's conning tower—dubbed the "lepre-con" for its diminutive size— and into his cocoon-like cabin. With only enough space for his body to recline and maneuver his arms and hands, he had to turn corkscrew-style when entering the small cuddy, first standing upright on the seat, stepping down into a slot to the right of the control panel, then pivoting his body in order to slide his feet down and under.

He twisted the full weight of his body under the panel and into position in his form-fitting seat—filled with a silica gel to control cabin humidity and provide more comfort. Parker rationalized if his favorite racers, Rick Mears and Michael Andretti, could squeeze into tight-fitting Indy cars for four hours or more a day, he wouldn't mind duplicating the process for the sake of science.

Aboard *Neptune*, everyone went about their duties with efficiency, yet no one spoke unless they had to. Launch equipment was checked and rechecked. Electricians monitored wires and connections. Software was screened for tampering and viruses. Ship radios, two-ways, and intercoms carried orders and requests from bridge to van, deck to bridge, van to sub, and back again. And divers were already in the water preparing for *Shelty* One to come over the side, making certain there were no obstructions—and that no one was in the water from the *A'isha*.

Having arrived in the middle of the night, the Libyan ship had pulled in a little closer, and anchored on bearing zero-one-nine, nearly three nautical miles out from the *Neptune*, over the sloping Newfoundland Ridge. Holt's crew kept a watchful eye with binoculars, and with sidescan sonar, for any activities that might warrant cautionary procedures.

The speaker above Parker's head crackled with day-to-day preparations from the control room. The safety check had gone smoothly and Parker, his mini-sub suspended between giant arms of the A-frame, awaited the signal to ride out over the fantail.

"Prepare for lowering," said Calder, his angular face reflecting back the array of console lights and monitor screens in the control room.

"Ready," said Parker.

Despite their nearby visitor, the launch countdown for *Shelty One* went without a hitch and, at 06:30 Parker soon found himself floating easily at the surface as the gyros kicked in to stabilize for pitch and heave of the ocean. Parker watched the cool waters splash around his viewports as the sub bobbed in the mild waves. With the sea calmer than usual, the launch was flawless.

Divers moved into position, all over his craft, making certain everything was in order. Muffled knocking sounds emanated around him as they performed their duties. Parker reflected on all the years spent in scuba gear.

Here I am, he thought, *inside my own scuba tank.*

For Parker, it was a landmark day for the field of deep submergence exploration, and a precursor of things to come. The lead diver gave a *thumbs up* sign, Parker pushed a bright red button to signal topside, and mothership released the umbilical cord.

Instantly, Parker felt a surge forward as the ocean's current wrapped its hands about the tiny submersible and pulled it away from any sense of security.

"Yeah!" he exclaimed, wishing this first abyssal launch hadn't been under such a dark cloud.

Then, the cycloidal jets took Parker and his new sub on its first true deep-water run.

In spite of the mission, he was where he wanted to be, as *Shelty One* slowly descended through the water's mixed layer. For the next 400 feet, temperature variations, outside and in, changed as quickly as a falling barometer during a summer's thunder storm. And the sea was bright with reflected and refracted light that danced about from the sun's surface-fed laser show.

At a thousand feet, Calder checked in from the control van.

"We're getting some breakup on sonar. Are you affected down there?"

They waited for an answer. "*Shelty One*, do you copy our breakup of sonar. You're fading in and out. Over."

Despite a tie-in with the military's digitalized SATLAS

blue-green laser network for satellite navigation and deepwater communications—the radio crackled with excessive static. Then Parker's voice broke through.

"Uh . . . *Shelty* here. You're breaking up on me, *Neptune*. Must be delayed biologics. I'll fine tune and see what I get. Sonar is affected. But I can get by for now."

"Roger. Scattering layer coming in at normal depth for this hour. Maybe the moon's confused the biologics and they're just hanging around."

Parker glanced out his viewport.

"Yeah. Still have luminescent diatoms and copepods flitting about. I've just caught 'em off guard."

"Lean, mean love machines," said Andy.

"One just floated by puffing on a cigarette," Parker smiled and checked his fathometer.

"Heading for three hundred fathoms. Over."

"Copy."

But Parker did not hear the last response.

At twelve hundred feet, *Shelty One* reached total darkness. In another hundred feet, the glow of millions of bioluminescent sea creatures played out their precarious lives until they either entreated a partner to join in the reproductive cycle, or ended up as the main course in a higher life-form's food chain. It was a tradition for Parker to stop briefly and admire this ever-present, miniature parade of lights—the smallest of God's electro-chemical light shows. He slipped Elton John's *The One* into his disc player and, as he watched the dancing plankton flash and sparkle to the beat of the music, he slowly pulled away and descended further into the abyss.

Miniaturization of the sub and components allowed the amount of oxygen to be condensed into a smaller space. Breathing in the sub would be more comfortable, since fractional distillation of oxygen compensated for the faster time the new cycloidal water jets helped the craft reach destination. The aquanauts could now fly to depths lower than those previously reached in less time than before, without the usual compression and decompression times needed in other submersibles. Trips such as this would have taken up to two and a half hours just to reach 13,000 feet below sea level. The *Shelty*, though, could reach that level in less than an hour.

Despite the addition of auto-charge, reverse-solar caliginous batteries, *Shelty's* headlights and sidelights remained out to save all possible energy for when it was needed the most on this refamiliarization and test run. The darkness could be overpowering to others. But to Parker it was an opportunity to plan ahead, to strategize and visualize what was to come.

The world had become Parker's laboratory. First attracted to the sea at age 17, aboard an old Marconi-rigged ketch to Tahiti, high technology now bridged the gap between innocent surface sailing, as a youth, and a new venture that would take him deeper into the yawning abyss.

Descending more quickly than before, yet with a purpose beyond Parker's rational mind, the mini-sub marked each new depth with a certain melancholy he had never experienced. And for the first time in many years, he felt a twinge of fear slip in. Promptly, he shook it off, forced a smile, and concentrated on the mission: To dive the *Titanic*, make quick observations for their next descent, then quickly return to the *Neptune*.

Static interference grated through the small cabin, "*Shelty* this is momma. We currently have you at nine-one-seven fathoms. Do you copy?"

"Copy."

"Sonar is clear for the moment. You okay?"

"Happy as a fish in a fryer," his mood kicked into higher gear.

"That's happy?"

"It'd be warmer than right now."

"Truer words were never spoken. Mark a thousand fathoms, a hundred atmospheres of pressure."

"Mark."

On this day and at these depths, Parker found himself appreciating company. It had turned colder and condensation formed on the walls of his cabin, as expected. His sub was progressing toward the initial goal without serious problems. And as he refocused on the positive, he allowed himself a moment of euphoria.

It was rare when bigger fish entered these depths. An occasional school of lantern fish or hatchetfish might pass by. But, with his outside lights off, he would take little notice. It would not be until he entered the deeper bathypelagic zone, between nine and twelve thousand feet, that he would encounter the big-eyed, larger-toothed, enormously jawed anglerfish, and the extended appendaged gulpers and viperfish. Some blind, some luminous, all of magnificent diversity.

Had Parker illuminated his surrounds in the mid-range depths, where few top-grazing animals other than the sperm whale inhabit the waters, he would have noticed an odd phenomenon. Schools of fish, that normally remained in the upper, lighted portion of the open sea—mackerel, herring, cod, and even small squid—were swimming in lower depths that would normally be off limits to their bodies. Their larger spination and specific body gravity would usually match the encircling water gravity and impede sinking below their normal level of habitat.

But, on this day, the gravity of the water itself had changed almost imperceptibly. Just enough to allow these animals to venture into the deeper mesopelagic zone.

If Calder, or any of the technicians in the control van, above, had meshed sonar, radar, Loran, and Sat-Nav through their sophisticated microprocessor, they might have noticed the anomaly. But they were not on a fishing expedition. And, unless a large pod of whales appeared too close to the *Shelty* for Parker's comfort, little attention would be paid to sea life.

Shelty One's fathometer measured off depth as the white submersible passed through chilled waters in absolute darkness.

Pressure readings continued to climb—already at nearly two thousand pounds per square inch outside the mini-sub's shell.

Parker adroitly shifted in his form-fitting seat and pulled on a sweater and a knit skicap for the remainder of the trip. He had put on two pairs of thermal socks prior to boarding. Cold was a hazard with which divers grew accustomed. It also kept them alert.

"*Shelty*. . .I've got you coming up on eighteen hundred fathoms. Any sign of your friend? Over."

"Sonar's picking up shadows below. I'm switching on lights."

As Parker approached the *Titanic's* coordinates, the turbidity of the water, from the previous day's storm, made it difficult to see out his viewports.

"Can't see visually, and sonar's acting capricious," he reported. "Like driving through Bakersfield in a heavy fog with my brights on."

"What'd you say? We're getting mostly static up here. Over."

"Ditto. Not important. May have to do an instrument landing. Coming up on two thousand fathoms."

Shelty approached the average depth of the world's oceans, 12,000 feet below sea level. The depth ranger continued to count off nautical measurements as the one-man sub and its captain descended farther into the dark abyss. At this point, over 6000 pounds per square inch of atmospheric pressure exerted itself on the tiny sub's casing and equipment, increasing by the minute the possibility of implosion if something went wrong.

Parker accelerated the craft downward.

Though gremlins seemed to affect it, a newer form of sidescan sonar developed by the Navy's deep submergence Submarine Development Group One, fed the sub new directional information, and provided Parker with a unique holographic view of the area.

Parker sat up straighter in his seat and focused on his control panel and sonar screen. "Just about there. Slowing down."

He circled the area as sonar picked up and then faded in and out on the expected object that loomed before him.

"*Shelty*, anything yet?" came a short call from *Neptune's Knot*. "Having trouble hearing you."

"This is *Shelty*. Your communications are breaking up, too. Sonar is erratic. But she's right in front of me. Nothing visually, yet. Should spot her any moment now."

"We're losing one word for every four we hear. Tracking has you about thirty-five yards south, southwest. Do you match?"

"Thirty-five? Yeah, that's a match, Andy. What's the prize?"

"You get to keep your sense of humor. Over."

Parker cut back on power as he approached the *Titanic's* bow section from the south, then eased the mini-sub slightly to the east along its starboard side.

"I'm in the field of plowed boulder droppings. The winds are clearing the water, at this level, and I can see them through my viewport. I'll repeat if you want."

"Got that."

Parker gently floated over a plowed up bed of rocks, dropped by icebergs over the centuries. It was a graveyard for more than ships.

"This is *Shelty*. The seabed is beginning to slope up. I'm just about on top of her. Mark coordinates at forty-nine, fifty-six, forty-seven West, and forty-one, forty-three, fifty-four North. Over."

"Mark and mark. GPS agrees."

The bow section of the *Titanic* appeared in the viewing window as a ghost might sneak up on its prey. As frequently as the scientist had visited the site, it never failed to catch him by surprise.

Hidden in the darkness, two miles from the surface, and covered by years of accumulating sediment and rust, the eerie bulk of the ship had suddenly and ominously loomed out at him as if it came from nowhere. The lightless and murky seabed was still contemptible and damning for anyone familiar with the terrain.

On each occasion Parker approached the *Titanic*, it was like

renewing his relationship with a kindred spirit. After years of study-
ing the ocean liner, from bow to stern and smoke stacks to keel
base, he had to take the opportunity to travel it's length . . . to say
"Hello old friend, it's me again."

For the next hour, at an elevation of 12,507 feet below the
surface—nearly as deep an abyss as Humphrey's Peak, in the San
Francisco Mountains of Arizona, is high—Dr. Parker surveyed
the entire length of the ship's bow section from port to starboard,
and cruised slowly over it's decking to the collapsed section, amidships. Then he moved out into the debris field and crossed to
the demolished stern section nearly a third of a mile to the south.

Parker knew he took too long. But it had been a prolonged
period between visits. And there was consolation that he could
genuinely miss Victoria, at the same time, and not have anyone
see his eyes water.

It was also past time to check in, topside. He turned down the
CD player and let *Night On Bald Mountain* take a back seat.

"*One*, here."

Neptune's control room speaker squealed out sounds similar to
those of beached whales.

"Yes, *One*."

"You might have guessed I'm slumming with an old friend."

Calder smiled before he pushed the button on his radio. He
looked at the crew in the control room and shrugged.

"No shit, Skipper. A little overdue for your call to Momma."

"Okay. I'm hereby chastised. Just give me five more minutes.
Besides, I need to do a quick survey for our exploration."

"Fine, Skipper. Just remember why we're here. Our neighbors
are keeping busy in the house next door."

"Up to no good already?"

"There's a flurry of activity over there."

Parker decided to postpone the survey until the second dive,
later that day.

"On my way up. Get subs two and three ready to join me after
lunch. And be prepared to check my electronics for these gremlins."

"Roger and out."

———

Ahmed Al-Salih came out of the rail car scolding his two accomplices in Arabic. They shouted back, hands flailing in the air. The FBI agents could not understand the words, but knew the men were venting their frustrations and anger on one another. The first sign the terrorist's plan was falling apart.

Al-Salih continued to shout at the other two and pointed toward the river. It was obvious they had been instructed to wash off the mud before getting another gun or entering the caboose. Mamun shut the Taurus' trunk and walked toward the river with Rahman.

Relieved their presence had not been discovered, Nakamura and Archer became more focused. Below, the two men started laughing once more, and their voices faded in the distance as the sounds of the river and the rising mist encircled them.

A muffled cry emanated from the rail car.

"We've got to get in there, Mike. Now's our best chance," she reasoned. "What time is it?"

Archer looked at his watch. "Seven forty-two. Backup'll be here soon."

"But we may not get the three of them apart like this again." She massaged her ankle, rested for several breaths, then pulled herself up and tested the weight on her left foot.

"Need help?"

Nakamura shook her head, winced from the sprain, but decided she could live with it. "I'll be okay."

She climbed up and rescued her Remington semi-automatic from the bushes, slung it over her shoulder—muzzle up—and warily moved up the hill toward the road. Archer looked back at the caboose.

"Hold on," he said.

Al-Salih came out of the rail car carrying two small overnight bags to the Taurus. He looked around suspiciously, unlocked the trunk and, without looking, threw the bags inside.

"Crap, they're leaving," said Archer.

"Vicky's in danger now." Nakamura thought quickly. "What if they meet the rescue team coming in on the road?"

"Dammit!"

The terrorist glanced toward the hillside, then returned to the caboose. The platform door closed behind him.

The agents were thankful the fog hid some features of the land. With as furtive a stance as they could produce, they carefully moved between the trees and bushes, and hoped Al-Salih would not spot them before they could get close.

"Cover me," said Nakamura. "I'm going to the back. Watch for the two at the river."

"Gotcha." Archer concealed himself in a grove of trees just up the road from the front entrance—with a direct view of the caboose and the path from the river.

Within twenty feet of the rail car Nakamura picked up a stone, crept toward the back platform, and tossed it on the metal step. She quickly limped for the front platform, moved quietly toward the door and listened. Nakamura heard steps receding toward the other end, and the back door opening.

Al-Salih set down a piece of luggage, stepped cautiously onto the platform, and glanced out toward the river. He couldn't see his two accomplices and wondered what caused the noise. Holding his XE-47 out from his chest, he looked down the side of the rail car. Then he moved to the other side and glanced to the end. Convinced something fell from the trees above, he relaxed and turned to walk back inside. He reached to pick up the bag by the pot-belly stove and saw movement at the other end.

Once—while killing time in an El Djazair movie house—

Al-Salih had seen two western gunfighters play out their scene in slow motion. As though he were in that movie, he saw his own enemy come through the rear door with a Sig Sauer aimed at his head. The moment slowed instantly as he screamed out Arabic curses and brought up his machine gun. But two 9mm bullets traveling at 1155 feet per second had already entered his heart and exited through his back, A third bullet passed between his eyes, through his brain.

Ahmed Al-Salih first slammed forward, then backward as the impact of each bullet caught him off guard. He reeled sideways, stammered unknowingly outside and dropped, suspended half-way over the platform railing. He never got off a shot.

Archer had heard the gunfire and saw Al-Salih as he faltered out the back door and collapsed. The agent raced to the front platform and turned toward the door.

"You need help?"

"Watch for the other two," Nakamura answered as she searched for Parker. "They should be coming up any minute."

Archer moved back to his original position and waited.

"Vicky! Where are you?" Nakamura favored her bad foot as she hurried through the rail car. She heard a hard bang come from behind the dirty-white horizontal door, as Victoria kicked it with all her might. Nakamura turned to the plywood door, unlatched it and saw Vicky Parker bound and gagged on the filthy mattress. She ripped the blindfold off Parker's head. Victoria's eyes showed the terror she had faced.

"Jesus, Vicky, let's get you out of here."

She helped Parker up. "This'll hurt me more." She grabbed the gaffer's tape over Vicky's mouth and pulled fast.

"Ow!"

"Sorry. We've got to move rapidly. Let's get these ropes off. Then we'll pull the dead one inside."

Victoria looked out the back door and saw Al-Salih's body hanging from the railing. She turned away, sickened by it all.

"You take care of him," Victoria stammered, still affected by the drugs. "I can get out of these."

"You're kidding."

"I can do it."

Nakamura raced to the back of the caboose, looked toward the river for the other two, grabbed the back of Al-Salih's pants, and pulled him from the railing. The body fell with a loud clump to the floor as she dragged him inside, looked around and opened the door to the out-of-order toilet. She stuffed him inside and slammed the door shut, then turned to help Victoria—only to find her totally out of the ropes.

"How'd you do that . . . where'd you learn to escape ropes like that?" Victoria rubbed her rope-burned wrists and held them high.

"Magic," she smiled feebly for the first time in a week. "Tell you the trick later."

"Let's go! We've got help on the way."

Nakamura grabbed a baseball cap off the floor and gave it to Parker.

"Put this on. Agent Archer is waiting outside."

Weak and exhausted, Victoria tugged the cap on. Nakamura grasped Vicky's arm and assisted her to the front of the caboose. As they started out the door, Nakamura saw the head of Atak Abu-Rahman rise over the embankment. She shoved Victoria back inside.

"The other way, quickly. They're coming up from the river."

Victoria stumbled and fell to the floor near a makeshift table. Maps and diagrams lay scattered about.

"Come on, baby. Don't fail me now," Nakamura grabbed Victoria by the waist. "What's this?" She picked up the papers. "A map of Philadelphia . . . and look at what's circled. My Lord, these must be bomb sites."

The agent stuffed everything she could inside her jacket and helped Victoria to the opposite door. They stepped off the platform, used the rail car to block the view of their retreat as they rushed past Archer, and moved up the hill toward the Cherokee. Archer held back to cover their escape.

Rahman and Al-Mamun had heard the reports from the gun. Uncertain of their origin, and having heard several distant shots from poachers during the past week, they were cautious not to overreact. Perhaps the buck had returned to the area and Al-Salih had shot it.

Al-Mamun took no chances and hurried ahead of Rahman. As he hit the top of the rise, he saw two figures dart past their car, and up the hill. He recognized the clothes on Victoria, noted Al-Salih was not with her, then saw a scoped Remington semi-automatic aimed in his direction.

———

An anomalous mist had risen from the North Atlantic waters, in the mid-morning sun, just before the day's second launch of the *Shelties*. With the warm Gulf Stream swept up from the south, meeting the frigid northern Labrador Current in the region of the Grand Banks, the area was notorious for heavy fogs. Yet, inconsistent with the course of the two flowing bodies, this fog seemed to rise out of nowhere. A fleshy ghost in appearance, it had floated over the sea like a heavy veil, on bearing three-five-eight, just four nautical miles north and slightly west of the *A'isha's* position.

Following Parker's morning dive, the fog seemed a harbinger of what was still to come in its quiescent, almost hushed and portentous state. But Cary avoided expressing his pessimistic thoughts for the moment. They needed to remain upbeat from here on out.

"It doesn't appear to be moving this way," he said, dropping his binoculars to his chest. "Hopefully it'll dissipate and burn off."

"At least the water's calm," said Holt. "Couldn't ask for smoother conditions."

"Speaking of which," Calder reminded everyone on the bridge.

"Are we ready?"

"Did you check radios after the problems with *Shelty One*?"

"Couldn't find anything," said Calder. "Must've been a permutation of the electromagnetic fields. Possibly those magnetic anomalies we found back in the eighties. Maybe flareups on the sun. Who knows. Whatever it was, it's gone now."

The door from the portside bridge wing opened. "Dr. Parker," said the crew chief, "Could I speak with you?"

"Certainly. Come in."

"Uh, out here, sir?"

Parker looked at the others, shrugged, and walked to the bridge wing. "What's up?"

"Sir, I checked our satellite dish wires and found them hanging loosely from their connections."

"You think the storm loosened them?"

"Uh, no sir. I believe someone's tampered with the equipment." He held out two metal nuts. "These here nuts . . . and the others up there like 'em . . . they were unscrewed and barely resting on top of the bolts. The entire dish could've toppled in the slightest breeze."

"The storm could've done that."

"I doubt it, sir. The nuts had been sealed. Someone broke the seals."

"Well, that'll explain some of our transmission problems, if we have other wires loosened in our equipment."

"And the U-bolt that was cut before you went overboard, yesterday."

Parker opened the door to the bridge and stuck his head inside.

"Andy . . . you and John want to come out here a minute."

The crew chief repeated his information. Parker requested that he be on guard and remain observant for the remainder of their mission. He dismissed the man to complete preparations for the triple-sub dive to the *Titanic*, then turned to Calder and Holt.

"Any thoughts?"

"You don't want to know," said Calder.

"No secrets. Just lay out what you're thinking."

"I've never trusted that son-of-a-bitch, Dupont. Wouldn't surprise me if he's getting back for what Bramson did to keep him from diving on his own."

"Yeah, but the U-bolt . . . and the test dive over Georges Bank? He wouldn't have done that to me . . . "

"Frankly, Cary," said Calder, "I think you're naive as hell."

Parker glanced at Holt.

"Don't look at me," said Holt. "I'd just as soon shoot him and save the trouble of guessing . . . but, I won't."

"Well, we're stuck with him," said Parker. "And I'd rather have him in a sub, where we can keep an eye on him, than up here wandering around, disrupting communications."

Calder gave Parker a skeptical look and let out a long sigh. "It's your call, partner."

———

"Where do you think you're going?" Al-Mamun screamed over the din of the Allegheny.

Archer held the terrorist in his gun's sight.

Nakamura faced Al-Mamun, with Victoria behind her.

"Go on," Archer indicated to Nakamura. "Get her up the hill. I'll hold them off."

"No," Victoria said, her voice wavering, "We'll stay here with you."

"Don't be foolish, Vicky," Nakamura turned to her. "Get to my Cherokee and lock yourself in. I'll be right behind you." She handed her keys to Victoria.

"Go. Now!"

Archer held fire, with Al-Mamun still in the cross hairs of his sight.

Confused by the aftereffects of the drugs, Victoria stood motionless.

"Please! You'll be safer up there," insisted Nakamura. "Mike can hold them off until the other agents arrive. Head up through the trees and I'll follow."

"I don't have the strength to make it up there," Victoria cried.

Archer turned to look at Parker. "You can make it Mrs . . . "

Victoria screamed as rapid fire rang out from the beach, below. Mike Archer yelped and dropped his shotgun as he grabbed his right temple and went to the ground.

Nakamura pulled Victoria out of the way and sat her behind a tree. Bullets ricocheted around them.

"Damn," Archer said, angry at himself for dropping his guard. His head throbbed with pain, but his hand had deflected the bullet that grazed his temple. He checked his bleeding hand and pressed it against his jacket, as he picked up his Remington and darted for cover.

"Take Mrs. Parker to the car," said Nakamura, "and radio for an ambulance. If you must, drive out to meet the H.R.T."

"What about you?"

"I'll be up soon."

Shots raced by them, again, barely missing Victoria's legs. Both terrorists sprinted toward them, wet from the river.

Nakamura got off several rounds and temporarily held them at bay. Despite his bleeding hand, Archer reached for his Sig Sauer and fired back.

"I'll cover for you, this time," said Nakamura. "Get out before you draw more fire."

With Victoria still in a daze, Archer and Parker slowly moved through the trees, then to the road. Archer watched the terrorists inching closer to Nakamura. Then he assisted Parker, as they moved up the hill.

Nakamura lifted the Remington to her right shoulder, twisted her arm through the strap for support, cross-haired Al-Mamun in her sight, and shot off a round. Seeing the rifle come up, Al-Mamun ducked for cover, but was grazed in the left arm. He dropped to the ground and rolled behind a boulder.

Furious, Rahman triggered his machine gun and splattered hardened plastic bullets around Nakamura. The FBI Agent retreated behind a larger hickory, took aim and shot back. The bullet ricocheted off the XE-47, at Rahman's chest, and he took cover with Al-Mamun, wildly shooting back as he jumped behind the large rock. Bullets ripped at the tree bark and Nakamura pressed closer to the ground.

"Ahmed!" screamed Atak Abu Rahman from his position just outside the caboose. "Ahmed!"

He shouted several phrases in Arabic. Then there was silence. Again, Arabic screams echoed past the rail car, followed by more silence. Suddenly, Rahman jumped from his position and raced for the back door of the caboose.

Nakamura rose and got off a shot, but missed as the terrorist found cover on the backside. Without warning, a large silver knife spiraled from behind the boulder and stuck the tree, narrowly missing the agent. She shot back at Al-Mamun, moved up the road toward her car, and turned every twenty feet to observe her adversaries and fire off a round to keep Al-Mamun in check.

Rahman stood tight against the wall on the rail car platform, afraid of what he might find inside. Slowly, he turned into the doorway and edged past the pot-belly stove.

"Ahmed, are you in here?"

Silence answered.

"My cousin, are you all right?"

He lifted the makeshift door that had covered Victoria's bunk. Nothing. He looked under the rickety table and into the dilapidated pantry. Then he saw the trail of blood leading to the old toilet door.

"No, Allah, please . . . I beg of you . . . "

He lifted the metal latch that had held the door closed over thousands of miles of cold steel rail. Rahman prayed to Allah once more. Then he opened the door.

Al-Salih's body rolled from the enclosure and fell over the feet of his cousin. His blank countenance stared up from the floor with a surprised, wild-eyed gaze—his face torn by the bullet and covered with blood, and his chest soaked as red as the rail car.

From outside, Nakamura and Al-Mamun heard a raging man scream to the heavens.

"NO!"

Silence followed again.

Then, as though a deranged entity had been released from the earth, Atak Abu Rahman flew out on the forward platform, wildly aimed up the hill and, in seconds, emptied an entire magazine load in Nakamura's direction.

"You bastards!" he screamed into the trees.

Filled with fury and indignation, and seething with rage, Rahman slammed another clip home, jumped off the steps, and ran toward the ridge road firing wildly in every direction. Bullets snapped into trees, off gravel, and near Nakamura's feet.

As she sprinted up the hill, pain in her left foot slowed her down. Two bullets slammed into her back, knocked her forward and, for an instant, took her breath away. But her vest absorbed most of the blows, as she gasped for air and sprinted toward Victoria and Agent Archer.

Below, Al-Mamun had raced to grab another gun. He lifted the Taurus' trunk lid, tossed out the bags, and discovered the remaining XE-47's were gone. He slammed the lid and ran into the rail car, where his fallen partner's gun had dropped to the floor.

"Praise Allah," he said as he grabbed the blood-spattered gun and jumped off the platform to help Rahman. He jogged up the road yelling curses in Arabic—alternately begging Allah for help.

Archer, weakened from loss of blood, assisted Victoria as she collapsed from exhaustion on the road.

"Just another hundred yards," he entreated. "You can make it to the car."

Shots echoed hideously through the trees, but Victoria's mind was still clouded from the drugs. She gasped for air and felt a heaviness in her chest, as the flight-or-fight instinct battled for control. Laboriously, she tried to rise as Archer leaned to give her support.

Dizziness overcame Archer, but he stood up to gain control.

"No sitting on the job," a voice yelled from the curve below.

Archer and Victoria watched Nakamura dart up the hill, one leg skipping to protect the sprain. Alternately, she fired back rounds of bullets, as shots were answered from behind.

"Thank God," Victoria cried, inspired with new energy as an additional burst of adrenaline hit.

Archer helped her up.

Nakamura reached them, grabbed Victoria from behind, and the three moved out, just as the babbling Rahman rounded the bend with his spraygun wide open.

Victoria cried out as bullets glanced off everything around them, and Archer held tighter to Parker's waist to keep both of them up.

Rahman stopped to ram another clip into his gun. Nakamura fired back to keep him down as she edged Parker and Archer into the trees.

"Stay here for God's sake. I'll be back." She looked down the road.

"Keep low," Archer instructed Victoria. He wrapped a hand-kerchief around his hand, pulled out his Sig Sauer and waited.

"Where the hell's our backup?" Nakamura yelled to no one in particular. Hoping to divert attention and draw fire away from Parker and Archer, she ran across the road to a larger clump of trees and rolled into the brush as the first terrorist approached. Bullets rained around her. She carefully took position, aimed her Remington short-barrel, and fired three rounds.

Each bullet ripped through Rahman's body, as the force of the shots sent him reeling backward toward his partner. Rahman's finger stalled on the trigger, sending shots wildly into the wooded area. Archer pressed his body over Victoria, using his own vest to shield her.

Al-Mamun stared at his fallen comrade, saw Victoria and Archer in the woods and fired in their direction.

Archer got off several rounds, but his control was weakened. Realizing the two were in trouble, Nakamura emptied her rifle, just missing the last terrorist. He held back, turned and retreated down the hill. She pulled out the Sig, took aim and shot off six more rounds. But Al-Mamun was beyond the trees.

Nakamura reloaded her guns, slung her rifle over her shoulder, and dashed across the road.

"You okay?" she asked, helping Victoria up.

"Just get us out of here," Victoria responded confused and dazed from the trauma.

"Can you move to the car?"

"With an assist . . . "

"Don't know what's happened to our terrorist friend," Nakamura glanced back down the hill as she helped Archer lift Victoria around the waist, "but I suspect he'll be back. Put your arms around our shoulders."

She looked at Archer. "How're you holding up?"

"I'll make it. Let's move out."

The three were exhausted as they rushed for cover across the dirt road, for the trees that opposed the bend below. They saw the top of the Cherokee—seventy-five yards up the hill —a welcome sight as they approached the flat-topped rise.

"Give me the keys," said Nakamura.

Victoria searched her pocket. "I can't find them."

"Which pocket?" asked Nakamura.

"The right-back. I think that's the one."

"Nothing's there." Nakamura tried her left side, while Victoria checked the front pockets. "Not here."

"Must've fallen out," said Archer.

"Shit!" said Nakamura.

Victoria began to cry.

"We'll be okay. Let's get to the car." The three limped up the road. Then Nakamura stopped. "I hear a car."

"I don't hear anything," said Archer.

"A car's coming."

"Maybe it's the rescue squad."

Nakamura listened intently. "Not likely. It's coming from below. From the river. FBI isn't here yet. There's been no shots fired to stop them."

"Who is it?" Victoria asked in panic.

"The knife thrower."

"Al-Mamun," Victoria confirmed.

"He's got the Taurus, heading this way. Come on. Quick!"

The three hastened toward the Cherokee as best they could—the two agents holding up Parker—using every ounce of adrenaline to reach their goal.

Tires were heard as they raced across gravel and climbed the hill. Both agents' hearts jumped. Al-Mamun could drive right on top of them.

"Damn, I should've shot their tires out."

They approached the Cherokee, and Nakamura pulled out her Sig Sauer.

"Stand back and cover your eyes!"

Nakamura aimed her gun at the front passenger window, covered her face, and pulled the trigger. The glass shattered and flew mostly inward. Nakamura reached through and pulled the door lock.

The Taurus was heard rounding the bend below. Then another sound emerged.

"There's a copter in the air," said Archer.

The three looked up but saw nothing beyond the trees.

"I told them no noisy equipment," Nakamura said, glad the helicopter was on the way.

The car radio crackled up front.

"Calling WF2D, this is WF12C. We're within sight of the caboose. Do you copy? Come in WF2D. Where are you? Over."

Nakamura ripped open the car door, unlocked the back, and looked at Victoria.

"We're gonna make this. Get in the backseat, lie on the floor, and watch out for glass." She pulled open the back door and grabbed an XE-47, as Archer helped Victoria into the car.

"Mike . . . you conscious enough to drive?"

"Have to be."

"Extra keys are under the seat. Get us out of here."

Archer pushed glass aside as he slid across the seat, felt around for the keys, and rammed them into the column. Nakamura slammed the back door shut, jumped up front and reached for the radio's handmike. The Cherokee's wheels spit up loose gravel and mud as Archer gunned it in reverse, twisted the car in an arc, and gave it full throttle.

"This is WF2D. We're in deep shit. Do you read? Better get here fast. Look for a dark gray Taurus—I repeat—dark gray Taurus coming up the hill north of the caboose, just east of the Allegheny. We're in the Cherokee. Copy?"

The radio crackled back, "Copy WF2D. We have air and ground. Should see you any minute. Have eye contact on something moving up the road between the trees. How many of you down there? Over."

"Hostage is safe with us. Hostage and WF9C need immediate medical. Get a couple of ambulances out here. One terrorist remaining in the Taurus . . . in the mood to commit suicide at all costs. Over."

"Roger."

They overheard the copter order medical assistance and direct ground cars on both roads leading into the camp from the split. Then Nakamura turned as Al-Mamun's car sailed over the rise—a trail of gravel and mud soaring into the air behind him. Above the tree line, two miles to the south, she saw the FBI's helicopter as it tracked the auto up the road.

Nakamura saw a gun emerge from the Taurus. Bullets sprayed across the road, sixty yards behind, getting nearer as Al-Mamun pulled closer to the Cherokee.

Then the gray car stopped.

Al-Mamun heard helicopter blades thrash at the sky. In his side-view mirror he saw the FBI chopper as it bore down on him. Suddenly, shots were fired from above—still at some distance.

The decision was made. Al-Mamun put a fresh clip into his gun, stomped on the gas, aimed his XE-47 out the window, and blasted once more at the escaping Cherokee.

Nakamura hit a dash button that popped the rear door window latch. She rolled over the front seat, past Victoria, climbed on the rear bench seat, and sent the rear window up out of the way.

"Here's a taste of your own medicine, jackass!" Nakamura yelled. She aimed the confiscated XE-47 at the oncoming car and pulled the trigger.

"Damn, this thing has power." Bullets ripped through the air and shattered half the terrorist's windshield. The Taurus bounced erratically over the rain-filled rutted road, but kept advancing. Bullets slammed at the Jeep's body and exploded its brake lights.

"Floor it, Mike."

"She's all the way down," he yelled over the engine, as he pulled the Jeep onto the dirt apron to avoid the bigger ruts. Tree branches and bushes tore at the car as Archer put distance between themselves and the terrorist.

Nakamura realized if the rescue squad hit the Ordnance Center explosives with stray bullets, the combustive force could take out the helicopter, instantly, and anything else nearby.

She replaced a clip, fired several quick rounds at Al-Mamun, then reached in her jacket pocket for the small black box—pulled from the Taurus' trunk.

"Hand me the radio," she yelled, and jumped toward the front, desperately holding onto the back of the seat as the car bounced across the road. Archer struggled to get her the microphone. She grabbed it and pushed Talk.

"WF2D, here. Pull back for a couple of minutes, fellas. Keep the copter a mile aft or more and hold up your cars. It's going to get hot around here."

"What's going on? Over," queried the helicopter pilot as he backed off on the throttle. The rotor blades could be seen floating up and turning to the south.

The Cherokee hit a large rut and bounced high in the air. The coiled mike cord instantly shot from Nakamura's hand. She was thrown against the side and hit her head on the window. Victoria's eyes showed panic and abject fear, but there was nothing Jenny could do to help her.

Archer caught the mike by its cable and handed it back to Nakamura as she forced herself upright. She competed with the road for balance and pressed Talk.

"WF2D, again. Stand by and stand back for a big boom. No time to explain. Over and out."

The Jeep put distance between itself and the Taurus, but Nakamura saw bullets skip off the road as Al-Mamun accelerated. She glanced at the small red button on the side of the box, placed her thumb on top of it, and wrapped her palm tightly around its base. Then she rushed back to the rear window.

Even with the blind spot the morning sun reflected off the Taurus' remaining windshield, Nakamura knew she was dealing with a madman. He would not quit until his mission was accomplished.

"Vicky, cover your head and stay down," she yelled over the seat. "Mike, hold that wheel steady."

Shots rang closer as Nakamura shielded herself behind the rear door and seat. She fired back at the terrorist. Bullets blew out his right front tire and entered the Taurus' grill above the engine. The Ford bounced high and nearly out of control, but shots still danced around the Cherokee.

Defiantly, her arm rose out the back opening, straight into the air, and Nakamura turned her hand to expose the black box to her adversary. Al-Mamun tried to identify the object held high, as he raced toward the Jeep. Then he watched Nakamura pull the black box to her face.

She could now see through the Ford's remaining windshield. And Al-Mamun's countenance expressed sheer panic when he recognized the Ordnance Center's stolen detonating device.

"Hold on everyone!" Nakamura yelled up front. "Mike, whatever you do . . . just keep this baby floored."

Nakamura placed the high-pitched whistle in her mouth and could not hold back a smile as she stared for one split second at the terrorist—now falling behind.

Abruptly, the Ford skidded in an attempt to stop—as the Jeep put considerable distance between them.

The Taurus slid sideways toward the ridge, and the driver's door flew open.

As Al-Mamun began to jump, Nakamura pushed the detonator's red safety button.

"Hold on . . . !"

She dived under the seat for cover, and blew intensely into the high-pitched whistle.

Eight contiguous explosions reverberated through the valley as the Taurus and its passenger were lifted into oblivion. A giant ball of flame reached out in all directions—pursuing the Grand Cherokee with its searing heat as the Jeep raced on an opposite course around a mud-slicked bend, behind a cover of thick hickory and walnut.

And fire rose two hundred sixty feet into the sky.

The force cut into gravelly sandstone like a laser through ice, and a fifty-seven foot crater was left behind. A heated cloud of muddy shale and black smoke followed close on its heels, scattering thousands of rocks and fine, quartz-grained pebbles over a square-mile area.

Multiple shock waves thrashed at the air, jolted through the woods, and flattened anything in their path.

The twisted frame of the burning Taurus shot out over the trees, rolled down the high ridge, and—in an immense plume of hot steam—slid off the embankment into the raging Allegheny.

"What the hell was that?" a voice on the radio kicked in. "Come in, WF2D. You all right? Over."

The helicopter avoided incoming shrapnel, bypassed the crater, and followed the road to the Jeep. From the air, the aftermath looked as if a large meteorite had slammed into the earth.

Archer slowed down the Cherokee, rolled it to a stop, and sat zombie-like at the wheel.

Nakamura climbed out and moved around to the front passenger side —her hands, face and strands of hair singed from the intense heat.

The radio blared, "Come in, WF2D. WF9C . . . are you okay? Do you copy?"

Dazed from the shockwave, Nakamura stared at the radio, trying to get back her senses. The helicopter again called for a response as it hovered over them.

Archer weakly handed the mike to Nakamura. Taking it, she looked above and pushed the Talk button.

"WF2D, here." She pulled off her cap. "You'd better call in the Forest Service to mop up. There's one big hole to fill. Any sign of an ambulance or two?"

"On their way. Should be here any minute. Over."

Exhausted, Nakamura sat limp on the edge of the rocker panel. Then, she called over her shoulder.

"Victoria?" There was no response. Nakamura climbed back inside and glanced at Parker, curled up on the floor. "It's over Vicky. You all right?"

Victoria turned her head and forced a smile. She had no energy to respond. The FBI agent reached over, extended her hands and helped her up to the bench seat.

Nakamura smiled reassuringly, "It's over," she repeated quietly. "It's all over. You'll see your girls soon."

Tears welled up in Victoria's eyes and ran down her ashen cheeks. "Thank you," she managed to say. Victoria placed her hand lightly on Archer's shoulder—thanking him without words—then sprawled out across the backseat. And for the first time in nine days she closed her eyes and began to relax. Relieved, Nakamura collapsed into the front seat exhausted.

The helicopter hovered over the site in an attempt to land. The voice on the radio persisted. "WF2D, do you copy? What the hell caused that explosion?"

Jennifer Nakamura hit the Talk button. "I'd call it poetic justice."

"Looks like a Nevada testing ground from up here."

"No heavy water—just the experimental plastic toy from that Kentucky Ordnance Center. And you know what?"

"What's that?" the pilot inquired.

"The damn thing works!"

It had taken twenty minutes to get medical help from Franklin to the site. Following Archer and Parker's treatment, and the wrapping and icing of Nakamura's ankle, FBI and CIA headquarters had been notified of the rescue and Parker's condition.

Both ambulances had picked up the main highway. Archer was evacuated in one—Victoria was asleep in the back of another. Jennifer Nakamura accompanied her as they headed toward Franklin's Northwest Medical Center. Parker would be placed under medical observation before a med-flight evacuation would take her to Brigham and Women's Hospital, in Boston, for recuperation and a reunion with her children.

The ambulance driver's radio was set low, with the local country station playing Gary Morris', *Wind Beneath My Wings*. The vehicle struck a pothole and jarred Victoria Parker out of a deep sleep. Mentally and physically drained, she remained still and relaxed. The humming of the engine soothed her frayed mind and body as they approached the outskirts of Franklin. She saw Nakamura strapped into a jump seat, next to her—dozing lightly. An attendant monitored them, nearby.

Victoria felt the warmth of the sun flicker through the roadside trees and into the side windows of the speeding ambulance, as it headed toward town. Her eyes casually absorbed kaleidoscopic reflections that bounced around her gurney. Then, swiftly—as though a hand had grasped her throat—from deep in her subconscious mind, images stirred. And panic gripped her heart.

Suddenly, like she had been dropped into a bath of ice, Victoria gasped out loud. Nakamura quickly awakened and turned to look at her. The attendant came to her side.

"You okay?" he said.

Frozen with fear, Victoria mouthed silent words that would not come out.

"Vicky, what's the matter?" said Nakamura.

Victoria became hysterical, trying to scream, but fear held her silent. Nakamura moved to her.

"My God, my God." Victoria thrashed from side to side, and her hands flew up to cover her face from what her mind had suddenly seen. The attendant prepared to give her a sedative.

"No!" Parker insisted. "No more drugs, please."

Nakamura stroked Victoria's head and pulled her close to her chest, like a little child.

"Whatever it is, Vicky, it'll be okay. We'll get you to the hospital." She started to let go, but Parker moaned loudly, then opened her eyes wide to stare at her. Parker tore at the safety straps, forced herself to sit up straight, and glared out the opposite window—her entire body shaking uncontrollably.

The attendant made an attempt to re-buckle the safety belt, but Parker resisted. Nakamura gently placed her hand over his, as if to say, "No need. She'll be all right."

"What is it?" Jenny said.

Parker turned to Nakamura, looking like she had seen an apparition, and slowly began to speak.

"Call Colonel . . . uh, Bramson at CIA. We've got to get through to Cary . . . he's in grave danger. They're *all* in terrible danger."

Nakamura saw that Parker was not hallucinating.

"What's wrong. Tell me so I can relay the message."

Parker began to hyperventilate. Nakamura held her hands to comfort her.

"Calm down, Mrs. Parker," said the attendant. "Breathe slowly. Lean slightly over and take it slow."

Parker desperately tried to compose herself and quell her fears. She took several deep breaths and let them out slowly to relax. Then she brushed her hair aside and turned to Nakamura.

"At one point," Parker was hesitant to speak, "tied up in that cubicle . . . uh, I think it was last week, I heard a car pull up next to the caboose. Someone got out, slammed the door shut, and talked with the terrorists, outside."

Nakamura waited for her to continue.

"He spoke with an accent," she went on. "I couldn't make it out. I was heavily drugged. I couldn't hear anything intelligible, but I knew he was different from the others."

Parker searched the depths of her memory.

"Go on."

"After a time . . . everything became silent. Then I heard steps on the platform and the door opened. He stood at the entrance for the longest time. I could tell because the caboose shook every time someone stepped through it.

"Finally . . . I felt it shake as he moved toward me. My wooden door creaked open and light spilled in through my blindfold. I struggled to see through the slit under my eyes . . . but I couldn't identify him.

"I felt his presence for the longest time . . . just staring. Never said a word. He must've stared at me . . . it seemed forever. For the first time in days, I could smell a clean man. He smelled pleasant . . . of cologne."

Tears streamed down Victoria's face as she recalled what happened next.

"He gently pulled back the tape from my mouth and softly stroked my hair and caressed my lips with his fingers. My heart pounded. For an instant I thought Cary had made a deal with the terrorists and had come to rescue me. Then he leaned into the cubicle and fondled my breasts, and kissed me on the lips. I was still drugged . . . and my mind went berserk with excitement. That's when I recognized his cologne. A familiar fragrance, but not Cary's. One I remembered from the past."

Suddenly, Victoria's mind flashed with suppressed images. Her entire body shook as she remembered more. And she sank to the mattress.

"When I realized it wasn't Cary, I bit his lip and spit at him."

"What did he do?

Victoria cried, "He slapped me . . . stuck the tape back over my mouth, and slammed the door shut."

"He said nothing to you?"

"Not a word," she sobbed. "I felt the car shake heavily as he stomped out, and . . . words were exchanged before he drove off. But I couldn't hear what was said because of the car's motor. Ever since that day, I've struggled to see his face . . . to recall the cologne."

"And now you know," Nakamura said softly.

Victoria shuddered again, not knowing if she trembled from fear, anger or both. "The accent . . . was French Canadian. It was Dupont. Henri Dupont. The cologne was his favorite. He always bragged about buying it wholesale outside of Cannes. It was the only fragrance he'd wear when he tried . . . "

Victoria sat up straight. "Henri and I nearly had an affair years ago. I was stupid for getting involved, but I cut him off. Nothing serious happened." She looked directly at Nakamura. "Dupont is the only one who'd have the nerve to visit me. Please, Jennifer, notify the authorities. Bramson's got to stop Cary from diving to the *Titanic*."

Nakamura released Victoria's hands, squeezed her arm for reassurance, and moved to the front of the ambulance.

"I need to uplink to a satellite. It's an emergency."

The assistant handed Nakamura a cellular phone.

Parker was extremely weak from exposure and the after-effects of the Nembutal. Exhausted, she slid down across the gurney from her upright position, and would barely remember Nakamura making contact with FBI Headquarters. Finally, she found a deep and profound sleep.

––––––

49° 56' 50" W, 41° 43' 45" N

THE *Neptune* monitored the *A'isha* and vicinity for sonar activity below the surface. Other than the three *Shelty-class* subs, launched thirty minutes before, no other submerged vehicles bounced reflections from the water.

Countdown and launch, for the *Titanic* expedition, had gone like clockwork as each sub was moved into place, lifted out over the ocean, and carefully lowered into the water. Calder went first, in *Shelty Two*. Dupont followed in *Shelty Three*. Then Parker in *Shelty One*. Never before had a trio of submersibles taken to the water together. This would be a ground-breaking adventure for all three oceanographers—regardless of the circumstances.

The cold already had a bite to it. Yet each man was accustomed to the experience. By 1000 feet—167 fathoms—each diver had donned knit ski caps and palm gloves out of habit. To Parker, it was no different than a cold day skiing at Snowshoe, West Virginia.

At eleven hundred fathoms, the outside water temperature measured thirty-seven degrees Fahrenheit but gradually decreased through the remainder of the Thermocline and stayed fairly constant—between thirty-four and thirty-two degrees—to the bottom.

Parker checked with topside at each milestone of depth. But as the three *Shelties* approached two thousand fathoms, they encountered the same trouble Parker had during his dive earlier that morning.

In the dense ocean water, communications between subs required digitalized and highly compressed voice transmissions sent over modified VLF and ELF frequencies. Frequency-agile trailing antennas and mounted loops received the digital codes, and the onboard computers instantly decoded them into voice messages.

Now, all communications and onboard electronics fluctuated between fully operative and sufficiently inoperative to make the dive uncomfortable.

"Damn," said Calder. "Is your sonar breaking up? I can only see you half the time. And my Sat-Nav system isn't cooperating. Over."

The transmission was garbled but could be understood.

"Affirmative," Parker said. "Keep our subs thirty yards apart, to be safe, until we figure out what's going on. No need to implode on one another. Over."

"Any ideas, Dupont?" Calder asked sarcastically.

"It is difficult to hear either of you," said Dupont. "My equipment is acting up also."

Parker was more than concerned about the electronics. Other than the problems during the test off Nantucket Sound, the equipment had performed admirably. It was bad enough the radios were acting up. But not to have control of the satellite navigation system or sonar was dangerous.

Any of the three subs could implode on impact with the *Titanic*, or with one another. The reality of that made Parker consider scrapping the mission until problems were overcome.

"Hello, Mother," Parker radioed to the *Neptune*. "Are you picking up our dilemma with the electronics?"

There was no answer.

"I repeat, *Neptune*. This is *Shelty One*. Do you copy electronics problems? Over."

"*Shelty One* this is Mother," radioed Holt. His message faded in and out with the static. "We're getting about half your conversations and call-ins. Did you fine-tune notch filters?"

"Long ago. We've attempted to trap the interfering signals on automatic and manual. Nothing discharges them."

"We're trying to figure out what the hell's causing it. Over."

"If you have any ideas . . . send 'em down in a basket," said Parker. "It seems about the only way we'll get them."

"If you talk as much as you normally do, we should get about what we need," Holt laughed to break the tension.

"I can't *hear* you," Parker anxiously joked back. That was the last bit of levity he allowed himself as the subs began their final approach to the gravesite.

"Maybe we should scrap," Calder suggested.

"We're here," said Dupont. "We should make the best of it, unless it gets worse. Besides, we may not get another opportunity. Who knows what the *A'isha* has in mind."

"Sonar's back. There she is, partner," Calder reported, picking up the imposing ship on his sidescan screen. "I have us about a hundred fifty yards out. Do you copy? "

"Copy. My sonar's working, too. Over," said Parker.

"Oui, there she is," Dupont could not help but feel the excitement. "I can see her. Over."

Parker was quiet for a moment, then hit the button on his mike. "Fellas, I was just thinking. We seem to be losing our communications and sonar simultaneously. When one has a problem, the other two experience the same complication. Right?"

Both answered in the affirmative.

"So it can't be our equipment. Copy?"

"Yes," radioed Dupont. "The odds for three subs with identical failures, at once, would be astronomical. Over."

"That leaves another possibility," Calder mused. "They're jamming from the *A'isha*."

"Mother, do you copy?" radioed Parker.

"Mother copies . . . barely," said Holt. "Must be some type of Japanese technology. We'll check it out. Over."

The three submersibles closed in on their target, intermittently losing contact with one another, and with the *Neptune*.

"Take it slow," urged Parker.

"Yeah," Calder agreed. "Want to make it back for dinner. Rather not *be* dinner."

"Take advantage of sonar, to move more quickly when you have it. But inch in if you lose it. Leave lights on so we can see one another, side-by-side."

"Roger," came from Calder and Dupont.

From a distance, the submersibles appeared to be large sea horses with bright lights attached as they moved swiftly—and on occasion slowly and deliberately—to inspect the *Titanic*. They approached the forward section of the ship on a course due north along the portside decks. Masses of hanging rust—rusticles, as Dr. Robert Ballard had dubbed them—glowed bright orange in their passing lights, and sea-polished brass twinkled back like stars in a bowl of sand.

"Bear on a course zero-two-eight toward the bows," said Parker. "Reduce to point-five knots. Over."

"Copy." And the submersibles edged forward on a heading slightly east, north-east.

As though three horses rode in unison over a once barren desert, the brightly-lit subs cast bizarre shadows against the roughly buckled and crimped bulkheads of an extraterrestrial vessel—a ship that had at once invaded and surrendered to this unwelcome environment.

Parker clicked on his mike. "She looks like a worn soldier after walking through a field of thick, orange mud."

"What?" Dupont radioed, "I lost you in the static."

"Just reminiscing, Henri. You wouldn't understand."

Parker led the expedition up and around the forward decks, carefully avoiding the davit for number-2 lifeboat, the remains from the dislodged number-1 funnel, and other projecting objects and cables. They surveyed the entrances and gaping holes where once proud and wealthy passengers entered for meals, entertainment, or conversation.

Then, following an unsuccessful attempt at locating the much sought-after safe on Deck B, Parker and Calder maneuvered through a large opening in the top of the *Titanic's* forward section, where the Grand Staircase entrance was once located. Dupont remained behind, ostensibly to assist when needed. In reality, he wanted to see what they might find.

Again, they came up empty handed, and Parker signaled the two subs to follow as they moved on to the starboard-bow side of Captain Smith's cabin—just aft of the wheel house, in the partially collapsed area of the officer's quarters. This was the final area suspected of holding the lost safe with the famous book and, possibly, other valuable treasures inside.

The subs paused forward of the Grand Staircase at a starboard entrance opposite, and just in front of, what would have been the wireless shack. The door led to the hallway of the demolished quarters.

During the calamitous journey to the bottom, the *Titanic's* bulkheads failed and pulled out and away from the cabin on both sides of the ship. A partially collapsed, precariously resting roof made it difficult for the subs to enter together. Presuming the remaining part of the roof was stable, only one *Shelty* could fit through the opening and lift away rubble with it's prehensile arms.

Any engineer worth his salt knew that many parts of the hull were now paper thin, from decomposition over time. And Parker's awareness of this fact concerned him more than the depths at which they were operating.

Parker compensated for the flow of the current as he attempted to pass the sub through the door, "feet first."

"Guide me from behind, Andy." Parker reversed the cycloidal jets to readjust the angle of his keel as it passed the darkened entrance.

"Doing fine," said Calder. "Hold position for another three feet, then edge your sail down three degrees to avoid the top door jam."

The previous day's storm caused the *Titanic's* cross currents, inside, to run faster than usual. They pushed dangerously at his sub as he attempted to clear the entrance. Even with the *Shelty's* cold interior, Parker found himself sweating profusely. He wished he'd had more time to test such maneuvers before taking this assignment. Silently, he cursed Colonel Bramson.

"Bear to port two degrees," Calder warned. "Watch it, Cary. The current's pushing you too close to . . . "

Abruptly, Parker's right thruster caught the door jam and the sub jerked hard against the rusted metal. The hull seemed to curse back as the lower half of his Shelty swung to the right and brought the upper sail hard against the left side of the entrance.

Primed for a worse-case event, Parker let up on the power. But the sub held its position, against the steel wall, without imploding. Sounds of the collision reverberated throughout the hull.

"Damn, I should have compensated for that." A rust storm encircled his viewport, and he was momentarily blinded. "Report damage when the dust clears. Over."

Calder combined his cycloidals and thrusters to replicate the effect helicopter rotors might have underwater. Holding his sub in place, he backwashed the rust particles from the vicinity.

"What's going on down there?" Holt called from above.

"I'm all right," said Parker.

"Just an unscheduled meeting with a bulkhead entrance." said Calder.

"Keep us informed. You got us on pins and needles up here. Over."

"Copy, John. Relax. Everything's okay." Parker knew Holt paced a trail back and forth on the bridge.

Dupont remained considerably behind and out of the way in quiet observation.

"Back out slightly and hold your position," said Calder.

"Any visible cracks in the shell's surface?"

Calder aimed his lights at the right thruster, then surveyed *Shelty One*. "Nope. Lucked out. The new diamond skins on these babies are tougher than alligators."

"Better be," said Parker as he cleared the entrance and found himself sharing the space with several curious grenedier fish.

Loud screeching and crackling split the silence of their cabins.

"This is Mothership," said Holt, "Seems the noise is with us to stay. Our equipment can't detect any direct jamming coming from the *A'isha*. However, we are picking up serious activity from their ship. Over."

"What do you see?" Parker maneuvered down a jet black hallway, toward the captain's cabin—his way lit only by the heavy candle power of the *Shelty*.

"Crew moving all over their decks. With their canvas, though, it's difficult to make out much. Live satellite pix from KH-14 shows a lot of activity around the stern. But with jamming—or whatever it is, the pictures are distorted and we keep losing the satellite feed.

"The *A'isha's* stern is turned away from us. And they've canopied another portion of the deck. Most of their activity on the fantail is blocked from view. Over.

"Cancel that 'over' . . . the *A'isha* just gave birth. We've got activity on sidescan, and Doppler confirms the launching garage is lowered over the fantail, below the hull."

Holt paused as he watched his screens.

"They're at seventeen fathoms. And . . . " he paused, again. "They have a launch."

"Only made out half of that." Parker cussed the static. "Is it a surface launch or sub? Over."

"They've launched their submersible. It's moving in our direction. . . .

"Yes, there she goes. Diving deep . . . and fast. Jesus, look at that baby go. Wait a minute. The damned thing is fading on our screens."

"It's that stealth resin and anechoic tiles," said Parker. "Check it's DR before you lose it. I want the fix on our visitor. Over."

There was silence as the topside crew scrambled to check the direction, time, and speed, for vectoring into a charted fix.

"Put out the welcome mat. It appears they're heading straight for you. ETA . . . seventy-five minutes or less," said Holt. "Hold on. Here comes satellite pix."

There was silence, again, as the crew waited for the photos to process. Parker used the moment to concentrate on moving his *Shelty* through a tight corridor, just outside the threshold to the captain's cabin.

Holt pushed the Talk button, "The picture's distorted, but it's a modified *Yoritomo-class* design, all right. Sleek little baby. Looks like a large stingray without the tail. Except for the two side thrusters and one at the stern, it's got stealth written all over it.

"I don't see prehensiles up front," he said.

"They're retractable," said Calder.

"Right," said Parker, as he inched his way through the open threshold to Captain Smith's demolished room. "And who knows what's hidden inside its skin. By the way, I'm in Captain Smith's quarters. Adjusting position."

"I'll leave you alone," said Holt. "We'll update if we lock on again. Over."

Calder clicked in, "We'll keep an eye out down here." Heavy static squeals returned and most of Calder's remarks went unheard.

Dupont patiently waited out his prey.

Parker's lights hit a large object in a collapsed corner of the cabin.

Is this the safe with the missing spoils? he wondered.

Shelty One moved through the rubble at a dead slow pace. The starboard wall and ceiling were dangerously close to toppling in and over the object. He decelerated and let the current carry the sub in for a closer look.

"Got a safe, here."

"Copy," said Calder from outside. Dupont was silent.

Shelty One scraped the floor, and dust kicked up in the shadowy darkness. The large, rusted repository hung precariously, just short of the bulkhead's open edge that was pealed away before impact.

"I can't tell if the safe or remaining bulkhead holds up the ceiling," he radioed. "What do you think, fellas? Is this the one that has it all?"

"We found little in the safes on our last dive," Dupont feigned interest. "Must be the one missing all these years."

"Got to be," Calder ruminated.

Parker closed in, contemplated how he would move the strongbox out for inspection, then called to his divers, "If the two of you position your subs on the starboard and fore-edges of the roof, near the collapsed end, and use robotic arms to brace it, I might be able to pull the safe out from underneath. Over."

"Roger that," said Calder.

Dupont followed as Calder moved around into position, each of them bracing the roof with their prehensiles to prevent collapse. The metal beams creaked, and the haunting sounds echoed throughout the silent tomb, as cycloidal jets were used to force pressure upwards on the roof.

Lights reflected brightly through giant fissures between the roof and bulkhead. And Parker could see Calder and Dupont's faces lit by their interior lights.

"Andy, pull your end up more. I need to get behind."

"Roger," the speaker clipped in short acknowledgement.

Like peeling a sardine can lid, Calder slowly pulled back on the weakened ceiling. Dupont's prehensiles held tightly to the roof, as he waited above for Parker to free the safe.

With caution, Parker methodically extended his prehensile arms toward the captain's safe—one reaching to the back for leverage, the other attaching to the handle for grip. He maneuvered his sub around the object.

"Ever so slowly, Parker," he said to himself as he increased his cycloidals and adjusted the throttle to reverse. Unhurried, he pulled the safe back toward the open end.

"Come on baby."

"Careful down there," Calder warned.

Parker glimpsed through the damaged roof. "Hold those ends tight. I don't want to end up flat as a doubloon."

Calder smiled through his viewport and flashed a quick look to *Shelty Three*. There was no reaction from Dupont.

Forced apart after decades of metallic arthritis and rust had set in their joints, the ceiling, severed walls and floor creaked loudly— as though begging to be left alone.

"This piece might pull back enough to come off," said Calder.

Parker detested the thought of ripping off any section of the ship, but the dive's duration was shortened progressively with the *Yoritomo* now on its way.

He gave in. "See what you can do."

Calder and Dupont made certain their grips were solid, as they increased cycloidals and reversed thrusters to pull back the ceiling. The aged, weakened roof fought against the reverse tension. But brittle, sulfur-laden steel gave way to the stress and the persistent cold—and cracked as ice. The two subs flew back with the release, still holding on to the large piece of roof.

"Drop it before it takes you into a bulkhead," said Parker.

"We're stabilized," said Calder. "Need to clear this piece out of your way. Henri, reverse thrust at point-one-zero knot and bring it behind the fallen bridge cab. We'll drop it there."

"Copy."

Shelties Two and *Three* maneuvered carefully across the starboard decking, clearing the area directly above Parker. But with the jarring of the roof line and the weight release against the safe, without warning, the safe shifted and skidded across the decomposing floor, pulling *Shelty One* with it. The sub hit the edge of the remaining ceiling and jarred Parker's hand off the controls.

"I'll be damned," Parker yelled out loud. "Andy drop that piece and get over here."

"But it might fall on top of . . . "

"Cut the crap. I'll get outta' the way. Dupont get over here."

The safe continued its slide to the low spot, and headed for the side bulkhead as the ceiling piece came down—missed *Shelty One* by inches—and splattered dust everywhere. A muffled crash echoed hauntingly through the hull and rose to the surface.

"This is Neptune," Holt called from topside, between the disruptive hissing, "what's going on? You okay?"

"One, here. Some unfortunate demolition on the roof line. But we're all right. We've located a safe. Over."

"Watch your step, fellas."

"Understood," said Parker, not having a moment for extraneous conversation. "Over and out."

Rust storm blindness slowed Parker, but he used his weakened sidescan to move through the debris and reversed thrusters in the direction of the safe. A scraping sound was heard as the large captain's safe came to rest in a clear, cramped section of the quarters. A deteriorated floor beam caught the heavy metal container and held it fast.

Within moments Parker regained control of the safe's awkward size and weight. And a large hole in the roof now cleared the way for Calder to move in.

The cycloidals and prop thrusters gave power enough for the *Shelties* to drag the safe from the debris. Calder got his prehensile arms underneath and assisted in lifting it out of the area. Inch by inch, the two carefully moved the steel safe from its former hiding place. Dupont made way, as Calder and Parker maneuvered it out from under the wreckage.

Squeals blew through Parker's cabin as he switched on the radio.

"*Neptune*, this is *Shelty One*. Do you read?"

"*Neptune*."

"John, have you been monitoring? The safe is out. I repeat... we have the safe."

"We copy. Congratulations. We've been following between static bursts. A heavier fog's returned about five miles north of us. But it's remaining upwind of our position. Over."

"We're moving the safe to stable ground. Anything else to report? "

"Zero on the *Yoritomo*. Disappeared off sonar almost the second it went underwater. We're not even getting shadow reflections . . . when sonar's working. The *A'isha's* quiet for now. But I want you to . . . "

Loud crackles filled their cabins. Their communications went awry and electronics were disrupted once more.

"Shit. There it goes again. John, do you read? *Neptune* do you copy? Over."

The static overwhelmed them and nothing else could be heard from above. "Those *A'isha* bastards are screwing us up," said Parker, but no one heard the comment.

Then, the hissing and squeals subsided slightly.

"Jeez," Calder complained, "that about blew my eardrums out. You okay, Henri?"

"I can barely hear you," said Dupont. "If you are talking about the static . . . I'm affected too." He secretly wondered how Ragem could cause the jamming.

"Can either of you hear me?" asked Parker.

"Barely," answered Calder.

No answer from Dupont.

"Look," said Parker. "We haven't a moment to waste. If you hear me, Andy, let's move this sucker to the Marconi roof before we totally lose communications. Copy?"

Calder radioed, "I couldn't copy your last remark. Over."

Parker repeated his message. "Copy?"

"Got enough. . . . You want her on top of the Marconi roof. Right?"

"Roger that. How's your sonar? "

"Sucks. I'm relying on visuals right now. Over."

"Same here.. Henri, if you hear enough of me to understand, move way back so we don't collide. Keep both of us in sight at all times. And watch for those bastards from above. Copy?"

There was a long interval. "I understand," said Henri, as he pulled back over the opening where an opulent, wrought iron and glass dome had once covered the first-class entrance and Grand Staircase. "I'm receiving about half the words. Most are clipped in the middle."

The ear-splitting sounds battered their senses. And sonar was useless.

"Roger, Henri. Turn off cabin speakers, plug in your headsets, and place them just behind the ear for bone conduction. That should cut down on direct static and squeals. And keep our mikes open to free our hands. Copy?"

Both answered in the affirmative.

"Repeat everything twice. Enough should get through. Make sense?" Parker repeated his own request. "Over."

"Roger. Roger. Over. Over." If nothing else, Calder would try to keep his sense of humor. Dupont responded in the affirmative.

If the other two had seen Dupont's face, they might have noticed visible concern about his inoperable electronic gear, at this depth.

"Andy," said Parker, "haven't got much time with the *Yoritomo* on its way. The current is blowing from the north. Set throttle at the first mark. I'll stay on the starboard side of the safe. You remain at port. I'll repeat that." And he did.

"Carry the safe to the center of the roof. Turn on all lights. We'll need everything we've got for visuals. Flash your strobe test button, once for 'stop.' Two for 'go.' Three flashes to 'slow down.' Hit your forward top light once for 'yes.' Twice for 'no.' I'll repeat." And he did.

"You with me?" Parker asked of Calder.

The subs were close enough to read lips through their front viewports. Calder gave a thumbs-up signal through the glass and flashed his forward top light once for "yes." Inside their cabins, the sonar screen's erratic glow gave the appearance of an electrical storm.

The two subs moved together at a crawl, as the safe was guided closer to the stable roof. Calder began to lose his grip. He flashed his strobe three times, and they slowed to an almost imperceptible speed. Alert to the danger, they inched past the forward davit for lifeboat No. 1, debris from the peeled-out quarters, and dangerous railing posts that jutted from the deck.

They moved at a snail's pace, as they crossed the stokehold vents, the first vacant funnel opening, and passed over the skylight for the officer's bath. Parker signaled to stop as they approached the Marconi roof.

"Move it out where the *Alvin* set down, before. Should be sturdy enough to hold. With me, Andy?"

"Copy, barely."

Dupont followed close behind.

As they edged out over the roof, with the Grand Staircase yawning wide just aft of their position, a deafening screech emanated over their headsets. Calder instinctively reached to adjust the volume, but his sleeve caught on the throttle and thrust *Shelty Two* slightly forward.

"Shit!" yelled Calder.

The sub lunged ahead and knocked Parker back. He lost control of the hydraulic arms and the weight of the safe shifted aft. The container dropped out of control toward the edge of the roof—

half floated and half rolled into the mouth of the Grand Staircase—and disappeared down the pitch-black void.

Seconds later, the safe hit the remains of the staircase, below,
and smashed through the weakened and rotting metal sub-deck-
ing. The structure collapsed in and consumed itself as the safe
forced more bulkheads to give way underneath. Another deck
collapsed and the crashing sounds continued, until the safe rested
on a stronger piece of superstructure at Deck C.

"Damn," Parker remarked over his open mike. "That was
exactly what we didn't want. We just tore her to shreds."

"I'm sorry," said Calder, his apology barely heard.

"Forget it, Andy. Couldn't be helped."

The down-rushing water caused a volcanic-like eruption of
rust to shoot up from below. With no place to go, it billowed to
the top with the current—in the shape of a mushroom cloud—
and enveloped all three subs.

"We've lost it," reported Parker. There's no way we'll retrieve
it."

"Our sonar's as gone as the safe," said Calder. "We couldn't
navigate down there, even in these subs. Too many loose cables."

"Everyone stay put. I repeat stay put until we have visibility."
Parker barely heard them respond.

"I'm sorry, Cary."

"Like he said, it could not be helped," mocked Dupont, a
note of derision in his voice.

"Easy for you to say, Mr. Mercenary of the year," Parker shot
back. "You're accustomed to ripping this place apart."

"Salaud," Dupont said under his breath, forgetting his mike
was still open.

"Oh, a bastard, am I? Listen, you jerk, if it weren't for me
you'd probably be sitting in a prison right now."

"Okay, guys," Calder jumped in. "This is not the time or, I
guarantee, the place for a disagreement."

Static cut in with a voice from topside. "What the hell's
going on down there?" Holt radioed. "You guys got the bends or

something?"

"Never mind, John. The safe just dropped several decks through the superstructure," Parker said—sarcasm still in his voice. "We're okay."

"Cut the crap, guys. It's bad enough we can't help you. Over."

"I apologize," said Parker. "I'm just a little pissed."

"Get over it."

You'll live to regret your remark, Dupont sneered to himself.

"Confirm positions," said Holt, "before we lose you."

"We're just over the grand staircase," said Parker. "Or what's left of it." There was a pause.

"Okay," said Holt. "We've got a partial fix on . . . " But the radio only blared out static.

Parker slowly pushed on his controls to inspect the collapsed area. As if in a black hole, cross currents that ran under and through the decks below, created a siphoning action that cleared the vicinity of sea dust and small objects tottering on the edge of the vessel's decks.

As the water cleared, it was evident what had happened.

"I'm going down to inspect the damage," said Parker. He adjusted downward thrust to move ever so slowly into the dangerously small and claustrophobic area. Maneuverability was at a minimum, as Parker did a slow three-sixty. He relied on his lights and the television monitor for visuals.

"I think I can make it down there," he reported back. Cameras revealed several sharp, jagged edges where the structure had been ripped through by the safe.

"I'll go down," said Dupont. "No reason for both of you to endanger your lives. Over."

"Not necessary," said Parker.

"Listen," said Dupont. "You two have plenty to live for. You both have families. I have none. I'll go in. If a bulkhead collapses, it'd only be me in there."

"No chance, Henri. Over and out," radioed Parker.

"Cary, he's right," said Calder. "It's too dangerous for anyone to go down there. In days past we would've sent *Jason* in to perform reconnaissance."

"Why do you think the Navy spent thirty million dollars developing these subs? One of us will fit . . . and it's my responsibility to go down there. Subject closed. Over and out . . . again."

———

The darkly-painted *Yoritomo* moved in on its target. On its way to the *Titanic*, its two-man crew monitored communications between the three *Shelties*, and attempted to interpret messages between *Neptune's Knot* and the mini-subs. With the radio disturbances, efforts to eavesdrop—let alone communicate with the *A'isha*—were just as difficult.

With sonar interference, the large-winged mini-sub still moved as gracefully as an eagle in flight, as it passed through the layers of intensely cold water in search of its prey. The sub cruised through the ocean at twenty-one knots, its two Japanese crew certain of their ability to conceal their arrival, as they searched for the *Shetland-class* subs.

They had reached nine hundred fathoms on their way to assist Dupont in locating the *Great Omar* and the jewels—or to relieve Dupont of them, if necessary. Prepared to do battle with anyone who might get in the way, the *Yoritomo's* crew had been instructed to do whatever necessary to achieve their goal.

With fewer but larger jets than the *Shelties*, the super conducting silent electromagnetic propulsion system had all the essential elements for quiet stealth technology. Even with stealth capabilities, however, the Japanese sub was as vulnerable to failed radio transmissions, through the "jamming," as the *Shelties*. Even *A'isha* could not communicate encrypted signals with its submersible when static was high. Their sonars and tracking devices were just as susceptible.

The crew was instructed to maintain radio silence throughout, to remain undetected, and to keep other surface ships from determining their mission. But the *Yoritomo's* radio acted as a scanning device, and they were able to pick up most intelligible communications between surface ships and other subs. A small, onboard computer kept track of each navigational fix and automatically compared itself with pinpoints sent from the *A'isha*.

Navigator Takeo Karoji looked up from his printout.

"Sir, we have a new line of position intersecting the *Titanic* since that last disturbance."

"Ah," Captain Zosho Shimizu grunted, looking away from the dark viewport to his assistant. "Have we regained our ground?"

"Yes, sir. The ship is directly below. Between static, we receive good amplification from it. We should pass twenty-one hundred meters within minutes, with just under seventeen hundred meters to target."

"Uh, huh," Shimizu grunted. The captain was deep in thought, visualizing how he would take out the two Americans, without causing their subs to implode. *It would be better to immobilize them*, he contemplated. *Then, recover the treasure.*

"Captain, another transmission . . ."

The two listened in. Parker's voice came over the speaker. The navigator turned up the volume.

"Piece of cake," said Parker, reporting his progress as he headed down through the collapsed roof of the once luxurious first class entrance.

Karoji and Shimizu looked quizzically at each other. *Piece of cake?* they mimicked.

———

"On my way down," Parker continued. All his lights glowed, and the cavernous ruins of the staircase shaft lit up like he were floating through an eerie ballroom—a surreal backdrop, not of this earth.

"So this is what *Jason* felt like when he was sent in here." He smiled and imagined Andy might be smiling, too. It left him when he realized he was at B-deck, where a once elegant light fixture dangled from its cord, providing life only to a feather-like sea pen. Now it was missing.

"Those bastards," Parker said out loud, not caring if Dupont was listening in. Henri had been one of them—one of the grave robbers who had pillaged the ship of any artifact that could be taken for private gain. Parker's blood ran hot as he recalled the ship's looting.

Hundreds of artifacts. The three ship's telegraphs, the cherub from the aft Grand Staircase, an empty safe filled *mysteriously* with jewels and wet money, when it was "opened" for TV cameras—coal brought up to be hawked like trinkets from a carnival. Greed had taken over and nothing would stop them. *Not even the United States Congress*, he reflected.

The captain's safe had landed on its side when it hit the deck, knocking the heavy rusted door loose on impact. The hinges broke off like brittle candy, and the entire contents spilled out on the inside door wall.

Parker's lights caught something that sparkled as he circled from back to front. *Is it brass reflecting back at me, or broken glass that floated in with the current?* he wondered.

Then, he saw them.

Almost as a mirage—as Shah Jahan would have witnessed from his Taj Mahal on a full-moon night during the days of the Mughal emperor—in the glow of *Shelty One's* powerful lights, the glimmering of hundreds of gems sparkled back at Parker from the missing jewelry. And projecting almost imperceptibly in the dark, underneath, was an oversized leather bag. . .its tie-string broken loose from the fall. A large rectangular leather-bound, double-tray, hinged box protruded from beneath—the type Bryon White had described that holds rare and valuable books.

It had to be the *Great Omar*!

Parker carefully pitched his sub downward for a closer look.

Much had been done to protect the book before shipping it to its American owner, Gabriel Wells. He recalled Stephen Llorayne's description of precautions taken and preparations made by Sotheran's Booksellers.

> "*The Rubaiyat of Omar Khayyam* was first placed in a leather-bound, lead lined teak case, double-tray box," he had said. "Few know this—perhaps just me by now— but the box was finished with another Peacock, copied from the *Omar's* cover, its tail spread wide, with a large ruby set in its eye.
>
> "The box was adorned with an unknown number of jewels," Llorayne had continued, "all set in the Peacock's tail. Emeralds they say. Then, they wrapped the box in several layers of thick paper, bound it with heavy twine in all directions, and covered it with three coats of candle wax to protect it from moisture and humidity . . . "

Almost subconsciously, Parker opened his radio channel and spoke in a restrained tone of voice. "This is Parker. I hope you copy. Listen carefully. The *Ruby* is here . . . I repeat, the *Rubaiyat* is here."

Enough of the broken message was translated for Calder, Dupont, and the *Neptune*. Then the *A'isha* and *Yoritomo*, received a preset signal tone from *Shelty Three*.

Calder hit his radio, "Did you get that, *Neptune*? Cary's found it. Do you copy?"

Communications deteriorated more quickly.

"Do we ever," whooped Holt. Ge- it up h-re, pr-nto, bef-re the fog gets w-rse, or the Yori---- gr-bs it from ---. Over."

But Parker had already shut off his channel to clear his head from the clutter of the disrupting and annoying acoustic airwaves.

———

Calder had been waiting patiently, in *Shelty Two*, above his partner—hovering in the confined space between decks, as a helicopter suspended over a black void—ready to assist if called upon. Dupont remained back over the collapsed roof of the gymnasium, just aft of the rusted boiler room vent, his lights off, ostensibly to save power.

"Cary, this is Andy. We need to clear out of here. Do you copy? Over."

"I don't think he hears us," called Dupont. "For that matter, can you hear me?"

"Barely," Calder replied, the hissing almost earsplitting. "*Shelty One*, this is *Shelty Two*. Do you read? Time's running short. We're expecting visitors."

Parker did not respond.

"I'm going down to see if he's okay."

"Parker asked us to remain here," said Dupont. "We need to be alert for intruders. You should come out of there, in case Cary must get out quickly."

Calder hesitated as *Shelty Two* floated in place, "Damn, I wish he'd answer us."

The holographic sidescans were useless, as all electronics continued to get worse. Calder punched in some numbers, but there was no change. "If it weren't for my lights, I'd be blind. I can barely see the stairwell walls."

Topside, a thick fog had rolled in from the north. The *A'isha* was lost from local surveillance, as the fog cut squarely between the two ships.

The satellite phone to *Neptune's Knot* was out, but the ship had received several written communications from Bramson. Each had broken up so much, none was intelligible.

It took time to translate the messages. But when treated as a cryptic note—a clipped word or two received over the STAR satellite, several lines with words missing in sequence via the FAXline, and an emergency radio patch with a passing freighter—when pieced together as a puzzle, a startling message emerged for *Neptune's* crew.

Holt glanced frantically back and forth between the different sheets of words, hoping to decipher the message.

"This would've been easier if it were encrypted in Navajo," Holt exclaimed to archivist, Harold Chapman. The two men painstakingly patched each complete or near-complete word side by side to make sense of the electronic gibberish. Then Holt's face grew taut as the fragments coalesced and the message hit home.

"Damn that son-of-a-bitch," Holt yelled, as he raced from the chart table to the ship's radio. The crew wondered what had set him off, but there wasn't a moment to explain. Chapman stared at the interpreted message, and his eyes widened with each word read.

Holt pushed the Talk button, to communicate with the subs, and squeals shot back like bullets from an AK-47.

"Shit!" He let up on the button and looked at everyone in the control van.

"Victoria's been rescued."

The crew let out a sigh of relief, but wondered why he was upset.

"That's the good news," Holt said as he opened the screeching radio line once more. "Dupont is in with the terrorists, and I'm not sure I can get through," he said above the crackling sounds, letting up on the switch once more.

"And how the hell can I tell Parker and Calder about Dupont's connection with the terrorists, without putting them both in jeopardy?"

Holt and his first officer looked around in despair. Chapman felt a twinge of guilt set in for siding with Bramson on Parker's involvement.

Silent panic took over and tension filled the control van.

"We can't take any chances," Holt said. "We've got to warn them. Discreetly . . . somehow." He pushed the button and a high pitched squeal filled the area.

"Parker, for God's sake, I hope you hear me. This is Holt. Over."

More static and squeals.

"Calder, do you read me. Parker, Calder . . . report in, please."

Without looking at anyone in particular he asked the crew, "Any status to report on the *Yoritomo*? How close are they."

"Can't tell, John," a reply came back, "they're as invisible as a ghost."

"Shit, keep adjusting that damned sonar. Try the computer. Keep on the satellite. Whatever you can do. We've got to get our eyes and ears back."

———

"I'm com--g out," Calder radioed to Dupont. "Do you c-py, Henri? Sta- clear of the hol-."

"You are coming out? I copied some. I'm just forward of the stairwell," he lied.

"Cald-r, P-rk-r . . . som-one ans-er me," Holt's anxious voice radioed from topside. "--n a-yone hear me?"

Dupont started to answer, but with the urgency in Holt's voice, he listened for what was coming.

"Andy h-re." Calder adjusted his thrusters and began to climb out of the collapsed Grand Stairwell. "We c-n barely hear --u. And Cary's g-t his radio off. What's up?"

"Andy . . . do you re-d me? We aren't copy--g you up h-re. If y-u can read me, I will continu- to broadcast --is message unt-l someone can interpr-t it. Over."

There was momentary radio silence. Dupont and Calder waited to hear the broken message.

"*Shel-- On- and ----ty T-o*," came the message . . . about every other word or syllable clipped or missing, "this is Joh- H-lt. List-- carefully. ----oria has be-- rescu--. I repeat, Victoria --- been r----ed. --ont connec--- to terrorists. I repeat, --pont con---ted to t-----ists. Ge- th- hel- out of the—. Do you copy? Over?"

Calder approached the outer lip of the staircase roof, illuminating the area around him. The black hole of the abyss quickly absorbed the light.

"Did you get that Henri? Too broken up for me. Cary, is your radio on?"

Dupont was silent. And there was no answer from Parker, though Calder could still see Parker's lights nearly three decks below.

"Henri, did you copy that message? Do you copy me for Christ's sake?"

Usually cool under pressure, his frustration mounted as he knocked his radio with his fist. "This damned piece of crap. . . . Why can't they give us equipment that works fifty percent of the time." *Shelty Two* glided to just above the Grand Staircase opening. "Copy that message, Henri? It was garbled crap for me."

There was no reply.

Dupont silently edged his cycloidal jets and the thrusters of his darkened *Shelty Three* into a slow, forward heading, using the bright lights from Calder's sub to direct him to his target. As Calder turned his sub, Dupont followed behind in an elliptical arc—a moon circling it's planet—careful not to be caught within the range of lights.

"I don't see you," Calder continued to look out the forward viewport to where Dupont had last reported his location. "Flash your lights so I know where you are," radioed Calder, as he slowly moved *Shelty Two* out and down over the decking, aft of the first-class entrance.

Shelty Three shadowed his moves, keeping well behind, hoping the sonar would continue it's erratic behavior. "Dupont . . . are you okay? Answer me. Do you copy?"

"*Shelty One* and *Sh--- Two*," Holt tried once more, while picking up bits and pieces of Calder's message to Dupont. It was obvious Calder hadn't gotten the message. "And-, this is Holt.L--ten carefully. ----oria has be-- rescu--. I repeat, Victoria --- been resc--d. Dupont connec--- to terrorists. Listen. I repeat, --pont is con---ted to ------ists. Ge- th- hel- outa' ther-. For God's sake, do you read me. Come in, *Shelties*. This is Mothership. An---er me, -ammit. Over."

Calder faced the bulkhead, stopped his cycloidals and held the thrusters at minimum, hoping to hear the message more clearly. Behind him, Dupont's *Shelty Three* aimed its prehensile arms straight out, like a football lineman ready to block, grab, and pull his opponent aside.

Suddenly, hit from behind, Calder's sub lurched ahead. Dupont grabbed Calder's submersible on both sides of the upright dorsal-fin, nudged the sub forward, and gunned his thrusters and cycloidals.

"What the hell . . . " was all Calder could say. He looked to his rear viewport and reached for his joystick to make a quick ascent. But it was too late. *Shelty Two* raced uncontrollably forward as a force pushed it toward the ship's outside bulkhead.

Before Calder could accelerate out of danger, his sub slammed against the outer gymnasium wall, and a headlight exploded on impact. The sub's recorder fell from it's base above and put a gash in Calder's head. Blood trickled down his forehead, and he fell unconscious over the control panel. Outside, loaves of crusted rust fell from the superstructure and enveloped the area in a massive rust storm.

Dupont's *Shelty* immediately shot straight up, to avoid implosion. None occurred. His intent hadn't been to cause one, but he couldn't be certain about the outcome. He was prepared to do whatever it took to get the *Great Omar*.

From C-deck, Parker heard the impact.

The collision caused the Grand Stairwell's rust to stir up in the moving waters, flow down the large cavity with the cold-water winds, and envelop Parker's sub. He looked up through the murky waters and viewed lights from what he presumed was Calder's *Shelty* directly above. He opened his radio channel.

Dupont hoped Parker would think him to be Calder, as he gazed up from below.

"Wh-t's goin- on up there? -- you copy? Wh-t struck the bulkhe-d? O--r."

Silence followed the static, though Dupont heard enough of the message to understand.

"A-dy? Henri? --- you all righ-? Over."

"We are fine," Henri finally radioed back. "I accidentally backed into a bulkhead. Appears to be no damage. Andy's right above you. He's fine. But his radio is as irritating as mine. I think it's off." He repeated the message, hoping the earlier communication, from above, would not be repeated.

"How are you coming?" asked Dupont.

"Repe-t the quest--n, Henri."

The noise fed back through both radios.

"Have you got the book? Over."

"Just -bout. But --- rust storm w-ll add time to clear. Should ascend -- abo-t ten minutes. Any sign of *A'isha's* cr-w?"

"No sign. Sonar's still not working."

"I'm going off," said Parker. "E--rything is g-rbled and th-s static is unb-arable. Over." Parker repeated himself.

"Roger that. Out."

Dupont could barely see *Shelty One's* lights and movement associated with Parker's search. But as the water cleared, an occasional glint of an unusually sparkling substance cut through. There was no question. Parker had, indeed, found the treasure.

Dupont decided to wait for the *Yoritomo* sub to enter their space, before making contact. It was fruitless to communicate with the electronics as disrupted as they were.

The northerly wind pushed Calder out over the bow section's collapsed edge. All but two of his battery controlled panel and console lights remained lit, as the sub floated gently down the portside promenade. It caught on a bent stanchion, turned with the current, then continued in its idle descent over the collapsed first-class lounge roof.

His keel scraped the decking where the missing compass platform once stood, amidships, kicking up a foggy trail of silt and rust as it slid past the jagged edges of the ship's midsection, on into an unflinching, tenebrous nothingness.

Within thirty seconds *Shelty Two* hit the sandy bottom, next to the *Titanic's* split-open bilge keel. A stronger north west wind picked up Calder's sub. And he was transported out to the debris field, where the *Shelty* settled in an anomalous eddy of currents converging on the site.

An occasional copper pot or pan, missed by earlier salvors, sparkled in his lights and glimmered back from the sand, as stars in a distant unknown firmament. A blind galathean crab skittered across the sea bottom as the sub began to revolve in place.

From the surface, Holt attempted to make contact, again. "And-, --ry, do you rea- me? Victoria has be-- rescued. I repeat, Dupont is connec--- with *A'isha's* terror----. For God's sake, do --- read me? Come in, *Shelties*. T--s is Mothership. Dupon-, if you can hear this, you -an't --- away -ith it. Do --- copy, Dup---? Answer me! Over."

Dupont had followed Calder's lights down, until certain Andy was out of commission, and there was no indication of life. The disabled sub's illumination flickered and cut through the dark abyss in alternating slivers of light—and turned in the revolving currents as though a haunted carousel on a distant landscape.

Three decks below, Parker had to decide. For years he had spoken in private and open forums regarding moral and ethical objections to plundering underwater gravesites. Particularly those not considered of archaeological consequence. Certainly the *Titanic* was historically significant, considering it's unique place in history. But it was not an undocumented ship of a previous century. And Parker had remained committed to protecting this site from salvors.

Now, before him, was the antithesis of all he had espoused and believed—and the motive to justify a reversal of his beliefs to satisfy his government. But was it that simple?

Was Bramson's assessment accurate? he wondered. Parker had seen terrorism's results firsthand, at Heathrow. And there was New York . . . and Oklahoma City's anti-government fanatics. It didn't take a genius to recognize a growing world-wide threat. *Should I have the power to decide the destiny of these artifacts? Can I bring them out, hide them somewhere else, or worse...do I have the right to destroy an historical work of art to prevent others from using it for illicit purposes?*

Here was a leather-bound container possibly holding one of the most beautiful works of art ever conceived by the mind of man. And treasure that could make pirates blush with envy.

What Parker contemplated went against the very grain of his soul. His emotions welled up as previous years of diving the *Titanic* flashed before him.

He had many opportunities to remove artifacts from the *Titanic*—but had withstood the temptation. In fact, it had not been a question for him to consider. Searching for antiquities from sunken treasures of seventeenth and eighteenth century ships, or earlier, was one thing. Salvaging gravesites of ships, where living relatives still existed to grieve, was another.

As Chairman of the United States Maritime Law Association— involved in discussions entailing ethics on the high seas—he now found himself at odds with all he had campaigned and crusaded for over the years.

He had written many briefs for the Comité Maritime International, defending ethical practices in Admiralty Law. There were several on environmental concerns and disposal of nuclear wastes. But, as important, were those questions of ethics that dealt with issues of salvaging underwater gravesites.

Now he was expected to go against every principle he had ever fought for in international courts. How would Bramson . . . how would *anyone* justify placing these articles on display, after the United States Congress fought to designate the *Titanic* an international memorial, banning any such artifacts from public display or for private gain.

He shuddered within and felt his soul sucked away by time, and opportunists. And he knew more were on their way—a different kind of thief—those who would despoil, sack, and devour what little remained from the *Titanic*, their ultimate purpose more repulsive than that of earlier salvors.

His decision was not coming easily.

It had been nearly ten years since *Titanic's* discovery, and on this day Parker felt every one of them as he brushed his blond hair back from his face, up and under his cap, and toggled off the joystick that controlled the prehensile arms. Then, he pulled a set of power-gloves over his hands and prepared to go to work.

A set of wires split off from each electronic sleeve and directly plugged into the console with one RCA-jack. The cycloidal jets were set to hover over the safe on autopilot. And the thrusters were adjusted to pitch the sub at a downward angle, just enough for *Shelty One's* robotic arms to reach the leather bag.

Then, as always, Parker switched on his digital recorder. He felt more like a coroner at an autopsy—as he described his experience for posterity.

"Today, I realize the distinction between that for which I've fought—the preservation of the *Titanic* as an international gravesite—and the need to protect its most valuable remaining artifacts from terrorists. Fanatics who, in the light of their life-long holy war, have gone to extraordinary lengths to make their point.

Parker hit a button labeled "Virtual Arms" and the fingered prehensiles came to life.

"Regardless of concerns, I've concluded that Ragem, or anyone who backs terrorism, can't be allowed to turn to the sea to finance their activities . . . and we must stop them."

He rehearsed with the delicate droid-like arms, then slowly moved them toward the safe's door.

There was little room to maneuver within the confined space of the mini-sub. To compensate for the wider expanse outside the cabin, the ratio for movement had been set at 9:1. Each arm could move, proportionately, nine inches for every one moved by a power-glove. Depending on preset ratios of torque to torsion, for the gimbal-joints, it gave tremendous flexibility for a wide range of activity.

He picked up recording where he had left off.

"If, for whatever reason, I don't make it back to the *Neptune*, I'm recording this message in the hope that someone connected with our mission will retrieve it."

With a precision not available before the *Shetland-class* sub, he reached his covered hands into the open space over his console. The robotic arms moved as gracefully as an East Indian dancer, with her expressive fingers and arms. Parker took precious time to get to know the gloves and their mechanical underwater extensions—while thinking of the consequences of what he was about to do.

"My personal beliefs haven't changed," Parker recorded, "despite today's actions. Still, before I allow Pandora to be transported topside, I'm compelled to satisfy our curiosity. Correct that...*my* curiosity, to assess whether this mission is justified."

Carefully, robotic fingers pushed aside diamond broaches, ruby and emerald pendants, and pearl necklaces spilled from the safe. Then, Parker deftly uncovered the large box, already halfway out of its leather bag.

"It's likely, once the book's container is opened, we'll find nothing. It's entirely possible that decades of water and microscopic organisms have devoured and destroyed most, if not all of the *Great Omar* . . . making our efforts useless.

"If, on the other hand, any of the book has survived, we're doing the world a favor. And we must do all we can to carry out the remainder of our mission.

"At all costs," he said quietly, and with resolve.

With his radio still off, the silence of the deep covered the area as a thick quilt. Parker concentrated for a moment, hearing only sounds that trespassed the ship. The soft humming of his thruster's props imitated sounds of a distant room fan on a hot summer's day; the haunting whoosh of the swift Labrador and North Atlantic currents, rushed through myriad holes in the ship's hull, as their ocean-river winds raced south to meet the powerful Gulf Stream; the occasional creak and moan of the *Titanic's* superstructure. And Parker's own breathing, as he took a long, deep breath, held it, then slowly released the air—feeling his heartbeat in the quiet of his cabin.

He pulled his hands to his chest, then down toward the console's underside, pinching his fingers together as though holding an object at two ends. The cybernetic fingers grasped the ends of the leather bag, lightly upending it. An inch at a time the rest of the book's protective box slid out onto the decking. The leather enclosure and it's contents appeared heavy, by the way it spilled toward the deck—implying the pages might still be miraculously intact.

He paused to take it all in, then delicately pulled the leather bag away from the box, setting it next to the jewelry. Parker stared in awe at the case that held the book, for which so many salvors had fought in courts to recover. At once he understood why.

Lights from *Shelty One* broke through the impenetrable darkness of two thousand eighty-three fathoms, exposed the rich goldleaf and jewels that glowed back at him, and heightened the effect.

The ruby eye of a peacock winked a brilliant crimson red. And reflections of bright, flawless emeralds danced in the waters from the peacock's tail. More of the box came into view and revealed reduced panels of Persian shapes and gold foliage taken from the binding's cover—designs reminiscent of *Kismet*—ironically the meaning of fate.

Parker looked, in awe, at what had become a symbol of fate—death for over 1500 unsuspecting people. He forgot about the outside world and, in the tranquility of the ship, the brightly lit submersible floated above the much-sought-after treasure, as an angel standing guard over protected souls.

As Parker placed his thoughts on the digital recorder, the video camera photographed what was before him. All the years of fighting the salvors, all the anguish of standing up on behalf of the dead—those who could not speak for themselves—came rushing at him. His voice came in reverent, measured lengths of words and syllables . . . chosen from the heart.

"I realize I and others have spoken against the raping of this ship. We've railed against pillagers or anyone who dared to enter this sacred graveyard for reasons other than observation or study."

All objectivity left him for the moment.

"But if only for today I allow myself the luxury of feeling what Frank Sangorski experienced as he let go of this beautiful treasure . . . his life's dream, then I can understand how he felt. How deeply he must have loved this work. For if the binding, inside, is half as beautiful as its casket, then Omar Khayyam should be smiling in heaven."

The decision was made. Parker knew he must quickly move on. Beyond the sub's viewport, the *Shelty's* robotic arms mirrored Parker's actions inside, as they reached toward the box. The scientist's objectivity returned, and he spoke quietly into the recorder.

"I've found the *Great Omar*. As expected, the binding strings and paper, and the protective coating of wax, were devoured by microscopic bacteria entering the safe and leather bag. However, as hoped, it appears the leather's tannin acted as an anti-bacterial agent. And the microbes found it to be not as appetizing as other organic matter. At least as far as the double-tray box is concerned. . .remarkably, the leather and jewels remain bonded in place.

"Beyond the jewel and gold encrusted leather binding, inside its protective box," Parker continued, "I suspect the standard pages of *The Rubaiyat of Omar Khayyam's Vedder Edition* have been destroyed by micro-organisms. I must admit, though, the weight of the casket appears to contradict me."

He smiled at the irony.

"I must also admit," Parker recorded, "that my interest has been aroused, and I'm overcome by a peculiar fascination with Sangorski's binding."

The prehensile arms were pulled back slightly, while the archeologist considered the appropriate manner in which to open the box. But as he moved the arms and stretched the cybernetic fingers to the edges of the container, a strong wind passed through the stairwell decking and pushed *Shelty One* aside.

Parker floated toward one of the bulkheads. He quickly pushed the "Virtual" button, killing the prehensiles, and grabbed the throttle to keep from hitting the ship.

Abruptly, the realization hit him. Opening the double-tray box, at over two thousand fathoms, could be disastrous in this bone-crushing atmosphere. The lead lining inside was all that gave the container its structural capacity to withstand the depths, and kept any remaining part of the *Great Omar* from collapsing within. Though the current had pushed him away, it was as if an unseen hand—a spirit of the ship—had said, "Not yet!"

Parker took a slow, deep breath. Having lost track of time, he stared through the upper viewport hoping the *Yoritomo* was still out of range. Then, he hit a ceiling button and a whooshing sound emanated from a vacuum-sealed, hydraulic "marsupial pouch" located just below the prehensiles.

Once more, the robotic arms went into action. Parker laid the bag nearby, knowing he could not get the case back inside. The cybernetic arms reached to the *Omar's* container, careful not to allow the box to slide open, as Parker stood it upright to get a better grip.

Again, he recorded his actions.

"The current is pushing the double-tray box toward the edge of the decking . . . close enough to drop toward the bottom of the ship if I make the wrong move. And I can't set the sub down for leverage, for fear the decking might collapse with any more weight beyond the safe."

From inside the *Shelty*, with precise movements, Parker held the top of the case with the right hand, while adjusting the left in preparation for lifting the *Omar* into the front-loading pouch.

"I prefer not to damage the covering and knock loose the gems," he added.

The right hand moved slowly as it slid down from the top, equal in height to the opposite set of mechanical fingers. Then, both hands grasped the container to pull the artifact up and into the pouch. Ever so slowly, Parker maintained a grip tight enough to hold the object, but light enough to keep from damaging it. Unable to wipe his brow, beads of sweat dripped into his eyes.

"I'm concerned the weight of the binding, in the upright position, will cause the casket's side panel to give way."

Moving only in centimeters, the arms lifted the small casket closer to the pouch's opening. Parker's hands and fingers cramped as he held the position on the prehensiles.

He gritted his teeth and focused to relax more, to maintain composure and muscle strength. His shoulder muscles twitched from the tension in his body.

Just when he thought he could hold on no longer, the *Great Omar's* box slipped over the threshold and into the pouch. The water's displacement acted as a cushion.

Cary slumped back into his seat, in near exhaustion, pleased he had accomplished the mission. Then he remembered the jewelry.

Quickly he reached for the leather bag, held it's top into the current, and opened it up with the other arm. Carefully, Parker stuffed as many pieces of jewelry as he could into the bag, concentrating mostly on the larger pieces to prevent Ragem from getting articles of considerable value.

"I feel like I'm robbing Tiffany's," he said to the recorder.

Then, as he prepared to close the bag, he noticed a small black case still hidden inside the safe—gold-stamped with "De Beers" on its face.

"My God, the Guggenheim diamonds." In awe of his find, he reached for the box, placed it in the leather bag, and decided not to announce it until certain of its authenticity.

Easier to lift into the *Shelty's* pouch, despite it's bulky contents, the bag slipped beside the book. Parker hit the button above his head. Another whoosh signaled the pouch's door was closing and water was draining from inside. The artifacts would be vacuum-sealed and safe until on board the *Neptune*.

Parker adjusted his thrusters, pitched the sub back slightly for a view to the top deck, but could no longer see lights from Calder or Dupont. He switched on his radio and was overpowered by the noise . . . and part of a communication from *Neptune's Knot*. Cary turned down the volume and hoped he could make out the message.

" . . . ---toria --- been rescu--. --pont ---nected to terrorists. Listen. I repeat, Dupont c----ted to --rr-------. Ge- th- hel- outa' ther-. Do you copy? -ome in, --elties. This is Mothersh--. Over."

Parker could not make it out.

"Andy, Henri, this is Parker. I don't see either of you. Where are your lights? Do you read me Andy? Dupont, flash your lights. What is John saying? Over."

Holt's message was repeated. Parker listened carefully.

He eased on the power to his cycloidal jets and began his slow and dangerous ascent toward the top deck, careful to avoid the jagged edges and hanging cables, encountered on the way down. As *Shelty One* glided up, Parker's subconscious mind interpreted the cryptic message.

"I'm coming up, fellas."

Inching his way to the top, Parker saw the remnants of B-deck, then A-deck.

The beautiful gold-plated light fixtures, that managed to survive the sinking, were now gone. So were the statues, cherubs, and nearly four thousand other artifacts taken from the ship over the years. Little was left to the imagination beyond the shell of the bulkheads and the encrusted rusting steel.

"Parker, is th-t -ou?" radioed Holt. "We thoug-t -- lost all thr-e subs. A-- y-u okay? Over."

"John, I'm not getting much. Try again. Where's Dupont and Calder? Over."

In a one-way conversation, anticipating trouble from the static, Holt carefully enunciated and spaced his words for easier interpretation. By the fourth attempt, Parker was overjoyed to hear Victoria was in good hands. But he was sickened from the news about Dupont and knew he was in serious danger.

What followed was a concern for Andy and a rising anger he was in no position to vent—under the circumstances. Now he'd be forced to act his way out.

"Mothership, I can't understand a damned word you're saying," he bluffed. "You'll have to wait 'til I return with this baby in my pouch. Over."

Parker heedfully rose *Shelty's* front viewport over the horizon of the top deck—where the giant glass dome once sat in all its grandeur. He slowly revolved 360 degrees, and vigilantly looked for his former and current partners. Without sonar, he relied on the video camera and screen to gain an advantage.

"Henri . . . Andy, where are you? Copy? Over."

Dupont maneuvered aft of Parker and waited in the darkness by the stokehold vent. *Shelty* One rose higher, then moved out over the gymnasium roof.

Parker's eyes were drawn to slowly rotating lights, out between the bow and the spilled coal field. He recognized its shape by placement of the lights and watched for the *Shelty* to change its heading. But the sub only turned in place. Parker presumed Calder was in trouble. Perhaps the *Yoritomo* had already arrived.

"Andy? Dupont? Who's south, near the debris field?" He waited.

"What's going on, Andy? Do you read me? Which one of you is out there? Over."

Without sonar, he couldn't see Dupont, hidden near the bulkhead, nor could he see the superstructure of the ship. Even his compass acted erratically.

He hit the unit with his hand, wishing it was Dupont.

Parker recalled the thump he heard earlier and knew it had to have been Calder's sub. But until he determined Henri's whereabouts, he could not react.

Dupont moved to the starboard side of the gym. His jets threw rust particles into the current, and the backwash passed through Parker's space, blocking his view. He now knew Dupont's—or the *Yoritomo's*—approximate position, just outside the range of his lights.

He maneuvered *Shelty One*, illuminated the area behind him, and waited for the water to clear. It was like driving on a foggy night with brights on—and no dimmer. Realizing he was vulnerable, Parker switched on all other lights for rear and side viewports, alternately glancing out each porthole.

Dupont decided to call Parker.

"Cary? This is Henri. Is your radio on? Do you copy?"

Parker waited to answer. His sonar ghosted momentarily as he watched Dupont move to starboard.

"Cary, can you hear me? This is Henri. Andy is in trouble. Someone hit him from behind. I think it was the *Yoritomo*."

"Where are you? I can't see your lights? Over."

"Off for security, since the *Yoritomo* arrived. I tried to reach you, but your radio was off. Andy was pushed out to the field. He hit some debris and they left him. I've tried to raise him but get no answer."

"Where's the *Yoritomo*?" asked Parker, seeing no sign of the terrorist vessel.

"Lurking out there somewhere," said Dupont. "I've clung near the bulkhead, hoping to fade into their sonar as just another piece of steel. You'd better do the same."

"We've got to help Andy," said Parker. *You son-of-a-bitch*, he wanted to add, moving toward Dupont's sub.

"But the *Yoritomo* could be anywhere."

"We can't just leave him."

"You've got the *Omar*?"

"And a leather bag full of jewelry."

"Pass them here. I'll take them topside while you assist Andy. Perhaps I can divert the *Yoritomo* for a while. Over."

Parker was getting closer.

"Andy needs us both. One to tow him topside. The other to keep an eye out for the *Yoritomo* during ascent."

"I should take the *Omar* before Ragem gets hold of it," Dupont insisted.

Parker moved directly in front of him.

"Need I remind you," said Dupont, "the terrorists want these treasures more than us." He backed toward the bulkhead. "And they'll do whatever it takes to get them. Over."

"Yes, it's over, Dupont. You got it right for once. *You'll* do whatever it takes, won't you?"

Parker moved within two yards of *Shelty Three*, stalking like a tiger going in for the kill. Dupont stood his ground.

"If you'd minded your business, Cary, this never would've happened."

"If *I'd* minded my..." Parker said incredulously. He stalked Dupont in a ninety degree arc. "Did I hear correctly? You'd have pulled this shit one way or another. And Victoria, you bastard. How the hell could you kidnap my wife . . . for God's sake Henri? She had nothing to do with this."

Dupont attempted to edge past Parker, but could not get by.

"I was against it Cary."

Each saw the other's face inside their cabins. Dupont had seen Parker angry before. Now his face expressed an anger even Henri had not witnessed.

"But you were in the way," Dupont continued. "They had to stop you. They thought you'd never come here. And Victoria would have been released . . . unharmed. Believe me. It's true."

Parker's tolerance for Dupont's lies gave out. "You bastard! You'll regret you ever heard of the *Titanic*, the *Omar* . . . or me."

Without warning, Parker toggled the robotic arms into an extended position, pushed his throttle forward, and jammed his sub into *Shelty Three*.

"This is for Victoria."

Parker forced Dupont hard against the gymnasium wall, and held him there. Dupont was shaken, but saw his opportunity—to break into Parker's front-loading pouch.

With his own robotic arms, Dupont grabbed the protruding top edge of the door and pulled back hard.

By the time Parker realized what Dupont was up to, the damage was done. Despite excessive pressure at 12,500 feet, the vacuum seal broke, water seeped into the pouch, and the door's hydraulics gave way.

"No you don't," yelled Parker, looking straight at Dupont's leering face. He slammed his prehensiles against Dupont's, turned off the lights, hit the throttle, and instantly ascended thirty feet above the deck.

Dupont killed his lights, watched his intermittent sonar, and saw a ghosting of *Shelty One*. He aimed his video camera in Parker's direction to obtain a better image. Parker did the same, to keep his eyes on Dupont's position.

"Turn the treasures over to me," said Dupont. "It's useless. If I do not get them, the *Yoritomo* will, I assure you."

"Not on your life."

Dupont set his cycloidal jets and thrusters for a full throttle ascent with a dead-reckoning to match slightly to port of *Shelty*

One. His sub moved to it's DR position, exactly where the computer had directed.

Reverse currents of water and minute debris shot past Parker's viewport and confirmed Dupont's presence. Parker reversed *Shelty One's* thrusters, shot out toward Calder's sub, and attempted to raise him on the radio.

Dupont followed.

"Andy, this is Cary. Get on the radio." He approached the slight incline of the field, and noticed Calder's sub rested against a set of davits.

"Andy, talk to me. Can you operate your sub? Acknowledge. Andy, do you hear me? Over."

Parker circled the sub, as Dupont observed and listened in from above. Cary looked into Andy's starboard viewport and saw Calder lying unconscious over his console. There was no movement.

While he was concentrating on Calder, without warning, Parker's sub was hit from the port side with a force that almost knocked the air out of him. Dupont pushed *Shelty One* back toward the sharp edges of the *Titanic's* severed bow, engaging his manipulators in a bear-hug grip that made it difficult to break loose.

Parker increased his speed for a quick ascent in an attempt to break free. He rose against the momentum of Dupont's velocity to avoid implosion against the jagged fringe of the *Titanic's* fractured midsection.

"Hank, you just couldn't leave the ship alone, could you. . . . without sucking every vestige of history from her." Parker struggled to pull on a Virtual Power Glove for more leverage with the robotics. "Of course, you don't give a shit about history, as long as a cash register rings."

Dupont used an arm to wrestle open the damaged pouch, sacrificing his grip on *Shelty One* for the ability to grab the *Omar*. He pried the door slightly open.

As the subs dangerously approached wreckage, Parker's submersible bobbed loose from Dupont's grip. He took advantage of the moment and jammed on the power. Within yards of the wreckage, *Shelty One* twisted ninety degrees to break Dupont's hold, then sailed up over the down-slanting perimeter of the wreck.

Parker flew the centerline of the ship, carefully avoided bulkheads and vent covers, and moved forward past the davits for lifeboats 1 and 2. He slowed over the Well-deck and stopped above the giant anchor chains, aft of the ship's prow.

"Dammit," Parker looked at his screen. Sonar gremlins had awakened once more. He dimmed cabin lights, turned the sub a hundred-eighty degrees, and glared into the black water. A small moving glow, from Dupont's viewport, sailed toward him as *Shelty Three* stalked the ship.

Parker knew his options were limited. He had the *Omar* and could make a run for the surface. But he would not leave Andy behind. He had to reach the debris field, rescue Calder, and somehow evade Dupont *and* the approaching *Yoritomo*— *wherever* it was.

With sonar inactive, Parker chanced going over the side, to get back to Calder. He switched off all but his console light and glided out backwards over the portside railing.

Though the *Titanic's* draft and freeboard had measured over a hundred feet, from keel to uppermost deck, there was only twenty-six feet to the bottom—at the point the bow had plowed into the ocean floor.

Parker watched his video screen to determine how close he was to scraping metal as *Shelty One* inched down the side of the rust-caked hull. Silt and rust particles clouded the camera's eye.

With a muffled thump, *Shelty One* touched bottom. Parker shut down his motors, to clear rust with the current. Then he restarted his thrusters, turned to starboard, and headed south.

The immense and sheer cliff-like dimensions of the *Titanic* confirmed the mini-sub's diminutive size. Glacial boulders, pushed aside as pebbles, emerged like asteroids flying in the darkness of innerspace. *Shelty One* crept past the riveted plates and the eerily intact portholes—and haunting thoughts returned. He pushed them out as every nerve in his body bundled in tight clusters, in preparation for any emergency.

Parker hugged the side of the ship as he passed the enormous black, gaping hole at the bilge keel. The torn, twisted carnage of metal plates jutted out where the *Titanic* had buckled and split apart on impact, at the collapsed end of the bow section.

Hoping Calder had regained consciousness by now, he had to help him, regardless of the situation. But without a cable and clasp, it would be difficult to latch onto *Shelty Two's* eyebolt for a tow to the surface.

Would the manipulator arm hold a grip on the eyebolt for two-and-a-half miles? Parker silently asked himself. *I'll never know unless I attempt it,* he decided. He waited quietly until it appeared Dupont wasn't nearby.

"Andy, this is Cary. Over." He waited.

"Andy, we'll get you to the surface. Do you read?"

Out of nowhere, Parker was startled by Dupont's sub, directly in front of him.

"Give me the *Omar*, Cary," radioed Dupont, "and you can rescue your friend."

"Go to hell."

"That's all I ask. Just give me the book. You keep the jewels."

"You're out of your mind, Hank. You're plumb crazy ya' know."

"Crazy or not, you'll never reach the top with that book."

"We'll see."

Parker switched on his bright lights. He expected to temporarily blind Dupont, and hoped to disappear in the crumpled superstructure where Dupont might find it difficult to follow. Parker shot out from the ship's hull, avoided the torn plating, and headed to the collapsed area of the bow section.

He saw little on his sonar and hoped Dupont still experienced the same trouble.

But Dupont was immediately behind.

Parker's sub rose straight up and maneuvered across the bow section. Relentlessly, *Shelty Three* tracked him up and around the fallen first-class lounge roof and down over the collapsed Number 3 funnel casing.

Parker descended past the gaping holes near B and C-deck's first-class staterooms and, without warning, his sub jerked to a halt. A motor whined loudly.

"Shit!"

Parker instantly killed all motors to prevent damage. He knew what happened.

"Well I'll be damned . . . as you so often say." Dupont hovered directly in front. "You've sucked in a loose cable, mon ami."

"Cut the crap, Hank. Which thruster is it?"

Parker's sub floated down, then collided with the deck. The weight of the submersible caused the decking to shift, and the winds of the current—forced through each collapsed deck—caused the sub to bob up and down like a cork caught in an eddy. The superstructure creaked and echoed in the abyssal silence . . . and both men knew it would soon give way.

"Not that it'll do you any good to know, Cary. You won't get out of this one."

Dupont's *Shelty* crept in measured lengths around Parker's sub.

"Your stern thruster is entangled in a fallen saloon deck cable. And the remainder of three decks is ready to come down from above that."

Knowing what thruster not to turn on aided Parker. He switched on the port and starboard thrusters to maintain balance and analyzed the obstacle he now faced. If he attempted to break off the rotted cable or to sacrifice the stern thruster, Parker could implode or be buried alive. If he did nothing, a chance for rescue was slim . . . all three *Shelty's* were in use.

"Look, Henri, do something honorable for once. Haul Andy

to the surface. Take the book. But help Andy. He doesn't deserve to die down here."

"Merci. A kind offer, but you aren't in a position to prevent me from taking the book." He maneuvered his submersible to Parker's starboard side to avoid directly facing him. "As for my replacement, Mr. Calder . . . it's unfortunate. But he is on his own."

"Listen, you son-of-a-bitch, if you think you can just walk away from this . . . you can't return topside without having everyone on your neck. Besides, if you make the wrong move and my *Shelty* implodes, you and I, the book and jewels, will scatter over half of Newfoundland Ridge."

"I'll take that chance, mon ami."

Through his side port, Parker watched Dupont's prehensiles reach out for the pouch that now hung more as a torn limb than a container. He attempted to push off Dupont with his own robotic arms, but the arc was too wide and he only succeeded in forcing *Shelty One* against the sagging decks of the *Titanic*.

The decking creaked loudly and dropped slightly.

"Don't do anything stupid, Cary. Your position is precarious enough."

"When I get out of here, Henri, you're dead in the water. There won't be an ocean you can enter without wondering if I'm right behind you."

"If you get out of here, I won't need the sea after today."

"You're too greedy to let it go."

"Not when the payoff comes all at once. And I need not wait for a government to rule on the sanctity of the treasure."

Dupont aimed the arms over the *Great Omar*, opened the robotic digits wide enough to grab its top, and moved in for the book.

But Parker used his own prehensiles to pull it out first. And the book dropped out toward the wreckage and floated downward.

"Salaud!" The move angered Dupont, as he raced below and slipped his prehensiles underneath. He grabbed the casket, midwater, then backed off a respectable distance from Parker.

"I'd not count on the *Sea Cliff* or *Turtle* to rescue you."

Parker remained silent in anger.

"They could never move them from Point Loma fast enough. And the *Mystic* and *Avalon* are both in drydock for retrofits."

Dupont deposited the artifact into his own container and hit the vacuum seal. With a whooshing sound, the book was now secure in *Shelty Three*.

"Nice try, Dr. Parker."

"If ever there was a curse on that book, Henri, let it now be on you."

Dupont laughed, almost diabolically. "Je m'en branle. Besides, curses are for the ignorant. That is, unless you count the curse that tied you to your cherished grave."

Dupont released ballast for a quicker ascent to the surface, and set his DR for the *A'isha*.

"Merçi, Monsieur Parker. Au revoir."

———

Diverted from its task force with the Second Fleet—originally enroute with an assembly of cruisers headed for wargames in the mid-North Atlantic—the *U.S.S. Standley*, *Belknap*-class guided-missile cruiser, pushed its eighty-five thousand horsepower, from two General Electric turbines, at thirty-three knots. Its heading, a point that intersected the *Titanic's* site.

After angry debate and charges of intimidation from third world countries, while in emergency session at The Hague, the International Maritime Organization had, with one affirmative ballot over the required two-thirds vote, ratified Resolution Number CMI-7002—the Revised Law of the Sea's *Undersea Gravesite Treaty* — for whose passage Parker and his colleagues had fought years to obtain.

Approved by the United Nations Security Council, the new

law granted the U.N. the right to assign designations to categories of international military, passenger, and certain classes of merchant marine ship wreckage; authority to monitor undersea salvaging, when approved under the auspices of the law; and to assign military intervention, and authorize the boarding of vessels suspected of pilfering ships designated as "official underwater gravesites, museums, or classified military sites."

The *Titanic* had been immediately classified as IW-1, for International Waters High Priority Protection from Salvaging. It was sub-categorized as a graveyard, but not an archeological site, due to its age—relative to the twentieth century.

Though too late to retroactively assign penalties to salvors who had previously ravaged the *Titanic*, any salvage action taken immediately following the vote would be treated as an infringement. Thus the "urgent and direct request for intervention" came into being—approved through the United Nations, with assistance from the CIA's director, Bureau Chief Colonel Bramson, and the chief of naval operations—and with the knowledge and approval of the NCA, NSC, and the President of the United States.

For this intervention and first test of the new law, gaining approval was even easier. Under the Act, the U.N. Secretary-General could invoke emergency powers to perform necessary surgical strike operations.

In a secret meeting between the U.N. Secretary-General, the United States Ambassador to the United Nations, and the White House Chief of Staff, Colonel Bramson shared the terrorist plot and the story of the *Omar*.

The book and jewels quickly became a secondary issue when CIA imaging specialist, Clyde Mitchell, privately displayed and analyzed their thermographic images—satellite photographs of the canisters suspected to contain nuclear and biological warfare agents.

It took only moments to convince the diplomatic representatives. A probable crisis, with potentially tragic world-wide consequences, could be averted—if the military could act swiftly in mid-ocean, before the canisters could reach highly populated areas for distribution.

Bramson had called over the secured line to apprise Holt of the new law's passage, and of the imminent arrival of the Navy's cruiser. A facsimile confirmed the message, due to continued transmission problems. The *Standley* was expected to board the *A'isha*, make necessary arrests, secure the dangerous canisters, confiscate any artifacts found on board, and, if necessary, impound the ship. Any resistance would be met with force.

"*Neptune*, this is the *U.S.S. Standley*. Do you copy? Over."

Holt jumped to his mike. "This is *Neptune*. We copy."

"*Neptune*, this is Captain Jim Robertson, aboard *U.S.S. Standley*. I understand you've been advised of our assignment. Approaching your coordinates and have you on radar on a DR of about sixty nautical miles. ETA at fourteen-three-five from the southeast, our bearing three-one-five. Anticipate problems? Over."

"This is Captain John Holt. Your presence is welcome. We're missing three submersibles at roughly two thousand eighty-three fathoms. One sub is suspect, under the command of a saboteur working with those aboard the *A'isha*. We believe a stealth Japanese submersible, from the *A'isha*, is currently in descent to the bottom—to remove valuable artifacts from the *Titanic*, or to transfer them from our submersible."

"Is Dr. Cary Parker down there? Over."

"Confirmed. And his partner, Andy Calder. The suspected saboteur is Henri Dupont, Parker's former partner."

"At what location do you have the *A'isha*?"

"Uh . . . latest range is about three point one nautical miles out at bearing zero-four-five."

"Based on our DR, those numbers match the other blip on our screen and SAIC SASS program. When was your last communication with your subs? Over."

"About two and a half hours ago, at fourteen-one-five hours, we received a broken message from Parker. We've experienced incessant difficulties with communications. It appears the *A'isha* has jammed transmissions. Transponders ineffective. Over."

"What channels have you used?"

"Tried them all. But four is our primary channel."

"Captain Holt. Hold for further orders. Over."

"Roger, *Standley*."

"Captain," *Neptune's* navigator turned to Holt, "that ship's got some fire power. I served three years on her sister-ship, the *Biddle*, before they rotated me out. They can fire Mark 46 torpedoes right off the side. And she's loaded with SAMs, Mk 141 Harpoon launchers, an Mk 42 5-incher, and two twenty millimeter Phalanx Mk 15 multibarrels. The *Standley* can knock the shit outta the *A'isha*!"

"I'm not sure that's their mission," said Holt. "But if they don't, I will."

"*Neptune*, this is *Standley*. Over."

"Go ahead *Standley*."

"Maintain status quo. Keep channel seven open for future directions. Copy?"

"Roger that Captain. Just get here as quickly as possible. Over."

———

Parker tried to free the jammed cable from the stern's thruster by reversing his motors a little at a time. Nothing worked.

"Wish the Navy hadn't sliced cable and rope cutters from our budget," he said out of frustration. If sharp blades had been attached to his thruster props and prop bearings, he might not have been caught in this dilemma.

Openly exposed to the Labradorian Current rushing over and through the *Titanic's* hull, the floating cable tugged on the wounded *Shelty* and caused it to whip up and down on the edge of the rotted deck. Parker was equally concerned with the whipping motion that could break off his stern prop, and with the possibility of the deck collapsing over him.

The radio's hissing sounded like TV snow after late-night station sign off. With each attempt to reach the *Neptune*, he was greeted with ear-splitting screeches. Cary turned down the volume and hoped he could break through to Holt. It appeared he was completely cut off from topside. At wit's end, Parker sat back in his contoured seat and composed himself.

An odd sound penetrated his cabin between the disturbances. "I must be hallucinating."

The sound came, again. It emanated from his overhead speaker—like a low pitched voice or moan—mixed with the static.

"Jesus," Parker sat straight up and adjusted the volume. The quick movement of his body weight caused the *Titanic's* decks to shift underneath.

"Andy is that you? This is Cary. Can you hear me? Andy, do you read?"

There was no response. Parker listened again. Nothing more. He thought his imagination was playing tricks, attached to a creaking cenotaph at two-and-a-half miles down.

Cary sat back, disappointed. Then a voice came over the radio.

"What a hangover . . . shit, my head hurts."

"Andy. Is that you."

"Is it me what?" Calder answered slowly. "That you, Cary?"

"Listen, Andy." Parker had a renewed urgency in his voice. "Keep your channel open. Are you okay? You've got to give me a hand. Can you handle your sub?"

"Which one . . . I see two consoles."

"Clear your head partner. We're both in deep shit. I'm caught on a cable at the end of the bow section. And its ready to plunge to the floor with me attached. Dupont escaped with the *Omar*, and the *A'isha's* emissary is due here to take us both out . . . forever."

"Mind if I take a raincheck?"

"Talk sense for God's sake. We're in trouble pal."

"Cary, I don't mean to complain, but I can hardly hear you. My head's split open, and blood's all over my cabin."

"Understand, partner. But start your motors. You've got to get over here. We both need to get topside."

Between the recurring noise, Parker heard activity from Calder's sub.

"What's going on, Andy? You all right?"

"I'm returning this damned piece of equipment to its nest. Let's screw it in next time. Okay?"

There was an interminable pause. Parker heard Calder cuss up a storm under his breath. Then, the muffled sound of electric thrusters pushing water.

"Where am I situated?" asked Calder. "I'm really disoriented. Electronic's are still going nuts."

"You're about ninety yards out, directly south of the bow, near the old fallen davit's location. Bear slightly northeast at zero-zero-two. If your computer works, set your DR for forty-one forty-three fifty-four North by forty-nine fifty-six fifty-one West. Throttle slow ahead. You should DR right to me. Got that?"

Calder slowly repeated and entered the coordinates, then looked out his forward viewport. "Flash your lights."

Parker responded.

"All right," said Calder. "I'll be right there."

He eased into the throttle, and *Shelty Two* moved toward Parker at less than a knot. Calder felt lightheaded but waved it off.

As he waited, Parker explained what happened with Dupont. Amazed, but not surprised at the news, Calder had always found it difficult to put complete trust in Dupont. But he blamed it on resentment or jealously on his own part.

"Your cabin lights are headed straight for me Andy. You're doing fine."

"The power's erratic." There was a long pause. "Come to think of it, so am I. We both keep fading in and out."

Parker observed Calder had recovered his sense of humor. "What do you expect after being knocked out?"

"Got a bump on my head the size of Mount Shasta."

"Cut all unnecessary power. Batteries are drained from sitting out there with your lights on. The caliginous batteries should recover now that your computer's on again."

Calder was close to blacking out, but dismissed the feeling. He pulled up his systems control module on the computer screen and adjusted the power conservation icon to its lowest setting. The screen dimmed with his lights, and the motors slowed slightly as *Shelty Two* crossed the gently sloping submarine canyon.

"That seemed to help," reported Calder, as his sub reacted more consistently than before. "Sonar's picking you up near the decking. Flash your lights once more so I can double-check range and positioning." Parker responded.

"Yep. I've got you, my pretty," Calder chortled.

"Just get me out of here, before the wicked witch of the Mid-East returns."

Calder's coordinates placed him within ten yards of the *Titanic's* collapsed decking. He cut his thrusters to bare minimum and edged toward Parker's sub.

"Coming aft to check your prop."

"Don't get hung up in this crap."

"Hold on for backwash. You might get whipped around a bit." Calder turned his lights low.

The wind pushed against Calder from the north, as he painstakingly skirted around Parker's sub. Careful not to get too close, he avoided other floating and hanging cables snaking in the water, aft of the old compass platform.

"Got a cobra pit back here."

Calder maneuvered between the open, sloping sections of Number 3 funnel casing, and closed in on the tail prop. But a wave of dizziness hit him. He was losing consciousness, and he forced himself to take a deep breath.

His sub hit the edge of B-deck.

"Dammit."

The deck creaked loudly, and a piece of debris hit Parker's sub.

"Sorry. Started to black out."

"Take your time to reacclimate," said Parker. "But not too long.

What do you see back there?"

"The angle of the decks won't let me in close. I'll have to lie in a prone position over your stern to get manipulators to the cable. It'll probably kick up dust."

"Careful, my friend."

Calder adjusted his thrusters and mini-jets, and *Shelty Two* found a face-down position above the decking, immediately over the entangled thruster. Calder's head throbbed as his sub assumed an angle nearly horizontal to the sea floor. He forced his attention on the task as waves of nausea overtook him.

Organic dust surrounded the *Shelties*, but enough had already blown away to make the cloud less opaque.

"Come on, baby," he coaxed. Calder aimed the robotic fingers of his right prehensile, grabbed for the floating end of the cable, and missed.

"Damn thing twists like a belly dancer." He reached the large strand and clamped the fingers tightly, five inches from the end. "This's worse than tying underwater knots at SEALS bootcamp."

Calder changed emphasis to the left prehensile, to pull the cable back.

"How're we doing, Andy?"

"Two feet of this stuff ran through, and a blade's caught a crimp in the wire." He pulled with his left prehensile and lifted and pushed with the right.

"Crap. I'm in motion. Didn't set for drift . . . "

Suddenly, the current pushed Calder into Parker.

"Hold on Cary." In his rush, he hadn't instructed his computer to compensate for the current's force. The two subs collided, and both *Shelties* pulled on the cable.

Tension created a force not exerted on the decaying hull since the last salvors had robbed the grave. The deck's superstructure creaked severely as the heavy weight of rotting steel plates slid away from the ship, collapsing downward as they moved.

"Were going for a ride!" Calder yelped.

With Calder's prehensiles still grasping the cable, both *Shelties* were propelled downward with the slippage. The force pulled the two subs together, and they struck with an intensity that signaled impending disaster. The split-second incident evolved into slow motion for them as they spent an eternity waiting for implosion. But the vessels held.

"Damn close," exclaimed Calder as the creaking subsided.

"Let go of the cable, Andy."

"The deck's weight on your thruster will tear it off," argued Calder. "I can hold this up and keep the weight off until we find a solution."

"If you insist, but I hate to rush you. A glimmer of light's coming from the south, out at the stern section."

"Can't worry about that. Got to get you untangled."

Before Calder could increase his thrusters, the weight on the cable tore a section of the funnel casing from the ship. It thundered to the next level, carrying the still-attached subs.

Again, the subs collided, but the ship's plates stopped short of falling to the next level as other cables held the casing, and the submersibles came to rest on top of the saloon deck.

"Yes!" said Calder. "The rotted cable tore off at the other end."

Intensity and amplification of the catastrophic sounds increased with the high pressure and echoed across the abyssal plain. Out at the debris field, just north of the collapsed stern, the moving lights paused, turned in their direction, then picked up speed.

"Give me a minute to pull this sucker out of here."

"No time," said Parker. "Let it go and get the hell out before the *Yoritomo* arrives."

"No way. We're in this together."

Parker increased his left and right thrusters for balance and throttled the cycloidals for a tighter hover. He waited to hit the stern thruster as soon as Calder gave the signal.

Calder used the force of the manipulators to pull his sub in.

"The *Yoritomo's* getting closer, Andy. How're we doing?"

Calder concentrated on the prehensiles. "Except for Toad's wild ride, I've still got both ends of the strand."

Ever so gently, Calder moved his right hand slightly up and to the left.

"Got to get this crimp past your blade. It's shorter on the right end."

Calder jerked up on the right end of the twisted cable to unhook it. As quickly as it released, he flinched his virtual-gloves to the left, and the prehensile, with cable, followed.

"She's out."

"How's it look?"

"Bent a little toward topside, but clean as a filleted mackerel."

"Clear the stern. I'm turning on aft thruster." Parker punched up his side lift props and gained more float. Then he switched on the motor for the stern prop. A loud hum followed, and his console light flashed a cautious yellow.

"The prop's jammed," said Calder.

"Knock the shaft. I'll move out to give more clearance."

Calder pulled behind Parker and grabbed the stern prop. He jiggled it back and forth then pushed the point of the blade to set it firmly in place.

"Try it now."

Parker re-started the aft motor, and the blade turned.

"Looks good."

"All right. Cut lights, drop weights and head for topside."

Calder turned off his lights. "What're you going to do?"

"Distract the incoming sub while you get a head start. They know I've got the jewelry and won't be concerned with you."

"Hell you say. I'm not leaving you with those bastards."

Parker knew Andy was stubborn. "Okay . . . get down to the bilge keel and use terrain masking to blend in with the hull. Maintain radio silence, but leave your channel open for my call."

"Be careful, for crying out loud." Calder reversed cycloidals and drifted out with the current, away from the sheared-off bow. He countered his direction to slightly north-by-north-west, cautiously moved in under cover of the bilge keel, and tucked his sub next to the silent and shadowless vestige of a giant rusting boiler.

Without lights, Parker moved up over the slumped roof of the first-class lounge, cleared a window casing in the gymnasium's wall where the roofing had collapsed, and floated down behind the bulkhead—his sub rising just enough to peer to the south. He cut power to bare minimum and waited for the *Yoritomo's* approach.

From his vantage point he watched the ghostly shadow of a manta-like vessel traverse the sloping plateau as it neared the bow.

They're still searching for Andy, believing him out of commission, thought Parker. *Maybe they'll think he drifted south with the current.*

Parker glanced at his sonar screen. It detected a weak disturbance to the southwest. The *Yoritomo* was true to form. Were it not for the running lights so brazenly displayed, he would not have recognized it on sonar and might have thought it to be a slight magnetic anomaly. Few would have paid attention.

Damn, they're confident.

The *Yoritomo* approached the coordinates where Calder had been stranded, circled the area, then hovered for a time. Slowly, it turned toward the *Titanic's* bow section. Then, as if a space ship had darted across the sky, *Yoritomo* instantly traversed the distance between the old davit and where Parker had been entangled in the cable. And its running lights went out.

Thanks to Henri, they know exactly where to look, Parker thought. He glanced at his sonar screen and realized the magnetic anomaly had become stronger.

"Fascinating," he whispered to himself. *It's got tremendous capacity to sneak up on its prey from a distance. But up close, beam-to, it can still give itself away if you know what to look for.*

Parker watched from his darkened cabin as the pitch-black *Yoritomo* stalked back and forth, aft of the bow section, obviously searching for the *Shelties*. He studied the design, thinking all along it reminded him of something else. Then it hit him. *George Pal's alien ships from Mars—his H.G. Well's film*, War of the Worlds. *That's what it resembles. A cross between the butterfly-shape of the manta ray and the center-rise, cartilaged, cow-nose ray.*

Parker's sonar picked up less electromagnetic visibility feedback from the *Yoritomo* when it aimed its nose toward him, at twelve o'clock, or receded from him with its tail.

Her EMV is at maximum when it banks, increases speed, or flies by with its beam facing me. But her stealth features function well, Parker ruminated.

The rubbery anechoic tiles, affixed to the *Yoritomo's* hull, absorbed most of the signals from Parker's sonar, converted the sonar frequency energy into heat, and minimized reflected echoes. Parker switched on his thermal imaging device attached to the video camera, looked at his monitor, and smiled.

"I'll be damned," he whispered to himself. "Gotcha' you son-of-a-bitch." The TID sensors picked up heat given off by the *Yoritomo's* anechoic tiles. The infrared heat generated by converted radio waves from *Shelty One*—fed back to him as video images— now made the *Yoritomo* glow in the dark on his screen. As long as Parker's sonar and thermal imaging device functioned minimally, there were few deep-water canyons or tributaries where the sub could escape, without being detected.

"Andy," he quietly spoke into his mike in as low a tone as possible. "Switch on TID. Keep RF operational and open at three hundred megahertz. Copy?"

"Copy," came back a whispered reply from below.

"Hopefully, they won't notice. Wait'll your monitor shows this baby heating up."

Parker watched the experimental sub disappear from view as it descended toward the ocean floor. "Maintain radio silence from here. Be on guard."

"Copy," the reply hissed in a brief bout with static.

Calder watched his video monitor from inside the keel section. When the *Yoritomo* passed in front of the camera, the TID uncloaked the visiting sub's shape. Calder held his breath as he viewed it on his screen.

Yoritomo passed by the gaping hole, cut between the ocean floor and the torn steel plating, then stopped, hovered, and reversed thrusters. As it backed up, it turned slowly to look head-on into the blown-out bilge section of the ship.

In the relatively safe darkness of the abyss, Calder realized the two subs were face to face and wondered if the *Yoritomo* had its own TID focused on him. With their running lights laid in three strips along the raised canopy, he could partially see through their viewports.

The TID's image reminded him of the F-117 Stealth Fighter, its angular fuselage tucked between highly swept wings. This was not a mini-sub by *Shelty* standards. With a wing span of nineteen feet and an overall length of nearly fourteen, nose to tail, Calder felt safe from direct attack inside the keel.

He zoomed the video camera in for a close up. On the monitor, two men carried on a discussion in the side-by-side cockpit. Both were Japanese. Not a surprise to Calder, since Arab terrorists weren't known for developing superior technology for the high seas.

Then, Calder watched both men put on sunglasses. Without warning, the equivalent of two-million candlepower nearly blinded him—as though daylight had cut through from above. The brightness was overwhelming.

Discovered, he fed his brightest lights back to the *Yoritomo* in a feeble attempt to piss them off. Still feeling relatively safe beside the giant boiler, he waited them out and shielded his eyes from the light.

They don't know if I'm the one with the jewels, Calder thought. *I'll lead them on while Cary gets topside.*

The *Yoritomo* turned to starboard, ascended above the *Titanic's* bilge opening, and flew over the steel plating that projected from the gaping hole. As quickly as they had taken position above, Calder heard the whining of a tube door open. A prehensile arm hydraulically telescoped from the sub's bow. It locked into place, and a bright red laser beam shot out from the robotic arm and cut across the plating. Cold sea water boiled at the point the hot light met the metal.

Calder knew three options faced him. The first was the possibility the steel plating would be cut, then dropped inward to crush him in his place. But that would cause implosion and be dangerous for both sides. The second was to remove the heavy plating to gain access to the jewels they thought he had. His third option was to break for open water.

Not wanting to get caught or give away Parker's position, Calder picked the third. He reset the battery icon to full power.

Parker had waited for a return visit from the *Yoritomo*. When nothing happened, he ascended from the carcass of the *Titanic's* gym. Just then, the entire aft portside lit up like the rising sun.

What the hell'd they do . . . steal Fenway Park's lights? He darted back into place, and prepared for another visit from the enemy. But the bright lights broadcast toward the southwest end of the bow. A bizarre—almost supernatural—shadow of the formidable ship's hull danced in the water behind him.

Then, Parker noticed a combination of rust and bubbles rising through the reflected light from beneath. And he knew Calder was in trouble.

Before the terrorists cut through the plates, *Shelty Two* burst out under the overhanging steel and headed from the ship.

"Don't fail me now," Calder said to himself. He pushed full throttle and headed north, his keel flying just feet above the sloping terrain.

Hearing Calder's remark on the open channel, but not yet aware of Calder's escape, Parker moved *Shelty One* to the gym's portside bulkhead and climbed out over the A-deck roof. He watched the *Yoritomo* pull in its laser torch, turn, and immediately give chase across the ocean floor.

Parker hit full throttle and followed, maintaining enough

distance to allow time to plan an assist. The TID imaging camera was more effective than sonar for tracking their location.

The *Yoritomo* used its Doppler for pursuit as it locked on to *Shelty Two's* every move.

Calder quickly turned to port or reversed direction in attempts to shake them off. But the Japanese submersible came about as quickly as he altered course.

"Hope they don't have ordnance," he said out loud.

Parker heard Calder and hoped he might catch the *Yoritomo* by surprise.

Calder shot across the abyssal floor, adjusted his diving planes, and plunged 300 feet below the sea bottom—where an elongated three mile earthen gash ran parallel with the continental shelf. He hoped to take cover in the dark recesses of the small ocean trough, but the *Yoritomo* crew left on their bright lights.

The oblong depression lit up in fast receding sections of terraces and outcroppings, as dark shadows melted into the mud, and pelagic marine sediments were quickly left behind.

Shelty Two held to the lower edges of outcroppings in the depths of the V-shaped trough. Calder hoped the larger sub would catch on a ridge too large for its wing span. But the *Yoritomo* tracked its prey with the diligence of a hawk and, with its sophisticated bottom-and-sidescan sonar, escaped the trough's jagged edges.

The canyon sloped upward and fed into a chain of volcanic sea knolls, as Calder burst into the open—the *Yoritomo* still in pursuit.

Calder banked steeply around a small sea knoll, overcompensated, and nearly ate mud until he corrected his position. By then the *Yoritomo* had closed the range and flown to his port side.

Calder decelerated, banked sixty degrees to starboard, and placed *Shelty Two* behind the terrorist's 3/9 line. As he flew just above, the *Yoritomo's* bow lifted straight up at a ninety-degree cut through the water, in front of him, then rolled a three-sixty over in a dive to his tail.

They were so close, Calder swore he saw both faces laughing as they shot past him.

Instantly, he executed a one-eighty to the rear. The *Yoritomo* followed as both subs sprinted, at thirty-six knots, past the rising series of knolls. Anticipating the other's moves, they darted in and out between the faults, folds and mantles of sediment that covered the perimeter of the extinct volcanoes.

Then Calder disappeared.

The *Yoritomo* continued its hunt, racing between the small seamounts, searching for any signs of the *Shelty*.

Suddenly, Parker's vessel hovered directly ahead. Startled, the *Yoritomo* cut straight up to avoid a crash, banked sharply to starboard, and came around to greet him from behind. Parker hit the transverse propulsors. His sub rotated in place to face them head on.

Thinking him to be Calder, they focused attention on *Shelty One* and ignored a blip on their sonar . . . where Calder had reappeared behind them.

The *Yoritomo* increased throttle as it approached Parker. He backed up to keep the focus off Calder.

Closing on *Yoritomo's* stern, Calder moved to its starboard thruster. He grabbed the prop shaft with the manipulators and held on tightly—throwing the tension adjustment on automatic.

The *Yoritomo's* crew felt a jolt and glanced out the canopy. Fearful the shaft would break off from parasitic drag, the *Yoritomo's* crew slowed to a crawl.

"Grab the other elbow, Cary."

Parker moved in and latched onto the portside shaft. It was an odd sight—both *Shelties* dragging alongside the large stealth submersible. The *Yoritomo* crew no longer laughed.

"Throttle up, Andy. Ten knots, in twos, on go. Over."
"Aye, Aye, sir. Happy to be aboard sir."
"Go!"

Both *Shelties* slowly pushed their throttles, two knots at a time, until each console read "10." The three subs picked up momentum and moved in unison as they approached the northern edges of the Sohm Abyssal Plain.

"Twenty knots, and ascend to sixty yards on go, my friend."

"Twenty knots and ascend to sixty it is, sir. Happy to comply, sir."

"Go!"

They picked up speed, rose two hundred feet above the floor, and tugged the $23-million manta ray along with their *Shelties*. The terrain climbed as they advanced on the outer tip of the Newfoundland Ridge, near the Laurentian Cone seamount.

The two *Yoritomo* crew members looked back at their unwanted guests. They were animated in their reactions and busy pushing buttons on the control panel.

The electronic gears of a small tube door were heard opening at *Yoritomo's* bow. Calder recognized the sound that preceded the laser cutting torch.

They watched the hydraulic arm extend from the tube and lock in place. And with the aid of gimbaled joints on the welding arm, it twisted in a one-eighty turn on its jointed axis and pointed aft.

Careful not to hit their own sub, a bright red-hot laser shot out at intermittent bursts over the top of the starboard wing and slowly approached Parker's *Shelty*.

"Increase to thirty knots on one, bank seven-five degrees to port on two, and descend to a hundred feet altitude on three," yelled Parker.

"Understood."

"Go one!"

The two *Shelties* boosted their speed to thirty.

"Go two!"

They banked heavily to the left, and G-forces caused the gimbaled laser to whip back toward the *Yoritomo's* bow. The laser cut a swath into its own canopy, nearly slicing through the viewports before it came to rest up front.

"Go three!"

The *Shelties* dropped to one hundred feet above the floor, their cycloidal jets easily carrying the large submersible down while maintaining their own equilibrium. There was no latitude for watching the expressions of the panicked crew as the *Yoritomo* was pulled toward the ocean bottom at high speed.

"Level with terrain . . .

"Now!" said Parker.

The subs ran parallel with the terrain, as the seamount came into view—and the laser cut its way through the water once more.

"Increase throttle to thirty-five knots . . .

"Now!"

"Uh, mon capitaine, there's a slight impediment to our course at twelve o'clock? We're about to become fish bait. Over."

"Roger that. Trust me on this one."

The *Shelties* had placed themselves in certain peril as they sped toward the basaltic volcano. The underwater mountain rose over three thousand feet above them, as the sea floor closed in below.

"How's Situation Awareness, partner?"

"SA's hot and on target. Ready when you are, but hurry," Calder said as the *Yoritomo's* laser approached his robotic arm.

This had to be the one moment where both called upon their ability to optimize Situation Awareness . . . that intangible force that separated them from the ordinary, helped them analyze and assess the encounter—exactly as it should be—then react instantly and with precision to multiple tasks.

"This is it, partner. If it doesn't work . . . see you in our next life."

"Shit," was all Calder could say.

"Counting down from three to one, cut all motors, jerk back on their thrusters while rolling zero-five to starboard, then jettison prehensiles. One move. Understood?"

In the bright light through his sideport, Parker saw a large knowing smile form on Andy's face. Calder threw a big thumbs-up sign.

"Three, two, one. Hit it!"

In one complete motion, both *Shelties* cut throttles to zero, twisted back hard on the *Yoritomo's* port and starboard thrusters with their prehensiles, rolled their subs five degrees to the right, and jettisoned their robotic arms—still hanging around the prop shafts. And the manta shot ahead, out of control.

"Get the hell out'a here," Parker insisted as they reversed position, and backed off a safe distance from any forthcoming shrapnel.

Instantly the *Yoritomo's* thrusters bent aft, weakening and tearing the vessel's surface skin. Propelled forward by momentum, the sub shot out over the rising blanket of sediment in an uncontrollable spin. The blinding glare from its lamps created a strobe effect as the rapidly spinning sub flew eerily across the ocean floor, its lights reaching for the muddy seabed and, alternately, the murky, pitch-black heights above.

The *Yoritomo's* captain gunned the throttle, hoping to obtain enough thrust to regain control. But drag from the bent props prevented the sub's recovery, and *Yoritomo* uncontrollably pitched and rolled as it flew toward the submarine mountain.

Parker and Calder watched the oversized manta defiantly careen toward the seamount, and lose altitude as it approached the rugged boulders and centuries of detritus that filled the surrounding incline.

"Better them than us," said Calder.

The loose thrusters caused the *Yoritomo's* hull to viciously shake. And it began to tear apart.

The hanging starboard prop shaft was the first to make contact with a boulder. As the *Yoritomo* rolled inexorably over the steep-banked terrain, it caught on the jagged edge of the volcanic debris and ripped off its thruster. The outer skin of the sub instantly separated from its starboard frame and, simultaneously, the entire vessel slammed into the mountain and violently collapsed inward with a fierce, implosive force.

The sub's lights extinguished, and the abyssal ridge was once more hidden behind a cloak of darkness.

High technology had met with the crust of thousands of years of decomposed marine sediment, as the *Yoritomo* abruptly compressed and devoured itself—injecting the water with a barrage of fragments—spewing metal, plastic, stones, mud, and human matter.

Mesmerized by what they had witnessed, Parker and Calder realized they were in jeopardy, as fragments rained around them.

"Retreat bearing two-zero-eight," Parker called out, and they pulled back farther from the site.

They listened to sounds from *Yoritomo's* impact rumble across the ocean floor and slowly fade in the darkness. Momentarily there was silence, and the tranquility of the deep seemed reassuring.

Then, from the undersea mountain, they heard a different rumbling. It grew louder as seconds passed, until the disturbance reverberated throughout the underwater valley and became a threatening roar. Parker recognized the timbre from previous experience.

And an avalanche of marine sludge cascaded down the side of the seamount.

"Drop ballast and get out of here," Parker insisted, "before the ooze buries us with the remains of the *Yoritomo*."

Static took over once more.

"What'd you say? This damned equipment's acting up again."

"I'm having trouble, too. Drop ballast and follow me topside. Over." Parker motioned through his viewport, pulling an imaginary chain and moving his thumb straight up.

Calder nodded.

They reached four hundred feet above the floor, and the

distorted hissing sound became almost unbearable. Parker noticed his altimeter indicated no further gain in ascension. In fact, his sub lost ground. His motors functioned, and no warning lights indicated trouble. He looked out his viewport and watched *Shelty Two* slip as well. Then, the altimeter displayed descending numbers as the subs lost buoyancy.

Parker glanced out the viewport, again, and saw something unusual rising around their subs.

"Andy, turn on your lights." He repeated the communication to overcome distortion.

Both subs switched on all halogens. Parker's mind clicked and a disquieting fear tool hold.

————

A wet Dupont climbed the steps of the *A'isha's* ladder—the *Great Omar* under his right arm. He was visibly worn when he climbed from *Shelty Three's* hatch. With the help of divers, he had jumped to an inflatable boat, next to the stolen sub. But his foot had slipped on the rubber siding and he fell into the water. Out of instinct, he tossed the *Omar* into the dinghy and grabbed hold of a safety line running the length of the boat. Divers helped him up into the inflatable, and then to the ship itself.

Faheed Al Mar Ragem stood in the shadows of the overhead tarpaulins, at *A'isha's* fantail, and watched the divers pull Dupont and his prize from *Shelty Three*. For one split second, Ragem considered leaving Dupont in the water, then thought he might still be useful. For now he would make other arrangements.

With the *U.S.S. Standley* approaching, Ragem's crew did not consider it a high priority to pull the mini-sub from the water. Tied as a horse to a railing, the white submersible was left to bob aft of port, like a floating toy. Rubber fenders were loosely arranged around its sides, to prevent damage against the ship. It would be pulled in later, if time allowed.

Dupont stood limply on the edge of the fantail and looked into the dark eyes of Ragem. He searched for an expression of approval, but found a hidden anger even he had not seen before.

"We have accomplished the larger mission, Monsieur Ragem." Dupont held out the rare book. "Here is the *Great Omar . . . The Rubaiyat of Omar Khayyam.*" Dupont stood firmly in place, at once proud of his accomplishment and relieved he had made it back alive. He held out the artifact as though it were a part of the Crown Jewels.

Ragem approached Dupont, and the terrorist's plain white galabiyya gave the appearance of a ship's ghost moving across the deck. His kaffiyeh headdress flowed in the late afternoon breeze, held tight by its headband.

Ragem pulled the *Omar* from Dupont's hands—his manner colder and darker than the Atlantic, itself. It was as if Ragem thought he had owned the book, and had personally retrieved it from the *Titanic.*

"Before you spend time with the book," Dupont stuttered, "I must get it into the electrolytic bath, or it will crumble to dust in a matter of days or even hours."

"I will decide what we do with the book," Ragem commanded.

"The *Omar* will be worthless if not stabilized immediately," Dupont shot back, surprising even himself. "You have waited this long, Faheed. . . . Over eight decades that book has been down there. We've planned this expedition for nearly a year. Certainly you are a patient man. What is another week or two?"

Ragem stood firm and in thought. "Insha'allaah," he finally said with a wide smile, accentuating the sharp features of his face. "I agree. We must get it into the bath immediately. Dr. Hirao will see to it."

It was now Ragem's decision, not Dupont's. And he presented the book to a man standing behind him. Caught by surprise, Dupont had not been told another scientist would be on board. Without a word, Dr. Hirao turned with the book and left for the ship's hold.

"Not even a 'thank you?'" Dupont inquired.

"You were paid to do a job, not to be thanked. The job was only half done. We have lost contact with the *Yoritomo* . . . and the jewels. Dr. Parker and Calder appear to be on their way up.

"Compounding the issue, Monsieur Dupont, is that Dr. Parker's wife may no longer be in our custody. Which leads me to consider why we have lost all contact with our operatives in America. We now have a Navy battleship heading in our direction. And they will probably attempt to board. Might it all center around your visit to Colonel Bramson at the CIA, and your subsequent visit to Franklin, Pennsylvania just before boarding the *Neptune*?"

The insinuations were more than Dupont would allow, under the circumstances.

"I am dripping wet because I just risked my fucking life and reputation to bring you the rarest book in the world from the bottom of the ocean, and you ask me if I planned all this? You think I enjoy the thought of implosion at four-thousand meters below the surface. You try it!"

He turned away before his anger got the better of him. Then he reeled around to face Ragem once more.

"I must get out of my wet clothes. I'd suggest you pull anchor and move from these waters before the United States Navy sends us all to the *Titanic*, for eternity."

"We cannot leave until we retrieve the *Yoritomo* and the balance of the treasure. If the Navy attempts to board, we will be ready for them."

"Don't be a fool. You can't match their power."

"We shall see."

Dupont was dumbfounded at Ragem's arrogance. But he knew the terrorist was not about to change his mind.

"Where is my cabin?"

Ragem ordered a crew member to lead Dupont to his room.

Dupont sat on the edge of his bed and peeled layers of wet

garments from his body. He heard the deadbolt lock click into place and jumped for the door. It would not budge.

Imprisoned in his own cabin, Dupont's anger reached its threshold and he pounded on the door.

"Ragem! Open this door, you bastard! You'll regret this. I promise you."

Dupont spun around to look for a way out. No portholes; no other exits. He searched the room and found nothing to pry open the door. In frustration, Dupont sat on the edge of his berth and stared at the floor. Slowly he regained his focus...as he waited for the right opportunity to escape.

———

Miles out from Newfoundland Ridge, the Laurentian Cone took on life. Slag-like refuse fell away from its side, enlarged the underwater slump, and rumbled down the geologic formation to find a low point.

"My God, it all makes sense," Parker said over his mike.

"What's going on?"

Parker barely made out Calder's question. Small bubbles encircled both subs as they floated above the seamount.

Another rumbling sound emanated from the ridge and the area of the slump grew wider. More sludge drifted down the side of the cone, and a larger volume of globules sprang from beneath the sediment. The silvery bubbles rose swiftly for the ocean's surface as they passed the *Shelties*.

"Andy, throttle to full, dive to fifty feet and head south. Quickly!"

He repeated it twice and indicated direction through the viewport. But their compass readings changed erratically between points, and they couldn't tell which way was south.

"Move out of these bubbles before they take us down. Then dive for the floor. Can you hear me, Andy? We've got to find that deep trough leading back to the *Titanic*. Over."

There was no answer through the blaring interference on the radio. But Parker saw Calder look questioningly through his portside window. Parker signaled "follow me" and hit his throttle.

He tried to raise *Neptune's Knot* on several channels, but to no avail.

Both subs were losing buoyancy as they intentionally descended toward the ocean bottom, throttled forward, and moved out of the stream of bubbles. Their small vessels' buoyancy returned as they headed where Parker hoped the tip of the deep depression would be found.

Following the small seamount chain, passed earlier, the two *Shelties* moved farther away from the larger cone and the slow-moving avalanche.

With the distorted radio noise partially subsiding, Calder attempted to communicate once more.

"What the hell was that? Is the volcano active? Do you read? Cary, what's going . . . "

"We've got to get topside, ASAP. That rumbling is not volcanic in origin." He checked his magnetic compass against the computer. It was inconsistent, but occasionally matched magnetic reading.

They located the edge of the deep trough and swiftly descended to escape the grasp of the rising bubbles. Disruption of the radio was intermittent.

"Those globules were frozen hydrates escaping from under centuries of sediment. We need to gain as much turf between us and that shit as possible."

"Hydrates," Calder thought out loud. "You mean methane?"

"Frozen methane." Parker answered, while the two subs followed the trail back to the *Titanic*. "It all makes sense, doesn't it? The recurring, dissipating fog on the ocean's surface yesterday and this morning, disruption of radio transmissions, confusion with sonar, bubbles rising from the seafloor. It's methane all right. Frozen gas hydrates have probably leaked from under the seafloor's crust for weeks."

"And we thought *A'isha* jammed our electronics. The current must've carried the gas in our direction."

"It still is," said Parker. "And we've got to get far away from it. All that slag needed was the *Yoritomo* to break it loose. It's approaching a blowout. If the avalanche scours away the layer of frozen hydrates, there's a chance an enormous pocket of pure gas is underneath."

"Can't it take out ships on the surface?"

"Just like the Bermuda Triangle. Once it reaches topside, in any sizable volume, its as volatile as a hydrogen bomb. If it ignites it'll melt down ships faster than a China Syndrome."

Parker had received a recent study, conducted by the U.S. Geological Survey, confirming what many scientists had suspected for years. When plants, organic droppings from sea life, or minute creatures fall to the ocean floor and decompose, methane gas is produced from the rotting deposits. Under extreme pressure thousands of feet below the surface, at or below temperatures of one or two degrees Celsius, it transforms to its frozen, crystalline equivalent known as gas hydrates or hydrate crystals.

Over the centuries, layers of frozen hydrates accumulate to thicknesses of a mile or more. Heavier crusts of sediment form over the hydrates and gas to hold them in. But, the report noted, when unleashed by underwater earthquakes, volcanic activity and other natural causes—or through the actions of man-made disruptions that break the natural crust covering the sleeping methane—the consequences could be disastrous.

Parker and Calder's subs hastily rose with the gradient of the ocean fissure as its tip reached sea floor level, and they headed toward the *Titanic's* bow. Soon they arrived at the old ship, and Parker felt a final twinge of despair.

"So long pal. May be a while before we return."

Making certain they dropped their weights into the sand, away from the ship, the two subs rose above the *Titanic* for the last time.

The radio interference partially subsided, and Parker searched for an unimpeded channel.

"*Neptune* this is *Shelty One*. Do you read? *Neptune* this is . . . "

"Where the hell have you been," Holt almost screamed into the mike. "We've tried to raise you for three hours."

"So good to hear your cheerful voice, John. Andy and I are on our way up...a little worse for wear. But we're the least of your worries."

"What's going on? Between loss of communications we've picked up distinct sounds on sonar...like explosions and volcanic rumblings. We thought you'd imploded down there."

"The *Yoritomo's* history. Unfortunately, that's the implosion you heard . . . against the Laurentian Cone. Over."

"Holy shit." said Holt. "And you're upset about that?"

"It was a beautiful piece of engineering, John."

"What's going on down there? A *Shelty* pulled alongside *A'isha*."

Despite poor radio contact, Parker explained how Dupont stole the *Omar*, deserted them, and left the *Yoritomo* to finish the job.

"But forget him," said Parker. "Are you still getting fog?."

"Comes and goes."

"When the *Yoritomo* hit the cone it caused a massive slump. The rumbling you've picked up is an avalanche of sediment releasing gas hydrates toward the surface. They've been leaking for some time now."

"That's what caused the fog?"

"Correct. And agitated water forms negative ions and sets up an ionic disturbance."

"And that screwed up electronics and communications . . . "

"Roger that." Parker checked his altimeter. "We're only up to thirteen hundred fathoms. Prepare to pull out right after retrieval. I'm aborting the mission from..."

Holt interrupted. "Hate to tell you, but we can't move until the Navy arrives. The *U.S.S. Standley* is due here, shortly, to board the *A'isha*. They want you along to identify Dupont, now that he's on board, and to locate the *Omar*. Over."

"Listen, John, I'm not experienced with gas hydrates, but I've seen films of entire oil rigs going down with absolutely no trace left. Just tell the Navy we may all have to clear out, fast, if we get a blowout down below. It's extremely unstable."

"I copy. Stay in touch. Over."

———

The unusual fog was now reported three and a half miles to the north of *Neptune*'s Knot, just past the *A'isha*. Though sonar monitoring was inconsistent, with high-powered binoculars it appeared to Holt that the *A'isha* had little going on. Its crew members occasionally wandered the decks, and checked for signs of the *Yoritomo*. But all appeared relatively quiet.

Holt, though normally steady and calm, paced the *Neptune*'s bridge like an expectant father waiting for the sea to birth twins.

With the immense quantities of released hydrates, additional negative ions discharged throughout the water and atmosphere. Communication became more difficult, and all electronics went berserk—particularly as the two *Shelties* approached the deep scattering layer.

Holt and the *Shelties* marked each one hundred fathoms of ascent by voice or signal—whichever got through first. Fifty percent of the check points made it. But conditions deteriorated to less than twenty percent by the time Parker and Calder reached five hundred fathoms.

"Sir," the chief communications officer interrupted Holt from another attempt to reach his subs, "The *Standley*'s calling in."

"Open her up."

The screeching sounds overpowered the bridge. Holt signaled the CO to take down the level and manually adjust the radio's notch filters.

"*Neptune*, this is *Standley*. Do you copy?"

"This is Captain Holt. We don't copy well."

"We have you in sight about six nautical miles out, due west from our position, with the *A'isha* about three miles due north of you. We anticipate pulling alongside in under ten minutes. Any sign of Parker and Calder? Over." The message was repeated.

Holt glanced out his starboard side and saw the approaching guided missile frigate.

"We have a visual on your cruiser. Good to have you in sight. Expect our subs to hit the surface any minute. Be advised to remain back from our position until we pull them in. Don't need any serious wave action. Copy?"

There was no answer. Holt repeated himself.

"Copy and understood. Will comply. Over and out."

Holt signaled the CO to switch off the channel.

The intercom crackled fiercely. "Captain," said the bosun, "*Shelty One* just hit the surface fore amidships. Starboard side."

Holt raced to the window and smiled with relief.

"Thank God."

"There's number two!" came a second call.

"Yes!" a resounding cheer went up around the ship.

"Get them out of there, pronto."

The suited divers were already in the water as the crew lowered the rubber, water-filled fenders over the fantail.

"Ready to come about. Let's place this baby right on their tails."

"Ready to come about sir."

"Bring her about to port."

"About to port, sir."

"Take her easy now lad. Don't suck them into our wake."

The cycloidals revolved the ship in place, to put its stern closer to the subs for recovery. The crane-like arms of the A-frame were extended out over the fantail, and the cable swayed like a pendulum, while lowering. The divers hooked up *Shelty Two* first, and signaled the surface control team to retrieve the sub.

The relatively calm sea simplified the operation. And by the time *Shelty One* settled in her crib, Parker was already out through the top of its sail.

The surface controller yelled directions to the crew as the winches hummed loudly and took up cable slack.

"You guys okay?" Holt shouted above the noise.

"Get Andy to the infirmary to check that head gash," Parker yelled back.

Calder waved them off. "I'm okay. Forget it."

"The hell you say." Parker pulled two crew members out of the crowd and attached them to both sides of Calder. "Make sure he sees the doc."

Parker looked at Calder and smiled, "Get your butt down there and check that mother out."

"Captain Holt," a voice hailed over the intercom. Holt moved to the speaker box.

"Holt here."

"Sir, the *A'isha's* got action over the stern . . . launching another submersible."

"Just what we need, "said Parker, "another sub in the water."

They glanced to starboard at the *U.S.S. William H. Standley*, now taking position a nautical mile northeast, between *Neptune* and *A'isha*. Nearly the size of two football fields, the frigate reclassified to cruiser status in 1975—would have dwarfed the two research vessels had it been closer to either.

"Notify the *Standley* of the *A'isha's* shenanigans," Holt ordered, "and tell them our subs are on deck."

"Sir, they're already paging you on the radio."

"Patch them down here."

Ionic disturbances played havoc with the intercom.

"This is the *Standley*. A launch is heading your way to meet Dr. Parker and Mr. Calder. We watched your haul-in. Are they ready for pickup? Over."

The radio squawked and screeched. Holt waited for a clear moment to be understood.

"Parker's ready, but the doctor's checking Andy Calder's head injury. He may not be available. Are you aware of action over *A'isha's* fantail?"

"We're monitoring. The captain has just warned them not to abandon ship. He's told them of our boarding party. Over."

"They may be going in search of the *Yoritomo's* remains," said Parker. He pulled off his ski cap and lifted his sweatshirt over his head. "They won't find anything."

Holt echoed Parker's remarks over the channel.

"They aren't going anywhere," said the voice over the radio. "I assure you."

Suddenly, a flash of light and a trail of smoke left the port-side forward end of *Standley's* aft deckhouse. The air resonated with a powerful whoosh, resembling the sound of a large bottle rocket, as a single Harpoon RGM-84-Delta missile hurled toward the *A'isha* from the SSM Mark 141 launcher.

Parker grabbed Holt's glasses from him, and Holt borrowed a pair from the surface controller. They watched the solid-fuel rocket booster propel the anti-ship missile from its launcher.

At flying speed it jettisoned the booster, and its Teledyne turbojet took over, powering the 488-pound payload across the stern of the *A'isha*. Radar coordinates sent it to within fifty yards off *A'isha's* fantail. And with a resounding explosive force, tons of water were sent one hundred feet into the air, then rained down over the rebel ship and crew.

"Sonofabitch," said Holt.

"Nice shot," said Parker.

"We have more of those suckers if we need them," said the communications specialist from the *Standley*. "Out."

———

The *Standley's* commander picked up the handset to communicate with the *A'isha*. His rugged face showed more years than he wished to admit. But shocking white hair complimented his blue-gray eyes, weathered tan, and solid frame, and gave him an air of distinction. He spoke clearly and succinctly into the phone.

"*A'isha*, this is Captain James Robertson of the United States Navy aboard the *U.S.S. Standley*. We are here to enforce United Nations mandate Resolution Number I-M-O-seven, one, zero, two, recommended by the International Maritime Organization and approved by the UN Security Council, effective immediately and retroactive as of seven days ago. I wish to speak with your captain."

There was a long silence.

"*A'isha*, do you read? This is Captain Robertson commanding the *U.S.S. Standley*. You are hereby ordered to stand down on your command, heave-to, and plan for a boarding party from the *Standley* within the next thirty minutes. Do you read, *A'isha*? Over."

The captain turned over the microphone to translators who gave the identical message in Arabic and Japanese. There would be no question of a misunderstanding or false accusations that might lead to an international incident.

"Captain," said Lieutenant Corcoran as he continued to monitor the *A'isha* from mounted, nitrogen-filled binoculars, "there's more scrambling on the aft deck of the *A'isha*. And sir . . . they're pulling canvas on several decks."

He refocused the glasses. "Sir, they're uncovering ordnance."

"On a research vessel," the captain said, not at all surprised. "Fancy that, son. Can you ID?"

"Checking, sir." Lieutenant Corcoran's glasses traversed the length of the ship, pausing occasionally where various crew members stirred.

"Sir, it appears they have old Soviet Strela portable missile launchers at the bow and stern."

The captain looked at his weapons specialist for confirmation. "Strelas."

"Nickname for Soviet SAM's," confirmed the WS, glancing through his own binoculars. "We call 'em Gremlins."

"Of course, a three-stager."

"Infrared heat-seeking guidance, sir, with a four mile range and an altitude of over three. Designed for surface to air.

Then he added, "Could be rigged to hit a ship."

"They're breaking open crates, amidships," said the lieutenant, "and issuing guns like candy."

"Appear to be Russian Tokarev pistols," said the WS. "Or Chinese knockoffs. Nine millimeters. And there's larger . . . looks like machine guns. Can't make out the model. They're unfolding collapsible butts."

The WS peered through the powerful binoculars. "Might be Czech Skorpion submachine guns, but something's different."

"Different?" the captain glanced at the WS.

"Hard to tell from here, sir." He pulled out a bulletin from a folder. "Could be this new hardened-plastic gun they've produced. We got a warning on them. Tests said they had a cyclic rate of over four thousand rounds per minute."

"Shit," Captain Robertson whispered under his breath. "That can do some damage."

"Damn straight, sir."

Helmsman, ahead one-third."

"Ahead one-third sir."

"And plot me a DR upside their ass."

"Plotting upside, sir."

"Have we a fresh x-ray of that hold full of canisters?" Robertson looked to the CS.

"Sir, can't pull it off our direct-feed satellite with ionics disturbing everything. But what images I've got imply they're still sitting quiet."

"Keep me informed of any changes." He turned to his Lieutenant. "Full alert, son."

"Full alert, sir."

————

The Navy ship was enroute toward the *A'isha*. Its launch had picked up Dr. Parker and his partner, once determined Calder was fit to leave sickbay. He would have it no other way.

With permission from United Nations to board any illegal salvage ship, the *U.S.S. Standley* prepared to take action to stop the terrorists. Orders were to secure the deadly canisters; recover the *Great Omar* and any other valuables taken from the *Titanic*; capture and hold the terrorist Ragem and accomplices; and arrest Henri Dupont. The *A'isha* would not be sent to a watery grave unless and until the primary objectives were accomplished, or until it was determined to be in the best interest of world peace to dispatch the *A'isha* and its crew all at once.

"Welcome to the bridge, Dr. Parker. Mr. Calder."

Captain Robertson introduced himself. The three men exchanged greetings as the admiral guided them to the window.

"We're within three minutes of boarding. That is, if there're no incidents beforehand. As you know, we'll take care of those canisters, but we'd prefer you to aid in identifying Dupont and the salvaged items. Particularly that book that seems to have everyone in an uproar."

"Happy to assist Captain," said Parker.

"We'll identify Ragem if he's on board. We have photos."

"Captain, we have a serious problem when we recover the *Omar*."

"What's that?"

"A special freeze-drying lab and an electrolytic bath. We've got to get the *Omar* back to our research ship, freeze-dry the pages to remove the water, then immerse the leather in solution, and pass a controlled low-level electric current through it."

"What's it do?"

"Breaks down compounds into basic elements and leaches salt and other contaminants from the book."

"Won't that damage paper and ink?"

"Actually, between freeze-drying, electrolysis, and a couple of other tricks, the *Omar* can be restored to near original state if we get to it quickly. We've already got the recovered jewels in a bath."

Robertson considered the request. "We'll assign our Seasprite helicopter to rush it back to your ship Dr. Parker. But what if you don't recover it quickly enough?"

"Any artifact, particularly paper exposed to air for a protracted period, will crumble to dust. Salts permeated over decades at six thousand pounds per square inch pressure are extremely corrosive when combined with oxygen and hydrogen in the air. Together they form hydrochloric acid, sulfides, oxychlorides and other contaminants. They'll destroy it in no time at all."

"You think that Dupont fella was smart enough to bathe it?"

"If anyone knows better, it's him," Calder confirmed. "We're as concerned about pulling it out, though, as we are about the interval between solutions."

"It'd be ironic, after all the years the book survived underwater, if it disintegrated before our eyes, wouldn't it . . . "

"It would be a tragedy," Parker said.

"Just understand our new priorities," said Robertson, "as a result of that volatile contraband the *A'isha's* transporting. Frankly, your book and the new treaty has given us an excuse to board their ship. But we'll be doing everything in our power to secure and stabilize the Pu239 and other agents, first. Then we'll find your artifact."

"Certainly," said Parker. "Wouldn't want it any other way."

A puff of smoke emanated from the *A'isha*, and a delayed report—broadcast across the ocean—signaled a shoulder-fired infrared-homing SAM had just been fired. Its pop-out control canards and tail fins engaged as its momentum picked up, and the conical, multifaceted infrared seeker window locked in on the *U.S.S. Standley*.

The lieutenant interrupted, "Sir, a Strela just launched off *A'isha's* starboard bow."

"Sound general alarm."

"Aye, aye, sir."

"Lock in coordinates and knock it down. Then take out their launchers . . . try not to sink her," the captain ordered with a calm demeanor, like flicking an annoying fly off his shoulder.

"Done, sir." The lieutenant turned and repeated the orders. The ship instantly came alive as the loud, intermittent BINGing alert echoed across decks and through corridors.

"A second Strela fired . . . " radar reported.

"You know what to do." The lieutenant responded accordingly.

The captain glanced out over the starboard bow, "Helm, steady course three-two-four."

"Steady course three-two-four, sir."

Within seconds, a Terrier RIM-2 surface-to-air missile launched from the forward deck, ahead of the *Standley's* bridge. It seemed to hang in midair for several moments, as it tracked the Soviet-made rocket, locked on and shot toward its assigned goal. An initial trail of smoke marked its flight. A second Terrier whooshed out from the hull.

The wait seemed interminable. Then the short-range missiles picked off their targets. Two fireballs lit up the afternoon sky, in succession, and reflected off the daytime waters midway between the ships. Everyone on the bridge breathed easier.

Robertson glanced at Parker and winked with self-assurance. "They're a nuisance. But its obvious Ragem is out of his league."

Parker and Calder were relieved.

"Was it just my head wound that made me think I saw the water light up?" said Calder. "Or did you see it too?"

Parker and the Captain looked at each other, then at Calder.

"The water lit up?" said the admiral.

"Like it was on fire . . . but it extinguished itself immediately. At least, that's what I thought I saw."

Parker glanced at the *Standley's* commander. "I watched the midair fireballs. Andy must've seen residual effects from methane that floated up from below."

Parker looked toward the water. "I was afraid of that."

"What?" said the captain.

"If we don't pull out of here within the hour, we could all be sitting on the bottom." Parker turned to the admiral. "Coordinate SAT-NAV with GPS, and clear all shipping lanes and air space from the region. We have a serious emergency developing."

"They'll want more explanation than that."

"It was a pocket of gas that lit up over the water."

"And if that's what I saw," said Calder, "it's a prelude to more pure gas on its way up."

"If the release gets worse, anyone coming into this area could be sucked into a floating time bomb of hydrocarbonic gases." Parker looked the captain straight in the eyes. "Heavy gas escaping and rising into the atmosphere can sink any ship or plane, especially if we get a total blowout below."

"It's extremely unstable down there," Calder interjected.

"Vessels can't float in this gas . . . large or small. And white-hot exhaust from jet engine planes, or even a small plane's electrical instrumentation can ignite the air like napalm."

"Holy shit," the captain whispered under his breath. "Are we talking Bermuda Triangle, here?"

"Exactly the same effect. It's happened in the North Sea, too. Entire oil platforms and their crews have disappeared with no trace, after a blowout. If a massive gas pocket opens up, turbulence from giant globules of methane can swamp this ship."

Robertson and his crew looked skeptically at Parker.

"I don't care how big this sucker is," Parker continued. "Compare it to pouring millions of gallons of chemical surfactant into the ocean. The gas becomes a dispersive, breaks down the molecular structure of the water, and changes it to a flat surface. In a highly gasified sea, any one of our ships could lose gravity and drop to the bottom like dead weight."

"In all my years I've never experienced this."

"It's a relatively new theory, but one that's been tested and documented on the open sea. Survivors are the exception. Have the crew monitor *Standley's* water line while you're boarding the *A'isha*. If you notice any loss of buoyancy, get the hell out of here. May I call the *Neptune*?"

"Certainly."

Parker ordered Holt to get *Neptune's Knot* out of the immediate vicinity as a precaution. Following that, Robertson ordered all other approaching air and sea traffic to avoid the area.

"Sir, take a look at this," an officer handed binoculars to the admiral.

"What is it?"

"The *A'isha's* hull, sir. She's listing slightly to port. And the last time I looked, her name was sitting higher in the water."

Robertson peered through the glasses. "Hummm," was all he said and handed them back.

"What d'ya think, sir?"

The captain glanced at Parker, who gave a knowing look. "Let me know if it drastically changes."

A series of flashes and reports emanated from outboard of the *Standley's* after deckhouse, as the 20mm Phalanx CIWS Mk 15 multi-barrel guns fired at the *A'isha*. All eyes turned to watch the results.

Within seconds, multiple explosions followed on the terrorist's ship. Through binoculars, the captain and his crew confirmed the portable missile launchers had been taken out. Surviving crew members left their posts and scrambled for safety. Some attempted to extinguish fires.

"Right in the kielbasa," Robertson said as he handed the glasses to Parker.

"You can inflict a little damage when you need to," whistled Calder.

"And with precision," Parker added, as he scanned the approaching target, now burning furiously in several locations on deck. "Check binoculars, fellas, and look at this."

The others aimed their glasses at the *A'isha*.

"The fires are drawing finger-like gas pockets from the water. See the wisps of white flames shooting up from different spots in the water? They're like invisible, ghostly fires you see when an Indy car crashes and burns."

"I'll be damned," whispered Robertson.

"Sir, ETA of two minutes," reported the navigator.

"Any radio contact with the captain yet?"

"Sir, I think we just got the equivalent of 'You fucking son-of-a-bitch' in Arabic."

Robertson looked at a translator. She nodded in agreement.

"Anything else?"

"No sir. They won't return our request to board."

"Give me the phone. We'll give them one more chance with a loud-hailer. Up close and to the point." The CO handed a phone receiver to Robertson and switched to the outside PA system. The captain looked at Parker.

"They can't say we didn't do everything in our power to communicate as peacefully as they'd allow us." He punched the Talk button.

"This is Captain Robertson requesting *A'isha* heave-to and stand by for peaceful boarding. This is your last chance to stand down before we come aboard."

There was no answer. The captain's message was repeated, followed by translations. The loud-hailer echoed between the two ships. Then a burst of gunfire erupted from the *A'isha* and glanced off the *Standley's* hull.

"Bring her alongside our afterdeck," ordered the captain, "so we can reach the *A'isha* from a similar level."

"Done sir."

"Keep both Phalanx guns aimed in her direction, and be on guard for sniping. They're not happy campers now."

"Done and done, sir."

"Every available man armed to the teeth as the boarding party crosses over. All crew and passengers on the *A'isha* are considered armed and dangerous. Understood Lieutenant?

"Understood sir."

"Boarding party ready?"

"Ready Captain."

"Fenders over?"

"Lowering now, sir."

"Better move the Seasprite into the garage, out of harms way . . . in case they've hidden more Strelas."

"Very well, Captain." The lieutenant called down to get the helicopter moved into its 01 deck hanger and to delegate other duties.

Robertson pulled a key from his pocket and held it up for Parker and Calder. "Here's your insurance."

They looked inquisitively at Robertson. He moved to a locker, inserted the key in a padlock and pulled the hasp. Inside was a cache of military-issue weapons. He pulled out three 92F Berettas, handed Parker and Calder a gun, and kept one for himself. He gave them three clips.

"Either of you fire a gun?" Robertson asked as he closed and locked the cabinet.

"Quite a bit lately," said Parker. "Not by choice."

"These are fifteen-rounders." He looked to Calder.

"In the service," said Calder. "Somewhere between marksman and sharpshooter."

"Good. But don't get too cocky. They're for protection only. Not authorized for use unless directly threatened or under attack. Understand?"

Parker and Calder gave a "wouldn't want it any other way" look, and nodded.

"All right. We won't destroy the ship unless they force our hand. Since you're here for identification purposes, don't board the A'isha until our men take and secure the ship. Understood?"

"Clear, Captain," Parker agreed.

"Our sailors will board from ship to ship, unless we're under too much fire. Hopefully we've taken out their heavy weapon capabilities. Otherwise, we'll scale their side from a launch. Then our teams will impound the canisters, capture Ragem, and locate the book."

"What about Dupont?" asked Parker. "Where does he stand in the line of fire?"

"He's now an accomplice. He'll be arrested and detained for interrogation. Considering he's traveled at will in and out of our country, he'll be treated as a spy. His passport will be confiscated and he'll have no diplomatic immunity."

"So he's in deep shit," responded Calder.

"That's an understatement."

The navigator turned to the captain. "Sir, coming up on the *A'isha*. She's sitting lower in the water now."

"Prepare to come alongside."

"Very well, sir."

"And, Lieutenant, aim hoses at those fires when we get close enough. Let's cool that hull down."

"Done, sir."

"Captain," said Parker, "Remember the hydrates and the need to get in and out as quickly as possible."

"I read you."

On the afterdeck, four men suited up in Hazmat gear. Sailors helped them step into and seal the awkward clothing around them, checking for tears or leaks in the material and adjusting their breathing apparatus. They looked more like astronauts prepared for a spacewalk, as they readied to cross over and enter the dangerous cargo hold.

Suddenly gunfire erupted from the *A'isha*, and sailors scrambled on all decks. Fire was returned as a battle erupted from the fantail and amidships, on board the terrorist ship, and from responding sailors shooting their Ingram M10's in quick bursts from the *Standley*.

Robertson surveyed the action with his binoculars. Parker and Calder watched from behind as the captain patiently assessed risks to ship and crew.

"We're cleaning up down there," the captain confirmed. "Should board any minute."

The firing became sporadic, then died out. Occasionally, a shot from a hidden sniper rang out over the ship's deck.

"Their bridge appears vacant. Anyone left has probably ducked below. Lieutenant, you'd better get Dr. Parker and Mr. Calder down to check it out."

"Yes sir." Lieutenant Corcoran immediately grabbed his Ingram M10, turned, and crossed over the bridge's threshold into the late afternoon sun. "This way, gentlemen."

The two scientists followed.

"Careful, fellas," warned Robertson as he closed the door behind them. "They may've boobytrapped the ship, so watch your step. Lieutenant, keep me apprised of what you find... particularly when you locate the canisters. I don't want to bring them on board. But we may have no choice."

"Yes, sir."

By the time the three men reached the outboard of the afterdeck house, several hawsers had been tossed and fastened to the *A'isha*, and armed sailors arranged a makeshift gangway that rose and fell with the sea.

The sailors had to at once cross the gangway, judge the jump-off distance to the *A'isha*, and protect themselves from sniper fire. Smaller swells than usual made the difficult crossing a little easier, as the research ship and the cruiser heaved and pitched against the grain in opposite directions.

Sailors in the boarding party assisted the Hazmat handlers across, as they maneuvered the gangway in their modern coats of armor. Armed guards shielded them from bullets that could tear the suits and render them useless in a hostile radioactive or biological environment.

Shots reverberated through various levels of the *A'isha* as sailors moved from stern to bow in one sweeping motion.

Lieutenant Corcoran, Parker and Calder watched the action unfold from the safety of the *Standley's* afterdeck. Sailors maneuvered around the research vessel's superstructure, checked and secured each area, then moved on in through the various bulkhead entrances.

"Gentlemen, I'll be crossing over," said the Lieutenant. "Wait here, out of harm's way, until I signal to come aboard."

"You bet," the two men echoed as Corcoran tucked the Ingram under his arm, predicted the heave, and quickly negotiated the crossing. He gave a friendly salute to Parker and Calder, carefully moved across the *A'isha's* fantail, and disappeared under a large canvas masking the deck.

Calder spotted movement near the *A'isha's* fantail. In the shadows, a figure skulked near an upper bulkhead and covertly attempted to move for a ladder to the lower deck.

Thinking it better to liberate Dupont, to join the battle, Ragem had released him from captivity. In the engagement with the *Standley*, Dupont had chosen to evade both sides and strike out for himself.

"There's Henri," Calder pointed to a distant catwalk near *A'isha's* portside.

"He's escaping," said Parker. "Cut him off."

"The admiral said not to get involved."

"Hell, we're not Navy. What're they gonna do . . . fire us?"

Both men negotiated and raced across the gangway, and jumped to the *A'isha's* deck. Parker extracted the Beretta from his rear pocket. Calder followed suit.

"You gonna use that on him?" Calder looked at his partner.

"Admiral said they're for protection only . . . if we're under attack or directly threatened."

"Right. Well, I'll be the first to shoot the son-of-a-bitch if you don't."

The two moved stealthily across the modified decking, careful not to attract attention from any of the remaining *A'isha* crew or terrorists. Parker indicated direction to Calder, as they maneuvered their way past cables, davits, the launching crane for the mini-subs, and crates surreptitiously covered with tarps.

It was apparent an old freighter had been quickly converted into enough of a research vessel to get by. Parker lifted a tarpaulin and saw multiple crate markings stenciled in Japanese, underneath.

"Talk about multi-cultural . . . " he mumbled.

Water poured onto the fires from the *Standley*, and smoke from the still smoldering decks hung in the air, making it difficult to breathe as they traversed the fantail toward portside. Then they came upon a dead terrorist, his finger frozen on the trigger of his XE-47.

"Obviously caught by surprise," whispered Parker.

Calder pointed to an entrance at the *A'isha's* submersible control station. Two other terrorists had been shot and lay crumpled at the door's threshold.

"Move on," Parker said quietly.

The two edged themselves between a stand of large crates. Just as they reached the end, Dupont stole across the portside deck and looked over the side. Parker stepped into his path and aimed the Beretta at Dupont.

"Give it up, Henri. You've lost the war."

Startled, Dupont froze in place. But believing his former partner wouldn't fire on him, Dupont looked to a hatchway, ducked and rolled to the door, pulled it open, and raced down the passageway.

Parker glanced over portside. Their abandoned *Shelty Three* was tied to the railing, with makeshift fenders attached. The small *Yoritomo-class* sub, the *Amagaeru*, floated nearby.

"He was leaving all right," said Parker.

They raced through the doorway in pursuit of Dupont and heard retreating footsteps. But echoes blended with rounds of shots fired in other parts of the ship, and it was difficult to determine Dupont's location.

The Canadian escaped down another corridor, passed over a threshold to an alternate hallway, and down steps leading to a hold, aft. Along with storage, the hold had been converted into a temporary lab to treat items recovered from the *Titanic*.

Dupont sprinted to the electrolytic bath table and cut the low current to the deionized solution. He pulled on rubber gloves, picked up the teak case, and removed two thin wires wrapped around it.

The *Great Omar* was inside.

Quickly, he poured purified water over the container, and sponged it off with a large towel. Then, he opened it up and did the same with the book.

Suddenly, the hold's door slammed open and crashed against the bulkhead. Unnerved, Dupont dropped the book at his feet.

"I know greed's a compulsive behavior, Henri," Parker aimed his gun, "but I never thought you'd go this far."

He moved toward Dupont.

"You don't understand," said Dupont. "Your philosophy is outdated, mon ami. This book should be saved for posterity."

"Saved for whom may I ask? You? To be sold to the highest bidder? Ragem . . . to trade for bombs and bullets? Or will Ragem sell it to Clayton Paul Taylor . . . that's it, isn't it? Taylor'll buy it from Ragem, through you, and place it with his plundered ivory tusks and other ill-gotten spoils."

Dupont cautiously picked up the book from the floor. He opened the cover to the front doublure, with its sunken panels and the 58th Stanza skillfully implied by the inlaid snake at the center of the Garden of Eden.

He rambled incessantly. "It's a miracle the book survived this long. The safe must have held its air-tight seal for decades, before water and microbes invaded and ate away any protective coverings."

An emerald, set in the snake's eye, over its ivory teeth, shimmered from the hold's subdued overhead lighting. It rested amidst multi-colored leathers and solid chased gold that depicted a bright sun shining through the foliage of an apple tree. Garnets and turquoise completed its emblematic depiction of life.

Dupont placed the *Omar* back in its casket. "Look at the leather. It's in remarkable shape."

In the dim light of the hold, Parker and Calder saw the captivating beauty of the special Vedder Edition, "crown quarto-sized" book—nearly intact—jewels still glimmering as they had aboard the *Titanic*.

Remarkably, except for being wet and probably deteriorating quickly, the *Great Omar* was everything it was reported to be.

"You think I'm greedy," Dupont continued nervously. "But I'm willing to share with an old partner. We can deal with C.P. Taylor and the other financiers. They want the *Omar*, and will pay any price. We can get it off the ship . . . place it on a mini-sub and retrieve it later. We'd be rich, Cary."

Calder turned red with anger.

"The three of us, Andy. You'd be wealthy beyond wildest dreams. I'll split it three ways."

"Go to hell, Henri," Calder jumped for Dupont.

Parker held him back. "Henri, the International Maritime Organization and the United Nations passed a joint Resolution Number IMO-Seven Zero Zero Two, enforceable by the Law of the Sea. It forbids recovery of artifacts from specified gravesites. Since the *Titanic* is now considered part and parcel within the definitions of the Resolution, you are hereby ordered to turn over all salvaged artifacts and surrender yourself to authorities."

"You sound so official, mon ami."

Parker stepped toward Dupont. "Give me the book, Henri."

"Not on your life," Dupont responded as he backed up toward the chemical bath table.

"Don't make me shoot, Henri. Give me the book."

"You won't shoot. We both know that."

"But *I* have no qualms about it, Henri." Calder stepped

forward—his gun aimed at Dupont.

"Turn the book over and hope they go light on your sentence."

"The book . . . she is mine now." Dupont held it tight against his chest, as much for protection as for avarice.

Parker grabbed for the *Omar's* case. Dupont pulled back, slipped, and fell into the chemical bath. The casket slid to the floor, and the table collapsed—spilling out solution.

Instantly, the table's electrical feed shorted in the solution, sparked, and ignited a pile of stored mosquito netting. And the fire spread to a stack of wooden crates.

Parker reached for the book.

"Damn you!" Dupont went for his back pocket.

Calder saw a gun emerge.

"Look out Cary!" Calder pushed his partner out of the way.

Blindly filled with anger—having been ambushed at the *Titanic* and left for dead—Calder fired two rounds at Dupont, who quickly rolled to avoid the shots.

Bullets ricocheted off the steel floor. Dupont turned, aimed, got off a shot, barely missing Calder's head, then ran toward the stacks of cargo.

Calder fired at Dupont. Dupont turned, shot back and hid behind the crates.

Parker pointed his direction to Calder, pulled around to get a better angle, and moved guardedly toward the stacks.

Calder slipped behind racks of stored electronic equipment and carefully maneuvered toward the opposite end of the hold.

Suddenly, shots rang out from the foresection and glanced off the metal hull. Silence followed as each became wary of the other's position.

Dupont moved to the foresection, unaware Parker was moving with him at the opposite end. Calder came from the other side.

"Not a chance in hell you'll get out of here, Henri," Parker shouted.

"We shall see," Dupont's hollow voice echoed through the hold.

Parker vigilantly traversed the hold and edged his way across the front of the stacks toward Dupont.

"You always had to have it your way Cary," Dupont babbled. "But your smug American attitude won't save you now." He reached out from behind the row of crates and fired wildly.

Parker ducked between the cargo.

Then, Dupont saw an opportunity and fired through the banks of electronic gear.

Calder screamed out and reeled back as a slug cut into his left shoulder. He regained his stance and stammered in Dupont's direction, his gun aimed high.

Noxious smoke and a rolling ship made it difficult for Calder to maintain balance. He backed up toward the entrance, lost consciousness, collapsed against the bulkhead, and slid to the floor—his gun still in hand.

"You bastard!" Parker reached the edge of the crates and confronted Dupont. He kicked the gun from Dupont's hand. Then Parker grabbed his arm, jerked him from behind the crates, and lunged at his chest.

They crashed into the stacks. A box tumbled from above and knocked Parker's Beretta across the floor of the hold.

Parker sent an uppercut to Dupont's chin. The stinging blow threw him hard against the bulkhead. He backed away from Parker, retreated down an aisle, out of breath, and rubbed his chin as he looked back at the angry scientist.

Then Dupont lunged at his opponent. Parker met him with a blow to the stomach. Dupont rolled into another stack, grabbed a box, and tossed it overhead. Parker dodged the box, and the heavy crate exploded against the floor.

With years of fury and anger built up over their soured partnership, both regained their stance and tore into each other.

Dupont laid a hard right into Parker's side. Parker grabbed the arm, twisted it around Dupont's back, and pushed him against the hull. Then he forced Dupont around and assailed him with punches to the stomach.

Parker grabbed him by the shirt collar and, with a series of rights, hammered him up against a pile of nylon ropes. But Dupont seized a crowbar from a nearby crate and menacingly swung the claw-end at Parker's head.

Parker ducked and came around as the crowbar missed, smashed through a wooden box, and stuck inside. Parker threw himself in a full-body tackle and collided with Dupont. Henri doubled over, screamed out in pain, and both men crashed to the floor.

Fire spread to the shipping containers and the hold filled with an acrid smell. Both men had trouble breathing. But Dupont sent his knee to Parker's groin and rolled away. He jostled the crowbar from the crate, thrust it at Parker as he came at him, and hit him squarely in the stomach. Parker screamed in pain, rolled forward from the force, and the air was knocked from him. Parker dropped limp to the cold steel floor.

Worn down and choking from the smoke, Dupont dragged himself across the hold to recover his gun.

Parker could barely move, but he realized what Dupont was after. Struggling to pull himself up, he grabbed hold of a crate, for balance, and desperately looked for his own Beretta. He gasped heavily for breath, as he moved down the aisle.

Then he looked to the hold's entrance. Coming through the corridor was Ragem and another terrorist. Each carried XE-47's.

"Oh, shit," he whispered as he searched for concealment. His foot kicked something. It flew across the floor and hit the bulkhead with a resounding crash.

Realizing it was his gun, Parker flung himself across the distance, grabbed the Beretta, and rolled against the wall.

Hearing the sounds, Dupont sent bullets in that direction.

"Harrison Ford makes it look so easy," Parker moaned to himself.

"Dupont?" Ragem yelled through the door, holding at the

threshold to avoid crossfire. "Are you down here?"

"Over here," he yelled from behind a row of boxes, afraid to reveal himself. "Parker's behind the third row of crates."

Ragem signaled his accomplice to take Parker.

"Where's the book, Dupont?"

The Canadian realized he was still in danger, and did not immediately answer.

"Monsieur Dupont. Where's the *Omar*?"

Ragem searched the area with caution as he moved deeper into the hold. But the smoke made it almost impossible to see.

"I'm losing my patience, Dupont. Have you got the *Omar*?"

"No." Dupont answered curtly. "It's on the floor somewhere."

"You asinine fool. It could be burnt to a crisp. Where is it?"

Dupont remained silent for a moment. "Near the collapsed table."

Parker listened to gauge positions of the approaching men. Footsteps reverberated between the aisles of cargo, but he could not determine location.

Without warning, a terrorist opened fire with his XE-47, one aisle over. Crates snapped as bullets indiscriminately ripped into them.

Shards and pieces of equipment from the crates flew by him like straw missiles in a tornado. Slivers penetrated his skin, and he pressed himself to the floor to avoid stray bullets.

More shots echoed through the hold as the terrorist rounded the corner at the forward end, and aimed down the cross-aisle toward Dupont. Then he burst into the aisle where Parker was hiding, and pressed the trigger.

But it was too late. Parker had rolled on his back—gun held up and ready. When the terrorist entered his territory, the XE-47 was aimed too high.

"Down here buddy."

Parker got off two shots. The terrorist flung backwards from the force of the bullets, shooting off several rounds wildly into the air as he hit the bulkhead and slid to the floor in his own blood.

Ragem searched for the *Omar*, heard Parker shout out, and aimed his machine gun in Parker's direction. He emptied his clip between the stacks.

Calder regained consciousness, lying on the floor in the shadows of the hold, weakened from loss of blood. He was jolted awake by the bursts of machine gun fire and remained silent in an attempt to determine who was in the fight. Occasional rounds of fire echoed beyond the hold, as Navy gunmen and terrorists exchanged gunfire throughout various parts of the ship.

Ragem located the teak case with the *Great Omar*. As the box was opened, Parker ran toward the terrorist—hoping to catch him off guard. But Ragem heard steps, turned, and shot off a volley of bullets in that direction. Parker jumped for cover as the bullets ripped into the cargo and diving supplies. Ragem secured the container and prepared to move topside.

Parker came around the back of the crates.

"Well, who do we have here?" Dupont surprised Parker, and shoved a gun into his back. "I should kill you on the spot."

Parker arched forward, pivoted on the ball of his foot, and came around in an arc. He knocked the gun from Dupont's hand, then came back with his knee to the groin.

Dupont bellowed and fell prostrate to the floor, grotesquely massaging his organs. Parker gasped for air, crawled to Dupont, and, with one powerful thrust of his fist, knocked his adversary out cold. Then Parker collapsed in exhaustion next to him.

Ragem had watched the two from a distance, not caring who would win. The *Omar* in hand, he turned for the exit to abandon ship, and felt a jolt of cold steel against his temple.

"You give a bad name to the good people of Islamic nations," Calder said in as firm and composed a voice as his weakened body allowed. He blocked the exit and a tired smile crossed his face. Operating on the periphery of collapse, Calder held on with a new flow of adrenalin as he leaned against the bulkhead.

Ragem remained frozen in place.

"No need to shoot."

"Shut up you maggot," Calder's anger rose. "You aren't worth shit the flies bring home."

Ragem's mind searched for an opportunity to escape. Calder knew his gun clip was nearly empty and didn't have the strength to pull out a reserve—nor would he have the opportunity.

Ragem held the *Omar* tightly. But he knew one wrong move and he would praise Allah from the abyss.

"The invincible Faheed Al Mar Ragem," Calder mocked. "Terrorist bomber . . . mastermind slaughterer of women and children." His rage kept him alive.

"Cary? You okay?," he yelled across the hold without taking his eyes off Ragem. There was no answer, and Calder turned his attention back to the terrorist.

"So this is the scumbag who kidnapped Cary's wife and held her hostage. The same man who wanted us dispatched to our watery graves..."

Calder weakened with each passing moment. Blood loss slowed him down, his left shoulder throbbed with pain and, in his stand-off with the terrorist, he had trouble holding up the two-and-a-half pound automatic.

Ragem noticed Calder's right hand shaking and, for an instant, his arm faltered. Ragem found the moment and pushed the *Great Omar* at Calder's shoulder.

Calder was knocked off balance, and his Beretta fired to the ceiling as it left his hand. Ragem pushed him aside and moved for the door. Calder jumped for Ragem's legs, pulled him down, and they crashed over the threshold.

Blind with rage, Calder used every ounce of energy to hold the man down. Ragem grabbed for Calder's throat, saw an opportunity, and rammed his fist into the open wound. Calder screamed in excruciating pain.

Across the hold, almost overcome from smoke inhalation, Parker heard Andy's cry. He moved toward the sounds of struggle.

Calder got up, tried to remain conscious, took a swing at Ragem with his only good arm, and missed.

Ragem came at Calder with a vengeance and slammed him against the bulkhead.

Calder was beyond pain. He winced as he hit the wall, then pushed himself off and came back at the terrorist with all his remaining strength.

Ragem dodged him, sending Calder reeling toward the storage racks. Parker intervened and caught his partner before any more damage was done.

"You!" Ragem sputtered.

"None other, asshole." Parker came around with a kick to Ragem's side. Ragem caved in and flew across the floor. Parker hurled himself at the terrorist, picked him up, and obtained enough leverage to throw a swift right to Ragem's head.

The terrorist lurched across the hold, slammed against a metal rack, and collapsed.

"Get up you bastard."

Ragem was dazed and Parker pulled back to Calder.

"You okay, Andy?"

Calder nodded slightly.

"Let's get you out of here."

Calder struggled to speak, "Secure Ragem and Dupont first."

"They're not going anywhere," he said breathlessly. "We've got to get you taken care of . . ."

"I'm all right." He leaned on the bulkhead and slid to the floor. "Secure them first. I need to rest a minute."

Parker watched Calder for several seconds, to make certain he would not black out.

"Do it Cary. I'm fine . . . really."

The French Canadian had regained consciousness. Parker grabbed Dupont by the back of his shirt, tossed him across the hold near Ragem, and threw a Beretta to Calder.

"Keep it on Dupont."

Parker moved toward Ragem, lifted an XE-47 off the floor, and straddled the incapacitated terrorist, who was on his hands and knees. He held Ragem by his hair, pulled his head between his legs, and placed the machine gun's barrel against his head.

"How's it feel to be at the receiving end of your own prototype weapon, Ragem? These work well. . .except when they overheat."

The terrorist remained silent.

Dupont stirred. Calder pushed himself away from his resting place, and shoved the pistol at Henri's forehead.

"Don't even think about getting up. I've got my French-tickler here."

Dupont froze in place.

"Only takes a split second for this to clear your mind." Calder edged the trigger back. "Kind of ironic, isn't it, Henri? Your greed has brought you full circle." He pushed the barrel firmly against Dupont's head.

"Expected we'd be microbial meals at two thousand fathoms, didn't you?"

Dupont wouldn't respond.

"Well? Didn't you?" He pushed the gun harder into Dupont, forcing him off his knees. Dupont winced but remained silent. "Answer me you son-of-a-bitch or I'll blow your brains across this hold."

"Andy," Parker yelled out. "Don't shoot him."

"Why not?" Calder quickly became unhinged. "He's a scumbag like the rest of 'em. Cary. . . . How can we let them live? These bastards kidnapped your wife. Left us both for dead. Ragem has slaughtered hundreds of innocents in the name of world politics . . . and you say don't shoot?"

"For God's sake, Andy, don't do it." Parker's scream echoed throughout the hold. "Let the Navy take over. If we pull the trigger we'll be as crazy as them."

"That's right," Ragem laughed. "Shoot him and you'll be as crazy as us."

Calder slowly turned in a daze toward the laughter. By degrees, he methodically left Dupont's side and moved across the cargo hold in the direction of Ragem—his gun hanging as limp as his wounded arm. Andy's eyes tautly focused on the terrorist.

Calder was in another world.

Ragem laughed again.

"You Americans are crazy. You think everything can be settled with a fight. But our holy war against you infidels will go on forever. We'll come in waves to your country. . .like tsunamis." He laughed once more.

Parker's thighs tightened on Ragem's head as he straddled the terrorist's shoulders. He prodded the XE-47 at his neck.

"Don't make me buy in to Andy's argument. My trigger finger's damned tired from all this crap."

Dupont had revived and saw an opening, as the focus shifted to Ragem. He backed into the shadows of the hold, and skirted around and behind the metal racks.

Calder moved like a zombie. His mind far from the *A'isha*—a smile frozen on his face.

Dupont edged toward the exit.

Calder's hand tightened, once again, on the 92F's oversized trigger guard. And Parker saw Andy's right arm muscles tense as his wrist lifted the gun.

Dupont avoided the preoccupied men, grabbed the *Omar*, and quietly slipped into the corridor leading topside.

"Andy," Parker said quietly.

Calder was silent as he moved closer.

"Andy think about what you're doing."

Calder slowly stepped toward his partner and shoved the gun's 4.9-inch barrel deep into Ragem's mouth. For the first time in his life, the terrorist's eyes opened wide with shear panic. He gagged from the gun's muzzle.

"Don't do it," Parker said calmly, attempting to reach Calder at another level.

"Look," Cary pulled the XE-47 from Ragem's head and rested it on his shoulder like a knapsack. "We'll turn him over to the Navy."

Ragem glanced up at Calder's blank and unyielding eyes. Then, the terrorist's eyes crossed as he looked down at the balance of the gun's cold muzzle.

Most of Ragem's victims never had time to think about impending death. Bombs had exploded around unsususpecting targets without warning. Bullets ripped into his political victims with deadly force.

Abruptly, the image of Ragem's wife and children flashed in his mind. He had faced death on numerous occasions, and had caused it on many more. Now he was confronted with the paradox of his own holy war . . . violence used as vengeance against violence perpetrated in the name of Allah.

The 9mm Parabellum automatic rested in Ragem's mouth.

"I'll bet you don't know much about this little beauty, Mister Gunrunner." Calder's words were void of emotion.

"It's reliability is flawless . . . fifteen rounds and bilateral." He forced his wounded arm over, shifted hands, and no longer felt pain.

"I can kill you with either hand." He switched back and laughed. "I may look like Swiss cheese, but I'm still ambidextrous as hell"

"Andy, listen to me . . . "

Calder was beyond reach. He glanced at Parker, as though staring at a blank wall, then back to the almost comical face of the terrorist—and Andy's smile broadened.

"In fact, this thing's got a special triple-safety feature you should have on your new gun. Let me demonstrate, Mr. Terrorist Slimeball." He paused. "In case you'd like to make a purchase on the black market . . . or use it in your next life."

He forced his left arm over again. "It's got a passive firing pin catch, with a safety slide that decocks the gun."

He pushed the safety on. "With its unique firing pin, there's no chance a falling hammer will ever break the safety barrier and accidentally shoot the shit outta' someone. Observe."

He pulled the trigger. Ragem twitched, but nothing happened.

"See?" Calder rambled. "Or I can switch it off . . . " and he did. "To kill . . . "

Then he reversed the safety slide, once more. "Or I can leave it on . . . so no one get's hurt. Excellent feature, huh?"

"Or not . . . " Calder pulled on the safety slide. Then the trigger.

The deadly silence was broken as a bullet entered the terrorist's throat, exploded through his lungs and heart, and burst out through his spine. Ragem fell limp to the floor.

"Jesus," Parker felt warm blood on his pant legs.

The pistol rolled and dropped off Andy's fingertips.

Parker watched in stunned silence as his partner calmly left the hold. Calder walked down the corridor, retraced his earlier steps from above, and climbed the stairs to starboard. Outside, he blankly walked to the railing, leaned over, and vomited any remaining anger and fear that had plagued him.

Two Navy seamen spotted Calder and approached to return him to the *Standley*.

"Sir, we've been ordered to clear out. We haven't located Ragem or Dupont and the ships are losing buoyancy from the hydrates. The *Standley's* pulling out in less than five minutes."

"I just shot Ragem. He's down in the cargo hold with Dr. Parker."

"And Dupont?"

"He's there too."

"We'll send some men down. Is Dr. Parker all right?"

Calder had to think. "Yeah . . . yeah, he's okay."

"Let's get you to a medic."

The sailors helped Calder across the decking, and radioed assistance for Parker.

In the hold, Parker realized Dupont had slipped out with the *Omar*. He stepped over Ragem and raced topside. As he reached the deck, Warrant Officer Kineta met him coming outside.

"Dr. Parker, we must abandon ship. Your partner's been evacuated to the *Standley*. We're leaving the plutonium and viral bacteria behind. . .too unstable to move right now." He noticed the blood on Parker. "My God sir, you need a medic."

Parker looked at his blood-soaked pants. "It's not me. I'm fine."

"Sir, the *A'isha's* sitting low in the water. We've got to return to the *Standley*. Follow me."

"Wait a minute. Has anyone caught Dupont?"

Kineta looked at him quizzically.

"The French Canadian. He just came up here with the rare book we're looking for."

"Not to my knowledge," said Kineta. "But we've got to move out, Dr. Parker. Orders are to withdraw."

Parker's eyes caught movement out from portside. He looked across the railing and saw *Yoritomo's* backup sub turning from the ship.

"That's him." Parker jumped to the railing and looked over the side."

"Who sir?"

"Dupont. He's in the sub."

Parker spotted their abandoned *Shelty Three* floating off the port quarter.

"We've got to stop him." Parker sprinted toward the stern.

"Sir we'll shoot it out of the water."

"No!" Parker turned to the warrant officer. "He's got the book. And more ordnance could ignite the methane creating an incendiary bomb around us. Use your radio. Tell them not to shoot at anything, and move out the *Standley*. I'll catch up later."

"But Dr. Parker we're under orders to . . . "

Parker climbed over the railing, stood on the edge of the gunwale, and dived overboard. The cold water was a shock to Parker's system, but revived him as he headed for the sub.

Kineta raced aft to the railing. He watched as Parker swam to the *Shelty*, untied the tether and threw off the rubber fenders. Parker delicately balanced himself, as he climbed in through the sail, and pulled the hatch closed.

Kineta knew Parker would not be called back.

The warrant officer grabbed the radio from his belt, notified the *Standley* of Parker and Dupont's departure, and gave the captain Parker's warning not to fire ordnance.

Kineta was instructed to take another seaman to the hold; confirm Ragem's status; leave him there, if dead; and, return to the ship immediately.

Kineta watched the *Shelty* rise up in the water, as it headed after the Japanese mini-sub. He looked out over the ocean, saw dead fish floating to the surface, and realized the *A'isha's* deck was now even closer to the water.

The ocean was, without a doubt, losing its surface tension.

In the distance, the sea appeared to be foaming. But on closer inspection the warrant officer noticed thousands of bubbles reach the surface. Mesmerized by a sight he had never witnessed, Kineta glanced toward the northwestern horizon.

The water churned and boiled like a cauldron—where larger, turbulent bubbles of gas surfaced in a frenzy to escape the abyss. Another bank of thick methane fog formed about five miles out and rolled-in closer to the *A'isha* and the *Standley*.

A blast from the *Standley's* loud horn broke Kineta's daze. He radioed for assistance and moved in toward the hold to confirm Ragem's death.

After taking remaining terrorists as prisoners and locating Ragem's body, Navy personnel abandoned the *A'isha*, leaving it behind with Captain Tarik and a skeleton crew to fend for itself. The *U.S.S. Standley* came about, slowly, and prepared to leave the immediate vicinity, to beat the fast-rising hydrates. They would monitor the *A'isha* until it could be brought under control —whenever sea-state returned to normal. The viciously churning sea water moved closer to the two ships, from the northwest, as the slump widened below.

"Captain . . . a report from the stern," said Lieutenant Commander Winslow." She's taking a dip sir . . . six feet above normal water line in typical seas."

"Ah, but these are not typical are they?" Robertson handed his binoculars to the lieutenant commander. "Look at this and tell me what you see."

The LC gazed out over the bow. *Neptune's Knot*, already distancing itself, was three nautical miles farther south from their position.

"Your report on sea conditions, Lieutenant?"

"Sir, the sea is rising slightly with one to two foot waves, average length seven to ten feet downwind, with occasional gusts between five and twelve knots."

"Enough of the weather report. Now look aft," said the captain.

The lieutenant commander looked north, over the stern. Then he quickly glanced south, across the bow, and back again.

"I'll be damned. Except for the bubbling waters on the horizon, it's smooth as glass just aft of the stern. Can't even find capillary wave action out there."

He thought for a moment. "Must be energy from the escaped gases that dissipate and absorb wave action . . . probably in an exchange of energy for heat."

"You remember your physics well. The water molecules are

dispersed by the film created by escaping methane. The film breaks down the density of the water and causes a dampening action on the waves. Any object floating directly upon it can lose ability to stay afloat."

Robertson turned to his navigator. "Let's get our tail out of this tank. Sonar, con . . . what's echo ranging on the *Neptune*?"

"Con, sonar, we have active echo bearing two-four-three, designate CR 31. Target follower uniform assigned."

"Range?"

"Three miles, sir."

"Helmsman, give me ten knots."

"Aye, ten knots sir."

"Course heading two-four-three."

"Two-four-three, sir."

Robertson watched, with some expectancy, and looked for the *A'isha* to drop behind as the *Standley* pulled out. But the guided-missile cruiser just treaded water.

"What the hell's going on?" Robertson said as he turned to his crew.

"Sir, we can't grab the water. We lack propulsion."

"Push her to fifteen knots."

"Fifteen knots sir."

Those on the bridge were dumbfounded as their 547-foot ship was held in the grip of the hydrates.

"Increase to full ahead at thirty-three knots."

"Full ahead, thirty-three."

The ship held fast in the water despite the full output of its engines.

"Sir, we've acquired another four feet of displacement. We appear to be going under," a report came from across the bridge.

"My God," Robertson said out loud, "Eighty-five-thousand horsepower kicking in with both G.E. turbines and all four boilers, and we still can't pull away?"

He looked out over the bow. The sea experienced two to three-foot crests a thousand yards out to the southeast. But in the immediate vicinity, except for the bubbling action, the water was like a mirror.

"Shut 'er down," he commanded.

"Shutting down, sir."

Robertson stood completely still, in thought, as he contemplated a course of action. He was a skilled pilot who knew the waters and unseen shoals of every port and ocean. But this experience baffled him. His crew waited anxiously for orders.

"We've got to reach that cresting water," Robertson pointed dead ahead. "Call General Quarters. Dump anything non-toxic overboard that carries weight. Get the message out. And give me flank speed."

"Flank speed sir."

General Quarters alarm sounded and the LC made the prescribed announcement.

Robertson watched the crew jump into action and the seamen cast off everything not bolted down. He had fought many battles over the years but never an enemy invisible to the eye—and to radar.

"Give me a serpentine course to grab water surface . . . if there's any left out there. Cut it back across fifteen degrees every twenty-five yards. Let's try whatever it takes to gain a foothold in this crap, even if we have to secure territory a yard at a time."

Imperceptibly, at first, the cruiser's hull began to move. The stern slid a degree to starboard, like a car losing traction on an icy road. Then, it took hold and the sharp stem of the ship's bull nose proceeded to slowly cut water. The *Standley* meandered through a course and zigzagged across the water, methodically picking up speed, eventually making headway.

"Three knots, sir." The giant turbines whined below as the props strained to propel over seventy-nine hundred tons of displacement to safety.

"Keep her coming," Robertson encouraged.

"We've got seven knots, Captain."

The ship had only traveled twelve hundred linear feet in slightly over ten minutes, but it was closing in on normal water.

"Sir, six hundred yards and we should be in the clear," reported the LC.

Robertson glanced back at the *A'isha*. It was not moving at all and was sitting much lower in the water, listing heavily to port. "Jesus, Parker mentioned oil rigs going down from these eruptions, but I've never seen anything like this."

"Thirteen knots sir."

The *Standley* gained momentum.

"Let's move this baby out of here. Hold her straightaway, son. She should take it head-on now."

"We're gaining back normal displacement, Captain. She's coming back up in the water."

"Where's the *Neptune* now?"

"Echo ranging bearing two-four-six."

"Adjust course heading two-four-six."

"Aye, aye, sir."

The ship jumped into its new course and headed toward the more typically cresting ocean. Within ten more minutes it cleared the gas-filled waters and moved out into the open sea.

———

Parker's *Shelty* had hit full throttle as it raced to catch up with Dupont. Not certain what he'd do, Parker could only hope to persuade Dupont to turn around.

The radio greeted him with massive crackles and squeals.

"Damn . . . I should've known," he said, in an attempt to find a channel less affected by ionic radiation.

"Henri. This is Cary. Do you read?"

There was no answer.

"Listen to me, Henri. You'll never make it through the escaping gas. Turn around. . .just get out of there. Do you copy?"

The radio crackled as it had before.

"Henri. Don't be a fool. Come around and forget the *Omar*.

Over."

Parker watched as the highly advanced mini-sub dashed across the sea toward the fog bank.

"Henri, if you enter a high concentration of methane, your electronics can trigger an explosion. For once, just do as I say."

Then his speaker carried a distant-sounding voice that faded in and out.

"H-drates is just a th-ory. No o-e has pr-ven it. Ov-r."

Negative ionic clouds became thicker, but Dupont pushed full throttle. He approached the dense fog thinking he would skim across the ocean—avoiding the dispersive results induced by the methane. But the churning, bubbling gas had deposited a thick film over the sea, broken down the water's molecules, and changed its density.

Parker watched the *Amagaeru* skim across the surface ahead of him. As moments passed, the manta-like sub had trouble staying afloat. Then Dupont veered off course, attempted to correct, and spun to a stop. The sub lost complete water gravity and was sucked closer to the rising methane bubbles.

It was obvious Dupont's sub had lost instrumentation and all sense of direction—much as the Bermuda Triangle had taken doomed planes, ships, and boats over the years. And the Japanese mini-sub began to sink in the churning waters.

"He's going to commit suicide," Parker yelled in anger, at once aggravated with himself for allowing him to escape. Despite Dupont's contempt for the sanctity of the *Titanic's* gravesite, and for his involvement with Ragem, Henri had once been a respected and admired scientist.

Parker radioed Dupont, once more, "Henri, don't waste your life over this incident. It's not worth it. . . . I'll try to guide you back. Over."

Suddenly, laughter drifted in and out with the deteriorated reception.

Parker's speaker crackled with communications attempting to break through. He couldn't tell if it was Dupont answering him, or the *Standley* or *Neptune*.

Then he heard Dupont.

"Au r-voir, -on ami," the detached voice said. "W- both go together, huh? Over and ou-."

Exhausted, Dupont was unable to fight any longer. Sucked into the perimeter of the churning waters, his vessel sank from view.

Parker barely saw the *Amagaeru's* tailfins as it sank half a nautical mile to the north. Saddened by the message, he could no longer dwell on Dupont's problems. He watched the *Yoritomo-class* submersible sink, then noticed water beginning to cover the *Shelty's* viewport. He pushed the throttle to maximum thrust and adjusted the ailerons to ascend above waterline. But the *Shelty* lost speed and slowly descended below the surface.

The radio spit back at Parker as he continued across the water.

"D-ct-r Par-er this is -ap-ain Rober-s-n. Get tha- sub o-t of the wa-t-r. Th-t'- an ord-r."

Parker understood enough to know it was an order from the *Standley* he would obey without question—*if* he could pull out. He was losing ground. *Shelty Three* was sinking fast and recovery from the grip of the hydrates became difficult.

He pushed the Talk button, "Coming around Captain. I'll confirm coordinates when transmissions settle down. Can you see Dupont? Over."

Static blared back.

With the constant noise, it was difficult to concentrate on the task at hand. Parker turned off his radio out of futility.

Parker's *Shelty* was immersed in water with little surface tension. Millions of bubbles surrounded his sub, like fingers pulling him down. Few electronic gauges worked and his monitors were immersed in snow. The rapidly deteriorating water would soon cause his sub to lose all buoyancy and *Shelty Three* would promptly sink to the bottom.

Parker initiated a one-eighty and gunned his jets and thrusters for a rapid descent from the surface. Using years of experience and innate judgment to manually reverse direction, he prayed he had not overcompensated in the maneuver. He cut a path, heading toward the ships, and down at a forty-five degree angle—away from the expanding gases and approaching chaos.

The U.S.S. *Standley* had pulled back six nautical miles from the *A'isha*, just north and west of the *Neptune*, in an attempt to avoid the affected region where flash point might occur.

"Captain," Lieutenant Commander Winslow entered the bridge. "Look at these seismic reports." He handed a file to his commander. "Had trouble pulling them off the satellite."

The captain glanced at the printout.

"Lord help us," he said, then reached for the handset. "Dr. Parker. This is Robertson. Do you copy? Over."

They waited for the atmospheric distortion to clear, hoping for a signal from the *Shelty*.

"Captain Robertson calling Dr. Parker. Do you read? Over."

More distortion, but someone was breaking through.

"Come on. Come on." Robertson impatiently tapped his fingers.

"Th-s -- *Shel*--. Ov-r."

Robertson was relieved. "We're getting nasty seismics from below. MIT, CalTech and Colorado Seismic Centers have all confirmed extensive activity in our coordinates. Clear out now. Over." He waited, then repeated the message.

"On --- way ---. Condit-ons --- deteri--ating r-pidly. Los-ng buoy-ncy, b-t speed hold-ng aga-nst meth-ne. Ov-rwork-ng cycloidals. Not c-rtain t-ey'll hold."

"Our navigator will feed coordinates for DR with your ship.

Copy?"

"Won't do m- -ny good, Capt--n. All nav-gati-n syst-ms are out. Ev-n backup. I'm fly-n- blind. -'m he-ding for bot-om, to avoid upris-ng bub-les. I'll contac- f-r co-rd-nates when - leave t-is muck. I'm mainta-ning - forty-five degre- ride down -- capture som- dist-nce betw-en me and a pos-ibl- explos . . . "

"Jesus! What was that?" the sonar coordinator yelled out. "Captain, we just had an enormous event on the bottom."

"What is it?"

"Whatever it is, its heading for the surface." The coordinator fine-tuned his dials and adjusted the distorted holographic imaging simulator on his screen. He couldn't believe what he saw.

"Looks like the stem of a nuclear mushroom," the coordinator exclaimed, dumbfounded. "We're losing sidescan. Son-of-a-bitch!"

Without warning, at two thousand seven-hundred fathoms below the surface, the final and largest slump released, carrying enough accumulated weight—from the mid-point of the seamount—to cause the sludge to plunge down the side and into a nearby canyon.

And over ten thousand square yards of underwater surface was uncovered.

The resulting violent eruption exposed thousands of years of decomposed sediment, released millions of cubic metres of frozen, crystalline gas molecules from chemical limbo—and, under high pressure, caused a mammoth underwater geyser of gas hydrates to disgorge and climb for the surface.

No one needed a speaker to hear the initial rumbling and the ensuing blowout, since highly compressed sound travels faster underwater. From two and a half miles down, a shock wave emerged as the immense column of frozen hydrates morphed into methane gas—by degrees, as it reached the warmer levels— and shot toward the surface at an explosive rate.

The shock wave raced up and across the ocean, hit Parker's sub with a jolt, and propelled *Shelty Three* uncontrollably through the abyss. Seized by the moving wave, the sub careened through the water as it tumbled and pitched forward.

Parker was helpless as his mini-sub plunged end over end.

Under extremely high pressure, tons of frigid sea water were pushed aside, and the giant wall of gas was injected into the ocean with an intensity and force that was felt for hundreds of miles.

And it climbed to devour anything in its path.

"My God, sir . . . better take a look at this," said the *Standley's* SC.

The commander moved into the darkened room and stood before the bank of consoles. "The methane?"

"Or the devil himself, sir . . . a column rising directly outta' the earth."

"How big is it?"

"We got a rising shaft the size . . . the size of three or four football fields." He glanced over his shoulder at the captain. "Sir, it's bigger than this friggin' ship."

"Speed?"

The SC turned back to the console, "Let me put it this way, sir . . . if I were riding its crest, the rapid pressure changes would give me the bends, and I would've imploded by now." He checked his deteriorating sonar screen.

"Echo ranging says it's approaching the surface at . . . " the SC confirmed his readings, " . . . somewhere around five hundred feet per second."

"That's less than thirty seconds before it breaks the surface."

"It's carrying its own ordnance, Captain."

"Ordnance?"

The SC pointed to his erratic screen.

"Sir, that thing's transporting all kinds of shit from below. See these blips? Giant rocks and boulders, I'd guess . . . I'd estimate the size of cars or even trucks. And this stuff here, sir . . . " he pointed to a spot on the screen, " . . . probably tons of mud and sludge, as the hole widens."

"Give me the radio," said Robertson. He pushed the Talk button, "Dr. Parker do you read? Report in Parker. Do you copy?"

The interference was impossible to overcome.

"Damn!" the captain slammed down his fist. "Get Parker back on the radio," he ordered. "This thing could take him out instantly, if it hasn't already." The CO clicked through several channels and called Parker.

"Have we got him on sonar?" The captain inquired.

"The eruption's too intense. Can't tell his sub from these rocketing boulders."

"Keep at it." He turned to his navigator. "What's the status on the A'isha? Is their crew holding on?

The intelligence officer had observed the A'isha since pulling away. "Sir, she's sitting on the leading edge of whatever's rising from below."

"We should've arrested every ass onboard," said the captain. "At least they'd had half a chance at surviving."

The crew on the bridge shrugged at the irony and continued monitoring at their stations.

"Any word on that Japanese sub?"

"Not sure. Transmissions indicated Dupont lost water gravity and was sucked below."

"If he isn't a large blip in the column, he soon will be," said the sonarman.

Robertson looked out through the panoramic windows and back to his navigator. "Helmsman, all ahead, flank speed. Maintain course and heading.

"All ahead, flank speed, Captain. Maintaining course and heading."

"Let's distance ourselves from that damned thing. CO, Con."

"Sir?"

"Radio *Neptune* and tell 'em to move farther out."

"There she blows!" the sonar technician exclaimed.

Everyone looked to the northwest, beyond the A'isha, where

the sea had been churning.

No one aboard the *Standley* was prepared for what came next. The powerful methane column hit the surface with an explosive force—cataclysmic as it had begun at the ocean floor. It rose over two thousand feet into the air—a once clear shaft of pure gas— now permeated with tons of sea life, and the primordial ooze, rock and underground boulders from centuries upon centuries, and layer after layer of sodden marl.

And the monstrous spout regurgitated and spit huge objects out of its towering spigot.

Rising ever higher into the late afternoon sky, the ancient effluent rained over the ocean like a hailstorm from hell, and underwater pressure spewed abyssal objects miles into the atmosphere. Rocks the size of missiles, and boulders the length of rail cars careened into the *A'isha* and plunged around the *Standley*. The ships took bombardments as if in a war zone.

Dupont had lost control of the Japanese sub long before the final eruption. Initially pulled in a downward spiral toward the ocean's floor, dementia gripped hold of every nerve and fiber of Dupont's being. Water density had altered so much, he hoped he was being rushed through a thaumaturgic tunnel that would lead to a quick death.

But that was not to be.

Drawn toward the abyss in a Mephistophelean sluiceway, Dupont and his sub had unwillingly descended past five thousand feet below the surface when the gigantic column of gas raced up to meet them from the bottom.

It took hold of his vessel with a ferocious grip and swirled the submarine atop its flue, like a small ship caught in a cyclone. Crazy with fear, Dupont had let go of the controls, and pulled the *Great Omar* tightly to his chest.

In his delirium, he had grown accustomed to the thought of an instant, painless death. But the column of gas had reversed the submarine's direction. Suddenly his body felt the accelerated effects of too rapid an ascent from the intense, deep-water pressures, as he headed back toward the lesser atmospheric pressures above.

Having initially descended too quickly and, regardless of technological advances that processed the sub's oxygen, the increased underwater pressure caused compressed nitrogen in his system to rapidly absorb in his tissues and body fluids. Without slow decompression to release his body's nitrogen, the abrupt reversal of direction as he shot toward the surface—and resultant decrease in water pressure—forced air bubbles to move into his bloodstream.

At first Dupont experienced a dizziness that compounded his confusion. Though intoxicated from nitrogen narcosis, in a matter of seconds the pain in his joints intensified unbearably. His muscles cramped, and every ounce of energy was forced from his body as he clutched at the *Omar* and waited for convulsions to set in.

Aeroembolisms lodged in his spinal cord and, as paralysis reached his limbs, the embolisms raced to his lungs. Finally, his eardrums burst . . . and he never heard himself savagely wail in pain.

Rocks and boulders struck as the *Amagaeru's* shell slammed through the ocean's surface and shot two thousand feet straight up. At once, aeroembolisms tore into Dupont's heart and brain. And blood vessels and tissue imploded as he convulsed to a death he wouldn't have wished on Ragem.

Dupont's body slumped forward, simultaneously punched several electronic buttons, and the console short-circuited and sparked.

As swiftly as the column broke the surface, it burst into a massive pillar of fire, spewed forth gas-embedded, fire-laden boulders, rocks and other debris, and created an inferno that raged with an anger only the devil could prescribe.

From the *U.S.S. Standley* it appeared the final reckoning had come. Though six and a half nautical miles from the site of the blowout, the roar was deafening.

The first shock wave preceded the rising gas and hit topside only seconds before the monstrous shaft pierced the atmosphere. A giant rolling wave stretched out in all directions as it first overtook the *A'isha* and moved on toward the *Standley* and the *Neptune*.

Observed through binoculars, the *A'isha's* remaining crew, thinking they could escape death, abandoned ship as the shockwave rolled the vessel nearly on its side.

They leaped overboard with only life jackets to save them. But the water density was too unstable. And every crew member slipped through the surface as though a beast had grabbed hold of their legs and jerked them under.

The seething waters had already reached the *A'isha*, and the ship listed heavily to port. Just after it had righted itself, the second shockwave hit—following ignition of the column. Methane surrounded the *A'isha* and the hull exploded. The vessel lifted high out of the water and, in twenty seconds, was inexorably drawn downward and vanished beneath the ocean's veneer in its own fiery demise.

Captain Robertson stepped out on the open bridge, portside, and viewed the conflagration through binoculars. It looked more like Mt. Vesuvius erupting than an underwater geyser. The air smelled acrid and sour.

Whipped by the currents and fire-stirred winds, the ocean's surface was ablaze with roiling, white-hot flames stretching from where the *A'isha* had once floated, to as far as the eye could see.

Robertson recalled his final days in Vietnam, where atrocities would have staggered the mind. But in his years of service... having witnessed all the destructive devices man had invented— from napalm and Agent Orange, and films he had seen on the atomic bomb—neither man nor Mother Nature had unleashed so terrible and powerful a battery of fire as he had witnessed this day in the Atlantic.

The captain released his glasses to the neck strap. The

continuous roar from the burning gas was unsettling. And he moved back inside.

"Any sign from Dr. Parker?" Robertson asked the CO.

"Nothing, sir."

"Sonar?"

The sonar technician shook his head. "Haven't given up, sir."

"No one sleeps until we find that submersible." The captain turned to the CO. "Get me their research ship."

"Sir, they just called in. Can't get a good signal."

The captain picked up the phone. "This is Robertson. Who's on the line?"

Both men struggled to hear each other. The conversation was garbled, but they persisted.

"This is Captain Holt. Any contact with Dr. Parker?"

"We lost him with the eruption. Too much going on down there. Over."

"Same here. Any ideas?"

"We've got fifty million in sophisticated electronics to enable us to find a pinhead on the bottom of the ocean," said Robertson. "But this has wreaked havoc with our systems. We can't even get a reading from SatNav. Over."

A long pause ensued. Then the speaker clicked in.

"How's Andy Calder?"

"He's heavily sedated in the infirmary. They've patched him up best they can."

"Gonna' make it through?"

"Prognosis is good, Captain. We'll dispatch him to Bethesda, by air, as soon as we're assured the air is flyable. Over."

The radio was silent—then a static click.

"Keep us informed if you pick up any signals. Over."

"Roger that. Over and out."

The mood aboard *Neptune's Knot* was tenebrous at best. Though the scientists and shipmates were prepared for difficulties and unexpected events at sea, the entire crew was exhausted from the ordeal. Nothing could have prepared them for what they encountered on this expedition. Nerves were threadbare. Bodies were worn. No one spoke unless necessary.

The silence reached out to the sea, despite the still burning waters.

Deep down, all hoped they might hear a familiar shout from their principal shipmate—a call over the radio, a cry from the water, a familiar blip on the sonar—something, anything.

They wanted Calder to pull through. And the unspoken thought that Dr. Cary Parker might be dead . . . lying somewhere out there within range of his second love, the *Titanic*, was left unsaid.

In desperation, Holt opened up another channel.

"Cary Parker. Do you read? Come in Cary. This is mothership, baby . . . come in. I know you're out there. Don't let me down."

For the first time in years, John Holt choked up. He took a deep breath and checked to make certain no one saw his damp eyes. Those on the bridge looked away to avoid the awkward moment.

Holt pushed the Talk button.

"Cary, this is John. I know you're out there. I feel you in my creaky ol' bones. And you're making them older and creakier. Give us a break. If you're in trouble signal us so we can help. Do you read? Over."

Piercing hisses answered back. Then, more silence. He punched the mike, again, and hailed Parker for the next hour.

———

Parker had no way of knowing how far the initial shock wave's impact had tossed him. When it slammed against his sub, *Shelty Three* was propelled beyond the extremely hot and agitated waters of the slump, and pushed clear of the immediate danger zone.

He would never know how long he was unconscious, or how close he came to imploding against an undersea guyot. But the thrust of the aftershock had reflected off the flat-topped seamount, pushed the sub in a direction opposite to the guyot's incline, and it came perilously close to the ocean floor.

Then, the *Shelty* regained partial buoyancy and held its level, even with the underwater turbulence.

Initially, the convulsive thunder-like sounds emanated from the belly of the Cone, and nearly deafened Parker as they bounced and reverberated off submarine mountains, through chasms and crusty gashes, and across the abyssal hills.

Pinned in his seat for five minutes, his sub flew out of control. His ears burned from the loud acoustic reflections, and he wanted to yell out in pain. But his stomach had contracted, and his breath was sucked from his lungs. Parker had no way to protect his hearing until the gyros kicked in and stabilized the sub. Only then could he turn off the radio and protect his ears with the headset. Then he blacked out.

Though the sub had distanced itself from the eruption, the rumble vibrated through the hull. Air inside the *Shelty* was heavier than usual. And a slight hissing sound persisted in the background, from somewhere underneath Parker's seat.

A constant ringing settled in his ears. Yet, in his unconscious state, Parker heard the faint sound of escaping air-mixture, and the urgency of it slowly pulled him back. As if drugged, he sluggishly extracted himself from a deep sleep. He willed his eyes to open, yet his body felt too lethargic to move his limbs. His head throbbed and he felt dizzy.

Parker recognized the beginning stages of carbon-monoxide formation in the cabin. He gazed at a flashing yellow light marked CO, and it confirmed his diagnosis.

This was not the first occurrence for him.

Hemoglobin, the bloodstream's oxygen carrier, had a much higher affinity for absorbing carbon monoxide than for oxygen. And Cary knew this. Excessive exposure to CO would shut down his body's ability for oxygen to reach tissue. If he did not react promptly, he would develop nausea, lose consciousness, lapse into a coma, and die of respiratory failure.

Shivering in his still wet clothes, Parker did not have the luxury for anxiety . . . or hypothermia. He focused each nerve and every synapse in his upper torso to respond to his call for help, as he exerted muscles in his arm to reach the computer keyboard.

Parker switched on the recorder to transcribe thoughts for the record. He brought it up to date with what he remembered, then rambled and fought to remain conscious. He fumbled for the computer's trackball and dueled with the keyboard to modulate the outside disturbance with noise suppressors. But his CRT screens were filled with electronic snow.

I've only minutes to cleanse my . . . hemoglobin, he struggled to think . . . *and reverse the effects of . . . of CO poisoning. And I need to . . . bring up the programmed icon to read oxygen . . . reserves.*

He waited for the icon to appear.

"The display screen . . . alternately pops in and out," he said, to reassure his mind and check alertness.

"Come on, dammit," Parker barely whispered as he skirmished between keyboard and trackball.

Then, the control panel icons window flashed in and out on the screen. He moved the arrow to "H²O AIR PURIFICATION" icon and clicked Return. It missed.

He waited for another flash of the icon and clicked again. A dialog box appeared. It read: *Air Processor Cycling — Interior Cabin Pressure Compromised — Carbon Monoxide Detected.* The word DANGER flashed off and on from his screen.

"Danger . . . danger . . . " he mimicked in near delirium.

Before the eruption, most cabin air had been routinely replenished and purified by an electric current passing through sea water, as it circulated through the cycloidal jet tubes. Oxygen atoms were separated from the hydrogen. And remaining oxygen came from recirculated air that passed through a lithium hydroxide bath—to filter out carbon dioxide.

The shock from the eruption had affected the processing unit for air. Now Parker had to determine the scope of any oxygen leak, and the level for which he had to compensate, with whatever remained functioning within the system.

Parker struggled to breathe, and clicked on the next icon. It brought up a series of electronic levers.

"Adjusting oxygen mixture," he said aloud, to reassure himself, " . . . increasing it to achieve five percent CO^2, carbon dioxide flow . . . to offset . . . effects of the CO as the dead air filters out . . . and recirculates."

Too much CO^2 could become a deadly mixture. And too much CO would be highly poisonous—and potentially explosive.

Parker reached below the console for the emergency supply tank manual-control valve. He nearly blacked out as he leaned underneath. But a louder hissing signaled release of pure oxygen in the cabin. He checked the gauge.

"Two hour supply. . . . But with escaping air mixture I've no idea how long the oxygen will last. At least its inside," he said, knowing if the leak had been outside—even the size of a pinhole— the sub could have imploded.

"Have to begin slow ascent. . . . Don't need nitrogen narcosis."

He had to reach the surface before any crimps in the hull could be compromised from outside pressure.

Parker used the thirty minutes it took to regain his strength for examining areas of the cabin that might have been structurally damaged. He checked viewports to determine if methane bubbles still encircled the hull.

Oddly, the sea appeared as though the *Shelty* sat just below the surface, with sunlight filtering through from above.

"One of the strangest sights I've ever encountered . . . " he recorded. "I'm quite a distance from the burning methane, but an ominous glow, from the fiery column of gas, has pierced the dark waters and turned perpetual night into day."

With the water less murky than before, and fewer globules to prevent him from safely traversing the waters, Parker felt confident he could make his ascent. The natural buoyancy of his submersible had returned. On its own, without steel ballast, the *Shelty* was already ascending ever so slowly.

An erratic, but rising altimeter agreed with his observation.

"Subterranean pressures were relieved by the blowout," he noted. "Not as much gas seeping into this quadrant."

In the distance, however, the frozen hydrates still escaped the earth in massive quantities. As they reached warmer elevations and lighter atmospheric pressures, the ice-bound molecules melted and rushed to the surface as explosive bubbles of gas. Though the currents funneled more methane and sediments farther out at steeper altitudes, the high-pressure gas column did not radiate as far outward, near the ocean floor, as it did above.

At eighteen hundred fathoms, Parker carefully pushed on the throttle, to check thrust, then adjusted for trim. The submersible propelled forward and remained stable. And Parker breathed a little easier.

He hit the navigational computer switches, glanced at the standby wet compass, and matched readings.

"Thank God," he whispered to himself, his teeth chattering from extreme cold.

He set a temporary dead reckoning toward the darker edge of the sea, engaged the autogyros, and turned on his radio, hoping to reestablish contact.

The noise was still intense and sonar picked up nothing. He needed coordinates from either of the two ships on the surface to set a manual DR for retrieval, before the air supply gave out. But without a solid dead reckoning, he was on his own.

He switched on the inertial navigation system and read the coordinates on his screen. The onboard computer had been fed the submersible's location seconds before the blowout. Now the accelerometer compared and measured the distances traveled, as written into its harddrive, and present position was determined. The coordinates calibrated a position south-southeast, about four and a half nautical miles from the original area of the event. Parker hoped to get topside safely, tie into the GPS satellites, and realign his coordinates.

He blew out his small ballast tanks, increased speed and ascended for the surface—this time reversing his forty-five degree angle as he rose, to distance himself farther from the hydrates.

Parker lifted the handmike, sat back, and scanned all radio channels as he broadcast his request for coordinates. He began a pattern of call-wait-call-wait, in thirty-second intervals, hoping his voice would eventually escape the villainous ionic disturbance that blocked an early rescue.

The *Neptune* and *Standley* rested ten nautical miles from the site of the blowout. Aboard *Neptune*, Holt continued his attempt to regain contact with their lost submersible. His voice left him nearly an hour before, but he refused to give up on his shipmate. Between sips of hot tea, to soothe his throat, he lay exhausted—flat out on a cot—and continued to call Parker.

"Captain Holt," an expedition staffer approached.

"Yeah," Holt whispered, his voice hoarse.

"The *Standley's* on channel seven. You want me to patch 'em through?"

"Is it Robertson?"

"I believe he's coming on."

Holt sat up on the edge of the cot. "Yeah, of course. Patch him in."

"Captain Holt . . . Jim Robertson here. Do you copy?"

"Copy."

"We've heard your calls. If it's any consolation, we know how you feel . . ."

"Been a long day," Holt's raspy voice interrupted.

"You'll be happy to know we've picked up an image moving on sonar...about 500 fathoms down, approaching our sector."

Holt thought for a moment. "Three thousand feet."

He looked at the crew and staff waiting anxiously on the bridge. "What's his bearing?"

"Coming in at bearing zero-four-one. Based on active echo-ranging, it reads about the size of a *Shelty* . . . and its making decent time. See anything yet? Over."

Holt's communications officer shook his head.

"Nothing here, captain. You sure you got him?"

"We're getting echo clutter from biologics and hydrates. But it looks quite solid. Can't be a whale and it's too big for plankton."

"Any communication breakthrough?"

"Still trying to get Parker on the line. He's either got radio trouble . . . or it's turned off. Or, he's on autogyro with no control."

Holt knew the "autogyro" remark referred to a dead man going for a ride. The thought knocked him down a notch.

"We'll keep trying and keep *Neptune* informed. My CO will give you modified coordinates by the minute, to lock in on him. Over."

Holt sprang to his feet. "That's the best news we've had all day. Over and out."

He dropped the mike on his cot and raced to the sonar screen. "You got him?"

"There's an object moving right here, Captain," the sonarman reported. He adjusted the coordinates and pointed to a sector on the screen.

"That's gotta be him," Holt's voice barely made it out, as he raced back to the mike and began hailing Parker, once more.

———

"Anyone home?" Parker inquired after he modulated the still persistent static.

"Hello...anyone out there. I'll talk with a porpoise. Just let me hear someone's voice. Over."

The emergency oxygen tank supply had dwindled fast, and the computer showed only a twenty-minute supply remained—with at least a forty-minute trip to reach topside. The oxygen-hydrogen air separator only partially kept up with the continuous leak.

"This is *Shelty Three*. Anyone left topside? Come in, *Neptune*. *Standley*...are you there? Over."

Parker was fatigued and chilled beyond any point he could remember. His body cried out for sleep, but he would not give in to the temptation. He remained awake to monitor the air. Weakened to the point of total exhaustion, his spirits were challenged by the elements and his inability to break through on the radio.

"*Shelty Three* calling *Neptune*. Over."

"Parker? Is that you, you son-of-a-bitch?" Holt radioed.

"Just me and the dead fishies," Parker answered, sounding drunk with languor.

"Where the hell you been?" Holt jumped back on.

"Hey, if I wanted someone to climb down my throat, I'd call Bramson."

"Sorry fella...we've been worried sick. We'll get ya' outta there. Don't worry about that. You sound sluggish. How's the air? Over."

"Pushing the big zero. Over...but not out."

Holt was concerned. "Listen, partner, stay on the radio. Understand? You'll be out of the drink in no time. You hear me? No time at all. Over."

"Sounds like a plan." Parker thought for a moment and pushed the button. "Am I on screen? Over."

The sonarman threw his thumb into the air.

"You bet. As clear as your voice is now. Over."

"How's Andy?"

"He'll make it...in good hands aboard the *Standley*."

Parker was relieved. "And Henri?"

"Dupont's fried rice."

"Like Krispies?"

"More like snap, crackle, bang."

Cary was silent for a time. There had to be a moment to properly mourn an old friend . . . even one irretrievably corrupt.

He spoke quietly, "I'd prefer to remember him the way he used to be. As my partner . . . when times were good," he almost whispered over the mike, and clicked off.

"Any sign of the *Omar?*" Holt inquired.

"Henri had it with him . . . "

"You saw it, huh?"

Parker silently pondered the choices he had made. "It was everything Francis Sangorski had envisioned and all Byron White had described," he said. "I should have left it aboard the *Titanic.*"

"You couldn't have known what would happen," Holt reassured. Both were quiet for a time, then Holt pressed Talk.

"By the way, Victoria sent a message. Over."

Parker's voice picked up noticeably, "What'd she say?"

"She said, and I quote, 'Tell him I'm ready to fall in love again' . . . whatever that means, sailor."

Parker was energized. He forced himself to sit up in the seat and smiled widely.

"Thank's, John . . . I needed that. Call her and tell her I'll be okay."

"Sure."

"And ask her to reserve our favorite window table at The Landfall. Have 'em stockpile a giant plate of Chatham scallops and the largest lobster they can find. I'm going to have an appetite when I get back."

"You got it, sailor. Over."

Cary parked his mike, rifled through the compact discs, and put Mannheim Steamroller's *Fresh Aire VIII* in the CD player. Then, he adjusted the oxygen controls, to conserve the supply even more.

Using his training in relaxation and slow breathing to buy time, he adjusted the cycloidals and thrusters, broke through the glowing bioluminescent sea-creatures gathered in the deep scattering layer, and headed for topside.

———

From a distance, Victoria heard thumping sounds in the air—getting louder with time. Her heart jumped as she moved to the kitchen window and looked up. She saw nothing.

Most air traffic avoided the area, though Coast Guard helicopters occasionally ventured into their space.

The sound bordered the property. Victoria froze as panic set in. *God, don't let it be them.*

Jennifer Nakamura walked in from the front porch and saw the terror in Victoria's face. She knew the psychological aftermath of her captivity would frequently return.

"It's a military copter, Vicky," said Nakamura, assigned to watch over the Parker family until the terrorist episode was put to rest. "It's one of ours. I can tell by the sound. "

For additional security, police officers had been posted outside—two in front, two in back.

Marlowe and Jessica Parker kept them all busy.

"Mom, Mom," Victoria heard Jessica yell from the front yard.

"Something's wrong," said Victoria.

"She's just excited about the copter, I'm sure."

"Mom, come here. Mom!" Marlowe called out, as she ran into the kitchen. "A helicopter's coming in over the trees," she said, out of breath. She turned about-face and ran out. "Come look."

Victoria glanced at Nakamura and both dashed to the front porch. Two officers raced from the backyard to investigate with their partners.

Agent Nakamura stepped to the far end of the covered porch. Victoria stood in the doorway clinging to her children.

A giant S-61 Sikorsky Sea King passed the tree line from the beach, crossed above the main drive from the road, powered down and hovered, menacingly, over the front yard.

"Too close to the trees and house," yelled Nakamura. "Can't land here."

Nakamura noted that no visible armament was present. The fixed landing gear, usually found on the Westland Commando version of the Sikorsky, was absent, and the craft was configured, instead, with at-sea stabilizing sponsons.

A knowing smile crossed Jennifer's face as she turned to Victoria.

"It's him," she yelled over the roar of the two GE T-58 engines. Nakamura crossed back to the Parkers, and hugged Vicky and the girls.

"It's your daddy. I'm sure it's him."

The SH-3H transport levitated above them for some time.

Victoria's heart was in her throat as she looked to the cockpit. The high-overhead sun created a blinding effect as it glistened back from the windshield. She barely made out the two helmeted heads of the pilot and co-pilot sitting side by side in the nose.

Victoria held the girls tightly to her side.

As the turboshaft engines whirred-up, the five-bladed rotor tilted its airfoils slightly, then turned several degrees to the left. The downdraft blew sand up from the grass and into the air, and everyone on the ground shielded their eyes.

The wide door of the Sikorsky slid open. Colonel Bramson waved and smiled from the open main cabin. The girls waved back.

Victoria bit at her lower lip, as a Navy crewman reached out from inside the cabin and grabbed the rescue hoist. He draped the heavy cable from its tip to inside the helicopter.

Then Victoria observed the figure of a man in the shadows of the cabin. When she realized it was Cary, tears welled up.

Parker secured his safety belt to the hoist, tugged on the cable twice, and looked down to his family.

Cary saw Victoria standing on the porch and waved. From the

distance he saw tears glisten on her cheeks—caught in the sun like reflected mirrors—as they traveled to meet her wide smile.

Colonel Bramson spoke to Parker, over the whine of the engines. Then they shook hands and Bramson stepped back.

The steel cable rose to take up slack, and Parker moved to the edge of the door. A Navy crewman yelled instructions into his ear and patted him on the back. Parker stepped off the edge and swung freely from the end of the cable. Then, the line slowly fed him to the ground.

Cary turned his head with each twist of the cable and resembled a handsome, pirouetting dancer from the Bolshoi—spotting in place—all the while his eyes on Victoria.

Nakamura took the children's hands as Victoria's courage moved her out of the doorway and off the porch. Her legs seemed paralyzed when she began her run to meet the husband she so loved. Then she found herself in a sprint across the grass.

As Cary's feet touched the ground, he released himself from the rescue belt and threw his arms tightly around his wife.

Neither remembered how long it took for Cary to descend and for Victoria to cross the expanse of the front grounds, though it had seemed interminable. Nor did they hear the loud whirring of the receding helicopter, while it turned and disappeared over Nantucket Sound.

For a moment, both were suspended in time—searching the patterns of their being—acting out and renewing, in milliseconds, and without saying a word, the love, companionship and trust rediscovered in the safe harbor of each others arms.

They clung tightly, and not a word needed to be said. Cary and Victoria wept until they were spent, then retreated inside with their family.

———

GLOSSARY

3/9 Line. With the nose of a sub representing 12 o'clock and the tail representing 6 o'clock, a line drawn from 3 o'clock to 9 o'clock position at its widest wing or hull span.

Abaft. Toward the stern from another direction.

Altitude-depth sonar.
Furnishes depth and altitude off the bottom to provide vertical navigation.

Anechoic tiles.
Act as a stealth muffler for sounds coming out of a submarine (ie. a reactor) or DSRV (ie. motors); also absorbs sonar energy, like a sponge, when sent from another vessel, thereby preventing the "rebound" from a hull necessary to identify the vessel.

ARPA. Advanced Research Projects Agency (U.S. Department of Defense). A top secret organization, funded by the government, that researches and develops extremely advanced, futuristic technologies and applications for military, satellite communications, and in some cases, civilian use. Located in Arlington, Virginia.

ATF. Bureau of Alcohol, Tobacco and Firearms.

AUV. Autonomous Underwater Vehicle (unmanned).

Beam-to. A ship's beam/side facing parallel.

Black SS Sat.
> Super-secret satellite, funded through a masked (black) budget in the National Reconnaissance Office.

Bottom-bounce.
> Below the Deep Scattering Layer.

Convergence zone.
> Usually thirty miles, where noise bounces off the DSL, then off the bottom, then off the DSL, and so forth.

DCI. Director, Central Intelligence at CIA. A member of the President's cabinet.

Deep sound channel.
> Where a vessel is looking for "noise," usually around a thousand to two thousand feet, to abyssal depths; where the sound is very pure, without interference from temperature, waves, planktonic creatures, or other noises that might disrupt sound radiation.

Doublure. The decorated inside of a book's cover boards. Lined with leather or other material.

DoD. Department of Defense.

DP. Dynamic positioning, through the use of satellite fixes, allows a ship to maintain its position "on station."

DSL. Deep Scattering Layer: millions of planktonic creatures cause an echo phenomenon at levels from 1,300 to 2,600 feet. Intersects with the Semi-Permeable Barrier (SPB).

DSRV. Deep Submergence Research Vehicle (also DSV).

DR. Dead reckoning estimation of position. Continuous-wave or pulse-type Doppler sonars used to display distance traveled or direction of travel for "dead-reckoning" purposes. A Doppler shift in signal frequency coming back from the seafloor can also determine speed, fore, aft, and athwartship.

EER. Explosive Echo-Ranging. Using acoustic energy in identification of underwater vessels by bouncing EER sounds off of targets. Generated by dispensing incredibly large, raw explosive sounds into the water, to sense and classify large numbers of targets, in "deep-sound channels." Can differentiate between granite seamounts and underwater canyons, new-metal vessels (like DSRV's or moving subs) and old rusting wrecks.

EFC. Expect Further Clearance (airport tower jargon).

ELF. Extremely Low Frequency. Radio wave bands from 300 Hz to 2 KHz, used most often, within limited depths, for communications between submarines and surface stations.

EMV. Electro-Magnetic Visibility.

EVOC. Emergency Vehicle Operator's Course (at Quantico).

Fathom. Maritime depth equal to 6 feet i.e. 100 fathoms = 600 feet.

FDS. Full Dive Simulator, built specially for use by oceanographers, marine biologists, and to train for secret military operations.

Finishing. In bookbinding, the last stage. Includes the gilding and tooling by hand, done by a "finisher," with the use of tools heated on a finishing stove.

Flyleaf. A leaf page, left blank at the beginning and end of a book.

Forwarding.
Work accomplished on a book between sewing and tooling and includes the rounding of the edges, placing of the backing, and putting in the cover boards.

Gilding. Placing the gold gilt (or other material and decoration) on a book, including the edges and covers.

GGNS. Gravity Gradiometer Navigation System.

GPS. Global Positioning System for satellite navigation. Satellites use an atomic clock for controlled time signals to submersibles, to transmit radio messages that contain exact details of their orbit. The INS, aboard the submersible, then calculates the length of time it takes for the signal to arrive from a series of satellites (usually 3 to 4 at a height of nearly 13,000 miles) to pinpoint their position on a chart, or through an onboard computer); GPS also serves hand-held satellite navigators for land use.

Head-to. A ship's heading directly into a wave, during a storm.

HOS. Horizontal obstacle sonar detects objects fore of a submersible.

HRT. FBI Hostage Rescue Team.

Illuminating.
Ornamenting a book through the application of gold, colors, jewels and other decorative materials.

IMO.   International Maritime Organization.

INS.   Inertial Navigation System. A modern version of DR, it is kept absolutely horizontal, pointing in a fixed direction by gyroscopes, regardless the attitude of the submersible. INS calculates location by measuring, within feet, the distance and direction the submersible has traveled from a starting point (fed into the system at the beginning of a mission). The accelerometer measures every movement and direction, while the computer determines exact distance and direction traveled, to establish present location. Because slight errors are cumulative, corrective instructions (realignments) are fed through radio signals from NAVSTAR (part of the GPS).

Interpol.   International Criminal Police Organization, with 136 member nations, whose police forces collect, screen and/ or exchange data to aid in resolving criminal cases of international scope.

Jim.   Armored suit named after the 1930's *Lusitania* explorer Jim Jarratt. It allowed divers to reach such depths and return to the surface without having to undergo the typical nine days of decompression.

Kilometer. A thousand meters, or nearly two-thirds of a mile.

ME.   Medical examiner, generally a physician assigned to determine the cause of death in a homicide or other crime scene. An ME must give permission for the removal of a body, before it may be taken to the morgue, for autopsy by the coroner.

Meter. Equivalent to 39.37 inches, or 1 yard and 3.37 inches.

NIMA. National Imagery and Mapping Agency. A consolidation of the numerous CIA agencies that previously processed and analyzed satellite photos and other imaging.

Mossad. Israeli intelligence organization.

Moroccos. Genuine leathers made only from goat-skins. The highest quality is usually considered to be Cape Goat Morocco. Levant, French, Niger, Persian, Swiss, Titling, and Turkey Moroccos are other types generally accepted for use in fine books.

MSC. Military Sealift Command.

NCA. National Command Authorities. The president, vice-president, or those authorized as alternates, who has the authority to authorize the use of nuclear weapons.

NSC. National Security Council. The president, vice-president, secretary of defense, and secretary of state.

Nippers. Also "band" nippers. Pinchers used to "rip up" the bands (the cord or tapes on which the books sections are sewn) of a leather-covered book in the process of forwarding.

NRO. National Reconnaissance Office; an extraordinarily secret agency spinoff from the CIA that builds spy satellites capable of obtaining extremely high resolution images,cutting through clouds with special radar, and eavesdropping on communications. Created in 1960 and classified above top secret, until 1992 its existence was officially denied.

NSA. National Security Agency.

NSY. New Scotland Yard, London, England.

OMEGA System.

Older type of underwater navigation, still utilized by some vessels as a backup system. Radio broadcast signals are detected from special stations set up in eight locations around the Earth. Broadcasting at very low frequency wavelengths (VLF), with signals that circle the earth, the synchronized signals are measured for receptive time differences between stations, allowing a submersible to measure its position within one to two miles.

Piezoelectric Ceramics.

Used in underwater sound projectors (sending transducers) and hydrophones (receiving transducers) to transform electrical signals into acoustical signals, and back again, in order to send and pick up information. Signal processing, with piezoelectric ceramics, projects electrical signals into the water as acoustic signals (through the projector). Then the information is extracted from background noise, by picking up acoustic signals and translating them into electrical signals (through the hydrophone).

PVT. Position, Velocity and Time through GPS.

Radar. Electromagnetic energy transmitted through air.

QQC-Multiplex.

> A multiplexed laser manufacturing process used to apply diamond coatings to industrial materials. In the QQC method, finely tuned laser beams interact with carbon dioxide to rapidly form a dense protective membrane of crystalline diamond, in less time, and at less cost than with older typical chemical vapor methods manufactured in a vacuum.

RF. Radio frequency.

RIB. Rigid hull inflatable boat.

RUC. Royal Ulster Constabulary. Northern Ireland's state police.

SAM. Surface-to-air missile.

SAS. Special Air Service. British stealth, counter-terrorist group.

SATLAS. Digitalized, electronic counter-countermeasure satellite laser communications system, utilizing sophisticated glue-green lasers capable of penetrating deep water, for very high speed transmission of data to deeply submerged submarines. Includes tactical voice scramblers.

Sinn Fein. Irish terrorist group fighting for independence from Britain.

SIOC. Strategic Intelligence Operations Center. The Command Center at FBI, where Ruby Ridge, Waco, and the World Trade Center was run.

Smooths.   Groups of low waves of water.

Sonar.   Electromagnetic energy transmitted through the water. Must be very powerful to travel through water, particularly when it must pass through the DSL or SPB.

SPB.   Semi-Permeable Barrier tends to reflect sound waves from around 1,200 to 2,000 feet. Intersects with the Deep Scattering Layer (DSL).

Surfing.   Running down the face of a steep wave in a high sea state; controlled or uncontrolled.

SWAT.   Special Weapons and Tactics Team.

TECHINT.
Technical information provided through intelligence services; raw data from satellites.

TID.   Thermal Imaging Device.

Tooling.   The process of using heated tools, and other implements, to impress, chisel, or attach the decoration to a book's cover, edges, doublures, flyleaves, and so forth.

Transponder.
A passive unit that does nothing until triggered by electromagnetic radiation or acoustic energy (in the case of underwater use). Responds when transmitted to from another transponder and radiates a directional or omni-directional pulse (a certain frequency of radar, infrared, or sonar) to provide directional, identifying, or other information in code to a nanometer (for example to a GPS satellite). In combat, pilots use pocket-size transponders to radiate identification, altitude, location and

other codes to prevent "friendly fire" incidents. Underwater, powerful transponders are used to mark, identify, and locate specific geographical sites, submersibles, shipwrecks, or military vessels. An array of acoustic transponder beacons provide the most accurate technique for precisely locating position, in a system of navigation that uses points on the sea floor to pinpoint DR.

U.G..   London's underground subway system; also referred to as the Tube.

Underwater Transducer.
Converts input signals into output signals. A sending transducer (projector) converts electrical energy (information) into acoustic signals. A receiving transducer (hydrophone) converts acoustic signals into electrical energy (information).

VLF.   Very Low Frequency. Radio wave bands from 3 to 30 KHz, used most often, within limited depths, for communications between submarines and surface stations.

VOS.   Vertical obstacle sonar determines the height of an obstacle in the path of a submersible.

WS.   Weapons Specialist.

Zodiac.   An inflatable boat.

———

ACKNOWLEDGMENTS

To my wife, Janette, for her loving and giving friendship and patience, and for her research assistance; to our family, Colleen and Kerri and Kenneth, for their support and belief in the dream; to Robert Gover, for mentoring and providing a caring attitude that pushed me past the mundane; to Mary Heyborne and Anne Mills for their kind assistance; to Alan Law for his encouragement and support; to Dr. John and Theresa Maestas, for their love, loyalty and friendship; to Janet and Robert Rutherford, for their timely encouragement and companionship during long hours of proofing; to Gary and Samantha Shlesser, for their friendship and technical assistance; to Reverend Paul J. Wharton, for his guidance and prayers; to all our friends in Candlewyck who kept asking, "Is it done, yet?"; to D.S.—and, you know who you are—for keeping me laughing while spinning your web of advice; to Dick Cady and James P. Munford for kicking me hard enough to make me notice; to John Snow; and Robert and Carol Caniglia for their support.

FOR TECHNICAL INFORMATION
AND ADVICE

I want to thank Dr. John Allen, Assistant Professor of Chemistry, WV State College; *American Spectator* Magazine; P. Jean Barile, Maritime Law Specialist; a very special thanks to Rosemary Barker, Manager, and John Sprague, Antiquarian & Literature, Henry Sotheran Limited, London; Jan Blake, Tony Rainbird, and Simon Nicol of Sangorski, Sutcliffe & Zaehnsdorf, Ltd., The Asprey PLC Group, London & New York; Mr. and Mrs. Stanley Bray; Barbara

Bowers, R.N.; Gary Browning, R.N. Glaxo, Inc.; Isolde Chapin, for her special kindnesses and advice "beyond the call;" Judith Dunn, London Times; Dr. Vernon Fletcher, Chemistry Department Chairman, WV State College; Joseph Foote, for his extraordinary advice and some great lunches; Mirjam Foot and Philippa Marks, The British Museum; Frasca International, Inc.; David G. Gallo, PhD., Woods Hole Oceanographic Institution; Martyn Goff, OBE, Chairman, Henry Sotheran Ltd.; Tawney Hall, Chemist, FMC; Colonel Joseph E. Halloran; John Hallquist; Russ Hanna; Chris Harrison, Tour Guide Extraordinary, London; Dan Heartwell, Navy Aviator; J.T. (Tim) Holland, of *The Crescent Review*, for generous encouragement and some more great lunches; Charles Horner, The Hudson Institute; Linda Hughett, for her terrific cheesecake; Tim Hughett, Air Traffic Controller, Indianapolis Center; Michael Garvey, EMT-P Deputy Director, Indiana State Emergency Management Agency; Steve Jekel, Jekel Moving & Storage, United Van Lines, Grand Rapids, MI; Jim Kessler, Resident Agency Director, FBI, Charleston, WV; Carolyn and David Crowley for their "hospitality on the Hill;" Office Max™; Bill Peckol, Chemical Engineer, Monsanto; Forrest "Dan" Reese, Jr. and David Mennenga, Frasca, International, Inc.; Barbara Ritchie, Chemist & Environmental Mgr, FMC, Lithium Division; Beryl Rupp; Donald Scott; Mary J. Scroggins; Linda S. Stern; Turchan Technologies Group Inc. and QQC Diamond Technologies, Dearborn, MI; Video Graphics Technology, Beaver, WV; David and Dottie Webster; Maryjo Wheatley, Woods Hole Oceanographic Institution; and others too numerous to mention, who know who they are —a special note of gratitude!

CRAIG O. THOMPSON

Biographical Sketch

Author, Craig O. Thompson, has led an exciting and eclectic life. He was born in Los Angeles, California, where he lived most of his formative years. Some college and a life-changing experience in Sri Lanka—as the first 18-year-old to serve overseas in the U.S. Peace Corps—was all it took for him to decide that an ordinary life would not do.

In his early years, Craig was honored with a special invitation to Washington, D.C.—by Vice President of the United States, Hubert H. Humphrey—where he was able to speak before the very first gathering of returned Peace Corps volunteers. Several years later, he received a letter of commendation from the Carnegie Hero Foundation for "courage in the rescue of accident victims," after he helped pull a woman and her children from a burning car just before it exploded.

A graduate of Northern Arizona University, Craig O.—as friends call him—holds a B.S. and M.A. in Education from the Center for Excellence in Education at NAU. He also holds college lifetime teaching credentials in Theatre Arts and Related Technologies.

Mr. Thompson taught 3rd, 4th, 6th and 8th grades on the Navajo Reservation, followed with over twenty-five years work in marketing and arts management. While an instructor on the Navajo Reservation, he co-directed the Navajo-Hawaii Cultural Exchange, a program—created with his friend, Ed McGrath—that was later honored in Congress and recognized twice in the *U.S.*

Congressional Record.

He worked for Lucille Ball, as Desilu-Paramount Television's post-production office manager during the days of the original *Star Trek, Mission: Impossible, Mannix,* and *The Lucy Show.* Craig was also the producer-artistic director for the Lucille Ball Studio Theater on the Desilu lot.

Mr. Thompson has spent most of his life in the arts management field as an arts presenter, fund raiser, and not-for profit arts management consultant. He has devoted time as an executive director and chief operating officer for several arts centers that produced professional repertory theatre series, mounted extensive art exhibitions, offered numerous art classes and seminars through a school of the arts, and represented the juried works of hundreds of artists. Each center served regional, national and international visitors.

As a freelance arts management consultant, Mr. Thompson has provided advice and information dealing with arts facilities, artistic bookings, performing artist and residency contract negotiation, fund raising and development, corporate and business grant application evaluations, and other areas that serve the needs of the not-for-profit arts sector and the corporate giving sector.

Mr. Thompson has been writing for nearly twenty-five years. He first started with poetry and lyrical pieces—encouraged by Poet Laureate and Pulitzer prize-winning Poet, Gwendolyn Brooks, and by renowned composer-pianist, Roger Williams. Further encouragement came from comedienne, Lucille Ball, after he attempted a script for *The Lucy Show* (Lucy personally read the script, rejected it, but told him not to give up writing).

Years of writing copy for regional and national advertising markets—and for public relations campaigns—rounded out his ability to express his ideas. As a member of the National Speaker's Association and International Platform Association, Mr. Thompson was published in an anthology titled *Star Spangled Speakers.* Following on the heals of these experiences, he moved on to larger literary pursuits.

Craig O. Thompson's first novel—*OMAR*—is actually his second.

The first, a science-fiction fantasy thriller, was put on hold when the idea developed for *OMAR*. Now, he is re-exploring the inner-workings of the science fiction plot while gathering research and other important character development and plot requirements for at least three more novels in treatment stage or at various levels of progress. He is also adapting two screenplays.

Mr. Thompson divides his time between enjoying all aspects of the visual, literary and performing arts to writing, skiing, and spending time with his family. His ultimate goal includes establishment of the St. Jude Foundation of Hope. . .to be funded through a portion of the revenue from his writings.

NOTICE OF SALE FOR THE *GREAT OMAR*

HENRY SOTHERAN & CO., 43 PICCADILLY, W., AND 140 STRAND, W.C. 9

JEWELLED AND OTHER ORNATE BINDINGS:

THE MOST MAGNIFICENT BINDING IN THE WORLD:

26 OMAR KHAYYAM, The RUBÅIYÅT of, translated by Edward Fitzgerald, *illustrated by* Elihu Vedder: THE ORIGINAL EDITION, royal 4to. magnificently bound by Sangorski and Sutcliffe in Levant Morocco, doublé; the outside covers and the doublures most lavishly inlaid, richly tooled, AND STUDDED WITH 1050 JEWELS SET IN GOLD; morrocco flyleaves, also richly tooled and inlaid; gilt edges.

NOTE:
A full description of *Great Omar* binding follows the above introduction

SIZE OF PARCHMENT—*Authorized by H. Sotheran & Co.*:
Minimum 8.5 inches by 14 inches on high-quality parchment

INQUIRE TODAY:
$ 19.95 (U.S.) Unframed, Plus S/H, and tax if applicable
$129.95 (U.S.) Ltd. Ed.—Framed, Plus S/H, and tax if applicable
(both versions include Certificate of Authenticity)

WRITE OR FAX FOR INFORMATION:
Brightwater Enterprises, LLC
P.O. Box 503, Dept. CP, Greenwood, IN   46142-0503 USA

FAX: 1-317-883-3603   **Email:** BrightPub@aol.com

Visit Our Website: www.brightwaterpublishing.com

Craig O. Thompson's *OMAR* Is Now Available At Special Quantity Rates For Corporate and Private Group Orders

Fund Raising—Premium Gifts—Employee Rewards—Customer Thanks

Let Us Create A Limited Edition For Your Special Needs

Brightwater Publishing will create hardbound, leatherbound or paperback editions to match your specific needs and budget. Here is a unique way to provide hours of enjoyment, thrills and suspense for your special clients, vendors, customers and employees.

Contact us today. To obtain more information: Email requests to BrightPub@aol.com. Or, write to BWP, Director, Group Marketing, Dept. QDCP, P.O. Box 503, Greenwood, Indiana 46142-0503 USA